# EXTREME MEDICAL SERVICES BOX SET VOL 1-3

## Academy Probie Year

Extreme Medical Services Box Sets
Book 1

## JAMIE DAVIS

MedicCast Productions

# Also by Jamie Davis

**Get a free book and updates for new books.**
**visit JamieDavisBooks.com/send-free-book/**

—

**Eldara Sister Series**

*The Nightingale's Angel*

*Blue and Gray Angel*

—

**The Huntress Clan Saga**

(A 6-book Urban Fantasy series starting with)

*Huntress Initiate*

—

**The Broken Throne Series**

(A 5-Book Dystopian Urban Fantasy

starting with)

*The Charm Runner*

—

**The Accidental Traveler LitRPG Series**

(with C.J. Davis)

(A 6-book Epic Fantasy Series starting with)

*The Accidental Thief*

—

**Lone Wolf Squadron Scifi Series**

(A multi-book space opera series starting with)

*Marshal the Stars*

—

Follow on Facebook for updates, news, and upcoming book excerpts

Jamie's Fun Fantasy Readers Facebook Group

# JAMIE DAVIS

# EXTREME MEDICAL SERVICES

Extreme Medical Services Book 1

**Extreme Medical Services Box Set Vol 1-3**

**By Jamie Davis**



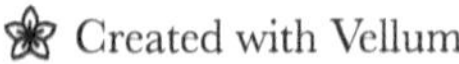 Created with Vellum

*To Amy, Chris, Mindy, and Saralynn. Maybe all my crazy stories over the years will come to something after all.*

*And*

*To my editor, fellow author, and friend Sam Bradley who helped make this book come to life.*

# Prologue

Dean couldn't believe what was happening. He was in a darkened bedroom lit only by a single overhead light and the flashlights of him and his partner. A struggle was taking place on the bed in the corner, accompanied by grunting, growls, and shouts of the two paramedics and their patient. A diminutive dark-haired female was wrestling with a large, snarling, furry creature on the bed.

"Get me the glucagon," Brynne Garvey said. "Right now!" Brynne is a lot stronger than she looks, Dean thought as he struggled to figure out how to reconstitute the powdered drug in the preloaded syringe. She was only about five foot two inches tall and her long, straight brown hair pulled back in a ponytail made her look younger than her 34 years.

"Probie. I. Need. That. Syringe,"she said through gritted teeth.

"I'm coming, I'm coming. I've never used one of these prefab syringes before." Dean finally got the syringe assembled and handed it to his preceptor. "Here."

"I can't do the injection. I'm a little busy here," she said as she grabbed one of the creature's flailing arms and pinned it to its body with one leg. She avoided the claws that had spontaneously grown out of the creature's fingertips. "You do it, Probie! It's time you stepped up your game and showed me why you got this gig to begin with." The struggle on the bed intensified as the snarling creature seemed to sprout more body hair and grew even stronger. "Do it! Glucagon! Now!" The last was almost a whisper.

Hesitantly, Dean stepped forward and injected the syringe into the hairy thigh of the creature struggling with his partner.

As the beast continued to struggle, Brynne muttered under her breath. "Humans are much easier to deal with."

A NORMAL-LOOKING MAN, wearing the same shorts and t-shirt as the creature Brynne had been wrestling with, was sitting on the edge of the bed eating a peanut butter sandwich.

"I'm sorry, Brynne. I must've dozed off after my insulin shot tonight."

"You've got be more careful, Bob," Brynne said as she zipped up the medication bag. "That's the third time this month. You're going to hurt someone one of these days. Here, sign this transport refusal so we can go." She handed the patient a tablet computer that Bob signed with a finger.

The paramedics picked up their gear and headed out to the ambulance. Dean climbed into the passenger seat staring straight ahead as his new partner and preceptor started the engine. The diesel motor growled to life. "So werewolves are…" Dean started.

"…real", she finished. "And whenever anything causes a lycan—and they prefer being called lycan—to have altered mental status, they lose control and shape shift. That is the cause of most attacks, by the way. They aren't that bloodthirsty. Bob's a CPA and a member of the Chamber of Commerce."

"And our job is to…" Dean started.

"…treat known or suspected Unusuals who need emergency medical attention." Brynne glanced over at him. "It's not all that tough. They're mostly human, but not. You apply human anatomy and physiology then diagnose the problem based on what you know about the type of Unusual you're dealing with."

Dean shook his head. "So I worked my butt off to graduate at the head of my class, aced my NREMT exam on the first try and I get rewarded by getting assigned to be a paramedic for monsters?"

"Unusuals!" Brynne said as she gunned the engine and pulled away from the nondescript suburban home. "Look, Dean, I know this is a bit of a shock to you. Believe me, I didn't ask to break in a new partner. The job is hard enough without dealing with a brand new paramedic unfamiliar with this type of specialized work. I was hoping to get paired with somebody who had some real street experience—someone who knows what kind of things we're likely to run into—but it looks like we're stuck with each other."

Unusuals…werewolf CPA, lycan…Dean's mind was trying to put it all in perspective.

She glanced over at him as she drove. She must have seen the shocked look on his face and shook her head.

"Say something. I need to know you're tracking what I'm telling you." After a pause, she raised her voice. "Dean, answer me."

"What do you want me to say?" Dean snapped back. "I finish school and start on what I think is my dream job —saving lives, making a difference—and now I'm - I'm… hell, I'm not sure what I'm doing!"

"You are saving lives and making a difference to people who don't need to be ostracized. You can apply for a transfer from the chief after this shift is done. For now you need to listen carefully to what I have to say or you're going to end up getting hurt. Worse, you could get me hurt." Brynne glared at him. "I need you to listen to me like you would any of your academy preceptors. On a call, do what I say, when I say it, without question. A lot of the folks we serve are a bit prickly about how the rest of society views them. We need to tread carefully. For you, that means stay right next to me and keep your mouth shut. When I ask for something from our kit or the back of the unit, you hop to it and get what I need. Got it?"

"Uh, yeah, I guess so," Dean replied. He looked out the window as the Elk City streetlights went by in the night, the overhead lights forming little pools of light surrounded by what he realized were too many shadows. Shadows that apparently really do have monsters hiding in them. He looked over at Brynne, "Tell me again just what happened back there. Clearly you've been to that house before and knew that guy."

"Bob is an okay guy," she began. "We didn't start to get calls to his house until recently. He and his wife are separated, and I think she used to help him treat his diabetes and keep his blood sugar levels even. Since she left we've been there a bunch of times to handle what dispatch alerts as an 'agitated subject'."

Brynne pulled the ambulance in to a strip mall parking lot and stopped in front of the Dollar Store. Putting the vehicle in park, she turned in her seat and looked at Dean. The overhead lights in the parking lot lit up the left side of her face. "Look, Dean, you must have some mad skills or you wouldn't have been assigned to this unit. You just need to take the stuff you know and apply it to a new situation. Unusuals are people just like us for the most part. Think of them as having a comorbid medical condition that affects the current problem they're having."

Dean felt a throb between his temples. He knew his first shift might be tough, but this was off the charts.

She continued, "In Bob's case, he's a lycan. He has a disorder that causes him to change form when he gets upset or loses control somehow. Most of the time lycans manage their whole lives without anyone knowing they're any different. The full moon thing is just a myth. It takes some medical condition or trauma to cause them to lose control and change. In Bob's case, we never went to see him before his marital situation changed. Now that his diabetes is out of control, he starts shifting the minute his sugar levels get low enough to affect his mental status. Normal people become anxious, agitated, sweaty, diaphoretic, and thirsty. Bob becomes a hungry wolf-man."

She stopped, the pause getting Dean's attention. He looked up from staring at his lap and peered at her, "But how am I supposed to know what to do for him?"

"What do you do for any diabetic with low blood sugar?" she asked. "What if you can't start an IV and give D-50? Then what do you do?"

"I give them glucagon intramuscularly, IM. The hormone makes the liver release sugar stores into the blood and…"

"…and gets him the higher blood sugar level needed to reverse the shift to wolf-man," Brynne said, finishing his thought. "You do know this stuff."

She turned back to the front and shifted the ambulance back into gear, then pulled out of the parking lot and onto Route 40. "Nobody gets sent to this station if they're an idiot. We don't need 'cookie-cutter' medics here who can only follow protocols. There are no specific protocols for Unusuals. What we need are true medical professionals who can apply what they know critically to a given situation and improvise when needed. Someone must've seen that in you or you wouldn't have been sent to Station U."

Dean fell into his own thoughts and looked ahead as they crossed through the green light at an intersection. "That seemed awfully dangerous back there. What about the old EMS mantra of 'scene safety' first and foremost?"

Brynne chuckled, "Well there are two answers to that. First, no scene is ever really safe. What that mantra means is to be aware of potential dangers and proceed as safely as you are able…" She held up her right hand to forestall his objection. "…within reason. I know there are situations that require us to call for special assistance before proceeding to the scene. For Unusuals, well, let's just say that the police have their own version of 'Station U.' Actually, we don't call them that often, which brings us to the second answer." She turned into an industrial park and headed back toward the last building. "Remember that extra set of vaccinations you got after you completed your class?"

"The Hepatitis B and tetanus boosters?"

"Those weren't Hep B or tetanus shots. At least that's not all they were. You got zapped with an experimental batch of the latest in Unusual prevention vaccines. Didn't you read the fine print in the release they had you sign?"

"Uh, no? Why?" he replied. "You mean they snuck them in without making me aware of what they were giving me? That's malpractice!"

"Possibly. No, probably," Brynne corrected herself. "I've been told it's covered under some Homeland Security thing. Anyway, if you'd read the whole release before you got your shot you would have realized you were opting in to 'additional vaccinations as required to perform your duties.'"

She shrugged. "I've never known anyone to have a negative reaction and I have seen what can happen to someone who gets exposed without them. All in all, you are better off with them." She turned the wheel as she pulled up in front of the bay doors at their station. "Hop out and back me in."

Dean popped his seatbelt off and jumped out, walking around to stand in the ambulance bay doorway as the garage door started to go up. She pulled the ambulance up, lining up the back end so she had a straight shot to back in. Dean saw her looking for him in her driver's side mirror. He checked behind himself and then slowly walked backward, directing her into the bay.

Brynne shut the unit down, jumped out and plugged the ambulance in to the shore line power plug hanging from the ceiling. Dean waited, then asked. "What next, boss?"

"We need to replace the glucagon we used, then write up our run report," she answered. "Let me show you how we get our drugs out of the provisioning machine in the back. It's kind of like a giant snack machine but instead of food, it dispenses medications."

She led him up to a big metal box with windows and doors in it. "Any medication we use is kept stocked in here. If it needs refrigeration or climate control, it's on this side." She gestured to the left side of the box with small, separate, windowed doors. "If it's stable at room temperature, it's on this side." She pointed to the right side of the machine. Dean saw familiar meds: epinephrine, atropine, bicarb.

Brynne pulled her photo ID badge off her uniform and swiped it in the machine, then entered a four digit code. "When we get you in the system, and you have your ID badge, you'll be able to do this, too. It automatically keys the med dispensed to your ID in the computer. When you start a patient care report you can pull up meds used and replenished."

She selected a letter-number combination and after a few seconds, a thump was heard at the bottom of the box. She reached down into an open bin in the bottom of the dispenser and pulled out a new dose of pre-constituted glucagon. "Go put this back in the med bag where you got the original dose, then meet me back in the squad room. I'll get started on the report."

Dean climbed into the back of the parked ambulance and looked around. It sure looked like a regular ambulance, he thought. He pulled the med bag out of its cabinet and replaced the boxed dose of glucagon. Turning off the interior light, he climbed out of the back of the rig and shut the doors.

"What have I gotten myself into?" he muttered to himself.

Dean thought back to the ceremonies for his paramedic class just a few days before. The Elk City EMS Academy class of new paramedics stood at the front of the room. They all looked out at their families and friends who watched as each of them was recognized for their achievements over the last two years. The program was an Associate's Degree program that culminated in the students testing for the National Registry Paramedic (NRP) certification. That certification, coupled with the passing of the Maryland State EMS protocols test, made them a licensed paramedic.

The group of forty-five had once been a group of seventy-eight. The rigorous testing and course load winnowed that down pretty quickly. They had completed hundreds of hours of clinical time including airway management and intubation practice on both cadavers at the state university medical school and time in the operating room assisting anesthesiologists with their patients.

They'd ridden on the road alongside experienced paramedics, learning the art and craft of caring for injured and ill people in unusual situations. It was often said that anyone could manage a difficult airway in a well-lit operating room or start an IV line in a vein with a patient stationary on a cot in the ER. It took a true artist to do that kind of work upside down in a ditch on the side of the highway at night. That was the life of the paramedic.

Dean Flynn had worked hard alongside his classmates with that one goal in mind. He stood a little apart from the others in the group. He had always wanted to be the best, not just good, but the best paramedic in the academy. That drive had put some distance between himself and his classmates as he expected the same drive from them, too. Most of them considered him aloof at best.

Dean had always wanted to be a paramedic. Ever since his own tumultuous ride in the back of an ambulance following a car accident at sixteen, he'd known this was what he wanted to do. He'd watched from the ambulance's front passenger seat as his girlfriend's life was saved, as that quick thinking, fast acting paramedic, worked his magic in the back of an ambulance speeding to the trauma center. Now all the hard work, the long hours studying, the working alongside real paramedics with street smarts was about to pay off.

Dean had heard that the top of each class got to pick their first assignment in the city. He'd thought long and hard about where he wanted to be. There was Station 1, located in the center of downtown. He'd get his share of high energy calls, with shootings, stabbings and other exciting trauma calls to keep him busy between the boring medical runs for the diabetics and asthma patients. He'd thought about picking one of the two stations near I-95 where it went through town. They got some pretty terrific car accidents there, which would test his skills and problem-solving abilities as he tried to extricate the victims from the twisted wreckage.

He was sure of one thing. He didn't want one of the outlying stations in suburban areas, where they were working on implementing some community paramedic and integrated health programs. These paramedics made house calls and didn't even get to transport most of their patients to the hospital. He'd done his rotations there and learned the importance of helping patients with chronic disease and minor problems stay out of the hospital. He knew that these stations were part of the new health care reform that was shifting high health care costs to the savings of prevention, but where was the fun in that? There was no glory in helping a diabetic patient keep his blood sugar even from day to day, was there?

Dean looked out at the crowd from the stage in the auditorium where he and all his classmates were lined up. They wore their light blue uniform shirts and navy cargo pants with the pockets for all the gear they would carry. He was average height at 5' 11" with short brown hair. He was thin and thought he looked good in his new uniform. He prided himself on being pretty fit, though not as muscle-bound as his classmate Jeff Jones. Jeff looked as if he could lift a car off a trapped patient all by himself. Dean had achieved his goal of being first in his class, getting top marks not only in his National Registry test but also on his grade point average and his clinical rotation scores. Even in the boring parts, like the community paramedic stations, he'd paid attention and tried to learn something from the medics he figured had washed up there at the end of their careers.

The Elk City deputy fire chief, who was chief of EMS, was now standing up and addressing the group of paramedics. He was talking about their call to serve the community, congratulating the family members and guests of the class for their support during their studies. Dean didn't have anyone out there in the crowd, so he didn't care what the chief had to say about support. He'd done this on his own, and he was proud of it. His mother had wished him luck but was disappointed in him not going to regular college to find what she thought of as a real job. His father, well, he was never around enough to say anything worthwhile or supportive anyway. Dean was standing there waiting for the chief to finish so the reception could begin, and they could all find out where their assignments would be. He'd ended up requesting Station 1 downtown because that was where he'd get the best calls and all the good trauma patients.

Deputy Chief Decker wound down the speech. He turned to look at the row of newly minted paramedics standing behind him and asked the crowd to give them a round of applause for their choice to be servants to their community. The applause was enthusiastic since this was the end of the ceremony. A few of the folks out in the audience even whistled and cheered. Then Dean was walking off the stage in a line with his classmates and into the reception in the cafeteria and student lounge. He chatted with a few of his classmates. Jill Manning told him she was hoping to get assigned to one of the community paramedic shifts and he wasn't surprised. Everyone knew that she eventually wanted to continue her education in healthcare and become a nurse practitioner someday. It suited her. She'd never really bought into the adrenaline rush that most of them wanted in this business of emergency medical services (EMS).

Dean wandered around, making small talk with the few people who would talk with him. He filled up his cup with some more punch from the refreshment table. His primary instructor, Mike Farver moved around the room with a collection of big manilla envelopes, talking to each of the students in turn and handing them one. Dean knew that in each envelope was their final scores and the badge they had earned to pin to their uniforms. That was the badge that said paramedic on it. The envelope also contained their new uniform patches and, most importantly, their new assignments and the name of their preceptor at the new stations. It was a formality in his case since everyone knew he'd picked Station 1 by now, and the top of the class always got their pick of assignment.

Mike was taking his time getting to Dean, though. He'd passed by and said hi when he first started handing out the envelopes but since then, the older paramedic instructor had not come over in Dean's direction. People and their families were starting to leave as the assignments were handed out, shaking hands or hugging each other before they left, wishing each other luck on their first days on the job next week.

At this point, Dean had pretty much figured he was going to be the last one who found out where he got assigned, and he was ok with that. Everyone else had people here to congratulate them and most were going out with family to congratulatory dinners and such. While he considered himself friendly with his classmates, he'd never gotten close with any of them and he didn't have anyone here to celebrate with anyway. The reception had pretty much wound down by the time Mike came over to Dean with the final manilla envelope. The deputy chief had left long ago, along with all of the other invited dignitaries. The catering crew was starting to clean up the tables and mess.

"Took you long enough," Dean said with a smile as Mike made his way over to him with his assignment. "I would have thought that I would get to go first."

Mike stepped over and shook his hand. "'The last shall be first, and the first shall be last,' my friend," he said smiling. "I wanted to have a few words with you in relative privacy before you got your assignment. You've been the brightest of my students in a long time, Dean. You've studied the hardest. You have a good handle on skills, and you're one of the best intuitive problem solvers I've ever seen. I want you to know that it's been a pleasure teaching and watching you grow into a fine paramedic these past few years."

He handed Dean the envelope. Dean could feel the extra bulk as he took it. The badge and patch were pushing the envelope out in places. Mike continued, "I just wanted you to know as you head off to this first assignment, you got picked for it because you're one of the best to come through the academy in a while." Mike put his hand on Dean's shoulder. "This is not what you expected, Dean, but it suits your unique skills and talents. Remember to keep an open mind and stay safe out there. You've got the skills to do this job the way it needs to be done." And then he shook Dean's hand again and walked away, grabbing his uniform coat and heading out the door to the parking lot.

Well, that was weird, Dean thought as he flipped the metal tabs on the manilla envelope and lifted up the flap to look inside. He reached in and slid out a stack of papers along with his patch and badge balanced on top. He sat down at one of the tables as the caterers continued to clean up around him, looking briefly at the silver badge that said paramedic on it. The patch looked a little different than expected which was weird. He thought all the Elk City paramedic patches were the same. It said EMS-U at the top, had a star of life in the middle and Paramedic at the bottom. There was a certificate of completion. His diploma for an associate's degree in applied science as a paramedic was in there along with another white sealed envelope with the Elk City letterhead on it. He quickly opened this one, tearing the sealed flap with his finger, careful to avoid a paper cut, and pulled out the paper inside. He unfolded it and read the letter.

"Dean Flynn, congratulations on your achievement and graduation from the city college paramedic program. This is your letter of acceptance to employment as a paramedic for Elk City and pending the receipt of your state paramedic license, will act as your proof of licensure. Please report on Monday morning June 2 to Station U …"

"Station U?" Dean muttered under his breath, his shoulders sagging a bit with disappointment. "Where the hell is Station U?"

TWO DAYS LATER, Dean had been driving around the outskirts of town as his phone's GPS took him to his new work assignment. He looked a little startled when the sedate woman's voice on his phone told him to turn left off of Route 40 into a rundown industrial park. "What kind of EMS station was in a dump like this?" he wondered aloud to himself. The directions took him to the very back of the industrial park, past buildings and warehouses, to the last parking lot on the right. He turned in as he saw the small sign on the metal siding that read "Paramedic Station U."

Dean drove his beat-up white Ford Ranger pickup into the lot and parked. There was only one other car in the lot, a small silver Nissan sedan. He glanced at his watch. Damn, he was late. He jumped out of the truck, quickly checking his reflection in the driver's side window as he shut the door. Dean wanted to make a good impression on his preceptor, whoever they were. Maybe he could work his way out of this backwater station and into something more exciting. He still didn't know what he had done that netted him this assignment.

He turned and walked up to the steel entry door. It had a vertical rectangular slotted window in it, and he tried to peek inside as he turned the knob. He walked tentatively into the squad room for the first time at Station U. Dean looked at the small woman behind the desk at the computer and said, "Hi, I'm Dean Flynn. I'm reporting for my first shift here."

Brynne looked up from the computer where she was working on a report and shook her head. "No freaking way."

Dean pulled a piece of paper out of his pocket and looked at it for second. "This is 'Station U' isn't it? It was a bit hard to find tucked away back here."

Brynne held up a finger and picked up her desk phone. She pushed a button on speed dial and waited while it rang. "Chief …" She waited while she listened to a response and got an angry look on her face. "Stop laughing, and what do you mean 'you knew it was me'?"

"I think I'm your new partner," Dean began, stopping at her upheld palm.

"So it's final?" she paused. "And I assume he doesn't know what we do?" There was another pause. "Chief, you owe me … again." Brynne hung up the phone. She sighed as she looked at Dean standing in the doorway. "Yes, you're my new partner," she said to him. "Sit down. We've got a few things to talk about."

# Chapter 2

He was still thinking about the events from earlier that night; of his first call with their unique patients, and meeting his new partner, as Dean walked back into the crew quarters.

Brynne glanced up from the computer screen and laughed out loud at the expression on Dean's face.

"How did you react when you saw your first real werewolf?" he retorted. "I didn't even know they existed for until now!"

"Oh, pretty much the same," she said with a chuckle. "You have to start thinking about them as any other patient. Most of these people just want to blend in with the rest of us and live out their lives despite their unusual situations and living conditions."

"If you say so," Dean responded.

"I do say so, and for the time being, that's going to be what you have to go on," Brynne said. "Look, despite what I said earlier, I don't intend for you to be a robot who follows me around and blindly does whatever I say. Sure, there will be some of that at first as you get used to what we're doing. You have to listen to me when it comes to patient care because there's much you don't know, and it's to ensure our safety. But we're going to be a team. So if an idea, no matter how hair-brained, comes up during a call, let me know. Just be ready to do a little thinking outside of the box." She turned back to the computer screen. "Let me finish up this report, and then I'll give you a chance to read it before I send it off to headquarters. Okay?"

"Okay," Dean said. He turned and headed over to the couch in the corner by the flat screen TV mounted on the wall. A bookshelf below it held the usual textbooks he might have seen in any EMS station around the country. There was an older edition of the same anatomy and physiology text he had used in paramedic school, along with a series of paramedic care textbooks. He also saw a lot of paperback novels and two different hardcover versions of what appeared to be Grimm's Fairy Tales.

"What's with the children's books?" He asked.

"Huh?" Brynne muttered, looking up from the screen. "Oh, those. Consider them patient research tools. Not everything in them is accurate, but a lot of the quirkier stuff is. It seems people have known about the Unusuals living among us for years, and that knowledge has made it into popular culture. The same goes for all the fantasy and sci-fi novels on the shelf. If you aren't already a fan, you might want to start reading some of them to get a handle on the type of things we may deal with on this job."

"Uh, okay?" Dean said. "What about movies? Are they any good for research? I'm not much of a reader."

"Some are, some not so much," she replied as she spun around in her office chair and got up. "It seems that, lately, Hollywood has been playing fast and loose with the standard legends and are coming up with their own variations. The Twilight movies are a good example of that. Some would say that Bella has ruined vampires for the rest of us."

Dean just stared at her. "Wait. There are vampires?"

"Yep and some of them would like to have a word or two with Stephenie Meyer, believe me," Brynne chuckled. "Look, Dean, calm down. Nothing's going to happen to you. They're just people. A little different, sure, but people none the less."

"If you say so," Dean said, picking up one of the hardcover Grimm's Fairy Tale books and starting to leaf through it. He shook his head. This was going to take some getting used to. "Do we ever go on calls with normal people?"

"Only if there's a mass casualty situation somewhere in the district. Then we're on call for anything until the MCI is dealt with. Most of the time we are only on call for Unusuals. We're the only EMS-U team in the city. We only get three or four calls in the course of a normal shift. That ebbs and flows of course. Some days there's nothing, and others we're running our butts off."

Brynne pointed to a doorway off the main squad room. "Back down that hallway are the bathroom and bunkroom. If you're on duty, you're allowed to grab some sleep. Believe me, the overhead alarm will wake you up with no problem if there's a call. We work twelve-hour shifts on the sixes for which I'm glad. Working twenty-four-hour shifts like they do in some EMS systems is just asking for trouble with medication errors and fatigue-based mistakes." She pointed over to the first computer of the two at the desk. "Take a look at the report and let me know what you think."

Dean rose and went over to sit in the black swivel chair. After a few minutes reading, he turned to Brynne. "There's no mention of his being a werewolf at all."

"Of course not," Brynne said. "If we started putting all that stuff in our reports, they'd lock us up! These reports are part of the medical record and can be queried by the courts. Official knowledge of the presence of Unusuals in society is highly compartmentalized. There are government sub-committees and certain judges who are in on it in case there is a need for a legal remedy. There are also docs at the hospital who know about it in case we need to take someone in, but for our so-called 'public reports', we write it up in strictly medical terms."

She pointed to the screen. "Click the EMS-U tab at the top of the report window." Dean did so and looked at the series of check boxes and drop-down menus as well as a short narrative section. Brynne continued. "That's where we put the Unusual information from our call. In this case, I selected 'lycan-Wolf' from the drop-down menu. That's it. Everything else can be written or marked in the regular electronic report. We responded to a call for a diabetic patient with altered mental status. The patient was agitated, and while physically restraining him, we administered glucagon IM to treat the problem. The patient signed a transport refusal, and we returned to the station. It's simple as that. We usually don't even stray from protocol very far, if at all."

Dean turned and looked up at Brynne as she stood behind him. "About that, I thought we were under the same protocols as the rest of the district units."

"We are," she said. "It's just that the medical director - who is, by the way, in on the secret - has given us permission to step outside of protocol for normal humans when necessary. We can call for a medical consult if we need it. If we do venture outside of protocol, we'd better have a good reason, and we have to document it in the EMS-U tab." Brynne smiled reassuringly. "Don't worry. It doesn't happen that often."

"Should I assume the 'U' in 'EMS-U' stands for 'Unusual'?" Dean asked.

"Yes," Brynne replied. "We're officially in the Emergency Medical Services - Unusual Division."

She walked over to the other side of the long desk, slid open a drawer and pulled out what looked like a squirt bottle of blue or black ink, a stencil and small paint roller. "I didn't get a chance to do this when you first got here since that call came in so quickly. Most Unusuals can see into the infrared and UV spectrums. Because of that, we mark ourselves so they can see that we are one of the good guys and they can let their guard down with us. This is a special UV/IR dye that is like permanent marker. It will be invisible to us unless we look under a backlight or with night vision goggles. It wears off after four days or so, so you'll have to do this again when you start each new shift rotation."

She squirted some of the dark ink on the small paint roller. "Hold out your hands, palm down." Dean hesitated. "Don't worry, this stuff is harmless. It's just like the stamps they use at nightclubs and amusement parks to mark you so you can come back in after you leave." He held out his hands as she had asked and she placed the stencil with the same shape as his shoulder patch on the back of his right hand. She rolled the ink over the stencil. It felt cold to the touch. The ink was dark blue at first but faded as it dried.

"So you do this every four days?" He asked.

"Most of us opt for the permanent alternative," she said as she returned the ink, stencil and roller to the desk drawer and returned with what looked like a standard flashlight. She clicked it on and shined the purplish glow of a black light on his hands. He could see the stencil outlined on the backs of his hands in a faint blue color. It disappeared when she took the light away. She shined the black light on the back of her left hand. Dean saw the same outline as his but the lines looked thicker and more substantial. "This is a tattoo you can get if you want. It's done at a special place where Unusuals get their ink. I'd wait until you think you'll last here, though. This job's not for everyone."

She put the light back in the drawer with the rest of the stencil supplies and closed it. "Let me finish up my run report and send it off to HQ. You can go out and start washing the bugs off the ambulance. There's soap, sponges and a bucket in the metal cabinet between the med dispenser and the sink." Dean got up and Brynne sat down at the computer again.

"And make sure you do a good job. The chief likes us to keep the units clean, inside and out!"

WHEN DEAN RETURNED from washing the ambulance, there was someone else in the squad room. He was about six feet tall, dark-haired and dressed all in black with black jeans, shirt and a black blazer.

"Dean this is my friend James," she said. "He dropped by to say 'hi.'"

James extended his hand and Dean took it in a firm grip. The hipster's hand was cold despite the warm temperature outside and in the office. He was struck by the intensity of the man's gaze. "It's a pleasure to meet you, Dean," James intoned with a slight southern drawl. "I hope Brynne has been nice to you on your first day. I know she has a habit of snapping at people, especially in tense situations."

"Uh, she's been great." Dean said. "First days on the job are always a bit tense, right? She's showing me the ropes."

"Oh, she likes ropes." James said with a laugh, dodging as Brynne launched a semi playful punch at his midsection.

"Hey," she said. "I have to work with this guy."

"Sorry my darling," James said. "I was just making a joke. Maybe all that experience with knots is because you dated a boy scout when you were younger."

Brynne laughed. "Like I would ever be caught dead dating a boy scout."

"True," James responded. "They're not your type, are they?"

Brynne dropped a few ice cubes in the cup and poured in a diet soda. She looked up at Dean, "Did you finish cleaning the unit?"

"Yes, I also put the stuff away in the cabinet and shut the bay door." Dean said. "Is there anything else that needs doing right now?"

"Not really," she said. "We've got the rest of the shift to pick up the squad room, vacuum and make sure the bunks are made up with fresh sheets. Why don't you take some time and do some research - watch one of the DVDs on the TV or do some reading? I'm going to walk James out. I'll be back in a minute."

"Ok," Dean said. "It was a pleasure meeting you, James."

"Oh, the pleasure was all mine." James said with what might be called a grin. "Brynne so loves breaking in new guys. I'm sure I'll hear all about it when I see her next. We'll no doubt meet again. Until then…"

"Sure," Dean said, "I guess I'll see you sometime soon." He watched the strange guy turn and gracefully leave the room. He'd always thought hipsters were a bit strange, but this guy had weird written all over him.

Dean heard the door close as the two of them went outside. He picked up one of the Grimm's Fairy Tale books and sat in the recliner. It looked 50 years old - maybe older - but was well taken care of.

He started to leaf through the pages and noticed there were handwritten notes in the margins. They were in different colored blue and black inks and the variation in the handwriting suggested they had been written by multiple people. There were comments like 'Clearly Mister Grimm never dated a witch,' or 'Don't turn your back on a vampire, ever!' He put the book down and looked at others on the bookshelf. There was Greek and Roman mythology, stories from India and the Far East, and several copies of Bram Stoker's Dracula. There was even a book on Native American folk tales. "What have I gotten myself into?" he said quietly to himself. That was becoming his mantra.

He looked up as the outside door opened and Brynne came back in. She nodded. "You're doing some research, I see."

"It's easy with all this material," Dean answered. "But I don't know the best place to begin. I never realized how many different stories and cultural tales there are out there."

"Just start with one and work your way to the next," she said. "You just pick a starting point. Some books you will like more than others. Don't forget to devote time to reviewing your medical stuff, too. It's also important. With you just out of school most of that stuff is still pretty fresh, but you're a professional now, and staying current is your responsibility."

"That's what my instructor used to say," Dean said.

"Who'd you have?" Brynne asked.

"Mike Farver," Dean answered. "Do you know him?"

"You might say that," Brynne chuckled. "He was my first preceptor here at Station-U before he moved on to the Academy. I should have figured he would have had something to do with sending me a rookie to break in."

"He told me to keep an open mind and listen to you."

"Well, I guess you'd better then," Brynne said. "I'm going into the bunkroom to catch a little sleep. The doors are locked. Make sure you leave the lights on if you decide to bunk out for a while, too. They're on motion sensors so they'll shut off on their own."

Dean watched her as she headed down the hallway to the bunkroom, then turned back to the bookshelf. Peering at one of the copies of Dracula, a dark-haired, pale-faced man with fangs looked back at him from the cover. It reminded him of the guy who was, apparently, his partner's boyfriend. He leaned back in the recliner and began to read the story he'd always thought of as fiction. Perhaps not.

Chapter 3

The remainder of that first night was uneventful and Dean eventually fell asleep reading the Bram Stoker novel. He was awakened by the sound of Brynne's voice from across the squad room. He jerked his head up, quickly wiping some drool from the corner of his mouth.

"Wake up probie," she said. "Man, I'm glad you didn't come back to the bunkrooms. I would have heard you through the walls. You snore like a freight train." She was seated at the computer in one of the swivel chairs. "The guys from the next shift will be here soon. Run out to the ambulance bay and make sure everything is straightened up in the back of the unit. I know we didn't have any calls after that first one, but it's always a good idea to leave the station in the condition you'd want it left for you."

"Got it," Dean said, jumping up. He stretched briefly then headed out to the bay after a quick bathroom break to throw some water on his face. Everything looked just as he'd left it, but he found a soda can in the cup holder of the cab. He dumped the contents out in the sink and put the can in the recycling bin. In the back of the ambulance he emptied the trash and put a fresh red hazmat bag in the can and replaced it.

He closed the doors to the ambulance, washed his hands, and walked back to the squad room door. He heard voices as he opened it. Walking in, he saw two paramedics named Bill and Lynne. They were chatting with Brynne. Bill was about five foot ten, balding and a little thick around the middle. He also looked to be around fifty years old – older than most people in this profession.

"I see you didn't break the new guy, Brynne," Bill said as Dean walked in.

"He's not a complete incompetent," Brynne said with a grin. "Mike sent him to us, so he's got some promise."

Lynne, seated in one of the two desk chairs, pulled off her glasses, and pushed a lock of curly blonde hair out of her face. It was clear to Dean she was at least fifteen years younger than her partner. She folded the newspaper she had been reading. "How is old Mike these days? He was one of the first EMS-U medics in Elk City you know."

"He's fine, I guess," Dean said with a shrug. "He was our primary instructor in the paramedic program. I always enjoyed his lectures. Listening to him was easy because he made the information seem real. He always had a story to go with the material and that helped us make sense of what we were supposed to be learning."

"It's too bad there were so many stories he couldn't tell," Brynne said with a conspiratorial grin.

"So true," Lynne agreed.

"Well, if he sent you to us, we should at least give you the benefit of the doubt," Bill said. "He pioneered this program with Doc Spirelli years ago. Until then, the Unusuals had to take care of themselves and make do with back alley medicine. The powers-that-be have always known about them, but didn't care to provide any kind of special services. Doc Spirelli over at Elk City Medical Center changed that when he started up this unit with Mike."

"Did Mike run the calls all by himself at first?" Dean asked.

"In the beginning, yes," Bill replied. "He had a chase car. Word got out quickly with the Unusuals that there were people in the medical community who felt they had a right to equal care and wouldn't out them. After about a year, Doc got funding from somewhere to put a full time "special needs" ambulance on the street. Now, there are six of us in the full-time rotation and about four more who pull some shifts part-time to fill in as needed."

Lynne jumped in. "When are you going to retire, Bill? You've been doing this almost as long as Mike has."

"I don't know," Bill said. "I guess I'll stop when I feel like I can't make a difference anymore. I like the work, I like the patients, and I like helping people. Hell, there are worse ways you can spend your time."

"Anything interesting last night?" Lynne asked. "Anything we need to be aware of?"

"Bob Jackson had another diabetic lycan episode last night," Brynne said shaking her head.

"What's that, the third or fourth time this month?" Lynne asked.

"Fourth, I think," Bill said. He looked at Dean. "Well, that's a good way to see what we deal with, eh?"

"It was certainly eye opening," Dean said. "I wasn't sure who – or what – Brynne was struggling with at first. As if the first shift isn't disconcerting enough ...."

"You should've seen him fumbling with the glucagon," Brynne said, laughing. "I'm wrestling this slobbering, drooling lycan in mid-change and he's shaking like a leaf in a January wind trying to get the needle on the syringe. It was priceless."

Bill clapped the newbie on the shoulder. "You'll figure it out, kid. You should've seen Brynne on her first call. She couldn't talk for a half hour afterward. She just kept saying 'They're real! All of them, they're real'." Bill laughed. "She'd just found out that not only were her childhood nightmares real, but now those creatures of the night were her patients." He nodded toward Brynne. "Look at her now. This is all second nature to her. Dean, you would be wise to follow her lead. Brynne has the intuition it takes to do this job, and I would guess you do too."

"I'll do the best I can," Dean said. "At least I know it won't be routine."

"All right," Brynne said. "That's enough. I don't need you guys telling my probie any more stories about me or artificially inflating his opinion of me. I can do that by myself. Come on Dean, I'll walk you out so these two won't keep you here all day. We have to be back in twelve."

Dean waved goodbye and followed Brynne out to the parking lot. The morning sun was just coming up over the warehouses and buildings surrounding them. She headed to her car, pulling her keys out of her purse as she went. "See you tonight, Dean," she said over her shoulder as she pressed the remote to unlock the doors. "You got lucky last night. It's not usually that quiet. I expect we'll be busier tonight. Make sure you are here a few minutes early so we can make sure Bill and Lynne can leave on time." He heard the engine of the little silver Nissan sedan fire up.

Dean got in his pickup and caught the image of his eyes in the rearview mirror. He stared back at his reflection and just shook his head. What had he gotten himself into – or more appropriately, what had Mike gotten him into? As odd as this all seemed, part of him realized it was a compliment being chosen for this unique position. What had Bill said about intuition? He sighed. It was his growly stomach rather than his intuition that told him he hadn't eaten in over twelve hours.

He stopped to pick up a box of donuts at the mini-mart around the corner from his apartment. It was a routine morning as people got their coffee and paid for gas at the counter. That's when he realized that last night changed how he saw the world. Were any of the people Unusuals? How would he even know? He looked up at a pretty young woman in her twenties staring at him. Actually, she was staring at the hand clutching the box of donuts. She smiled, brushed her long brunette hair away from her eyes, nodded, then turned and left. He watched her get into her red sports car by the gas pumps and pull away.

The clerk called him with a level of impatience in her voice that suggested he didn't hear her call him the first time. He snapped his head around and muttered an apology as he put the box of donuts on the counter to be scanned. As he did, he looked at his hand. Of course. The young woman could see the stenciled stamp that

Brynne had put there last night. He had just met an Unusual. He quickly paid the clerk for the donuts and headed out to his pickup, suddenly self-conscious of the invisible marks on his hand. He looked around as he walked to his truck. Who else was around him that could see the mark? What kind of creatures were they? The world was suddenly a very different place.

Dean climbed back into his truck and drove around the block to his apartment. Parking on the street, he headed up the outside stairs of a detached garage next to a single-family home on a side street. His place was above the garage owned by Mr. and Mrs. Baxter, a nice retired couple. They liked having a paramedic living on the premises. He also got a break on rent for doing odd jobs around the place for them. That reminded him, he needed to mow the lawn in the next day or so.

He unlocked the door at the top of the stairs and went inside. At least home was the same, he thought to himself. Unless there was a ghost lurking around somewhere, he was alone with his thoughts. He put the TV on the morning news to catch up on what was happening around Elk City. He sat on the sofa, kicked off his shoes and put his feet up on the battered coffee table. Grabbing a glazed donut out of the box, he zoned out to the familiar voice of the female news anchor droning on about something or other.

He'd become a paramedic to get into the action. Based on the single call of the first night with Brynne, he knew he was in for some unique encounters. Maybe his patients wouldn't be the typical gunshot victims seen by crews in other central city stations, but he couldn't help but be intrigued by the population of patients he would be seeing. He had always liked a challenge and there was certainly a challenge in dealing with patients out of myth and legend. He rubbed absently at the back of his hand where his invisible stamp was located. His grandmother had always said to be careful what you wish for. You might just get it. He dozed off thinking about her prophetic words.

Chapter 4

The next two nights were busy for Dean and Brynne, but, if he didn't know his patients were Unusuals it wouldn't have been obvious. They had chest pains, stomach upsets, and minor bumps and bruises from motor vehicle accidents. One call stood out as two vampires fought over a girl, but the end result of bruises and cuts that needed bandaging was very routine.

Brynne had him doing the reports by the end of the second night, and he liked writing the narratives. It gave him a chance to get some perspective on what he was doing. One thing he noticed though was that none of the patients wanted to go to the hospital. Even the chest pain patient, who Brynne said was a Rakshasi, a sort of magical creature from India, didn't want to be transported. They ran her through the heart monitor routine, checked her twelve-lead ECG for ST elevation and used the i-Stat portable labs to run the blood work. When it came back negative for troponin levels, Brynne told her to call her doctor in the morning and call them back that night if it happened again.

The question was on Dean's mind when they returned to the station. "Brynne, what's up with us not taking any of these patients

35

to the hospital? I mean I get that they're different but why? Are they so supernatural they can heal themselves?"

"Most of the people who call 911, even the Unusuals, don't need to go to the ER. They just need someone to tell them whether their emergency is really an emergency or if it can wait until they see their doctor the next day." Brynne pointed to the screen where he was working on the Rakshasi's report. "In this case, I would have liked to have taken her in but most Unusuals distrust the hospital. They have a real fear of what might happen to them if they get in there and their "Unusual" talents are discovered. It's not too much of a stretch to think about how they might end up becoming some doctoral student's science project. They all have stories about the secret government labs that are used to cut up Unusuals and see what makes them what they are. It may not be happening anymore, but I'd bet it has happened in the past, somewhere."

"We have to balance that fear with whether they need to go in or not. There is also the need to notify the hospital ahead of time so that the nurse and doctor assigned to them would keep their status in confidence."

"I guess that makes sense", Dean said.

Brynne continued. "There are always at least one doctor and one nurse on duty at ECMC who are part of our team. There is a list of other trusted people from medical specialists to imaging and lab techs who are called in to treat an Unusual. The patients get a private room that's fairly isolated in case something weird happens like one of Bill's diabetic episodes." Dean nodded as he envisioned Bill running down the hallway half-man and half-wolf. Not pretty. "They go to great pains to cover for an Unusual so they are kept safe and the rest of the hospital population doesn't feel threatened."

Dean swiveled around in his chair. "So what do we do when we know they need to go?" he asked.

"Doc Spirelli's cell phone is programmed into the dispatch system, and I have it in my cell phone too. The Unusuals respect and trust him. Generally, if he tells them they have to go in, they listen – but not always. Ultimately, it's their decision just like anyone else."

Dean nodded. It was the same answer his preceptors gave him when he asked about how to convince a reluctant patient to go to the hospital. Any patient ultimately had the right to make their own health decisions – Unusual or not. It was up to the paramedic to make sure they were fully informed about the possible consequences to their decision.

Dean went back to the chart he was working on, pulled up the i-Stat blood work that was automatically uploaded to the unit in the ambulance and added it to the patient's chart. He had to admit that the technology was pretty cool here. The tech was even better here than the standard units in the city. Brynne said it was because of the grant funding for the "Unusual unit". Everything was automated to make patient charting easier. There was an iPad tablet in the back of the ambulance to keep the patient chart on when on the scene. The heart monitor and other electronic gear all reported and connected to the system as well. Ironic that a station stuck in the back fringes of an industrial park was the best funded in the city. He put the finishing touches on the narrative, "painting a picture of the call" as Mike had told him in the academy.

He was just getting ready to turn it over to Brynne to read when the tones dropped. He listened as the radio's speaker alerted automatically and the dispatcher's voice was clearly heard. "Medical box U-843. Allergic Reaction. 634 Bridge Road." Simultaneously, the printer next to the desk printed out a sheet of paper with the call information, address and box number.

The box number related to the old system when they had fire department call boxes around the city that would call into the local fire station when pulled. The fire department would respond to that particular box and then would follow the person there to the emergency or, in some cases, follow the smoke to the fire. Now the boxes were a reference to the specific geographic area of the city. Once you got to know the numbers, you could get a general idea of where you were headed while your partner programmed the GPS to get a more specific location.

Dean closed the screen and hopped up, heading to the door to the ambulance bay, which Brynne was holding open for him. She jumped in the driver's seat as he walked around to the passenger side. The garage door of the bay was already on its way up as he climbed in. He glanced at his watch - 5:30 AM. Damn, they were almost done with the shift and he was tired, but duty called. As Brynne pulled the ambulance out into the parking lot, he picked up the radio's microphone and keyed the mic saying, "U-191 responding."

"U-191 responding" the dispatcher parroted. "Switch to med channel 1 for additional."

Dean switched the radio frequency to the correct channel. While the initial dispatch was on an open channel, all calls were then routed to a secure, trunked radio channel for the rest of the call. He keyed the mic after double-checking the correct frequency. "U-191 on med channel 1."

The dispatcher came up immediately. "U-191, respond for a male subject in the parking lot of the Jiffy Mart complaining of a severe allergic reaction, unknown cause. The patient will be seated in a gold minivan."

"U-191 copies," Dean responded and hung up the mic on the dash. "Any idea what this one is, Boss?"

"Nope." she said. "I guess we'll see when we get there."

For 8 minutes, Dean watched the lights reflect off the windows of businesses and noticed the wailing sound of the siren at night had a mournful quality. He also noticed Brynne was a good driver, stopping at each red light or stop sign and acknowledging "due regard" for the safety of others before driving on through.

As they pulled in to the Jiffy Mart parking lot on Bridge Street, Dean scanned the area. Scene safety was the first responsibility, and while it was moderately busy with people coming in to get their morning coffee on the way to work, there was nothing out of the ordinary. He pointed to a gold minivan parked along the side of the building. The windows were tinted dark and in the early dawn light there was no way he could see if anyone was inside.

Brynne pulled the ambulance up beside the minivan as Dean keyed the mic and said, "U-191 on location."

Brynne put the unit in park and climbed out. Dean did the

same. As his feet hit the ground, a short, plump, middle-aged and shirtless white guy jumped out of the driver's door of the minivan and shrieked "Thank God you're here." He dashed to the side of the ambulance, opened the side door of the ambulance box and jumped in, shutting it behind him. Dean was too stunned to move. Brynne went to the back of the unit.

"Well, get the gear out probie!" she said. "Don't just stand there with your mouth open."

He gestured at the ambulance door. "No need to move the gear, the patient just loaded himself."

"What?" She crossed over to the ambulance's side door. Peering in the window on tip toe, she let out an exasperated sigh. "I didn't recognize the car, but I should've guessed." She peered at Dean. "Well climb on in. Let me introduce you to Gibbie. His name is Gibson Proctor. He may look middle aged, but he's a vampire who's been around more than six centuries." Dean grasped the door handle, quirked an eyebrow at Brynne, opened it and climbed in with his preceptor close behind. As Dean sat down in the captain's chair at the head of the cot, Brynne climbed in and sat in the bench facing the patient.

The patient had stripped off most of his clothes and appeared to be covered in some kind of glitter which was flying everywhere. The glitter decorated noticeable hives popping up all over his torso. Gibbie, as Brynne had called him, ripped open a ten pack of four by four gauze and began to wipe frantically at his skin. He looked up at Brynne and Dean. "Thank, God! Thank, God! Thank, God! Brynne, you've got to get this stuff off me. It's itching like crazy. It's killing me."

"I don't know about that," said Brynne looking him over. "Gibbie, calm down. Getting yourself all worked up is only going to make the reaction worse." She looked at Dean. "Get a bottle of sterile water out of the cabinet behind you. I'll get some more gauze. There should also be a few folded white towels in with the sheets and pillowcases for the cot. Get them, too." She turned back to their frantic patient. "Good Lord, Gibbie what is this stuff?"

Brynne said as she too, began to wipe the glittery cream off him as best she could.

"It's sunscreen, okay. I was trying to impress my new girlfriend. She's all into those old Twilight books, and I thought I could impress her by showing that I can sparkle in the sunshine, too." He started blubbering as he looked around. "Oh my God! We have to get out of here. She works night shift here at the Jiffy Mart and gets off at 6. I was going to surprise her by standing by her car as the sun came up. Sparkling the way she wants me to. Now it's all ruined!" He started sobbing and whimpering as he continued to swab at the glitter cream on his chest.

"Gibbie we can't do anything or go anywhere until we get this stuff off of you," Brynne said. She took the bottle of sterile water from Dean after he wet a white hand towel with it. She poured some into the plastic gauze packaging, grabbed a few with her gloved hand and began wiping Gibbie's chest off. The hives were getting worse which was making Gibbie start to scratch at his chest and arms.

"Okay, Probie, what's next?" She asked Dean as she continued to wipe down the patient. There was glitter everywhere. The ambulance was going to be a righteous bitch to clean later.

"Right," Dean said aloud. "Allergic reaction. Moderate to severe. 0.01 milligrams per kilogram of epinephrine, up to 0.5 milligrams max single dose. He's over 50 kilos so he gets the max single dose. Give 0.5 mg Epinephrine 1:1,000, intramuscularly?" His voice going up at the end of the statement as he looked at his preceptor quizzically.

"Yep," she responded. "Do it. And make sure you double check the dose." She continued to wipe at the frantically scratching vampire, trying to get as much of the allergen off his skin as possible.

Dean got the med bag out and unzipped the top. He swabbed the top of the medication vial with an alcohol prep, inserted the needle, and pulled the medication out of the vial. He then turned to the shirtless patient and swabbed his shoulder with another alcohol prep, glanced at the syringe barrel one more time then slowly injected the medication. Gibbie yelped a little. Dean drew out the syringe, snapped the safety cover across the needle and dropped the syringe in the sharps box next to him. Gibbie was already rubbing the injection spot so Dean didn't need to do that to help hasten absorption into the muscle.

Brynne's voice broke in to his concentration. "What's next?" she asked him. "Epi's on board but what else can you do or should you look for."

"Okay, right. Uh, sir," Dean turned to his patient. "Are you having trouble breathing? I mean, do you breathe? I'm not familiar with your background."

"Do I breathe?" the vampire said, astounded, his voice getting higher and more frantic with each word. "Do I breathe? Brynne, honey, what have you gotten me into here? You let this know-nothing cretin treat me?"

Dean flinched at the man's reaction but in his mind it was a valid question. Vampires actually are dead, aren't they?

"Calm down, Gibbie," she soothed. "It's only his second shift. He's on the right track and we got the important medicine in you. You should be feeling better soon." Brynne turned back to her partner. "Dean, to deal with the histamine release, causing the hives, what should you do now?"

"Oh, right," he said. "I need to get an IV started then administer 25 mg IV diphenhydramine." He glanced at the patient. "I should also consider albuterol/ipratropium inhaler via nebulizer for breathing difficulty, uh if there is any breathing difficulty."

He turned again and began to get out an IV solution bag and tubing. Pulling the tab on the bottom of the 1,000-milliliter bag of saline, he then pushed the hollow plastic spike on the end of the tubing into the exposed tube in the bottom of the bag. He pinched the drip chamber to fill it from the bag as he held it up. Brynne took the bag from him and slipped the hole in the top of the bag's flap over the metal hook in the ceiling. She stood up and offered him the other seat so he could get better access to start the IV line. Dean shifted to the offered seat, reached over and tied an elastic tourniquet just above Gibbie's elbow.

Brynne spoke up, "His veins are flatter than you're probably used to. Think 'dehydrated 80-year-old woman' and you'll get the right idea. You've got this Dean."

Dean started looking for a vein on the back of Gibbie's hand then worked his way up to the forearm using his eyes and gloved fingertips to palpate for a vessel. He thought he found one he could both see and feel as he lightly pressed down, sensing the spongy feeling of the vein. Wiping the area off with another alcohol prep, he reached over and, looking at the IV box, thought to himself, 'dehydrated 80-year-old woman,' huh?

Selecting the thinner 22 gauge IV needle he slid the cover off, hovering the tip briefly over the forearm, then at a slight angle slid the needle with the IV catheter into the arm. He watched the chamber at the base of the needle looking for the flash of blood that signified success, and was surprised to see dark red blood fill the small chamber. He hadn't been sure if vampires had blood in their veins or not. Now he knew. He pressed down on the arm just above the insertion point to stop blood from flowing out of the tubing as he withdrew the needle leaving the hollow plastic catheter in place inside the vein.

Brynne handed him the end of the IV tubing she had primed and he attached it to the end of the plastic catheter. He got the clear IV dressing that Brynne handed him and laid it down over the site where the IV catheter entered Gibbie's arm. Lastly, he assured the IV was running properly into the vein and not into surrounding tissue.

Satisfied, he looked up at Brynne. "Twenty-five milligrams IV diphenhydramine next, right?"

"Right, but what else do we need to do?" She asked. "I'll get the med drawn up for you. What else haven't we done yet? Think basics."

Dean thought for a moment before he came up with the answer, "Consider oxygen, IV's done, now monitor." Brynne nodded and he began to gather the electrode leads and sticky patch electrodes, attaching four of them to Gibbie's upper arms and ankles. Turning on the heart monitor, his own heart rate spiked when he saw the rhythm. Ventricular fibrillation, a lethal heart arrhythmia. Damn, he needed to shock this guy, except he was awake and talking to them. One of his instructor's famous phrases rolled through his mind. 'Treat the patient, not the monitor.' He looked over to see Brynne smiling at him.

"Vampires don't have pulses," she said. "That's why you see V-fib. Sure, in a normal human, it's a sign of cardiac arrest and one of two shockable rhythms. In a vampire, it's completely normal. I'm still not sure how their circulatory system works or how the blood moves around, but you should be able to run the diphenhydramine in and it will get where it needs to go."

Brynne finished drawing up twenty-five milligrams of diphenhydramine and handed the syringe to Dean. "That's twenty-five milligrams of diphenhydramine from a concentration of fifty milligrams per milliliter so you should have ..." she paused for him to finish.

He looked up from the monitor and the alarming heart rhythm. "Uh, right, so twenty-five milligrams of the drug is half an mL, right?"

"That's right," she nodded in agreement. "Remember, this is a slow IV push so take it easy."

Dean checked that there was half a milliliter in the syringe then screwed the syringe hub on to the port on the IV tubing and began to slowly depress the plunger. It seemed to take forever.

Brynne finished up wiping what glitter sunscreen she could from Gibbie's arms and torso. "I have to say, Gibbie, you have outdone yourself this time. This is a first even for you," she said with a smile. "Where'd you pick up this stuff?"

Dean perceived that vampires didn't blush, but Gibbie still looked embarrassed. "I found it in the back of a magazine for Cosplay folks. You know the folks who dress up like cartoon and manga characters?" He shifted as he tried to scratch an area on his shoulder he couldn't quite reach. "Brenda's such a fan of Twilight and was so excited that she found a real Vamp to date. I thought I'd treat her to her own sparkly hero boyfriend. I figured I'd be able to take the early sunshine and not get burned with the sunscreen on.

Then I could sparkle for her just like Edward." He shook his head. "This is embarrassing, Brynne. I can't wait for the Twilight thing to blow over. Every century it's something new. This Twilight phase is almost as bad as the 40's and 50's were when everyone was expecting us to have Bela Lugosi's Romanian accent. I got so tired of the whole 'I vant to suck your blood' thing, I thought I was going to scream."

"Well you should feel better soon but you're probably going to want to go into the hospital and get some steroids on board just in case that reaction is worse than it looks," Brynne said.

"No, I'll be alright," Gibbie said. "The itching's starting to feel better already. You know vampire constitution. I just need to get home and get some rest. I spent all night coming up with the perfect romantic touch and now it's all ruined. I just want to forget the whole thing."

There was a tap on the doors to the back of the ambulance. Dean looked at Brynne and his patient. The younger paramedic got up and opened one of the doors partway. A woman's voice from outside was heard.

"Is everything okay?" A woman's voice asked. "I just got off work and saw you here with your lights on next to my boyfriend's van."

"Brenda," Gibbie cried. "Don't come in, I don't want you to see me like this."

"Gibson, is that you?" Brenda stuck her head into the doorway, looking past Dean. "My dearest, what happened?" She pushed the door open and climbed in, rushing over to sit on the cot next to Gibbie. She looked from Dean to Brynne with raised eyebrows. "Is he alright?"

"It's nothing my love, just an allergic reaction to something," the vampire told her as he reached out to hold her hand. "I was being foolish."

She looked around at the glitter, coating everything in the back of the ambulance, and what little remained on her boyfriend. "Did you do this for me?"

Gibbie nodded sheepishly.

"How romantic," she said throwing her arms around him and showering him with kisses, oblivious to the awkwardness of the situation and the two onlookers. "You don't have to dress up to be my man, Gibson Proctor. I love you just the way you are." She looked at Brynne. "Is he okay now, can I take him home?"

"I think he'll survive," Brynne said. "There's some paperwork to fill out, but I think he's on the mend." She winked at Dean as the two lovebirds embraced.

DEAN AND BRYNNE watched the minivan drive away, followed by Brenda in her little hatchback. Brynne playfully punched Dean in the arm. "Well, that's part of your initiation done with at least," she said with a grin. "You've now met Gibbie."

"I take it we see him a lot?" Dean asked.

"Often enough," she answered turning to climb back in the unit and put things away. "Put us back in service and then come back here and help me get the rig in order. We've got to get this glitter cleaned up."

# Chapter 5

They returned to the station and signed off the shift. Dean headed home to his apartment, musing about his first week on the new job. He surprised himself by smiling with a sense of accomplishment, as he thought back over the week. The new paramedic had been sure he wasn't going to like his first assignment out of school.

Dean spent his three days off refreshing his knowledge base. Mike had always impressed on their paramedic class the need to continue learning after they graduated. He sure hadn't thought he'd need the refresher so quickly, though.

This wasn't actually a refresher since learning about the quirks and lore surrounding the populations of Unusuals was kind of new to him. Sure, he knew the big stuff that everyone knew like how vampires can't be out in the daytime and werewolves shift on the full moon, which wasn't true. Brynne, though, had told him to focus on the little details in the books that weren't such common knowledge. It was that little-known information that might be the clue to figuring out a medical issue or how to treat a specific kind of Unusual in the field.

Dean sat with his laptop and began to search the net to see what classic horror films there were. Brynne had told him to concentrate on them since the newer versions of monsters, vampires and were-wolves took too many liberties with tradition. The new producers and scriptwriters tried to make up new legends for the stories. The older ones seemed to stick to the most common, and therefore probably truer legends of monster stories. Dean stopped and thought about it for a moment and made a mental note. They weren't monsters, they were Unusuals and, based on his limited experience so far, people just like him.

He typed classic horror into the search box and started adding some movies to his list. He found the Mummy with Boris Karloff, Bram Stoker's Dracula by director Francis Ford Coppola and the 1929 silent vampire classic, Nosferatu. He also listed the ones he could check the local library for if he couldn't find them on Netflix or Amazon. There was An American Werewolf in London, the zombie classic Dawn of the Dead, Bride of Frankenstein and the Spielberg classic, Poltergeist. He checked the list and seemed satisfied. That should get him started.

He changed into some shorts and his Streetlight Manifesto t-shirt and headed back to his bedroom to get some sleep. He would start digging into his movie research list after he took a nap. Working midnights seemed to sap him more than working days did. Maybe there was something to that medical research he had seen on the effects of shift work on the physiology of humans. As he lay down in bed, he found himself wondering if it affected Unusuals the same way? He fell asleep pondering that question.

Dean spent the next three days in the routine of sleep, gym, library, and research. It had been fun watching some of the old black and white classic monster movies. The library had quite a collection for loan and he'd taken as many as they'd allow. He also got himself back on a day schedule - sort of - in time to return to day shift.

He showed up at work about five minutes early, ready to start his day and watched a fancy, silver sports car with dark tinted windows pull up. After a moment or two, Brynne hopped out of the passenger side. She was wearing a turtleneck under her uniform shirt and looked a little flushed. She looked at him and said, "What are you staring at Newbie?"

"Aren't you going to be hot in that?" he asked. "It's supposed to be in the 80's today."

"I'm always cold and we usually have the AC blasting," she answered. "Don't worry about me, worry about the job."

"Yes, ma'am!" Dean said holding the door and trying to peer into the darkened windshield of the sports car. "Bye, James," he waved and then went inside. The sports car revved the engine once and then pulled away.

"I'd advise you to leave James alone," she said as they went inside. "He's a nice enough guy most of the time, but he can be the jealous type."

"I'll keep that in mind," Dean responded.

Bill and Lynne were grabbing their stuff as the two entered the squad room. "Did I hear 'lover boy' speeding off in his fancy car?" Bill asked. "Brynne, I don't know what you see in that guy."

"Leave her alone, Bill. She's a big girl," Lynne countered.

"I know, I'm just saying the whole thing puzzles me," Bill said. "I just don't see it. But, to each their own, as they say. Adios, muchachos. I've got a bed at home calling my name."

"Yeah, me, too," Lynne said. "See you guys!" She left as Bill held the door for her. Dean and Brynne were alone in the squad room.

"Look, Brynne, I didn't mean anything by it saying goodbye to James like that," Dean said.

"Forget about it," Brynne said with a wave of her hand. "I'm grumpy this morning. I didn't get much sleep the last three days and I'm tired. I don't want to say the 'Q' word and jinx us but I sure hope it's a below average day shift."

"Do you want me to do the vehicle and bag check while you rest up?" Dean asked.

"No, I'll help out," she said. "I'm supposed to make sure you know what you're doing and you might miss something we need, though usually Bill and Lynne leave things in good order." The two of them went into the bay and began going over the ambulance, double checking the supplies in the med bag and all the cabinets. As Brynne had said, all was in good shape.

Dean was considering a cup of coffee but the first tones of the day dropped as they were coming back into the squad room. "Medical Box U-301, sick person, 1273 River Road at the community pond picnic area."

Brynne took the driver's seat and Dean jumped in the passenger side. He was looking forward to when she would let him drive. It was always a thrill to operate an emergency vehicle with lights and sirens. He picked up the microphone as she pulled out. "U-191 responding."

"U-191 Responding, switch to med channel 2," returned the dispatcher's voice.

Dean switched the radio over to the med channel and keyed the mic. "U-191 on med channel 2."

"U-191," the dispatcher said, "Respond for an unresponsive adult female found by work crews at community pond. A crewmember will meet you at the parking lot entrance. No additional information at this time."

"U-191 copies," Dean said. "This is on the other side of town. It almost makes sense to send another unit until we can get there."

Brynne accelerated up the onramp for I-95 northbound. It was the fastest way to the other side of the city. "We can't be sure what kind of Unusual we're dealing with. A regular crew would be in over their heads. I hate that we're the only unit for these calls when we have to drive fifteen minutes to get to the patient. I've asked for them to place another Unusuals unit on the other side of town to get better coverage, but they say that there just isn't the call volume to justify it. Let's hope we don't have a cardiac arrest by the time we get there."

They pulled into the parking lot in the park next to the community pond about thirteen minutes after they left the station. True to the dispatch instructions there was a guy in jeans and a t-shirt with muddy work boots and one of those hi-visibility neon orange and yellow vests on. His hard hat was in his hands as he ran his fingers through his hair.

He started talking as soon as they got out of the vehicle. "We found her down by the edge of the pond. We're pretty sure we didn't hit her with any of the equipment. Eddy was backing up in the Gradall excavator when he saw her in the grass."

"Where is she now?" Brynne asked as she walked around the vehicle.

"We didn't move her," the guy said. "She's all the way on the far side of the pond."

"What pond?" Dean asked, looking at the broad, muddy basin in front of them with a small pool of water in the middle. "Where's the water?"

"We're draining the pond to fix the outlet system," the worker said. "It's gotten clogged with debris and we needed to drain most of the water out of it to get to it."

Brynne went to the rear of the ambulance. "Let's pile the gear on the stretcher and roll it over there. I don't want to drive the ambulance around there and risk getting stuck." She opened the two rear doors, released the stretcher from its locking mechanism and pulled it from the back of the unit.

Dean came over and started placing the bags on the stretcher. "I've got the med bag, BLS bag, oxygen and airway supplies."

Brynne climbed in the back, grabbing the heart monitor off the shelf and the portable suction machine from its charger. She placed them on the top of the stretcher, taking a moment to secure the monitor in place with one of the straps. "Let's go."

With Brynne at the head of the stretcher and Dean at the foot, the two began rolling the stretcher across the uneven ground around the pond's banks. They found a group of construction workers clustered around one of the pieces of equipment. Two of them were kneeling next to a woman who looked to be in her early 20's. She was dressed in what looked like a short pale blue nightgown, thin and slightly see-through.

Brynne spoke up, "Who's in charge here?"

"I am, ma'am." A tall man in his 40's stepped forward. "I'm Jim, the foreman. Eddy said he didn't hit her and it doesn't look like she's hurt, but we can't wake her up."

"Okay, Jim," Brynne said. "I need you to clear most of the guys out of here but you." She gestured to the big Gradall machine. "The guy who can run this vehicle should stay in case we need to move it."

She and Dean moved over to the woman on the grass. She didn't look injured from what they could see. Brynne reached into her pocket, pulled out a pair of exam gloves and put them on. "Dean, you get a set of vitals and put the heart monitor on her while I do a head to toe exam."

Brynne knelt down next to the girl, touching her on the shoulder and giving a gentle shake. "Miss, hello, are you alright?" There was no response. She used the knuckles of her hand to rub the woman's sternum and got a groan in response. The woman's hand came up and brushed feebly at hers to push it away. "Alert to painful stimuli only," Brynne reported to Dean. She carefully ran her hands through the woman's dark hair, gently lifting the head up as she did so. She checked her gloves for blood as she pulled them away. Lifting each eyelid in turn, she shined her penlight in them then moved it away. "Both pupils equal and reactive to light," she said.

Dean hooked up the automated blood pressure cuff and hit the button on the heart monitor to start it inflating. While that ran, he started connecting the leads from the heart monitor to the woman's arms and legs. Once all four were connected, he looked at the heart monitor's screen and the lines started bouncing across it. "Sinus tachycardia at 156," he said aloud. "Blood pressure is," he paused briefly to look at the monitor as the numbers stopped changing. "Blood pressure is 92 over 48."

He picked up her wrist and palpated a pulse with two fingers, watching the monitor screen to match the beats on the screen to what he was feeling under his fingers. Her pulse was difficult to detect, no matter how he moved his fingertips around. "Pulse is weak and thready." He checked his wristwatch and watched her chest rise and fall. "Respirations, 26 and pulse ox 96."

Brynne continued her head-to-toe check for signs of injury. She checked the back of the neck, the rib cage, sternum, abdomen, and hips in turn. The whole time, she watched both the patient's face for signs of grimacing in pain and frequently checking her gloves for signs of blood. She moved down to the legs and bare feet, before moving back up to the arms.

"No sign of injury," Brynne said. "Let's roll her. I want to get a look at her back." Together, they carefully rolled the woman up on her side and scanned her back. There was no sign of bleeding or other injury. They laid her back down in the supine position. "Okay Probie," she said. "Thoughts?"

Dean thought for a moment then picked up her hand and gently pinched the end of her finger at the fingernail, watched the color change and counted in his head. He looked in her mouth at her tongue and pulled her lip out gently, looking at the skin inside. Finally, he pulled up at some skin on her forearm closest to him. It stayed pulled up briefly like a peaked tent.

"Severe dehydration is my best guess, boss," he said. "She's got signs of shock with altered mental status. Capillary refill time is four seconds. Mucous membranes are dry and skin turgor non-existent with tenting." He looked around. "My only question is how did she get here? The guys on site swear they never saw her when they first got here. They said she just appeared. Since we're here, I guess there's an Unusual connection somehow. You didn't find any sign of injury or bleeding so we're not looking at a vamp attack, right?"

"You're right," Brynne said. "If I were to guess, I think she's the Naiad tied to this pond."

"The what?" Dean asked.

"Naiad, a water fairy," she answered. "Look at the pond. My guess is when they showed up this morning and started pumping out the pond to clear the drain field, she got caught unawares. Usually she could have, well, detached herself from the pond and not been affected so much." She looked up at her partner. "So what do we do?"

"Okay," he began. "Her oxygen sats are ok, no O2 needed right now. I've got the monitor hooked up. IV access next with a bolus of fluids to get her hydrated. We should also get her back to the unit since it's hot out here. That might contribute to dehydrating her, plus how she's dressed, or should I say, undressed is getting too much attention from these guys."

"I agree," Brynne said, nodding. "But we can't move her farther from the remaining water in the pond until we get fluids in her. You start the IV. Remember to go large, we need to get fluids in her quickly. I'll get the IV bag spiked and ready."

Dean got the IV pack out of the side of the med bag that had all the supplies to get a line started. He tied the elastic tourniquet off a few inches above her elbow and then got out a few two by two gauze pads, two alcohol prep swabs and selected a 16 gauge needle to establish the IV access. Turning back to the patient, he gently palpated the antecubital space on the inside of the elbow, feeling for the big veins there.

"Brynne," Dean said. "I'm having trouble finding the vein. Maybe she's too dehydrated?"

Brynne came around to his side of the patient and handed him the IV bag. "Finish getting this set up while I take a look." She knelt down next to the woman's side and checked her arm, looking and feeling with her fingertips. "There," she said holding her finger on the spot she found while she picked up one of the alcohol preps Dean had already ripped open. Lifting her finger up, she swabbed it in a circular motion.

Dean handed her the 16-gauge needle catheter he'd selected. Keeping one hand holding the arm, she pulled the needle cover off with her teeth, spitting it onto the ground while she pulled the skin tight with her thumb just below the spot she'd found. Advancing the needle in at nearly a forty-five-degree angle at first, she then leveled it out, watching closely for the flash of blood in the chamber. There it was. She advanced a few millimeters more then slid the plastic catheter forward off the needle as it slid back with a click, safely stowing it in the housing. Dean attached the IV tubing from the bag, rolling the valve all the way open to allow full flow of fluid into the vein. Brynne taped off the IV on the patient's arm to hold it in place, then stood up.

Brynne looked at him. "How much fluid do we give her?"

"Twenty milliliters per kilo," he answered. "She's small so I'd guess forty-five or fifty kilos so nine hundred or a thousand Mls. Pretty much the whole bag." He nodded toward the bag of normal saline he was holding.

"Okay, we'll run about five hundred milliliters in and then check her vitals again," Brynne said. "Mr. Foreman," she called to the leader of the construction team.

He came trotting over. "Yes, ma'am?"

"I know this is going to seem strange," Brynne began, "but can you hold off pumping out the rest of the pond for about fifteen minutes? It's our protocol when on a construction site that all work stop until we clear the scene."

"Uh, I guess so," he said, taking his hard hat off and scratching his head. "Only 15 minutes? I've got a lot to try and get done today and the boss wants us to finish up and get the pond filling again before the end of the day."

"15 minutes," Brynne said. "A half hour, tops. Just until we get her loaded into the back of the ambulance. We need to get her stabilized first."

"What's wrong with her?" he asked.

"Not sure," she said. "She's not awake yet so we're just treating symptoms. We'll know more when we get her back in the ambulance."

"Okay," he said. "Let me know if you need anything else. I'll go shut the pumps down for a bit and give the guys a break." He laughed. "It's not like they're getting anything done right now anyway with all the excitement." He walked over to his crew, giving some order and gesturing to the pumps still chugging away on the far side of the pond basin.

Given the size of the IV line Brynne had started, it didn't take long to get half of the liter bag of fluid into the patient. Dean, holding the bag up over his head, knelt down and pressed the button on the heart monitor to start another blood pressure reading. The pulse rate had come down to 126 and her respiratory rate was down to 20, possibly showing that her body wasn't working as hard to get blood around to the various organs and tissues. The blood pressure came back as 104 over 54. All signs were good.

Dean heard a sound and looked over as the patient's eyes fluttered open. "Wha- what happened? Who are you?" she asked looking up at him.

Her eyes were a deeper shade of blue than Dean had ever seen before. "You're doing alright," Dean said, reassuring her. "We got called here when the construction crew found you here next to the community pond in the city park. I think you're dehydrated so we've started an IV and are giving you some fluids. Can you tell me your name?"

"Jaina," she said, then looked around with fear in her eyes. "The pond. I can't feel it anymore."

Brynne knelt down on the other side of her. "I'm Brynne and this is Dean. We're paramedics. The construction crew is here doing some cleanup and are temporarily draining the pond." She laid a hand on Jaina's chest when she suddenly tried to sit up. "Easy does it! You don't need to be alarmed. They're planning on refilling it after they get the overflow drain cleaned out."

"Oh," the diminutive Naiad said. "That's why I got so confused so quickly. I didn't know they were starting the work this morning or I could have prepared myself."

"Okay," Brynne said. "We're going to give you a little more fluid and then we'll get you up and move you to the ambulance."

Jaina turned her head and looked at the bag of fluid Dean was holding, now only half full. A look of concentration crossed her face, and Dean was astounded as the saline fluid in the clear plastic bag began to disappear quickly. "Ahhhh," the Naiad gasped as she closed her eyes, a smile on her face. "That feels good," she said, smacking her lips. "Though it's a bit salty for my taste."

The bag hung empty in Dean's hand, completely dry. He looked at Jaina and Brynne. "Would you like some more?" he asked as he smiled at her.

"I've got a few bottles of water in the ambulance," Brynne said. "Why don't you let us take you back there and we'll try and get you back to normal, or at least as close as we can until your pond is filled up again."

"That sounds good," the Naiad said, trying to sit up. "Whoa, I'm still a bit dizzy." She laid back down again.

"You need to take it easy and let us do the work," Brynne said. Dean turned and put the empty IV bag on top of the med bag then got up to help Brynne unload the rest of the gear from the stretcher. They put it down to its lowest position and rolled it up next to the patient on the ground.

"Dean and I are going to help you sit up and then move to the stretcher, Jaina," Brynne said. "Do you think you can help us out with that?"

"I think so," Jaina responded.

"Okay," Brynne said, nodding to Dean as she put her hand under Jaina's shoulder and helped prop her up to a seated position. Then the two paramedics each took a side and, lifting under the patient's arms, boosted her up to sit on the side of the stretcher. Dean brought the head of the stretcher up to a semi-reclining position and helped her lay back as Brynne raised her feet up. They put the seat belts on her to secure Jaina on the stretcher. Dean carefully put the heart monitor on the stretcher and secured it next to her legs. He then asked the foreman Jim and the Gradall operator, who were still hanging around, to help carry the bags for them while they wheeled the stretcher back toward the ambulance.

When they got to the ambulance and loaded Jaina into the back, Brynne took the remaining bags from the workers and thanked them for their help. She packed them away and then climbed in the back with Dean and the patient.

Dean was handing Jaina a water bottle as Brynne stepped up into the back of the unit via the side door.

"How do you feel?" Brynne asked, sitting down in the chair by the head of the stretcher.

"Better, thanks," Jaina replied. She held her hand up to her forehead. "I think they caught me by surprise. By the time I realized what they were doing, they had drained too much water from the pond for me to make up the difference. I had no time to tear myself away from the connection to the water." She opened up the plastic water bottle and downed the contents in one go. She put the bottle down next to her and held her hand out for more. Brynne handed her another bottle that quickly went the way of the first one.

Brynne glanced at the screen of the heart monitor. Jaina's vitals were looking better now that she'd gotten some fluid on board. "I'm glad we were able to help," she said. "Can we take you to the hospital to get checked out and make sure your labs are good?"

"No," Jaina replied. "I'm good now that I'm awake and able to take care of myself. I'll be fine." She handed the empty bottle back to Dean. Her touch lingered on his arm while he took it from her. "I would like a few more bottles for the road, though."

"No problem," Dean said, reaching into the cabinet at the foot of the stretcher for two more water bottles. "Is two enough?"

"Yes, thank you," Jaina replied taking the bottles.

"I just need you to sign this transport refusal and you're all set to go," Brynne said, holding up the iPad for Jaina to sign. The woman scrawled a signature on the line with her finger. Brynne handed her a paper with some printed and handwritten information on it. "This is a sheet with some basic instructions for you and advising you that you have the right to call us back if you need us, even if it's just after we've left." She caught the woman's eye. "I'm serious, Jaina. If you feel worse, call 911, and we'll come back and check you out. We can give you more water or even take you to the hospital if needed."

"Thanks, I'll keep that in mind," Jaina said. "But I am feeling better now. I'll be okay."

Dean helped her unbuckle the stretcher's seat belts and then opened the back doors, climbing out and turning to offer a hand to the Naiad. Jaina jumped down nimbly from the back step. She didn't look shaky at all anymore. She thanked the paramedics and walked around the back of the ambulance towards the pond. Dean turned to say something about being careful but the woman was nowhere to be seen. He spun around and then looked up at Brynne, who gave a little chuckle.

"Fairies who don't want to be seen, can't be seen, Dean," she said. "It goes with the whole supernatural thing. It's one reason I suspected who she must be when the construction foreman said that it was like she just appeared. When she suddenly went unconscious from the severe dehydration she lost control of her magic or mojo or whatever you want to call it, and 'Poof' there she was."

"I think I'm gonna take a little while before I get used to all this Unusuals have magic and stuff thing," Dean said shaking his head. "She was cute though."

"I figured you'd noticed," Brynne said. "Just don't get in the habit of dating former patients or Unusuals in general. It leads to complications most of the time."

"Really, Brynne?" Dean asked. "You're telling me not to date Unusuals?" He stopped himself even as he thought that he was not the one wearing a turtleneck on a warm day. She was clearly covering up the hickey or whatever else she didn't want people to see on her neck. He didn't dare say that out loud, though. It was none of his business.

"I'm not having this conversation with you, Dean," she snapped. "Just take my word for it. It's not for the faint of heart. Leave it at that." She turned and left him standing there as she stepped down from the back of the unit and headed back toward the driver's seat. "Put fresh sheets on the stretcher while I get on the radio and put us back in service. You never know when we'll get another call."

Dean stood there for a moment, watching her walk away, kicking himself for stepping over a line. Her private life was just that, private. It was hard, though, for EMS partners to avoid learning a little too much about each other. Dean had seen his share of rocky relationships without one of the significant others being a probable vampire. Still, she was the boss and certainly knew a lot more about this than he did. Maybe she knew something he didn't. He climbed into the back of the unit and remade the stretcher for the next call. He heard her on the radio in the front seat, calling dispatch. Hopefully, she'd forget he ever said anything about it. He didn't want to get on her bad side.

# Chapter 6

They headed back to the station on the other side of town in silence. When they arrived, they cleaned out the mud and dirt that had been tracked into the back of the ambulance, all without saying a word. Dean went in and started on the report while Brynne sat down in one of the recliners and looked at something on her phone.

By lunchtime the tense silence was driving Dean nuts. He finally spoke from where he was sitting by the computer checking his email. "Brynne," he said, turning to look at her where she sat in the recliner. "I apologize. If I stepped over a line, I didn't mean to. I had no intention of hurting your feelings or making things awkward between us."

She put her phone down in her lap and looked up at him. "I shouldn't have delved into the subject of dating Unusuals myself if I didn't want to have that conversation with you, Dean," Brynne said. "Just trust me. It can get pretty complicated. Just be careful."

"You, too, Boss," Dean responded. "I'm sure you know what you're doing and all but I remember some things from a class I had once on relationship violence and …"

"It's not like that at all," she interrupted. "Look, I don't want to talk about this with you or anyone else. Everything is fine, okay?"

She got up and plugged her phone into the USB charger on the wall by the desk. "Look, apology accepted," she said, "and thank you for your concern, but there's nothing to be worried about. Deal?"

"Deal," Dean said.

"It's time for lunch. Any thoughts?" Brynne asked.

"I don't know," Dean said. "What are you up for?"

"Let's hit that salad place out on Rt. 40. You can get a sandwich there if you don't want a salad."

"Sounds like a plan," Dean said, wondering if this was the end of the discussion.

AS WAS USUALLY the case in the EMS world, you order lunch and the next call comes in. The two paid for their meals, grabbed the bag of food from the counter, and headed out to their ambulance. Dean put the bags behind the seat as he climbed into the passenger side. The call was for a choking subject and it wasn't far away. Brynne hit the lights and Dean turned on the siren as his partner drove the unit out of the strip mall and back out onto Route 40. Turning right, they headed down two lights and turned left onto a winding road on the outskirts of the city. It lead to a lane with a group of ramshackle mobile homes in various states of disrepair.

"I'll take the lead on this one, Dean," Brynne said. "Just watch and keep your eyes open." She pulled up next to a trailer. "Bring in the portable suction and the oxygen/airway bag. Watch your step coming into the trailer. Most of them are falling apart and there are probably holes in the floors."

She jumped out and started up the steps toward the rusted screen door. Dean got out and retrieved the suction and oxygen bags. Brynne had already gone inside. As he stepped up on the makeshift cinder block steps, he slipped the straps of the oxygen bag over his right shoulder. He cradled the portable suction in the crook of his right arm as he reached for the screen door.

He entered a dark room with a musty, moldy odor just in time to see his partner standing behind what looked like a dead guy, administering the Heimlich maneuver. The guy's eyes were sunken in, and his skin was mottled and blue in tone. She pulled back sharply once, then a second, third, and fourth time. With a gasp, something flew out of the guy's mouth and struck him in the chest followed by something else. Dean stepped back with a disgusted groan as he brushed at his chest with his free hand. He reached into his pocket, fumbling to put on some gloves as Brynne released the man's midsection from her embrace and stepped from behind him.

"Is that better?" she asked. The man groaned at her but nodded. Then he looked confused, stuck two fingers in his mouth fishing around as if looking for something then started scanning the floor at Dean's feet. Dean looked down and there, on the floor next to his left foot was what looked like a tongue and a lump of chewed food.

"It that his tongue?" Dean asked. "What the ...?"

"Oh, good," Brynne said as she walked over. "Freddy's always losing that." She bent over and picked up the detached muscle with her gloved hand. "Do you want me to wash it off first?"

Freddy held out his hand with a shake of his head. Dean noticed that there were two fingers missing from his right hand. He took the proffered tongue, blew it off and then unceremoniously shoved the whole thing back into his mouth. He poked around with the forefingers of both hands for a bit, obviously trying to position it. When he pulled them away, he offered a gap-toothed grin to Dean and croaked, "That is better. Thank you, Brynne."

"What happened Freddy?" Brynne asked. "I thought you said you weren't going to let that happen again?"

"I tried to be careful but I just wanted to have a brownie." It was hard for Dean to make out the words that came out of the guy's mouth. It was a wonder that he could talk at all considering he had a loose tongue - oh - and was clearly dead.

"You know you shouldn't eat anything." Brynne admonished. "You're dead so you can't digest it anyway."

"But," the dead man's voice groaned. "I can still sort of taste things. I used to be so good at cooking and tasting things. I miss that, Brynne. I really do." She nodded in sympathy as he continued. "I decided that I could make a small batch of brownies and try just one." He turned and ambled into the kitchen at one end of the trailer home, stepping around a foot-wide hole in the floor. Dean and Brynne followed. Once there they looked around at what had to be the filthiest kitchen Dean had ever seen. There were pans and pots everywhere with rotted bits of food in them. The sink was piled high with dirty plates and more pots and pans. Flies buzzed around the rotten food and the trailer's occupant.

Freddy picked up one square baking pan with what looked like fresh brownies in it. One corner piece had been removed. "See," he said. "I just had one."

"Freddy," Brynne said putting her hand gently on the guy's shoulder. "I know you used to be a pretty good chef, but you're dead now. You can't do all the things you used to do no matter how much you want to. I'm not always going to be this close to come bail you out."

"I know. I'll try," Freddie said with a sigh. "I just wish I had more opportunities to cook again."

"We've all told you that you're welcome to come by the station any time and cook a meal for us," Brynne offered.

Dean turned to look at her and stared at his partner, dumbstruck.

"What?" she asked, looking back at him. "Don't knock it until you've tried it, Dean. Freddy here was once one of the best chefs in the country. Why, if he were still alive and cooking today, he'd have a cooking show on the Food Channel for sure."

"Really?" Freddy asked. "You think so?

"Absolutely!" Brynne answered. "Why don't you plan to come over tomorrow evening in time for shift change. We are still on days and I know that Brook and Tammy, who are both coming on tomorrow night, would love a home cooked meal after they missed the last feast you cooked for us."

"I would love to," Freddy choked out. "Thank you. I'll stop by tonight after dark and leave a shopping list for you. Just a list of some of the things to pick up. I'm going to make something special for you, Brynne. It's going to knock your socks off!"

"I can't wait," Brynne said. "In the meantime, no more brownies! Okay?"

"Okay," he answered, walking them to the door. "Thank you again. Both of you."

The paramedics stepped carefully down the rickety, cinderblock steps and headed back to the ambulance. Brynne walked around to the driver's side while Dean went over to the side compartments to replace the oxygen bag and portable suction. He turned and climbed into the passenger seat. They were just about to pull away when the screen door slammed open and Freddy shuffled out holding up a zipper baggie of brownies as he came up to the passenger side of the ambulance. Dean put down the window.

"I thought you'd appreciate these since I can't." Freddie croaked, handing the baggie through the window to Dean. "Thank you for coming and helping me out again. I'll see you both tomorrow night." He stepped back and let the ambulance pull away, waving goodbye.

Dean leaned out the window. "Thank you," he called, then sat back, closing the window again. He was just about to shove one of the brownies into his mouth when Brynne reached over and batted it out of his hand.

"What do you think you're doing?" she asked. "Are you crazy? Don't eat that!"

"But the way you were talking back there …." he said, suddenly confused. "All that 'you are a great chef, Freddy' and 'cannot wait to have you cook us dinner, Freddy.' I assumed they must be pretty good."

"Did you see that kitchen?" she asked. "He always offers us snacks when we come help him out. That doesn't mean it's a good idea to eat them." She shook her head. "You're a pretty good medic for the most part, Dean, but I keep forgetting that you're still a newbie at this. It is one thing to have Freddy come over and cook for us in our kitchen with some supervision to make sure he doesn't lose something in the sauce. It is quite something else to have something a zombie made in that disgusting excuse for a kitchen." She glanced over at him. "I thought you would have had more sense than that."

Dean grinned. "I guess it was pretty stupid. But in my defense, you had me completely flipped out and turned around when you offered to have him come cook for us."

"Oh, you just wait and see, Newbie," Brynne said. "You just wait and see. He's going to come and cook the kind of meal that a guy on a paramedic's salary can rarely afford. The last time he came over and cooked he made us fresh tortellini with a homemade marinara sauce that I still have dreams about."

"What happened to him anyway?" Dean asked. "I assume he's a zombie or undead."

"Zombie's right," Brynne answered. "It's a sad story. He was dating a girl who was dabbling in some dark magic when he decided to cheat on her. She created a zombie potion of some sort and then tricked him into drinking it. Then she shot him five times in the chest after informing him that he would come back as a member of the undead. She ended up going to prison for the rest of her life and he ended up in that trailer for the rest of his unlife."

"But it looks like he's slowly disintegrating," Dean said.

"Yes, that's true, unfortunately," Brynne said. "He'll slowly rot away and eventually die, or whatever it is that zombies do since he's already dead. Our job is to help occasionally reattach things to him that fall off and keep him from ending his existence early by choking on the food he can no longer eat." She pulled up next to a dumpster in the industrial park next to their building. "Toss that baggie in there and then we'll park and go inside to finish our lunch."

Dean tossed the baggie of brownies into the open dumpster. He again got the impression he was never going to figure out all the nuances of this job or get used to the surprises it held in store. Maybe he hoped he never did.

ON THE WAY back to the station, Brynne drove by the hospital to pick up some supplies for the station. They went into the supply closet where Brynne loaded Dean up with an armload of gauze and other assorted first aid items. As he was standing there, he heard a melodious voice behind him.

"Brynne, are you going to introduce me to your new partner? I heard you had a new probie to break in."

Dean turned around and saw the girl from the convenience store, the one who had seen the stamp on his hand the week before. She was dressed in light blue scrubs, and her badge read Ashley Moore, RN, BSN.

Brynne laughed aloud. "Ashley, you have no idea! Dean, this is Ashely Moore, one of the charge nurses here in the ER. Ashley, meet Dean Flynn, our newest initiate into our little world."

"Welcome to the club, Dean," The nurse said with a smile. "I think we've run into each other before. You were getting donuts, I think."

"Uh, right. Um, yeah, they were donuts." Dean stammered as he tried to free one hand to hold out and shake her hand.

"Hey, probie," Brynne said with a chuckle. "Don't drop anything. Just say hello."

Ashley laughed along with Brynne. "Don't mind me. I was just checking to make sure you guys found everything you needed. Was there anything that you couldn't find, Brynne?"

"Nope, I got everything on my list."

"Alright. "Well, it's nice to meet you, Dean. Tell Brynne to bring a patient by once in a while and not to be such strangers." The young ER nurse turned and walked back around to the nurses' station.

Brynne snapped her fingers.

"Dean. Yo, Dean. Wake up and pay attention to what you're doing."

"Oh, sorry Brynne. I had just run into her before, off duty, and hadn't expected to see her again here of all places."

"Well, you'll see her again. She's here all the time." Brynne said.

"Come on, let's get this stuff out to the ambulance and get back to the station."

As they walked out through the automatic sliding doors to the ambulance bay outside, Dean stole a look over his shoulder and caught Ashley glancing in his direction. She smiled and turned back to her work.

# Chapter 7

The meal that Freddy made for the four paramedics the next night in their station's tiny kitchen was truly amazing considering what the dead chef had to work with. Station U's third shift team of Brook Barnes and Tammy Haines entered to the smells of fresh pork chops with cornbread and herb stuffing. There also real potatoes au gratin, not the boxed crap, and green beans topped with a honey glaze and toasted, slivered almonds.

The paramedics sat down to eat while the chef watched. A crooked smile was the best he could do to express his pleasure. It was easily one of the best meals Dean had ever eaten. It was almost sacrilege that they ate such a fantastic meal on styrofoam plates with plastic forks and knives. The pork was so tender that it hardly took any effort to cut and the sauce, with a slight hint of apricot, literally topped it all off perfectly. Satiated, Dean slid back in his seat at the small table and shook his head in disbelief. After seeing the kitchen disaster in Freddy's home yesterday, he found it hard to believe that the same cook could turn out something so refined.

He raised his can of soda to Freddy. "My compliments to the chef."

"Here, here!" his co-workers replied in unison. A gap-toothed smile grew on Freddy's mottled face.

"I appreciate the opportunity to cook for you guys once in a while," Freddy said in a raspy voice. "You make me feel almost alive again."

"The pleasure is all ours," Brook said. "I can barely boil water safely so having an occasional restaurant quality meal here at work is a big bonus."

There was a sound of a car horn from outside and Brynne checked her watch. "That must be James," she said, standing and grabbing her purse. "Time to go." She looked over at Brook and Tammy. "We bought the ingredients, you clean up and give Freddy a ride back to his trailer?"

"Sure, although we might just have to make a run to the store and see what he can come up with for dessert," Tammy laughed.

"Just make sure it's not leftover brownies," Brynne said.

Brook smiled. "Oh, we heard. We'll all avoid the brownies. Although, we heard that the newbie here almost ate one."

"Hey," Dean said with mock indignation. "It was an honest mistake."

The horn sounded from outside, longer this time. "Uh, I really gotta go," Brynne said rushing for the door. Brook and Tammy exchanged a glance.

"Bye, Brynne," Tammy said. "Say hello to James for us. Tell him we'll come looking for you if you're late tomorrow morning."

Brynne waved them off, then left. Dean turned and looked around. "I can give Freddy a lift home," he offered. "It's sort of on my way."

"That would be great, Dean," Brook said. "We've got quite a bit of clean up to do and we should do it now in case we get busy with calls tonight. Thanks."

"Ok then, Freddy," Dean said. "You're coming with me."

The deceased chef shuffled toward the door. "Thank you for the opportunity to get into a real kitchen again," he said. "It was a pleasure."

Dean strode across the parking lot outside their nondescript station and clicked the unlock switch on his remote key. The pickup truck's lights blinked once. He walked to the driver's side and waited as Freddy slowly walked over.

"Uh, Dean?" Freddy asked. "You're going to have to open this door for me. My fingers are too brittle to operate the handle without snapping off."

"Oh, right!" Dean said, jogging around the front of the truck. "Here you go, sir!" He opened the door with a grand gesture.

"Thank you," the zombie murmured as he slid into the passenger seat.

Dean returned to the driver's side, started the pickup and pulled out onto the road through the industrial park. It was already getting dark as they pulled onto Route 40. It was silent for the first five minutes or so as they drove.

"You know," Freddy started. "You're not the only one worried about Brynne and James. A lot of us are more than a little worried about them."

Dean glanced over at his passenger. "That came out of the blue. What do you mean?"

"I mean that James is really old school. He considers himself better than the rest of us. And I don't think he thinks of most humans as anything more than a snack. He says he's turned over a new leaf in the last hundred years, but most of us don't think he's caught up with current reality. He's still stuck in the time of feudal overlords and serfs."

"What does that mean?" Dean said. "Do you think he's hurting her?"

"I'm not sure," Freddy said with a creaky shrug. "I used to think she could handle herself, but sometimes I wonder. I said the same thing to her old partner Zach. He said he was going to look into it but then he left town suddenly. I was surprised because he seemed pretty sure that something strange was going on with the two of them. I got the impression he was going to try to do something about it."

"I've never heard about her old partner at all," Dean said. "I just assumed he'd been reassigned."

"Not that I know of," Freddy said. "From what I heard he just didn't show up for work one day and then they got an email from him that he had to leave and take care of family out of town. When they went to check on him, his apartment was cleaned out. His super said that a moving truck had come and cleaned the apartment out at night. There was an envelope with enough cash inside so that the rent was paid through the end of the lease and the keys were left on the counter inside."

He shrugged again. "We all thought it was kind of weird. Zach was a city employee and he didn't seem like he would have had the money to pay a couple of months' rent in advance like that. It was just strange, that's all." They rode in silence for a bit longer, then they were in front of Freddy's trailer.

"Thanks, I guess, Freddie. The problem is, what do I do with what you just said?" Dean asked as he slid the gearshift into park. "I'm so new at this job, I positively squeak. I'm not sure from one day to the next what I'm doing. I wouldn't begin to know what to do about something like this."

"Well you don't want to confront James head-on or antagonize him in any way," Freddy advised. "I'm sure he doesn't deal well with things that don't go his way. Everyone in the Unusual community knows that. You should be careful. It's just that we're worried about her. Brynne's changed a lot in the last few years since she started hanging out with James. She's told me it's nothing to do with him, but I don't know."

"Thanks for the heads-up, Freddy," Dean said as he jumped out and went around to let Freddy out of the passenger side. "I appreciate it, and you can let your friends know that I'll try to keep an eye on her as best I can."

"Just be careful," Freddy warned. "Like I said. James is an old school vampire, you know – feudal lordship and respect and all that. He thinks he's at the top of the food chain socially and in reality. To him, she's not just his girlfriend, she's his property. I don't think he would just let her go with a 'fare thee well'." He took a few steps to the house trailer then turned. "You're a good kid and everyone already says you seem like a good guy to have around when there is trouble. Do not go out there and get yourself injured, or worse, missing like Zach. That's all I am saying." Freddy turned and shuffled up to his door and inside. Dean stood in the pool of the pickup's headlights in the growing darkness.

Dean stared at the closed door of the trailer for a bit before turning and getting back into his pickup truck. He backed onto the road and drove back towards the highway. Freddy had given him a lot to think about. He had a feeling that something was not right with James and Brynne. Now he had some confirmation. Still, he couldn't act on a suspicion. Brynne was able to do her job and take care of herself, and if she didn't want help, he couldn't force it on her. That would be just as bad as whatever James was supposedly doing to her. He was just going to have to watch and see if there were overt signs – not just his hunch and the word of a zombie chef. He couldn't go tell the shift commander that his immediate supervisor was in danger because she was dating a vampire. Heck, he couldn't even be sure the lieutenant knew about the Unusuals anyway. He'd gotten the impression that beyond a very tight circle of people, the real purpose of Station U was where you put the rejects and weirdos.

Dean just couldn't figure out who he could turn to. Then a thought occurred to him. Maybe Mike Farver was the answer. Mike, his old paramedic school instructor, could be the right person. Mike was a founding paramedic member of Station U. He might know what to do with a troublesome vampire or how to handle it with Brynne.

Dean started putting together a carefully worded email message in his head as he drove back to his apartment. He had to be cautious, making sure the message got the idea across without alerting any others who might see it to what was really going on at Station U. That might just end up with him locked in a psych ward for a few nights. That was not a desirable outcome for this situation and it would leave Brynne unguarded. Dean was so engrossed in his thoughts that he didn't see the headlights of the darkened SUV behind him or realize that they might be following him home.

# Chapter 8

After he got home that night, Dean tried to compose the email he intended to send off to Mike Farver. He couldn't figure out how to state the problem as he didn't have any proof. He hadn't seen any physical signs of injury. He deleted the e-mail – for now. He decided to keep his eyes open and see if he could come up with proof of danger to his partner. He would watch Brynne and learn what he could about both her relationship with James as well as the best ways to treat their patients.

The only thing that stood out over the next few days was that Brynne continued to wear the turtleneck despite the warm temperatures. The calls were routine. They dealt with chest pain, respiratory distress, and the occasional assault. In cases where police were involved, Dean noted the same two or three police officers were dispatched with them. They seemed to be the equivalent to the Station U ambulance crews. Brynne knew them all by name and introduced Dean to them so they would get to know him.

It wasn't until they moved back to night shift that he saw James again. He was working on a patient care report from a call earlier that evening when the door to the parking lot opened and James swaggered in. Dean was surprised because that door was supposed to be locked. James either had his own key, or there was some vampire talent he didn't know about. The station wasn't a home or other residence so they couldn't deny him access. He'd learned about vampire lore from Brynne and found vamps couldn't enter a home unless invited in by the homeowner or other permanent resident. That was good news. He felt safer in his own apartment now.

James met Dean's stare as he crossed to the recliner where Brynne was sitting. "Hello my dear," he said to his girlfriend. He bent down to give her a kiss. It lingered a little longer than was proper in a public situation, Dean thought to himself.

"What are you doing here, James?" Brynne asked. "I didn't expect to see you tonight. You said you were traveling for a few days."

"I am getting ready to leave," James responded. "I wanted to see you again before I left. I also wanted to let you know that I have left Rudolf in charge here while I'm gone. If you need anything, you let him know and he'll take care of it."

"I'll be here, too," Dean interjected. "I'm sure we can cover anything that might come up."

"I'm sure you are up to the mundane challenges you might expect, Dean," James retorted. "I'm talking about the non-mundane things that crop up from time to time. When the cat's away, the Unusuals will play, as the saying goes. When those problems crop up it is best to let us deal with it, in-house if you will."

"I'll keep that in mind," Dean said. "Where are you off to anyway?"

"Personal business," James responded. "I need to return to Europe and deal with some things that have cropped up." He turned to Brynne. "It is entirely possible that this is a distraction to get me away from my home base. If so, Rudolf will be ready to deal with things until I can return."

"I'll let folks know to contact him if there is any trouble," Brynne said. "I suppose you need to go. I'll walk you out to your car." She got up and crossed to the door arm in arm with James.

Before they walked out, James turned to Dean. "I do appreciate your willingness to help out and watch over my dear Brynne, Dean.

I'm sure you will do anything in your power to protect her, too. I thank you for that." It sounded almost sincere.

Dean nodded in reply.

The couple was in the parking lot for about ten minutes before Brynne came back into the squad room. Dean was just finishing up his report and hit the send button on the screen to shoot it off to the hospital and headquarters with his electronic signature.

"What am I going to do with you, Probie?" Brynne asked as she entered the squad room. "You don't want to get in a pissing match with James, believe me. Just let him play his games his way. I can handle myself without your help."

Dean turned in the desk chair to look her way. "What was up with all that 'Rudolf will watch over things' stuff? It's like he's the king of Elk City or something."

"He is," Brynne said.

Dean started to laugh but stopped. "Wait, you're serious."

"Dean, the Unusual population is a very old and established group of world citizens. They've coexisted with humans for thousands of years without being known as anything more than legend and myth by the bulk of the population. They've done this by governing themselves. Because their government is so old, it is kind of like a feudal system. They have leaders, sub-leaders, and vassal subjects."

"So, James is the king?" Dean asked.

"He's more of a Baron actually," Brynne said. "His area covers a fifty-mile radius around Elk City. Most of the areas are led by a vampire or other higher order Unusual that craves order. A Minotaur rules Washington, DC and its surroundings."

"So what is it that James does as the leader of the Elk City Unusual population?" Dean asked.

"He makes sure that no one draws undue attention to themselves for starters," Brynne said. "Anonymity is key to their being able to coexist peacefully with humans. Anything that threatens that anonymity is cause for action by the Unusual leadership. He also acts as Judge for high and low justice when there is a dispute between Unusuals in the region."

"Why don't they just take their arguments to court like the rest of us?" Dean asked.

"That's a remedy they might use for a dispute with a normal human." Brynne replied. "But when they have a dispute with each other, they turn to the local leadership for a judgment. It's much faster than human courts, and the decisions are final. There are rarely appeals to the decisions of the local Barons. You have the right to appeal but if you choose to bother the higher authorities at the national level and you lose your appeal, the consequences can be severe. It deters all but the most desperate cases from going higher."

"So they're a sub-government hidden within our own democratic government?" Dean asked.

"Yes, although they're also active in human politics as well." Brynne said. "There are enough people in the human leadership that know about Unusuals that it behooves them to vote and pay attention to what we're doing politically as well."

Dean thought about that. It made sense to pay attention to what the leaders in your area were up to if you were a human and he guessed it was a good idea to pay attention to that for Unusuals, too. "Who's Rudolf, then?" Dean asked. "Is he another vampire?"

"Rudolf is a lycan, a werewolf, who is James' second in command. He'll be our contact should we need to deal with an Unusual problem beyond our limited abilities."

The alert tones dropped, startling them out of their conversation. "Medical Box U-265, Respiratory Distress, 57 Quartet Drive," intoned the dispatcher as the printer began whirring and spit out the sheet with the address and additional information. Brynne grabbed the paper as the paramedics jumped up and headed out through the doors to the ambulance bay. Brynne handed the sheet to Dean as she headed to the driver's side.

"You're going to have to let me drive at some point, Brynne," Dean laughed.

"Maybe tomorrow," Brynne said.

"Maybe never," Dean muttered under his breath.

Dean climbed in as Brynne started the engine. He picked up the mic and put them on the street. "U-191 responding."

"U-191 responding," repeated the dispatcher. "Switch to med channel 1 for additional."

Dean switched the radio over to the secure, trunked med channel. "U-191 on med channel 1."

The dispatcher's voice came back immediately. "Respond for a 22-year-old woman complaining of respiratory distress."

"Copy dispatch, U-191 out." Dean said, replacing the mic on the dash. He made a mental note to continue the conversation they had started earlier. He wanted to delve into this topic more. Just when he thought he had the Unusuals figured out, something else cropped up.

Chapter 9

It took them 8 minutes to get to the quiet suburban neighborhood of small, single-family homes. As Brynne turned the ambulance left on to Quartet Drive, Dean started reading numbers on the mailboxes and the house numbers when he could see them. "It's going to be on the right side of the street," Dean said noticing that the odd numbered houses were on his side of the road.

"There it is," Brynne said. They saw a person frantically waving on the front lawn of the ranch style house. She pulled the ambulance up to the front of the house. When she came to a stop, Dean jumped out and began pulling bags out of the side compartments on the unit. He shouldered the oxygen and airway bag then grabbed the med bag and started walking across the broad yard to the front door. Brynne caught up to him with the heart monitor clutched in one hand and the portable suction bag in the other.

As the paramedics approached the front door, a man in his twenties met them on the front porch. "She's in here, she can't breathe!" he told them as they approached. He pulled the screen door open and held it for them as they walked into the house. On entering the living room at the front of the home, they saw an attractive red-haired young woman in her twenties. She sat on the edge of the sofa, her hands on her knees, slightly leaning forward as she struggled to lift her torso up to allow complete filling of her lower airways. Dean recognized this was called the tripod position, and it was not a good sign. She was struggling to breathe and was pale with a slightly blue tinge to her lips. They could hear wheezing of her labored respirations from across the room. On the coffee table in front of her were several medication inhalers and a portable home nebulizer with tubing that led to a mask.

Dean put the bags down on the floor next to her and started to pull out a non-rebreather mask and tubing from the oxygen bag. "Hi, my name's Dean," he said as he worked. "We're going to do what we can to help out, okay?"

"She's Lydia," the man said. "Her asthma is acting up. This is the worst I've ever seen it."

Lydia gasped out one word at a time. "I. Tried. My. Nebu. Lyzer. Treatment. But. It. Did. Not. Work."

"Here," Dean said, holding the non-rebreather mask up to her face with oxygen set to fifteen liters per minute. He stretched the elastic band around her head to hold it in place. "That should help a little bit while we get some other things set up."

Brynne set the heart monitor down on the coffee table in front of Lydia and turned it on. She connected the blood pressure cuff to the machine, wrapped it around Lydia's arm, pressing the button to start inflating the cuff for a reading. She also slid the pulse oximeter probe sensor over her index finger and plugged that into the monitor. Dean could see the 88 percent value. Not good. Brynne placed the earpieces of her stethoscope in her ears and held up the bell in one hand. "I'm going to listen to your lungs, okay?"

Lydia nodded and Brynne reached around the woman's back, lifting her shirt up and sliding her hand under. "Wheezes at the top, diminished breath sounds in the middle and nothing at the bottom." Brynne looked up at Dean. "So, Dean, what's next?"

"Nebulized combination meds," Dean said confidently. "Albuterol and Ipratropium, two point five milligrams of Albuterol and five hundred micrograms of Ipratropium via nebulizer mask." He turned to the oxygen bag pulling out the neb mask and tubing.

Then he unzipped the medication bag, reached in and pulled out two plastic ampules, which he put in the nebulizer mask. Taking the non-rebreather mask off Lydia, he replaced it with the nebulizer mask and attached that tubing to the oxygen cylinder, setting the flow to ten liters per minute. The chamber began bubbling, sending a cool mist of medication up into the mask for the woman to breathe in.

"I need you to try to calm your breathing down," Brynne said. "I know it's hard but try. We need to get that medication as deep into your lungs as we can. Listen to my voice and try to breathe in as I count to five, hold it for a second, and then breathe out." Her calm voice started counting slowly holding Lydia's eyes as she worked with the struggling woman. The technique started to work. The combination of Brynne's tone and the medicine seemed to have the desired effect.

"Dean," Brynne said. "Start a line but just attach a saline lock at this point."

"Right," Dean said. He unzipped the front pouch of the med bag and pulled out the IV pouch. He tied an elastic tourniquet off just below the elbow of Lydia's left arm and selected a vein in the middle of her hand that looked good. He wiped the skin, then picked up a 20 gauge IV needle.

"Just a small pinch," he said as he took her hand, pulled the skin tight with the thumb of his right hand and advanced the needle with his left. "There. Got it!" he said to himself. He picked up the saline lock and carefully screwed the hub nut on securing the end in place.

After applying the dressing on top of the insertion site and taping the rest of the tubing down securely to her wrist, Dean looked up at Lydia. Her color was already much better, and her breathing was less labored. Brynne was still helping her concentrate on her breathing, and Dean looked around, thinking about what to do next. His mind went through the mantra. O2, IV, monitor … He looked at the heart monitor and realized it wasn't hooked up yet. He reached into the back pocket of the heart monitor case and counted out four sticky electrode leads then unzipped the side pocket containing the wire harness for the four primary heart leads then attached them. He then looked at the monitor where the heart rhythm was starting to manifest on the screen.

"Sinus Tachycardia," Dean said aloud. "At 134. Pulse ox reading is now 92." He looked at Lydia and saw that she seemed a little more relaxed. The nebulizer mask was starting to sputter intermittently, a sign that the medication supply was running out. He thought she still needed to go the hospital and get checked out. Dean was also curious about what kind of Unusual the patient was. Dispatchers never said, probably because they didn't know, and Brynne had given no clues. Lydia looked completely normal, at least normal with a chronic respiratory illness like asthma.

"Lydia," Brynne said, anticipating Dean's thoughts about treatment. "You're looking better, but I think you still need to go to the hospital." She gazed at Dean, "Let's switch her to a nasal cannula for now and discontinue the neb treatments."

Dean nodded and took the spent nebulizer mask off Lydia, then reached in to pull out a nasal cannula. He was in the process of removing the cannula from the plastic wrapper when Lydia spoke. Her tone was captivating … literally … and he sat staring at his hands as she spoke.

"You all are so helpful," Lydia said. "I want to thank you, but I'm not sure I need to go to the hospital. You could just stay here and help me out. Right, Dean?"

Dean looked up from his hands to Lydia. Jeeze! She was beautiful. Why hadn't he noticed that before? Her voice was so entrancing and melodious, how could he consider telling her no. "I would be happy to stay here and attend to you, Lydia," Dean said. "You only have to say the word."

Lydia's husband was staring at her, aghast, "Lydia, I can't believe you're doing this again." He held up a hand. "I want nothing to do with it." He turned and stormed out.

Brynne looked up at her partner in alarm. "Aw, hell no!" she shouted and started digging around in the med bag on the floor. "Crap, crap, crap!" she stood up and bolted out the front door. Dean couldn't understand why she was so rude to their hostess.

After all, Lydia was generously offering them an opportunity to stay here with her, which was obviously a better idea than taking her to the hospital. And anyway, if he stayed here he could keep listening to her lovely voice. She was humming a tune now, nothing he recognized but a lovely melody with a steady up and down cadence that —.

Suddenly a loud clanging broke through the melodious humming and Lydia shrieked, covering her ears. Dean looked up at Brynne, standing in the center of the room. How had she gotten there? She was just sitting on the couch a second ago. And what was that she was banging on with a drumstick? She stopped for a second and then held out her hand.

"Dean, twist these up and put them in your ears," Brynne ordered. He reached out for what she was handing him, confused but obeying. He stopped though as soon as Lydia started talking again.

"You come to my home and make that infernal noise when I'm talking?" Lydia said. She covered her ears again when Brynne started beating on the metal box again. Dean shook his head to clear his thoughts. It wasn't a metal box. It was a cowbell, like from a drum kit. Where had she gotten that?

"Dean," Brynne shouted over the din of her banging. "Come over here. Pick up the two pieces of beeswax you dropped, twist them up and stick them in your ears." Dean stood up, took a few steps and picked up the two orange lumps off the floor. They were sticky and soft and he rolled them, one in each hand between his thumb and forefinger and then inserted the column of wax in his ear canals. The din of the cowbell taps was not as sharp as soon as the two earplugs were in place. As soon as Brynne saw that he had done as she asked she stopped the banging.

She looked at Lydia, "Lady, you've got a lot of nerve trying to charm my partner. We came here to help you."

"I just don't want to go to that nasty hospital," Lydia pouted. She looked at Dean and sighed as she saw that she was no longer having the desired effect. "I thought you two could just stay here and take care of me until I felt better."

"You need to get to the hospital and get a steroid follow-up shot. We don't have those, and that's what you need," Brynne said. "And just for the record, we're happy to help you out in any way you need. You don't have to turn on your charms and try to coerce our male paramedics that way. You're new in town, right? I don't think we've been here before or there would have been a note to take precautions. We didn't know you were a siren. Did you check in with our headquarters or your own leadership when you got here?"

"I don't like all those formalities," Lydia said. "I'm always afraid the information will get into the wrong hands. I didn't want to call 911 anyway. It was my husband's idea. I think he was feeling bad because we had a fight, and whenever we have a really bad argument, the stress always triggers my asthma."

"Well I'm glad we came," Brynne said. "Even though you tried to hijack my partner. You were in bad shape." She reached into her pocket. "Look, here's the number of our ER medical director, Doc Spirelli. He can help you out, and he'll keep your secret. If you promise to get your husband to drive you to the ER, you don't have to go with us, but you do have to go. You need a course of steroids. That asthma attack has secondary effects that are going to catch up with you in an hour or so."

Dean stood there, still slightly confused as to what just happened. One minute he was trying to get the patient ready for transport and then Brynne teleported to the center of the room and was banging a cowbell.

Lydia's husband walked back in. "I can take her," he said. "I'm sorry I didn't warn you. As sick as she was, I really didn't think she'd turn on the charm while you were here helping her."

"Well we'll know from now on so we'll come prepared," Brynne said. "Remember that the next time you need help from us and decide to try anything funny. Still, no lasting harm was done, right Dean?" She looked at him and chuckled. "He'll be alright, he's pretty good at following instructions, as you have seen. I'll talk him through what happened. No harm, no foul." Brynne set the cowbell and drumstick down and pulled the iPad tablet out of the side pocket of the med bag. "Here, let me get you to sign our transport refusal and we will get out of your hair. If you need us, you can always call us back. But, you are not going to be here because you are going to the emergency room, right?" She looked at Lydia's husband as she offered the screen to Lydia to sign with a scribbling sweep of her finger tip. The man nodded. Satisfied, Brynne then put the iPad back in its pocket and started to clean up their gear. Dean was still standing in the middle of the room, just watching the events going on around him, a bit dazed. She finished packing up the gear, then started hanging the bags by their shoulder straps on Dean until everything was accounted for. She kept the cowbell and drumstick for herself.

"Dean, you head out to the ambulance," Brynne said. She was still watching the siren closely. She clearly did not trust her. Lydia had proven how quickly she would resort to using her powers when it suited her. "Lydia, I just want you to know that we always have a woman along on this particular ambulance team. We are happy to serve you when you need help, but you should know that we won't let ourselves be taken advantage of." She held eye contact with the siren for a few moments. "Do we have an understanding?"

"Yes," Lydia said, waving her hand in the air as if she were shooing an annoying bug. "I was not going to hurt him, and I would have let him go once I was feeling better."

"He's not your medic, he's mine!" Brynne said with a feral grin. "I'm responsible for him, and he's still too new to know how to watch his own back. That's why I've got his back for him. Just remember that."

"Whatever," Lydia said. "I'm done with you now." She used a shooing gesture of her hand to punctuate the remark.

Brynne watched her walk back down the hallway to the bedrooms, then turned and left with a shake of her head. She grabbed Dean by the shoulder where he still stood with all the gear draped on him, confused. She led him out to the ambulance and started to help him stow the bags in their compartments.

"You okay?" she asked him, putting her hand on his shoulder.

"What happened back there?" he said, trying to make sense of it. "One minute I was checking a heart rhythm on the monitor, and then I was standing there and you were banging on that stupid cowbell. I vaguely remember you telling me to stick something in my ears, then you loaded me up and sent me out here."

"Lydia, our patient," she began, "is a siren. You know, the mythical creatures that lured men to their deaths on the rocks from ships at sea. Her voice is like a super hypnotic aphrodisiac to men. As soon as she was able to speak normally, she started to turn on the charm and get you to comply as her own personal paramedic. I should have been paying more attention. With certain types of calls, the dispatchers get a cue from the higher ups via the computer to send us responding on 'Omega' status that alerts us to take special care. We have a bag with a few special tools in it for just such occasions. I would have brought it in if I realized we needed it. My mistake."

She walked over and pulled open the passenger door for Dean. "Climb in. My guess is that you are going to be a bit fuzzy for a half hour or so." Dean watched her glance back at the house behind her before walking around to the driver's side of the ambulance with a shake of her head.

As she climbed in behind the wheel, he asked her, "What was that you had me put in my ears?"

"Beeswax," she answered as she started the unit and pulled back into the street. "For some reason, it's the only thing that works on sirens. I think it has something to do with some kind of residual resonant 'buzzing' trapped in the wax from the hive that stops the siren's voice from getting through. Regular earplugs, headphones and other similar things just do not work."

"It's obvious I needed hearing protection because you were making all that racket on the stupid cowbell," Dean asked. "Where did that come from, anyway?"

"All part of the emergency kit," Brynne said. "Something about the tones of a standard cowbell breaks through the spell, reversing some of the effects. It drives the siren nuts, too. They hate it. Based on that fact alone, I have a theory that the Rolling Stones' 'Honky Tonk Woman' is really about a siren in a southern bar. No proof, of course, but that cowbell opening and then the continuous beat of it throughout the rest of the song would drive a siren nuts, and that makes me think it's true."

"So, I was under a spell, and you used a cowbell to break it," Dean said, a sudden thought occurring to him. "Oh, no!"

"That's right!" she said, grinning ear to ear. "You had a fever and the only cure was …" Dean groaned and then joined her. "… More cowbell."

# Chapter 10

The incident with the siren really shook Dean up. He'd learned in school about being situationally aware and keeping scene safety in mind, but they never discussed a sneak attack by a siren. As Brynne drove them back to the station he kept mulling over the question of how he was supposed to protect himself, or his partner, when he couldn't recognize some dangers when they were staring him in the face?

When they got back to the station, he got out and helped Brynne back the ambulance in, then started methodically repacking the bags and restocking the used medications from the dispenser. When he was done, he sat on the rear bumper. He enjoyed the peace and quiet of the ambulance bay. After a bit, he walked over to the squad room door and went in. Brynne was at the desk on the phone. He heard her talking to someone.

"I didn't think I would need to call you either, Rudy. The issue needs to be dealt with, though. There's an unregistered siren living over off of Quartet Drive. She said she doesn't like to deal with all the red tape, which I could care less about one way or the other. The problem is that she can't seem to stop trying to charm guys. She got my partner before I could stop her, and I would still be there trying to snap the spell if I hadn't found the cowbell so quickly."

She paused for a moment, listening. "It's not funny Rudolf. I'm responsible for him, and he's still too new to know what is going on most of the time. I just need you to talk to her and make sure she knows how things play out around here. James said to call you if there was any trouble. Well, this is trouble, and I need you to take care of it."

She listened some more then said, "Thank you, Rudy. I appreciate it. All right. See ya."

She looked up at Dean as he approached the desk. "What's up? Are you okay?" she asked.

"I'm still pondering what happened earlier," Dean said. "How am I supposed to prepare for things like that when they are completely out of my realm of knowledge? I don't like being blindsided like that."

"Sit down," Brynne said, gesturing to the chair next to the recliner she was in. "As far as scene safety goes, that's mostly my job right now, especially when it comes to Unusuals. A couple of things in our system broke on this particular call. You should be thinking about it so you can learn from it. We both should. We need to make sure we don't make the same mistake again, right?"

Dean nodded and she continued. "But there is no reason to blame yourself. Like I said earlier. I should have picked up on the fact that something was out of whack. We knew it was an Unusual response, but I wasn't familiar with the home or neighborhood so that meant they were new in town or had a new problem they couldn't deal with on their own. Apart from whatever algorithm that the computer and the higher-ups use to pick our calls for us, she wasn't someone I was familiar with. Based on all of that, I should have brought the emergency kit in with me."

"What's in the emergency kit?" Dean asked. "Besides beeswax and cowbells?"

Brynne stood up. "I should have showed this to you sooner. Let's go and see." She led the way to the ambulance bay, then took him to the cabinet just behind the driver's door. The cabinet held road flares, a tool box, wheel chocks and other odds and ends. Dean had never paid a lot of attention to it because the items in it were rarely used. She popped open the door and pulled out a black hard plastic Pelican case. She put the case on the ground, undid the four flip-up latches, and opened it up. The inside of the case looked like something out of a spy movie. It was lined with foam, including the lid. Slots had been expertly cut in the foam in various shapes and sizes, and in the slots rested assorted bottles and vials. He saw what looked like a dog whistle, a cross and a Star of David. Set into a recessed area in the lid with a velcro strap holding it in place, were the cowbell and the drumstick Brynne had used to break Lydia's spell.

"So," Brynne began, crouching down next to the container. She pointed to the cowbell and drumstick in the lid, then to a paper-wrapped block the size of a jumbo pack of gum. "There's the block of beeswax I used." She started pointing out other things, occasionally lifting a glass vial or metal tin to show him. "We have holy water, of course. There's a priest or minister who comes by and re-blesses it for us periodically to maintain its potency. This tin contains dried African termites which I've been told are the only cure for the bite of an Impundulu or African vampire spirit. Never had to use them, and I never want to," she continued with a shudder. "There are various holy symbols to make sure we cover all the bases. The important thing with those is that you select the one that matches your beliefs or heritage or it won't work on those Unusuals who have an evil side."

"Like vampires?" Dean asked. "Gibbie doesn't seem evil, but I guess they aren't all like that."

"Yes," she said with a sigh. "Like vampires. They can all be warded off by a boldly presented holy symbol that's been blessed by a priest of the religion in question. It has to do with the fact that they feed on the life energy of living beings. Nowadays most get their blood from legitimate sources or survive on animal blood. But occasionally, we get a case where one is feeding on humans, and we need to be prepared for that." This time Dean shuddered.

She pulled out what looked like a small med kit from one recess. "This is the medication kit of particular Unusual remedies." She unzipped the pouch and Dean saw medication vials inside with the familiar caps that had the rubber membranes so you could draw off the med with a syringe and needle. "There's liquified wolfsbane in here for the odd lycan bite. We're vaccinated, but the public isn't so if we get a patient who's been bitten, we can usually ward off the infection with this if we get there in time."

"Does it work just on wolf forms or does it work on all animal lycans?" Dean asked. "You said there were others."

"I think the name wolfsbane comes from the fact that the plant was known to work on wolf lycans, but it works on them all." She pointed to a small vial. "There's liquified garlic extract." We use that on cardiac arrest patients who have a suspected vampire bite. It doesn't revive them, but it will stop them from changing after they die if we fail to resuscitate them successfully."

"I don't see any stakes or crossbows," Dean observed.

"We aren't the police, and it is not our place to carry weapons," she said. "When the situation is dangerous, we stage somewhere away from the scene or remove ourselves as best we can and get to safety. There is a team of cops who deal with Unusuals who don't like to play nice. There's also James and his leadership group. They do a good job of policing Unusuals, too. We get the necessary tools to protect ourselves and our patients, but no weapons. It gives the wrong impression, and I think makes us think in the wrong direction."

"So you don't think medics have the right to carry weapons?" Dean asked. He knew this was a hot topic among some EMS circles.

"My opinion is if you want to carry a gun on the job, be a cop or a soldier," Brynne said. "We're healers and healthcare professionals. It is not our place to be fighting battles or dealing death." She looked at Dean. "Are you one of those EMS providers who thinks we should all have concealed carry permits in case a patient becomes combative?"

"No, not me," Dean said raising his hands. "I was just asking that's all. With all the weird things we've encountered I just wondered what we would do if attacked by something we couldn't handle."

"Look," Brynne said. "I know that you're a little shaken up by what happened tonight. I understand, I really do. But the system worked. We had the tools we needed to protect ourselves, and we did our jobs to help the patient. The fact that the patient was a manipulative, psycho bitch with delusions of grandeur is beside the point. We don't have to like our patients. We do have to treat them and do it safely for both ourselves and them. Understand?"

"Yeah," Dean replied. "I guess you're right. Tonight did kind of freak me out, though. I've never been in a situation where I had no control over what happened." He met Brynne's eyes. "I guess I owe you a thank-you, Boss."

"You owe me a lot," she said, "but not for this. We both have a lesson to learn from tonight's events. I need to think, and remember that you're still new. You can't protect yourself because you haven't learned how to be aware of Unusuals' powers in play. There's a possibility - even a probability - that you could have gotten yourself out of that situation back there if you'd realized what was happening early enough. No spell or power works instantly, so, in the future, if you notice something out of place or weird happening or you don't feel right, tell me. If I'm not around, just get up and leave the situation until you figure it out."

Dean quirked an eyebrow. "Isn't that patient abandonment?"

"Safety first," Brynne said. "You cannot help the patient if you're incapacitated, right? So protect yourself and your partner first, and then the patients, and then bystanders, in that order. Got it?"

"Got it," Dean said. "I guess I just need some time to process everything that happened tonight."

"You also might need to talk to a professional," Brynne said. "I'll call headquarters and get the number of a service we use. You can even do it over the phone if meeting in person isn't convenient." Dean started to object, but Brynne held up a hand. "Look, we can't do this alone, and there's a support structure that is specifically put into place to help us manage the bad stuff we see on this job. You learned about this in school, Dean. You just have to apply what you learned to yourself. There is no shame in asking for help or in getting that help. It doesn't mean you're weak or can't cope; it's about learning to cope. That takes some help sometimes."

"I just never thought I would have to deal with anything like this," Dean said. "I always thought that critical incident stress would be something that happened to someone else."

"Now is not the time to be all macho, Dean," Brynne said. "You might need some help dealing with tonight's situation. No big deal. Look, if you cut your finger on the job and needed stitches to make it better, you would go do that right?" She looked at him and he nodded. "Think of this the same way. It is like stitches for your brain. You had something happen tonight, and you need to work through it in order to be at your top form the next time something happens."

She shut the emergency case and snapped the latches down. "Here," she said. "You put this back and I'll go in and call HQ and get that number for you. It is part of your benefits package and it doesn't cost you anything." She got up and left him alone in the ambulance bay as she headed to the squad room.

Dean stared at the black case on the concrete floor next to the ambulance for a long time. He wasn't used to feeling this way. He'd been completely helpless back there at Lydia's house. He didn't understand why someone whom he was helping would turn around and try to control or hurt him like that. It was not something he'd been prepared for. He particularly didn't like how it had him second-guessing everything now. He wasn't sure how it was going to affect him on the next call, or the one after that. Would he freeze up or not be able to think clearly because he was afraid of what might happen to him? How would that affect his ability to care for his patients or protect his partner? He had a lot of questions that needed answers, and he wasn't sure if there were any way he, or anyone else could answer them.

Dean finally stooped down and picked up the case on the floor, placing it back in the compartment in the side of the ambulance. Shutting the door, he wondered, not for the first time why he had been selected for this particular position. It would have been much easier treating regular people. Maybe he wasn't cut out for being a paramedic at all. The door opening to the squad room behind him interrupted his thoughts.

"Dean," Brynne said. "I found that number for you. Come on in. It's open around the clock, twenty-four hours a day so you can call and chat with them now."

"I think that might be a good idea, Brynne," Dean said turning her way. "I'm questioning that I'm the right person for this job right now. Maybe you should call someone in to relieve me until I get this figured out."

"Let's not worry about that right now," Brynne said. "You come in and call. I'll make sure that HQ knows we're out of service for a little bit. They generally have backup in place for us if we need it and right now we need it."

Dean followed her into the squad room. She handed him a sticky note with a phone number on it.

"See," she said. "It is even toll-free. I also think you might want to talk to your instructor, Mike. I dropped him a quick email letting him know you might be calling. He helped me out a lot with something similar to this when I was still pretty new. It's something we all run into from time to time on this job, and not just here on the Unusual side of things. Regular medics get stressed out by things they see, too."

Dean took the number from Brynne and looked at it. He couldn't figure out why he was feeling reluctant to call. He knew he needed help but taking that step felt like an admission of weakness.

"Dean," Brynne said breaking through his thoughts. "Call the number. Talk to them and tell them what you're feeling right now. It is all perfectly normal. We're not getting any more calls tonight until you do it. Sit down, pick up the phone and dial the number. After that, do what you want, but tonight your job is to talk to the person on the other end of that line. I'm going back into the bunk room if you need me. Come get me when you're done talking to them if you want." She left the room, picking up her book from the recliner on the way by.

Dean walked over to the desk chair, pulled it out and sat down. He picked up the phone, glanced at the sticky note in his other hand

and dialed the number. He sighed as it started ringing. After the second ring, it picked up.

"Hi, this is Rebecca, is this Dean?" the voice on the other end asked. She sounded very pleasant.

"Uh, yes. Yes, this Dean," he said.

"I was told to expect your call," Rebecca said. He swore he could hear her smiling. "I understand you had a rough situation tonight. Why don't you tell me what happened."

As he discussed the incident, it seemed like a weight was lifting off of him. Could it be some other kind of magic? Well, magic or not, he felt better. He may survive this after all.

## Chapter 11

The conversation with Rebecca was just what Dean needed. They talked for about an hour and he felt noticeably better after he got off the call. She warned him that this type of counseling for first responders was just the first part of treatment. He was going to need to follow up with her later that week. They set up an hour-long appointment in her offices across town for that Wednesday, his next day off. He was surprised to discover that he was actually looking forward to it.

He checked his email while he was in front of the computer and found a message from Mike Farver. Mike wanted to catch up with him for a cup of coffee at the end of his shift on his way into the academy. He said he'd come by at six and pick him up. Dean replied back that he'd be looking forward to it.

Dean decided not to bother Brynne in the bunkroom since she was probably asleep. There were still a few hours left until the end of the shift. He decided to catch up on some more reading and see if he could be better prepared the next time he encountered a patient like Lydia. Rebecca told him it was not his fault. She'd also said it might help him to be more confident if he learned more about the community and culture of the unique patient population he dealt with. He went over and picked up a book "The Heroes, Gods and Monsters of Greek Myth." Lying back across the length of the sofa, he started flipping through the stories until he found one about sirens. He'd be prepared for Lydia or others like her next time.

He woke up with a jolt as the door to the parking lot slammed shut. "Hey Newbie," Bill said as he walked in. "Slow night?"

"Uh, we had one call," Dean said. "It was … interesting."

"Those are the best kind, my friend," he said, laughing. "Hi, Brynne!" Dean turned to see Brynne walking out from the bunkrooms.

"Did Dean tell you about our night?" she asked.

"No," Bill said, setting down his coffee on the desk. "I just got here. He said you had one call."

"We ran into a new siren in town," Brynne said. "Lydia was her name. She had a pretty bad asthma attack, but be careful if you go there. She wanted to keep Dean as her own paramedic for a while. I had to convince her otherwise."

"Oooo," Bill said. He looked at Dean. "It's great to have women fighting over you, isn't it, kid? Did she get to break out the cowbell and beeswax?"

"Uh, yeah," Dean said, "it was a little too weird for my taste though. I prefer normal dating. You know, dinner and movie before I get a spell cast on me.

"I got zapped by a siren once a few years back," Bill said. "I even dated her off and on for a while. Nice girl, but a bit too high on the crazy-hot scale."

"The world is littered with women who could say the same thing about you, Bill," Lynne announced from the door. "What brought that up anyway? You guys have a run in with a siren last night?"

"Yeah," Brynne said. "Dean got his first taste of the darker side of Unusuals."

"Patients, no matter whether they're human or not," Lynne said, "can catch you by surprise anytime, anywhere. Keeping up your guard all the time is impossible. That's why we have partners to watch our backs. Hey, by the way, I think I saw Mike pulling up as I came in."

"Oh, yeah," Dean said. "He's here to take me out for coffee, and I guess I get a pep talk after last night's events."

"Mike's the guy to do it," Bill said. "Hell, he invented this job. He knows more about dealing with Unusuals than anyone else out there, except maybe for Doc Spirelli of course."

Dean put the book he'd fallen asleep with back on the shelf. "I guess I'll go meet Mike and see what he has to say. You guys have a good day. I'll see you tonight." He left the squad room and went outside to the parking lot. The sun was shining and it looked like it was shaping up to be a great day. Mike sat in a marked Ford Explorer with the Elk City EMS shield on the doors and emergency lights on the roof. He walked to the passenger side, opened the door and climbed in.

"Dean," Mike said, holding out his hand. "How the heck are you? I've been checking in with Brynne and she says you're doing a great job. She says you've got some good skills and instincts for this unique type of patient care."

Dean took the offered hand and shook it. "I've had better nights, but I guess that's why you're here."

Mike smiled. "I would have been checking in on you soon anyway. I make a point to do that with all of my students a month or so after school is over. I want to make sure that their preceptors are treating them right." He started the SUV and pulled out of the parking lot. "I did throw you to the dogs out here at Station U. I never had any doubts you were the right person for the job, but I probably should have prepared you better for the specifics of what you were going to run into here. You remind me of me when I was starting out." He turned onto the main drag of Route 40. "You okay with diner food? I know a really good place called 'Hanks' near here if that's okay with you?"

"Diner food sounds good," Dean said. "I'm hungry after that night shift."

"You'll find that when something supernatural happens to you, it takes a lot of energy to recover from it," Mike said as he drove. "You'll likely be hungrier than normal for the next few days."

They talked about some of the other students in the class but stayed away from anything about the previous night's activities. After about 10 minutes on the road, they pulled into the parking lot of a beat up diner modeled after the old train diner cars.

"Don't let the outside fool you," Mike said. "Trust me, the food is excellent. Everything you order here is good."

"I'll take your word for it," Dean said. "I don't think you'd try to poison me."

Mike laughed as the two of them walked up to the diner's door. Mike held the door for his former student as they both walked in. Mike nodded to the hostess and headed to an empty booth in the back corner. That was interesting, as the rest of the place was packed and there were others waiting for a seat.

"I come here a lot and I called ahead and had them save this spot for us. It'll give us more privacy," Mike gestured for Dean to sit down. Dean slid into the seat and picked up the plastic laminated menu as Mike sat down across from him. It was typical diner breakfast fare, and he thought maybe the creamed chipped beef on toast looked good with two eggs over easy on the side.

"Like I said," Mike reminded him. "Everything here is good." He didn't look at the menu. "I usually get a short stack of buttermilk pancakes and a side of sausage links. Do you see anything that looks good to you?"

"I think I'm going to get the chipped beef with gravy and a couple of eggs," Dean said.

Mike raised his hand and a waitress came over. She looked a little tired but greeted them with a smile. Her name tag read Daisy. "Hi Mike! Who's your friend?" she asked.

"This is one of my former students, Dean," Mike said. "Dean, this is Daisy."

"Hi," Dean said.

"So," Daisy said. "What'll you have?"

"The usual for me," Mike said and looked at Dean, quirking an eyebrow. "And the creamed chipped beef for Dean, with two eggs on the side." Dean nodded in affirmation.

After she left Mike looked at Dean. "So, how are you really? Last night must have been quite a shock."

Dean met his mentor's eyes. "I'm a little overwhelmed, honestly, and freaked out. I won't lie; last night shook me up." He looked down at his hands. "Mike, I've never felt so helpless. And the worst part was that I didn't even know I was in danger or would have cared about it if I did know. Lydia was in control and I thought that was fine. It wasn't until Brynne came in beating that cowbell that I knew something odd was happening. I really don't remember much of it. I remember starting an assessment, then Brynne was leading me out to the ambulance."

Mike nodded as he listened, a slight smile on his face. "I understand," he said. "I really do. I got jumped by a vamp my first week on the job and that was back when we were first getting a handle on the type of things we needed to do. Doc Spirelli was riding along with us at that point and had to threaten the guy with the crucifix that hung on a chain around his neck. When we got back to the station, I was ready to quit on the spot and go work for my brother-in-law in his construction business. The doc talked me off that ledge. I'm still here."

"I guess I kind of feel the same way," Dean said. "I'm not sure this is right for me. Don't get me wrong. I really do enjoy the challenge of getting the medicine right and the puzzle of assessing these patients is intriguing. But I'm still not sure it's worth it."

They paused the conversation for a minute as Daisy came back with their drinks. She set a steaming mug of coffee down in front of Mike, then put Dean's water and diet coke down. "Your food should be out soon, she said.

Mike waited until she had stepped away and then asked, "I heard you set up an appointment to talk with Rebecca?" Dean nodded. "She's awesome, I think you'll like her."

"I talked with her on the phone last night," Dean said. "She helped, some."

"That's good, Dean," Mike said. "You have to understand it's a process. You're not going to forget this all in a night or even a single counseling session. The trick now is to decide whether or not you're up to continuing on the job right now."

"I guess if I was a cop," Dean said. "I would get desk duty for a few days."

"And that is a choice," Mike offered. "I'm here to talk to you so that together we can come up with an option that works for you. You should know that Lydia, the siren you ran into, will not be bothering folks that way anymore."

Dean looked up. "You didn't …?"

"No," Mike laughed. "We didn't bump her off or anything. We don't work that way. She's new in town so we had some folks stop by and have a chat with her and her husband. Did Brynne tell you about the special Unusuals police unit?" Dean nodded and Mike continued. "We work with a few select police officers. There's at least one on every shift. They stopped by and explained to Lydia the way things work here. Not every place has the services we provide. Most Unusuals have to protect themselves from the humans they live among as best they can. Think of their powers and abilities as a sort of defense mechanism that helps them survive alongside us."

"Brynne also contacted Rudolf," Dean said. "She had his number from James to help deal with problems if they came up. The way she talked, they handle these things internally."

"They do," Mike agreed. "Still, Brynne needs to take things through official channels. Her relationship with James doesn't give her the right to go around her supervisors when something like this comes up. I guess I need to have a chat with her about that. We contacted Rudolf, too, since we knew James was out of town."

"I just don't know what led Lydia to do what she did to me," Dean said. "We were there to help her. Why did she turn on us?"

"It's like I told you back in school when we were talking about drunks and drug abusers," Mike said. "You can't know what drives them to be the way they are, and because of that you have to be careful to treat them with the same compassion as you'd give any other patient. You can't get mad at them or try to take revenge on them on behalf of society."

"I remember that lecture," Dean said. "You used that old Native American proverb about not criticizing people until you had walked a mile in their moccasins."

"Good," Mike said, smiling. "I'm glad you remember. That's part of the lesson here. I don't pretend that what this Lydia did wasn't bad. She was wrong and we have dealt with her both officially and unofficially through Rudolf. The part of the job you have is to try and understand is why she might be driven to manipulate you that way. What happened to her in the past that made her not trust the medical system or people associated with the government? Does that make sense? It doesn't forgive what she did. It does try and explain the why, understand?" Dean nodded. "Good, because the food's here."

Dean turned and looked over his shoulder to see Daisy approaching with a large round tray balanced on one hand and steadied with the other. She lowered the tray and let one edge rest on the table. She set the plates in front of them. The food smelled delicious and Dean's stomach growled.

"Wow," Daisy said with a chuckle. "Was that you?"

He laughed, too. "I guess I'm hungry!"

"Well, you came to the right place," she said. "I'll check back on you in a few minutes."

Mike and Dean ate in silence for the next few minutes. Mike was right, the food was excellent and there was something about breaking bread with his old instructor that helped settle his fears a bit. It was a reminder that life was still going on around him. Before he knew it, he was finished with the meal, literally cleaning his plate of the last remnants of delicious gravy with a piece of toast.

"I told you it was good," Mike said. "Do you feel better?"

"I do," Dean said. "Thanks, Mike."

"No problem," Mike said. "We can do this again. Anytime you need to, just call me. Okay?"

"Deal," Dean said. "Though I hope this kind of thing doesn't happen too often."

"Look, Dean," Mike said. "This is a critical incident. It could happen to anyone whether you're a regular medic or work in EMS-

U. The unusual circumstances surrounding your situation don't matter as much as the fact that you had a traumatic event. It could have been the death of a sick kid, or a bad motor vehicle accident. We all have triggers that can affect us out of the blue. When that happens our job is to seek out the help we need. We can't stop these things from affecting us in the moment or immediately afterwards, but we can control how we respond to those effects. You've got my support, Brynne's and your other co-workers as well as a whole support network of people like your new counselor, Rebecca. Use that support to get your feet back under you."

Mike dropped a few bills on the table. "Come on, I'll drive you back to your car so you can get some sleep."

As Dean drove home later, he thought about the conversation and realized he was no longer pondering what he did or didn't do to cause the situation the previous night. He wasn't blaming himself as much. He figured that was part of what Mike was trying to achieve with their breakfast conversation. He would have to bring that up with Rebecca when he saw her in two days.

# Chapter 12

Two days after the incident with Lydia, the siren, he met Rebecca in person. Her offices were downtown in a high-rise suite. He parked in the underground garage and opted to walk up the stairs to the lobby rather than to use the elevator, as was his habit. He was a little anxious about the meeting. He wondered again if his reaction was a sign of weakness. He knew intellectually that it was not, but there was still a part of him that wondered about his own inner strength.

Once in the lobby, he found the building directory on the wall next to a bank of elevators. He saw the name he was looking for, CISM Solutions, located on the 7th floor. When the elevator arrived he waved to let the others enter first and then stepped on, asking the man nearest to the panel of buttons to push the seventh floor for him.

He was thinking about what he would talk about with Rebecca as the elevator car stopped at the third, fourth, and fifth floors before arriving at seven. He stepped off the elevator into the hall-way. The sign for CISM Solutions was next to the second door on the right. He walked over to it and walked inside.

The waiting room was empty, and there was no one at the reception window when he entered. He wrote his name and time of arrival on the clipboard; then he sat down in one of the four chairs lining one wall next to a coffee table with a few scattered magazines on it. He saw two recent EMS magazines. He opted to browse his phone's social media feed while he waited to be called. He could hear the murmur of voices behind the wooden door across the room from where he sat. The soft music from the speakers in the overhead ceiling kept him from understanding anything that was said, which was the point, he supposed.

After about ten minutes of waiting the door opened, and a man and woman came out. "I'll email you a reminder about your next appointment, Ian," a woman said.

"Thanks, Rebecca," the man said. "I'll be there." He walked to the exit and left.

"You must be Dean," the woman said extending her hand. "I'm Rebecca." She was a lot younger than he expected, maybe in her mid to late twenties. She had shoulder length red hair, wore a navy blue woman's business suit and slacks with a white blouse. She had some jewelry on, but not much. Dean stood up and shook her hand.

"Uh, yes, I am," he said. "I guess I'm in the right place."

"Come on back, Dean," she said, smiling. "Let's go into my office and get to know one another for a bit." Rebecca led the way to the door and gestured for him to enter first. There was a desk and chair in one corner next to a window, as well as a small love seat and chair combination with an end table in the corner between them. There was a box of tissues on the table. He paused for a moment when he saw that. God he hoped he didn't end up needing to use them.

"Go ahead and have a seat anywhere, Dean," she said as she sat down in the chair at the desk.

He sat in the cushioned chair rather than the love seat, and looked around the room at diplomas and credentials on the wall. The proof, he supposed, that she was qualified to do this job. She turned, picked up a file from the desk, and laid it on her lap as she opened it. "I think I have all your information here, and I have my notes from our call the other night. I want to remind you that this is confidential. You also don't have to worry about them finding out anything we talk about here. The only thing I'm obligated to report is whether you might need reassignment or a change of pace for some reason. Also, you should know that the visit is covered by your employer so you don't have to worry about paying."

"Okay," Dean said. "I guess that's a good thing."

"It is," Rebecca said with a smile. "I notice that you were assigned to Station U right out of school. That's quite an honor. It usually means your chief and instructors thought highly of you."

"I wasn't sure what to think when I first got there," Dean said. "I didn't know what to expect, but it's been okay."

"I know quite a bit about the subject of 'Unusuals' as you call us, Dean, so you can speak freely here," Rebecca said. She laughed as he looked up with surprise at her admission. "I'm a Muse, Dean. Traditionally we inspire artists and musicians to create, but I found that I could use my talents a bit differently. Because of my connection I can help people use their creative minds to see many different potentials. In an artist, that potential is what could be wrought from a block of marble or put on a blank canvas. I like to inspire people to be better people, to see what they could potentially become and then help them live up to that potential."

"I'm not sure I'm comfortable with you using some kind of mojo on me," Dean said, holding his hands up in front of him. "That's what has me coming here in the first place."

"Oh my goodness, no," she said with a little giggle. "Muses don't work that way. I can't do anything to you at all. Let's just say that as we talk, I will see answers and options that may not occur to you, and I'll bring them up to see if they resonate with you. Eventually, we'll find a way to resolve what is bothering you. But in the end, it all comes from you. Muses help people become the better person that is hidden inside them. It all comes from within. Does that make sense?"

"Uh, I guess so." Dean still wasn't sure he was comfortable having his counselor be an Unusual.

"Look, let's make a deal," Rebecca proposed. "We'll talk for an hour or so. Afterward, if you think it will work out between us, great. We can keep working together. If you're still uncomfortable, no worries there, either. I can easily transfer your file to another counselor. The advantage of having me as your counselor is that we can talk freely about some of the things you encounter. You won't have to beat around the bush about your patients' strange abilities or habits. How does that sound?"

"I guess that's fair," Dean said.

"Excellent." She smiled. "So, let's talk a bit about what happened with the siren the other night. You've had a few days to get some perspective and give it some thought. Tell me how you feel about it now."

Dean did most of the talking and Rebecca asked occasional questions. The hour was up before he knew it. He wasn't sorry he came, and he wished he could stay and talk with her longer.

"So, Dean," Rebecca said as she put his folder down on the desk behind her. "I think this was productive, but more importantly – what do you think? Shall we continue or would you like me to help you find someone else to talk with?"

"I guess we can keep working together, Rebecca," Dean said. "This wasn't that bad."

She laughed. "I'm glad it wasn't horrible."

He smiled back at her. "Yeah, it wasn't horrible."

"Let's meet up again in a week," she offered, pulling out a tablet computer and tapping on it. "What is your schedule like next week on Tuesday evening?"

Dean pulled out his smartphone and checked his schedule. "I'm back on days starting Monday, so I'm off at six."

"Excellent," she said. "I'll put you down for seven that night. And remember – if you need to talk sooner, you can call and we can find a time to squeeze you in before then. Do you need me to write that time on an appointment card or do you have it on your phone?"

"I've got it," Dean said as he finished tapping in the information on his calendar app. He stood up. He really did feel better. "I guess this wasn't as bad as I'd feared."

"Well that's good, Dean," Rebecca said. "It may not always be completely painless, but together we can sort this out for you. I'll help you get back to a place where you won't question or second guess yourself." She stood and opened the door for him. As Dean walked out, he saw that the next person was in the office already.

"Thanks, Rebecca," he said as he walked into the reception area. "I'll see you next week."

She nodded at him and walked over to the woman waiting in the chairs. Dean let himself out and paused for the elevator to go back down to his truck. Mike had told him to keep an open mind and that he wouldn't mind the counseling, and his old mentor was right. Rebecca had lightened the load on his mind. He still had questions, but he no longer feared that he wouldn't find the answers. Rebecca the Muse had inspired him to start believing in himself and trust in his own abilities again. He could do this.

# Chapter 13

He had a few more days off, then he was back at work covering nights. The calls were pretty routine for the most part, and Brynne trusted him more and more with handling patient care on his own. The two of them sat in the station house checking on updates from the online management and scheduling system. Elk City EMS headquarters used the system to keep in touch with each station, and every member of the system was expected to check in regularly and sign off electronically after reading the notes and updates posted there.

Dean was reading a research paper on recent opioid overdoses where the heroin was laced with fentanyl, causing a respiratory depression situation that was extremely difficult to overcome when treating those patients. He wasn't sure if he'd encounter it, but he guessed there were Unusuals who were drug abusers just like everyone else.

"Brynne," he said. "I'm reading about this new fentanyl-laced heroin. It's certainly kicking the butts of our colleagues running calls for the regular population. I haven't seen much drug abuse in our calls so far though. Do Unusuals use drugs like other people do?"

"Sure," she said. "We just haven't run in to any yet. Mostly they're into the club drugs like ecstasy and the synthetics like bath salts. I guess you've just been lucky so far. When dealing with Unusuals, the treatment parameters are similar to humans. I'll look up and email you a link to an EMS podcast I listen to that covered club drugs recently."

Brynne turned in her chair and looked over at him. "How are you doing, anyway?"

"I'm fine," Dean said. "Really, I'm fine. I am working through it. I just need to go through the process. The counselor you and Mike hooked me up with seems great and I think she has me on the right track."

"Good," Brynne said. "I'm glad to hear that. I just wanted to tell you that I'm sorry. I didn't pay close enough attention to what was going on. I'm supposed to be the one that keeps you from getting into that kind of trouble and I didn't."

"Boss," Dean said. "If I've picked up anything from this experience, and from Rebecca and Mike for that matter, it's that you can't second guess yourself after the fact. It doesn't do any good. It happened and what you did was recognize the problem and fix it. If you hadn't done that I don't know what would have happened. I could still be there as Lydia's personal paramedic. If it makes you feel better I could say 'apology accepted' but I don't think that's the right answer either. All we can do is the best we can with what we know. You didn't know she was a siren. When you found out, you took action. The way I look at it, you didn't make a mistake."

"Well," she said. "I'm sorry that it happened the way it did."

"Hey," Dean said, laughing, "me too. I don't want anything like that to happen to us again, but I guess that would be wishful thinking."

"Yeah, that's true," Brynne said.

The tones sounded and interrupted their discussion. The voice of the dispatcher came over the radio. "Medical Box 421, injured subject. 699 Breton Way."

"Time to go to work," Dean said, hopping up and heading to the ambulance bay door. "Gonna let me drive, Boss?"

"Not on your life, Probie." Brynne laughed. "Let's do this."

The call took them up to a residential neighborhood and a large Victorian home that had been converted into apartments. The additional information from dispatch had come back that there was a male subject with an arm injury located on the south side of the building outside. It was already late and dark out, and their scene safety radar was up as they pulled into the parking lot next to the building.

"I'll grab two flashlights, Dean," Brynne said putting the gearshift in park. "You grab the oxygen and splint bag."

Dean keyed the radio, "U-191 on location at Medical Box 421." Then he jumped out of the passenger side of the ambulance and opened the doors to pull out the bags. A voice spoke right behind him and caused him to jump.

"Dean," the voice said. "You have to help me. I think she's trying to kill me."

Dean spun around with a yelp to see Gibbie standing behind him. He was cradling his right arm in the other, and the right forearm was clearly misshapen. "Jeez, Gibbie, don't sneak up on a guy that way."

Brynne came trotting around the back of the ambulance, shining a flashlight on the two of them. She relaxed when she saw who it was. "Oh, it's you Gibbie," she said. "What happened?"

"Brynne, honey," the excited vampire said. "I think Brenda is mad at me. She tried to kill me."

"Oh, you think that I'm mad at you, do you?" Another voice came from the direction of the front porch. A woman approached them. "Did you think you could just come flapping into my bedroom window after you'd been with that tramp, you … you two-timing vamp man-whore!"

Brynne diverted the flashlight to shine on the woman, Gibbie's girlfriend Brenda. "Dean, get him in the back of the unit and see what you can do for him," Brynne said. "I'll deal with her."

Dean popped open the side door of the ambulance and helped Gibbie climb inside, then he jumped up behind his patient and shut the door. He directed Gibbie to sit on the cot while he sat down on the side chair next to him. "Gibbie, tell me what happened."

"I really have no idea, Dean," the vampire began. "I don't know what's got her so upset. I was flying over in my bat form to visit like I usually do. Brenda had her window open like usual until I got there. Then she slammed the window down on me. She caught my wing between the window and the frame. She opened it again to yell at me and I fell down outside in the bushes like some kind of rubbish. I shifted back to human form right away. I think she broke my arm. That's why I called you."

Dean looked at Gibbie's right arm. The lower portion of the arm just above the wrist had a lump that just didn't belong there. "I think you might be right, Gibbie," Dean said. "Let's see what we can do. Can you tell me how much pain you're having, on a scale of one to ten with one being very little pain and ten being a lot of pain?"

"Ten, Dean! Definitely a ten," Gibbie said. "I mean look what she did. She tried to kill me."

"Okay," Dean grabbed a chemical cold pack out of the cabinet, broke the pellet inside and shook it to mix the chemicals so that they started to chill. "Here, put this on that bump. That'll start helping with the swelling and will also help with the pain."

He got out the IV kit and got the supplies together to start an IV line in the uninjured hand. He got the line in place and attached the IV tubing to the catheter in the vampire's arm.

"Gibbie, I'm going to give you something for the pain. Do you have any allergies to morphine?"

"No," Gibbie replied. "Do you think she'll let me explain myself? I can't lose Brenda, she's the love of my life."

"I don't know, Gibbie," Dean answered. "But Brynne's out there with her, and she'll find out what's going on with Brenda. Let me try and help you. We'll find out what is going on with her when we're done with taking care of you, okay?"

"Alright," Gibbie conceded.

Dean pulled out the pre-filled syringe of morphine and, pinching the tubing above the port, attached the syringe and carefully and slowly administered two milligrams of the drug into the IV line. He detached the morphine syringe and then rolled back the valve on the tubing to allow the fluid to flush the drug into his patient's system. He watched Gibbie's face as he administered the drug.

"We'll let that start to work, and if that dose doesn't take the edge off the pain, I can give you some more," Dean said. "Now let's look at what I can do to stabilize that arm so it won't move around and hurt you even more." Dean took the chemical ice pack off gently and checked the area of deformity and swelling on the vampire's arm. It was definitely broken. He went over to a cabinet at the back of the ambulance and selected a short padded board splint and carefully placed Gibbie's injured forearm on top of it. He got a roll of cling gauze and began to wrap the arm carefully to the splint. Dean knew he was supposed to check pulses in the affected limb after applying the splint but since the vampire had no pulse he didn't bother with that part of the process.

"How does that feel, Gibbie?" Dean asked. He was admiring his handiwork, but ultimately it was the patient's comfort level that was paramount.

"Better," Gibbie answered. "It doesn't hurt as much."

"Okay, let me make a sling so you can keep the arm still," the paramedic said. "I also think you're going to have to go into the hospital. I don't know how your super healing thing works, but I don't think you want the arm to heal crooked. Doc Spirelli is going to have to set that bone so it's straight. Okay?"

Gibbie nodded, and Dean got out a triangular bandage to fashion a sling to support the arm on the way to the hospital. When he was finished tying the sling in place, he checked that the arm was supported properly. Everything looked good.

"How is the pain level now on a scale of one to ten?" Dean asked.

"It's about a six," Gibbie said.

"Okay, I can give you some more morphine." He picked up the narcotic syringe and attached it to the port in the IV tubing again, then he slowly began pushing another two milligrams.

As Dean was administering the drug, the back door of the ambulance opened and Brynne climbed in, closing it behind her.

"Boy, Gibbie, she sure is pissed at you," Brynne said. "I got her to go back inside but what did you do to her? She's convinced you're cheating on her."

"I don't know, Brynne," Gibbie said. "I couldn't come over the other night because I was a little hung over after a bit of a feeding frenzy. A friend of mine got some fresh blood from the blood bank, and we stayed up all night drinking."

"Is that friend of yours a woman?" Brynne asked.

"Well, yes, but nothing happened," Gibbie replied. "Josie is like a sister to me. We've been pals for over two hundred years. She's got this cushy job working for the Red Cross and gets access to the blood bank from time to time, but it was nothing for Brenda to be jealous of."

"Well," Brynne said. "I don't think she sees it that way."

She looked over at Dean. "What's the deal with the arm?"

"I'm pretty sure it's fractured," Dean replied. "It has swelling with deformity. I've given him four milligrams of morphine, and that's taken the edge off the pain. I think he needs to get into the hospital to get it set properly before his vamp healing starts forming it in a crooked position."

"You're probably right, Dean," Brynne said, nodding. "Okay, I'll drive. You stay back here with Gibbie and call it into the hospital, so they're expecting us. Remember to use his apparent age. No need to freak them out with a patient who is older than the country we live in." Brynne opened the back door and hopped out. As the door closed behind her, Dean helped his patient turn and lay down on the stretcher so he could buckle him in. He lifted the head of the stretcher up to a reclining position and then moved to the captain's chair at the head of the stretcher to access the med radio there. He attached his own seat belt as he felt the ambulance start to move forward.

Picking up the microphone from its cradle, he dialed into the direct channel to Elk City Medical Center and keyed the microphone. "ECMC this is ambulance U one-nine-one. How do you receive?"

After a pause, a voice came back over the radio. "We receive you loud and clear, U one-nine-one. Go ahead."

"City, we're enroute to your facility with a 50-year-old male with a suspected fracture of the right forearm. I have the arm stabilized and have administered four milligrams of morphine for pain. The patient is conscious and alert."

"Received U one-nine-one. Do you have a set of vital signs for us?" the voice asked.

Dean winced. How did he relay that his patient didn't have vital signs as a member of the undead community? "Uh, I'll have that for you on arrival. Unable to obtain vitals at this time."

"Roger, U one-nine-one. Vitals on arrival. What's your ETA?"

"We should be arriving in about ten minutes," Dean said. "I will contact you again if there is any change in status. U one-nine-one clear."

"Received, U one-nine-one. We'll see you when you get here. City clear."

Dean put the mic back on the cradle and reached around the head of the stretcher to put his hand on Gibbie's uninjured left shoulder. "How are you doing, Gibbie?" he asked.

"I'm fine, Dean," the vampire replied. "I'm just worried about Brenda. I don't know how to impress upon her that she's my number one girl. I would never cheat on her."

"I don't think that's the problem," Dean said. "She seems to be worried about who's number two, three and four. You are probably going to have to come up with something pretty big to make it up to her."

"I think you're right, kid," Gibbie said. "Do you have any ideas? What do these modern gals like?"

"You should have this locked down, dude," Dean said. "Believe me, you don't want to take advice from me. I'm a complete idiot around women I like."

"Well I have to think of something," Gibbie said and then he started blubbering. "I cannot lose her. She's the best thing that ever happened to me. I'll just die if she breaks up with me."

Dean continued to listen as they made their way to the hospital, occasionally making reassuring sounds and gestures while Gibbie ranted about his relationship failures. Dean checked on his patient's pain level one more time, but he reported that it was nearly gone and was more like a dull ache.

Dean smiled as they made their way across town. The aged vampire was beginning to grow on him. In fact, this job was beginning to grow on him. He'd been disappointed when first assigned to Station U as he was sure it was a punishment. But the jobs were interesting and challenging, and even the patients offered something of a thrill ride with their Unusual quirks and traits. The crew he worked with were all top-notch paramedics. They were true health care professionals. Brynne was a great preceptor and, despite the challenges of the job and the incident with Lydia, he thought that this was a good fit for him.

"We're here," Brynne called from the front of the ambulance as Dean felt them pull up onto the ambulance ramp outside of Elk City Medical Center. He stopped his daydreaming and unhooked the IV bag from the ceiling hook. He then dialed back the rolling valve to close off the tubing so no more fluid would flow and laid the bag across the top of the pillow behind Gibbie's head. Then Dean moved to the back of the ambulance as Brynne opened the back doors. He hopped down, and she reached over and unlocked the stretcher's undercarriage from its position. With Dean at the foot of the stretcher, they wheeled it up and into the emergency room entrance.

They pulled the stretcher up to the nurses' station and waited for the middle-aged nurse there to look up from her work on the computer.

"Is this the broken arm?" she asked, looking up. "Oh, hello Gibbie. I didn't know it was you." She shifted her gaze to Dean. "Take him over to exam three. I'll be right there to take your report."

Dean and Brynne wheeled Gibbie to the room the nurse indicated, then helped him move over to the hospital bed. Dean hung the IV bag on a stand next to the bed and readjusted the rolling valve to the point there was just a drop in the drip chamber every few seconds.

The nurse who checked them in came bustling in the room. "So, what do we have today with Mister Proctor?" she asked.

Dean looked up, "Suspected fractured arm due to a fall or getting it caught in a window, take your pick. We gave 4 milligrams of morphine and splinted the arm at the point of deformity."

"Carol, it was awful," Gibbie said to the nurse. "Brenda, my one true love, slammed the window down on me, and I was just hanging there. Even if the arm heals perfectly, I don't think I'll ever be the same again."

"I'm sure you'll be fine, Gibbie," Carol said. "I'll have Doc Spirelli come in and take a look. He should be able to set it for you and you'll be as good as new." She turned to Brynne and Dean. "We've got it from here, guys. Thanks."

The paramedics backed their stretcher out of the exam room and wheeled it over to where the linens were kept. They stripped the sheets off the cot, sprayed it down with disinfectant, made it up with fresh sheets and pushed it out to the ambulance. Another job well done, Dean thought.

## Chapter 14

Brynne and Dean were on the way back to the station when the next call came in over the radio. "U-191 respond to assist ambulance 792 with a cardiac arrest. 26 year-old female. CPR in progress. 462 West Front Street."

Dean picked up the mic. "U-191 responding, 462 West Front Street." He reached over and switched on the lights and keyed the siren as Brynne pulled into the left lane and prepared to make a U-turn back towards downtown. "I guess we're just the next closest unit?" he said to Brynne. "Is that why they called us to assist?"

"Could be that, but it might be something else," she said. "That location is near a bar that a lot of Unusuals hang out in so keep your eyes open. They might need our Unusual talents."

The location was only a couple of blocks away and they saw the lights of the other ambulance as they approached the scene. They pulled up behind the other unit, parked, got out and started to push their way through the crowd to an alley between two buildings. On the right was a bar with a sign that read Wicked Moon. On the left was a 24-hour drug store. As Dean was moving to the edge of the crowd he glanced to the side and saw James Lee, Brynne's boyfriend. The vampire met Dean's eyes and smirked, mouthing the words, "too late."

"Hey, Brynne, did you see ..." Dean started to say to his partner.

"Yeah, I saw him," Brynne said. "Keep your eyes open. Something is going on here that might require us to do something strange. Be ready to distract the other crew if I tell you to."

"Right." Dean said.

They approached the edge of the alley where two paramedics were in the process of performing CPR on the young woman. She had that pale look that a patient gets when their heart stops beating and pushing blood around the body, or when you're a vampire, Dean thought. Brynne came up and addressed the senior medic on the code who was managing respirations with a bag valve mask while his partner pumped away on the chest compressions, counting out loud. "What do you have, Ray?"

"Hi Brynne," the other paramedic said as they approached. "She was found collapsed here in the alley. Bystander CPR was started when they realized she was in cardiac arrest. She's in PEA on the monitor with a sinus bradycardia showing but we haven't had a chance to do anything else but continue CPR and get her hooked up to the monitor."

"Okay," Brynne said. "Dean, take over compressions and give him a break. I'll take over respirations while you guys get IV access and get some epinephrine on board." Dean waited until the paramedic doing compressions finished a round of thirty compressions and then jumped down and started pumping on the chest. He focused on his technique as he'd been taught.

Brynne knelt down at the girl's head and began using the bag valve mask to breathe for her, sealing the mask to the girl's mouth and nose with one hand, maintaining an open airway and squeezing the bag with the other while watching for chest rise. "Dean, let's go to continuous compressions and asynchronous respirations." Dean stopped counting and switched to doing continuous compressions at a rate of one hundred per minute. Brynne started her smartphone CPR metronome app to help Dean with the pacing and delivered a breath every thirteen compressions with the bag valve mask. While she was doing that, she examined the young woman carefully from her perspective at the head and Dean saw a change in her expression.

"Dean," she said quietly, and turned the girl's head to reveal her neck to her partner. He glanced down and saw two neat puncture marks on the side of her neck near the junction with the shoulder. Alarmed, he looked up and met her eyes. He realized he was slowing down his compressions so he refocused his attention to listening to the smartphone metronome beeps while his mind raced. The girl was in a pulseless electrical activity rhythm which indicated that there was something that was inhibiting the effective pumping of blood outside of the heart muscle itself.

Brynne had just narrowed the cause down to two choices, trauma or hypovolemia, a loss of blood. Both could be related to a suspected vampire attack. They couldn't do anything until the other medics got an IV line in place. This girl needed a fluid bolus to raise her blood pressure, assuming she had any blood left. They didn't carry blood products on their units, which is what she really needed, but a bolus of IV saline might help give her enough volume to revive her long enough to get her to the hospital. Dean was finishing up his first hundred compressions, already feeling the fatiguing effects.

The other paramedic team was working quickly. Ray, the team leader, had the intraosseous gun out which would drill a needle directly into the fibrous center of the bone in the patient's ankle allowing them to quickly get fluids and medications into her. She was wearing a short skirt so getting access was easy. Ray's partner was preparing the IV fluid bag and tubing to attach to the IO needle catheter when it was ready. Ray took the end of the IV tubing from his partner and attached that to the intraosseous access point. His partner had wrapped a manual blood pressure cuff around the fluid bag and pumped it up until he saw the drops start to fall in the drip chamber on the tubing. The paramedic holding the bag of fluid handed it to a police officer standing nearby while he got out the med bag.

Now that they had IO access, they could start administering drugs for the cardiac arrest. Brynne and Dean switched positions as they pushed the Epinephrine in. He checked for a carotid pulse while looking at the monitor. No pulse detected. Dean thought of a way to get them to infuse fluids without revealing what he and Brynne had discovered. Usually hypovolemia was due to massive trauma but since there was no sign of bleeding, they had to come up with another reason to explain it.

He continued compressing the bag of the bag valve mask, focusing on breathing regularly as the other paramedic did her turn of continuous compressions. Brynne said. "She must have been in that night club and may be overdosing on ecstasy. She might be severely dehydrated or hyperthermic. Try a volume infusion."

Ray looked up from where he knelt at the foot of the patient. "That's a good thought, Brynne." He looked at the patient again. "She's probably about one hundred twenty pounds so we'll say fifty kilograms. Do it Brynne," he said to Dean's partner. Brynne pumped up the pressure on the cuff around the bag of fluid the officer was holding until the saline in the drip chamber started flowing continuously.

The team kept going on compressions for another minute, then the other paramedic, Dave, asked Dean to swap out again. Still no pulse and no sign of a change in rhythm. She asked Ray to bag the patient while she got the airway kit out of the other medics' bags and got set up to intubate. She got out the video laryngoscope, then got set up to drop a tube into the girl's airway. After passing the tube, she used a small syringe to inflate the balloon securing the end of the airway in place. Ray attached the end tidal capnography sensor to the end of the tube. He bagged the patient a couple of times watching the ET CO2 numbers on the heart monitor. Using one hand, Brynne placed her stethoscope in her ears and listened bilaterally in the lung fields. "I hear lung sounds and nothing over the epigastrium. Tube placement is confirmed by capnography and auscultation," she said then took over bagging for Ray.

Dean swapped out compressions with Dave, the second paramedic from 792. Man, CPR was hard work, he thought. He looked up at Brynne. "What's next boss?" he asked. "Are we due for another round of Epi?" She nodded and a glance at Ray confirmed it so he pulled out another pre-filled syringe of epinephrine and assembled it. Brynne gave the BP cuff another couple of pumps to increase the pressure on the bag as it emptied its contents into the girl. Dean attached the syringe to the port in the IV tubing and pushed the drug into the patient.

A minute or so later, as they continued to work, Ray spoke up. "Hey, I've got a spike in the capnography reading. Check a pulse."

Dave stopped compressions and checked a carotid pulse. "I think I've got one," he said. His brow furrowed as he concentrated on feeling the girl's neck. "Yep, I'm sure. It's faint and thready, but it's definitely there."

"Okay," Ray said. "Let's get the stretcher and move her to the ambulance."

"Dean and I will go get your stretcher. Come on Dean," Brynne said taking her partner by the arm. The two of them started towards the other unit to get the stretcher. "Okay, we'll let them take her into the ER. We need to get a dose of garlic extract on board when they're not looking, though, to counteract the vampire bite. We'll write up our version of the report when we get back to our station. The hospital needs to know she has a suspected vampire bite in case she doesn't survive. They'll have to take further steps to keep her from turning."

Another voice sounded from behind them as they approached the back of the other crew's ambulance. "You should have let her be. She wanted this." Dean and Brynne spun around and saw James standing behind them.

"Did you have something to do with this, James?" Brynne asked quietly as she turned and kept walking. The crowd was watching them so she didn't dare say anything too loud. "You told me you were finished feeding on people," Brynne said in a low voice.

"It has nothing to do with you, little one," he said in a condescending tone. "This was an arrangement with a friend to whom I owed a favor."

"What friend? Her?" Brynne said referring to the patient.

"No one, and I said it is not your concern. I will not have you cross me on this, Brynne. It's an obligation I had from many years ago," James said.

"You can't just go around biting women and killing them. We'll have to report this to our superiors," Dean said, defiantly. He wasn't sure what they could do about it but he was sure this was not the first time it had happened.

"Ah, the baby bear has some fangs after all," James sneered. "Do not dabble in things you do not understand, Dean, my boy. This is not merely some siren you're tangling with."

Dean stopped in the street next to the other ambulance and looked at Brynne. "You told HIM about it?"

"No, I didn't, but he asked because word gets around in the Unusual community," Brynne said. "Rudolf probably told him when he got back from his trip. Look, we've got to get the stretcher and get her to the hospital." She turned to James. "This discussion is not over, James. This is not fifteenth century France. You cannot go around biting anyone you feel like, whether there was some arrangement or not."

"We'll see, little one," James said. "We'll see." He turned and walked into the crowd, disappearing from view.

Dean opened the doors to the rear of the ambulance and reached in to unlock the stretcher undercarriage from its position in the back of the unit. Brynne watched the crowd where James had disappeared a moment more then turned and helped Dean lower the wheels to the ground. Dean looked at her across the stretcher. "He's dangerous, Brynne," Dean said. "I don't know what you see in him. Does he have some sort of control over you?"

"Drop it Dean," she snapped. "Focus on the job at hand. I'm a big girl and I can handle James. You get the stretcher out. I'm going over to draw up some garlic extract from our emergency kit. We're going to have to find a time to get that dose into her without Ray and Dave suspecting anything or seeing what we're doing."

Dean closed his mouth but knew he wasn't going to drop the topic. There was something going on here he didn't understand and his partner was deep in the middle of it. He unloaded the stretcher and was turning it around as Brynne returned. She was holding a capped syringe, which she carefully put in the cargo pocket of her duty pants. Dean pondered what he could do about James as the two of them rolled the stretcher back to the girl and the other two paramedics. The girl still had a pulse when they returned but Ray was still bagging her so she still needed assistance breathing. Dave was attaching another bag of saline to the IV tubing. The first bag was empty. He pumped the blood pressure cuff up again to continue infusing more fluid. Dean and Brynne lowered the stretcher and moved it up to the girl's side.

"Here, Dave," Brynne said. "Let me get that. You help Ray and Dean get her ready to be moved to the stretcher." The other medic handed her the IV bag and turned to start prepping the patient. Dean stepped between him and Brynne to block the view as she pulled the loaded syringe from her cargo pocket. She uncapped it, screwed the syringe hub onto a port in the IV tubing and quickly pushed the dose of garlic extract into the patient. The crowd wouldn't think anything unusual was going on. They would just see a paramedic giving a drug to a patient.

Once that was done, they carefully lifted the girl onto the stretcher along with the heart monitor, oxygen tank and IV bag. They then cleared the way through the crowd as Dave and Ray rolled her back to their ambulance. Dean opened the rear doors of ambulance 792 and then helped Dave load the stretcher after Ray climbed inside ahead of it, still operating the bag valve mask.

"Do you want one of us to ride along in case she goes into arrest again?" Brynne offered.

Dave shook his head. "We're only two blocks from ECMC here. Why don't you just follow us there?" He shut the rear doors as Ray was getting himself situated in the back of the unit. "I'll signal you to pull over and help if we need you to." He turned and climbed into the cab's driver's seat.

Dean and Brynne watched them leave the scene. The crowd dispersed now that there was nothing else to see. Dean climbed into the passenger side of their unit, stripping off his gloves while Brynne climbed up behind the wheel. She pulled out and started to follow the other unit to the hospital. They rode in silence. Dean started to speak but she stopped him with a held up hand.

"Put us back in service," she said curtly. "We'll talk about this back at the station. Let's help them get into the hospital and situated first."

Dean contacted dispatch and notified them that they were clearing the scene and heading back to Elk City Medical Center.

<hr>

# Chapter 15

<hr>

The drive back to the station was quiet. Brynne looked like she was ready to kill someone and Dean wanted to make sure that he didn't get in the way when she blew up. James had all but admitted to biting and nearly killing that woman and then he acted like it was no big deal. He was taken back to his conversation with Freddy, the zombie chef, about James and wondered if he needed to follow-up on his instincts and contact Mike about this. He thought that Brynne was in over her head and that James was bad news. The events that occurred tonight just backed up that assumption.

He was still thinking about it when they arrived back at their station. As they got out and restocked the ambulance, he noticed again that Brynne wore a turtleneck despite the weather. Was she just cold-blooded or was she letting James drink from her? Was that what was making her so angry, or maybe afraid? She didn't seem the type to scare easily, but after seeing that girl close-up maybe she saw herself. Maybe she could see the danger she was in by dating someone like James.

They went back into the squad room to do their patient reports from the two calls. They sat down at their computer workstations and started to work. Finally, Dean couldn't take the silence anymore.

"Brynne," he said as he leaned back in the desk chair. "We have to talk about what happened back there with that girl and James. Shouldn't we call the police or headquarters or something? That girl was almost murdered. She still might die."

"We don't have any evidence of wrongdoing on anyone's part," she said after a bit. "James' statements to us were casual enough to be considered harmless by a court of law. It would be our word against his. He's been doing this for too long to get caught that way."

"But you think he did it?" Dean confirmed. "He bit that girl."

"Yes," she said, gritting her teeth. "I think he did it. He knows how I feel about it and he did it anyway."

"Oh, thank God," Dean said. "I was sure you were letting him bite you, too." Then he saw her self-consciously put her hand to her collar. "Wait a minute, you are, aren't you? You're letting him feed off you?"

"That's none of your business, Dean," Brynne snapped. "What I do in my free time with other people is not a workplace concern. Period."

"Don't give me that," Dean said, raising his voice. "I saw that girl. She almost died … hell, she could be dead now. That could have been you. You can't let James put you in that kind of danger. You have to stop and break this off with him. You don't want to end up that way, do you?"

Brynne paused and took a breath. Then she turned to look directly at him. "Dean," she said quietly. "There is more going on here than you know. That girl wanted to be bitten. She wanted to be bitten and then die so that she could have a chance to come back as a vamp. That's what James was talking about. The arrangement he alluded to had to do with her paying some sort of tribute to be turned. The fact that he did it is something he told me he wouldn't do anymore. He told me he wasn't that kind of vampire anymore."

"Clearly he was lying," Dean said. "He seemed almost proud of it. In any case, something happened with the plan. She ended up in the alley."

"Something must have gone wrong," Brynne said. "Maybe she

changed her mind and tried to get away. I don't know. I just don't know."

"Brynne," Dean said softly. "We have to tell someone. Something has to be done."

"James knows they screwed up," Brynne said. "There must be an explanation. Why else would he have stuck around, right? I have to talk to him about it and get his side of the story. Maybe he was forced into it and didn't want to admit it in front of you. Let me have a couple of days to sort this out and find out what happened. Then, if there is not a better answer, I'll make the call myself. Okay?"

"I don't know, Brynne," Dean said. "There has to be some sort of report made tonight. We have our charts to turn in. Headquarters dispatched us to that call for a reason. They have to know that there is some connection to our work here at Station U. If we don't turn in a report, we'll have some explaining to do. I just got this job. I don't want to lose it over a missing report or falsified records."

"You will not lose your job," Brynne said. "I'm your preceptor, so it is on me to make sure that the proper paperwork gets filed. Let me deal with this. There has to be some explanation. I'll get it and report it to headquarters. Okay?"

"If you say so, Boss," Dean said. "If you say so." He really didn't know what else to say to her. She was in charge, and that was that. She could make the call. The problem was, he wasn't sure she was making the right call. When he was in school, he was told that there would be occasions that he would not agree with other providers' calls in the field, but he had always assumed that would be a medical issue. This was something else altogether. This was attempted murder, or maybe an assisted suicide. He was not sure. Either way, he couldn't be a party to a cover up of something like that. Still, he guessed he owed her something in the way of thanks. She'd bailed him out of that Lydia situation, and she was his supervisor. He decided he would write up his own version of the night's events and keep it on hand in case he needed to turn something in later on.

"Will she live?" Dean asked. He knew they had gotten a return of spontaneous circulation, but that didn't mean that she wouldn't die in a day or so from organ failure.

"I don't know, Dean," Brynne replied. "Maybe. She's young, so she has that going for her. The intensive care unit at City is excellent for post-cardiac arrest care. They will have implemented therapeutic hypothermia as soon as she arrived. That gives her the best chance of getting out neurologically intact. I texted the nurse at the ER, Carol, of the dose of garlic extract we gave in the field and our suspicions. She'll make sure that girl gets the care she needs."

"If she doesn't live, will she - change?" Dean asked. "I mean, she was bitten, we know that. Does the garlic extract work every time?"

"That may be something of a gray area," she said. "Technically we brought her back, so she didn't die from the bite itself. I'm sure they'll give her whole blood at the hospital. That might hold off the change when coupled with the garlic dose. I'm just not sure. I'll know more when I talk with James. He has a lot of questions to answer, and I'll get a firm answer on that one, too."

"I guess he has the tall, brooding type going for him?" Dean asked.

"Are you asking what I see in him?" Brynne challenged. "Why would I, dedicated to saving lives, see someone who is so opposite to that goal?"

"Look, Brynne ..."

"He's not a monster, Dean," she said firmly. "He's just a man. He's older than usual, sure, but when you get to know him, he's just like any other guy."

"Except he's a vampire," Dean said. "And he might have almost killed that girl."

"I'm not sure he sees it that way. If she had successfully changed, would she have been dead? To him, he was doing her a favor."

"I'm sure drug dealers look at it the same way," Dean said.

Brynne sighed. "I don't think that's fair. He was making her stronger, forever young. She'd never get sick or die in a normal way."

"She'll also never get to see the sun again," Dean said. "She would be a predator, who could end up believing she could feed unchecked on humans without regard to their lives. You already said that James is, how did you put it, 'old-fashioned?' Maybe she was going to be an old-fashioned vampire, too."

They were silent for a few minutes. Then Dean spoke very quietly. "You don't want that type of life, too, do you?"

"I think that's none of your business, Probie," she replied. "I think we've talked enough about this subject. Why don't you go out and check the inventory in the drug dispenser and make a list of what we're likely to need soon? You can forward that list to the lieutenant since you feel like you have a need to talk to headquarters."

Dean's shoulders slumped. He felt like his partner was in trouble here, but he was at a loss to figure out a way around it. He'd agreed to give her some time to investigate the situation with the girl this evening. In the meantime, he was sure that he should have sent that email off to Mike a few weeks ago after Freddy warned him about James.

He got up and walked out towards the ambulance bay, grabbing the inventory clipboard off the hook by the door on his way. He decided to spend the rest of the shift doing some busy work so he didn't have to be around Brynne. There was nothing else to say that hadn't already been said. Anything else would just lead to an argument. One thing he didn't want to do was shut down their avenue of communication over this. He still had a lot to learn from her and he hoped she would still feel comfortable talking to him about this situation in the future. In the meantime, he pulled out his smartphone and shot an email off to Mike asking to meet for breakfast after work that morning. Maybe he would have some insights.

Dean worked through the rest of the night doing odd chores around the station and avoiding talking with Brynne. There were no more ambulance calls. At 6 AM, James pulled up out front to pick up Brynne in his fancy car. He sat outside and beeped his horn. He could imagine the smirk of victory on James' face. The idiot raced his engine as Brynne got in the car, then peeled out. Dean stood and watched them drive away, then he went back into the station to talk to Lynne and Bill. Maybe they would have some insights. He was just about to enter when he heard the sound of the alert tones. Damn, they had a call. Well, maybe he could catch them later that evening by showing up a little early for the next shift.

He headed over to his truck. It was then he noticed the black SUV idling on the street at the end of the building. The windows were tinted dark so he couldn't see inside. It seemed as if he had seen one like it some other times, both here and in his own neighborhood. Was it the same one? This whole thing from last night had him creeped out, and now he was getting paranoid. They could just be there for another of the businesses in the industrial park. Dean stood and stared at the vehicle for a while, and it pulled away from the curb and drove off. He hoped he was getting himself worked up for nothing.

Dean hadn't heard from Mike about meeting for breakfast, but he was hungry so he decided to stop at Hank's Place for a nice meal on the way home. He watched the sun starting to rise as he drove off from the station. Maybe a new day would bring answers to his questions about the situation with Brynne and James. Daisy was working and showed him to a booth. He was in the same back corner booth that he and Mike had met in. He was perusing the menu, trying to decide on how hungry he was when someone sat down across from him. He looked up and his blood froze in his veins.

"Hello, Dean," James said in his southern drawl. "I think it's time we had a little chat, don't you?"

# Chapter 16

Dean was startled when he looked up at James sitting in the booth across from him. "You shouldn't sneak up on people that way," Dean said with false bravado. He was freaking out on the inside and glanced around to see if anyone else had noticed the vampire suddenly appear. And how was he able to go out during the daytime?

"My apologies," James said. "Call it a bad habit. I find that people who might avoid talking with me are less likely to be successful if I just show up." He grinned without showing any teeth.

Daisy, the waitress walked up then. "What can I get you two?" she asked, holding up her pen and order pad.

"I'll have a black coffee, and my friend here will have a ..." James paused looking at Dean intently. "He'll have a grilled cheese sandwich and a diet soda."

Dean just stared at him, a little bit of terror creeping into his mind as he realized how apparently vulnerable he was right now. James had submitted his order for him like he'd read his mind.

"Okay," Daisy said. "I'll be right back with your drinks, guys."

James held his gaze as the waitress left them alone again. "A little parlor trick, nothing more," James said with a chuckle. "I can sometimes see the things on the top of someone's mind, and you were just reading the menu. It's nothing more than that I assure you. I can't see deeper thoughts, which is why we have to have a chat."

"I'm sure you know that it makes people uncomfortable when you do it, though," Dean said defiantly. "I would think that etiquette would dictate you avoid reading someone's mind without their permission."

"It's not really mind reading," James said. "I just saw a few images is all. It comes with living so long among humans in this form." He gestured to himself. He was dressed in black jeans, a black button-down shirt and a black sports coat. James was definitely playing up the look.

"Brynne told me you had some specific concerns about the incident you witnessed tonight. I decided to seek you out myself and have a little talk. I want to answer your questions if you have any."

"I have a lot of questions, James," Dean said. "But how do I know you won't put some vampire mojo on me to make me forget. We saved that girl's life, although I get the idea that you didn't want us to."

"I will not lay a charm on you, Dean," James said. "In fact, I cannot. Not unless you let me feed on you. It is the blood, you see, that builds that particular connection."

"So what's to stop you from feeding on me to gain that ability?" Dean asked. "I can't possibly stay here all day. Eventually, I'll have to leave, go home or somewhere else where I'm vulnerable. You've already proven that you can do pretty much anything you'd like."

James sighed. "Dean, I really am trying to fit into this new, civilized world of yours. Sometimes I am more successful than others, but in this case I assure you that you are completely safe. I am here to talk with you, answer your questions and ask a few of you. Fair enough?"

Dean stared at him. The tension was broken by Daisy's arrival with James' coffee and Dean's soda. He waited until she left again, then looked at James and nodded. "Okay, fair enough."

James took a sip of coffee and set the cup down, leaning back in the booth and putting one arm up on the back. "You first, Dean. I feel like you are fairly bursting at the seams with questions for me."

"Well," Dean didn't know where to begin then decided to jump right in starting with the details of the cardiac arrest call. "What was up with that girl last night? Did you bite her, drain her?"

"Yes," James said matter-of-factly. "She asked for the favor, had paid the proper tribute, and the community had agreed that she was an appropriate member to join our number. Unfortunately, when we thought she was incapacitated and on her way to death, she became disoriented and wandered away from where we were keeping her, awaiting her transformation. By the time we realized our mistake, she had already gotten outside and collapsed there. Bystanders called 911 and started CPR on her before we could get to her and carry her back upstairs." He chuckled. "Kudos to you and Brynne by the way. I truly thought you were too late to revive her. Your quick thinking and the bystanders doing CPR saved her life, though that is not what she wanted."

"If she lives to get out of the hospital and seeks you out," Dean asked. "Will you do it again?"

"Eventually, yes," James said. "It is what she wants. We will ask her again to be certain that her wishes have not changed. These things, however, are usually final decisions. I do not think she will change her mind." He paused to sip at his coffee. "I will not be the one to do it this time. I've delegated that responsibility to another of our number following my discussion with Brynne. I was unaware of how strongly she felt about my involvement with these types of things."

"Are you sure it wasn't just because you got caught?" Dean asked. "I'm sorry, but I can't see you being all that conscientious about it, especially since you made a prior arrangement with Brynne not to do something like this."

"Let us just say it was an unfortunate decision that I regret," the vampire said. "It was necessary at the time due to some favors I owed another of my kind. I have advised that individual of the change in plans and they have accepted my explanation."

James took another sip from his coffee and continued. "Dean, we Unusuals like to police ourselves without undue involvement from the humans around us. This particular situation got out of hand and risked exposing something about us that we would prefer be kept under wraps for the time being. We have reported it to the proper authorities along with providing all the documentation and affidavits concerning the woman. They verify that she was being turned of her own free will. They've accepted it. Unfortunately, you and Brynne are upset about my involvement with it and will probably not let it go. I am here to set the record straight with you. I'll do the same with Brynne later."

"Are you going to work some mojo on her memory?" Dean asked. "I know you've fed on her blood, so the connection you mentioned exists there."

"I would regret having to do that, Dean," the vampire said.

"I notice you didn't say you wouldn't do it," Dean snapped. "Do you think that's okay? Are you afraid she'll break up with you or something?" Dean felt bolder. "You know James, you sit here and talk to me like you're all civilized. You say that our superiors know about what happened, and everyone is okay with what was going on, but you still feel it might be necessary to charm your girlfriend over it. Pardon me, but that doesn't make any sense at all."

"What goes on between Brynne and I is our business, Dean," James said curtly. "I will not change her memory unless I think it would be for her own good. I will not apologize to you for what I might do. It is between her and me."

"That's convenient," Dean said. "You will answer my questions, but not about what concerns me the most, your potential control over my partner."

"She is an adult, Dean. Let us just say that she entered the relationship with her eyes wide open. She knows of my powers and abilities. She has allowed our relationship to progress in certain directions. Sometimes we need to keep secrets from those we love because we don't want to hurt them. Certainly you have kept things from those with whom you've been in a relationship?"

"But I didn't charm them or mislead them after they had discovered the truth of something I'd done," Dean said. "That's just wrong, James. It's wrong!"

"Well, you are a better man than I am, Dean," James said with a wave of his hand. "I've lived a long life, hundreds of years in fact. I think that when you get some perspective you will discover that it is not all so black and white. There is, in fact, quite a bit of gray area in there."

Daisy arrived with the food just then, and the tension broke a little again as she set down Dean's grilled cheese sandwich with chips and a pickle wedge on the side. Dean thought for a bit while he took a bite and chewed. James just sipped his coffee and waited patiently. After a few bites of his sandwich and a sip from his soda, Dean looked up and met James' eyes. The vampire stared back at him impassively.

"So you admit to nearly killing the girl in a botched vampire turning, or whatever you call it," Dean began. "And you admit to the possibility of charming my partner to make her forget about it because she doesn't like you biting other girls. Am I right so far?" James nodded. "What do you expect me to say to you or do after that kind of realization? I can't let you hurt my partner, and I can't let you go around assisting in the suicide of people who think they will have a better life as a member of the undead."

"Let me address the second point first if you don't mind," James said. "The woman would not have died. She would have changed to be one of us. That is not assisted suicide. Call it … call it an alternative lifestyle choice." Dean started to interject, but James forestalled him with a raised hand. "You are new to our culture, and the life that you never knew existed right alongside your happy little human existence. What happened there is legal and, as I have already said, has been reported to your superiors. Contact your chief directly if you don't believe me."

"And my first point?" Dean asked. "Do you think that Brynne deserves to be treated this way?"

"As I've said," James said. "That matter is between Brynne and me. I have admitted that I may have overstepped my bounds there. If I charm her, it will not be permanent, and she will eventually remember that I clouded her memory. When that happens, if it happens, I will have to deal with the repercussions. What I don't want is for you to cause more trouble before then. Let us deal with it. As long as you and I come to that understanding, I think we will get along fine. If not, well …"

Dean just looked at him for a while meeting his gaze. His insides were roiling. He was at the same time terrified, angry and disgusted. It was strange, scary and a little exhilarating. Another thought occurred to him, and he decided to jump in since he was already in hot water.

"While we're being honest with each other, James, can I ask you another question?"

James nodded.

"What happened to my predecessor, Zach? I've heard rumors that he crossed paths with you and that his departure was sudden and suspicious."

James laughed aloud, throwing his head back. "Well, you are fearless, aren't you?"

"Answer the question," Dean said.

"Okay," James responded. "Zach and I had a similar discussion once upon a time. He also didn't like the way I was treating his partner. After the discussion, he decided that this work was not for him, and he moved on to a more normal position in another town."

"So you didn't have him killed?" Dean asked. He figured he was in for a penny, in for a pound.

"No," James said, suddenly dead serious. "I don't operate that way, at least not anymore. There was a time I would have been more direct, but I really am trying to be civilized here, Dean. I'll admit that I did encourage him to leave, but nothing more. As far as I know he is living happily ever after in a town on the other side of the state."

"But no one has seen or heard from him since," Dean said. "Do you expect me to believe he just moved away without a trace?"

"Mike Farver and your chief know where he is," James said. "Ask them if you don't believe me. I assure you that no harm came to him at my hand or from those I know." The conversation paused again as Daisy returned to ask if they needed anything else and to leave the check on the table.

"I think this conversation is over, Dean. I've had my say, and you have had yours. I think we will just have to agree to disagree for now. I will say this. I have been honest and straightforward with you here this morning. It is not in my nature to bare myself this way, but Brynne thinks very highly of you. In fact, I think very highly of you. We need open minded and intelligent partners among the normal humans to watch out for us when we need assistance. It's a better world for all that way." James paused to pick up the check and stood up next to the booth. "I'll pay for your meal. I ask that you think on what we talked about and understand that while I am trying to live in this new world, I am still a very old world man. I do not like people meddling in my personal affairs. I will not take lightly to such intrusions in the future. This chat is my way of setting the bar, as they say, to where we stand."

"And where do we stand, James?" Dean asked, standing as well.

"I'd like to think we stand for the best interest of Brynne Garvey and for the community around us, Unusuals and Normals combined, Dean." James said. "And I know what is best for my Brynne. You are her coworker, and I appreciate your concerns. However, I am hers, and she is mine in a way that you couldn't understand. I know what she needs and doesn't need, and I'm sure she has the same feelings for me. As I said, I'll deal with the repercussions of my own actions with her. All I ask is for you to stay out of it in the meantime." James glanced at the check in his hand, pulled out his wallet and dropped the check and a few bills on the table.

"Aren't you going to burn up or something going out in the sunlight?" Dean asked, looking out diner windows at the brightening morning sky.

"I'm old enough that it would take several minutes of direct noontime sunlight to adversely affect me." James said. "I assure you, I'll be fine." He glanced out the window, chuckled and walked away. Dean watched him go, his appetite was suddenly gone. He wasn't sure what he was going to do.

He left the diner more than a little shaken by his encounter with James. Somehow the vampire had come across as almost civilized … almost. There had been an undertone to the conversation that had been, well, creepy and frightening. James had not openly threatened him. He'd made the request to leave the Brynne situation alone seem reasonable, at least a little bit.

Dean checked his email to see if Mike had responded back to his request to meet up, but he still hadn't responded. He did have a request from a Nigerian prince to transfer some money to a U.S. bank account. Based on how he felt after the conversation with the vampire, that scam email might have a better chance of being true than believing anything James had to say.

He sat in his pickup truck for a long time in the parking lot at Hank's Diner just thinking about the situation. He was sure that Brynne needed some kind of help, but James had assured him she was in no danger. But what was to stop James from charming her, again and again as long as it suited him? What Dean couldn't get out of his head was that James had all but said aloud that he had drunk from Brynne. She'd acted as if it was no big deal but if it gave her vampire boyfriend some sort of control over her, it was a bad idea.

Dean finally came to the conclusion that there was nothing he could do until he got a chance to talk to Mike and verify some of the things that James had said. He started the truck and headed home to his apartment. There was nothing else to do until he could talk to Mike. Lost in his thoughts, Dean again missed seeing the black SUV that pulled out behind him and followed him home.

# Chapter 17

The next day Dean could not sleep, so he had all day to think about the previous night's encounter. His restless thoughts during the day kept him distracted from getting anything done. He tried doing some laundry and picking up around his apartment, but he always ended up sitting down and staring at the wall of his kitchenette. He mulled over what he was going to do about James and Brynne.

He finally got an email back from Mike. He was away at a conference and wouldn't be back for a week. If there was a problem that he couldn't talk to Brynne about, he suggested going to Bill or Lynne about it. That was really no help since Bill and Lynne were off for the next two days, and he didn't know how to contact them aside from their work email addresses. Did he reach out to one of them or did he wait and see what Brynne was like over the next few days?

Eventually, the clock made the decision for him. It was time to go back to work. He changed into his uniform and headed out to his pickup. This time he noticed the black SUV with the dark tinted windows parked along his street and watched in his rear-view mirror as it pulled out behind him. Great, James was having him followed by his henchmen. Apparently the vampire's promise to leave him alone if he left this situation with Brynne alone was all a bunch of crap. He watched them follow him and was going to confront them directly when he got to the station parking lot, but they drove past the entrance to the industrial park where the station was.

Dean was fuming when he pulled into the lot at the station. He saw James' sports car pulled up in front of the building and watched Brynne get out, say something from outside the passenger door, laugh and go inside. Dean jumped out of his truck and strode across the parking lot to confront James before he drove off. In the twilight of dusk, Dean saw the driver's window roll down as he approached revealing James' pale face behind the steering wheel.

"James," Dean said angrily as he approached. "You said you'd leave me alone and yet you have your goons follow me around from my house to here in that black SUV."

"Dean," James said calmly. "I have no idea what you are talking about. I assure you that I don't need to use anything as mundane as a black SUV to have you followed. I have access to the whole pantheon of Unusuals at my command."

"What?" Dean said, confused. "Well, who is following me then?"

"I don't know," James said with a smile. "But it's not me. Perhaps you owe someone money? If you need a loan or something, I'm sure I can arrange favorable terms for you. I am a man of some means after all."

"I don't think I want to get into your debt, James," Dean said. "We both know that would be a bad idea."

"Dean," James said smoothly. "You act like I'm some sort of mobster goon. I'm a businessman who is not above helping out a friend of a friend who is in need. Also, I just thought you'd want to know I told Brynne the truth after our chat. I realized that you were right. I shouldn't have considered charming her about the girl. She's ready to talk with you when you get inside. She can smooth everything over for you." He glanced at his watch and looked at Dean. "You had better get inside. You are going to be late for work. I'll be around if you need to chat again. Just let Brynne know and she will get in touch with me."

Dean stood there as James put the window back up and pulled out of the parking lot. He watched the vampire drive away, revving his engine again as he left. He was more confused now than he had been when he left the diner that morning. It was like James had listened to reason and suddenly done the right thing. Could a leopard change its spots? Dean didn't think so. He crossed the rest of the way to the entrance to the station and went inside. Maybe Brynne could shed some light on the situation.

Brook and Tammy were packing up to leave when Dean got inside. They were animatedly chatting about their night with Brynne as Dean set his stuff down. Apparently, they had gone back to Lydia's house to manage another asthma attack, and she had asked about Dean. She wanted to personally apologize to him. They giggled at this. He was not amused.

"Lighten up, Dean," Brook said. "She seems really sorry for unleashing her vocal charms on you. And, you have to admit she's pretty hot. You could do a lot worse."

"I don't think dating a former patient is such a good idea," Dean said. "Anyway, isn't she married? That guy with her was her husband, right?"

"Who said anything about dating her?" Tammy said, which brought howls of laughter from the other two.

"Very funny," Dean said. "Brynne, I think I'll go out and check the gear and do the shift med check." He nodded to Brook and Tammy. "Ladies, I'll leave you to your gossiping." They burst into laughter as he walked through the room shaking his head. He headed out to the ambulance bay and started going through the gear for the night. A few minutes later he heard the door to the squad room open, and Brynne was standing by the open back doors of the ambulance. She looked up at him where he was bent over the med bag with his checklist open on the iPad.

"They didn't mean any harm, Dean," Brynne said. "I don't think they realize the effect that situation had on you."

"It's fine," Dean said. "There's just been a lot going on over the last few weeks. First that thing with Lydia and then this situation with the cardiac arrest the other night." He looked over at her. "You know that James came and had a chat with me over my meal at the diner this morning, right?"

"He told me," she said. "I'm not sure what you have against him, Dean, but you have to get over it. He's my boyfriend and what I do on my private time is my own business."

"This has nothing to do with you and him together," Dean said. "It has everything to do with his involvement in the cardiac arrest with that girl. He said just now that he worked the whole thing out with you. Is that true?"

"He and I have dealt with the situation," she said.

"Did you know that he all but told me he was going to change your memories about the call and have you adjust our reports on it based on that influence?" Dean countered.

"Let me deal with this, Dean," she said firmly. "I know there are some strange things going on from your point of view, but you're too new to this job to understand. Just let me handle it. James and I have been together for over four years. I know how to deal with him."

"I'll let you handle it as far as it goes, but I'm going to write a version of my impressions of the call and submit it as an addendum to the patient care report." He defiantly met her eyes.

"That's your right," she said, "but it's not necessary. Headquarters is completely aware of the situation so you would just be wasting your time." She turned and walked back into the station's squad room. He watched her go and heard the door to the ambulance bay shut behind her.

The rest of the shift passed again in relative silence. Dean sat at the computer and drafted his version of the cardiac arrest call but didn't attach the document to the official record yet. He was still not sure of the right course of action to take. He needed to talk to Mike, and he was out of town for the rest of the week. He considered emailing it directly to him, but then changed his mind after a quick review of the service's HIPAA electronic security policy. The email was not secure, and he would expose himself to disciplinary action or worse if he sent out patient information over that route of communication. Instead, he saved the document locally on his account and plugged in his thumb drive to keep a copy for himself.

Later, as they were riding back from their first call of the night, a Wiccan with food poisoning from spoiled eye of newt, he brought it up again. "Brynne, I'm not trying to make trouble. I just really don't understand," he said. "Just tell me how you're alright with how James planned to manipulate you."

"I am not alright with it at all, Dean," she said, "but, I'm not talking about that with you. I said I'll deal with it and I will, but it is a personal matter between James and me. As far as the official report goes, everything is on the up and up. The patient did give her consent to be in that, uh, situation, and while you might not choose that option, she did make that decision and we have to respect it."

"Well if everything is alright, then why did James feel like he had to do what he did?" Dean asked.

"He panicked," she said. "He comes from a different time. Back in his early days such things would have wound up with him being chased by villagers with torches, pitchforks, and sharpened stakes." Brynne held his gaze for a moment then looked away. "I won't lie to you. I'm pissed at him for doing what he did, but I also understand why he did it."

"Aren't you afraid that what he was planning to do with you was, well, abusive in some way?" Dean asked. "I'm just worried that he's exerting control over you somehow. You may not be reacting normally, and how would I know if you weren't?"

Brynne glanced over at him. "Believe me, I'm acting normally, Dean. Let's just say that I've taken precautions to make sure that he doesn't do anything like that to me. I will not be a position to be influenced like that again. I made that clear to him and I think he won't try it, but I'm also not leaving myself open. I've sought what you might call professional help, and no vamp can threaten to charm me like that."

"Is it something I can get, too?" Dean asked. "I'd like all the protection I can get after recent events. I don't even know what is dangerous to me anymore. I feel like my sense of scene safety is kind of a joke right now."

"Don't stop trusting your instincts," she said. "They're good. They alerted you that something was up with that cardiac arrest call and they alerted you that James was up to something. All were true. Your instincts were dead on." She stopped as they arrived back at the station. "Hop out and back me in. We'll finish talking about this when we get back inside."

# Chapter 18

Dean jumped out as she pressed the button to raise the garage doors. He helped her back the ambulance into the bay safely. Then he hooked up the electric line to the side of the ambulance box and headed into the squad room just in time to see a figure in dark clothes run out the other door to the parking lot. A quick glance showed the desks in disarray, papers all over the floor and the room a complete mess. He shouted at the person as he ran across the room, pushing the door to the parking lot open and watching as that same black SUV sped away from the station parking lot. He tried to get a look at the license plate, but they were gone, disappearing into the night too fast for him to make out the letters and numbers.

Brynne came into the squad room just as he returned. "What the …?"

"I just chased some guy out of here. He was dressed all in black like some sort of ninja," he said. "He sped off in a black SUV. I'd swear that's the same black SUV I've seen around for the last few weeks off and on. I thought at first they were with James, but when I asked him about it, he denied having anything to do with them."

"James wouldn't do something like this," Brynne said. "He could just ask me if he wanted information." She walked over to the pair of desks and the computer workstations. "It looks like they were trying to pull the hard drives out of these but couldn't get the cases open. The filing cabinets are still locked."

Dean walked over to the break area. "They tore apart the bookshelf and dumped our small collection of tomes and legends on the floor. It's like they were looking for something in particular."

"I'll call this in. We should probably get the police involved," Brynne said. "You check through the rest of the building and see if you can find anything else that's missing."

"Maybe they were looking for drugs or something," Dean proposed.

"Why look in here, then?" she asked. "They would have been trying to break into the med dispenser out in the bay if that were the case. It's like they were after patient information or something. There are some hate groups out there that target the Unusual population."

Dean looked at his desk and quickly checked his pockets. "Oh no," he said rushing to the messed up desk and moving papers and books around.

"What is it?" Brynne asked.

"My thumb drive," he said. "I think I left it plugged into the computer. I was keeping a record of my call reports on there and had a copy of my version of the cardiac arrest call complete with my suspicions about James' involvement."

"That's not good, Dean," Brynne said. "Why would you keep an unencrypted copy like that in your personal collection? That's protected patient information, Unusual or not."

"I just wanted to keep track of what I was doing. I only had the last few days of calls on it." He looked up at his partner. "I upload it to a secure cloud-based server when I'm home, but I hadn't updated it for the last several days. There were three or four run reports on there as well as the cardiac arrest report."

"Okay, we'll deal with that later," she said. "I'll call dispatch and report the break in. You keep looking around and see if there is anything else missing."

It didn't look like the intruder had made it back into the

bunkrooms or bathroom of the station. He, or she, had just focused on the office and squad rest areas. He wasn't sure what to do next. He remembered his class on dealing with medical crime scenes and decided not to clean anything up until the police had come and gone. He walked back into the main squad room area and saw Brynne talking on the phone.

"They're sending a police unit over - one that specializes in Unusuals so we can talk to them freely," Brynne said as she hung up the phone. "They've put us out of service for now. We're to continue to inventory anything that's missing but try not to muck up the crime scene any more than necessary."

The two cops arrived in about five minutes. They said the door looked like it had been forced open and that they would probably have to get it repaired before it would lock correctly again. A crime scene unit showed up, and a tech came in and looked around. He dusted the computer and desk for fingerprints, as well as the inside and outside of the door. He said it all looked smudged like the intruder was wearing gloves. Dean couldn't remember if he saw the intruder wearing gloves or not. He closed his eyes, trying to picture what the person looked like as they ran out the door. He couldn't get a clear picture in his mind.

The police stayed for about two hours interviewing him and Brynne separately. They also got fingerprinted by the crime scene tech to rule out their prints from any others that were found. The tech said they'd have to get the other regular Station U paramedics printed as well to rule them out. Dean pointed out that they were all fingerprinted for their background check when they entered the academy. The tech said that it would save time to get them locally and not have to go to the state and FBI databases to request them.

It took about two hours for each of them to give their report both to the police and then writing it all up for headquarters to review. It was well after midnight and Dean was suddenly very tired. He'd gotten into this job for the excitement of it, but lately that excitement had gotten pretty stale. A sleepy maintenance guy was the last person to show up. He attached a new deadbolt lock to the door and screwed in a receiver for the bolt on the metal door jam.

He handed Brynne two sets of keys for them and the next shift, and said he'd get more made the next day when he came in for his regular shift.

Now that the door was repaired and the squad room straightened up, Brynne called headquarters on the phone and put them back in service. Dean just sat down and looked around. That SUV he'd seen earlier obviously was following him. It bothered him. James and Brynne had both skewered the likelihood that James had anything to do with it. James could arrange to have him followed in much more covert ways. So who were they and what did they want from him and from the station?

"Penny for your thoughts?" Brynne asked as she came over to the recliners and sat on the edge of the couch across from Dean.

"Wow," Dean said, "The last time I heard that it was from my grandmother."

"Are you saying I'm old?" Brynne asked, dangerously.

"No, I'm just saying that the 1970's called and they want their catch phrase back," Dean said with a chuckle.

"It seems like you're back to your old self," Brynne laughed. "Are you feeling better?"

"I guess so," Dean said. "I'm just tired of all the excitement. This has been more than I bargained for when I took this job."

"C'mon, Dean," Brynne said. "Excitement and adrenaline are what this job is all about. They don't call us adrenaline junkies for nothing."

"That's a different kind of excitement," Dean pointed out. "We come in and deal with someone else's excitement. We bring order to the excitement. It's not supposed to happen to us."

"True," Brynne agreed. "Still it gives us a sense of how our patients feel about things. Maybe it's a good thing for us to have our own emergencies from time to time to give us some perspective."

"Maybe Brynne, but I've had enough excitement focused on me." Dean said. A pensive silence was followed by the jarring sound of the tones on the radio.

Chapter 19

"Ambulance U-191, respond for an injured subject at 49th and Main Street," came the voice over the radio. The printer chattered to life as it began to spit out a page with the response location.

Dean grabbed the page off the printer and headed for the unit in the ambulance bay. Brynne checked the new lock on the parking lot door and then followed him out to the ambulance. She started up the unit as Dean climbed in on his side. He keyed the mic and put them responding, turned on the lights and activated the siren. He switched to the med radio channel.

"Ambulance U-191, you are responding for a 52-year-old male involved in an assault. The subject will be located in the office of the Rusty Cue Pool Hall at that location. Police are on the scene, and report assailant has fled the premises. You are safe to proceed in. No additional information at this time." the dispatcher said.

"Ambulance U-191 received. Proceed in. The scene is safe per police on location," Dean repeated back. He looked at Brynne. "Well, that's pretty cryptic. It could be almost anything."

"Yeah," she said. "The police don't like to put out too much information over the radio - even over secure channels. When we get there, you grab the trauma bag and oxygen bag. I'll jump in the back and get the heart monitor and med bag." She steered the ambulance up the ramp onto I-95 to head downtown and hit the gas.

The trip downtown took about eight minutes. It was after two o'clock in the morning and traffic was light. It was just after closing time for the bars and most of the people had cleared out of the downtown bar district by the time they arrived. There were two police cars out front. One young officer was just coming out the front door of the pool hall, and he looked a little green around the gills.

"I'm glad you guys are here," the younger cop said as they passed him on the way to the door. "That's more than my limited first aid training can handle."

Dean gave Brynne a look and reached out to hold the door for her. As the two paramedics entered the large central room, they heard a familiar voice coming from way in the back. "If you would just hold this end, officer, I can help myself and pull it out," they heard Gibbie say. They quickly crossed the room. As they turned the corner into the office, they both stopped and stared. Gibbie sat there on the corner of the manager's desk facing two police officers who both looked completely out of their element. The patient had the broken half of a wooden pool cue sticking out of his chest.

Gibbie looked over and saw them standing there with their jaws hanging open. "Well don't just stand there, doooo something," he shrieked, his voice climbing an octave as he said it. "I can't sit here all night. I have to go and see what got Brenda so upset this time."

The older of the two police officers looked at him. "This Brenda, she's the one who did this to you? Do you have an address for her?"

Gibbie responded to the officer with pursed lips then turned back with a pleading look at the paramedics.

Brynne set the monitor down on the floor, followed by the med bag and walked over to the middle-aged vampire with her gloved hands held out in front of her. "Gibbie, I want you to calm down and sit very still," she said quietly. "That pool cue has got to be sitting right next to your heart, and you know as well as I do what will happen if so much as a splinter gets in there."

She carefully reached out and held the end of the cue still and stable at the point it entered Gibbie's chest right through an old "Frankie Says Relax" t-shirt. She looked over her shoulder at Dean. "Get that shirt cut away, and then get the monitor on him. I want to see what's going on with his heart."

"Don't you dare cut this shirt off young man," Gibbie shouted. "I got this at their U.S. concert tour back in 1984. I got to go back-stage and meet the band. It was fabulous."

"Gibbie," Brynne said, sternly. "You need to sit still and calm down right now. Dean is going to do what I told him to do, and you are going to let him. Do you understand?"

"But Brynne, honey…" he began.

"Don't 'Brynne, honey' me," she said. "Dean, do it and try not to move him while you do."

Dean got out his trauma shears from his pants pocket and started to carefully cut up from the bottom to the point where the pole jutted out of the T-shirt. Then he cut carefully around the obstruction and up to the collar. Gibbie groaned and whimpered. When Dean was done, he slid the shirt off like a jacket. Now that the chest was exposed, and Brynne stabilized the impaled pool cue, Dean connected electrode stickies to the wire harness of his heart monitor and attached them to Gibbie at the upper arms and ankles. He turned the monitor on and took a look at the screen. He saw a run of ventricular fibrillation as he'd expected in a vampire but then he saw what looked like two or three organized sinus rhythm beats before it turned back to V-fib.

"Brynne did you see that?" he asked.

"Yeah, I saw it," she said. "Normal sinus rhythms are not good in someone like our friend Gibbie." She looked at the vampire and got his attention. "Gibbie, this thing must be resting right up against your heart. The monitor is showing your heart with a bad rhythm every few beats. If that rhythm takes over, there will be nothing we can do for you, so you have to stay really still, do you understand?"

Gibbie nodded, biting his quivering lower lip. Then he quietly asked, "Can't you just pull it out, Brynne?"

"There's no way of knowing what additional damage that would do, Gibbie," she replied. "So here's what we're gonna do. I'm going to sit here with you and hold this very still while Dean goes out to the truck and gets the tool box from the driver's side bin on the ambulance." She looked at Dean. "Got it, partner?"

"Got it," Dean said. He went back out through the pool room to the rig. The young cop he and Brynne had passed on the way in was standing outside waiting when he came out.

"That's super weird, ain't it?" The cop said. "He's sitting up and talking and all with that pool cue sticking right through him. All he would tell us over and over again was that we had to find his girlfriend and that it was all a misunderstanding. We're looking for her, but I don't think he should be the one to talk to her when we find her. She must've been really pissed to do that to him."

"I think he has that effect on people," Dean said. He went around to the driver's side of the ambulance, opened the compartment door behind the driver's seat and pulled out the toolbox. It was kind of heavy, and he wished Brynne had told him what specific tool she needed. He came back around the back of the ambulance, and the cop was waiting.

"Is he gonna live?" he asked. "I can't believe he's just sitting there talking like that."

"We're going to do what we can for him," Dean said. "If we can help it, we're not going to let him die," or whatever you called it when a vampire left this life.

Dean went back through the pool hall and into the cramped office where the two police officers stood and watched dumbfounded as Brynne stabilized the impaled pool cue in Gibbie's chest. Dean set the toolbox down next to the heart monitor and popped the lid open.

"What next, Boss?" Dean asked.

"Under the top tray is a small folding hacksaw," Brynne said. "While I hold this pool cue really still, you're going to cut the end off just past my hands so we can maneuver him more easily in this room. You get that ready to go. Before you start cutting, I want to alert ECMC about what we have so Doc Spirelli can get the trauma team squared away. He's got to pull in a few favors to get the right people in the hospital this late without anyone freaking out about what they'll see. Dial the portable radio to patch us through to the Elk City Medical Center ED and hold it up where I can talk."

Dean had already gotten the folding hacksaw out and assembled it to its open position. He put the tool down and pulled the portable radio from its clip on his belt. He keyed the mic button and held it up to Brynne's face. "This is Ambulance U-191 calling ECMC with a trauma alert. Can I please speak to the Station U doc on call?"

"Received One-Nine-One. We're getting the doctor now," The nurse on the hospital radio said. "Stand by."

"Standing by," Brynne replied.

She looked at the cops. "We've got this if you want to go out and do some crowd control. When we bring him out, we're going to be in a hurry. The two officers looked relieved and hurried from the room.

"U-One-Nine-One go ahead," the radio squawked. "This is Doc Andrews."

Dean keyed the mic for Brynne again. "Doc, this is paramedic Garvey. Pick up the handset and go to private mode, please." She waited a moment, heard a click, and then continued. "We have an apparent 52-year-old male vampire with a wooden pool cue impaled in his chest just medial to the mid-clavicular line. He is conscious, alert and oriented. I have the object stabilized by hand at this time. We have him on the monitor, and it shows V-fib with occasional runs of normal sinus rhythm. The pool cue is too long to move safely, so we're going to cut off some of the length before we transport. We'll call in before we leave the scene to alert you that we're enroute. Do you request any additional information?"

"No additional information needed at this time. Use extreme caution when cutting the object, Brynne. The runs of normal sinus mean it is already in contact with the heart. Consider IV fluid bolus for blood loss."

"Understood, Doc," she said. "We'll be careful and will have fluids ready to flow. We'll call when we're on the way. U-191 clear." Dean lowered the radio and reattached it to his belt.

"Okay, Brynne," Dean said, picking up the saw. "Are you ready for this?"

"Yep," she said. She looked at her patient. "Gibbie, this is going to be uncomfortable. I need you to sit really still, okay?" The vampire nodded.

Dean set the saw blade on the pool cue about two inches beyond where Brynne's hands gripped it, holding it steady. Using slow, smooth strokes, he began to draw the fine toothed blade back and forth, letting the tool do the work and trying not to put downward pressure on it. It took what seemed like for forever, but he made steady progress and eventually broke through the other side leaving him holding the thick end of the pool cue. Brynne gripped the remaining six-inch stump left protruding from Gibbie's chest.

"Okay, now we can get ready to move you to the ambulance," Brynne said. "Dean, you get some cling rolls and gauze pads out. There's surprisingly little blood, but I think the cue's smooth round side is sealing against the skin. Let's pack some gauze around the wound then use the whole cling rolls to stabilize the object in place, wrapping around his torso to secure them. How's that sound to you?"

"I think that will work," Dean said. He unzipped the trauma bag and retrieved a ten pack of four by four gauze pads along with six four-inch wide cling gauze rolls. He opened the pack of gauze squares and handed them to Brynne, who folded them in half and began to layer them in a criss-cross pattern around the wound. She created a layered round gauze wall around the pool cue pressing them firmly up against the wood. Dean opened two more gauze cling rolls and began wrapping the strips of long gauze around and over the stabilizing packing and then around Gibby's back and torso until he was satisfied that the packing was secured.

"What do you think Brynne?" he asked, perusing his handiwork.

"I think that will do, Dean," she responded. "Any other ideas before we move him?"

"I think we need to immobilize his whole torso," Dean

suggested. "I think the KED is probably the best option. Then we can move him and lay him down on the stretcher without bending or twisting his torso."

"Good idea. Run and get it and the stretcher," she said. "I'll sit here with Gibbie."

Dean ran out to the unit and opened the back to retrieve the stretcher. He rolled it around to the side and opened the long tall doors that held the backboards and KED, the Kendrick Extrication Device. He placed the green bag with the KED in it on the stretcher along with a long backboard and the bag of straps and clips used to secure a patient to the backboard. He rolled the stretcher back into the pool hall, parking it by the entrance to the office.

He picked up the bag with the KED and went inside. He noticed she'd taken the time to start an IV on him and was attaching the bag's tubing to the catheter secured to the patient's arm.

"Okay," he said taking the device out of the container and unfolding it. It looked like an inverted capital T. It had wide wings at the base to wrap around the torso then an extension that went up behind the neck with two smaller wings that were intended to wrap and secure the head in place. The device was stiffened by metal rods. When properly secured, Gibbie should be able to be moved without twisting or bending his upper body at all, minimizing the risk of shifting the pool cue's splintered end still inside him.

Dean had always liked the KED and thought it was a better option to move an injured patient than just using a long backboard. He placed the opened KED against Gibbie's back and carefully lifted his arms while wrapping the wings around each side in turn. The wings didn't fully wrap around him, just coming partially around to the front, which was good, since it would have pushed against the wooden stake if it had reached all the way around. He undid the three colored straps and applied them to immobilize the torso.

"That was good thinking, Dean," Brynne said. "I'm not sure I would have thought of the KED for this application, but it works. Okay, Gibbie," she said to their patient. "We're going to help you stand up and move over to the stretcher. We're going to do all of this slowly, without twisting you or moving you unnecessarily. You're going to stay calm and help us, right?"

"Okay, Brynne, honey," he said quietly. Dean thought he sounded frightened. "Whatever you say."

"I brought a backboard but I think this will do by itself," Dean said. "What do you think?"

"I agree," she said, nodding. "Okay, Gibbie, we're going to work together and move as a unit over to the stretcher. I'll count to three, and I want you to slide slowly forward on the desk until your feet touch the floor. Dean and I will be on each side of you, holding your body still." Dean stood on one side and grabbed the carrying straps on the KED on his side. Brynne did the same on hers. She glanced at the heart monitor, the wires still attached to Gibbie as she counted down. "Three, two, one, nice and easy," she said helping him to slide to his feet and stand up. "Okay, hold it there for a sec." She had seen a couple more runs of normal sinus rhythm on the monitor as they moved him, but the rhythm settled back into his "normal" of ventricular fibrillation once they stopped. The change made her nervous, but they had to get him to the trauma center. He needed surgery.

"Now for the next step," she said standing next to Gibbie. "One step at a time. Make sure you stand up straight and move your legs only. The KED should help you keep your upper body still. We'll be right here with you." The paramedics began walking with their patient across the room and to the door where the stretcher waited for them. They turned him around, so his back was to the stretcher at the midway point, the mattress lowered to knee level and helped him sit straight down. Working together, they helped Gibbie swing his legs up onto the stretcher while they used the KED's handles to turn him so he was sitting up on the stretcher with the back brought up to support him. Dean attached the straps securing Gibbie to the stretcher and put the side rails up. Then with him at the base and Brynne at the head, Dean pressed the button for the motor to raise the stretcher up to his waist height so they could comfortably roll him out to the ambulance.

They loaded Gibbie into the ambulance after rolling him outside without a problem. Dean climbed in back with his patient, while Brynne went back inside with a few of the cops to get the rest of their gear. Dean hooked the IV bag on a ceiling hook and put the heart monitor back in its locking cradle.

He picked up the mic from its hook on the wall next to the med radio and keyed the button. "U-191 to Elk City Medical Center Trauma, how do you read?" He waited for a moment for someone to pick up on the other end.

"We read you loud and clear," came the nurse's voice.

"Patient is extricated to the ambulance, and we will be enroute momentarily," Dean said. "Impaled object is secured in place and patient's torso is immobilized to minimize internal movement. Our ETA to your facility is approximately 5 minutes."

"Received, One-Nine-One. The trauma team is ready for you when you arrive. ECMC Trauma clear."

"U-191 clear," Dean said. "Alright Gibbie, I think the hardest part is over, now we just need to get you to the trauma surgeons to get that thing removed."

"I hope so," Gibbie said. "It's weird, it doesn't hurt all that much. I'm just worried about Brenda. She was so upset, and it is not like her to be so jealous."

"Do you have any idea what caused her to freak out and ram a pool cue into you?" Dean felt the ambulance begin to move.

"I don't know," Gibbie said. He tried to shrug but winced, realizing he couldn't do it all trussed up the way he was. "She's been so strange lately and doesn't want me talking to other women. All I did tonight was laugh at the waitress's joke when she brought our drinks to the table where we were playing pool. Brenda started shouting that she was tired of all my flirting and the next thing I knew I had this pool cue in my chest, and she was flailing at me with her fists. It took three people to haul her off me."

"I won't say I'm any kind of relationship expert," Dean said, "but you need to find yourself a new girl, Gibbie. She's doing nothing but getting you hurt, in more ways than one."

"I know," the vampire said, sighing. "But do you know how hard it is for a guy stuck in middle age to find a girl these days? It used to be that if you had some means, even if you looked like me, they'd be lining up. Now, heck, they want you to be rich and look good. It's just not fair."

"How old are you?" Dean asked. "If you don't mind me asking."

"I was originally born in Germany in a town called Lauenburg on the river Elbe in 1619. It's near Hamburg. I was the son of a cobbler and entered the trade myself, taking over the business when my father died. I had a wife and son who died of a fever that struck the area in 1658. I started hanging out in beer halls to try and forget what I had lost and then I met a woman who seemed more alive than all the others I had known. For several weeks, she met me each night in the beer hall."

"One night she agreed to come back to see my meager shop. She wasn't what she seemed, though. Once she had me alone, she revealed her true self and attacked me. I didn't even resist. I wanted to die and being attacked by some sort of monster seemed an appropriate way for me to go and join my family. But she had other plans for me. She needed a place to stay in Lauenburg, and my shop fit the bill. She kept me alive, feeding off of me from time to time while I kept up appearances and ran the cobbler's shop. She tired of me after a few years, though and decided to move on. She offered me an option. I could turn and be like her or she'd just leave, and I could live out my miserable life as I had before."

Dean saw Gibbie's eyes glance his way. "You can see what my choice was." He smiled. "It hasn't been a bad existence. I had to move of course. People notice when you don't age like everyone else, but overall I've had a good time. I came to the Americas almost a hundred years later, in the 1760's. It was getting too crowded in Europe, and I was running out of places to go and blend in around Germany and Prussia. I paid a shipping company to send a crate of shoes to the new world, and I packed myself inside for the voyage. I could subsist on rats and occasional snacks on the below-decks crew for the months it took to make the Atlantic crossing. It was all quite exciting." He chuckled. "Now I'm as American as you or Brynne."

"That's quite a tale, Gibbie," Dean said. "I bet you've seen a lot over the years. The Revolution, the Civil War and slavery ending - the whole history of this country. It must have been fascinating."

"Oh, it had its exciting moments, I guess," Gibbie said. "But I'm a homebody at heart, and I can't say I like excitement all that much anymore."

Dean laughed out loud but stifled it when he saw the frown on his patient's face. "I'm sorry, Gibbie. I'm not laughing at you, but your life lately has certainly been exciting for someone who describes themselves as a 'homebody,' don't you think?"

"Well," the vampire said sheepishly. "I guess everyone needs a little excitement once in a while."

Dean heard Brynne talking on the radio up front and he looked up through the front windshield to see them pulling up to the ambulance doors at the hospital. "We're here," he said. "See, we got you to the trauma center in one piece. They'll have that stake out of you soon enough." He unhooked the IV bag from the ceiling and laid it across the top of the pillow behind Gibbie's head. He made sure the tubing was out of the way of the wheels and unsnapped the heart monitor leads from Gibbie. He left the stickies in place so the hospital could hook back up to them when they got inside.

Brynne opened the doors, and Dean did one last safety check of all the tubing and wires, then said, "Alright, we're good to go." He jumped down and helped get the stretcher out of the ambulance. They rolled Gibbie feet first up the ramp and into the hospital ER. The trauma team, headed by Doctor Andrews, was waiting for them inside with a stretcher. After a brief update from Dean and Brynne, they carefully transferred the patient over using a slide board, then the team took Gibbie off to surgery. The two paramedics made up their stretcher with fresh sheets and a pillow from the cart by the ambulance bay doors.

"I got quite an earful from Gibbie about his past on the way here," Dean said as he tucked in the sheet under the stretcher's mattress. "He told me all about how he was turned and how old he is. I guess I didn't appreciate how the way he was acting might be a reflection of his past."

"They're just the same as us, Dean," Brynne said. "They aren't monsters, just different. And they have some great stories to tell. Sometimes I learn about things that never made it into history books or movies. I always try to learn something from our patients. It not only makes me a better paramedic, I think it makes me a better person."

They loaded the stretcher and headed back to the station. Dean thought about the event-filled few weeks that had passed by so quickly. He'd started fresh out of school thinking he knew everything there was to know about emergency medical care. He'd been told that he still had a lot to learn from his instructors and preceptors, but he was so confident, so over-confident really, that he didn't realize what they meant.

The theory of caring for sick people and the actual implementation of what he'd learned in school were two very different things. This was especially true with the challenging patients he found himself caring for as part of Station U's team of paramedics. He knew now how little he really knew and realized how far he still had to go to be the type of paramedic and health care professional he wanted to be. He'd also come to another conclusion - he definitely wanted to stay part of Extreme Medical Services, EMS-U.

Dean turned to Brynne. "I want to thank you for being patient with me as I learn the ropes in this job, Brynne. I know a few weeks ago when I started out you weren't exactly excited to have me assigned with you."

"It's no problem, really, Dean," Brynne said. "You've done everything I asked you to do, mostly without question. Mike did the right thing recommending you to come and join our crew right out of school. I questioned the wisdom of that in the beginning, but you've proven yourself. You're naturally a critical thinker, and you take what you know and apply it to new situations as well. The trick now is to keep an open mind and keep learning. I've found that every time I think that I'm getting a handle on learning this job, something new comes along and pulls the rug out from under me."

"Understood, boss," Dean replied. "I don't have any delusions that I'm in any way ready to do this job on my own, believe me."

"Good," Brynne said. "Let's keep it that way for a while."

They returned to the station and restocked the unit then worked on the report for Gibbie's injury. The shift was almost over and they still had some of the night shift chores to do so they got to work. Brook and Tammy showed up on time just as Brynne and Dean were finishing their chores. Dean was tired, so he checked with Brynne to make sure they were done and then signed out and headed to the parking lot. There was a folded piece of paper on his truck under the driver's side windshield wiper. Dean looked around as he approached the vehicle, but there was no one in sight. He reached over and picked up the paper, unfolding it.

"Dean, we need to talk. You are in the middle of something very dangerous. Call me." The note was signed with the name Zach and had a phone number scrawled below the name. He slipped the note in his pocket, climbed in the driver's seat and headed home. Great, just when he thought he had a handle on things, he gets a cryptic note from some guy he didn't know. He was tired and needed to sleep. Maybe he'd call the number when he woke up in the afternoon.

Dean got home to his apartment and went right to bed. Try as he might though, he couldn't get to sleep. His mind kept going back to the note from the mysterious Zach. He kept going over and over in his mind trying to figure out who it was. Then it hit him. He sat upright in his bed. Zach was the name of Brynne's previous partner, wasn't it? That had to be who it was. It made sense that he would know where the Station was and know the cars in the lot well enough to know which one probably belonged to the new guy.

He reached over to his phone and picked the slip of paper up from the nightstand. It was still early. Should he call now or wait until later in the day? He decided he was never going to get to sleep if he didn't resolve this, so he unfolded the paper and keyed in the number on his phone. The phone rang a few times until a man's voice answered.

"Hello, Dean. I'm glad you called," the voice on the other end of the phone said.

"You must be Zach, Brynne's former partner, I guess?" Dean asked.

"Very good. You got it on the first try," Zach said. "Someone picked the right guy for the job when they assigned you to Station U."

"Well, Zach," Dean said. "I'm really tired. You know how it is getting off a busy night shift. I couldn't sleep, though, with the cryptic note you left hanging over my head. Why don't we get to the reason you left the note and what you need to talk with me about?"

"I'd rather not say what I have to say over the phone," Zach said. "I thought we could meet for a cup of coffee and a bite to eat. I have some information that you might need in your current assignment treating the special patients you have."

"Well, I'm beat right now," Dean said, "So how about connecting later this afternoon?"

"Perfect," Zach responded. "Do you know the Pizza Guy sub shop over on Grand Avenue?"

"Yes," Dean said.

"I'll meet you there this afternoon around 4:30. Does that work for you?"

"Ok, 4:30 it is," Dean replied. "How will I recognize you?"

"I know what you look like Dean," Zach said. "I'll introduce myself when you come in. See you then." He hung up the phone.

Dean put his phone down on the nightstand and lay back in bed staring at the ceiling. How did Zach know who he was if they'd never met? He was never going to sleep with all of this mystery rattling around in his head. He picked up his phone again and scrolled through the screens. He opened Pzizz, set the sleep-inducing app to run and to wake him up at three PM. Soft music began, and a soothing voice started coaching his mind to fall asleep. He focused on the voice, trying to take his mind off of the thoughts racing through it. Fatigue finally won the battle and after about ten minutes he drifted off to sleep.

---

# Chapter 21

---

Dean woke to the Pzizz app alarm at three PM feeling refreshed and ready to face the challenges ahead of him. The app's gentle self-hypnosis coaching seemed to do that for him every time. His concern about the upcoming meeting with Zach seemed exaggerated. What did he have to fear from a previous member of his station's crew?

He had an hour to get a shower and do some blogging before he had to leave. He liked to share his thoughts in his online diary. He didn't relate any sensitive information, but shared his impressions of his progress in school and later on the job at Station U. It was a way for him to break down his experiences and make sense of them, and he truly thought it helped him through his paramedic school program. It wasn't much more than personal ramblings, but he hoped to change that as he became more experienced.

He showered and dressed in his uniform since he probably wouldn't have time to come back before work at six. With a half hour left, he sat down at the dinette table, opened his laptop and logged in to his blog at WannabeMedic.com. He never knew exactly what he would write, but something always came to him. He started talking about how he was finally fitting in at Station U. The call last night with the special trauma situation contributed to a sense he was starting to work within a comfort zone with his special patients. Brynne's appraisal that he had come up with a good idea using the KED to transfer the patient to the stretcher felt good, too. He concluded the blog post with a final thought: he wondered what new challenges awaited him at the station and how he would be called upon to improvise treatments based on his knowledge, skills and intuition. He didn't post anything about the special nature of his patients. He just posted about things he learned about himself and patient care in general.

He glanced at his watch and realized that he needed to get going. He closed up his laptop, grabbed his wallet and keys and headed out to the appointment with Zach. This day was going to be interesting, that was for sure. His curiosity had his mind racing as he backed out of his driveway and headed down the road to the highway.

Dean pulled into the parking lot in the strip mall where the Pizza Guy restaurant was located on Grand Avenue. He was about ten minutes early and he looked around to see if anything or anyone looked familiar. He checked his email and social media accounts on his smartphone then decided to go in on time rather than sit in the parking lot not knowing who he was looking for. A tap on his truck window startled him, and he jumped a little as he turned to see who it was. He didn't know the guy who stood there but had a good assumption. He was older than Dean, maybe in his late twenties. Zach was also taller at six foot two, and had sandy blonde hair. He was wearing jeans and a green, collared golf shirt. Dean pushed the button to put down the window.

"Hi Dean, I'm Zach. I saw you sitting here on my way inside and thought I'd come over and introduce myself."

"Um, hello, Zach," Dean stammered. "I'm sorry, you startled me."

"I apologize," Zach said. "Let's go inside."

"Sure," Dean answered, "Give me a second, I'll be right in."

"Okay, see you there." Zach crossed the parking toward the building entrance.

Dean finished the email he was writing and closed up his truck. Once inside, he took a minute to orient himself to the unfamiliar surroundings then saw Zach seated in a booth at the back.

"I'm so glad you could join me, Dean," Zach said. "I wanted to meet the guy who replaced me at Station U. By the way, how do you like it there?"

"It's challenging, that's for sure," Dean said. "I have to say it certainly took some getting used to." Dean looked at the other paramedic and asked, "I have to know. How did you know who I was?"

"I still have contacts at Elk City Fire Department EMS. I knew they'd have to replace me with someone, but I didn't think they'd throw a brand new medic fresh out of school into the lion's den," Zach said. "I'm sure it was quite a shock to find out you were going to treat the worst of society's monsters for a living."

"I don't know about that," Dean said, cautiously. He didn't like the cynicism he was sensing from the other man. "I think they're just people in need just like us. They're different, but that doesn't make them monsters. Most of the ones I've met are pretty much unassuming."

"You don't see how they're subverting our culture from within?" Zach asked. "They've been living alongside humans for thousands of years, taking advantage of us, living off of us like parasites."

"That's a bit strong, Zach," Dean said. "That hasn't been my experience at all."

"Not even with the siren and her attempt to control you?" Dean knew Zach had to have seen his startled expression. "I know about that situation and how you ended up having to get some counseling for it. Are you sure now they're all so innocent? If they have nothing to hide, then why don't they become open members of society?" He stopped as the waitress came over to take their order and waited until she walked away. "Don't you wonder what kind of control they must have over our leaders if they've been able to hide successfully for all these years?"

"Maybe they're just scared of people misunderstanding them," Dean offered. "And who told you I'd been to counseling? That's supposed to be private."

"I told you, I have my connections," Zach countered. "Look, my goal isn't to alienate you. It's to make you understand the danger you're in - that we all are in with these creatures living among us." Dean started to protest, but Zach raised his hand to stop him. "You're not the only person who had a bad run-in with one of your Unusual patients. I had one, too, and I was lucky to survive. Your incident with the siren was relatively mild by comparison. Let me ask you, did they send you to that mind reading muse, Rebecca?" Dean nodded. "I thought so. They do that so that you won't spread the word out about the Unusuals living among us."

"Zach," Dean said carefully. "I don't know what your run-in was or how it changed your outlook on the job. Frankly, I don't want to know. What did you call me here for? It wasn't to reveal that you know all about me because that's just creepy, and doesn't really make me want to stay and talk with you, let alone share a meal with you."

"I called you here, Dean, to try and save you." Zach said. "You can't know the danger you're in. Brynne is completely blind to it because James has her wrapped around his vampiric little finger. She can't see the risks when they're right in bed next to her. But you, Dean, are in a position to do some good and maybe save Brynne in the process. I tried, and she completely rejected what I was trying to do. I knew I had to get out when James threatened me if I kept trying to get between him and Brynne. So I resigned and left Elk City EMS to work alongside some people who are trying to do some good and not covering up the mess these monsters are making in our society. Something has to be done. In order to do what we need to do, we need someone on the inside who can help us expose the creatures among us. People have a right to know who their neighbors and co-workers really are, don't you think?"

Dean was dumbfounded. When he thought about meeting his predecessor at Station U, this was not what he had expected to hear. This was the most paranoid rant he'd ever heard. His own interactions with his patients didn't leave him feeling this negative. For the most part, they seemed to be normal people with some unusual abilities. They were the creatures made out to be monsters in legends and horror movies, but aside from a single incident with one misguided individual, they had treated him with respect. Clearly, Zach didn't see it that way, and he suspected that it was knowledge of his interaction with Lydia the siren that made this guy think he would be of like mind. What was he supposed to do about it?

Zach answered his question without hearing. "Dean, I know this is a lot to take in. I was overwhelmed when I was first contacted and asked to help build a safer society. It didn't make sense to me in the beginning either, but over time I began to see things their way. I think you might too."

"I don't know, Zach," Dean started. "I don't think I'm the right person to have this conversation with. Perhaps you should contact someone with a little more authority than I have about this."

"I don't expect you to make up your mind right now," Zach said. "I just want you to keep your eyes open and see what's really going on in this community. Later, you might feel differently. Will you do that?"

"Uh, I guess so," Dean said. He was uncomfortable and wanted to get out of this awkward conversation.

"I have one more favor to ask," Zach said. "I'd like to ask that you don't tell Brynne or anyone else that you talked with me, at least for a little while. She and I didn't part on good terms, and she might think less of you if she knew you and I met."

Dean thought for a moment. It wouldn't hurt to keep this meeting to himself for a little bit. At least he could wait until he found out what the end game was. "I guess I can agree to that, at least for a short time," Dean said. "I don't think about Unusuals the same way you do, but I'll keep my eyes open."

"That's all I'm asking," Zach said with a grin, leaning back in the seat. He looked up, and Dean saw the waitress arriving with their food. She set the plate with two slices of pizza down in front of Dean along with a soda in a hard plastic cup. She slid the plate with Zach's cheeseburger and fries in front of him and set his Coke down on the table.

"Can I get you anything else?" she asked.

"I think we're good," Zach said. "We'll call you if we need anything."

The two paramedics watched her walk away and began to eat. Dean thought as he chewed. This was all very strange and smacked of something more sinister, but Zach had made it seem almost reasonable. All they wanted him to do was to keep his eyes open to abuses of the system by his patients. He had seen one such situation with the girl in cardiac arrest after a botched attempt to turn her into a vampire. He had also been directly affected by Lydia the siren when she tried to charm him.

Zach didn't bring anything else up about Unusuals, steering the conversation around to Dean's time in the academy paramedic program. He asked about instructors who were still there teaching and what Dean thought of them. Dean answered but was focused on Zach's earlier statements. He wasn't comfortable with the extreme position Zach seemed to have. If he hadn't had the experiences he had over the past few weeks, it was likely he would have disregarded him completely. Dean would keep quiet about it, at least for a little while. He needed time to make more sense of it. Was he being recruited for some "anti-Unusual" movement?

They finished their meals quickly. Paramedics rarely ate slowly, a side effect of always being called away to respond during meals. In this case Dean just wanted to leave. Dean put a ten-dollar bill down on the table to cover his part of the meal. Zach put two fives down and they headed toward the door.

"Dean," Zach began as they stood on the sidewalk in front of the restaurant. "Thank you for keeping my confidence on this. Think about what you're doing and when you're ready, give me a call. You have my phone number. You can call me if you want and we can meet again. Otherwise, just keep your eyes open. I think in time you'll see what is going on under the surface. I'll be in touch."

"Okay, Zach," Dean said. "I don't think like you do on this subject, but I'll keep our little meeting to myself for a little while. Fair enough?"

"Fair enough," Zach said.

They shook hands and headed off to their vehicles. Dean sat

down in his pickup truck and couldn't shake the feeling that he'd done something wrong. He probably should tell Brynne about this meeting but he'd promised to be silent for a short while, and he didn't see any harm in that. What could possibly happen in the next few days?

## Chapter 22

When Dean entered the squad room for his next shift twenty minutes early, he saw Brook and Tammy, who looked up from the chairs where they sat in front of the TV.

"Hey, Probie," Tammy said.

"What brings you into work early?" Brook asked.

"I was out and about and decided that it didn't make sense to go all the way home first," Dean answered. "Anyway, I wanted to talk with you two about something. If that's okay?"

"Sure, Dean," Tammy said. "What's on your mind?"

"I had a run in with James. I wanted to see if you two had any insights about how to best deal with him. Can I take him at his word?"

Brook shared a conspiratorial glance with Tammy, then Tammy nodded. Brook turned back to look at Dean. "Don't you think you should check in with Brynne about this? She's your field training officer after all."

"I can't talk to her about this," Dean said. "She may be my FTO, but she's also his girlfriend. That may cloud her judgment about him. The fact is, James talked to me one-on-one after a call that raised some questions, and I began to have my own questions about the work we're doing. Frankly, he scared the crap out of me."

Tammy chuckled, "He has that effect on people, that's for sure. What did he say to you?"

"He didn't threaten me or anything if that's what you mean," Dean said. "He basically told me that I should wait until I understood the Unusuals' culture and way of handling things before I took any action regarding what I saw on that call. He also told me to deal directly with him if I had a problem and he would explain things to me." Dean glanced up from looking at the floor. "He also said he meant me no harm."

Dean looked at them, but they just stared back at him, allowing him to continue. "The thing is, I get the sense that he's pretty old fashioned about how he deals with things. He's like the Baron of Elk City or something, which means that he's still living in the type of feudal culture that he used to live in hundreds of years ago. Is he a nice guy who deals with things in a reasonable fashion, or is he some feudal overlord who does whatever he wants because no one can stop him?"

The women shared a glance as if to decide who should answer. "That's a loaded question," Brook said. "It has two parts. I'll address the last question first. James is in charge of the Unusual population in and around Elk City. He's the final answer for anything that needs to get done, and they will listen if he gives an order, so, in that sense, he's a feudal overlord. But, he is ultimately a man of his word. If he says he means you no harm, he means it. If he says you can come to him if you have any problems with any of your patients, believe him. He'll deal with it. That might be because you're Brynne's partner, or it might be because you represent an important resource for his subjects. Does that make sense?"

"I guess so," Dean said. "So he can do anything he wants, but he's an honorable man, er, vampire."

"Exactly," Tammy said. "The other thing to remember is that while the Unusual population has to listen to him, we have our own hierarchy and leadership. We don't have to listen to him at all, and he and his kind depend on our leaders to take care of them and keep their secret so they can go on living among us. It's a two-way street."

"So you don't think that it's weird that the bogeymen of our childhoods live side by side among us?" Dean asked.

"No," Tammy chuckled. "Not anymore. I sure thought it was weird in the beginning, though. When I first got this assignment, I was completely weirded out by some of the things I saw - things I just take in stride now."

"Me, too," Brook said. "I used to get nightmares from some of the patients we ran into. Not because of anything they did to me or anyone else, but just because of who they were. I ended up getting some counseling about it and realized that they were just people. They have families and businesses and jobs, and just want to go about their lives without anyone messing with them. They pay taxes, too, which is why Doc Spirelli organized the first Station U unit here. They had the right to have access to emergency care like anyone else, and so the EMS-U system came into being here in Elk City."

"So you haven't seen any of them abuse their powers or take advantage of normal humans?" Dean asked.

"Nothing more serious than what happened with you and the siren, Lydia," Brook said. "She is really sorry, by the way. She did what she did out of fear and misunderstanding rather than any sort of malice. She moved here from down south where the population is not as progressive as we are here in the more urban areas of the country."

Dean thought on that in light of what Zach had talked with him about earlier. It didn't really match up with what the ex-paramedic said. It did, however, match up with what he had seen with his own two eyes. The patients were all genuinely thankful for the care they rendered. So what was it that Zach had against Unusuals? Were his concerns of imminent danger really valid? His attention was pulled to the door when Brynne entered.

"Hey Dean, hi ladies!" Brynne said in a cheerful voice.

"Hi Brynne," Tammy said. "Why so chipper? Did you get a good day's sleep or something?

"I'll bet it was more like 'or something'," Brook interjected. "Just look at the grin on her face." The day shift paramedics burst into laughter at the blush that crept up Brynne's face. They laughed even harder when they saw Dean's look of discomfort.

"Sorry, Dean," Tammy said. "Girl talk should be meant for girls' ears only."

"Yeah," Brook said. "Don't write us up for hostile work environment."

"I think I'll go and get an early start on the bag checks in the ambulance," Dean said. "I'll leave you ladies to your private talk."

He crossed the room to the ambulance bay door and left them to their conversation. The diversion was actually good. He didn't want to talk with Brynne right now because he still needed to wrap his head around everything he had learned today. He climbed into the ambulance and began to go through the bags with the iPad checklist.

Dean was almost done with his checklists when he heard the door to the squad room open. A few moments later, Brynne showed up outside the open rear doors of the ambulance. "Sorry about the direction the conversation took back there, Dean. Sometimes girls will be girls."

"I'm a big boy, Brynne. I can handle it." Dean said with a smile. "I really did want to get a head start on the inventory."

"Are you almost done?" Brynne asked. "What can I help with?"

"I've only got the trauma bag to go through and I'm finished. Maybe you could check out the Med Dispenser and see if we need to order anything from the hospital."

"Sounds like a plan," Brynne said. "I'll get right on it. Then we can make a pick up later when we're out of the station."

The beginning of shift chores went quickly, and they were soon back in the squad room. Brynne was checking through the shift email that went out to each crew alerting them of news, training opportunities and medication changes, and Dean was reading a book on Egyptian mythology. He heard her sigh as she stared at the screen.

"What's up?" Dean asked, looking up from his book.

"Have you checked your email from headquarters?" Brynne asked.

"No," Dean said, "Is there something important?"

"There's a warning from headquarters to us from the police investigation division that there have been unprovoked attacks on members of the Unusual population. They're urging us to be very careful approaching scenes where an assault might have occurred because of reprisals against us for rendering aid."

"Why would someone do something like that?" Dean asked.

"There are groups out there who are afraid of the unknown, Dean," Brynne said. "While most normal people live blissfully unaware that the Unusuals live among us, there are a few who know the truth. Among them are some who think that we're letting monsters live among us who will eventually do us harm."

"Have you ever met someone like that?" Dean asked. "Are we in danger just because we provide emergency aid to them?" How we are to protect ourselves?"

"Your predecessor, Zach, had doubts about what we do, Dean," Brynne said. "He was never comfortable caring for our group of patients. Eventually he decided he wouldn't do it anymore. One day he refused to care for a vampire patient who had a drug problem. He would feed on junkies until he overdosed. Zach said that we should let him die because he was a danger to the human addicts he fed on. It didn't matter if the relationship was consensual, Zach thought it was unnatural. Let's face it, Unusuals behaviors are unnatural by human standards. That was the final straw from head-quarters' standpoint. You can't just refuse to treat a patient you don't like whether they're a different breed, race, or because they smell bad. That's abandonment, and it violated his license."

Dean was suddenly uncomfortable. His earlier conversation with Zach sent a chill down his spine. He agreed with some of the points that Zach had made. Did that put him at risk for losing his job? He liked the work, but he had some reservations about the way the Unusuals lived and the powers they wielded. Was having that conversation with Zach justification for firing him?

"You alright, Dean?" Brynne asked. "You zoned out."

"It's just that I'd never thought about it that way." Dean responded. "It seems a stupid reason to lose your job." He paused as a thought occurred to him. "Um, do you think Zach's mixed up in these attacks on the Unusuals?"

"No," Brynne said. "I just don't think he was up for this kind of work. Some people aren't. I don't think he'd actually hurt anyone. But, there are people out there who do horrible things based on misguided beliefs. We should make sure we're prepared for something unusual on our calls."

"Isn't that the very nature of what we do here at Station U?" Dean said with a smile.

Brynne laughed. "Yeah, I guess it is. Still it doesn't hurt to be cautious. Remember to keep your eyes open."

They both jumped up as the tones sounded over the squad room speakers. "Medical Box 231, burn victim, 3521 Martin Highway." Dean grabbed the dispatch paper as it came off the printer and headed out to the ambulance bay. Brynne jumped up into the driver's seat and started up the diesel engine as Dean headed around to the passenger side.

He climbed in and put them responding, and then switched the radio channel over to the appropriate med channel to get the additional information. The dispatcher came on almost instantly. "U-191, respond for a thirty-four-year-old female victim of an assault. Severe burns reported by bystanders. Fire and police also enroute. Use caution as you approach."

"Received, respond with caution." Dean hung up the mic on the dash. "What do you think we're getting into here?"

"I don't know," Brynne said. "You know where the fire extinguisher is in case the assailant is still around and decides to set fire to anything else, right?" Dean nodded. "Hopefully the police get there before we do and can lock down the scene."

# Chapter 23

It took them 10 minutes to get to the location of the call. The fire engine and police cars lit up the scene with their lights. Brynne pulled up near the fire engine but parked in such a way that she could still pull out without backing up when they had to leave. There were two firefighter EMTs next to the engine's cab and one of them stood up as they arrived to wave them over. Dean grabbed the med bag and oxygen airway bag from the compartment on his side while Brynne walked around and climbed in the back to get the heart monitor and the trauma bag.

Dean headed over to where the two firefighters were and saw what he thought was a pile of black rags on the ground. Then it moved, and he saw cracked red and raw skin underneath the charred clothing. Damn, this was bad. He caught a whiff of the sickly sweet smell of burned flesh, and his stomach churned. They already had a non-rebreather mask on her, hooked up to their portable oxygen tank from the fire engine's first responder kit.

"What happened?" Dean asked as he swallowed hard and knelt down next to the moaning patient.

"Bystanders said that someone just walked up to this woman and doused her with some kind of fluid from a can then flicked a match at her," the first firefighter said. "Could have been lighter fluid or gasoline. An arson investigator will be able to tell us when he's done with his investigation. Her clothes caught fire quickly, and she started screaming and trying to pat out the flames. Another bystander knocked her to the ground and had her roll around to smother the flames, and someone else grabbed a fire extinguisher from that coffee shop and used it on her. The fire was out when we arrived. We were just starting patient care when you guys got here."

Dean was staring at the patient, unsure where to start first when Brynne came up to stand next to him. Her gasp told Dean that she had just seen the extent of the patient's burns. He looked up at her. He was out of his element here. He shouldn't have been but this was more than he could handle on his own.

Brynne looked down at him and must have seen the look in his eyes. "One step at a time, Dean. Just take it one step at a time." She knelt down on the other side of the patient and started talking to her. "Hello, my name is Brynne, I'm here to help you. Can you tell me your name?"

The woman turned her charred face toward the soothing voice next to her. Her mouth opened and she croaked out "Vanessa."

"Okay, Vanessa," Brynne said, "my partner Dean and I are going to do some things to make you feel a little better. Then we're going to take you to the hospital, all right?"

"All right," Vanessa rasped. "It hurts so bad."

Dean looked at her right arm and saw that the burns were less severe there. "Brynne, I think I can get IV access on this side."

"Okay go for it, but if you can't get it, we're better off going straight to an intraosseous infusion route," Brynne said.

"Understood." Dean began gathering his supplies to start an IV. The firefighters were well trained. As soon as they heard what the paramedics intended to do, one of them came over and started prepping a bag of normal saline for the infusion, attaching the IV tubing and flushing out the air. Dean looked at the arm and knew he wasn't going to be able to clean the skin very well around the IV site but he made a few passes with the alcohol preps he had pulled out. He selected an 18 gauge needle which was the largest he thought he could get in the vein he'd identified. He removed the safety cover and started to insert it gently into the area. He was rewarded almost instantly with a flash of blood in the chamber at the top of the IV catheter assembly.

Dean looked up at the firefighter standing next to him holding the IV fluid bag and took the end of the IV tubing. He carefully attached the IV tubing in its place. He rolled the valve wide open and saw the fluid flowing through the drip chamber, then taped down the tubing and catheter so it wouldn't dislodge.

He left the fluid flowing wide. Extensive burns caused a fluid shift within the body and Vanessa was going to need a lot of fluids over the next twenty-four hours. He judged that she had second and third degree burns over sixty to seventy percent of her body.

Brynne had hooked up the blood pressure cuff and had gotten a set of vitals. She was in the process of hooking up the heart monitor leads so Dean thought about what he could do next. Vanessa's groans reminded him that pain management was next on the list. He got out the morphine. He wasn't going to have enough morphine on hand to deal with this patient's pain adequately, but he could at least get started. "Brynne, I've got IV access and I'm going to start pushing some morphine, okay?"

"You do that," Brynne confirmed. "I need to get ready to secure her airway. She sounds like she has some airway burns." She looked up at the firefighters and said, "Could one of you call dispatch and tell them that we'll need a paramedic supervisor with supplemental pain meds to this location. Also, have them notify ECMC burn unit that we have a patient with approximate 70 percent burn surface area coming in."

The engine's lieutenant nodded and turned away, speaking into the microphone attached to his shoulder. Dean double-checked the dose of morphine in the syringe. He attached the syringe hub to the IV tubing and slowly started pushing the drug into the patient. "Vanessa, this is Dean, Brynne's partner. I'm giving you some pain medication now. Hopefully it will take the edge off the pain you're feeling."

As he slowly depressed the plunger, he looked down at the

patient's charred face, watching for a reaction. He saw a flash of silver around her neck and a pendant of a pentagram on a chain. It looked like it was partially seared into her neck. He got Brynne's attention and she looked down to where he was gesturing. He thought it was a holy symbol for a Wiccan. He mouthed the word "Wicca" to Brynne. She nodded in agreement. It didn't change anything from a treatment perspective, but it would be pertinent information based on the warning email they had received from headquarters earlier. He glanced around to see if he could spot the police he knew were nearby. Maybe they should know. Then he froze as he saw Zach standing there. He made eye contact with Dean, shook his head no and then backed away into the crowd. Brynne's voice shook him back.

"Dean, what are you doing? We've got work to do, stay with me." She said. "We need to get ready to RSI her. I'm afraid that airway is going to close up." Brynne referred to the practice of rapid sequence intubation where a series of drugs were administered to a patient, sedating them so they could have a breathing tube inserted even though they were conscious. Dean helped Brynne draw up the meds and got the bag valve mask ready to breathe for Vanessa when the paralytics started working.

They had the tube successfully in place when the shift supervisor pulled up in his chase car. Brynne motioned for one of the fire-fighters to take over compressing the breathing bag every eight seconds and stood up to talk to the assistant chief walking towards them.

"Hi, Ari," Brynne said. "I just RSI'd her. She's burned pretty severely. I'd estimate the burn area to be around seventy percent. Dean got the IV and has already pushed ten milligrams of morphine. We'll probably need more at some point."

"That's all right Brynne," Ari said. "I heard the call and was heading over anyway. What happened?"

"Someone apparently doused her in lighter fluid or gasoline or something like that and set her on fire while she was walking down the street," Brynne said. "Police and fire were on scene when we arrived. Do you think that it has something to do with the alert we got this evening about attacks on Unusuals? She's wearing a Wiccan holy symbol. It could be nothing, but I'd rather be safe than sorry."

"I'll tell the police watch commander about your suspicions," Ari said. "If this is the beginning of some sort of trend, we need to have a coordinated response between the agencies, especially since it might be Unusual related."

Dean called out to Brynne, "I think we're ready to get her packaged and loaded into the ambulance."

"Be right there," Brynne said. "One last thing, Chief. I think I saw my ex-partner Zach in the crowd but when I looked up again, he was gone. I don't think he noticed that I saw him, but I thought you should know that he was here."

"Let's hope that was just a coincidence or that you were mistaken," Ari said. "The last thing we need is to have one of our own doing this sort of thing. We've worked too hard to gain their trust to have it all blown by a whack job who should never have been assigned to Station U to begin with."

"Let's get the patient squared away at the hospital and I'll take care of coordinating the investigation with the police. I'll also call the local coven and tell them that one of their own may have been injured. They might be able to supplement the medical care in some way."

Brynne nodded, and the two of them separated as the chief headed over to the police sergeant on the scene and she turned back to help Dean get Vanessa ready to transport. He and the firefighters had the situation pretty well in hand. She checked the vitals on the monitor and re-evaluated how Vanessa was doing with the intubation and meds.

"Dean," Brynne said. "Since I had to RSI her, you're going to have to drive the rig. Are you up for it?"

"I can do it," he said trying not to grin. "We're going right to the ECMC Burn Unit?"

"Yes, you'll have to call ahead and tell them we're on the way," Brynne said. "I'll bring one of the firefighters along to assist with ventilating the patient. Just take your time and get us there in one piece. Safety before speed, right?"

"Right," Dean responded. He could barely contain his excitement. Brynne was right, though. When driving, he had the ultimate responsibility to get the patient and his crew to the hospital in one piece.

The two firefighters had brought the stretcher from the ambulance and positioned it by Vanessa. With Brynne and Dean's help, they carefully lifted her up and onto it. Brynne took a moment to check and make sure the breathing tube was in place after moving the patient. She checked the in-line capnography reading and listened to the patient's lungs before nodding to them to keep moving.

The team slowly rolled the burned patient over to the back of the ambulance and loaded her inside. Dean held the door open while Brynne climbed inside. She turned and looked at him. "Remember, Dean, slow and steady wins the race."

"I got it, boss," Dean said. He slapped the closed back doors of the ambulance and walked around to the driver's side. His phone buzzed in his shirt pocket, and he absent-mindedly checked the text message as he climbed up and sat down behind the wheel. And then he froze.

The text message read: Dean, I know you saw me. Don't tell Brynne I was there. I'll explain later. You need to know the whole story before you make up your mind. There's a reason this all happened. Remember you are a part of this now. - Z

Dean felt stunned. Somehow he'd gotten mixed up in something that was rapidly turning into a disaster that he didn't know how to extricate himself from. He knew one thing for sure. He couldn't go to Brynne with his suspicions because Zach might implicate him in some way and then he'd lose the job of a lifetime. He couldn't risk that. He put the phone back in his pocket after deleting the message with a swipe of his thumb and shifted the ambulance into gear as he carefully pulled out onto the street and headed off to the hospital. He hoped he would figure a way out of this mess before anyone else found out about it. He decided as he neared the hospital that he needed to talk to Mike Farver about it. He'd know what to do.

# Epilogue

Zach watched the ambulance drive away with the witch in the back. He was pretty sure they had gotten the job done on her. Not even that bitch, Brynne Garvey, would be able to bring her back from the brink of death. The thing that worried him the most was whether Dean would keep his mouth shut about seeing him at the scene. It could bring up some inconvenient attention at a time when the Cause didn't need it. He was willing to sacrifice himself if that was what it took, but he didn't want to do so without a good reason. He thought there was still time to get to Dean, and to get him to keep quiet, one way or another.

He turned and walked around the corner and down the block, away from the crime scene and pulled out his phone, selecting another number to text. He tapped as he walked, choosing his words carefully. Even though it was a burner phone, he didn't want a search warrant of the account to turn up anything incriminating. The leadership in Elk City had a lot of resources in their bag of tricks, and that didn't even take into account the things those freaks in the monster community could do. He sent that message off and kept walking for a few more minutes until a large black SUV pulled up next to him. He looked around and then climbed up into the passenger seat. Mike Farver looked at him from behind the wheel.

"Well?" Mike said.

"I don't think she'll live, but we might have to take some steps to follow-up at the hospital," Zach said as they drove off. "There's another problem, though. The new guy saw me in the crowd. I sent him a text to keep it a secret until I could explain myself, but I'm not sure if it worked or not."

"I hoped that he would have been on our side by now with everything he's seen," Mike said. "I picked him for this job specifically because I thought he could be our man inside after you botched the job. Now you tell me you got noticed and that the witch isn't dead?"

"There's still time to fix it, Mike," Zach said. "I'll make it right, I swear."

"I know you will because you know the consequences of failure," Mike said with a deadly tone. "I don't have to tell you what the others would think if you can't hold up your end of the bargain." Zach didn't answer, just stared straight ahead as the older paramedic drove off into the darkness. "No worries, Zach. Perhaps I need to have another impromptu meal with Dean and see if I can find out what he knows. Then we can decide how to handle him."

READ on for a preview of book 2, *The Paramedic's Angel*

JAMIE DAVIS
THE PARAMEDIC'S
ANGEL
Extreme Medical Services Book 2

# JAMIE DAVIS

# THE PARAMEDIC'S ANGEL

## Extreme Medical Services Book 2

# Chapter 1

Dean Flynn steered the ambulance through the nighttime traffic of Elk City. The howl of the siren and the reflection of the flashing lights off the buildings cleared the traffic ahead of him as he drove to the burn unit of Elk City Medical Center. In the back with his partner Brynne, he had a female patient who had been attacked, and set on fire by an unknown adversary. His identification of her as Witch, a witch in common terms, made her his Unusual patient, and he was determined as ever to do whatever he could to save her life. In the recent months of his probationary period with the paramedics of Station U, Dean had learned that the creatures of myth and legend existed and lived alongside their human neighbors. The Station U paramedics were tasked with providing medical care to those Unusual patients.

The woman in the back was suffering from significant burns. He had worked with Brynne, his partner and mentor, to start IVs and get her some pain management. They had placed a tube in her throat to help her breathe through her burned airways, and now he was driving the ambulance to the hospital, lights flashing and siren blaring, to get her to the burn center alive. He checked the rearview mirror and saw Brynne hunched over the patient in the back, working to cut away the remainder of her charred clothing. A firefighter from the engine that responded to the fire sat at the head of the stretcher, occasionally squeezing the bag that delivered life-saving oxygen to the patient's lungs.

Dean returned his attention to the road and checked his speed, knowing that even with lights and sirens, he had to obey traffic signs and signals, proceeding through intersections only after he had ascertained it was safe to do so. The instructors in emergency vehicle operations courses called it "Due Regard" for traffic laws. What it meant to him was that he had the responsibility to get his patient, and his crew, to the hospital in one piece. Getting in an accident along the way would not accomplish that goal.

He turned the final corner and saw ECMC, Elk City Medical Center, lit up bright against the dark nighttime sky down the street. He had never been in the Burn Center entrance. It was on the opposite side of the building from the emergency department, but he knew where it was. As he approached the dedicated ambulance parking at that entrance, Dean picked up the radio's microphone, and keying the button to transmit, said, "Ambulance U-191 arrived at ECMC."

"Ambulance U-191 arrived, ECMC, Oh-Two-Thirty-Seven," the dispatcher replied with the military time of arrival over the speaker.

He backed into the parking spot, checking his mirrors often. He had only ever done this in practice at the academy. This was the first time Brynne had let him drive. She claimed this critical patient for herself because of the difficult airway management issues the burn patient presented.

"We're here," he called over his shoulder into the back, as he put the vehicle gear lever in park and engaged the parking brake. He unbuckled his seat belt and climbed down from the cab, heading back to the rear and opening the doors. Brynne was detaching the IV bags from their ceiling hooks. The firefighter from the engine crew squeezed the airway bag, breathing for the patient every eight seconds. Dean could see him counting under his breath in between squeezes, the way he'd been taught.

"Ok," Brynne said, grabbing the heart monitor from its rack and placing it carefully on the stretcher next to the patient's legs. She had covered the woman with a clean sheet up to her chin. "We're going to take our time and make sure we aren't moving her unnecessarily. I don't want to dislodge that tube in her airway."

"Got it," Dean said, nodding. He gripped the base of the stretcher and unlocked the mechanism that held it securely in the back of the ambulance. Brynne climbed down next to him and turned to assist. Dean looked at the firefighter in the back still focused on his job. "We'll go slow, you just focus on the breathing. I'll take over for you when we get this far so you can climb down, and then you can resume, Okay?" The guy nodded as he squeezed the bag one more time and then stood up, bent over the head of the stretcher to do his job.

Dean started to roll the stretcher out of the back of the ambulance, taking the weight of it as he did so. When the undercarriage cleared the back of the vehicle, he pressed the button that electronically lowered the wheels to the ground. He turned over control of the foot-end to his partner and he went to the head of the cot to take over squeezing the bag while the firefighter climbed down. Once that job was returned to the firefighter, Dean took over controlling the head of the stretcher, and they wheeled their patient through the automatic double doors and inside the ECMC burn center.

⊏⊐

INSIDE THE BURN CENTER, a nurse came forward right away to take their report. Brynne filled her in on the details of the patient, what little they knew. She covered their assessments and interventions as they followed the nurse to a broad, open treatment room. There were several doctors, residents and nurses there waiting for the patient.

They carefully transferred the patient from the cot over to the hospital's ER stretcher. A respiratory therapist took over squeezing the airway bag from the firefighter while the nurses hung the IV bags from poles at the corner of the hospital cot. Brynne answered a few more questions while Dean detached the heart monitor from the patient, and then they backed off to let the hospital's burn team do their work. He wheeled their ambulance stretcher back into the hallway.

"That was a tough call, I came over to see how you guys were doing," a familiar voice said. Dean turned to see the nurse, Ashley Moore, from the emergency department standing there. He had run into her at a convenience store soon after he had started his job at Station U. He had caught her staring at the back of his hand during that encounter. The back of the right hand was where all the paramedics from Station U put an ultraviolet ink stamp that declared them as paramedics for the Unusual community. Since only Unusuals could see in that spectrum, he knew she was one of them but he had yet to figure out what kind. Dean had discovered she worked in the ER here at ECMC as a nurse, and he looked forward to seeing her there whenever she was working.

"It was a bad one, Ashley," Brynne confirmed. She looked around to make sure no one was close enough to hear. The fire-fighter had headed back out to the ambulance deck, probably to wait for his crew to come by and pick him up. "Someone sprayed her with lighter fluid, or something like it, and then set her on fire. It might be a hate crime related to her being Witch. She's got seventy percent second and third-degree burns, and we had to intubate her to protect her airway. I think it will be touch and go."

"Has anyone tried to contact her coven?" Ashley asked.

"Chief Ari was going to do that," Brynne said. "I hope he gets them. Maybe there's something they can do to help her."

"How're you holding up on this one, Dean? This incident is a little more than the usual ambulance call for you guys," the nurse asked him. Her green eyes sparkled in the fluorescent lighting of the hospital hallway, or was that just his imagination?

"I'm fine; I guess," he said. "It was a rough call, sure, but it's a lot rougher on her than us," referring to the patient inside the treatment room. "I'll be ok, all things considered."

"Well, I heard you guys on the radio coming in and thought I'd come over and say hi," Ashley said. "Dean, if you ever need to talk, maybe over a cup of coffee or a glass of soda sometime, I'm available." She turned and headed back down the hallway towards the emergency department. Dean watched her go until she turned the corner at the far end of the long hallway.

"Earth to Dean, Earth to Dean," Brynne said, adding some radio static sound effects. "Yo, Probie!"

"Uh, sorry," Dean stammered. "I got distracted, should we get the unit back in service?"

"Yeah you were distracted alright. That Eldara Sister has your number, I think."

Dean blinked in surprise. "She's your big sister? I didn't know. She looks younger than you."

"Not elder sister, you goof," Brynne laughed aloud. "She is an Eldara Sister, an actual angel on earth; and she is most definitely not younger than me. Come on, let's get the stretcher made up and put the ambulance back in service. I'll fill you in on the Eldara on the way back to the station.

▭

ONCE THEY WERE LOADED up and driving back to the station in the ambulance, Dean notified headquarters that they were back in service. Then he could wait no longer. His curiosity about Ashley and the knowledge that she was an Unusual as he had suspected was burning him up inside. He looked over at Brynne in the driver's seat.

"Well?"

"Well, what?" she asked, glancing over at him, smiling.

"Well, what is an Eldara Sister?" Dean asked.

Brynne laughed. "Wow, you must really like her." He started to splutter a complaint, but she cut him off. "Okay, okay, enough torture. The Eldara are rumored to be the oldest of the Unusual races, older even than the oldest of the vampires. Some say they are the messengers of the gods or the God, depending on your perspective. It's said they are the source for the mythical angels of biblical stories. Ashley, specifically, is an Eldara Sister. They are a group renowned for their healing powers. I've seen no evidence of anything strange with Ashley and her patients, but that is what they say about the Sisters. She just seems to be a really good nurse by all appearances."

"I've never seen anything about the Eldara in any of the books," Dean said referring to the extensive library of myths, legends and fairy tales back at Station U.

"I hadn't heard anything about them either and wouldn't have known about Ashley if James hadn't mentioned her after an encounter he had with her at the hospital."

James was Brynne's vampire boyfriend. As far as Dean was concerned, the jury was still out on him.

"James told you about her?" Dean said.

"Yep," Brynne replied. "Apparently he was nearly blinded by her halo when he first ran into her."

"Her halo? I didn't see anything," Dean said, his curiosity piqued further.

"Yes, her halo. But I don't think you or I can usually see it. It's more of an aura thing that other Unusuals can see."

"So she's like, thousands of years old?" Dean said, trying to wrap his brain around the concept and whether he imagined things when he had thought that she might like him.

"Oh, at least," Brynne chuckled when she looked over at him. "Kind of makes her the ultimate cougar, doesn't it?"

"Really funny, Brynne. Really funny," Dean retorted. "You should talk. James is at least a thousand years older than you."

"About sixteen hundred, if you want to know the truth of it," she said. "The real question is do you like her? I say that because I think she likes you. That's not the first time she's turned up when you and I came in with a call. I asked Tammy and Brook about it, and they said she never just drops in when they bring a patient to the hospital."

"I suppose I do like her, as far as I know her," Dean said. "So what do I do? Is there protocol for talking to her?"

"What are you talking about?" Brynne asked. "You already talk to her."

"I mean, if she's this ancient being, there must be a tradition or a culturally different way to approach her, right?"

"Dean," Brynne said. "If I've learned anything from dating James, it's that you have to live in the times you are in. Long-lived Unusuals have adapted to changing times and morals. At least, most of them do. It's part of who they are. They aren't stuck in the ways of the past. She already asked you out. Take her up on it. Go out for coffee or a soda and bite to eat after work. You can call when you get back to the station. I'll bet she picks up the line at the nurse's station herself."

"Why would you bet that?"

"Because," Brynne said. "Unless I miss my guess, she's counting on you calling her because she likes you, too. I'll bet you, say, washing the ambulance for a whole week, that she picks up."

"You're on," Dean said. He thought about it, and he didn't think Brynne was right, but he also wouldn't mind losing this particular bet. He stared into the night thinking about what he would say on the phone as his partner drove back to the station.

<hr>

# Chapter 2

<hr>

Back at Station U, in the run-down industrial park on the edge of Elk City, the paramedics parked their ambulance and went about their duties after a call. Since Brynne had taken the lead on patient care, she went into the crew quarters to complete her patient report on the computer. Dean took care of the tasks needed to restock the ambulance and put the unit back in readiness for the next call, which could come at any time. He took his time and even scrubbed the bugs off the windshield before closing the outer garage doors on the ambulance bay and going into the crew's squad room.

Dean looked at the phone on the desk as he walked in, then thought maybe he should make up the beds in the bunk rooms with fresh linens while he was thinking about it. He was stalling. Deep down he knew it. He had lots on his mind following that call tonight with the burn victim. It had been an intentional attack, and he had seen Brynne's former partner, Zach at the scene. The former Station U paramedic had arranged a meeting with Dean a few days before. He had tried to enlist him in an underground movement against Unusuals. Was the ex-paramedic involved in the attack in some way, or was it coincidence? Brynne had noticed him, too, but she hadn't talked about that on the way back. She had steered away from the horror of the previous call, choosing instead to rib him about Ashley. He looked back at the phone again.

"My bet still stands, Probie," Brynne said without looking up from her workstation where she was still going through the documentation from the ambulance call. "She'll pick up. You just need to call."

What if Brynne was wrong, and Ashley was just being friendly? "I don't know, Brynne."

"What don't you know?" Brynne asked, spinning around in her desk chair to face him. "Do you not know if you want to wash the ambulance for me for a week, or do you not know if you like Ashley?"

"Of course I like Ashley," he blurted out without thinking. He paused, gathering his thoughts. "I mean, what's not to like? She's pretty, funny, knows what I do, and still talks to me."

"Fine, call her, and the bet is off whether she answers or not," Brynne offered. "Either way, you need to make that call. I don't want you pining around the station for the next two days about the one that got away."

Dean looked at the phone, then at Brynne, and then back to the phone. He picked up the handset and his finger hovered over the speed-dial for ECMC emergency department's number. He paused a few seconds, then pressed the button.

Brynne got up and crossed the room to the ambulance bay door. "I'm going to do a quick inventory," she said as she left the room. "I'll be in here if you need any help."

Dean was about to shout a snappy retort, but a woman's voice picked up on the other end of the phone line.

"Elk City Medical Center Emergency Department, Nurse Moore speaking. Hi, Dean," Ashley said from the other end of the line. "I'm glad you called me."

"Uh, yeah, sure, no problem," Dean said. How had she known it was him?

"You were calling for me, right?" she asked. He swore he could hear her smiling over the phone line.

"How did you know it was me?" he asked. Could she read his mind?

"Caller ID on this end," she explained. "You still haven't answered my question."

"Uh, yes, I was calling for you," Dean answered. "I wanted to take you up on that offer for something to drink after work. I could swing by the hospital and we could, maybe, go somewhere downtown?"

"I actually get off at five AM," Ashley said. "I think you're on until six, right? It might make more sense for me to meet you over there."

"Uh, it's not in a great part of town. Do you know where it is? Maybe it would be better if I met you somewhere," Dean countered.

"Aren't you sweet," Ashley chuckled from the other end of the line. "I know where you are, and I can take care of myself. I'll see you at six when you get off work. You pick the place for a nice breakfast, okay?"

"Sounds like a plan," he said. "See you later." She said goodbye on her end, and he hung up the phone. That had worked out alright. He stood, looking at the phone where it rested on the desk.

"Dean," Brynne called from the doorway to the ambulance bay. "We're about to get a call; I got a heads up from headquarters on my cell."

Even as she finished talking, the familiar tones sounded on the radio speakers set in the ceiling. The musical tones were followed by the female voice of the dispatcher. "Ambulance U-191, proceed to 1231 Main Street, Sabatani's Restaurant for a trapped subject."

Dean headed out to the ambulance bay where Brynne had already started up the rig and was sitting in the driver's seat waiting for him. No time to think about the phone call with Ashley. Such was the life of the paramedic. Duty always interrupted life. He climbed inside and picked up the radio mic as they drove out into the night. "Ambulance U-191 en route."

———————————————

# Chapter 3

———————————————

They drove downtown in the ambulance, the lights and sirens announcing their passage through the nearly deserted streets of the early morning hours. The dispatchers didn't give a whole lot of follow-up information en route. All they knew was that a male patient of unknown age was trapped somehow in an apartment upstairs from Sabatani's restaurant. The restaurant was a prominent downtown eatery. The dispatcher said that fire department rescue would only be dispatched if requested. Dean liked Sabatani's. They gave paramedics, firefighters and police officers a discount, and the food was delicious.

Brynne pulled the ambulance to the side of the street near the location and found a middle-aged woman standing on the sidewalk outside the restaurant, wringing her hands. She walked up to Dean as he climbed down from the ambulance cab.

"I just didn't know what to do," she said, tears in her eyes. "I've never seen anything like it, and I didn't know what to do. Mr. Algar, the owner, said to call 911 and ask for Station U."

"That's alright, Ma'am," Dean said as he opened the side cargo doors on the ambulance, pulling a few bags from their compartments. "What happened?" Brynne came around from the driver's side, listening to the woman as she attempted to describe what was going on.

"I always knew there was something special about Mr. Algar," she began. "He's such a great landlord, and he always shares leftovers from the restaurant with the tenants in the building. But I always thought it was strange that he lived in the smallest unit in the building when he could have the largest. It was his building after all."

"Where is Mr. Algar now?" Brynne asked, interrupting the woman.

"He's upstairs, in his apartment," she said. "His legs ... well, I've never seen anything like it. He is just trapped. I heard him calling for help through the wall. He was banging on the floor with his fist, trying to get someone's attention. It woke me up, and when I went over to his apartment, he had dragged himself over to the door and unlocked it, but had been unable to do anything else. I don't know how to describe it. You just have to see it for yourself."

"I think that would be best," Brynne said. She looked at Dean. "Let's leave the stretcher down here for now and see what we have first." She took one of the bags from Dean as they followed the woman inside. They entered by way of a nondescript door next to the main entrance to the restaurant, climbed a set of stairs up to the second floor, walked down the hall and through an opened doorway to the narrow hallway on the right. As they entered the room, Dean saw right away what the woman had been saying. He had never seen anything like it either. On the other hand, that was pretty much part of a paramedic's job description, especially at Station U. There, on the floor by the door, was the top half of a man. That was it. At his waist, his body suddenly narrowed down to about one inch in diameter, and disappeared into a narrow-necked ornate glass bottle located on the floor behind him. His face was red, his brows furrowed with pain, and he was gasping for breath.

"Kristof," Brynne said to the patient as she entered, taking in the scene in front of her. "What happened?" Clearly she knew the half-man, half-bottle creature on the floor.

The woman stood in the hallway behind them. "Can you help him? What happened? It's just weird."

Dean turned to her. "Thank-you for calling us Ma'am. Why don't you give us some privacy with Mr. Algar and we'll see what we can do to help him. We can take care of things from here." He walked with her as she moved to her door, the next one down the hall.

"How can you help him?" she asked. "It's like he lost his legs."

"Let us take care of it and see what we can do," Dean said. "I'll let you know if we need any more help. Thank you again for calling us." He waited as she shut the door to her apartment before heading back to the patient and his partner. Kristof was explaining the situation to Brynne as she knelt down next to him, taking his vital signs.

"… I must have hit my head on the table when the bottle tipped over and fell as I was heading into my room to get something," the man was saying when Dean came back in the room. "Since I was in mid-shift in my form, I was half in and half out of the bottle. Now I can't feel my legs at all, and I can't shift in or out of gaseous form to get free." Dean recognized him now. He was the manager or owner of the restaurant. He had seen him on the occasions when he had gotten dinner here.

"Dean," Brynne said. "Meet Kristof Algar, owner of Sabatani's. He's a Djinn, a genie in common terms. He has gotten trapped half in and half out of his bottle."

"Can't you just wish yourself out of the bottle?" Dean asked.

"I grant wishes, I don't get them myself," the trapped Djinn said.

Dean thought for a moment, looked at Brynne, who shrugged back at him. She turned back to the patient.

"Kristof," she asked. "What if I just offered a wish to get you out myself?"

"I wouldn't trust it," Kristof answered. "My magic is wild magic and unpredictable at the best of times. Even a simple wish like that could be taken in some weird literal way and only make things worse."

Brynne scratched her head, thinking. "You said you can't feel your legs. Do you think they returned to solid form when you were unconscious? Could we just pull the bottle off you?"

"I tried that, Brynne. The bottle, well, it's a portal to another dimension. It's where I come from. It's bigger on the inside. I think my legs are normal sized on the inside and then squeezed down to the opening. It's plugging the gateway, like a cork." Kristof explained. "I think that's why it feels like my legs are asleep, like when you sleep on your arm funny, and it gets all numb and limp?"

"We could break the glass?" Dean offered. "That would free up the opening and allow everything to expand back to normal."

"That might work," Brynne said. "I'm concerned with how long he's been trapped this way. Kristof said he came upstairs to get something at about 6 PM?" She looked at her patient, who nodded in agreement. She glanced at her watch. "That means he's been wedged in there for about nine hours."

"You're thinking compartment syndrome?" Dean asked. It made sense. When people became trapped by a heavy object, as in a building collapse, their limbs get squeezed, and blood flow stops. If you free them too quickly, the rush of blood frees up hours of cellular waste and toxins from the crushed area. It all rushes back into the body and can cause major organ damage, cardiac dysrhythmia or even death.

"That's what I'm thinking," Brynne confirmed. "We can break the bottle, but we've got some things to do first to get ready to manage the return of circulation to his lower extremities." She turned back to Kristof.

"We're going to work this out, Kristof," she said to her patient. "We need to take care of a few things first so that suddenly freeing you doesn't flood your system with toxins unprepared."

"Whatever you say, Brynne," the trapped Djinn said. "I trust you."

<hr>

IT TOOK the two paramedics about fifteen minutes to get everything in place for their trapped patient. Eventually they were ready to try their plan to free him. They had him hooked up to the heart monitor. The monitor showed a sinus tachycardia on the screen; a normal rapid heartbeat that you'd expect to see in stressful or painful situations. They had two IVs set up, one flowing into each arm, with the two fluid bags suspended from a chair they had pulled over for the purpose. They had an array of medicines and syringes laid out next to the patient, in preparation for counteracting the expected toxic effects of the sudden return of blood flow to his legs.

Dean knew the goal was to protect the heart from a flood of potassium released from crushed cells and to keep the kidneys working, unclogged by cellular toxins and low blood pH or high acid levels. They had sodium bicarb drawn up and ready to administer for that problem. He looked over at Brynne on the opposite side of the patient.

"Ready to go?" he asked.

"I think so," Brynne replied. She looked at Kristof. "Ok, we are going to do this, Kristof. Dean's going to use that hammer and crowbar to attempt to break the neck of the bottle right at the top. If all goes as planned, you should be suddenly freed from the bottle's portal and your legs will return to normal. We've got medicine to give you if we see a problem from your lower legs getting blood flow back."

"Whatever you say, Brynne," the patient said. "I trust you."

"Okay, Dean. Let's do this."

Dean checked one more time to make sure that the area on the carpeted floor where the legs should reappear or expand, or whatever, was clear of any obstructions. He then picked up the curved crowbar and the ballpeen hammer they had retrieved from the tool box on the ambulance. He set the teeth of the crowbar at the top of the narrow bottle's neck, hefted the hammer once to adjust his grip and then rapidly struck the top of the curved portion of the crowbar above the bottle. There was a crash and tinkling of broken glass, along with a strange whooshing sound, like air rushing from a giant soda bottle. Then suddenly, the legs of the patient appeared stretched out below his waist, which had returned to normal size as well.

"Oh my God, that hurts!" Kristof said between gritted teeth. "I can't move them either. They're still numb."

Brynne picked up a syringe and connected it to the IV line on her side. "Here's something for your pain, Kristof. Dean, you go ahead and slowly push the bicarb we measured earlier."

Dean started depressing the plunger on the syringe he had already attached to his IV line in anticipation of this. The two paramedics started running through their planned course of treatment and managing their patient as he slowly got the feeling back in his legs.

It took about an hour. During that hour, they ran some labs with their iStat portable blood testing unit, checked in twice with the hospital for advice from the doctor there, and tried unsuccessfully to get their patient to agree to go to the hospital and get checked out. Most Unusuals avoided trips to the hospital, even though there were a core group of doctors and nurses there who kept their secret while treating them. Ultimately he refused transport, but did agree to drink plenty of fluids for the next few days and to check with them or go to the emergency room if he felt light-headed, had unusual back or abdominal pain, or chest pain. Kristof was up and walking again before they left, albeit gingerly, and he escorted them to the top of the stairs as he bid them goodbye and thank you.

"How are you going to explain this to your neighbor?" Dean asked as he picked up their bags and slung the straps across his shoulders.

"I'll think of something," Kristof said. "If worse comes to worse, I'll have a Witch cast a memory spell on her. I don't think it will come to that, though. Mrs. Jenkins is a sweet old widow, and I have my charms." He smiled at them and winked.

Brynne laughed and shook her head. "Just be sure you call us back or go the emergency room if you start feeling bad, alright?"

"I will, Brynne, I promise," Kristof said as the two paramedics started down the stairs and back out to the waiting ambulance on the street.

# Chapter 4

As they arrived back at the Station U parking lot, Dean was still thinking about the last call with Kristof. It was almost the end of their shift. As Brynne drove the ambulance into the lot at the back of the industrial park, Dean saw nurse Ashley Moore, in the early morning light, leaning against a small red, vintage sports car parked next to his pickup.

"Looks like your breakfast date's here," Brynne said. She pulled the ambulance up next to where she was standing and pushed the electric window switch to put the driver's window down.

"Hi Ashley," Brynne said. "Follow us over to the garage door to the ambulance bay and you can come in that way."

"Okay," Dean heard Ashley say as Brynne drove away over to the doors. Dean keyed the overhead doors and then hopped out to help back her into the garage bay.

He saw Ashley walking over as he crossed behind the ambulance to the driver's side. He waved and then turned his attention to watching Brynne's face in the side view mirror as the ambulance started beeping, signaling it was backing up. Ashley stood and watched him as he walked backward, guiding the ambulance into the bay to park. She then followed it into the open garage entrance.

"Hi Dean," she said. "I heard you were out on a call when I left the ER, so I waited for you to get back. Are you still up for breakfast?"

"Uh, yeah, I mean, yes, absolutely." Dean was mentally kicking himself for stammering. Get it together, dude, he told himself. He walked over to the door to the crew quarters and opened it. "If you want to wait in here, I need to help Brynne get the unit together and then I have a report to write. If that's okay?"

"Sure," she said, coming over, smiling. "I'll be waiting." Her hand touched his where he held the door knob, as she passed by.

"I won't be long," he said, letting the door close behind her.

Brynne was standing by the driver's side of the ambulance cab, hands on her hips, shaking her head. "She must really like you, Probie. You're a mess. I've got this out here. You go in and get your report finished. Bill and Lynne will be here soon to relieve us." She plugged in the landline power cord to the side of the ambulance to keep everything inside charging and powered, and then climbed inside to replace the supplies they used. Dean shrugged and went inside the crew quarters.

Ashley was looking over the books in their small bookshelf of Unusual reference materials. It was a varied collection of fairy tales, ghost and horror stories, as well as a few books on mythology. There were even a few gaming tomes like an old Dungeons & Dragons Monster Manual. She picked up one of the books, he couldn't see which, and sat down on the love seat.

"Don't worry about me, Dean," she said. "Get your work done. I can wait."

"Okay," Dean said as he sat at his computer workstation across the room. "I won't be long. I just have to write a report on that last call." He logged in to his account and started working on the report while Ashley waited across the room, reading quietly.

Fifteen minutes passed, and Dean was doing a final check on his written narrative in the electronic patient care report when Brynne came in from the ambulance bay. She said a quick hello to Ashley on the love seat, and then sat down at her computer. Dean put the finishing touches on his narrative and electronically sent the report to Brynne for review. He got up and glanced at his watch. It was five-fifty-five AM. The next shift – Bill and Lynne, should be there any minute. As if on cue, the door to the parking lot opened and the two paramedics walked in. Bill was older and balding, about five feet, ten inches tall. Lynne came right behind him, a few years younger and 5 inches shorter than Bill.

"Hi guys," Lynne called. Then she saw Ashley sitting on the love seat reading. "Oh, hello Ashley. What are you doing here?"

"Hi Lynne," the nurse said, looking up from her book. "Dean's taking me to breakfast this morning. I couldn't refuse such a gracious offer."

Dean knew he was blushing again, confirmed by Bill's laugh as he glanced in his direction. He came over and clapped him on the shoulder with one hand as he passed. His mock whisper of "Good job" was heard by everyone in the room.

"Okay," Brynne said, getting up from her spot by the desk. "Leave my probie alone. Only I get to abuse him like that." She looked at Dean. "Dean, I got the report. Everything looks good. You and Ashley can take off."

Ashley got up and put the book she was reading back on the bookshelf. "Shall we go, Dean?"

"Uh, yeah," Dean stammered, again. "Do you want to follow me? I thought we'd go to Hank's Diner."

"No," Ashley said. "I'll ride with you, and you can bring me back to my car later. It's not far from here, right?"

"No," Dean said, "I mean yes, I mean. Uh, yes, you can ride with me and no it's not far." He opened the door to the parking lot and held it open for her.

Ashley laughed, winked at Brynne and headed outside with Dean following close behind. He thought he caught a whiff of a floral perfume as she passed by. It made him smile as he followed her out.

THE TWO OF them drove to the diner in his pickup truck. Dean had to do a quick clean-up of the passenger side, throwing some empty cups and other trash behind the seat before Ashley could get in. He was a little horrified, but she seemed not to notice, or at least not to care.

When they got to the diner five minutes later, a waitress showed the couple to a booth at the back of the tiny dining room. Dean looked at the menu she gave him even though he knew what he wanted, since he didn't want to stare at Ashley where she sat across from him. When he made eye contact with her, his stomach did flips, and he stopped thinking clearly. What did someone talk about with a being who was centuries older than you?

He stole another glance, looking over the top of his menu at her as she perused her breakfast choices. Of course, she didn't look centuries older. She looked his age, in her early twenties, with piercing green eyes and dark flowing hair. He'd thought that was her age when he first saw her all those weeks ago in the convenience store. He had caught her noticing the invisible UV ink stamp on the back of his right hand. Ever since that encounter, he had not been able to get her face out of his mind. When he had discovered she worked at the ER as a nurse, it had been great news. By then, he had given up trying to find her again, though he had tried hanging out at the convenience store in hopes of running into her.

Ashley had taken the initiative, as Brynne had pointed out. She seemed to make an effort to talk to him whenever their paths crossed at the hospital. He was never comfortable asking girls out. Even with Brynne's urging, it had taken Ashley's offer to meet up sometime that kicked him over the edge, so he had finally gotten up the nerve to ask her out. Now, though, he was at a loss for what to talk about. He wanted to know so much about her but didn't know where to start.

"You can ask me anything you'd like, Dean," Ashley said, not even looking up from her menu. "I'm sure you won't say anything that will surprise me."

"How did you…?" Dean started to say, looking up in surprise.

She laughed, meeting his eyes with hers. They seemed to sparkle again in the fluorescent light of the diner booth. "It's nothing super-natural, Dean. A girl just has her ways of knowing what a guy is thinking at times like this."

"I don't know where to begin, Ashley," Dean said. "There's so much I want to know about you. How long have you been a nurse? What brought you to Elk City? Do you like dating younger guys?" He paused and groaned, his face flushing a bright, cherry red color. He smiled at her in embarrassment. "Did I just say that?"

Ashley giggled, "Yes, yes you did. All I can say to that question is that youth is a state of mind, not necessarily a state of being. That's how it is to me at least. Do I seem too old for you?"

"No, not at all," Dean answered carefully.

"Then I'm not," she said. "As for your other questions, I've been a nurse, of one sort or another, all my life. You might say it's what I was destined to do. I came to Elk City about four years ago when your Doctor Spirelli first implemented this new health care program for Unusuals. I was curious about how it would work, so I came and got a job in the Emergency Department at ECMC to see what was going on."

"What do you think of the program?" Dean asked. "I'm still new to the whole thing, but it seems to do a good job of helping people in need."

She smiled. "I like that you call your patients 'people.' It shows that you are open-minded about things. It's a very attractive trait."

"What else would I call them? That's what they are, just differ-ent," Dean said. He thought about Brynne's former partner Zach and his view of Unusuals as monsters who needed to be exposed, hunted and run out of town. He wondered what people like him would say, overhearing this conversation? He pushed that thought out of his mind as the waitress arrived to take their order.

Dean ordered two eggs, over easy, with a biscuit and bacon on the side, and a diet soda to drink. He waited patiently while Ashley looked at the menu one more time. She ordered a waffle topped with fruit and whipped cream, and orange juice and water to drink. After the waitress had left Ashley asked him a question.

"What about you, Dean?" she asked. "Why did you become a paramedic?"

Dean told her about his experience in a motor vehicle accident in high school where paramedics saved his girlfriend's life right in front of him. It had impressed him.

"I guess I just want to do that kind of work," he said. "You know, the kind of work that matters in the world."

"But the work at your station is more like primary care than paramedic care," Ashley said. "It's not exactly the kind of stuff that other paramedics see and bring into the ER."

"You're right about that. When I first got assigned to Station U, I thought I had done something wrong and was being punished," Dean explained. "After a while, though, I found that I saw things that were much more exciting than knife and bullet wounds. I also think that the Station U paramedics have a lot more autonomy than other paramedics in the Elk City system. I don't see it as a bad assignment anymore. I guess I see it as an accomplishment and a reward for hard work in school."

"I think you're right, Dean," Ashley said. "You know, I hear good things about you on both sides of the doors to the ER. The other nurses and the doctors see you as a promising young professional, and the Unusual community is saying the new paramedic with Brynne is a good guy to have respond when you need help."

Dean was a little embarrassed. "I'm just trying to do my best. I have a lot more to learn before I get as good as Brynne at knowing what's going on with a patient at any given time. She seems to know almost intuitively what kind of Unusual we have as a patient, and how we should treat them."

"Brynne has the advantage of having James Lee as a boyfriend," Ashley said. "He has taken her inside our community and has showed her things that few humans have ever seen." Dean snorted at that and shook his head. Ashley raised an eyebrow. "You don't like James, I take it?"

"Let's just say the jury's out where he is concerned," Dean said. "I'm not sure he's all that much of a good guy. I'm pretty sure he's feeding on Brynne, and that's just not right."

Ashley shook her head. "You should not be so quick to judge James, Dean. What goes on between two consenting adults is their business, right? He has seen many horrible things in his long life. In some cases, I'm sure he's done things that he's not proud of, but he's not an evil creature out of the stories on the bookshelf at the station. He's a man who is trying to do the best he can in the times in which he lives. He's adapted quite well to modern times and conventions. Much better than some do."

"What about you?" Dean asked. "Have you adapted to modern times?"

She laughed again at that question. "I think I adapt very well. But you have to understand, there's a difference between James and I. He's a human who was changed into being an Unusual. His cultural background is still human. I am different. I have always been an Unusual. Since Creation, I have been part of a cultural background separate from humans. I don't have the baggage that people like James have."

Dean thought about that for a moment and then asked the question he had been holding back. "Can I ask you what it's like being an Eldara? I've tried to look up information about you, but I can't seem to get a handle on it."

"Once upon a time, and even now at times, we are the intermediaries between humans and their gods. We represented the supernatural world manifested in the human reality. Some of us, like me, were given a purpose and sent into the world to follow that purpose, wherever it would lead us. In that way, we spread the message and information we were created to deliver. I'm a healer. I always have been. I've lived among humans as a midwife, a nurse, a wise woman, a whatever-was-needed to teach the healing arts to someone. I've traveled far and wide, settling for a time wherever I felt there was a need for me. That's what brought me here. I'm needed. I can detect it."

"Needed for what?" Dean asked.

"I don't know," Ashley shrugged. "I'll know it when I see it, just like I'll know what to do when the time comes. That's just the way it works."

"And in the meantime, you're a nurse in the ER," Dean said.

"A darn good one too, if I do say so myself," Ashley said with a smile.

"So why me?" Dean asked, fearing the answer. "Am I part of your assignment?"

She laughed aloud. "No, Dean. You're not part of any hidden assignment. At least, I don't think so. But there's nothing that says I can't have a little fun along the way, and you're the kind of guy I like to hang around."

The food arrived then, and the conversation paused while they started to eat. The more he learned about her, the more he liked her, but he was bothered by the transient nature of her tasks. Would she get her assigned task here done and just leave? He didn't want that. He wanted her to stay at least a little while, maybe even longer. He liked Ashley Moore, the ER nurse. He wasn't sure he wanted her to turn back into Ashley, the Eldara Sister, and suddenly fly away to another assignment.

Their conversation turned to the mundane. Dean learned that Ashley lived in a downtown apartment above a storefront, not far from his ambulance call at Sabatani's earlier that morning. He told her of his apartment above a garage, the elderly couple who were his landlords, and how he helped with chores around their house. They continued to chat easily about everyday things all the way back to the Station U parking lot where Dean pulled up next to her red sports car. It was an old red MG convertible, but it looked in pristine condition. She said a quick goodbye and leaned over to deliver a brief kiss that left him breathless. She smiled at him and giggled again, before she hopped out of his pickup.

He waited until she had gotten in her car and started it up before he pulled away, heading home to get some sleep. As first dates went, he thought it was about perfect. He was already looking forward to the next time they could meet up. She had given him her cell number and told him to call her when he knew his schedule next week. He continued thinking about her laugh and the way her green eyes sparkled as they looked into his. Even though the night had started out with that horrible burn victim, the day had brought him something to look forward to. Such was the lot of a paramedic, he thought as he drove home.

Chapter 5

The next few days went by quickly with what passed for routine calls in Station U. There were some odd cuts and lacerations, a few chest pain and shortness of breath cases in the elderly residents of the Unusual community, and more of what passed for the usual Unusual ambulance call. Dean was distracted through it all by daily texts he had started getting from the ex-paramedic, Zach, who wanted to meet up with him again. Dean didn't respond. He wasn't sure what he could say or do that would get him untangled from being involved with the fanatic. Zach wanted to expose the Unusuals living among the human community and brand them as evil monsters. He knew that Brynne had seen Zach at the scene of the burned Witch victim too, and she had reported it to the assistant chief on the scene who oversaw Station U. Would she think less of him if she knew he had been in contact with the guy?

On top of all that distraction, he found himself thinking about Ashley all the time. What would she think of him if she found out he had some ties to this underground human movement against Unusuals? They were a hate group. He didn't hate anyone, but he might be found guilty by association. He liked the ER nurse. He liked her a lot. The challenge was that he didn't know who to turn to for advice in this situation. He supposed he could go to Mike Farver, his academy instructor and former Station U paramedic, but would Mike be disappointed in him, too? He could not talk to his critical incident stress counselor Rebecca about this either. She was a Muse, an Unusual herself, and would probably kick him out of her office for not reporting his meeting with Zach immediately.

At the end of the second stint on day shift, he returned home, still not sure what to do. He parked his pickup on the curb in front of the two-story residence with the detached garage. The second-floor apartment over that garage was his home. He walked around to the stairs up to his apartment door and turned the key to let himself in, but the door popped open. He must not have shut it all the way when he left that morning. He tossed his keys on the counter in the kitchenette and was kicking off his shoes when a familiar voice spoke up from across the room.

"Hi, Dean. You've been avoiding me," Zach said from his seat on the couch on the other side of the room.

Dean spun around, startled. He spotted the former paramedic lounging on the sofa as if it were his own apartment. "How did you get in here? I didn't tell you to meet me here. What if someone saw you?"

"Relax, Dean," Zach said rising. "No one saw me, and you didn't tell me much of anything. You haven't responded to any of my texts. I was going to wait outside, but you must have forgotten to lock your door. Since it was unlocked, I decided that you'd prefer me to wait inside, out of sight, rather than waiting around outside where people could see me."

"That's beside the point," Dean said. "I don't have anything to say to you. I don't want anything to do with you, or the people you're associated with. I have seen what you do."

"How was I supposed to know that, Dean?" Zach asked. "You haven't responded to my text messages. I told you the other night that I wanted to talk with you and explain why I was there. I know you saw me in the crowd when that witch was burned. You should at least give me that much respect."

"That girl was an innocent person who didn't deserve what

happened to her, Zach," Dean said. "I notice that you don't deny being associated with those who attacked her. Did you dump the lighter fluid on her yourself? Did you flick the match?" Dean paced the floor in his small kitchenette. "I can't believe you dragged me into this mess."

"That witch-girl was no innocent, Dean," Zach said coldly. "She was using her magic to manipulate people for her own gain. She was hurting humans and no one was doing anything."

"So you admit to attacking her?" Dean stood there aghast. "How could you do that? You're a paramedic, a healer! At least, you used to be."

"I heal HUMANS, Dean," Zach said firmly. "I never signed up to take care of monsters living among us. Monsters like that witch who was charming people to drain their bank accounts and set herself up in luxury. I have proof of what she was doing, but no one in authority would have believed a word of it. What was I supposed to say?" Zach assumed a pose, raising his right hand and said, "Your honor, I know she cast a spell on people to get them to empty their bank accounts and give their money to her."

"You know there are authorities who could deal with things like that, Zach," Dean retorted. "You must have worked at Station U long enough to learn that much."

"Sure," he sneered. "And you should know by now that it's all about sweeping the problems under the rug to keep people ignorant of the dangers walking the sidewalks downtown beside them."

"Well, you weren't as sneaky as you thought you were, Zach," Dean said. "Brynne saw you there and reported it to Chief Ari." He held up his hands in a pose of innocence. "I didn't tell her, Zach, but you'd better be on your guard because they have to be looking for you in association with this case. I should turn you in myself. I don't know why I don't call the police right now?"

"You won't call on me, Dean," Zach said coldly. "I documented our little meeting in my journal. I am writing all about this crusade we are on. I wrote about how you were interested in helping me, helping The Cause. They'll find it if I get arrested. At the very least, it will implicate you as an associate of mine. You'll be lucky if you only lose your job and your paramedic license." He pointed a finger at Dean as he continued. "You'll keep my secret, just like you'll keep this conversation to yourself, because deep down you know I'm right. We can't keep living in secret alongside the monsters of our nightmares. People need to know, or better yet, we need to get the monsters to leave and go somewhere else."

Zach picked up his jacket from the couch and put it on. He crossed the small living room to the kitchen where Dean stood rooted to the floor. Dean could smell his foul breath, he was so close. "You'll stay quiet, and you'll answer me the next time I text, or I'll leak your involvement in the attack on the witch. You've chosen your side in this battle, Dean. I'm not letting you back out now."

Dean stood still, staring straight ahead as the other man left the apartment. He heard the door shut behind him and the footsteps heading down the stairs. He stood alone in his apartment for a long time in the gathering darkness as night fell. He didn't know how he was going to unravel himself from this. He didn't know who to turn to or where to seek help. Dean was lost in these thoughts when his phone buzzed on the counter next to the keys. He saw Ashley's contact info pop up on the screen. He stood there watching the phone buzz until it went to voicemail, as tears welled up in his eyes. He was going to lose everything.

<hr>

IT WAS HOURS LATER, as Dean sat on the sofa staring into the darkness of his unlit apartment, that he was startled by a light tap on his door. He looked over at the door but didn't rise to answer it. The tapping came again, followed by a voice.

"Dean, I know you're in there," Ashley said. "I can sense you inside."

Dean had let several calls from her go to voicemail over the last few hours. He guessed she had decided to come find him. Did Brynne give her his address? Hell, he didn't care.

The doorknob turned, and Dean realized he hadn't locked the door after Zach left. It pushed inward, and a figure entered the darkened room, silhouetted against the doorway by the moonlight. Did he see the shadowy outline of wings around her? She shut the door behind her as she stepped into the apartment.

"There you are," she said, crossing to where he sat, sitting next to him and resting a warm hand on his knee.

Dean looked away, not wanting her to see he had been crying. Her Unusual eyesight in the darkness was likely as good as his in broad daylight. What was she doing here, anyway?

"I could tell you were in some kind of trouble. I sensed something was wrong. When you didn't answer my calls, I decided to come find you," Ashley said, as if in reply to his unasked question. "By the way, if you're trying to hide, you're doing a bad job of it. Your apartment was the first place I checked."

"Ashley," Dean said, "I don't know if it's a good idea that you're here. I'm not necessarily the right guy for you, at least not right now."

"I'm a big girl, Dean," she replied. "I don't enter relationships lightly, and I don't pick the wrong people. What's going on?"

"I'm not sure I can tell you," Dean said. He turned to look at her sitting next to him. He could see the look of concern on her face. "I'm not sure you'll want to be around me if I tell you."

"Dean," Ashley said, cupping his cheek with one hand, using her thumb to brush away a tear as she did. "You have to tell me what is bothering you. I know now why I came to Elk City, why I was sent here. It's you. You're central to what I'm to do here, and I have to make sure that you get the chance to do what it is that you're supposed to do."

She reached an arm around him and pulled him closer until he was resting his head on her shoulder. She held him there, speaking quietly. "Tell me what is going on, Dean. Start at the beginning and don't leave anything out. I won't leave you, no matter what you tell me. I'm here for you. I know that now."

Almost before Dean knew it, he was talking in a stream of words that wouldn't stop. He talked about how he had wanted to be a paramedic, about his dreams of being the best, about his disappointment with the assignment to Station U, and then his realization that he liked it there and had become attached to his patients. Then he opened up about his meeting with Zach after he voiced his concerns over Brynne's relationship with James. He told her that he felt tied to the ex-paramedic in some way, and perhaps his lack of reporting that tie was responsible for the horrible attack on the Witch woman a few nights before. He told Ashley that he was afraid for her. If she got too close to him, would she become a target of Zach and his ilk?

All in all, he talked for over an hour about his fears and concerns. Ashley just listened, occasionally stroking his hair or squeezing his hand where she held it in her own. As he finished telling her everything, the two of them sat in the silent darkness of his apartment for a time. He looked up at her and searched her face for a hint of how she was feeling. She smiled and leaned forward, planting a gentle kiss on his lips.

"See, Dean," she said. "I'm still here. You didn't scare me away. You have done nothing wrong. Having a meeting with Zach or being cornered in your apartment by him threatening you, does not make you guilty of anything. It does tell us that he is scared of what you'll do next, and he's trying to influence that decision. What we have to do now is to figure out what Zach and the others with whom he is associated in this 'Cause' are up to. Then we can try to keep them from doing anything else to harm humans or Unusuals."

"Shouldn't we report this to someone?" he asked. "I'm not able to do anything to stop this on my own."

"Of course you should report it," Ashley said. "But you also need to keep doing what you're doing, to go out and treat your patients. I think that is what Zach is afraid of. You are tied to this somehow. I know that now, and what you do day to day, in your job as a paramedic, taking care of all of us, is going to figure into how this all works out. I don't know how or why, but you have a part to play."

"So, what - I go back to work, and at some mysterious point in the future, I'll know just what to do to fix all of this? That sounds ridiculous."

Ashley laughed out loud. Her merriment filled the air. "Oh,

Dean, have you learned nothing in your reading of the tales of our kind? Most of those stories have humans in them who do just that. It's why we're tied together, to live alongside each other, human and Unusual. Our lives are inexplicably intertwined, and each of our existences relies on the actions of the other. Something bigger than you and Zach is at work here. I don't know what it is, but this is why I came here. It is why I was drawn to you. Together we'll find the source of the problem, and together we'll find the solution."

Dean was glad she was confident. He wasn't so sure. It all seemed too much for him to deal with as a new probationary paramedic. He didn't have her unwavering belief in destiny and divine missions. Still, he did have her, and that was strangely comforting even as he had his doubts. He knew he could keep doing his job. He could continue to take care of his patients. If that was all he had to do, he could keep doing it. He soon fell asleep on the couch, next to Ashley, comforted by her presence and thinking about what that mysterious task could possibly be.

## Chapter 6

The next morning when Dean woke up, Ashley was gone. For a short time, he wondered if it had all been a dream, but a handwritten post-it note stuck to the middle of the kitchen counter announced that she had an early shift at the ER. She said she'd call him later. He smiled to himself as he read the note. The sunlight coming in the apartment through the windows seemed brighter somehow, and that seemed to lighten his spirits. He got some breakfast and went about his daily routine, including mowing the grass for his landlords, Mr. and Mrs. Baxter. They were a nice elderly couple who liked having a young man renting from them and helping out around the house in exchange for a break on the rent.

He spent the next few days doing some chores, as well as helping Mr. Baxter clean out the garage downstairs, before he returned to work on night shift. Ashley's schedule was busy, and they talked and texted often, but were unable to see each other again as soon as he would have liked. He hoped he got the chance to see her on a trip to the ER since she was working nights this week. She had promised to come by the next morning, and they could make breakfast together at his apartment after work. He was looking forward to seeing her.

Dean pulled into the Station U parking lot a little before six PM for work and looked around for any suspicious black SUVs that might indicate Zach or his friends were following him. That had been how Zach had tracked him down before. He didn't see any other cars around. Nothing but a beat up white Chevy van parked on the street alongside the building. He grabbed his gear and went inside the station. Brook and Tammy, the day shift paramedics, were there when he walked in. Brook, a tall, thin blonde woman in her mid-twenties, was working on one of the computer workstations at the U-shaped desk to the left. Tammy, a brown-haired mother of four in her later forties, was seated in one of the recliners reading a book.

"Hi, guys!" Dean called as he came in. Brook looked up briefly and waved from where she was working on the computer. Tammy looked up from her book, smiling.

"You're in a good mood, Dean," she said.

"Yeah, I guess I am," Dean said, setting his duffle bag down on the coffee table in front of the love seat.

"It wouldn't have anything to do with your new girlfriend would it?" she jabbed, smiling.

"It might," Dean said, "But I don't kiss and tell."

"So there has been kissing?" Tammy asked. "Come on. Why do you and Brynne have to be so mysterious about your special friends? Some of us have rather mundane home lives. We need to live vicariously through you guys."

"What's that about living vicariously?" Brynne asked as she came in from the parking lot.

"Dean's been kissing Ashley, but won't tell us what it's like to date a real angel," Tammy said getting up from the recliner and stretching her arms out behind her. "I shouldn't say it, but it's been a quiet day, Brynne. In fact, we haven't had much come in all week since that bad burn victim you had the other night. Bill and Lynne said the same thing about their night shift runs over the last few evenings."

"Ugh, Tammy," Brynne said in an exasperated tone. "You know better than to use the 'Q' word."

"There's no other word for it," Tammy said, defending herself.

"It's like our patients are laying low and not calling us. Have you heard anything from James? I wondered if he knows if there's anything going on."

"No, not that he's mentioned to me," Brynne said. "He's been preoccupied by something else going on, but I'll ask him. Maybe it's just a natural lull in the action. There is nothing wrong with that."

"No, I guess not," Tammy said. She grabbed her purse from the desk nearby and headed towards the door. "I need to get home. It's parent-teacher conference night, and that always leads to some surprises. I'm meeting my husband at the school later, and I need to make sure the kids are settled and working on their homework before I head over there. See ya!"

Brook grabbed her stuff and followed her partner out the door with a wave. "Yep, I'm out of here, too. Have a good night, guys."

Brynne walked over and put her purse in the top desk drawer, leaned over and logged-in to her workstation before she turned around with her hands on her hips, looking at Dean.

"Well?"

"Well, what?" Dean asked.

"Well, tell me about Ashley," she said. "You guys must've had a good breakfast date. She texted me for your address while you were off. I can only guess that meant she was planning on dropping by."

Dean felt his face flush and Brynne laughed.

"I knew it!" she said. "Good for you, Dean. You need a good woman in your life to keep you straight."

"I'm not talking about this, Brynne," Dean said. "I'm a gentleman. Ashley and I are getting along and are planning on seeing each other again. That's all I'm going to say."

"Ok, fair's fair, Dean," she said. "I don't share my private life with James with anyone either. I know that dating an Unusual comes with some secrets. Still, if you need to talk about it, I'm all ears."

"There is one thing I need to tell you, Brynne," Dean started. He didn't know how to broach the subject other than to jump right in. He crossed the room and sat in the desk chair opposite hers. "The other night, I know you saw your ex-partner Zach in the crowd. I overheard you talking to Chief Ari about it. I saw him, too."

"How do you even know what he looks like?" she asked. "He was long gone before you got here. That was the first I'd seen of him since he left."

"Zach contacted me and asked me to join him, to pass him information on our patients." Brynne stiffened at this but didn't say anything as he continued. "He's mixed up in some group called "The Cause" that wants to expose the Unusuals in our community. He calls Unusuals monsters, and he wants them gone from Elk City."

"Why didn't you tell me, or the Chief, or Mike at the Academy?" Brynne asked. "Zach's bad news, Dean. He got really jealous of James and me. He thought our dating was an abomination. His words, not mine."

"I didn't know what to do at first, and I was shocked by some, uh, aspects of your relationship with James. I didn't know how I felt about that," Dean said. "I should have said something. I know that now. Maybe that burn attack would never have happened. He all but admitted to me that he had something to do with it. He said it was because she was Witch. He claimed she was using her powers to take advantage of humans and steal money from them."

Brynne waited when he paused, searching for the words to explain what he needed to get off his chest.

"Brynne," Dean continued. "He came to my apartment a few nights back, after our last day shift, and threatened to expose me as part of their movement. He claimed that he had evidence that could tie me to him, and he wanted to me to keep working with him. I have tried to avoid him, but he was waiting in my apartment, when I got home from work."

"You should have called me, Dean, or called the police," Brynne said.

"I know, but I was too upset by all of it," Dean said. "That's when Ashley came to find me. She said she could tell I was in trouble. She was the one who urged me to talk to you. So, here I am. What do I do?"

"I'll report this to Chief Ari," Brynne said. "Not to get you in trouble. He's aware of The Cause. That's the group that Zach is tied up with. They are determined to root out the Unusuals in our community and drive them from the area. I'll tell him that Zach is trying to draw you in and that you reported it to me. That should clear your name. In the meantime, don't have any contact with him and report to me if he tries to confront you again as he did at your apartment."

"I will," Dean assured her. "I just don't think that he's done with me. I get the feeling that he's got some way to use me in this situation. That he wants me to do something, to take some direct action against you and James and our patients."

"That may be true," Brynne said. "You need to keep telling me what's going on. Another thing, too. Don't let him know about your relationship with Ashley. That could make her a target. I don't know if he knows her identity as an Eldara, but he might. Tying her to you might give him leverage over you. We don't want that."

"She says that I have a part to play in the situation with Zach and The Cause," Dean said. "Ashley was sent here for a purpose, and now she thinks that I am tied in to that, somehow."

"Did she say what she knows?" Brynne asked.

"No, she acted like she was discovering her role as things went along," Dean said. "She just had a feeling."

"That sounds typical for the Eldara," Brynne said with a snort. "They're the Gods' messengers, but deciphering the divine meaning of a message is tough even for them. At least, that's what James has told me. They're less messenger and more like a change-agent than anything else."

"That sounds right, based on what she was willing to share with me," Dean confirmed. "Ok, so what next?"

"Next, I contact the chief," Brynne said. "Then we just do our jobs. I'm going to ask James about what Tammy said, about things being slow lately. Maybe he knows if there's something going on that's keeping the Unusuals from calling us. If there is something, he'll tell me and maybe there is something we can do about it. For you, Dean, reach out to Mike Farver. He might have some insights on this. He was doing this before I was, and he might know more about the Eldara than I do. I shouldn't talk to him directly. We have some history that is uncomfortable. Shoot him an email and see if he has time to meet up with you instead."

"I'll do that," Dean said. He was glad to have something to do and know that there was a plan in place to back him up. He turned around in the desk chair and tapped in his login information to the workstation in front of him. He clicked on his secure company email account and opened up a new email to Mike, his old Academy instructor. Mike was not just a knowledgeable instructor; Mike was a former Station U paramedic. He knew a lot about Unusuals and could offer some insights into his situation. Dean was clicking the send button on that email to Mike when the first call of the evening came in.

The tones alerted on the speaker overhead in the squad room. "Rescue Box 734, pedestrian struck, in the vicinity of 1322 Hopewell Road."

The two paramedics jumped up as one and headed out, Dean following Brynne through the door to the ambulance bay. She walked to the driver's side as usual, and Dean crossed around and climbed into the passenger seat. He reached up and keyed the garage door opener while his partner fired up the rig's diesel engine. As they pulled out into the parking lot, Dean picked up the mic and put them on the street responding.

"U-191 responding, Rescue Box 734." He reached up to close the garage door and checked in the side view mirror to make sure it was coming back down as they drove away to the call. He then reached down and switched the radio over to the response channel and waited for the dispatcher to contact them with any additional information from the scene as they sped through the darkening streets and night fell on Elk City.

## Chapter 7

The dispatchers didn't have much additional information to offer on the patient as the two paramedics sped through the night in the ambulance. All the dispatcher had to say was that it was a female victim found on the side of the road after an apparent vehicular hit and run. The patient was alive but unresponsive. The dispatcher also reported that another, unidentified responder was already on the scene. That caused Dean to look over at Brynne with a confused look on his face. Who could that be? She just glanced his way with a raised eyebrow and kept driving.

It took them seven minutes to get to the location, and as they pulled up on the scene, they saw other red flashing lights in the night. Dean was surprised to see they were coming from a beat-up, white Chevy van pulled off the side of the road. There was a little portable, suction-cup mounted, rotating flashing red light mounted to the roof out the driver's side window. The curly cord stretched back inside, and Dean guessed it plugged into the old van's 12-volt cigarette lighter plug. He'd seen such lights in catalogs used by local volunteers and security services.

Dean and Brynne had gotten to know each other well enough to have a routine for their calls at this point. Dean jumped out of the passenger side on their arrival and pulled out the trauma and oxygen bags from their side compartment. He knew Brynne would climb in the back and grab the heart monitor/defibrillator. Because they were on the side of the road, he took a moment to don a reflective, fluorescent yellow vest too, before he proceeded to find their patient. He was not prepared for what he found as he rounded the parked white van.

There, in the tall grass on the roadside, was the twisted body of a young female. She looked young, based on what he could see from the light of the van's headlights. Bent over her, apparently treating her wounds, was a heavyset person wearing a light blue uniform-style shirt with no collar insignia or shoulder patches he could see. The person was wearing navy blue cargo pants similar to his own, and the pockets appeared to be bulging with first aid supplies like bandages and trauma shears. He approached and asked what was going on. The other responder turned and looked his way.

"Oh, Dean, it's you. Thank God!" Gibbie, a middle-aged vampire, said. Gibbie had been a frequent patient of theirs since Dean had started on the job at Station U. He was usually simultaneously frumpy and flamboyant. He was not, to Dean's knowledge, an EMT, paramedic, or any other kind of first responder.

"Gibbie," Dean said. "What are you doing here?"

"I'm trying to help this fairy girl, what does it look like I'm doing?" Gibbie said frantically. "She's all busted up with a broken leg, and it looks like one of her wings is messed up although it's hard to tell because she's got it folded under her shirt."

"Okay, Gibbie," Dean said, taking control of the scene, the way he'd been taught. "I'm here. Step back and let me have a look at her."

The vampire stood and stepped back as Brynne approached with the heart monitor. "Gibbie, what the hell are you doing here?" she asked. "And what are you wearing?"

"I decided I could help you guys out, Brynne honey," the frumpy vampire said. "I got myself a scanner and some equipment. This way I can lend you all a hand on your calls with Unusuals."

Brynne continued past the vampire wannabe to the patient. She was shaking her head. Dean started working on his patient assessing her injuries.

"We'll talk about this later, Gibbie," Brynne said.

A car sped by the scene, coming dangerously close to all of them on the side of the road. Dean looked at his partner. Even though they were wearing reflective vests, that car had come too close for comfort.

"We need some traffic control, Brynne," Dean said.

She looked around and started to key the radio mic clipped to her uniform's shoulder. Then she stopped and seemed to change her mind. She turned and looked at Gibbie where he stood next to his van.

"Gibbie," she called. "Did you, by chance, get any road flares when you were getting your van equipped?"

"I sure did, Brynne," he said, bouncing on the balls of his feet excitedly. "I have a whole case. I picked them up from online."

"Ok," Brynne instructed. "Light some up and deploy three of them in intervals back to about 50 yards on either side of us in both directions. Then take a flashlight and flag down traffic coming this way to slow them up. Got it?"

"Got it, Brynne!" Gibbie said, his voice rising to a squeak in excitement. "Oh boy, oh boy, oh boy." He sped off and disappeared around the back of his beat-up van.

Dean meanwhile finished his head to toe trauma assessment. He had a female in her late teens or early twenties. She was dressed in a summer dress and both her lower legs had open fractures, consistent with being struck by a car. Gibbie had apparently applied Quick-clot gauze to the open wounds to control the bleeding, and that had slowed the bleeding significantly from what had been happening before the dressings were applied, based on the amount of blood soaked into the ground around her.

He rolled her gently towards him, supporting her head and neck with one hand, and checked her back. He found a crumpled pair of wings. She groaned in pain but didn't wake up or speak. He contained his surprise when he saw the pair of wings. They emerged from between the girl's shoulder blades above the sundress. They were multi-paneled like an insect's folding wings. The left one was clearly broken based on the way it bent at the connection between the shoulder blades. There was no bleeding on the back, so that was a minor injury compared to the leg fractures and any internal injuries she had.

"What have we got, Dean?" Brynne asked.

"Female, I'd say she's about 19 apparent age," Dean started. "She's responsive only to painful stimuli and has visible bilateral open tib/fib fractures, bleeding currently under control. She has a …" He paused for a moment, searching for a description. "She has an apparent left wing fracture at the base but no other injuries or visible bleeding. Based on the mechanism of injury, I suspect internal bleeding and a possible head injury. We need to get her to the hospital."

As Brynne looked over his shoulder, she said, "Good job on the Quick-Clot gauze on the open wounds, Dean. That was fast."

"That wasn't me, Brynne," he said, hooking a thumb over his shoulder to where the vampire was waving his flashlight frantically and nearly jumping in front of cars to wave them aside. "Gibbie had that done before we got here."

Dean looked around and said, "I wonder who called us? I didn't see any cars pulled over but Gibbie's van. Maybe the people who hit her called and then left?"

"Maybe," Brynne said. She stood up and flicked on her flashlight, shining it into the woods and brush on the side of the road. She called out, "If you're still here watching us, it's okay. We're going to help your friend. You can come out."

"Is it safe? I wasn't sure when the vampire came," said a tiny voice above them.

Brynne took a step back and shined her light up in the tree branches overhanging the road. Dean looked up, too. Crouched on a branch about ten feet up was a small, shadowy form. Brynne's light revealed a girl about the same age as the one he was treating.

"It's alright," Brynne repeated. "You can come on down. It's safe. The vampire's with us. He's helping."

The girl stepped off the branch into mid-air. Dean shouted and lurched to his feet to catch her. He stopped when he saw her wings unfold behind her, and she fluttered gracefully to the ground. She walked closer and knelt down beside her friend's head, the wings folding out of sight against her back. Dean noticed that their delicate laciness blended in with the dress and looked like part of the dress's ruffles when folded. He wasn't sure he'd have known they were there if he hadn't just seen them.

"What's your name, sweetie?" Brynne asked.

The girl brushed her curly, platinum blonde hair out of her face, tucking it behind a slightly pointed ear. "I'm Anuja, Anuja Drinkwater," she said in an airy voice. "This is my sister Jamila. We were walking home to the Barrens when this car came around the curve very fast. I jumped out of the way, but they hit Jamila. They stopped a bit down the road for a moment, then sped off and just left us here." She started crying. She touched her sister's face, stroking her cheek with a fingertip. "Is she going to be alright?"

Dean crouched back down and gripped her free hand to comfort her. "We're going to do our best. You did the right thing calling for help." He turned to Brynne. "Do you want to get the collar bag and backboard?"

"Got it," she said. She moved the monitor up next to the girl on the ground. "Get her hooked up to the monitor. We'll get IVs in the ambulance on the way." She left to get the stretcher and other gear.

Dean hooked her up the heart monitor and saw a sinus tachycardia of 142 on the screen. No surprises there, he thought. She's in pain and lost some blood. The blood pressure was 136/82, again not surprising given her injuries. It was not bad, she must not have lost enough blood to crash her blood pressure.

Brynne came back with the head and neck trauma gear and the stretcher. Dean didn't think much of backboards for anything but lifting devices anymore. They were not terribly effective body splints, though they had been used that way for over fifty years. The fact was, the body was pretty good at splinting itself in most situations as far as back injuries went. Still, it was easier to lift the girl onto the stretcher after putting a cervical collar on her and carefully moving her onto the backboard. She groaned a little as they lifted her, but that was all. The two paramedics tried to be gentle.

Dean climbed in the back of the ambulance after they loaded her inside, and started two IVs in case her blood pressure dropped and he needed to give Jamila fluids. He planned on splinting and finishing the dressings Gibbie started on her legs on the way to the hospital. Anuja climbed in the front with Brynne's urging to come along with her sister. Brynne got in the ambulance and pulled into the road, pausing briefly to call out the window to Gibbie, who was still animatedly directing the traffic and stopping cars.

"Don't forget to put the road flares out before you leave, Gibbie," she called, and pulled away with the lights and sirens blaring. Dean looked out the rear windows as the vampire was illuminated in the night by their flashing lights. He was waving at them as they sped off into the darkness toward the trauma center at ECMC.

———

BRYNNE MADE sure the ride to the hospital was both smooth and fast. Dean was able to bandage and splint Jamila's lower legs before they arrived. Her vital signs remained stable on the way. He called the hospital on the med radio to alert them of the trauma patient inbound, using the code that the patient was part of the Unusual population so that the appropriate ER staff could be arranged.

As they pulled up on the ambulance ramp, a team of nurses and doctors waited for them to take the injured fairy girl right into the trauma assessment room and then probably surgery. Brynne opened the back doors, and Dean saw Ashley dressed in her scrubs, standing off to one side with the other members of the trauma team.

Dean unhooked his patient from the monitor and laid the IV bags on the stretcher mattress next to her after shutting the valves in the tubing. Doc Spirelli was on tonight and came right over to help Brynne pull out the stretcher and lower the wheeled undercarriage.

"Any changes since you called in, Dean?" Doctor Spirelli asked, looking in at the tiny patient on the stretcher.

"No changes," Dean said, shaking his head. "The vitals are stable, and I was unable to find any other injuries other than the ones I listed on the radio. She did not regain consciousness and is still responsive only to painful stimuli."

Dean and Brynne rolled the stretcher over to the hospital gurney there. With help from a few nurses, they lifted Jamila over to the gurney using the backboard that was still beneath her.

"Ok," the doc said. He turned to the trauma team as they moved the patient towards the double automatic doors to the hospital's emergency department and trauma rooms. "We'll do a full trauma work up …" he continued talking as they went inside.

Ashley hung back, smiled at Dean and turned to look at Anuja, who was looking at the doors through which the trauma team rolled her sister. Dean introduced them to each other.

"Anuja, this is Ashley Moore," the paramedic said. "She's a nurse here at the hospital. She'll take you inside and get some information from you about your sister."

The fairy girl turned to look at Ashley and her eyes widened. She bowed deeply, touching her hand to her forehead in what looked like a salute. "Eldara, I'm humbled that you would arrive to help my sister. It is such a pleasure to meet one such as you."

Dean looked on in amusement. That was certainly interesting. He thought Ashley was pretty special, but that was obviously for just mundane reasons. There was something else going on here with his new girlfriend and the Fae child.

"It is my pleasure to meet you, Anuja," Ashley said lifting the girl out of her bow with a hand to her shoulder. "Let us maintain human appearances here at the hospital. I assure you, I'll take no offense. Come inside and tell me about your sister and what happened. Then I'll find out how she's doing for you." Ashley turned and winked at him and led the girl inside.

Brynne came over and tapped him on the shoulder. "Hey, help me get the stretcher made up so I can put us back in service."

"What was all that about?" he asked as he helped with the sheets.

"I told you," Brynne said. "She has a halo, an aura that is clearly evident to the other Unusuals. James told me that he recognized her for an Eldara Sister immediately after he first met her a few years ago."

"Wait," Dean said, stopping what he was doing. "You mean you weren't kidding when you said she had a halo? Like a real angel-style halo?"

"Yes, Dean," Brynne said rolling her eyes. "You are such a guy. You don't listen very well. She's an Eldara, a messenger of the Gods. They are the basis of the angel myth. For all we know, she could have been one of the heavenly hosts singing over the birth of Jesus Christ."

"I heard you but I thought you were kidding," Dean said. "I didn't think you meant that she actually glowed with some sort of divine light."

"You'll have to ask if she can show it to you sometime," Brynne said, climbing into the back of the ambulance rig, cleaning up the bandage wrappers and putting things away. "She can probably turn it up so you can see it, too. I would suspect that she can do something like that. It would explain why we think of angels as having halos or auras today."

"I would feel weird asking her to do that," Dean said.

"Why?" Brynne asked. "One of the perks of dating an Unusual is watching them do weird stuff. It's like a magic show, but better, because it's real."

Dean thought about that as they finished picking up the trash from the call and wiping down the stretcher and surfaces in the back. The two paramedics climbed out after cleaning up and shut the rear doors of the unit. Brynne jumped in the driver's side as Dean got in his familiar seat on the passenger side. Something else occurred to him.

"What are we going to do about Gibbie?" Dean asked.

"I don't know," Brynne said as she pulled the ambulance out onto the street and started back towards their station across town. "It was a good thing he got there before us. He did stop the bleeding before we showed up. Without that she might have been a lot worse off. He also did a passable job at traffic control, but I hesitate to encourage him. He doesn't have the training and could get himself or someone else hurt."

"Could we get him the training?" Dean pondered, thinking out loud. "The Fire Department has an auxiliary, and the surrounding volunteer companies still have volunteer EMTs."

"Hey, that's a good idea," Brynne said. "We could hook him up with the ECFD as an auxiliary member. Maybe he could even get EMT training. We'd just have to find him an evening class. I'll call Chief Ari about the auxiliary thing and Mike Farver at the academy about EMT training."

"There is always CERT training," Dean suggested. He referred to the federal government's Community Emergency Response Team training meant to serve a community in the event of a disaster. The training included disaster preparedness training and some basic first aid. They also learned some basics of light search and rescue activities.

"That's a good idea, too," Brynne said. "One of those should work and will help make sure Gibbie learns the right way to do things instead of him running around freelancing like he did tonight."

"Where did he get all that gear, and the quick clotting impregnated gauze?" Dean wondered.

"Probably online," Brynne answered. "You can get all that stuff on Amazon, the uniform shirt, pants, trauma shears, and even the quick clot gauze. I used it to put together an emergency kit for my apartment and car."

"Really?" Dean said. "Can you get a good commercial tourniquet? I've always thought I should have one in my glove box just in case."

"Dean, you should know by now. There's very little you can't buy on the internet," Brynne said chuckling. "Put us back in service in case they need us for another call."

Dean picked up the mic and called dispatch to alert them that

U-191 was back in action after the call and wondered what else he could get on the internet for his personal first aid kit. It probably wouldn't be a bad idea to check out what was available to have on hand just in case. He continued to think about it as the ambulance sped off into the night of Elk City.

Chapter 8

One thing Dean found waiting for him when he returned to the station was an email from his former teacher, Mike Farver. Mike wanted to meet up for breakfast and check in on how he was doing after that night's shift was over. Dean was glad to hear from his mentor. He was looking forward to the opportunity to check in with him about his run-in with Zach. Mike would be able to counsel him on how to proceed. He trusted him.

The rest of the shift went quickly. There were a few routine medical calls for some elderly patients in the Unusual community. The remainder of the night was spent doing paperwork and chores around the station. By the time morning arrived, Dean was ready to go to breakfast and see his former academy instructor.

The next shift paramedics showed up, with Bill and then his partner Lynne arriving. The two were an interesting pair. Bill was older and balding, in his late fifties. He had been a paramedic for a long time. Bill had been one of the original Station U paramedics with Mike Farver. Lynne was a little younger, in her early forties. She had been instrumental in early programs to set up community paramedic outreach in the Elk City region. That had been why she had been tapped to move to Station U, where another underserved community needed attention.

"Hey, Dean," Bill said as he came in followed by Lynne. "How was your night?"

"It wasn't too bad," Dean said. "We had a pedestrian struck first thing last night, but the rest of the shift was pretty slow. Brynne's in the ambulance bay doing a final check on the gear for you guys."

"I heard the pedestrian struck call on the scanner at home," Lynne said. "That was out by the Barrens. We need to get a program in place out there for some wellness visits. There are some kids there who could use some attention instead of always waiting until they get bad enough to call an ambulance." She looked at her partner. "Bill, maybe we can make a run out that way and check in with August, the unofficial mayor of the Barrens, about doing that during day shifts a couple of times a week, when we can get away."

"I'm up for that," Bill said. "August always gives us some of his home-made beer to bring back with us. That stuff is good, like something from the Old Country."

"Good to know you have your priorities straight, Bill," Dean quipped.

"You have no idea, Probie," Bill replied. "If you get out there and see him, don't turn him down. It is some truly excellent brew. Better than the piss-water beers most mainstream American brewers make. I keep telling him that he should start up a micro-brewery. He just laughs and says he makes just enough for himself and his friends. He doesn't want to make more."

Brynne came in from the ambulance bay into the squad room. "Make more of what?"

"Bill was going on about August Beche's strange brewing capabilities," Lynne said.

"It is good stuff," Brynne said. "James gets a case or so every time he brews a batch. He keeps it around for special occasions." She glanced at her watch as she heard a horn sound from the parking lot outside. "That must be him now. James said he was going to pick me up. Gotta go. Have a good shift, guys. See you tonight." She grabbed her purse and jacket and headed out the door to the parking lot.

Dean watched her leave, wondering if James was planning on a snack from his partner before bed. He must have had a sour look on his face because Bill noticed it right away.

"Dean, dude, you have to let up on this whole 'James the vampire dating your partner' thing," the older paramedic said as Dean continued to stare at the door to the parking lot. "Brynne can handle herself. She's doing nothing she doesn't want to do."

"I know, Bill," Dean said, turning and looking at the elder medic. "It just creeps me out."

"Speaking of dating an Unusual, how are things with you and Nurse Ashley, Dean?" Lynne asked, changing the subject. "I heard you two had a date. I've been waiting to ask you what it's like dating an actual angel?"

Dean blushed and stared at the floor in embarrassment. Bill clapped him on the shoulder. "Don't you listen to her, Dean. She just wants to think about it as one of her soccer-mom novels where the guy falls for the angel and all sorts of steamy, girly romance ensues. She's a hot nurse, and that's all we care about, right?"

"Uh, well, I don't know if I'd put it that way either, Bill," Dean said, uncomfortable with that characterization of the relationship that was developing. "I think she's great, and I hope we can see each other again. That's all."

"Don't listen to him, Dean," Lynne said. "Ashley's a nice girl and a good match for you. Don't you let lecherous old men like Bill ruin your love life."

Dean laughed as Bill made a face of shock at that description of his temperament. "Moi? Lecherous? I don't know what you mean?"

"Yeah, right, Bill," Lynne replied. "Try that innocent act on someone who doesn't know what a letch you are."

Dean picked up his jacket and slipped it on over his uniform shirt. "I think that's my cue to leave. I'll see you two in twelve." He headed out the door as the other two paramedics said bye and got to work on their shift. He was enjoying getting to know the crew better at Station U. They weren't just good paramedics. They were good people, and becoming good friends. He liked the way they looked out for each other. Maybe that was as good a reason as any for him to stop being concerned about his partner's relationship with a vampire. He'd have to think on that. Perhaps Mike would have some thoughts on it, too. He had been Brynne's partner before moving to the Fire Academy to train new paramedics.

He hopped into his pickup and backed out of his space in the parking lot, leaving the run-down industrial park that was home to Station U and heading to Hank's Diner, where Mike was meeting him for breakfast.

---

THE DINER WAS BUSY, but Mike was already there when Dean arrived and had grabbed a booth. Daisy, one of the waitresses, said hi as Dean entered. He saw his mentor sitting at the back and walked over while he waived back at the waitress. Mike was sitting in the booth looking over the menu. He glanced up as Dean approached.

"Hi, Dean," Mike said warmly. "It's good to see you."

Dean reached out to shake Mike's hand as he slid into the booth opposite him. Daisy came over and got their drink orders. Mike must not have been waiting long, he hadn't ordered his coffee yet. Dean didn't want any caffeine since he was going to be headed home to bed soon. He ordered a Sprite and grabbed a menu from where it was stashed behind the condiments at the end of the table, while she went to get their beverages.

Mike waited while he looked at the menu and when he set it down, spoke up cheerfully. "So, how have you been? It's been a few weeks since I've talked with you."

"It's been good, mostly," Dean said, qualifying his response.

Mike raised an eyebrow when Dean said "mostly" and probed right away. "What's that mostly part? Is there something that isn't as good as the rest?"

Dean thought for a moment about how to approach this. Daisy returned with their drinks, coffee for Mike and Sprite for him. He used the break while she took their orders to keep thinking. He watched her leave and looked back at Mike.

"I don't know where to start, Mike. There's been so much going on," Dean said.

"Why don't you start at the beginning," Mike said. "What started you down this path to worrying about your work?"

"I think it mostly has to do with a call we had the other night. There was a patient attacked with burning lighter fluid, or gasoline or something. It was a pretty rough call, and I saw someone there who I wondered might be involved with it," Dean said.

"You saw Brynne's old partner, Zach," Mike said, watching Dean's eyes.

"Yes. How did you know?" Dean asked.

"I still keep in touch, and I hear things while at the academy," Mike responded. "Do you think Zach did it? Burned the witch girl?"

Dean looked up and paused at the term "witch girl." That sounded a lot like the way Zach had talked about her. "She was Witch, it's true, but that's no reason to do that to her."

"So you've talked with Zach about this?" Mike probed.

Dean stared at the cup of soda in front of him for a while before answering. "Yeah, I have talked with Zach a few times, and he's mixed up with some anti-Unusual group called The Cause. He seems to think I would side with him and help identify and target our patients for them. He's threatened me with exposure to the Chief, tagging me as a member with him if I don't help."

"Don't you sympathize with some of what Zach said?" Mike asked. "It's not necessarily bad to have doubts about what you see going on at work, if you think something is wrong."

"I've already told you in the past, I have problems with James and Brynne," Dean said. "I don't like what goes on between the two of them. I don't think it's healthy. But that doesn't mean that I would use that to justify random attacks on our patients."

"I'm not saying it does," Mike said. "I'm just helping you talk through your feelings a bit. I knew Zach when he worked for the

Fire Department. I helped train him in the academy, like you. I don't think he would do something like that without good reason."

"What do you mean, Mike? What could possibly be a 'good reason' for doing something like that?"

"I'm just saying there are opposite sides to every issue out there," Mike answered. "If you have no evidence that Zach did anything wrong, it's probably not a good idea to implicate him. I know from the Chief that Brynne saw him there. Your additional information about some crackpot things he said, or ideas he's told you about would only serve to make him look even more guilty."

Dean leaned across the table and whispered urgently, "I don't just think he's guilty, Mike. I heard him all but admit he had something to do with that attack. He knew too much about the girl and made some accusations about her magic activities that were affecting humans."

Mike leaned back in his seat and looked at Dean for a bit. The pause was further interrupted by Daisy's return with their breakfast. She set their order down and, after checking it over, laid the bill down on the table, too.

"I'll get that when you're ready," she said. "Enjoy your food."

Dean watched her move on to another table and then looked back to Mike. His mentor was starting in on his food, and motioned with his fork at Dean's plate to do the same. He picked up a piece of bacon and chewed while thinking about the conversation so far. It seemed as if Mike was defending Zach, but that couldn't be right. He had a sudden thought and, as he swallowed his mouthful of bacon, it was as if a lead weight settled in the pit of his stomach.

"Dean," Mike said between bites. "You're still pretty new to Station U. I know you've seen some interesting things. I also know you've been through some tough situations, like the time you were charmed by that Siren. Surely you can see some of why Zach feels the way he does. I'm not necessarily condoning anything he may or may not have done. I'm just saying that some of his feelings may be valid."

The probationary paramedic took another bite while he pondered the shift in the situation. He kept eating, keeping his mouth full so he couldn't politely answer while he thought of what to say. If Mike was on Zach's side, then he might be part of The Cause, too. Was that possible? He had always thought of Mike as the perfect paramedic, the model to which he aspired when he was in the Academy. This revelation of another, less attractive side of his mentor was jarring. He finished his food while the awkward silence continued. Mike just sat there watching while he finished. It was just the way he used to wait quietly for an answer back in the Academy. Mike's patience while waiting for the answer to a tough question was legendary with his students.

Dean looked up and decided just to ask him. "Mike, do you agree with Zach's position about the Unusuals? Do you think they are a danger to our community?"

"What do you think, Dean?" Mike asked. "That's the question at hand. I think you already know the answer to your own questions. I want to know if you are up to the challenge of being part of something bigger than you are alone. Something that has been going on for longer than you can know. This isn't just a conflict in Elk City, Dean. It's a battle for the good of humanity. You've got the chance to make a difference here and choose the right side. If you don't, then it could be the end of everything you've ever wanted or dreamed of doing."

Dean picked up his drink and took a sip. God, what did he do? He suddenly wished he hadn't met Mike for breakfast. His whole world seemed to be crashing down again, and he felt like he did when Zach confronted him in his apartment. His mentor and the paramedic he aspired to emulate the most was just as twisted as Zach was. Did he have no one he could count on that could be trusted?

"Hi, Dean. Hey Mike," a familiar voice said. "Mind if I join you guys? I'm famished."

Dean looked up and saw Ashley standing there, in her navy blue scrubs and a light jacket. She motioned to Dean to slide over, and she sat down next to him. She was like an answer to his prayers. Again.

"Hello, Ashley," Mike said, coolly. "What brings you here, all the way across town from the hospital?"

"Oh, I was heading by when I thought I saw Dean's truck." She slipped her hand into Dean's, interlacing her fingers with his. He gripped her hand back, giving it a grateful squeeze.

Mike's eyes narrowed at that exchange. "I see," he said, staring at their clasped hands for a moment and then paused, glancing at his plate. "Well, I think that's that. I'm done eating, and I don't want to get between the two of you. Dean, you need to think hard about what I said. You don't want to end up on the wrong side in this." He stood up, glanced at the check and dropped a few bills on the table next to it. "That should cover my portion. I've got to go."

Dean turned his head and watched the older paramedic leave. Ashley switched sides to sit across from him, taking Mike's empty seat in the booth. She didn't release her grip on his hand. A little squeeze of his fingers returned his attention to her.

"How did you know?" Dean asked, shaking his head. "I just thought I needed someone, something to get me out of that conversation with Mike before it went too far, and then there you were."

"I told you, Dean," she said, her quiet, calming voice washing over him like a gentle wave. "I now know why I'm here, and who I'm supposed to help out. I'll never be far away anymore when you need me."

"Ashley," Dean said, hardly daring to say it out loud. "I think Mike's part of The Cause, too. He's tied up with Zach somehow, and he wants me to take sides in some upcoming conflict."

She squeezed his hand in support. "And have you chosen a side in this conflict?"

He looked at where her delicate hand held his tanned, weathered one in hers. His eyes tracked up and met hers. Those deep hazel green eyes seemed to go on forever. He knew the answer to that question. "Yes. Yes, I have."

Chapter 9

The rest of the day went fast for Dean. Ashley stayed while he finished eating, but had to return to work for a few hours so they said their goodbyes with a kiss in the parking lot, and the promise they'd see each other again, soon. He was tired and wanted to get home. He needed to get some sleep before he had to return to night shift later that evening. He was just getting in the door at his apartment when his phone chirped with a text message from Bill at work.

It read, "Freddy wants to make dinner for us tonight - Bring a date! Dinner at 5 PM."

Freddy was a former chef, turned into a zombie by a jealous ex-girlfriend who happened to be a voodoo priestess. He couldn't cook in a restaurant anymore since he lost random body parts without feeling it. He couldn't even taste or eat food. But despite all that going against him, he was still one of the best chefs Dean had ever had the pleasure to meet. He regularly offered to cook a meal for the Station U paramedics, usually after they came by to help reattach some lost body part onto him. Dean had first met Freddy when he was choking, and Brynne's Heimlich maneuver launched a blackened, rotting tongue across the zombie's broken down trailer. The next night, Freddy made a five-star restaurant meal in their little kitchenette at the station. Dean was looking forward to having another excellent meal again tonight.

He glanced at the text message again. Bill had texted "… Bring a Date!" He wasn't sure if she was available, but he shot a quick text off to Ashley, inviting her to meet him at the station tonight at five o'clock. She didn't text right back. So he got ready for bed, looking forward to a decent meal that single guys, especially paramedics, rarely got. He fell asleep thinking about food.

---

DEAN WAS EXCITED and a little anxious as he drove into the Station U parking lot in the back of the industrial park in which it was located. Ashley had texted back an excited "Yessss!!!!" at his request to meet at the station for dinner. He was happy to see her but a little nervous at having her there as his guest in front of all of his co-workers. He decided it wouldn't be that bad since all of them had known Ashley from the hospital emergency department for longer than they had known him.

He saw Ashley's car already there; her red MG convertible pulled in next to Bill's Ford SUV. He pulled his pickup in next to her car and hopped out to head inside. That was when he saw the car parked next to Bill's. The silver Lexus belonged to James, Brynne's vampire boyfriend.

Dean walked up to the door in the side of the metal building that housed Station U and glanced through the rectangular glass panel in it, seeing James and Ashley talking together just inside. He pulled the door open and went in. Ashley turned when he entered, crossed the room over to him and slipped an arm around his waist, giving him a quick kiss. She was dressed in light blue scrubs so she must have to work again that evening.

"Heading to work after this?" Dean asked.

"Yep," she replied. "I'm on again tonight from seven to seven."

James walked over. He was tall, dark haired, wearing black

skinny jeans, a white t-shirt and a black sports coat, a typical hipster look. "Hello, Dean," James said. "It's been a while since we've had the chance to chat."

Dean took the cool hand in his and shook it firmly. He didn't bother to try the macho hand-squeeze. Only a fool played that game with a vampire. "Hi James," Dean said. He looked around and didn't see his partner. "Where's Brynne? I would have thought she would have driven over with you."

"She had a meeting with the Chief this afternoon," James said, glancing at the Rolex on his wrist. "She should be here soon."

The two were interrupted by the sound of a raspy voice behind them. "Hors d'oeuvre?" Freddy asked lifting up a plate. It held small scallops, wrapped in bacon, skewered by a toothpick.

"Oooo, yum!" Ashley said, reaching across between James and Dean, grabbing a toothpick with one of the appetizers and popping it in her mouth, sliding it off the toothpick with her teeth. "Mmm-mmm, that's really good," she said. "Dean, you have to try one." She grabbed another from the proffered plate and held it up for him.

"Yes, Dean," James said, grinning. "Do try one."

Dean leaned forward and took the bite that Ashley offered him, a little embarrassed. His embarrassment was forgotten as he chewed the bite-sized seafood and bacon appetizer. It was delicious. The sweet taste of fresh scallops was combined with the salty bacon, and a marinade that caused his mouth to water. He thought about having another.

"Oh, good Lord," Brynne said from the doorway behind him. "She's feeding you bites of food now? Ashley, we have to have a discussion about spoiling my probie like that."

"He's your probie, but he's my boyfriend," Ashley said, giving his waist a squeeze where she had her arm around him. "I'll spoil him if I want."

Brynne laughed as she finished coming into the squad room. She clapped a hand on Dean's back and crossed to James, giving him a quick kiss. She reached over to Freddy and took one of the scallop bites off the plate. "Freddy, it smells awesome in here," she said as she popped the scallop in her mouth. "And this is delicious. I can't wait for the main course. What are we having?"

Bill spoke up from across the room. "Kristof at Sabatani's heard Freddy was making us dinner and sent over a delivery with a whole boatload of fresh ingredients from his restaurant. Freddy's whipping up a Frutti de Mar with linguine and a garlic butter sauce. Sorry, James."

"No worries," the vampire said. "I'll just be having the wine anyway. You all enjoy the food. I'm here for the company."

Freddy set the plate of scallops down and shambled back to the kitchenette area of the squad room. "Dinner is almost ready," he croaked. "It'll be ready as soon as the pasta is done."

Bill and Lynne were still technically on duty, and they were wrapping up their daily paperwork at the computers on the other side of the room. As Freddy shambled away, it left the two couples alone to talk together. There was an awkward silence. It was broken by James who looked at Dean and raised his glass of wine.

"I suppose, based on Ashley's announcement of your relationship status, that I should welcome you to the club," James said.

"The club?" Dean asked.

"There aren't that many human-Unusual relationships out there," James clarified. "We tend to keep to ourselves, or only have transient interactions with the humans around us. Ashley's choice of you says something about you that I did not know before."

"And what is that?" Dean asked, his eyes narrowing in suspicion.

"That there is more to you than meets the eye, is all," James said. "The Eldara are very discerning in their interactions with humans. If she chooses to associate herself so closely with you after all these years of living here in Elk City, I'm inclined to offer you a level of trust that I wouldn't ordinarily give." He held up a hand, palm forward. "I know we have not gotten along well in the past, but I'd like to offer a chance to start over fresh for both of us, if you'll take it."

"Okay," Dean said, not sure where this was headed. "I guess we can do that." He looked around meeting Brynne's eyes, then looking at Ashley, who nodded. Dean reached out and took the cool hand in his again, and shook it firmly.

"Good," Ashley announced to the two of them. "This had to happen, but it had to come from the two of you, without interference. There is something coming, a significant event that will require you two to work together. It's important that you develop an understanding with each other."

Brynne looked at Ashley in alarm. "What do you mean 'something is coming?' That sounds ominous, Ashley."

"I don't know, yet," Ashley said. "It's only a feeling right now. Kind of like an itch between your shoulder blades, where you can't reach it. All I know is that Dean's involved, integral to it. Tonight's interaction confirmed that somehow he and James need to get together at some point to solve a problem."

"Ah, typical Eldara cryptic pronouncements," James said. "Just once, could you Eldara give us the information up front so we know what we're supposed to do?"

"That interferes with free will, James," she said.

"What's free will got to do with it?" Brynne said. "If something is coming, that sounds like a prophecy of some sort. Doesn't that mean that it's already spelled out?"

"Free will is everything, Brynne," the Eldara Sister explained. "Without it, the earthly creatures would just be pawns of the Gods. Toys with no true direction of their own. It all comes down to choice. The Gods might direct an action be taken, even urge it, coerce it in some way but the choice to act or respond in a certain way always lies in the individual. That is the basis of free will."

"I can offer direction based on what is revealed to me," Ashley continued. "But, the decision to do something with that direction or inspiration is still up to you. You have to decide what is the right thing to do." The last sentence she seemed to direct at both James and Dean. "That is why it was important that the two of you get past the animosity you bear towards each other, or at least start to do so. I don't know why, yet. I only know that it was an important step in the right direction to solving a future challenge. Free will means that you had to arrive at that choice to overcome your differences on your own, which you did, so it's all good for now."

"Well a brief handshake doesn't make James and me instant friends," Dean said looking at the vampire, who nodded in agreement.

"You don't have to be friends, gentlemen," Brynne said. "Ashley means that you have to get along and respect each other when you're together. Be polite, at least. Right?"

"Exactly," Ashley said. "The friendship will come later, I think."

Dean wasn't sure about that last statement, but he was willing to rethink his notions about James if that was what Ashley wanted. There were things about him he didn't like, and he still didn't trust him much, but Ashley and Brynne seemed to trust him. That would have to be enough for now, he supposed.

Freddy broke the tension of the moment announcing that dinner was served. The zombie chef had laid out all the items for dinner on the counter next to the stove so they could dish up their food buffet style. He stepped back to make room for his hungry friends. Dean and Ashley headed over instantly, Dean letting Ashley go first while he looked over the spread. There were fresh bread sticks, and the pasta was tossed with what looked like more scallops, shrimp, and fresh lump crabmeat in a creamy white sauce. There were also salad greens and a homemade vinaigrette.

"Freddy," Dean said, taking it all in. "You've outdone yourself again."

"Thank you, Dean," Freddy rasped in response. "It always feels good to cook again, and you guys are the only ones who will eat my food."

Bill came over to get in line behind Dean. "I'll keep eating it as long as we do a check to make sure you're not missing any fingers or a random ear or something."

They all laughed at that as Freddy bowed at the comment. "Everything is accounted for paramedic Bill. I checked."

Things quieted down, and everyone made small talk while they ate, or in James' case, drank. Dean focused on eating his fill since he and Brynne were on shift soon. The rest of them could take their time. It was as good as it looked and smelled. He listened to Ashley share some humorous nursing stories from the ER as everyone laughed along. He watched her closely, from where he sat next to her. He'd had girlfriends before. This felt different, though. It was closer somehow. It was intimate already, even though they hadn't slept together yet, well at least not that way. She offered him support in a way that he couldn't define. She had come to his rescue twice now when he had needed it. Oh yeah, and she was freaking hot. He smiled to himself, and she looked his way and winked as if she knew what he was thinking. Maybe she did. He decided he didn't care all that much. Maybe he was joining a new sort of club after all, as James had said.

The cleanup from these meals traditionally fell to the crew coming on shift, and that meant Dean and Brynne, so as everyone was finishing up, they started gathering up the leftovers and putting them in containers so that people could take some home. Freddy had made enough for an army, and there was plenty for all of them to take home a meal for the next day. It was getting close to six, and Bill and Lynne were packing up their gear. Bill offered to give Freddy a ride home, and they all headed out to the parking lot, James walking very quickly to his car and getting behind the tinted windows in the weak evening light of sunset. As old as he was, more than a millennium, James was able to stand short periods of sunlight, if only for a few minutes, though it was painful. Brynne followed him over to his Lexus and leaned in at the driver's window to say goodbye.

Dean walked Ashley out to her car as well. She threw her arms around him and planted a solid kiss on his lips. "I'm proud of you, Dean," she said. "I know it was hard for you to make peace with James." The softness of her lips on his lingered in his mind as she pulled away and climbed into her little classic sports car. "Can I see you after work? I'll bring something for breakfast by your apartment."

"That sounds like a great idea," Dean said. He wanted to see her alone again. He longed for another opportunity to be close to her.

"Great, I'll see you tomorrow and maybe tonight if you bring any patients in to see us in the ER." She started her car and backed out of her spot, driving off with a wave of one hand above the convertible's windshield.

Freddy came out then with Bill. Dean thanked the chef again for his excellent meal. The older paramedic helped the fragile zombie open the door to his SUV and climb inside. Dean watched as they pulled away from the station, and then he went back inside. Brynne followed close behind him. Neither of them saw the black SUV pull out from the street and follow Bill's Ford out of the industrial park.

# Chapter 10

Dean and Brynne had a slow start to the shift. That was good since they had the clean up to do from Freddy's dinner. Afterward, they spent an hour or so doing the regular start-of-shift chores before settling in for the night in the squad room. Brynne was scrolling through her email across the room at her desk, and Dean sat on the couch reading a book on mythological creatures when his phone chirped. He glanced at the screen and saw a number he didn't recognize. Whoever it was had sent him a text. He opened the phone screen with a swipe of his thumb and froze.

"Your zombie friend pays the price for your failure to join us. The Cause."

He was about to go over and show Brynne the message when the alert tones sounded on the overhead speaker. It was followed by the voice of the Dispatcher.

"U-One-Nine-One, respond with the fire department for working house trailer fire. Bystanders report residents trapped inside."

"That's not good," Brynne said getting up and heading to the ambulance bay, she grabbed the printout as it came out of the printer on the way to the ambulance. "Hey, this looks like it's near Freddy's place in the Barrens."

"I was afraid of that," Dean said coming over to meet her at the door. He showed his phone screen.

She read the screen. "Shit," she cursed. "Let's get over there."

A minute later they were rolling out of the industrial park, headed toward the Barrens, the trailer park on the outskirts of town inhabited by many Unusuals, including their friend Freddy. The diesel engine whined as Brynne pushed it to its limits on the night-time city streets. The lights were flashing, and the sirens were blaring from the roof of the ambulance cab to signal their passing. They listened to the radio as the first fire engine arrived on the scene to report the trailer was fully involved. In other words, it was engulfed in flames. The two paramedics looked at each other. If anyone were inside, there would be no rescue at that point. They knew the firefighters would just contain the blaze, keeping it from spreading to neighboring structures, fighting the fire from the outside.

Within ten minutes, they were approaching the area of the trailer park and could see the glow of the fire on the horizon in the darkness. The vents in the ambulance cab transmitted the smell of the smoke as they approached the scene. The flames leaped twenty to thirty feet in the air over the trailer. The fire had burned through the roof and could be seen in the broken windows and through the remains of the front doorway. Firefighters were surrounding the burning structure, using their firehoses and streams of water to control the blaze. Dean checked in with the fire officer in charge over the radio to alert them that the ambulance had arrived.

"Received, One-Nine-One," the incident commander responded on the radio. "Stage away from fire ground. No survivors reported at this point."

"Understood," Dean said grimly. "U-One-Nine-One on location, staging." He looked at Brynne as she put the gear lever in park leaving the ambulance about one hundred yards away from where the firefighting operations were taking place. "What do we do?"

"We get out and set up in case any firefighters need assistance, since we're the only ambulance here," she said. "We don't know that Freddy was inside, and I'll keep hoping until they find his body."

Dean looked around and saw a familiar white van parked off to one side under some trees, also away from the action. "Hey, isn't that Gibbie's new van?"

"It might be," Brynne said. "I wonder if he knows anything about what's going on?" She looked at Dean. "Let's check. Grab the portable radio. I'll get the flashlights out of the utility compartment."

The two paramedics got out of their ambulance and headed over to the white van. There was no one inside it, but it did look like it was Gibbie's van. They walked around it and shined their flashlights in the windows. It was empty.

"You don't think he went in and tried to save Freddy on his own, do you?" Dean asked.

"I sure hope not," Brynne said looking at the fire engulfed trailer. A noise from the trees behind them caused them both to spin around and shine their lights into the darkness. A white-clad figure darted behind a tree there.

Brynne stepped forward, shining her light at the ground near her feet instead of into the trees. "Hello? We're here to help out," she said. "Do you know what happened to the man who was driving this van?"

A small voice came from the tree as they approached. A face peeked around the trunk. "Paramedic Brynne Garvey, is that you?" Dean recognized her. It was Anuja, the fairy girl they met when her sister was struck by a car a week ago.

"Brynne, it's…" Dean whispered.

"I see her," Brynne said to her partner as she turned to answer the girl in the woods. "It's me, Anuja," Brynne said in a calm voice. "Do you know where the man from this van is?"

The girl stepped from behind the tree and pointed to a spot in the woods. "He was injured trying to get into the zombie's trailer. I remembered he helped my sister, and I got some friends and we carried him to the woods away from the fire."

"Show us," Brynne said. "Dean, get the basic bag, oxygen and burn kit. I'll shine the flashlight back toward you so you can follow the beam to me."

"Got it," Dean said. "Be careful." Brynne headed off as Dean turned to get the gear from the ambulance. He loaded up with the bags and came back to the edge of the woods. He saw the light of his partner's flashlight about twenty yards into the trees. He hurried over to where she knelt on the grass next to a large tree. Leaning up against the trunk, moaning in pain was Gibbie. His hands were severely burned, and he held them out in front of him while Brynne assessed them.

"I tried to get him, Brynne," Gibbie cried. "I know he was your friend. I heard the call of a fire and when I got here, I tried to open the door but it wouldn't budge. I could hear him yelling inside, but I couldn't get him."

"The men who set the fire nailed the door shut," Anuja said. "We were playing nearby in the woods when we heard shouts and banging. Two men held the door to the trailer closed while another hammered nails into it. Then they lit a bottle of something on fire and tossed it through a window. I used my cell phone to call the fire department, but they took so long to get here. The vampire arrived first and tried to enter."

Dean noticed other white-clad forms in the trees around them. They must be Anuja's friends. "You and your friends did the right thing helping Gibbie out and finding us, Anuja."

"Gibbie, I'm going to pour some sterile water over your hands to cool them down. They are still warm from the burns," Brynne said. Dean got out the liter bottle of sterile water from the burn kit, handed it to Brynne and then started opening some gauze and rolled bandages. He watched as Brynne poured the water over the vampire's burned and tattered hands. They still had smoke rising from them in places until she poured the water over them. She used some of the gauze pads he handed to her to pat his hands dry and then some others to cover the burns, wrapping the gauze-covered wounds with the rolled bandages.

"Gibbie," Dean said. "I'm going to give you something for your pain. It's only a little morphine, but it should take the edge off of it."

"Dean, it was awful," Gibbie said, tears in his eyes, "I tried to help him. I could hear him yelling inside, and I tried as hard as I could."

"I know you did," Dean said. "Sometimes in our line of work you do your best, but it's just not enough. It is not your fault; it's just the way it is."

Dean opted to give the first injection in Gibbie's shoulder. They could start an IV once they got him back to the ambulance and on the way to the Burn Center. While Dean did that, Brynne keyed the mic on her shoulder from the portable radio.

"Ambulance U-One-Nine-One to command, we have a patient with burns to his hands here. We are going to treat and transport."

"Received One-Nine-One," the fire incident commander said. "Do you need any manpower assistance over there?"

"Negative on manpower," Brynne replied. "We will be able to transport on our own."

She released the mic where it was clipped on her lapel. "Gibbie, can you stand on your own? Do you have any injuries other than to your hands?"

"I can stand up," Gibbie said with a groan. "It's just my hands." The vampire started to stand and swayed on his feet.

"Whoa," Dean said. "Take it easy. Let us help you." He gripped the portly vampire under the arms and lifted with Brynne on the other side, steadying him. Gibbie stood up straight and stayed still for a moment, swaying a little in the arms of the two paramedics, then he steadied himself. He was wearing his uniform outfit they had first seen the other night when they encountered him on the roadside with Anuja's sister, Jamilla.

"Dean, can you handle getting Gibbie back to the ambulance?" Brynne asked. "I want to talk to Anuja and her friends, and I think they'll react better to just me."

"Sure, Brynne," Dean said. "I've got this." He pulled one of Gibbie's arms gently across his shoulders, careful of the bandaged hands. The two of them started back towards the ambulance parked about 50 yards away.

Dean had Gibbie settled on the stretcher in the back of the

ambulance and an IV started by the time Brynne came back to the unit. He was able to get some more morphine on board before Brynne opened the rear doors to check on them.

"I'm good here, Brynne," Dean said. "You can start on the road to the ECMC Burn Center."

"Got it," Brynne said closing the doors on the back of the unit. Dean heard her climb into the front seat and report them as en route to the hospital before she pulled away from the orange-lit fire scene. The flames were lower now that the firefighters had arrived and started to knock down the fire. Dean watched that glow recede into the distance as the ambulance sped off into the night. He turned his attention to his patient. Gibbie was just staring out the back of the ambulance. He was clearly upset, but Dean thought he was lucky to be alive. If the flames were that bad when he arrived at the trailer, he could have become trapped inside trying to rescue Freddy if the door had not been nailed shut. It was ironic that the efficiency of the members of The Cause, (that had to be who was responsible) kept them from catching and killing two Unusuals instead of just one. He still couldn't believe that Freddy was dead.

"Gibbie," Dean said softly. "There was nothing you could have done. The door was closed, nailed shut, if what the fairy girls told us is true. You did your best. If the door wasn't closed, you might have been overcome going inside to rescue Freddy. You're a vampire, and you have some strengths, but you're not invincible."

"I know, Dean, I guess," Gibbie replied. "I just wanted to help out, to do something, you know? Do something heroic, like you and Brynne do."

"I hear you Gibbie," Dean said. "But you have to understand that Brynne and I have a lot of training to go along with our skills. You are trying to do something for which you have no training. That might change soon, though. Hopefully, if all goes as planned, Brynne and I are going to try and get you some EMS training."

Gibbie looked over to him, meeting his eyes. "You mean that?"

Dean nodded. "I do. We do. If you want to continue to help out like you have been, there are rules you need to follow, and training you need to have. We'll help you get that training if you want it. First, though, we need to get you back in one piece."

"I would like that, Dean," Gibbie said. "The training, I mean, I want the training. I like how you and Brynne are giving back to our community. There should be some of us giving back, too."

"I'm glad to hear that, Gibbie," Dean said. "There are some programs out there to offer civilians training in first response and disaster aid. Do you think you could round up two or three others who would like to train alongside you?"

"I think so," Gibbie said. "I just need to get over this first." He held up his bandaged hands.

"It's no hurry," Dean said. "We'll need some time to gather the resources to teach the class. I don't think we can use the regular CERT instructors. They don't know about Unusuals. You get well, and get your list of interested friends together. I'll work with Brynne to figure out how we can get your training done."

"That's great news, Dean," Gibbie said excitedly. "These burned hands won't hold me back for long. I just need to feed and spend some time regenerating. Burns don't heal completely in vampires but aside from some scars, I'll be as good as new in a week or so. It's going to be great! Me, responding right alongside you and Brynne!"

"Hold on there, dude," Dean said holding up his hands. "Part of the training is going to be following a chain of command and knowing when to respond, and when not to respond. If you just show up at the wrong time and place, you can get in our way and cause more harm than good. Let's just get the training squared away, first. Then we can look into how and where we can collaborate."

The conversation continued all the way to the Burn Center. Gibbie was excitedly explaining how he was going to help, and Dean was carefully pointing out how the middle-aged vampire had a lot to learn about how emergency operations worked. The good thing was that the conversation distracted Gibbie from his painful injuries. Distraction was an effective pain management tool, too, Dean reminded himself as he realized they had talked all the way to the hospital. He prepped his patient to take inside as Brynne backed up to the ambulance entrance. Distraction also helped with grief, he thought as he remembered Freddy. Brynne popped open the doors to the rear of the ambulance, and the two paramedics rolled their patient into the emergency department and up to the burn center.

—

SOON THEY WERE ROLLING the newly cleaned and made up stretcher back into the ambulance bay to load it onto the ambulance. As he waited for Brynne to open the back doors, his phone chirped in his pocket. He absently glanced at it and froze. It was a text from Zach.

"I wonder if he knew it was his last meal? You've made your choice, The Cause has made theirs."

Tears of rage and guilt welled up in his eyes. Was this all his fault? Did Freddy die tonight because of him? Brynne noticed his reaction and raised an eyebrow in question. He held out the phone and showed her the screen of Zach's text.

"Damn," she said. "We've got to report this. I'm sure they know that it was arson, but this is a different matter. This makes it some sort of a hate crime. Come on. Let's get loaded up and get back to the station. I want to call headquarters on this and talk to the chief. This cannot go out over the radio."

Dean nodded. This was too volatile to be broadcast over the open airwaves. This was signaling the start of a war.

———————————————

# Chapter 11

———————————————

The next few days were a whirlwind of meetings, investigatory events, and ambulance calls. The Elk City police detective and the fire department arson investigator both wanted to see the text conversations with Zach on Dean's phone. He was worried they might implicate him in some way, but Brynne had looked at them and said he had nothing to worry about. Brynne also told him that James had been in some high-level city meetings about the potential for more attacks and violence directed at the Unusual community. She said James' biggest concern was to maintain secrecy about the community. The Mayor was worried that the Unusuals might take some action on their own part. Their carefully crafted joint society and community was unraveling.

All the Station U crews were pulled together on two different occasions for additional scene safety and situational awareness training. While there was no evidence that The Cause was going to target humans, there was a fear that one of their paramedics would get caught in the crossfire. Ashley told Dean that the hospital had done some drills and there was a constant security presence in the ER now that hadn't been there before. Everyone was very much on edge. Dean had asked if there would be any funeral for Freddy but

Brynne said that there was no body recovered. The zombie chef had burned to dust in his fragile, partially decomposed state. That made him sad. He felt like he needed to do something. He ate the leftovers from Freddy's last meal almost reverently, savoring each bite.

He was just finishing up the last bite when there was a tap at the door to the parking lot. Dean got up to answer it and was stunned to see Freddy standing there.

"Freddy," Dean shouted. "We all thought you were dead."

"Rumors of my demise were slightly exaggerated," the zombie's raspy voice sounded even worse since the fire. He shambled into the room.

Brynne came running over at Dean's shouted greeting and grabbed the undead chef in an earnest but gentle hug. "What happened? Where have you been?"

"I was able to open the back bedroom window after I realized that I couldn't leave by the front door. I lost a few fingers forcing the old window jam to work but I made it out ahead of the fire. I took off for the woods and hid in an old-hollowed out tree trunk for the last few days. Whoever wanted me dead might still have it in for me."

"What are you doing here?" Dean asked.

"I don't have anywhere else to go. That trailer was so beat up and run-down that it was abandoned. That is the only way I could live there," Freddy said. "I was kind of hoping you guys would have some ideas. I could stay here and cook and clean for you guys, kind of keep up the quarters while you all are out on calls."

"Wow, Freddy, I don't know," Brynne said. "We might be able to work something out, but if headquarters ever found out you were living here they'd have a hissy fit over it."

"I'm not really alive so I wouldn't be living here anyway," Freddy explained. "I don't sleep so I could just hang out on a permanent basis, at least for a little while."

Dean looked at Brynne and caught her eye. "A little home-cooked food every shift might be a welcome addition to our station, eh, Boss?"

"I'll have to run this by the other Station U medics before it becomes anything like a permanent set-up," Brynne said. "Still, you can't just be outside in the elements and scaring the residents. You can stay for now."

Freddy gave one of his hideous, gap-toothed grins and moved over to the kitchen area. "I'll whip something up for you both, you will see. You won't be sorry I'm around."

Dean just shrugged and went along, grateful that the undead chef was still around after all. He could tell from the way Brynne stared after the zombie as he shuffled over to the kitchenette in the station, that she felt the same way.

There was some more good news later in that shift. Headquarters approved getting some training together for Gibbie and his newly assembled crew of Unusual first responders. The middle-aged vampire had gathered four other like-minded Unusuals for the class and Dean and Brynne were assigned to do the CERT training. The CERT program was laid out by FEMA, the Federal Emergency Management Agency, and there were grant funds to pay the overtime needed for the instructors. Dean had to admit the extra money was good, and he was excited to share his knowledge with the students in the class. It also felt good to be on the other side of the student-teacher relationship for a change.

---

THE FIRST GROUP of Unusual CERT students was an eclectic group, most strange in some way, just like Gibbie. There was a teenaged female werewolf named Marian Gregory. There were twin Dryads. Dean had learned they were some sort of tree fairies of Greek myth. Wim and Dora were both shy, but said they were determined to do something to help their community. Dean and Brynne were surprised to see a name they recognized on the class list. Kristof Algar, the Djinn, who owned Sabatani's restaurant. He told both of them at the first class session that he wanted to be ready to help a patron or employee at his restaurant in case of an injury.

Freddy joined in the classes, too, and made light snacks for the group while they learned.

They held the classes at Station U rather than the academy, as was usual, so they could talk freely about Unusual topics and work those special discussions into the class structure. The class was held on Tuesday evenings from seven to ten, and it lasted for seven weeks. During that time, Dean and Brynne continued their regularly assigned duty schedule except on those Tuesday evenings. Then they were covered by the day shift crew until ten, when they took over the ambulance again after class. The CERT class was as fun for Dean as he hoped it was for the students. They covered disaster preparedness, fire and disaster medical operations, and some light search and rescue operations. They also covered CERT and disaster response structure and organization.

When the seven weeks of CERT training were completed, the Chief came by the station to award the new Unusual CERT team their certificates and congratulate them on completion of the course. He also told Dean and Brynne that he was encouraged by their initiative in getting this program off the ground for the Unusual community. He hoped this would go a long way to smooth things over after the attacks perpetrated by The Cause.

There had been no other attacks or overt activity since the fire. The intense police and arson investigation seemed to have driven The Cause members underground. Zach had probably destroyed his phone and gotten a new number because they had been unable to trace the other one. The detective told Dean to be on the lookout for new texts and contacts from Zach, or others in The Cause. Dean and Brynne had told the Chief about their suspicions that Mike Farver was involved with The Cause somehow, but nothing had changed there. He was still teaching in the academy. Brynne told him that the Chief and investigators had looked at Mike for a link to The Cause, but there had been no apparent connection to Zach or the fire. If Mike was involved as more than a sympathizer, he had covered his tracks well.

Once the CERT class was done and the investigation had died down, things went back to normal. Dean was glad for the return to the regular routine. Teaching the class had been fun but it was a lot of work prepping for each class. He hadn't been able to see Ashley as much as he wanted either, primarily because of the increased workload for both of them. She was planning on meeting him after the day's shift for dinner. It would be the first chance they had to see each other in over a week. He couldn't wait, but of course he had to. Their date was after his day at work, and soon the tones sounded overhead on the speakers to alert them for the next call.

"Medical Box 634, Ambulance One-Nine-One respond for female overdose patient, 1237 Highpoint Road."

AS THEY PULLED out of the station, Dean put them on the road via the radio, and switched to the med channel to get the additional information from dispatch. The only information the dispatcher had was they were responding for a female in her twenties, discovered unconscious on the side of the road by some bystanders. Dean operated the siren as Brynne wove the ambulance through the afternoon traffic to the scene of the call on a street that bordered a tree-lined park. There were several people around a girl laying on the grass near a tree, next to the sidewalk. The two paramedics grabbed their gear and headed over to her.

"We were doing our daily walking laps in the park," said an elderly man. "We found her laying there in the grass, unconscious. We thought maybe she was a kid who'd had too much to drink last night but we couldn't wake her up at all, so we called 911."

Dean knelt down next to her, smelled the acrid odor of urine, and looked at the large wet patch extending from the crotch in her blue jeans. She was barely breathing so he put a mask with oxygen on her face while he continued his assessment. He checked her eyes and saw pinpoint pupils and excessive tears forming as he was watching. It was weird. It was like it was a poisoning, not an overdose. He said as much to Brynne while he attached the heart monitor, which showed a slow heart rate called bradycardia. He had to wipe her chest and arms down to get the sticky patches to attach because she was so sweaty.

"Let's call the poison center and medical control and get them to check this out. They might be able to help us identify the problem," Brynne said. She pulled out the portable radio and keyed the mic. "Dispatch, patch the poison center and ECMC medical control into this channel for a consult."

They continued to assess the patient while they waited for the radio patch to be completed.

"Ambulance U-One-Nine-One," the dispatcher said over the radio. "You have poison control and ECMC ER on the med channel."

Brynne handed him the radio for the consult. "Poison Control and ECMC," Dean began. "I have an apparent 22 year-old female found unconscious in a wooded park by bystanders. She has a pulse of 42, blood pressure of 90/40, respirations of 6, and pinpoint pupils. She is not alert and has voided urine. There are no overt signs of trauma or drug abuse on assessment. We currently have her on oxygen and an IV established and are preparing to assist with ventilations."

"One-Nine-One, this is the poison center. Is she diaphoretic?" a voice said over the radio.

Dean remembered the sweaty state of his patient when attaching the heart monitor patches. "Affirmative, Poison Center, she is diaphoretic."

"Is there any sign of pesticides nearby? Maybe a can of spray or something like that?"

"No, nothing like that in the vicinity, Poison Control. We are in a park and not near any residences," Dean replied.

"My recommendation would be to administer two milligrams IV Atropine to this patient every five to ten minutes and transport immediately to the hospital for further monitoring and treatment. All the signs point to an organophosphate poisoning," the poison center voice responded.

"This is ECMC medical control," came another voice. "I

concur with assessment and treatment. Recontact as necessary en route."

"Received on two milligrams Atropine IV every five to ten minutes," Dean repeated the orders. "Will transport to ECMC presently."

He looked around and then at Brynne. Organophosphate poisoning usually meant pesticide exposure. "Where did she get into pesticides?" he asked. "I don't see anything around here in the park." Brynne shrugged as she pulled two pre-loaded Atropine syringes from the med bag beside her on the ground.

The elderly man who was one of the couple who found the girl spoke up. "I think they sprayed the trees here last night. We complained about how bad the mosquitoes and other bugs were getting in the evenings," he said. "I don't know how she got in that spray unless she had rubbed the leaves all over her, or spent the night in the tree or something."

Dean and Brynne's eyes met as he said that last bit. Dean nodded. It might not make sense to the older gentleman but it sort of made sense to him and his partner, especially if this girl was a Dryad. The tree nymphs, or wood fairies, were bonded to specific trees in a wooded area and actually lived in them, although Dean wasn't sure how that worked. If she had been inside when the trees were sprayed, it was possible she got gassed by the passing cloud of pesticides from the trucks doing the spraying. It didn't change their treatment, but it confirmed the poison center's initial diagnosis.

Brynne started slowly administering the IV Atropine while Dean went back to the ambulance to get the stretcher. When he returned with it, Brynne was finishing up the first syringe of the drug. He started getting ready to lift the small girl onto the stretcher as soon as Brynne was finished the second syringe, completing the two milligram dose. Together the two paramedics lifted her onto the stretcher and gathered up all their gear, stacking it around the patient before taking her back to the ambulance for transport to the hospital. As they were loading her inside, Dean noticed her starting to stir, her hand coming up to her face to push at the oxygen mask there.

"You're ok," he said, reassuring her. "I'm Dean, a paramedic. We found you next to the trees and think you were injured by a pesticide spray last night." Her eyes fluttered open. He leaned over so she could see him, and smiled down at her. "It's going to be alright."

"I-I feel so tired," she said in a weak voice.

"That's normal," Dean reassured her. "What's your name? Do you remember anything from last night or early this morning?"

"I'm Daphne," she said. "I remember hearing the trucks, but I didn't pay any attention to them. I hear traffic going by my tree all the time. You think it was spraying the trees with something and that's what did this to me?"

"They sprayed for bugs overnight," he said. "The effects of the spray they probably used matches your symptoms. That's our best guess, and you seem to be responding to our treatments for that problem, too."

She nodded and closed her eyes. Dean checked the monitor. Her heart rate was faster and her breathing was approaching normal. He checked his watch and got two more Atropine syringes ready to give her at the ten minute mark. That would be right before they arrived at the hospital. They could treat the symptoms for now, until her body processed the poison out of her system naturally.

▭

THEY WERE MOVING the girl from the stretcher to a hospital gurney when Ashley came into the ER room.

"Hi, Dean. Hi, Brynne," she said cheerfully. "What do we have today?" She logged into the computer workstation on the wall while she talked.

"This is Daphne," Dean said. "She's a Dryad. She was in her tree when a municipal pesticide spraying program blasted her tree with a suspected organophosphate insecticide. She's responded well to two doses of Atropine two milligrams IV. The last dose was just about five minutes ago."

The ER nurse typed the information into the workstation's

health record program. When she was done she looked up at Dean. "We still on for dinner tonight?" Ashley asked.

"I'm looking forward to it," Dean said. "I've got an invitation to Sabatani's from Kristof after he was in our CERT class so I think I'll take him up on it."

"Sounds good to me," Ashley said. "Ok, let me get Daphne here squared away and I'll see you tonight." She winked at him, smiled and turned her attention to her patient while the paramedics rolled the stretcher from the room.

Brynne muttered under her breath just loud enough for him to hear, "If you two get any sweeter when you're together, you're going to give everyone around you diabetes."

Dean chuckled to himself. He didn't care. He was happy when Ashley was around. She made him forget everything that was going wrong in his life. She made him forget The Cause, and Mike and Zach. He just hoped it stayed that way.

# Chapter 12

Dean went right home after work, showered and changed. He looked in the mirror and thought he had done a pretty good job of cleaning up. He had shaved, put on his best jeans, and ironed a long-sleeved gray and white checked button-down shirt. He slipped on his white sneakers, grabbed his keys and headed out to pick up Ashley at her apartment downtown. This was their first real night out in a restaurant that wasn't a diner or a hospital cafeteria. It was a real date, and he wanted everything to be perfect. All of their meetings up to this point had been grabbing a meal before or after work at Hank's Diner, or the coffee shop at the hospital. This date had to be memorable he decided.

He also hoped their relationship moved forward in other ways. The question was, how to approach an angel about something physical like sex? She was an excellent kisser but Dean was about kissed out. He respected her too much to push anything, so he had resolved to be patient. But, it had been eight weeks since they started seeing each other officially. He just couldn't figure out how to approach the subject with her. Ashley didn't seem the one to be all proper, and she had a mischievous streak and a wicked funny sense of humor.

Mrs. Baxter, his landlady, was watering the garden in front of her house when he came down the stairs from his apartment above their garage. She looked over at him and smiled.

"Big date tonight, Dean?" she asked.

"I'm taking my girlfriend Ashley out to Sabatani's downtown," he replied.

"I've seen you two together the few times she's come over," Mrs. Baxter said. "You treat that girl nice, Dean. She's a keeper."

"Yes, Ma'am," Dean said with a laugh. The Baxters had taken him under their wing and often treated him the way he imagined his own parents might treat him, if they had been around, and if they actually cared. He decided he liked the attention.

He got in his pickup truck in front of the house, returned Mrs. Baxter's wave of encouragement, and headed downtown from his residential neighborhood on the outskirts. His landlady had nothing to worry about from him. He fully intended to treat Ashley nice. He thought she was a keeper, too.

The drive to Ashley's apartment took only about 15 minutes, and he pulled up in front of the building where she lived. He was looking for a spot to park when she stepped out the front door, waved and walked over to his truck. He thought he cleaned up nice, but that was nothing compared to Ashley. She wore tight-fitting blue jeans that clung to the curve of her hips, accentuated by the way she walked in the tan heels she wore. Her burgundy top hung loosely down to just above her hips, and she wore a collection of necklaces made of different sized wooden beads that nestled down into the hint of cleavage he could see above her blouse. Damn, she looked nice. Yep, he thought with pride, looking around to see if anyone he knew was nearby to see his amazingly hot date. She was going out with him tonight, and everything felt nearly perfect.

He jumped out and ran around the pickup to open the passenger door for her. She quirked an eyebrow at the gesture, smiled and climbed into the truck. He crossed back around to the driver's side and got in. He checked his mirror and pulled out into traffic.

"Thank you for getting my door, Dean," Ashley said. "I like a man who hasn't forgotten the little things like that of manners."

"Well, it is our first real date night out on the town," Dean said. He glanced over at her as he drove. "You look really nice tonight."

"Thank you," she replied with a demure smile. She rested her hand on his thigh, and he dropped his right hand down to hold it as he drove, steering with his left. It was nice riding with her; it felt right somehow. They continued crossing town to the restaurant district while chatting about their day. Ashley told him that Daphne, the Dryad they brought in to the ER, was going to be fine. The docs were keeping her overnight as a precaution to monitor her, but they expected a full recovery. He was glad to hear it. It had been a little touch and go until they had figured out what was going on. He remarked on it.

"It's funny how much we end up being detectives on the job," Dean said. "We don't always know what's going on, and then you throw in the Unusual side of things. It becomes a huge challenge. I like it, but it leaves me worried about what could happen if I make the wrong decision."

"It's like that for us in the hospital, too," Ashley agreed. "The patients who can talk to us don't always tell us the truth, only what they think we need to know. Sometimes they outright lie to us, even though we are just trying to help them. The unconscious patients are just as much a mystery to us in the beginning as they are for you." She gave his hand a squeeze.

Dean glanced over at her as he was driving. She always offered him a perspective that shored up his concerns in a positive, non-confrontational way. He liked that about her. She genuinely liked helping people. It was one of the things he found so attractive about her. He checked their location and realized they were getting close, so he started looking for a spot to park, eventually opting to use a parking lot across the street from the restaurant. He paid the attendant as they pulled in, and then selected a parking space near the back of the lot. Dean jumped out to help Ashley down from the passenger side, but she had already gotten herself out by the time he got there. He shut the door behind her as she walked towards the sidewalk.

They crossed over to Sabatani's and entered the restaurant. It was bustling and busy, but he had made a reservation directly with Kristof, and he walked up to the hostess station to check in. She looked up and smiled as he approached. It was Anuja, the fairy girl from the roadside accident and the fire scene.

"Well, hello, Anuja," Dean said. "I didn't know you worked here?"

"I have only been here a short time," she said. "Just a few months. It is good to see you under better circumstances, though." She turned to Ashley as she followed him up and nodded her head and shoulders in a quick bow. "Eldara, it is good to see you as well. If you both will follow me, I will take you to your table." Anuja picked up two menus and a wine list and headed into the restaurant, gesturing for them to follow her. She led them to a corner booth near the back and pulled out the table a bit so they could more easily slip into the booth. The fairy hostess slid the table back into place, and set the menus down in front of each of them in turn.

"Your server will be with you shortly," Anuja said. "Enjoy your meal." She bowed slightly to Ashley again before she turned and walked back to her podium at the entrance.

"It's nice dining with royalty," Dean said with a chuckle as he picked up his menu. "I wonder if I treat you in a manner that befits your exalted station."

"Oh, stop it," Ashley said chastising him. "You treat me just fine. The other Unusuals just treat the Eldara that way because there aren't many of us roaming the earth at any given time. Plus, it's rare to have us living among them. They treat us with respect because our arrival often signals some significant event is on the way."

"But you've been living here for what, four or five years?" Dean asked. "That's what Brynne told me anyway."

"I've been here just over five years," she said. "I came at the beginning of the Station U program as soon as I heard about it. I'm a healer, Dean. That is my purpose in the world. I travel around and help human healers navigate through significant events they find themselves facing. Eventually, I will move on to another pending event, to lend help where it is needed."

"Oh," Dean said sadly. He had hoped she would be around for a while.

"Hey," Ashley said. She leaned over and bumped him with her shoulder. "None of that. I'm here now and plan to be for some time to come."

"But, eventually, you'll leave," Dean said.

"Yes, Dean, I'll leave," she said. "But 'eventually' to an Eldara can be a long time."

Dean looked at her, trying to figure out how long she had been on the earth. She must be so old. "Do Eldara, uh, live forever?" he asked.

"Are you asking a lady how old she is, Dean?" Ashley asked with a chuckle. "You should know better than that. Time doesn't hold the same meaning to us as it does to humans and most of the Unusuals. We appear, do our jobs and then transition back to a period of waiting. But the waiting does not pass for us as normal time does, so it as if an instant passes between our assignments."

"Do you talk to God to get your assignments?" Dean asked, curious. He had never been a religious person, but he had been to church on occasion, and his interaction with the patients of Station U had created a curiosity about things bigger than he was.

"No, Dean," she said. "Talking to God is a privilege reserved for humans and mortal Unusuals. It is something special you have. You can have a relationship with the divine that we cannot. We are their servants, their messengers. Instead of talking to God, we get a feeling, a direction to go somewhere or do something. You would call it a nudge. Once there, we must follow our instincts to solve the problems we face, in support of the humans who asked for divine assistance."

"So you're the answer to a prayer?" Dean asked. "I certainly believe it. You're an answer to mine."

"It can be a single prayer, or it can be a collective request for assistance," she said. "I think my presence here is more of the latter. The relationship with you is a nice perk of this particular assignment, though." Ashley slid closer to him in the booth as she went back to perusing her menu.

Dean went back to looking at his menu as well. He was distracted from reading it with her leaning against him. He thought about everything he had just learned about Ashley and the Eldara. He was still thinking about it when the server showed up to check on their readiness to order. Dean hated to make people wait, so he deferred to Ashley while he quickly made a choice of the chicken parmesan over spaghetti noodles with red sauce. He relayed his choice to the server after Ashley ordered the fresh fish of the day in a garlic butter sauce, with capers.

Kristof, the owner, came over as the server left. Dean had gotten to know him very well over the course of the last seven weeks in the CERT class. It was Kristof's invitation to Dean and Brynne that made the paramedic bring Ashley to the restaurant tonight to take advantage of the Firefighter/Paramedic/Police discount he offered.

"Dean," Kristof said as he came over. "How are you? And you bring such exalted company with you? You are truly a lucky man."

"I'm fine, Kristof," Dean replied. "Have you met Ashley Moore, from the hospital?"

"I have not had the pleasure, although I had heard there was an Eldara Sister living in Elk City," the restauranteur said. "My lady, it is a pleasure to serve you and have you grace my humble establishment."

"The pleasure is mine," Ashley said. "It is a lovely place, and I can't wait to taste the excellent food you must serve here."

"I will check back with you later, Eldara, to make sure you were satisfied with your choice," Kristof said with a bow. Some of the patrons, humans obviously, looked in their direction, wondering who Dean and Ashley were to get such treatment.

"Thank you, Kristof," Dean said. "I know the food here is excellent. I'm sure we'll be pleased with our choices."

The owner of the eatery left them to themselves as the waitress returned with their drinks. Dean had ordered a Sprite since he was driving that evening. Ashley had ordered a cosmopolitan.

Ashley raised her glass to Dean as she picked it up. "To a wonderful evening and good company!" she said.

Dean raised his glass and touched it to hers with a clinking of crystal. He approved of her words but wondered what the angel meant by 'good company.' What that all he was?" He took a sip of his soda while he pondered the question.

Their conversation turned to mundane dinner conversation about their days, and then to challenging Dean to see if he could pick out the Unusuals clustered among the restaurant's staff and patrons. He was surprised how his skills were developing. He spotted the vampire and date because she wasn't eating anything, just drinking what looked like a particularly dark red wine. The gentleman with her seemed a little nervous but ate a regular pasta meal. Others he couldn't quite place. He didn't know what variety of Unusual they were, but was pretty sure they were of a mythical nature. Ashley confirmed his suspicions, or told him when he was off track. Overall, he did quite well with that particular game.

Their dinner came, and Ashley raved about her fresh fish, the Branzino, a Mediterranean variety Dean had never heard of. His chicken parmesan was excellent as well, and the two of them fell silent as they devoured their dinners. He offered her a bite of his chicken, and she slid her plate over so he could try the fish. He wasn't a fan of fish, but the Branzino in garlic butter sauce was pretty good. He might even be tempted to order that the next time he was here.

The two of them passed on dessert as their dinners had filled them nicely. When the waitress brought the check by, Dean reached for it out of reflex, but Ashley quickly leaned across the table and snatched the folder containing the check from in front of him.

"Hey," Dean protested. "I've got that. I planned for this."

"I know what paramedics make," Ashley countered. "Besides, I have resources I've set aside over the years. I'm not poor."

"I thought you appreciated an old fashioned kind of guy?" Dean asked. "You complimented me on opening your door."

"There's a difference between good manners on a date and outmoded systems of patriarchal control that makes the man think he always needs to pay the check," she responded. "I have little need for the money I make at the hospital. Let me spend a little on you." She looked over the check, took a credit card out of her purse and placed it in the folder. The waitress came over and took it from her when she held it up. Dean caught a look at the color of the card as Ashley slipped it into the folder with the check.

"Was that an Amex Black Card?" Dean asked incredulously. He had heard of, but had never actually seen the mythical credit card issued by invitation only to the wealthiest of the American Express card-holders.

"I told you, Dean," Ashley said. "I don't have much need of money. I have lived a very long time and accumulated substantial assets. It enables me to do what I do without encumbrances, like needless worrying about finances."

"I feel like I hardly know you, Ashley Moore," Dean said. "Every time I think I have you figured out, you drop another curiosity bomb on me."

"Women like to be mysterious, Dean," she purred as she leaned in close to him. "It is what keeps the men coming back. If you're interested in digging a little deeper, let's head back to my apartment. I have a thing or two to teach you about me."

Dean blushed, which made Ashley giggle and give him a hug. He found himself waiting impatiently for the waitress to return with the check. He wanted to find out what else his angel had in store for him that evening.

## Chapter 13

The buzzing woke Dean from a sound, satisfying sleep. He was curled up around Ashley's sleeping form in her apartment. She woke as he stirred next to her.

"Sweetie," she murmured. "Your phone is buzzing."

Dean groaned and rolled over in Ashley's bed to paw at the top of the night table on his side of the bed. He felt his phone and held it up to squint at the phone's screen in the darkened bedroom. It was four o'clock in the morning. The caller ID said it was his partner, Brynne. He noticed earlier calls listed on the screen from headquarters. He must have missed them. Wiping the sleep from his eyes as he propped up on one arm, he swiped the screen to answer the call.

"Go for Dean," he said as his voice broke a bit with the early morning lack of warm-up.

"Dean," he heard Brynne on the other end of the line. "Where are you? I went by your apartment to check on you after the all-call for Station U from headquarters. You weren't there, and I started to fear the worst."

"I'm fine. I, uh, stayed over at Ashley's tonight," he explained.

"What's up? Why the all-call?" He sat up in bed as he realized that something serious was going on.

"There was a fire at Sabatani's tonight," Brynne said. "It's bad, and I knew you had gone there with Ashley." She paused for a bit. "It was another attack, Dean. An anonymous email was sent to headquarters with a picture of you and Ashley at dinner talking to Kristof. We all thought you might have been there when it happened." Ashley had rolled over in bed, and he felt her warm skin press up against his bare back as she leaned in to rest her chin on his shoulder.

"We're both fine, Brynne," Ashley said. She had clearly overheard his partner's frantic voice coming from the phone in the quiet room. "Do you need us to respond somewhere? Is there a call into the hospital? I don't have anything on my phone." Dean toggled the phone to speaker mode and set it down on the dresser as Brynne answered Ashley.

"Oh, hi Ashley," Brynne responded. "I don't know what the hospital is doing. There are some injuries. Mostly it's smoke inhalation and minor burns. It was late, at the end of the evening, when two men threw Molotov cocktails into the entry foyer. The staff there saw them light the bottles from outside and cleared out the area before they threw the firebombs into the restaurant. The staff were able to evacuate most of the patrons through the back, but Kristof and a few others tried to fight the fire with the restaurant's fire extinguishers before the firefighters arrived. They all had some injuries."

"Okay, well we're fine," Dean said. "Do you still need me to report in?"

"Call in to HQ," Brynne said. "Based on the photo they received, they just wanted to make sure you were safe. The Chief is there, and he'll tell you what they want you to do. I'm glad you're both alright. Sorry I had to wake you."

"No worries, Brynne," Dean said still shaking out the cobwebs in his sleepy brain. "I'll call in and talk to Chief Ari and see what he wants me to do. Thanks for calling. Bye."

He touched the End button on the screen to stop the call and turned to Ashley, momentarily distracted by her naked form lit by the streams of moonlight coming in her apartment windows. Good Lord, she was beautiful. He reached out to stroke her shoulder absently as he thought about the information Brynne had shared with him. Someone had been stalking the two of them, and then firebombed the restaurant where they had been eating. Did that mean they were here, outside as well?

He left Ashley's embrace and padded in bare feet across the hardwood floor of her bedroom to look out the window through sheer drapes to the street below. There was no traffic, and he didn't see anything unusual, but then again, he wasn't sure he knew what he was looking for. He turned to look at Ashley still sitting on the bed watching him.

"You heard everything Brynne said?" Dean asked. "You heard about the photograph of us at dinner sent in to Headquarters after the attack?

"Yes," Ashley said. "You need to call in and tell them you're okay." She picked up his phone and held it out to him. "If you wait too much longer, they might have the police trace your GPS and come knocking here directly."

"Yeah, you're probably right," Dean admitted. He crossed back to the bed, took the phone from her and tapped the screen to call HQ back. He keyed the speaker phone function again so Ashley could listen in. The line was picked up immediately. They must have had caller ID on the line because the voice on the other end knew it was him.

"Dean," the voice said. "Dean is that you? Are you alright?" It was the voice of Chief Ari, the director of EMS for the Elk City Fire Department.

"Yes, Chief. It's me. I'm fine," Dean answered. "I just got off the phone with Brynne. She filled me in on what happened. Do you need me to come in?"

"No, stay where you are," the Chief said. "Just tell me where that is. We want to send a police unit over to check out your location and make sure it's safe."

"Uh, okay," Dean said. He looked at Ashley. He didn't want to involve her in this, but she nodded and mouthed the words "It's okay."

"Okay, I'm at 581 Fremont Street, downtown," Dean said.

"Is Nurse Moore with you as well?" the Chief asked.

"I'm here as well, Chief," Ashley said before Dean could answer. "We're both fine."

"Good, I'm glad to hear it," the Chief responded. Dean could hear the relief in his voice. "You both just stay put until the police get there and check things out. We're still conferring on what to do next. We'll have a plan on how to handle this soon. We're working with hospital administrators, too, since this might involve a member of their staff. Stay put for now. I'll be back in touch when I have more information."

"Okay, Chief," Dean said. "We'll hang tight and wait until you get back to us." The Chief said goodbye and hung up. Dean looked at Ashley. "Well, that puts a damper on a rather nice evening."

"Just 'rather nice?'" Ashley asked with a sly smile. "I thought it was way better than that." She swung her legs off the bed, placing her bare feet on the floor. "I suppose we should get dressed. The police are probably going to want to lay eyes on us to make sure we're alright." She started walking across the floor, picking up the items of clothing she had discarded as Dean had removed them the night before. She slid on her panties and slipped on her bra. Dean started looking around for his clothes in the pile on the floor. Ashley hooked a toe in the waistband of his boxers and flipped them up to him with a flick of her knee. Soon they were both dressed again and sitting on the edge of the bed in the dark room.

"I'm sorry to drag you into this, Ashley," Dean said.

"You didn't drag me into anything," she replied. "I told you. This is why I'm here. This conflict is important. In some ways, it feels bigger now than just a problem in Elk City. There's something else in play here. You're part of it and I'm here for you, but there's more."

"I'm glad you're so confident," Dean said. "I'm kind of freaking out inside."

"I understand that," Ashley said. "I just have faith in something higher. I know that I have a purpose because I've been an instrument of change many times before. I'm not saying it will be easy, or without sacrifice, but it's always been worth it in the end."

"Faith," Dean repeated. "I always thought of that as something some minister on TV talked about. You talk about it as if it's real."

"Oh, it's real, Dean," she replied. Ashley slipped arm around him, gently rubbing his back with her hand. "Faith as tiny as a mustard seed can be used to move mountains. It's true. I've seen it."

"I don't know, Ashley," Dean said, looking into her eyes. "I've never had much faith in anything higher than me. Certainly not like you are talking about."

"That's why I'm here, too," the angel replied. "I'm here to restore your faith. I'm here to restore faith for many people, and you're going to help me."

Dean got up from the bed and crossed to the window, looking outside up and down the street. He didn't see anything this time either but he was worried for their safety.

"Do you see anything?" Ashley asked.

"No, but I'm not sure what I'm looking for," Dean responded. "I'm concerned about our safety. Someone could have followed us here from the restaurant."

"Nobody followed us," Ashley said. She sounded very confident.

"How can you be sure?" Dean asked.

"It's a perk of the job," she said. "The Eldara are hidden unless we wish to reveal ourselves. I wanted privacy, and I have always masked myself when returning here. You were masked with me when we left the parking lot downtown. I'm sure no one followed us."

"What, we turned invisible or something?" Dean asked. He had learned over the past few months at Station U that some things he previously thought were impossible were very possible. But invisibility?

"Not invisible, just… let's just say that we were not worth noticing," she answered. "If someone had looked our way, they would have been distracted by something else as we passed by. I have used that technique for a long time to secure my home. It's habit by now. It's important to have a sanctuary. I've learned that over the years."

"So this is like the 'Bat Cave' or Superman's Fortress of Solitude?"

Ashley giggled. "You're too cute, Dean," she said. "Sure. If you want to think of it that way, then yes. Question, though? If I'm Batman, does that make you Robin?"

"Hey!" he said. The door buzzer below sounded and interrupted his comeback line.

Ashley crossed to the door of her apartment in the living room. Dean followed. She keyed the intercom. "Yes?"

"Elk City Police, Ma'am," the voice downstairs replied. "I'm sorry to bother you. We're looking for a city employee, paramedic Dean Flynn?"

"He's here; we're fine. Come on up." She pressed the door release for a few seconds and then let go.

"If there's some sort of distraction field, how did they find us?" Dean asked.

"They weren't sure they were in there right place, even though you gave the Chief the exact address," Ashley explained. "If I had said that you weren't here and that I didn't know you, they would have returned to their station and reported that they couldn't locate us."

There was a knock at the door. She looked through the peep-hole. "May I see your identification, please?" she asked through the door. She continued to look through the peep-hole and seemed satisfied with what she saw because she stood back and unlocked the door, opening it.

Two uniformed police officers and a detective with his badge showing clipped on his belt stood outside. The detective spoke first. "Detective Kineally," he said showing his photo identification in a flip-open wallet. He slid the ID back in his pants pocket. "Ms. Moore, Mr. Flynn. I'm here to check on your well-being. You were told to expect us?"

"Yes," Dean said. "I talked to my Chief. He told us you were coming. Is there anything we can do?"

"No," the detective said. "I just needed to lay eyes on you and verify you were alright. I'm going to leave Officers Burke and Platt here outside your apartment building for the rest of the night," he glanced at his watch. "As much as is left, anyway. They'll leave when they see you leave."

"Is there any information on who is responsible for the fire?" Dean asked.

"Nothing concrete," Detective Kineally said. "Although, there was a security camera recording across the street that may have seen the individuals involved before they put their masks on. We'll catch them. These types always make mistakes." He looked from Dean to Ashley. "Okay, I've seen you both. That'll satisfy the higher-ups. If you need anything or have any trouble, Burke and Platt here will be just outside in their patrol car."

"Thank you all very much for your concern," Ashley said. "We'll let you know if we need anything." She closed the door and turned the lock as the police officers and detective started to head downstairs to the street.

Dean watched her turn to face him and lean back against the door, striking a dramatic pose. "Oh, I do declare. Here we are trapped in this apartment," she said in a mock southern accent. "Whatever shall we do for the next two hours until we have to leave for work?"

Dean smiled. He was falling in love with this woman. There was no doubt about that. He could feel it more each time they were together. "I'm sure we can think of something Ma'am," Dean said advancing towards her. "Don't you worry. I'm a trained medical professional."

She laughed in delight and ducked under his reaching arms, racing past him back to the bedroom. He chased after her, shutting the bedroom door as he went through it. This was definitely not a Batman and Robin situation.

# Chapter 14

Dean's return to work at Station U that morning was more eventful than he would have liked. The police officers outside of Ashley's apartment followed him as he dropped her off at the hospital, and then continued tailing him until he arrived at the Station. He noticed another patrol car there in the parking lot, although this one was empty. He waved at the officers, who had been outside of Ashley's apartment, as he climbed out of his pickup. He walked over to the station doors, used his key to unlock it and went inside to the squad room.

There was another police officer seated in the station in one of the recliners. He looked up as Dean entered, noticed his uniform, nodded and went back to looking at the tablet computer he was holding. Brynne was already there, and Bill and Lynne were packing up their stuff to leave. Freddy was in the kitchenette whipping up breakfast. It filled the squad room with delicious smells of food that had his mouth watering.

"Hi guys," he said. "Exciting night, I guess?"

"Dean, you have no idea," Bill said. "We've had police following us everywhere since the fire. Luckily we didn't have any calls. I'm afraid we'll scare away some of our patients."

Lynne came over and nodded to the police officer on the recliner. "Officer Waters is here watching the station. His replacement will come by around lunchtime."

Dean went over and the officer set a plate of what looked like a western omelette down to reach up and shake his offered hand. "Dean," he said, "Dean Flynn."

"I recognized you from your photo," Officer Waters said. "We've had people looking for you most of the night. I'm Rick." He picked up his plate and took another bite. "I have to say, you paramedics have it nice here. You have your own live-in chef and everything."

"Freddy is in-between homes for a while, and we couldn't just have him out scaring kids on the street."

"That's for sure," the officer replied. "I'm just glad nothing happened to you. After that photo of you and your date came in to Headquarters following the fire, we weren't sure what had happened."

"We're both fine," Dean replied. "We didn't even know anything was wrong until my partner finally got through to me on my phone. I'm a pretty sound sleeper, so I didn't wake up for the other calls."

Bill and Lynne were headed out to the parking lot to leave, and Rick got up to follow them and check on things out there. Dean looked at his partner across the room after the officer left the squad room.

"What's happening out there, Brynne?" Dean asked her. "This is crazy. Does James know anything?"

She looked up from where she was sitting in front of the computer. "He's been talking to police and fire department leaders, as well as the Mayor. They've all assured him that they will protect the Unusual community," Brynne said. "James isn't taking any chances, though. He has beefed up security for his properties and Rudy has called in outlying members of the pack for additional support." Rudolf, or just Rudy to his friends, was James' second in command for the Elk City area. He was also a werewolf and the pack leader for the region.

"James is most worried that there's going to be an open

confrontation that will get caught on someone's cell phone video and posted on the internet," she continued. "Some of Rudy's pack are making statements that they'll do whatever they have to do to protect themselves. You can't blame them." Her phone chirped, and she glanced at it and froze.

"Damn."

"What?" Dean asked. "Is that James?"

"Yeah. He just sent me some still frames of the surveillance or security video from last night before the fire," Brynne said. "Here, take a look." She turned her smartphone screen and showed him a photo there. Dean instantly recognized his paramedic predecessor in this job, Zach, and some other guy, dressed all in black on a stretch of sidewalk downtown.

"Well, that seals it," Dean said. "If Zach's involved, there's now a tie-in to me." He shook his head and looked away. Was all of this somehow his fault? If he had handled things differently when Zach first reached out to him, would events have turned out differently?

Brynne must've been channeling James' mind reading capabilities. "Hey, Probie!" she said sternly. "This is not your fault. That guy was messed up and he will answer for it. He should have never been put in this job."

"Well, I was supposed to be his messed up replacement," Dean said. "We know that Mike's tied up with this somehow even if the Chief isn't sure. He recommended me for the job. Clearly he thought I would follow in Zach's footsteps."

"And yet you didn't," Brynne consoled him. "You're a good paramedic and a decent guy. Mike miscalculated his play on this one. My guess is that he thought you'd be bitter about being assigned here after graduating first in the class. He probably hoped that would turn you against the patients when you found out who they were. He was wrong, right?"

Dean nodded. Mike might have been right in his assessment about his student being bitter, except that Dean liked a challenge, and the patients here were even more challenging to treat than normal humans. He not only had medical problems to treat, but he also had to wrap his brain around their Unusual nature as part of formulating a plan of care. It also helped that Brynne was so dedicated to her work, and was a good preceptor for him as he continued in his probationary period.

"What turned Mike against this job?" Dean asked. "Based on what everyone says he was the best Station U paramedic there was. I thought he just moved on to the academy as part of a promotion, but now I have to wonder."

"Mike was my preceptor when I started, and later my partner," Brynne said. "There was a point early on where we were getting resistance from the Unusual community about getting treatment from human paramedics and doctors. That changed when I showed up at an accident scene involving James and Rudy. There were injuries, and I handled not only the injuries, but protected their identities and Unusual nature."

"James decided that he needed to take the initiative to introduce the Unusual community to some of us," she continued. "I started shadowing him on his rounds as their leader. I helped manage several tough medical issues that had been going untreated. The stories of what I and the other medics at Station U were doing started to spread through the community of Unusuals and we started getting more calls." Brynne shook her head. "The problem was that James and I became close during that time frame. Mike didn't like it, in much the same way you didn't, but even more protective. He refused to let me live my life, and he eventually confronted James about it."

"That couldn't have gone well," Dean speculated. "What happened?"

"It should tell you how far James has come in modern times," Brynne said. "He listened to Mike's concerns, and tried to explain to him that everything was fine. When the concerns turned to open threats, I turned to the Elk City leadership and filed a formal complaint of discrimination and bias. From what I've heard, Mike didn't even deny it. But, he'd been on the job too long, and had too many friends in high places, so he didn't get fired. He was sent to the academy under the pretense that he was burned out from the streets. Unless he does something overt, his job is protected by the union, so unless he screws up again, he'll retire there. The good news is that he's an excellent instructor. You certainly turned out okay."

"Yeah," Dean thought aloud. "He's a great instructor. I thought the best of him and respected him."

"It's hard when you realize that your heroes are human, Dean," Brynne said. "I used to respect him, too. I guess in some ways he still has a lot to offer to emergency medical services as an instructor. But he's also a bigot, and he's mixed up in this whole thing somehow. As long as he works at the academy and headquarters, he's got a pipeline of information about what is going on, and he can funnel that info to Zach and others in The Cause. The Chief suspects it, but can't convince Mike's other friends at HQ and City Hall of that fact. So, he stays - and more importantly, he stays in the loop."

They just stood in silence for a few moments until the quiet was broken by the police officer's return from the parking lot.

"All set out there," Rick said as he came into the squad room. "You guys mind if I put something on the TV? We don't usually get to watch the tube during the day shift."

"As long as it's not 'The View,' I don't care," Dean joked. He looked at Brynne. "I'll get started on the shift checks on the gear and the ambulance." She nodded and went back to her work on the computer. Dean went into the ambulance bay still thinking about how screwed up this whole situation was. All he could do, all he had the power to do, was to keep his head down and do his job. Ashley seemed to think that, at some point, him doing his job was going to be the thing that shifted the situation here in Elk City one way or the other. She had told him that he just needed to keep doing what he was doing, and when the time came, he'd know the right thing to do. It was a good thing she had such faith in the higher order of things. He only had faith in her, but maybe that was how it was supposed to be. Still he wanted to be out of his probationary period and be a full paramedic.

He started in on the medication checks, looking at expiration dates and counting to make sure they had the right amount. He always thought such redundancy was pointless. He knew Bill and

Lynne had done the same thing in the last hour of their shift to make sure everything was stocked up before they left for the day. But, he guessed that being careful and methodical was part of the job, so he kept on going. He was finishing up that job when the first call of the day came in over the ceiling speakers.

"Medical Box 724, Ambulance One-Nine-One, respond for emergency maternity at 1267 Ridge Road," the dispatcher's dispassionate voice said over the radio.

Dean zipped up the last bag he was checking and stowed it back in its compartment. He was climbing down from the back of the ambulance and shutting the doors when Brynne came in from the squad room. As usual she headed to driver's side, and he turned and went around to climb into the passenger side of the cab. He put the ambulance on the street with dispatch via the radio as she pulled out through the parking lot and then activated the lights and switched on the siren. Then they sped off to the call.

Dean was excited. He'd seen a baby delivered during his hospital rotation, but this might be his first chance to deliver a baby himself. It was surprisingly rare for paramedics in most systems. Most mothers made it to the hospital before the baby was ready to come. Now and then, though, they got the opportunity to assist in a birth. He shifted in his seat as Brynne drove, running through the important steps he remembered about the process of childbirth in his mind.

THE LOCATION WAS in the Barrens trailer park, part of the large community on the outskirts of which Freddy had lived in his broken-down trailer. Brynne parked in the gravel lot near their location. The narrow dirt roads between the trailers didn't allow enough room for the ambulance to navigate safely. They needed to bring everything they might need in one trip, since they didn't want to walk back to get anything in the middle of an emergency.

Brynne pulled out the stretcher from the back of the ambulance while Dean started gathering bags and equipment and stacking it on top. They had the heart monitor, drug bag, pediatric bag, two maternity kits, and the oxygen and airway bag, plus Brynne grabbed an extra set of sheets and a few towels from the cabinet in the back. When they both had done a mental check of everything, they locked the ambulance doors and started around to the trailers down one row. Brynne knew her way around here pretty well, but they didn't need to find their way alone. An older woman was waiting by the wooded lane between the mobile homes for them as they approached.

"Good day, Paramedic Brynne," the woman said with a slight bow, saying the name almost as a title of nobility. "Our midwife is away tending to another birth, and we have need of your services once again."

"Dean, this is Helena Beche," Brynne said, introducing the woman. "She and her husband August are the leaders of the Barrens community. Helena, this is paramedic Dean Flynn."

"Greetings Paramedic Dean," the woman said, again with a slight bow. "Please come with me and I'll show you to the girl. I fear her time is near."

Dean grabbed the rear of the stretcher while Brynne took the head end. They guided it carefully over the uneven ground as they followed Helena down the narrow lane between the trailers. Dean could see occasional faces peering out from behind curtained windows, and sometimes a child peeking from behind a tree, but there was no one but the three of them out and about which was strange considering the midmorning hour.

"Where is everyone?" Dean asked aloud, wondering about the lack of activity.

"Yes, Helena," Brynne said. "I can't help but notice that your folk are not out and about their business on a beautiful day like today."

"They are still very wary after the recent events, Paramedic Brynne," Helena said. "They are afraid of doing anything to draw attention to themselves after the fire set here by the human attackers. It is bringing back stories the old ones tell of the days of fear and intolerance of many years ago in the Old Country."

Dean pictured old black and white movies with angry mobs chasing monsters with torches and pitchforks. Clearly there was still a strong cultural memory of that persecution. These people had faced it all simply because they were different. The homes in the Barrens were largely inhabited by the Fae or fairy folk. They possessed none of the strong defensive survival traits that other Unusuals, like vampires, werewolves, and similar predatory types exhibited. The Fae's existence relied on their ability to hide and blend into their surroundings.

The trio continued to walk down the gravel pathway between the rows of mobile homes in the trees, until they came to one where a man with a worried look on his face stood on a small wooden porch outside the front door. Helena called to him as they approached.

"Erich, I have brought the paramedics including Paramedic Brynne Garvey," she said, gesturing to Brynne and Dean. "You know of her abilities as a healer. She will help your wife with her birth."

The man bowed deeply, relief showing on his face as they approached and started up the three steps to the porch and the front door of the trailer home. The paint was faded and peeling on the door, and Dean noticed that several of the boards on the porch floor looked like they were rotted halfway through. He and Brynne grabbed a load of gear from the stretcher they left parked outside on the grass, and picked their way carefully up the steps and through the door inside.

There was a woman on a beat up, brown couch, groaning and breathing heavily. She was obviously pregnant, and her belly's size suggested that she was near full term. A new contraction gripped her as they entered, and she grabbed at the arm of the couch tightly with one hand while the other clutched at her stomach. She let out a howl of pain. Dean checked his watch and noted the time the contraction started. He was supposed to take the lead and he stepped forward, setting his bags down next to the couch and kneeling next to the woman, taking her hand in his. Brynne started taking some of the gear out of the bags behind him.

"Ma'am, I'm Dean Flynn," he said. "I'm a paramedic. This is my partner Brynne. Can you tell me your name?"

"I'm Nura," she said through gritted teeth. The contraction must have started to subside, and she relaxed a little.

"Okay, Nura," Dean said in a soothing tone. "We're going to help you out. How many weeks pregnant are you?"

"Forty-one," she said. "I'm very ready to have this child, Paramedic Dean." Nura managed a weak smile.

"How many times have you been pregnant before this and how many times have you carried the babies to full term?" Dean asked. Brynne was putting a blood pressure cuff on Nura's free arm and starting to take vital signs.

"This is my fourth time with child," Nura said. "I have been past forty weeks with each one. All three of my children were born strong and healthy, Paramedic Dean. I wish the same for this one." She bit off the last word with a groan and released his hand as she clutched at her belly again. Dean checked his watch. It had been just over two minutes since the last contraction. Things were moving fast. Brynne was taking care of the gear and getting vital signs, so Dean continued to focus on the pregnancy and imminent delivery.

"I need to check and see if the baby is coming yet, alright?" he asked. Nura just nodded. The woman was wearing a nightgown, and he lifted it up. She was not wearing any underwear, and as the contraction progressed he looked at her vaginal opening, watching as about a four-centimeter circle of the top of the baby's head appeared, as the woman's uterus pressed the baby down into the birth canal.

"She's crowning," Dean said to Brynne. "I can see the head. She's not breach."

"Good," Brynne said. She was now attaching the sticky patches for the heart monitor to Nura's chest and abdomen. "You've got this Dean. I'll have your back. Remember she is Fae, so the biggest thing is to make sure the cord doesn't get tangled on the baby's wings."

He shot her a glance and realized she wasn't kidding. Dean looked back to his patient. "Nura?" he asked. "Do you feel like you have to push?"

Nura nodded as the contraction faded. Dean looked down and watched as the head disappeared back up into the birth canal a little bit when the contraction passed.

"Okay Nura," Dean said. "Before the next contraction, Brynne is going to start an IV to give you some fluids if you need it. I think this baby is going to come very quickly. You are almost there."

Dean quickly put on his gloves and opened the maternity kit they had brought. Mom would be his patient, and when the baby was born, he would hand it off to Brynne while continuing to focus on the mother. He laid out the contents of the kit on the floor next to him using the big plastic wrapper as a drape to keep the contents off the floor. There was a soft, rubber bulb syringe for suctioning the baby's airway, a pair of umbilical cord clamps, a pair of sterile scissors for cutting the cord, and a large absorbent pad with a plastic backing that he unfolded and slid the edge up under Nura's buttocks. This would help catch some of the fluid and secretions during birth. There was also a paper gown for him which he slipped his arms through and pulled up to his shoulders. It closed in the back, but he didn't bother to try and tie it behind him, just snugging it up over his shoulders. He also donned a paper face mask with a clear plastic eye shield jutting up from it. It would do the job of covering his face and eyes during the birth.

"Nura, with the next contraction I want you to bear down and push with it, okay?" Dean said. His patient nodded. She immediately let out a groan, signaling the coming of the next contraction. Dean knelt between the woman's outstretched legs and watched as the top of the baby's head appeared again. "I see the head, Nura, keep pushing," he encouraged.

The baby's head suddenly popped through the expanding vaginal opening, and Dean grabbed the bulb syringe from the packaging on the floor next to him. As Nura relaxed when the contraction eased, Dean used the syringe to suction out the baby's mouth several times, then doing the same with each nostril. The baby's skin was still pale and bluish and showed areas covered with the white pasty vernix that coated and protected newborns' skin in the womb. He looked at Nura.

"Nura," he said. "The head is out so the next push should finish the birth." She nodded and groaned as the next contraction came along quickly. She hunched forward around her abdomen and began to push again. Dean tilted the baby's head downward gently, working with the mother to ease the top shoulder out for delivery. It popped free as did the lower shoulder when he eased the head upward. Then the baby stopped, amniotic fluid leaking out around the baby's form. This was odd, he thought, quickly assessing the situation. His experience and education told him that once the shoulders were through the birth canal, the rest of the baby just sort of slid out. Something seemed to be holding things up.

"Remember the wings," Brynne said quietly, encouraging him to think it through.

Dean looked at the baby as it was wedged one shoulder up and one down in the vaginal opening. He gently manipulated the head and upper body forward to his right to look at the baby's back. As he did so, the tops of a pair of wings appeared. They looked paneled like a butterfly's wings might when folded and wet. There, pulsing across the top of the wings, where they attached between the shoulder blades, was the umbilical cord. He hooked a finger under the cord and eased it over the top of the wing tips and the baby slid free into his grasp followed by a gush of the remaining amniotic fluid. He used a towel that Brynne handed him to dry off the baby, wrap it and hand the newborn baby girl off to his partner now kneeling next to him. The baby started to cry almost instantly, which brought a smile to his face. The cord still extended up into the mother, remaining attached to the placenta.

He looked up at Nura and said, "It's a girl, Nura. Everything looks good."

The mother sagged back into the couch cushions, exhausted from the effort of birth. Dean looked over at Brynne, who was wiping the complaining newborn and putting the tiny diaper that she fetched from the pediatric bag on the baby. Dean picked up the two plastic umbilical cord clamps and attached them about five centimeters from the baby with about two centimeters between them. He looked around for the father who was standing just behind him. He picked up the scissors.

"Dad?" he asked. "Would you like to cut the cord?"

He nodded and leaned forward over Dean's shoulder, taking the scissors, and with a few sawing cuts, severed the tough cord connecting the mother to baby. He handed the scissors back to the paramedic as he stood up. He had a rather pleased grin on his face. Brynne had finished wiping and drying the baby and now that the cord was cut, handed her up to her mother who had pulled down her nightgown off her shoulders to nurse her newborn baby girl. Dean knew the skin to skin contact and early feeding solidified the bond between mother and baby, plus the early breast milk was rich with immune system boosting antibodies and nutrients from mom.

"Good job, Dean," Brynne said, clapping him on the back. "You just delivered your first baby!"

Nura looked at him, gratitude shining from her eyes. "Thank you, Paramedic Dean," she said. "With your permission, I would like to name her after you."

"You want to call her Dean?" he said in surprise.

Nura chuckled quietly. "No, Dean is a boy's name. We shall call her Flynn. That is also your name, is it not?" she asked pointing to his nameplate pinned on his uniform shirt.

"I would be honored," Dean said, taken aback by the gesture.

"Flynn it is," the father announced. "Come, we must celebrate!" He crossed the small living room into the kitchen and opened a cabinet. He took out an earthenware jug followed by four pewter mugs. He poured some of the amber liquid from the jug into each of the mugs and brought them over, two in each hand. He offered one to Helena, one to Dean, and one to Brynne, keeping the last for himself.

"To baby Flynn," the proud papa said. "May she grow up to be a paramedic and serve as well as her namesake." He raised his glass in salute.

Dean looked at Brynne. She smiled. "Just a sip, Probie," she said. "This stuff is overpoweringly strong. Trust me, I know." She raised the mug and then took a sip before setting it down on a nearby coffee table. Dean copied her motion and took a sip, surprised at the sweet taste and pleasant burning flavor of the Fae beverage. It didn't taste that strong, but he knew better than to doubt Brynne's instructions. He nodded to the father, and then set his mug down next to his partner's on the table.

He turned his attention back to his patients and marveled at the tiny, newly unfolded wings, drying in the air, extending from the baby's back. Nura had pulled up a blanket to cover most of Flynn's body, but left the upper back free to give the wings room to quiver and twitch as the baby nestled and nursed at her mother's breast. He pushed a button on the heart monitor to take another blood pressure and briefly checked under her nightgown to see if the bleeding had stopped. It had. Her blood pressure was slightly elevated at 136/90, but that was likely due to the excitement of the recent childbirth.

Dean set to cleaning up some of the mess from their equipment and supplies. He heard the father talking to Helena saying how excited he was to see the birth of the baby. Apparently, the regular midwife pushed all the men from the room when their wives were giving birth. Dean got the impression that Erich was going to be the talk of the community's other fathers, since he had been present at the birth of his daughter.

Brynne asked Nura if she thought she needed to go to the hospital to get checked out.

"No, Paramedic Brynne," she said. "There is no need. The baby is healthy, yes?" Brynne nodded, and Nura continued. "I am fine as well. We will be alright here at home."

"Okay, Nura," Brynne said. "You can always call us back if you or baby Flynn have any problems." She looked at Helena to make sure she had also heard and understood.

"I will be staying with her until the midwife returns, Paramedic Brynne," Helena said. "We will call you if we need further assistance before then."

Brynne seemed satisfied because she started to disconnect the IV line from Nura's arm and detached the sticky pads from the heart monitor. Dean continued his clean-up as well. The maternity kit came with a red biohazard bag for the purpose of gathering all the soiled trash and waste from the birth. He finished up as Brynne was done packing up the rest of the gear. He did one last check around him for anything he had missed and then stood.

The two paramedics picked up their bags and equipment and headed out to their waiting stretcher outside. Saying a final goodbye to the home's occupants, they started the trek back to their ambulance.

"Congrats, Dean," Brynne said. "That was your first birth, right?"

"Yep," he said. "It was pretty amazing, I have to say. It's much different than just watching from across the room like I did in clinicals at the hospital."

"Yes, it is," Brynne agreed. "You got to also witness the birth of the first fairy paramedic."

"What, you think the mother was serious?" he asked.

"The Fae take such pronouncements at significant events very seriously," Brynne said. "I wouldn't be surprised if we see her application come through the academy in eighteen years or so."

Dean thought about that as he and Brynne got back to the ambulance and put their gear away. He climbed into the passenger side and got on the radio to put them back in service. Then he looked at Brynne.

"Where will she put the wings?" he asked.

"What?" Brynne said.

"In her uniform, when she's a paramedic," Dean said, clarifying his thought. "Where will she put the wings?"

"Ah," Brynne said with a wink as she put the ambulance in gear and started to pull away from the trailer park. "Don't you know by now, Dean? Girls never give out their secrets. We all have our ways to do what we want to do, even fairies."

# Chapter 15

Dean spent the rest of the day glowing with a sense of accomplishment and euphoria that he had never felt before. While he had seen childbirth, even witnessing it up close in his hospital rotations while in the academy, participating in it and physically holding that newborn in his hands left him feeling emotions for which he was unprepared. Brynne seemed to humor him, at least she didn't chastise him when he kept bringing the whole scene up again and again. To top it all off, they had named the baby after him. It was like having a child of his own. Well, sort of.

He had never really thought about having a family before. His relationship with Ashley was great, but he got the sense that Eldara didn't reproduce, or at least not like humans did. They had the equipment, of that he was certain, but he thought that was more likely so they could mingle with humans without attracting attention. Dean thought he should ask Ashley about her background and learn more about her, but whenever he did, she changed the subject back to him. She always said that she was fascinated with humans and that learning about them never got old for her.

Dean hopped out of the ambulance when they returned to the station, and helped Brynne back the vehicle safely into the ambulance bay. She hopped out when she was done and plugged in the landline power cord to keep things charging inside while it was parked. Dean went to the storage closet to get a new maternity kit to replace the one they had used at the scene. When he came back out, Brynne was standing there holding something for him in her outstretched hand. It was tiny and flashed gold in the overhead fluorescent lights.

He reached out and took it from her to examine. It was a small gold stork pin. The stork was in flight, and had a wrapped baby suspended from its beak. He looked at Brynne, he had noticed a similar pin on the breast pocket of her uniform next to her name tag.

"You earned it, Probie," she said. "Good job back there. You did everything right, and we were rewarded with witnessing one of the miracles of life that we medical professionals have the rare privilege to see." She took the pin back from him and stepped up to pin it on his pocket next to his name tag, just like hers.

Dean looked down at his uniform shirt. The tiny pin made him feel proud. He took out his phone and snapped a selfie, pointing to the pin. Brynne laughed as he took the picture.

"What?" Dean said suddenly self-conscious.

"Oh nothing," Brynne said. "You kids and your selfies." She walked away shaking her head, chuckling to herself.

"You're just jealous," Dean said to her as she walked away. "I already looked good in this uniform. Now I look even better!"

"Yeah, yeah," she said without turning around. "Finish restocking and get your documentation done, Probie. We could get another call at any time." Brynne pulled open the door to the squad room and left Dean standing in the ambulance bay with a silly grin on his face.

Dean looked at his phone, examining the picture and then sent the photo and a text message to Ashley. "I delivered a baby! Woo Hoo!" he wrote. He knew she was working and wouldn't be able to text back right away, so he climbed into the back of the ambulance and started putting the replacement supplies away. His phone buzzed after a bit, and when he looked at it, he saw a photo of Ashley giving a thumbs-up. He smiled and put the phone back in his pocket. He couldn't wait to tell her about how he felt, but that would have to wait until they were both together and alone. It was good to have someone who worked in the medical field and with Unusuals to talk to after stressful days. He decided it was just as important to have someone with whom to share the victories.

He finished up the restocking and went back into the squad room seeing the police officer still parked on the recliner where they had left him. Dean had forgotten about the events of the previous night in the midst of the delivery of the baby. Now it was all front and center again.

The cop looked up and gave him smile. "I understand congratulations are in order, Dean," he said. "Kudos, and better you than me. I never want to do that. One of my fears is I'll pull a speeding car over and find a pregnant mother inside ready to deliver. I'm glad it was you and not me."

"It was awesome, Rick," Dean said. "You should have been there. The mother was already starting to push when we showed up."

"La, la, la, la," Rick said, putting his fingers in his ears and talking to cover up the sound of Dean's voice. Dean and Brynne started laughing. Even Freddie chuckled a little from over in the kitchen area. Cops were weird. They were simultaneously a lot like paramedics and yet completely different from them at the same time.

"How can you guys run around doing the things you do all day long and not be ready for this type of thing? You're not the only police officer I know who's squeamish and can't stand the sight of blood," Brynne said. "What's up with that?"

"You guys are the ones who signed up for the blood and guts," Rick said. "I wanted to protect people from bad guys. That's all. Heck, that's why I'm stationed here right now."

"And you're doing a fine job," Dean said, laughing.

"Yeah," Brynne agreed, smiling. "Let us know if we can get you anything."

"Well, I am a little hurt you didn't call me and ask if you could bring me a coffee from the donut shop."

"What and no donuts to go with it?" Dean said.

"I hate donuts," the police officer said. "They give me heartburn."

"You must be the exception that proves the rule, then," Dean observed.

"Cops like donuts for the same reason you do," Rick said. "They are portable and quick to order. You don't get your hopes up for a sit-down meal and then get another call that makes you miss your dinner. Donuts are grab and go."

Brynne walked over from the desk. "So, for future reference, what do you prefer instead of donuts?"

"I love a nice bagel with cream cheese," the police officer said. "Simple, classic and easy to eat on the go."

"I'll file that away for the next time," the female paramedic said. "We will be getting lunch in a little bit. I wonder what Freddy has in store for us?"

Rick looked over to where she was pointing and nodded. "Another gourmet meal for the hardworking paramedics at Station U, I'm sure."

They all laughed as Dean sat down at the computer to start writing up the birth of the baby at the trailer park. He had to document it as two patients, but the system allowed for that in cases of pregnancy he found. When he selected the drop-down menu for emergency maternity, it asked him if there was a delivery and then later popped up a separate window to document the baby's condition. He linked it to the call number from dispatch, and it asked him if he wanted to tie his report to the one Brynne had already started. She had done a report based on her patient care for the newborn. The system was well-designed, and he was able to finish both reports in a pretty short time frame.

He pushed back from the desk and looked around. This was his station and his job. He knew he was lucky in many ways. First, he was lucky to be in a job he had always wanted to do. Second, he was lucky that job was rewarding in ways that he could never have believed before he started here at Station U. Finally, it had led him to good friends in his colleagues and especially in Ashley. He had had girlfriends before, but the link to Ashley was stronger than he had ever felt before. Was it something to do with her Eldara nature and powers? He didn't know what it was that she could do. When he asked her, she just said she was there to support and help him. She seemed to be able to sense when he was in trouble, and find him when he needed her.

Dean pulled out his phone and looked at the photo she had sent him in response to his earlier text message. Her smile and the twinkle in her green eyes both filled him with warmth and more than a little desire. He wrote a hasty text message offering to make dinner that night for her at his place. She worked until seven, and he was off at six. He said they could eat at about eight. He slid the phone back in his pocket knowing she'd respond when she got a chance. He keyed open his email and worked on checking up on medical updates sent out by headquarters to all the paramedics to keep them up to date on their knowledge.

The phone buzzed in his pocket, and Dean stopped reading the article on closed head injuries. Pulling his phone from his pocket expecting a message from Ashley, he was surprised by a text message from Gibbie, their self-appointed vampire first responder.

"Dean, if you're available, call me. I have a problem - Gibbie."

Dean paged through his contacts and tapped the number to call his former CERT student. The vampire picked up immediately on the other end.

"Dean, thank God you're available," Gibbie said in a frantic tone on the other end of the phone. "I've got a problem, and I think I'm going to need you and Brynne."

"Okay, Gibbie," Dean said. "Calm down. Shouldn't you be calling 911 if you need us?"

Brynne turned around in her desk chair to look at him as she overheard the phone conversation. She quirked an eyebrow at him in question. Dean held up a hand as he listened to the voice on the other end of the line. He hung up the call as he stood and put the phone back in his pocket.

"I think we need to go," Dean said. "Gibbie's gotten himself into a situation and needs some assistance."

"What does he need?" Brynne asked, getting up. "We can't just go joyriding around in the ambulance every time a friend needs help carrying some groceries or moving some furniture."

"I'll fill you in on the way," Dean said as Brynne followed him into the ambulance bay. "Suffice it to say if we don't help him out, it could end up as a dispatched call. We'll call it a prevention detail."

THE AMBULANCE DROVE down the residential street, Dean watching the street numbers on the mailboxes tick by. They had gone out on the road, notifying dispatch that they were on a public service call, such as when they helped an elderly patient who had fallen out of a wheelchair, but had no injuries.

"It's that one," Dean said, pointing at the ranch-style house set about fifty yards back from the road on the left. The mailbox read thirty-two, matching the address from Gibbie's cell phone GPS map.

"I think there's an alley around to the back of that row of homes," Brynne said as she drove past the house. "That will be our best bet. There's his van parked across the street."

Dean saw Gibbie's beat-up white van parked on the right as they drove by. It marked the location and also seemed a little out of place parked in front of homes with well-manicured lawns. Brynne continued past it and then turned down a side street that led to the rear of the homes on the left. That led to a narrow alley that Brynne expertly pulled the ambulance into, driving down the lane. Dean was glad they hadn't seen anyone. This was the kind of neighborhood whose residents would come to see why an ambulance was at a neighbor's home.

There were tall fences along the backyards here and detached garages. They drove until they were even with the back of the rancher they had noted from the front. Dean checked the map that Gibbie had sent him by text link.

"This should be it," Dean said. He keyed the phone function and dialed the vampire's number. He put it on speaker phone so Brynne could listen in, too.

"Dean, I can hear your engine. I'm in the back yard in the princess house," Gibbie said.

Brynne looked out her window. She could sort of see over the fence and saw the top of the plastic playhouse castle in the backyard nearby.

"I see it, Gibbie," Brynne said. "The question is how we get you out of there. The sun's pretty high. You're going to get burned pretty badly if you just run for it."

"I'll get out and see if the gate's locked," Dean said. "If it isn't, I can bring you a mylar rescue blanket to wrap up in. That should keep the sun off of you."

"Oh, Dean, you're a Godsend," Gibbie said. "I'm afraid some kid's going to come out and play back here and find me. Then what am I supposed to do?"

"Just hold on and let me see what I can do with the fence," Dean said. "Be back in a sec."

He left the phone with Brynne to soothe the frantic, trapped vampire while he checked on the gate. The fence was a six-foot tall wooden palisade style with a wooden gate in the middle of it. Dean walked over to the gate and tried the outside latch. It opened, and the gate swung inward a little when he pushed. He pulled it closed and returned to the driver's side of the nearby ambulance. He climbed on the step outside the driver's door as Brynne put the window down.

"Gibbie," Dean said through the window. "The gate opens. I'm going to get the rescue blanket and bring it to you, but you be ready to high-tail it out of there. I don't want to get caught having to explain why I'm trespassing in someone's yard."

"Okay, Dean," Gibbie said over the speakerphone. "I'll be ready."

Dean stepped down from the driver's step and went to one of the back cabinets that opened to one of the first aid bags. He dug around and pulled out a folded mylar emergency blanket in its plastic wrapper. He opened the plastic and took the shiny silver folded packet over to the gate, opening it again. He pushed it open enough to slide through, looking up the back yard to the house. He didn't see anyone in the windows, but that didn't mean there wasn't someone watching. He scanned the large yard and saw a plastic playhouse castle for small children. He jogged over to it.

"Gibbie," he said. "Are you in there?"

"Yes, Dean," the voice from inside said.

"Here," Dean said. "Here's the mylar blanket." He held his hand in the window closest to him and saw a pale, meaty hand snatch it from him. "I'll be back in the ambulance. The back doors will be open for you. Hurry up."

"I'm coming, just let me wrap up," Gibbie said from inside.

Dean headed back to the ambulance, opened the back doors and barely had a chance to step aside when a silver reflective shape zoomed past him into the back of the ambulance. He laughed even though he was startled and shut the door. He walked back over and shut the gate before climbing back in the passenger side of the ambulance. The paramedic looked down the passage to the back of the unit to see the vampire sitting there, wearing his improvised first responder uniform shirt and pants.

"Thank you so much, Dean and Brynne," the chastened vampire said.

Brynne spoke up first, glancing over her shoulder at the vampire in the back as she drove back around to the front of the homes. "Gibbie, we need to talk about this. What was the first thing we talked to you about in your CERT training?"

"Scene safety," the vampire said quietly.

"That includes situational awareness," Brynne said. "Like knowing when the sun is starting to come up. How many hundreds of years have you been a vampire? Isn't that Vampire 101?"

"I thought you older vampires were able to withstand some sunlight for a short period of time?" Dean asked.

"That might be true for those as old as James," Gibbie said. "I'm only a few hundred years old, and I'd have been a flaming mess by the time I had gotten to the van."

"Well that's good information to know," Dean said. He thought Gibbie was a flaming mess most of the time.

"Gibbie," Brynne said. "What did we say to you about free-lancing like this? You can't just be out trolling for emergencies to take on."

"I'm allowed to be out driving around if I want. I just got out to patrol on foot and enjoy the night air," Gibbie said defensively. "I have some training, and I would not do anything that I didn't know how to do. I know the most important thing to do is to call 911 and get you guys on the way. But I also know that in the meantime, I could be making a difference with a patient, if only keeping them calm and telling you what's going on when you get there."

"That might be true," Dean said. "But if you're going to do this, you need to make sure you are back in your van and safe before sunrise." He looked outside as Brynne pulled the ambulance up next to the driver's door of Gibbie's van. "We're here. Your van's out the side door of the ambulance."

"Thank you again for rescuing me," Gibbie said. "I promise. I'll be more careful next time."

Dean heard the side door on the ambulance open and close and saw a flash of silver as Gibbie dashed into his van, closing the door, hiding behind the tinted windows. Dean waved as Brynne pulled away.

"Get on the radio and put us back in service, Dean," Brynne said. "We've done our extra good deed for the day."

Chapter 16

The next few days were routine. There were the normal sick calls
and a few minor injuries, but no further attacks from The Cause.
That was a relief to the paramedics of Station U. Dean and Brynne
moved to night shift for the weekend and they prepared for the
increased activity in the Unusual community that always brought.
And then they sat and waited as all EMS crews did. The police
detail at the station had been pulled after a few days, but everyone
was still on edge. Brynne had said that James was spending most of
his time, as leader of the Unusuals in the Elk City region, tending to
the concerns from his community about the human attacks on
them. Some wanted to move away. Others wanted to take some sort
of action to protect themselves and their loved-ones. It was four
hours into the shift on Friday night when the first call came over the
speakers in the squad room.

"Medical Box 843, Ambulance One-Nine-One respond for an
animal bite, 1259 Hopewell Road," said the voice over the radio.

Dean jumped up from the couch where he was sitting watching
TV, and followed Brynne out the squad room doors into the ambulance bay. He climbed into the passenger seat and called into HQ

over the radio to put them responding. As they sped off through the night, Dean looked over at Brynne.

"Animal Bite?" he asked. "What do you think? Maybe a lycan attack?"

"Possibly," she said, concentrating on the road ahead in the darkness. "Do me a favor. Text James and tell him that we have a possible lycan bite. Give him the location. He'll know what to do." She gave him the number as he pulled out his phone.

Dean sent the text message and James responded almost immediately. "I've been monitoring the scanner. Rudy will meet you there," the Vampire texted in reply. Rudy was James' second in command and, as leader of the area werewolf pack, he would be able to handle any rogue lycans in the area, if that was what this was.

They continued to the call, on the road leading to a suburban residential district that was bounded by a large patch of woods on one side of the road and homes on the other. There was a crowd of ten to fifteen people on the lawn of the home at the specified address as the ambulance pulled up. Dean jumped down, looking around carefully. If there was a rogue lycan around, he didn't want to get surprised by anything. He grabbed the trauma bag from the compartment and started across the lawn to the group of people huddled around a teenaged boy of about sixteen or seventeen sitting on the grass. He was holding his arm left arm in his lap. It had a very savage bite that had torn skin and muscle open to the bone on that forearm.

"Excuse me, folks," Dean said. "Let me through." He pushed his way through the group of mostly teenagers and knelt down next to his patient. The bleeding was bad, but the bite must've missed the arteries in the arm because there was no spurting blood. He quickly pulled out an absorbent gauze pad and handed it to the boy. "Here, press this on the wound. Tell me what happened."

"I was just hanging out with my buds here on the lawn. Then this wild dog came out of the woods across the road and just attacked me. Then it took off and ran back into the woods. It was weird."

"You weren't just minding your business," an angry voice came from across the yard. Dean looked up and saw a group of girls huddled around another figure on the grass there. Was there another patient?

"Brynne," he called to his partner walking over from the ambulance with some more gear. He pointed to the other group he hadn't seen at first. "There's another victim."

"She's not a victim," the boy in front of him said with a laugh. "That's just Leeann. She is just upset because we were talking to her. She doesn't like it when we talk to her."

Dean finished assessing the bite. It was serious but isolated to the forearm. The absorbent trauma pad he had applied was impregnated with a rapid clotting formula, and the bleeding stopped almost instantly. He wrapped the pad in place with a roll of gauze.

"Stay here while I go check on the girl," Dean said. "I'll be right back."

"Don't worry about her," the boy who was bitten said.

"Yeah, she's just strange. You know, weird, and begging for attention like she always does," said one of his friends standing around in the group.

"Well, I need to check on her. You're fine for now. Sit still. I'll be back in a minute." Dean got up and started across the yard to where Brynne was kneeling next to a girl of thirteen or fourteen, seated on the ground sobbing with a few other girls sitting next to her. They had their arms around her. Brynne was talking to her, asking questions.

"What happened, sweetie? Are you hurt?" Brynne asked. She held the back of her hand out in front of the girl's face, and Dean realized she was revealing the normally invisible tattoo that only creatures with exceptional vision in the ultraviolet spectrum could see. He had an ink stamp of the same emblem that he applied regularly to do the same thing. The girls all stopped their talking for a moment staring at the back of Brynne's hand and then up at her face. They looked over to Dean as he approached, and he held his right hand up to his chest, exposing the back of his hand to them as well.

One of the older girls leaned in and whispered, "Bobby and his friends are always giving Leeann a hard time when she walks home from her babysitting job up the street. This time, they got in her way and wouldn't let her walk by on the sidewalk. She was crying, and when one of the boys, Jeremy, grabbed for her arm, she screamed. That was when the …" She paused and looked around to make sure no one else was nearby but their group. "… That was when the wolf came out of the woods and bit Jeremy. He bit him until he let go of her," she whispered.

"And all of you are her …?" Brynne asked looking around at the group of girls.

"We're her half-sisters," the oldest girl said. "We're the Dryads of these woods. Her father and our mother live in a home in back of the lane across the street."

"Do you know the lycan who attacked the boy?" Dean asked quietly.

"He lives in a shack back in the woods," another of the sisters said. "Mom and Dad say he's just a hermit, and he has never bothered anyone before."

"And I'll make sure that he doesn't do something like this again," a voice suddenly said behind Dean. He spun around in alarm. The paramedic swore because he had just looked behind him, and no one had been there. Now he saw a tall man with broad shoulders, his scowling, bearded face lit by the porch lights of the house nearby. The girls saw him and all bowed briefly with a nod of their heads.

"Rudy," Brynne said. "Did you hear?"

"Yes, Brynne," the tall man said. Dean realized this must be Rudy, the werewolf and second in charge of the Elk City Unusuals. "I know the man they speak of. He is a gentle one, and I cannot believe he would have taken any action unless the girl was in some sort of danger. But he cannot go around biting anyone. Especially not right now. Have you administered wolfsbane to the boy?"

"Not yet," Dean said. "I wanted to get the full story first."

Rudy growled. "Please make sure you do so. I do not want such impulsive and rude scum like that boy in my pack."

"I'll get to it right away," Dean said. "Brynne, can you give me an idea of the dose? It's not exactly in the protocols."

"I'll come with you and help you out," his partner said, rising from where she knelt among the group of girls. "Leeann, I will be right back. You stay here with your friends."

The two paramedics went back to the ambulance and opened the contingency kit. It was a black Pelican case stored in its compartment with various antidotes and protections from Unusuals for the paramedics and their patients. Dean knew that he had received a series of vaccinations when he started the academy that covered the various blood borne pathogens he was likely to encounter on his job. That included protections against vampire and werewolf bites. Of course, they didn't call the vaccine that. It had been hidden in the fine print of his vaccine series as "other vaccines as determined by the Elk City Fire Department." Brynne pointed to a vial nestled in one of the foam cutouts in the container. Dean looked at it and saw it was Wolfsbane Extract for IV/IM use.

"Start an IV so it'll get into his system faster," Brynne instructed. "That will be quicker than a shot in the arm. The dose is five milligrams. That is just five milliliters since the concentration is fifty milligrams in fifty milliliters."

"I don't like that kid," Dean said. "He doesn't think he did anything wrong when he accosted that girl with his friends."

"We don't get paid to like them, Dean," Brynne admonished him. "We just get paid to treat them."

"Yeah, I know," Dean replied. "I hope he's afraid of needles, though."

Dean took the vial from the case and closed the contingency kit. He walked back over to the where the boy, Bobby, and his friends sat or stood on the lawn. Brynne headed back over to the girls. Rudy was nowhere in sight.

"Bobby," Dean said as he walked up to the group of boys. "I'm going to have to give you some fluids and some medicine to help with your injury. Your friends can stay with you for now, but I need them to back up a bit."

The teenagers stepped away from Dean's path as he approached and knelt down in the grass next to his bags and his patient. He opened up a bag of IV fluid, inserted the IV tubing and primed the fluid down to the end of the tube. Then he got out his supplies and handed his small pocket flashlight to one of the boy's friends.

"Hold that and shine it on his arm while I do this," Dean said. The other boy nodded as he took the light from the paramedic. He turned back to Bobby. "Don't move."

"Okay, Bobby," Dean said. "You're going to feel a pinch." He picked up the IV needle and inserted it into a vein in his uninjured arm. He attached the tubing and made sure the fluid flowed freely before he drew up the wolfsbane extract in a syringe and administered five milliliters of the preventative medicine into the IV tubing, flushing it through with the fluid from the bag above it.

"What's that?" Bobby asked in a smart-assed tone. "You have to tell me what you're doing. You can't just give me medicine without telling me what it is!"

Dean was liking this kid less and less. "You got bit by a wild animal. You could get very sick from that bite, so I'm giving you something to combat the germs you might have gotten from the bite. They'll probably give you more at the hospital when you get there."

"So it's some sort of antibiotic?" One of the boys asked.

"Yep," Dean said. "Something like that." It wasn't technically a lie even though the preventative treatment was more like a vaccine from a plant extract than a traditional antibiotic. He cleaned up his mess, so he didn't leave trash from his EMS kit on the lawn and repacked his bags. He looked over at his patient.

"Do you think you can walk to the ambulance?" Dean asked.

"The damned dog bit my arm, not my legs," the boy snapped at him.

"Okay, then," Dean said evenly, not reacting to the kid's temper. "Let's walk over there and we'll get you situated in the ambulance. We need to take you to the hospital and get that arm looked at. At the very least, you're going to need some stitches." He stood and waited for Bobby to stand, too. Then the two of them walked to the waiting ambulance. Dean watched the boy carefully, not wanting him to fall if he suddenly started to faint from loss of blood or the adrenaline draining from his system as the night's events calmed down. Brynne came over and grabbed the gear bags from Dean as he climbed up behind his patient. She closed the door behind him.

Once inside, Dean had Bobby sit on the stretcher, and he buckled him in place using the stretcher straps. He hung the IV bag from one of the fold-down ceiling hooks. Then he sat down in the chair at the head of the stretcher and picked up the iPad mounted there to enter information into his patient report. It would automatically send the information to the computer system for the department, and he'd be able to finish it back at the station.

He heard Brynne climb in up front and then felt the ambulance start to move on the way to the hospital. He hooked up the blood pressure cuff to his patient's good arm and pressed the button on the monitor to automatically take the vital signs from that device. As it pumped up, he briefly counted the boy's respirations and noted that value. Bobby was lucky that it was just his arm that was injured. The doctors would probably be able to stitch things together again and with some physical therapy, he'd be back to being his normal jerky self in no time. It was a shame there was no cure for that.

Dean thought about Rudy and his response to the situation. If the Unusuals were starting to be proactive with any perceived attacks on their kind, it could turn into a bloodbath, especially if the vampires and werewolves decided to start taking direct action. The werewolves were rumored to be more hot-headed, but the vampires were the true apex predators in the Unusual population. If they started trying to hunt down members of The Cause to take retribution, it could be bad. The police and City Hall would not be able to ignore such attacks on humans.

Maybe that was what The Cause was trying to get to happen, he thought, some sort of race war. If the human government had to take some sort of action, it would drive the Unusuals underground or risk exposing them all to the human community. They'd be forced to move away or be discovered living among the general population. Dean pondered this all the way to the hospital, interspersed with answering the questions from his patient about where they were and how close they were to the hospital. Brynne would have some things to say when he told her about his thoughts on the escalating situation. She could warn James, if he hadn't thought of it already.

He felt the ambulance turn up and onto the ramp for the hospital. He disconnected Bobby from the equipment and patient monitor while Brynne backed them in and was ready to help the boy up and walk him into the hospital. Dean wondered if there would be more werewolf bites to be dealt with in the near future as they walked the boy inside to get his arm tended to.

## Chapter 17

When Dean and Brynne returned to the station from dropping Bobby off at the hospital that night, they were greeted by James and Rudy in the parking lot. The two Unusual leaders were leaning against James' silver Lexus parked between Brynne's Nissan hatchback and Dean's pickup. Brynne backed the ambulance into the ambulance bay with Dean's assistance and then she went to let the two men into the squad room, leaving Dean to restock the gear. He didn't have much to grab since the supplies he used were relatively easy to carry. He strolled into the squad room to hear James talking to Brynne and Rudy.

"… I know there needs to be some restraint, but we can't go around completely defenseless either," the vampire leader said.

"James," Brynne explained. "This incident tonight had nothing to do with The Cause and their vendetta against you all. This was just some teenage boys acting like jerks. It was wrong and definitely assault, mind you, but it wasn't a terrorist incident." They all nodded to Dean when he entered the room from the ambulance bay and kept talking.

Brynne looked at Rudy. "Did you find the lycan responsible for the bite?"

"I did," the werewolf leader said. "It was Old Ebner Cutress. He's mostly harmless and keeps to himself. He doesn't even come to pack meetings anymore. I or one of my other pack-mates check in on him once a week or so to see if he needs help or anything. I honestly didn't think he could change anymore. It takes a lot of strength and older lycans can die trying to change once they reach a certain age and frailty."

Dean was surprised to hear that particular piece of information. He guessed it made sense, given the few painful transformations he had witnessed.

Rudy continued. "I talked with Eb about what happened. He said he's been out for several nights and witnessed the girl coming home past the boy's house. The boy usually just talks trash to her about his manhood, but tonight he had some friends with him, and it apparently made him braver. When the boy grabbed the girl and she screamed, Eb said he just got mad at them. He knows he shouldn't have shifted like that. And he should not have attacked the kid, but he didn't do any lasting harm and the boy let go, which is all he wanted him to do."

"You told him that he can't ever do that again, right?" James said to his lieutenant.

"I did, but not before he said the same thing to me," Rudy said.

"Wait a minute," Dean said. "This guy attacks a boy, nearly bites his arm off, potentially infecting him with Lycanthropism and all that's going to happen is the werewolf gets a slap on the paw?"

"Dean," Brynne said, laying a hand on his shoulder. "This is being dealt with through the proper channels."

"The Pack will pay the boy's medical expenses, anonymously of course," Rudy said. "You were able to administer the wolfsbane extract in time to keep the transformation virus in check, and continued infusions at the hospital will complete the cure. The old man was defending a girl being attacked and maybe eventually raped. He used an appropriate level of force, a single bite that succeeded in freeing the girl, and then he left. It was he who called 911 and alerted authorities that it was a Station U call."

"Based on all of that, Dean," James said. "We, Rudy and I, believe that it was justified to defend the girl."

Dean just looked at the two Unusuals standing there. He wasn't sure what he expected to happen, and sure, the boy was a colossal dick, but that didn't excuse what happened. Or did it? He wasn't sure. He was again tied up by his intense dislike of James. Rudy, he hardly knew, and he seemed an alright sort of guy, aside from willingly taking orders from James. Was he taking his dislike of James out on this situation?

"Dean," Brynne said. "What if the old guy had come out and told the boys to let go of the girl and hit Bobby on the arm with a baseball bat, breaking his arm in the process but getting him to let go?"

"I suppose that might be better," Dean murmured.

Rudy spoke up. "Dean, I've known Old Ebner all my life. He's never bitten any human, ever, to my knowledge. He was extremely upset that he had to do so this evening. He said the boys ridicule him and make fun of him all the time. He knew that if he came out in human form that they wouldn't listen to him. This was the only way he could think of to protect the girl and get her to safety. I trust him. You and I don't know each other very well, but I tell you and give you my word, it was a measured, calculated intervention to protect that girl, nothing more."

"And he's never bitten anyone before?" Dean asked. Rudy nodded. A thought occurred to him and he blurted it out before he could stop himself. "How do you all reproduce if you don't keep biting new people every few years?"

Rudy laughed out loud, his baritone voice filling the squad room. "How do you think? We have babies like everyone else."

"But …" Dean started, shocked by the werewolf's response.

"The virus inhabits our cells and gives us the ability to change," Rudy said. "It passes from mother to child but doesn't manifest until near the end of adolescence. We usually homeschool our teenagers for that reason. If you think average teens are bad, lycan teens are outright dangerous. Sometimes, a person is infected by a bite from one of us who is unable to control themselves, or has gone rogue for one reason or another. In those instances, if we can't get to them with wolfsbane extract in time, we shepherd them through the transformation and bring them into the pack."

Dean thought for a moment, and another thought came to him. "So it can also be sexually transmitted? Like other blood borne pathogens? How do you protect humans from that?"

"We take giving someone our disease very seriously, Dean," Rudy said. "We either date amongst our pack or nearby packs, or we take precautions. There are a few lycan/human marriages out there. Most are pretty successful, but the human spouse is vaccinated against Lycanthropy just like you and Brynne are."

"Wow, I guess you do learn something new every day," Dean said, taking in all he had learned. "Of course, on this job that is an understatement."

"Dean," Brynne said. "The bottom line is the boy's going to be okay. The investigation is proceeding and the girl is going to be alright, too."

"I talked with the police chief myself," James interjected. "He agrees with the self-defense argument. He also has sent a police unit to interview the girl and the other boys who were there. I don't think she or her parents want any trouble in the neighborhood, which is why they will not press charges. But the detective is also going to have a talk with the boy's parents and impress upon them that his assault on the girl could be sent to the district attorney for review based on the initial statements from Bobby, his friends, and the girl. Hopefully, the harassment ended tonight."

Dean thought about what James had said. Did he have to be so reasonable? Dean wanted to think of him as a monster and not some benevolent leader who took good care of his community.

"What about the next time?" Dean asked.

"What next time?" Brynne countered.

"I heard you when I came in," Dean said. "You were talking about this as a response to The Cause. So what will happen the next time someone steps out of line with an Unusual? That's what you all are worried about, right?"

"It is," James said. "There are some in our community who

think we should be more actively defending ourselves against attacks from The Cause. The attempted execution of Freddy was what woke many of the community up. He is well-liked in the Barrens. There's a fear that we will be exposed and openly hunted as we were during the middle-ages before we went completely underground and lived in hiding for the last several centuries."

"That won't happen," Dean said. "This is America. You can't just hunt people because they're different."

"Can't you?" Rudy said, leveling his gaze at the paramedic. "It wasn't all that long ago that, in parts of this country, the death of a person of a certain color was looked upon as no different than killing an animal. What will those same closed-minded humans do when they see there are monsters and nightmare creatures living among them now?"

Dean was uncomfortable because he knew they were right. Even now, more than fifty years after the civil-rights movement of the nineteen-sixties, there were strong racial tensions in the United States. That tension boiled just under the surface in some places and boiled over when racially-charged situations occurred. What would happen when a whole new minority group was exposed living among them? He just shook his head.

"This program is proof that those racial and prejudicial under-tones are changing," Dean said. "We are giving Unusuals medical care right alongside humans. It's working."

"But we're not doing it openly, Dean," Brynne said. "It's all hidden from their view because of what they might say or do if they knew the truth."

"You know it can't stay hidden forever," Dean said.

James nodded. "There have been times when the secret has been exposed in history. Some places and times were more enlight-ened than others in their response. Our fear is that in the current American xenophobic outlook towards foreigners, there will be a political backlash. Right now, only the President, House and Senate leaders, and national security and military leadership know about us. It is a closely guarded secret. I presume that the same or similar is true in other modern countries. At least that's what I've heard."

"We can't risk having something blow up here in Elk City exactly because of the successes of the Station U paramedic programs," James continued looking from Dean to Brynne to Rudy. "Do you understand, Rudy?"

"I understand and I'll do my best to control the pack," the werewolf said. "You should know there are those who want us to patrol and search for Zach and all his accomplices."

"I would like nothing more than to do that myself," James said. "I'm afraid that we can't afford the public outcry, and the back-channel outcry that would happen if we did that. I've assured the police chief, and the mayor, that we will abide by all laws and rely on their investigation to progress to a successful conclusion."

"I certainly hope they do so soon," Rudy said. "Eventually, The Cause is going to attack somebody who can defend themselves. And if they do defend themselves, it will likely be in a spectacular fashion. When that happens, all hell is going to break loose. Speaking of which, I need to check in on a few of my more hot-headed pack mates to make sure they know I'm watching them. Shall we go, Boss?"

James nodded in agreement. He leaned over and kissed Brynne goodbye, nodded to Dean and followed Rudy out the door to the parking lot.

Dean waited for the door to close and said, "I still don't know what you see in that guy."

"He grows on you," Brynne said. "I didn't think much of him at first either, but I've seen him working with his people and he cares deeply for them. It was that interaction that showed me what he was like under all the brooding vampire exterior."

"If you say so," Dean said. He felt like he needed to change inside. He wanted to be more like the kind of guy that Ashley thought he could be. She thought it was important that he and James come to some understanding. Maybe tonight was a beginning of that. He was included in the plans and the back-channel discussions for a change. They had listened to him, and been patient with him when he didn't understand something.

He still didn't like James much, but he was starting to feel something else. It took him a while before he recognized it as a sort of respect growing in him for the vampire's leadership and restraint. It couldn't be easy to stand by and let the humans take over the investigation and protection of his community. He and his other leaders were certainly powerful enough to deal with a problem like The Cause on their own. Of course, it would be a bloodbath, which would be a win for The Cause and a loss for the Unusuals. James understood that and was working hard to keep a rein on his followers, and let the regular human channels of justice work through the problem.

Dean's thoughts shifted back to Ashley, as they so often did since they'd started seeing each other. There was still the feeling she had expressed that he was somehow supposed to be the lynchpin of this situation's resolution, and that James would also be involved. It was annoying she wasn't able to tell him more. But she didn't communicate directly with her higher powers. At least not like Dean and Brynne did over the radio to dispatchers. All she could tell him was that he and James needed to get along, and that he would need her support through all that was coming. It was the fact that he hadn't reached the conclusion of this quest yet that made him most nervous. He was starting to think that something awful had to happen first. Something even more awful than what had happened to Freddy or the restaurant. Something that was going to happen soon.

# Chapter 18

The next several nights had a few chest pain calls, a couple of respiratory distress calls, and a mummy who needed rewrapping with fresh bandages. Dean chuckled to himself as he thought back about that last one. He had certainly come a long way to think that fixing the bandages on an ancient Egyptian mummy was a normal EMS call.

The work was followed by a few days off that coincided with a break for Ashley, so the two of them took advantage of their time off to leave town for a few days. Ashley wanted to go to a mountain lake a few hours away to the west. She had a nurse friend who had a cabin there that they could use for a few days. Dean was looking forward to a break from the tension in Elk City. Everyone, including all the paramedics, waited for the next attack by The Cause. Local police were trying to track Zach and the other arsonist down, but they had no luck so far. It would be good to get away from Unusuals and work for a change.

On his first morning off Dean looked around his apartment and double checked his duffel bag. He had his razor and other essentials, a couple of changes of clothes, and a pair of swim trunks. Ashley was picking him up in her MG, as she insisted his pickup truck was not appropriate for a vacation road trip. His phone pinged, and he glanced at it. Ashley was downstairs in the driveway. He grabbed his wallet, duffle, and phone. He locked the apartment door behind him and headed out to meet his girlfriend for a much-needed trip away.

HE HAD to admit that traveling in the small vintage sports car was a joy. The top was down and the sunny day made it perfect travel weather. He looked over at Ashley. She insisted on driving, saying that no one but her had driven the car since she bought it new over forty years before. It reminded him that she was older than she looked. The funny thing was that she didn't act that way. She had a joy for life and a vivaciousness that matched her apparent mid-twenties age, rather than her near immortal age. He supposed that her joyful response to everyday living was part of what drew him to her. She was the most down-to-earth person he had ever met, which was strange given her true nature was anything but down-to-earth.

He watched her as she headed west on I-70. Her ponytail was pulled up through the back of the baseball cap she had put on which served to keep her hair from blowing in the breeze as she drove. The nursing lamp logo on the front of the cap fit her as well as any sports team's logo would. Her sunglasses covered her green eyes, but he could imagine them twinkling with delight at being out on the open road. It was difficult to talk with the top down, but he didn't mind. It was nice just to enjoy the view as they drove, listening to Ashley's choice of what she called "Classic Road Tunes" on her phone plugged into the modern car stereo system she had installed in the dash.

He had to admit the songs were awesome for their road trip. The current tune was Tom Cochrane's "Life is a Highway." That seemed particularly appropriate. He was on a highway in his life right now, and he was driving it, though sometimes it seemed to be driving him. He thought of what life had driven his way recently in the way of Ashley, Brynne, his new career, and the unique patients he had the privilege to care for. It wasn't what he had expected, but it was certainly something he was glad to have in his life now.

Ashley flipped up the turn signal, and Dean looked over as they exited the highway. They were at the exit for the lake and should be at the lakeside cabin soon. He didn't know what to expect, but Ashley had said they'd have all the comforts of home. It was rustic in its setting only. That was fine by him. He had never understood why people camped when there were perfectly good hotels nearby. He enjoyed the outdoors but didn't look forward to sleeping there, at least not when there was a place with a solid roof and walls nearby. He watched as they drove down into a mountain valley, and he could see the lake, reflecting the sunlight in the distance. Their cabin was on the lake itself, and was supposed to have a boathouse with a couple of canoes and a small fishing boat with an outboard motor. They were going to have a great time here.

After about ten minutes, she turned the car down a tree-lined road that turned into a gravel lane at the end. A moment later they were pulling up to a quaint cabin set among the tall pines that bordered the lake. Dean looked around as he got out of the sports car. It was cooler in the shade of the tall trees. It was quiet, too. The soft pine needles that blanketed the ground meant their footsteps made virtually no sound as they walked from the car with their bags, to the front porch of the cabin. There were a few wooden chairs on the porch facing the lake, and he saw that they were positioned to watch the sun setting over the lake in the evenings.

Ashley put the key in the lock and opened the cabin's front door. She giggled a little with delight as she walked inside and spun around, her hair flying out behind her as she turned. "This is perfect," she announced. "I so needed to get away for a few days." She reached over and pulled Dean to her embrace. Dean dropped the bags he was carrying and wrapped his arms around her.

"We needed to get away," Dean agreed, planting a kiss on her lips.

"Yes," she agreed, "We did." She broke the embrace and pulled him towards the stairs. "Let's check out the upstairs. There's supposed to be a skylight in the bedroom."

Dean was barely able to reach behind him and push the door closed as she tugged his arm to follow her up to the bedroom. "Shouldn't we grab the bags and bring them with us?" he asked as he followed her.

"You can come down and get the bags later," she laughed. "I have plans for you first."

Dean shrugged and left the luggage behind. He wasn't about to argue with her. He liked it when she had plans for him.

▭

IT WAS GETTING dark when Dean returned downstairs to get their bags. He padded across the darkened room grabbing their two bags, his gym duffel bag, and her small wheeled carry-on suitcase. He snagged her purse and his cell phone from the counter, too. He paused to lock the door and look outside. He stopped when he saw a gathering of forms in the shadows of the trees. They looked human, but all were facing the house as if waiting for something.

"Uh, Ashley?" he called.

"What, Sweetie?" she answered from upstairs. "My purse is down there on the floor near my suitcase I think. Can't you find it?"

"I found it," Dean said. "I'm talking about the guests we have out front." He heard her walk across the wooden floor above to the front windows. Dean watched as the gathering forms outside all looked up suddenly, and one smaller figure in the group, a child he thought, pointed up to where Ashley must be looking out the window.

"Oh, I see," he heard her say. "I'll be right down." He waited in his shorts, standing there watching the crowd of about fifteen outside. They weren't doing anything, just standing there watching the house. It was kind of creepy. He turned as he heard Ashley come down the stairs. She was putting her hair up in a ponytail again, and she had pulled on her jeans and her t-shirt though she hadn't put on her shoes. She tossed Dean his t-shirt and pants.

"Here," she said. "Get dressed and we can go out. This must be a reception from the local Unusual community. I wasn't sure who all lived up here, but they are likely traditionalists, so leave the talking to me."

"Is everything ok?" Dean asked as he pulled on his jeans and slipped his t-shirt over his head.

"Oh, it's fine," she reassured him. "They're most likely the Dryads and Naiads of this valley, the forest and water nymphs, and based on their simple clothes, have probably been living up here in these mountains for hundreds of years. They must've seen us arrive, and I didn't mask my aura, so they probably recognized me right away. I just need to talk to them and introduce you. That's all." She opened the door as he finished zipping up his pants. "Shall we?"

Dean nodded and followed her out onto the porch of the small cabin. When they emerged, the group in front of them bowed. A young girl came forward with a bundle of fresh-picked wildflowers. She handed them to Ashley, her eyes wide and then scampered back to stand behind a woman who must be her mother. A man next to the woman stepped forward.

"Greetings, Eldara," he said. "I am called Thomas. We are honored with your presence among us. Please tell us the reason for your visit and we will endeavor to assist you in your mission."

Dean watched as Ashley smiled and raised the bundle of flowers to her face, inhaling the fragrance. "My mission here is to enjoy the peace of your forest, vale and lake," she said, looking at the trees surrounding the cabin. "It is truly a beautiful place. You are all to be commended for your excellent stewardship."

The group bowed. Dean realized they must be in awe of having a being of their myths among them. He wished he could see the light, or the halo, or whatever it was that supposedly surrounded her. It must be beautiful.

The little girl tugged on her mother's dress, "Will she tend to Zora, Mama?" She looked from her mother to Ashley.

"Hush, child," her mother said and then returned her attention to the Eldara standing in front of them. "I apologize for the child's impertinence, Eldara. She does not yet know her place."

"There is no need for an apology," Ashley said kindly. "Who is Zora? If there is something I can do to help, I will try."

The dryad woman bowed. "She is my eldest daughter, Eldara. She was caught as a tree was felled by humans. Her injuries are severe."

"Wait here," Ashley said to the group. "I will go with you to see her and do what I can to help her." She turned to Dean and gestured for him to follow her back to the cabin as the group waited under the trees outside. Once inside she spoke.

"Dean look upstairs and see if you can find a first aid or emergency kit. This is the vacation home of an ER nurse, so I'm sure she has stocked up on some supplies somewhere. I'll look down here." She started towards the bathroom under the stairs while Dean headed up to the bedroom. He arrived at the top of the stairs to what was essentially a loft above the first floor of the small cabin. There was a small built-in closet against the far wall, and he checked there first. It was empty other than coat hanger hanging on the rod, and a few spare blankets on the shelf inside. He turned and checked under the queen sized bed in the center of the room, as well as in the chest at the foot of the bed. Other than a few more blankets, a pillow, and some DVDs, there was nothing.

"I found the first-aid kit!" Ashley called upstairs. Dean came back down.

"There was nothing upstairs but a few blankets and a spare pillow," Dean said as he returned to the first floor.

"Erin is an old trauma nurse," Ashley said holding up a zippered gym bag. "I knew she would have squirreled away a disaster kit, or medical supplies of some kind. Everything we will likely need is in here. Come on."

Dean followed her out the door as she returned to the group of Unusuals clustered in front of the cabin. She walked up to the little girl still holding onto her mother's skirts and knelt down to the girl's level.

"Will you and your mommy take me to see your sister?" Ashley asked. "My friend and I will do what we can for her, if it is within our power."

The little girl curtsied, smiled and grabbed Ashley's hand, starting to pull her off into the forest away from the lake. Dean followed the group of Unusuals gathered around them as they walked through the woods down a small path Dean could hardly see as the sun started to set. He was a city boy and was sure he would get lost out here on his own, so he stayed close to Ashley and the little girl as they hurried off down the trail. He couldn't help but think this was the way every horror movie started.

After about a twenty minute walk, they arrived at a shack set up against a hill. As they got closer, Dean realized it was built into the hill itself. The moss had grown over the wooden roof shingles, and vines hung down the sides of the small building's facade. He would not even have noticed it if he were hiking nearby.

"Is your sister inside?" Ashley asked as they approached.

"Yes, Eldara," the little girl said. "Zora tried to stop the men from cutting the tree down. They pushed her away, and she fell as a limb dropped from above. It struck her on the legs. The men just left her there and ran away when she was hurt."

"We tried to help her ourselves, Eldara, but I fear our healers are not up to the task to save her," the mother said, tears in her eyes. "Will you try to do something?"

"Of course," Ashley said. "My friend is a healer from Elk City to the East. He and I have worked together before. May I bring him with me inside to see your daughter?"

The mother looked at Dean skeptically, and the man who had first addressed them spoke up.

"It was a human who did this to her," he said angrily. "They have never helped us before, why would one of their kind help us now?"

"Have you heard of the tattooed ones?" Ashley asked. "The new group of humans who heal rather than harm?"

The man nodded.

"Show them your hand, Dean," Ashley said. "The stamp is still fresh enough."

Dean held out his right hand, showing the back of it to the gathered Unusuals. He turned and held it up with his palm toward his face and the back of his hand outward so all could see the Station U stamp with the ultraviolet ink that marked him as a paramedic for the Unusual community. There was a gasp from the crowd.

"So it is true," the man said. "I had not believed it, but had heard the rumors of the human healers who moved among our kind, helping the sick and injured."

"It is true," Ashley said. "He may be able to help me tend to Zora if you let him."

The Unusual man nodded his assent, and Dean took the bag from Ashley as she led him inside the shack's rickety door. It was dark inside with only the light of a flickering oil lamp shining on a table in the center of the room. Zora's mother picked up the lantern and led them to a back hallway that Dean realized was cut into the hill. It led to a series of rooms. At one doorway, the woman pushed the door open and Ashley entered the dimly lit room, followed closely by Dean.

There was another lantern on a small table and an old wooden bed with what looked like a straw mattress across the lattice of ropes crisscrossing the bed's frame to hold the mattress up. There was a sickly sweet smell of rot in the room, and he saw the blackened crust of blood on the bandaged legs of the teen-aged girl huddled on the bed. She moaned quietly but didn't look up as they entered. She seemed oblivious to their presence. He could tell by looking at her that she was in bad shape. Ashley knelt down beside her as she opened the bag Dean handed her. She pulled out a blood-pressure cuff and stethoscope.

"Dean," Ashley said. "Put on some gloves. There are some in the kit, in a zipper baggie. Peel back those bandages and see what the injuries to her legs look like. We need to clean her up at the very least." The nurse wrapped the blood pressure cuff around the girl's arm and laid the stethoscope's bell against her arm below it as she pumped up the cuff.

Dean found the gloves in the bag and noticed the abundance of trauma supplies inside including IV bags and tubing and a suture kit. He pulled on the gloves and started to peel back the bandages from the leg closest to him. The injury was high on the legs at the mid-thigh, as if something had come down across both of them simultaneously. He felt the heat coming off the wound through his gloves. The girl's skin was hot to the touch. She was septic, he guessed. A massive infection from the wounds was coursing through her system.

The more he unwrapped, the worse the smell got in the room, as the putrid wound was exposed. He found a similar wound on the other leg. Whatever had struck the legs, whether a tree branch or the tree itself, it had packed significant force. Both femurs were broken and had cut through the skin from the inside. The thigh bones had been reset by someone, but the wounds had become infected and had putrefied. Although he had never seen gangrene before, he had seen photos in school and on his Figure1 medical mobile app. The skin was blackened around the wounds. There was a flow of yellow pus from the openings in the skin, and red streaks stretched up under the skin towards the girl's groin. This was bad. He wasn't sure if a full trauma team could save her legs at this point. They might not have been able to even save her life.

Ashley finished taking her vital signs and was grim-faced as she, too, assessed the wounds. Dean caught her eye and quirked an eyebrow upward. "What do you think?" he whispered.

"I think she needs a lot of help, and I'm not sure she would make it all the way back to Elk City if we moved her," Ashley replied. "She's septic. Her blood pressure is so low I can't read it. Her respirations are rapid and shallow, the carotid pulse is rapid and thready, and her temp is over 105° Fahrenheit."

"I can start an IV and try to get her pressure up with fluids, but she needs antibiotics, Ashley," Dean said.

"I know, but maybe," she said, pausing as she dug in the bag. "Yes!" the nurse exclaimed. She pulled out a vial of powder and a small bag of fluid taped together. "Erin, you're a paranoid genius!"

"What is it?" Dean asked.

"A broad spectrum antibiotic in powdered form," she explained. "It would last virtually forever and just needs to be reconstituted with sterile water. Erin, my friend, packed this bag with things that would last. I'll start working on this, you get the IV started and get her some fluids."

Dean turned back to the bag of supplies and pulled out a one-liter bag of normal saline solution, tubing, and an IV catheter needle. He assembled the bag and tubing, handing it off to Zora's mother telling her to hold it up so the fluid would drain through the tubing. He cleared all the air out of the tube and then turned to start the IV with the needle. The girl's veins were flat because of her sepsis and dehydration, but he was able to find one and inserted the needle, getting a small flash of blood to show he had connected. He attached the tubing to the plastic catheter hub and started the fluids flowing.

Ashley was still mixing the antibiotic, so he turned to see what he could do next. He decided to work at cleaning out the wounds. He got a small bottle of sterile saline and some four by four gauze pads out of the supply bag, and started irrigating the wound and cleaning out the pus and infection as best he could. He had seen a wound care nurse at work in one of his hospital rotations and knew that packing the wound with damp sterile gauze would help the opening heal more cleanly. He opened another pack of sterile gauze pads and poured the remainder of the sterile saline in the plastic packaging wetting down the gauze. He put on a fresh pair of gloves from the bag and then carefully packed the wound from the bottom up. He covered the wound with some more sterile gauze dressings and wrapped a new fresh bandage around it to hold the packing and dressings in place over the wounds on both legs.

His girlfriend had already piggy-backed the small IV antibiotic bag to the tubing of the other, larger saline bag, and the medication was flowing into the girl's veins now. Ashley looked down at the job Dean had done bandaging the wounds on the legs and nodded in approval.

"Is it going to be enough?" Dean asked her quietly.

"I don't know," Ashley responded. She closed her eyes and laid her hands on the girl's legs over the bandages. He watched her brow furrow in concentration and a light sweat broke out on her head. A gasp sounded from the doorway behind him and from the girl's mother, still holding the IV bag for her daughter. Dean couldn't see what they were seeing, but Ashley was doing - something. He watched as the red streaks on the girl's legs retreated back towards the bandages and disappeared underneath them. Zora's breathing became less ragged and slowed some, too. Whatever his angelic girlfriend was doing, it appeared to be working. Suddenly, Ashley let out a long sigh and sagged to her knees in exhaustion. Dean caught her as she slumped over.

"Hey, are you okay?" he asked in alarm, stroking her hair back from her face. She was flushed and sweaty, as if she had just returned from a workout.

"Wow! I haven't done that in a while," she said. "It takes a lot out of me. I think she'll be alright now. I was able to draw some of the infection out of her wounds. The antibiotic will take care of the rest." Ashley looked up at him and smiled. "I'm glad you were here. Take me back to the cabin. I need to rest." She collapsed and fell asleep in his arms.

## Chapter 19

Dean needed help to get Ashley back to the cabin. Zora's father, Enric, and another man helped him carry the exhausted Eldara Sister back to the cabin in the woods. Once they got her settled in the bed upstairs, Dean came down to find Anya, Zora's mother, busy in the kitchen of the large open room that made up the downstairs of the cabin.

"Anya," Dean said. "Thank you very much, but I can take care of getting dinner together. I think Ashley is going to sleep for a while."

"It is nothing," the Dryad woman said with a wave of her hand. "The Eldara Sister used her power to heal my daughter, and I will not have her or her companion left to fend for themselves. You sit and rest yourself, Paramedic Dean."

He thought it was amusing that she used his job as a title. He looked around and decided to go back upstairs and sit with Ashley. She had looked quite pale when she collapsed in his arms after doing whatever it was she had done to halt the spread of the infection. He pulled a chair next to the bed where she slept, opened a book on his phone's reader app and started it, occasionally glancing up to check on her. He didn't know how long he had been sitting there when Anya came up the stairs with a plate of food and a glass of cold beer.

"Paramedic Dean," she said. "You must eat something to keep up your strength. I made some roast venison with gravy, roasted potatoes and some fresh biscuits."

Dean's mouth watered as he smelled the plate of food. She came over and set it down on the bedside table. He thanked the woman, putting his phone away and picking up the plate and a fork.

"I have made a simple broth for the Eldara," Anya said. "It is on the stove. If she awakens before I return in the morning, simply heat it up to a simmer and then give her some spoonfuls to sip until she has gathered her strength. Our legends say that such healing is taxing for the Eldara. We are very fortunate she chose to use her power to help our Zora."

"I know Ashley would not have had it any other way," Dean said. "She always tries to help people."

"Of course she does," Anya chuckled. "It is her nature. To do otherwise would be to deny who she is. But it could have drawn her to the other side, healing Zora when she was so close to death. I would have not wanted her to send herself away on our behalf when she may have other, more important tasks here to accomplish."

Dean was confused. "I'm sorry," he said, seeking clarification. "What do you mean – 'send her away', and the 'other side'? Was she in some sort of danger?"

Anya seemed confused. "Paramedic Dean, I do not understand," she said. "You are the companion of an Eldara, a most honored position, and you do not understand such things?"

Dean shook his head. "I'm sorry, but I do not. Ashley and I are friends. Perhaps more than that now, but she has never told me of her powers, or of any danger in using them."

Anya bit her lower lip in consternation. "I have overstepped myself, I fear. It is not my place to explain such things to you. Perhaps you are not her companion, but a protected one instead. You must ask her for the explanation." She turned to go back downstairs. "Do not forget the broth I made. I will return in the morning.

One of the men will remain outside during the night should you need anything. Goodbye, Paramedic Dean."

Dean watched as the woman proceeded down the stairs, then turned his gaze to Ashley. What had she done back there in the shack? Had it put her at risk for — something bad to happen to her? He settled in to watch over her tonight while she rested. He took her pulse and counted her respirations while he sat there. She seemed fine from the aspect of her vital signs, but she barely stirred when he lifted her wrist to check the heart rate. She was in a very deep sleep, at least he hoped it was just sleep. The night passed slowly around him as he watched her on the bed.

<hr>

"DEAN."

Startled, Dean sat up suddenly in the chair where he had been sitting next to Ashley. He must have dozed off. He looked up and saw her staring at him from the bed. A wan smile on her face betrayed how weak she was.

"Dean," she said again. "Have you been here all night?"

He glanced at his watch. It was nearly dawn. "I wanted to make sure you were okay." He remembered the broth on the stove downstairs. "Wait here, I'll be right back." The paramedic rushed downstairs and turned the knob that fired up the gas burner under the pot on the stovetop. He lifted the lid and picked up a spoon from the ceramic spoon rest next to the stove, stirring the liquid as it warmed. When it started gently bubbling he turned the burner off and looked around the kitchen cupboards and drawers until he found a ladle and a mug. He filled the mug about halfway and then returned upstairs with the mug and soup spoon.

Ashley opened her eyes as he approached. He sat down again next to her. Dean stirred the broth in the mug to help cool it some more and leaned forward. "Here is some broth that Anya, Zora's mother, made for you. She said you would need it after what you did for Zora." He lifted the spoon over to her lips and she took a tentative sip. Her eyes brightened as she tasted it. He smiled and got her another spoonful to sip. She finished about half the mug's contents that way before she said she'd had enough. He set the mug down on the bedside table and used a napkin to dab a spilled drop from her chin. She smiled as he did it.

"Thank you, Dean," she said. "Though, I'm supposed to be the one taking care of you, not the other way around."

"I like taking care of you, Ash," Dean said. "It shouldn't just be one way."

"No," she murmured. "I suppose not."

"How do you feel?" Dean asked. "You still look pale and pretty weak. Are you all right?" He didn't know how to approach talking with her about what the Dryad woman had let slip the night before. He was worried about her and mostly about losing her so soon after he had found her.

"I'm weak, but I will be alright," she said. "I just need a day or so of rest. I have not done that in some time, and I forgot how taxing it is."

"What, exactly, did you do? Anya talked about you going away to the 'other side' or something? What did she mean by that?"

Ashley chuckled quietly. "So many questions, Dean. Do you never stop trying to learn?"

"It's just something that Anya said last night about you using your powers to help Zora," Dean said. He took Ashley's hand in his and squeezed gently. "Did you do something that could have hurt you?"

He looked at Ashley, meeting her gaze and she held it for a time before she sighed and answered him. "Dean, it's difficult to explain. I was never in any danger, but I have a finite amount of life force when on the earth in corporeal form. I have some limited ability to heal, but when I do so, it uses up some of that corporeal life force. If I use a lot at one time it makes me weak for a few days. If I use too much, I will lose my corporeal form and have to return to the higher planes to regenerate."

"So you could have died?" Dean asked, concern and a little bit of anger shading his voice.

"No, Dean," she said wearily. "I cannot die here on earth in corporeal form. But, if I use up the life force that keeps me here on earth I would return to my spirit form for a time before I could come back."

"How long would that be?" Dean asked, afraid to hear the answer.

"Dean," she said, laying her other hand on top of his where their two hands clasped on the bed. "For you, it would be a long time, a hundred years or more. But to me it would be but an instant."

"So I could have lost you back there," Dean said defensively.

"No," she replied firmly. "I knew what I was doing and I used my power judiciously."

They were both silent for a while. Dean pondered what she had said. He didn't want to stop her from being who she was, but he also didn't want to lose her to some higher plane.

"Dean," Ashley said softly. "I want you to understand. You shouldn't be concerned for me. It's supposed to be the other way around. I am supposed to watch over you.

"Sorry, Ash," Dean said. "I'm a guy. I'm not built that way. I'm supposed to protect you."

"You'll get over it," she said, smiling up at him. "I'm human in this form, but the Eldara are not of this earth. We are visitors, messengers, healers and guardians. I'll be fine. After all, I've been around for a very long time."

"How long is a long time?" Dean asked. He wasn't sure if this was crossing a line or not, like asking a woman her age, but he was curious.

"I first took a corporeal form to help a woman who was a healer in what you would have called Mesopotamia in present day Iraq," Ashley said. "Let's just say it was a very long time ago. Since that time I've returned to help other healers find a solution to a problem, or navigate a crisis in their communities many times."

"Is that why you've come here as a nurse," he asked. "Because you're a healer?"

"I guess I've always been a nurse, as you call the job," Ashley said. "It's a name that has gone through many changes over the years. Now we call these caring healers nurses but in the past they've been midwives, wise ones, or elders. The name does not matter. It is the focus on communities of care, and healing of the whole person that defines the people I'm drawn to."

"So that's how you see me?" Dean asked.

"You and all your colleagues at Station U," she replied. "You are all focused on helping a community that is not getting the services they need. You are healers."

"So, why me?" Dean asked. "Why not Brynne, or Bill, or one of the others?"

"You're important to what's going on in Elk City, Dean," Ashley said. "I am drawn to the person to whom I am called to help. It's why I was in that convenience store when we first met. I got the urge to pull in there and get something, and while I was there, I saw your hand with its Station U stamp."

"So you knew you were here to help me from that moment?" Dean asked.

"I had already been here for a few years but had not been able to figure out who I was here to help," she said. "I was getting pretty frustrated. So when I saw you, I thought that you might be the right one, finally, but not one hundred percent sure. I knew I'd see you eventually at the ER or elsewhere at the hospital so I didn't approach you there. When you came to the ER the next time I was on shift, though, I knew it was you."

"I think I knew I was supposed to meet you, too," Dean said. "I couldn't get your face out of my mind ever since I ran into you at the convenience store. Later, when I saw you at the hospital, I was so happy to learn you were a nurse at the ER. It meant that I would see you again."

Dean thought for a moment then looked up at Ashley.

"So, do you end up dating all your charges?" he asked in response to an impulse.

"Why? Are you jealous of my past lovers?" she said with a little laugh.

"Well, I'm just asking how it all works," he stammered. "Are you here to stay? When will you leave?"

"Sweetie," she said giving his hand a squeeze. "I'm here now, and I don't plan on going anywhere anytime soon. Let's live in the moment and enjoy each other's company while we're together. I've met and spent time with many wonderful people over the years. Enjoying their company in the time I have with them is the lesson I've learned."

Dean realized that was likely the only answer he was going to receive from her. He shouldn't be worried, but seeing her this weak made him uncomfortable. She was his angel, his Eldara and he didn't like knowing that she was at risk from using her healing powers. He didn't want to contemplate that she could be sent away for a long time, never to be seen again, at least not by him. It was not something he wanted to think about anymore. Ashley must've sensed that as well, because she changed the subject.

"Dean, honey," she said. "Can you get me some more of this yummy broth? I think it is helping me gather some strength. Then maybe we can cuddle up here in bed and watch a video? Erin said there were few romantic comedies in the chest at the foot of the bed."

Dean nodded, took the mug from her and went to get some more. He resolved to enjoy the time he had with her and treat every day as if it might be the last he had with Ashley. Someday he might be right.

# Chapter 20

Ashley recovered from her weakness following healing Zora over the next few days. She spent the first 24 hours in bed, sleeping most of the time. She and Dean passed some of the time watching a few classic romantic comedies on the TV using the DVDs stored in the loft bedroom at the cabin. Anya returned during the day and made a meal for them, and while she was there with Ashley, Dean returned to check on Zora's wounds and infection. She was remarkably better. The red streaks no longer showed on her legs, and when he checked under the dressings on her wounds, the wounds were pink and healthy looking. Clearly they were well on their way to healing.

Dean spent some time the next day showing Anya and one of Zora's older sisters how to dress the wounds with clean gauze and bandages, and he left some of the gauze and bandages from Erin's cabin stash of hospital first aid supplies. When he returned from seeing their patient the last time, he was surprised to see Ashley up and walking carefully around the cabin's first floor. She was still pale but seemed to be feeling a lot better. They only had the remainder of that day together at the cabin. The two of them had to return home to Elk City that evening. They both had to work the next morning.

Ashley spent most of the day sitting on the porch in one of the Adirondack style chairs, watching the lake and the trees in the gentle breeze. Dean brought her a blanket from inside to cover up if she needed it, but the weather was pleasantly warm, not too hot, so she opted not to use it. The remainder of the day went quickly. While she watched from the porch, Dean packed up their bags and loaded up the little bit they had brought in Ashley's MG. Eventually, it was time for them to leave, and Dean was thrilled when Ashley told him that he could drive the car back to Elk City. He was concerned that she still didn't feel well enough to drive it herself, while simultaneously excited about driving the classic car.

As the time came for them to leave at dusk, Dean helped Ashley to the car. The Dryads and a few others of the Unusual community of the lake valley came to see them off. Anya and Enric both came over and gave them a basket of gifts for their return home. Dean peeked under the cloth napkin covering the basket and saw some fresh blueberry muffins, and what looked like a few wood carvings. He and Ashley thanked Zora's parents, and Dean set the basket carefully on their bags behind the front seats in the two-seater sports car. Dean checked on the cabin to make sure it was locked up one last time and then climbed into the driver's seat. They waved to the onlookers as they drove back down the gravel road towards the highway. While the trip had not been what they'd expected, Dean was glad they had been able to help the girl, and he had learned a lot more about Ashley and the Eldara. He was still worried about her, but she said a good night's sleep in her own bed would give her the additional rest she needed to be ready to go back to work.

They were on the interstate highway, driving back to Elk City about an hour later when he heard Ashley gasp in the seat next to him. She had been looking at her smartphone as soon as they got back on the highway. They had been in a pretty sketchy coverage area at the cabin and their phones didn't work.

"Dean, you'd better check in with Brynne tonight when you get back," Ashley said. "There's been another attack by The Cause."

Dean nodded to his phone on the console between them. "I'm driving. Check my messages."

Ashley picked up his phone and scrolled through the two days of text messages that had rolled in, then checked the voicemail. Dean glanced over at her as he drove, her look going from concerned to grave as she listened. He wanted to hear for himself, but he'd never be able to hear the speaker on the phone driving with the car's convertible top down. He waited while she finished listening to the messages. She laid the phone down in her lap.

"The Cause has been busy while we were gone. They attacked a counselor who works for the county. I think you know her. Her name is Rebecca." Dean shot her a concerned glance. "I don't know the details, but she was assaulted as she left work the night we left on our trip. She was alive when they took her to the hospital, but it must've been pretty bad. In reaction, some of Rudy's pack must have decided to start patrolling on their own to protect the community and hunt for the attackers. One of them was seen changing, and part of it was caught on a kid's cell phone video. He posted it to the web, and there's all kinds of uproar going on about some sort of wild animal on the loose in the city attacking people."

"Damn," Dean said. He had thought that their two days away would give him a break, but with Zora's injuries and tending to Ashley it had not been as relaxing as he had hoped. Now he was returning to a real mess back at the station, and to top it off, Rebecca, the counselor who had once helped him cope with the stress of his new job, had been attacked. She was a Muse, an Unusual who used her powers to inspire humans' innate creativity. In her case, Rebecca was a professional social worker and counselor who worked with first responders who had trouble dealing with difficult work situations. She used her energies to inspire her clients to find solutions to dealing with their jobs and life situations. Now she had been attacked.

Dean knew that Zach had known about Rebecca and her connection to him. Zach had mentioned her derisively when they had talked in the past. The former paramedic was stepping up his attacks on people Dean knew. That was starting to get worrisome especially with his newfound concerns over Ashley. He had thought of her as kind of an invincible guardian angel, but now he knew differently. She was as vulnerable as any human would be to attack. If she were to find herself in a situation where she was forced to defend or protect herself, she might expend so much energy that she would leave the corporeal world for what might as well be forever, at least from his perspective.

He glanced at his watch. They were still two hours from home, but he didn't want to drive any faster than he was already. He banged his hand on the steering wheel in frustration. It was all getting worse, not better. What was he supposed to do to resolve all this? Ashley had assured him that he was integral to the solution to what was going on in Elk City, and that James was also involved. Somehow the two of them had to do something that would bring the situation to a head and tip things one way or another. She had told him that he should just keep doing his job and be himself because that was what was important, but he wanted to take some kind of concrete action and stop what was happening in the city.

These attacks couldn't go on forever before the general public was drawn into them. Now with the video of the werewolf changing on camera, the public was starting to get involved. He needed to see that video for himself. It was probably a cell-phone video, and shot at night from a distance. The quality was likely not that good, but it still must be pretty spectacular. He had seen the transformation of a werewolf in person and knew what a shock it could be to the uninitiated.

Ashley laid a hand on his shoulder, distracting him from his grim thoughts. "It's going to be alright, sweetie," she said. "Just get us home in one piece and we'll get back to work on solving this together."

"You're right," he replied. "But I can't help but think that there is something I'm missing, and that somehow I'm the center of what's happening now. First Freddie, then the restaurant, and now this attack on Rebecca. They are all connected to me."

"Not just you, Dean, but to all the Station U paramedics," Ashley reminded him. "You need to remember that this is focused on the whole program. Someone is trying to discredit it and to keep you all from doing your jobs serving the community. If the Unusual community sees calling the paramedics at Station U as putting a target on their backs, they are going to go back to trying to treat themselves and not get the medical attention they need. That is unacceptable."

Dean thought about that and all the patients he had helped over the months since he had started at Station U. He also thought about how he had resisted the assignment and wanted to be elsewhere. The patients in need had attracted him, though. He wanted to be where patients needed his skills the most, and the Unusual community was a huge underserved population in the Elk City region. He thought about this and about what the general public might do if they knew of the people living among them who would be seen as monsters from their nightmares. He didn't think they would be as accepting as he had been in the beginning.

The two of them drove down the interstate, with the sun setting behind them. They were heading back to the city, back to their jobs and responsibilities. In some ways, too, they were heading back into the unknown. Dean couldn't get rid of the sense of dread that something bad was coming. The thought picked at the corners of his mind that before they could solve this situation in Elk City, he was going to be at the center of a storm. The thought scared him more than just a little, but he continued to drive back to the city, back to his duty, back to the job.

# Chapter 21

Dean's first day back after the lake trip with Ashley started bright and early as always. He headed into the squad room at Station U and noticed a different vibe immediately. Bill and Lynne were packing up their things, but without the usual banter that accompanied the end of a typical shift. Dean said hi as he entered but got nothing more than a nod from Bill and a brief wave from Lynne in acknowledgment. Brynne didn't even look up from her seat at the computer where she had settled to log in to the daily updates from headquarters. Even Freddie merely waved a half-hand at him in greeting and went back to work making the shift's breakfast in the kitchenette.

Bill and Lynne left, and then the station was silent except for the tapping of the keys from Brynne as she worked on the computer. Dean shrugged and started on the beginning of shift checks of the gear in the ambulance bay. It felt good to be back doing something constructive. He had not slept well the night before. He had dropped Ashley and her car off when they returned from the trip the previous evening. She needed to sleep alone in her apartment and get some rest. He used an app to grab a ride-share car from there back to his apartment where he spent most of his evening staring at the ceiling, lost in his thoughts.

Now, back in the familiar confines of the station, he jumped into the work as a way to keep himself occupied. Dean realized that the station had become a kind of home and it felt right to be here, doing this work. When he finished up the tasks in the ambulance bay, ensuring he and Brynne were ready to respond to any calls, he went back into the squad room to see what Brynne had planned for the day. He thought it might be a good idea to make a supply run to the hospital, and use that as an excuse to check on Rebecca's progress while they were there picking up drugs and bandages.

Brynne looked up when he came in the room and turned the computer monitor his way so he could see it. "Have you seen this?" she asked.

"What?" Dean asked as he walked over looking at the screen. The screen showed a classic black and white movie photo of a vampire with his fangs sunk into the neck of a beautiful starlet. Words had been added to the image though, and as he read them he knew why she was concerned.

"The Monsters Live Among Us," the words in the photo read. When she saw he had seen that, she scrolled down to the image at the bottom that was previously hidden on the screen. There, below the feeding vampire photo and caption, were a series of photos that included James, Rudy, Kristof and other prominent members of the community. Dean recognized some as Unusuals he knew. The others were well-known businessmen and women in the community.

"That's bad, Brynne. Where'd you get it?"

"It's posted all over social media," she answered. "People are sharing it and following it up with links to the werewolf video. You heard about that?"

Dean nodded. He had taken some time to look it up online when he got back to his apartment. It was grainy and dark due to the low light level at night, but he recognized the transformation of the werewolf in the distance, although it could be explained away as a hoax with special effects.

"I saw it last night when I got back to my apartment," Dean

said. "I didn't recognize the individual, but it appeared real enough."

"It was Desmond Levann," Brynne said. "He's a member of Rudy's pack. James is furious, both that he was so careless in where he shifted, and that Rudy's pack was out hunting at all."

"Yeah, but it's easy to call it a cheap knock-off horror video," Dean said. "It's terrible visual quality, and the whole thing could have been faked. That's what I would think if I didn't know better. I saw a local news item on the TV that made fun of it."

"I saw that, too," Brynne said. "But it's a basic violation of the rules for members of the pack to change without first carefully checking to make sure no one is watching. He didn't do that. Now with this photo making the social media rounds it's only a matter of time before someone makes the wrong statement at the wrong time, and someone starts to connect the dots. James texted the link to me after a reporter called his office for a comment on his being called a monster online."

"I'll bet he loved that," Dean quipped.

"He didn't respond," Brynne said. "I'm sure he pawned it off on his assistant, Celeste. She gets paid a lot to handle such annoyances. The problem is that this photo, plus the werewolf video, equals trouble if anything else public happens. The chief just sent us an announcement that we are to do everything possible to ensure our patients' privacy while in the public eye. It's not like we weren't doing that already. You'll need to acknowledge receipt in your email inbox, by the way. It's an official Station announcement in the system."

Dean crossed over to the other computer workstation and sat down to log in. He saw the email from the Chief. He quickly scanned the email. It was just what Brynne said it was. He sent a receipt reply back and then looked through his other emails. He stopped when he saw one subject heading and who had sent it. Mike Farver sent him an email with the subject "We Need To Talk." He opened the email. Mike simply asked to meet again at the diner one night after his shift this week. Mike called it his last chance to do the right thing before it was too late. Dean wondered what that meant.

Mike was still working at the academy teaching, but the chief and other leaders were aware that he had possible ties to The Cause.

"Brynne," he said. "Mike Farver emailed me." He turned to look her way as she swiveled around in her chair behind him. "He wants to talk with me 'before it's too late.' What should I do?"

"I don't know, Dean," she replied. She spun around to face him. "Part of me says you should go so you can learn what he's up to. But another part worries that this could be a way to set you up for a fall in some way." Brynne pursed her lips in thought for a few minutes before proceeding. "Let me talk to James and email the Chief. They may want to do something to watch you so nothing happens."

"He wants an answer by one o'clock this afternoon," Dean said. "Could they have a timetable?" He thought some more and said, "I'll wait to see what the Chief says, but I'm inclined to say yes. This can't go on the way it is. We need to stop The Cause from trying to get in the way of our programs helping the Unusual population. Ashley worries that some of our patients will stop calling for help if they see themselves as potential targets. Now, with this outing of their leadership on social media, it's only going to get worse. Maybe we can get ahead of it if I meet with Mike. He might let something slip about their plans."

"Ashley's right," Brynne said. "Our ambulance call volume is off by about twenty-five percent and headquarters thinks it's due to the attacks on people associated with us at Station U." She thought for a moment more and then nodded. "I'll tell the Chief that I recommend you meet with Mike, but I'll go with you. I haven't talked with my old partner in a while. Maybe I can talk some reason into him. I should have suspected he would be part of this, but I honestly never thought he'd take his personal issues and go this far."

"I thought he was sent to the academy because he was such a good paramedic and instructor," Dean said.

"He is a good paramedic, Dean," Brynne said. "Or he was. Mike was chosen for the original Station U crews because he was so good at his job. The problem started when he became way too overprotective of me after I started dating a vampire. He couldn't get past my choice to date James. I think he had always seen me as a daughter figure. He didn't approve of my choice in boyfriends."

"He's not necessarily alone in that thought, Brynne," Dean reminded her.

"That's not the point," she said. "You've gotten over it, mostly. Maybe he still has those parental feelings for me. It may make him more open to telling us something during the meeting at the diner. That's why I'm coming along. Well that, and to keep you from doing or saying anything stupid."

"Okay," Dean said turning back to his screen. "I'm going to email him back and let him know that I'm coming to meet him today after our shift. I won't tell him about you coming. Maybe the surprise will help."

There wasn't time for the conversation to continue because right after he sent the email reply to Mike, the first call of the day alerted on the overhead speakers starting with the musical tones that alerted their station's radio system. The dispatcher's voice followed the tones.

"Medical Box U-821, chest pain, 1235 Telegraph Road." The male dispatcher's voice said.

Dean and Brynne grabbed their jackets and headed out to the ambulance bay to respond to the chest pain patient. There'd be time to formulate a plan for the upcoming conversation with Mike later in the shift, Dean thought, as they drove out of the station and onto the streets of Elk City.

***

THEIR CHEST PAIN call turned out to be an elderly Rakshasi - a Hindu spirit in human form, who looked like she had a heart attack. Although known as man-eater demons in the lore, she seemed nice enough from what he could see. The heart monitor showed an abnormal waveform called ST-Elevation, and the woman's symptoms of chest pain, shortness of breath, and profuse sweating all pointed to a heart attack even if the heart monitor hadn't showed it.

Dean knew that only about half of all heart attacks showed up right away on the heart monitor.

He started the blood work in the portable iStat device in the back of the ambulance while Brynne started them on the way to the hospital. He suspected that her labs were going to show high enzyme levels that signified heart damage based on what he was seeing. He continued treating her with oxygen and additional nitroglycerin to ease the chest pain. He was watching her cardiac activity on the heart monitor and ran another diagnostic strip to see if the ST-elevation had progressed and gotten worse. He was looking at it when an alert sounded, and his eyes darted to the monitor. The uneven rhythm of ventricular fibrillation showed on the screen, and that meant she had slipped into cardiac arrest. He briefly checked her for responsiveness then immediately attached the defibrillator pads to his patient's chest, then charged the heart monitor to deliver a shock.

"Brynne," he called up to the front of the ambulance. "I've got a cardiac arrest. Initiating code procedures."

The monitor finished charging up, and he made sure he wasn't touching the patient, then pressed the shock button to deliver the stored charge to the Rakshasi's heart. Her chest heaved with the sudden contraction of the chest muscles fueled by the electric charge. Dean waited a few seconds for Brynne to finish pulling over the ambulance before he could safely stand up and start CPR. He began with compressions and opted to do a full two hundred compressions over two minutes since she had just been breathing, and her lungs were still full of oxygenated air. Brynne climbed in the back with him as he continued the compressions.

"One shock delivered," Dean said, already out of breath from the exertion. "I'm on the first set of compressions following the shock."

He watched as Brynne grabbed the drug bag from its shelf and started gathering the meds for a cardiac arrest. He was nearly finished his first two hundred compressions when the woman's hand moved, and her eyes fluttered open. He stopped and looked to see that she was breathing. As he stopped compressions, the heart monitor showed that the heart rhythm had returned to sinus tachy-cardia, a rapid heart rate but not one that was lethal and needed a shock. The initial shock of her lethal heart rhythm had worked and reset her heart's organized contractions.

"I thought I'd lost you there for a minute," he said to the patient as he pressed the button to check her blood pressure and run another diagnostic strip. Brynne drew up some meds to be given and hopefully stop her from going into the fibrillation rhythm again.

"Ow, my chest," the woman said, putting her hand to her breast bone. "It hurts. What happened?"

"Your heart stopped, and I had to start CPR and shock you," he watched as Brynne pushed the anti-arrhythmia drug into the IV tubing that lead to the patient's arm. Then his partner clapped him on the back in support of his good work and left the back of the ambulance to head back up front and continue the drive to the hospital.

"Did we stop?" the woman asked.

"Yes," Dean said. "There's no way for me to do effective CPR bouncing around in the back of a moving ambulance. It's not all that safe either. Our protocol has the driver stop and come back to help with CPR. Now that you're back awake and talking again, we can finish our drive."

"Well, I guess I should thank you," the Rakshasi said. "I wasn't going to call you. I was afraid it would identify me to those awful humans who are hurting us. But the pain was so bad, I couldn't wait any longer for it to get better."

"You did the right thing," Dean said. "Chest pain and trouble breathing are two things you don't want to fool around with. They aren't likely to get better on their own and often are signs of serious trouble. You rest right now. I've got you, and we're almost to the hospital." Dean continued monitoring her closely, but the lethal arrhythmia did not return. He was glad. It could just as easily gone the other way and she would have died.

He was still thinking about how close a thing it was, even after they had dropped her off with the critical cardiac care team in the emergency room. He and Brynne were wiping down the cot as they always did between patients when Brynne looked up at something behind him and said, "Jeeze, Ashley, you look like hell."

Dean turned around and saw Ashley coming towards them. She still looked pale and her eyes had a sunken appearance. She had clearly not taken his advice to stay home and take another day off.

"Ash," Dean said. "I thought you were going to stay home and take it easy."

"You thought that, Dean. I never said it," Ashley replied. "I always planned on coming in. The rest of the nurses are short-staffed most of the time as it is. They don't need me calling out. It's not like I'm infectious."

Brynne snorted, "I'm not disagreeing with you, Ashley, but you look awful. You should have taken lover boy's advice. What's wrong with you if you're not sick?"

Ashley briefly explained what had happened on their trip to the lake two days ago. Brynne's eyes grew wide at the description of the girl's injuries and even wider when Dean chimed in and described what Ashley had done to halt the spreading infection.

"Damn, Ashley," Brynne said. "I knew you Eldara were powerful, but that must've been pretty impressive."

"It's not without a price, as you can see," Ashley said with a wan smile.

"We had to carry her back to the cabin, and she stayed in bed for the whole first day afterward," Dean told his partner. "I was really worried about her. She says she'll eventually regain her strength, but I don't want her to go around doing things like that regularly."

"He doesn't need to worry about me, Brynne," Ashley said. "I can take care of myself. I just can't draw on my power without paying a price, albeit a temporary one. All Unusual powers come with a price. I'll be fine."

"If you say so, Ashley," Brynne said. "Still, maybe you should take it easy a little longer."

"I've taken to doing routine tasks like drawing blood and doing triage for the day. That will keep me from the most strenuous work," Ashley said. "Another two or three days and I'll be as good as new."

Dean pulled her to him in a brief hug and gave her a peck on the cheek. "We've got to get back in service, but I'm glad you came out to see us. I'll come by later after work and check on you. We have a meeting after work, but I'll only be an hour or so late."

"A meeting?" Ashley asked.

Brynne spoke up. "Just a work thing. It's going to be boring but hopefully not too long."

Dean shot her a glance about the lie but said nothing. He gave Ashley another hug and then the two paramedics rolled their stretcher back out to the ambulance. When they got outside, Brynne spoke up.

"She didn't need to be worrying about the meeting with Mike," she said. "She wasn't going to talk us out of it anyway. You can tell her about it later if we learn anything interesting. Otherwise, she never needs to know."

"Look at you being all top secret and stuff," Dean said as he loaded the cot into the back of the ambulance and slid it into place.

"It's all about the 'need to know' my friend," Brynne said. "Come on, let's grab a snack on the way back to the station, my treat."

## Chapter 22

The rest of the shift was uneventful with only a few other routine ambulance calls. The two paramedics were able to spend some time talking about their plan to confront the former Station U paramedic, Mike Farver. They knew, based on Dean's earlier conversations with Mike, that he was somehow involved with The Cause and the attacks on Unusuals in the Elk City area. They didn't have any proof other than their suspicions. But based on those suspicions, he might even know where Zach was, which would help the police put a stop to the attacks.

When Bill and Lynne returned to take over that evening, Brynne followed Dean over to Hank's Diner, near the station, to confront Mike. Dean saw Mike's marked fire department SUV parked in the parking lot when he pulled in, and he got a tight feeling in his gut at the upcoming conversation with his former mentor. Mike had embodied everything that a paramedic was supposed to be as Dean's one-time instructor, and Dean had strived to meet his approval when in the academy and afterward at Station U. The discovery that he was somehow connected with The Cause had been a huge letdown to the new paramedic, and he was still struggling with that realization.

Dean parked in a slot that had an open parking space next to it, and Brynne pulled her Nissan sedan in next to his pickup. Dean got out and waited for her to emerge from her car, then walked up to the diner entrance next to her. As he did, he realized she was his new mentor. That sudden realization helped him reconcile some of his feelings about confronting Mike there.

The two of them entered the diner, and Dean saw Mike seated at a booth at the rear. He also saw the surprise register in Mike's eyes when he saw Brynne was with Dean. The two paramedics walked back to the booth and sat down across from Mike, Dean sliding into the booth first.

"Hello, Brynne," Mike said. "It's been a while." He glanced at Dean but didn't say anything, turning his gaze back to his former protege and partner.

"Yes, it has," Brynne responded. "You know, Mike, I thought that you were through all of this drama about our patients at Station U when you moved to the Academy."

"You thought I'd forget they existed simply because the Chief moved me to the Academy?" Mike asked. "If anything, it made me more aware of the danger we faced. The danger that you faced."

"So you're still mad about me choosing James against your wishes, is that it?" Brynne asked. "You have to let this father-figure, over-protective streak go, Mike. It's time."

"How could I, when you were in danger every time I let you go home to that blood-sucker," Mike hissed. "Then, after I got moved to the Academy, I started getting pictures sent to me of the two of you together on dates. They came from an anonymous contact who also feared for your safety. I knew I had to act. Luckily my new friend had other contacts and plans to help me out. He just needed my help to get the ball rolling."

"So you're not involved with this alone?" Dean asked. "You have somebody you're working with, doing these horrible things?"

Mike looked at Dean, and Dean felt very small, like a child who had spoken up during a grown-up conversation. The elder paramedic said nothing to him and turned his attention back to Brynne.

"I'm not alone in my concerns about these creatures living

among us, Brynne. I was fine in the beginning when they were just seeking medical treatment, but when I realized the true dangers, the dangers they posed to you and impressionable people like you, I could sit by no longer."

"I'm not a child, Mike," Brynne snapped. "I can make my own choices and decisions, and live my own life. I don't need or want your help."

"Like I said," Mike replied. "I'm past that now. You're beyond saving. You're gonna end up one of them, and there's nothing I can do about that. I have to worry about the safety of the rest of us." He turned and looked at Dean. "This is your last chance, kid. You can get out of this and save yourself. I know you've gotten mixed up with one of them, too, but it's not too late. Has that Eldara nurse got you so far under her spell that you can't leave?"

"I'm not under a spell," Dean responded defiantly. "I'm just not okay with hurting people to prove a point."

"First, they're not people, Dean. They are monsters and nightmares come to life." Mike corrected him, his voice taking on an edge. "Second, sometimes you have to cause some temporary pain to treat a problem. You use a needle to give medicine. You have to cut to remove a tumor to treat the cancer. That's what I'm trying to do." Dean just stared at him in disbelief. The former mentor continued. "But, it's clear from your defiance you've made up your mind, or it's been made up for you." He moved from the booth's bench seat across from them and stood up. "Either way, I think it's too late. I have tried to warn you both, and you both have decided not to take my advice. A change is coming. It's coming one way or the other. You can get on board, get out of the way, or get run over by it. It's your choice. I'll no longer be held responsible for the consequences."

Brynne and Dean watched in silence as Mike turned and strode away. Brynne shifted to the now unoccupied seat across from Dean and looked at him.

"He's even worse now than when he got transferred," Brynne said. "He hates all of the Unusuals now, not just James, just because they're different."

"And because he doesn't like your boyfriend," Dean added.

"Yeah, but you didn't particularly like James either," Brynne said. "It doesn't make you want to go out and kill people just because they are linked to him."

They paused their conversation as the waitress, Daisy, came over to take their order.

"I saw your friend leave, is he coming back, do you want me to wait to take your order?" Daisy asked.

"No," Brynne said. "He won't be back. We'll order now. I'll have the chicken tender dinner and a diet soda."

Daisy looked at Dean. He was not sure he felt like eating, but he ordered anyway. "A grilled chicken barbecue sandwich with fries and cole slaw. I'll have a Sprite to drink."

"Great, I'll get that started and be right back with your drinks," Daisy said as she flipped her order book closed and walked away.

Dean watched her go and then looked at Brynne. "I can't say I like James a lot. Maybe that has to do with his personality. Maybe it has to do with his - his feeding habits." Brynne pulled at her characteristic turtleneck's collar absently when he said it. Damn, that burned at him. Obviously James was biting her, but she seemed none the worse for the wear. Brynne started to say something, but Dean held up his hand to stop her.

"I'm not arguing the right or wrong of it, Brynne," Dean continued. "It's your life, and it's none of my business. I don't like it, but I'm not going to fight you about your personal choices." He watched as her tension relaxed. "Ashley says he and I need to get along to stop all of this. Somehow, James and I are linked to this. She just has a feeling. I mean, jeez, what good is being a messenger of the Gods if you can't be more specific with your messages?"

Brynne laughed aloud. "What does Ashley say when you ask her that question?"

"She says it's part of human free will," Dean replied. "She says that the higher planes all agree to keep hands off humans and let them make their own choices for major decisions. While they sometimes take sides, they have to act on the periphery. That way they offer humans the options to make decisions they hope their worshipers will make. In the end, though, she says it has to be up to us."

"So what have you decided?" Brynne asked. "Are you going to put aside your feelings and work with James?"

"I have to, don't I?" Dean said. "If I have a chance to stop these things from happening to innocent people, I have to do it. I just wish I knew what I was supposed to do. It would make life so much easier."

"Me, too, Dean," Brynne said.

Daisy returned with their drinks, and they sipped at them for a while in silence. Dean continued to think about how he could have idolized Mike so much and ended up being so wrong. It bothered him that he had made that mistake.

"What are you thinking about now?" Brynne asked.

"It bothers me that I looked up to Mike and tried to be the type of medic he would be proud of," Dean said. "It turns out that I couldn't have been more wrong about that. He is just awful. What does that say about me?"

"Don't beat yourself up," Brynne consoled him. "Mike is still an excellent paramedic and a really good instructor. You learned your trade from one of the best. I would never have tagged him as being behind all of this, and up until this meeting tonight, I sort of denied it was true. He was a good guy, once. You have to look at it as two separate things. Kind of like one side is his professional side, which is excellent and appropriate, and one side is his politics, which are screwed up. You can learn a trade from him and gain the skills you need without getting mixed up with the other side."

"But I am mixed up with it, aren't I?" Dean asked.

"In a way, yes, you are," Brynne said. "But you have chosen the correct side, while he has chosen the side that hurts innocent people. Like I said, I would never have pegged him as being part of this, even knowing how much he disliked my relationship with James." The two of them were silent for a time after that, lost in their thoughts as they waited for their food. Brynne broke the silence after a bit.

"James had an idea that you may or may not like," Brynne said.

"He thinks you and Ashley should move into an apartment in his building downtown where you can be guarded under his security network. James owns an apartment and office building downtown. He has the whole building and keeps furnished apartments for Unusual VIPs who are in town for meetings and such. He and I live there, too. There wouldn't be any danger to you while you were under his protection."

"Brynne," Dean said. "I don't want to live downtown. I like the suburbs where I am now. Besides, I could never afford the rent on a place like that while paying a lease on my own place."

"He's offering it for free, Dean," Brynne answered. "James knows what you and I make as city employees. He just wants to keep you safe so that you can be around to make that decision Ashley says you need to make."

Brynne paused briefly before continuing. "There's another side to this as well. There's Ashley to consider. You don't want her hurt in any of these attacks, do you?"

"Of course not," Dean said his voice rising with anger. "What would make you say something like that?"

"Mike knows who she is, Dean. He's made the connection to you, and that means that he could put a target on her to get to you. If you move in downtown, she'll likely follow to be closer to you, to offer what support she needs to in order to help you."

"I've expressed concern about this to Ashley after the arson at Sabatani's," Dean said. "She insists that she can take care of herself."

"Do you believe her?" Brynne asked.

"I did until this past weekend," Dean replied. "After seeing her become so weak following the trip to the lake and healing the Dryad girl, I'm not so sure. She could not even walk on her own right afterward, and if someone had attacked her then, I don't know what she could have done to stop them." Dean pondered a moment, thinking again how helpless Ashley had been. "I'll talk with her about it. If she comes because of me, then I'll think about moving."

"I'll let James know that you are thinking about it," Brynne said. "He'll hold two apartments open for you guys in case you decide to come in. He'll even make sure they're on the same floor." Brynne finished the last with a wink and a grin.

"I don't know if she'll go for it or not, but I'll ask," Dean said.

Their food arrived, and the two paramedics dug in immediately, as emergency medical providers usually did by habit since they were often called away suddenly during meals. There wasn't much else to say between the two of them. They had become very close in the months since Dean left the academy and came to Station U.

Brynne had demonstrated for him a level of professionalism and poise in difficult situations that he had not known existed, and he was glad that he had developed another mentor in the absence of Mike Farver. She was now the paramedic he most wanted to emulate. Her caring approach to patient care was evident in every call, and her knowledge and commitment to learning more every day set the bar very high for him to reach, which was just fine with him. He had always striven to be the best. They finished their dinner in relative quiet, with only some small talk about work and the community, then left to go their separate ways, each heading home for the night. Brynne made one more pitch about the apartment downtown before she got in her car and drove off. Dean thought about it as he drove home, wondering if he or Ashley were in danger or not.

---

# Chapter 23

---

Dean drove home from the diner and thought more about the confrontation with Mike. There was no doubt now that he was involved with The Cause. He had also alluded to the fact that he had someone else working with him in the organization. That meant that there was someone in charge above Mike, running the whole thing. That was new information, which was at least, a little bit of good news. He and Brynne had hoped to get some new information out of Mike during the meet up at the diner after work. Bringing Brynne along had been a good idea.

He arrived home at his apartment above the garage and saw Ashley's car parked out front. She had a spare key so she must have let herself in. Dean parked his pickup and grabbed his gear and stethoscope and headed up the exterior stairs to his door. It swung open as he approached, and he saw Ashley there inside. She was sitting on the couch smiling at him as he came in. She still had signs of the physical toll the use of her healing powers had on her. Her eyes still had circles underneath, and her color was still a bit pale. He wanted to chastise her for not going straight home after work, but he couldn't bring himself to do it. He would have missed her if she hadn't come over.

"Good, you're finally home," Ashley said as he came into the room and set his keys and work stuff down on the counter. "What happened? Did Mike show up?"

"Hello to you, too," Dean quipped, surprised. "How did you know we met with Mike?" He wasn't mad at her for finding out, but he did wonder how she knew. She smiled, walked over and threw her arms around him.

"I'm glad to see you, of course," she purred in his ear as she squeezed him in a hug and then stepped back. "I've just been dying to hear what happened at the meeting. James texted to see if I had heard anything about it since he hadn't heard from Brynne. I got the sense that somehow it was important, not just for you and Brynne, but for all of us, so I came over."

"We found out that Mike is not in this alone," Dean said. "Someone is helping him, and The Cause, in the attacks. Someone who brought him into The Cause in the beginning when he was moved to the Academy. That happened after an incident with James and Brynne a few years back."

"That's interesting. That would be just after I came here to Elk City," Ashley said. "I wonder if this is something that is part of a larger movement instead of just something locally here in Elk City? Did he say anything about that?"

"He didn't say anything like that," Dean said. "He seemed to focus on the problem as he saw it here." He crossed the apartment and sat down on the couch. Ashley came over and sat next to him, leaning against him as he lifted his arm and pulled her close. "I have to wonder, though, who this other mystery person is? Mike's pretty highly placed in the Elk City Fire Department, and his history as a former Station U medic gives him access to information about the whole community that another person in his position wouldn't ordinarily have."

Ashley placed her hand on his chest as she leaned her head on his shoulder. "It has to be someone else highly-placed, or somehow aware of the Unusual community in some other way," she said.

"Well, who else knows about the Unusuals living among the human population?" Dean asked.

"There are those humans who have been invited in, either because of their affinity for us or because of their position in higher levels of government," Ashley explained. "There are always those who just figure it out. You know, they have a quirky neighbor, so they start paying attention to their quirks and strange behaviors, and it suddenly dawns on them what is really going on next door. Usually, when that happens, if their reaction is negative, the Unusual neighbor just moves away. Everyone after that just assumes the person was crazy or was making up their stories about us."

"Yeah, but that doesn't explain the animosity that this other mystery person has for Unusuals," Dean said. "There has to be a reason for them to back and support The Cause, and people like Zach and Mike." He thought for a moment about the patients he had encountered in his work as a paramedic at Station U. He thought back to one human patient they treated near the beginning of his tenure where a young woman was being turned to a vampire, and the process was botched, requiring him and Brynne to resuscitate her. He wondered what her family might think about it.

"Maybe it's a family member of a human tied up with Unusuals in some way," Dean thought out loud. "That's why Mike got mixed up with this. He got involved because of Brynne's involvement with James. He didn't approve. So what if there's a group of humans, family members and loved ones of those who are mixed up with the darker side of Unusual communities?"

"That might make sense," Ashley said. "There are those who cross the line in the way they deal with humans, abusing their powers. Some brag about taking advantage of humans for their own gain, or worse, for sport. Every group has their rotten apples."

"I don't know how we're going to narrow this down," Dean said shaking his head. "There are so many possibilities."

"Don't beat yourself up over this, Dean," Ashley said as she soothed him. "You just found out about the presence of this other person above Mike who's orchestrating The Cause. We need to keep looking. Something will turn up about it. We need to be patient and keep doing what we are doing."

"But that won't stop the next attack on you, or me, or anyone else we care about," Dean said. He remembered something else that he and Brynne had discussed at the diner. "Brynne and James had an idea that might help us stay safe while we figure all of this out."

Ashley raised an eyebrow in question as she looked up at him. "What did they come up with?"

"Brynne suggested that in order to keep you and me safe while all of this plays out, we could move into some apartments that James has downtown," Dean said. "Apparently he has a whole building that has apartments and offices in it. He has a security team there and can keep us safe. I just worry that since The Cause is targeting Unusuals who are close to Brynne and me, that you might be a target, too."

"Dean," Ashley said. "I told you, I can take care of myself."

"I know you think you can," he responded. "I also know that there are those who would like to hurt me and any person close to me. I couldn't bear to have anything happen to you. You're still weak following what you did for Zora at the lake. What is going to prevent someone from taking a stab at getting to you?"

"I don't think it's me we need to worry about, Dean," Ashley said. "You are the one who is the most important player on the chess board right now. We need to protect you. I think you are too exposed here in this apartment, so maybe you should move in temporarily downtown and then we can see what happens."

"I won't move without you, too, Ash," Dean said. "If I'm important to this situation, then you're important to me. I'll move if you'll move with me."

"Are you asking me to move in with you?" Ashley asked with a sly smile.

"Uh, no, uh," Dean stammered. "I mean, I only meant … There are two apartments. You'll have your own place."

Ashley giggled and hugged Dean. "I'm just teasing you. I know what you meant."

"Yeah, well, I'm serious," Dean said smiling at her. "I'll only move in at James' apartment building if you come with me. I have to know you're safe, too."

Just then there was a thump from the porch outside the door to

Dean's apartment. It sounded like someone fell on the stairs up to the landing. Dean got up and went to the door to look out the window, He didn't see anything, but he couldn't see down the stairs, so he unlocked and opened the door to see if something had fallen from the roof. As he unlocked the door and went to step outside, the door pushed in against him, and a figure rushed inside, knocking Dean to the floor in the kitchen.

Dean rolled over and looked up to see a dark figure rushing at Ashley. Dean quickly climbed to his feet and rushed over to her, then stopped as a voice sounded and sent ice to his soul.

"Stop, Dean," Zach's voice said. "If you come any closer, I'll kill her."

Dean stopped, his fists clenched as he watched Ashley struggle briefly with Zach. He stood behind her. He had her arm wrenched behind her back and a large folding pocket knife opened and at her throat. It glinted in the dim lights of the apartment and looked razor-sharp.

"Zach," Ashley said calmly as she stopped struggling. "You don't have to do this. I know you. You're a good paramedic, and this isn't something you want to do. You're being influenced by someone else in this."

"Shut up, Bitch!" Zach snapped, pressing the point of the knife closer to her neck and drawing a pinprick of blood. "You are not going to use your spells to charm me like you have Dean. He's beyond hope because of you. That's what Mike said, and I believe him now that I've seen the two of you together."

Dean stood there, his body rigid, feeling completely helpless. His mind spun through possible solutions as he watched Zach hold that knife at his Ashley's throat.

"Zach, what do you want?" Dean asked. He decided to try and talk through this since he wasn't some kind of superhero, and didn't have any military or defensive training to disarm a knife-wielding maniac.

"I want to tell you that you have chosen the wrong side in this fight and that you can still make the right decision," Zach said.

"And you think that this is going to change my mind?" Dean was incredulous that Zach thought this would work. He seemed desperate, out of control, which was different from the Zach he had met previously. "Zach, this doesn't make any sense. We are just trying to keep people safe and help people. That's why you became a paramedic, too, just like me."

"I'm nothing like you, Dean," Zach snapped. "I would never fall under a spell like you have from one of these creatures." He twisted Ashley's arm where he levered it up behind her back, making her wince in pain. She didn't say a word, just meeting Dean's eyes.

Dean didn't know what to do. He stood rooted to the floor in the kitchenette area of his small apartment, just a few feet away from the former paramedic holding Ashley captive. He wasn't sure what was going to happen, but he knew he couldn't just stand by and do nothing. And yet there wasn't anything he could do but talk. Could he convince Zach to back down? He had to try.

"Zach," Dean started, trying to talk the other man down. "Something is wrong. This is not like how you were acting the last time you and I talked. What happened?"

"Everything happened," Zach snapped. "I'm a hunted man. That video of me after the Sabatani's fire is playing everywhere. My photo is in the newspapers and playing on twenty-four-hour news channels. To make matters worse, Joe, the guy who was with me, turned up dead in my apartment. Someone killed him, and I think they are going to kill me, too. The Cause doesn't like failures and no one I know in the group will return my calls for help."

"So why don't you turn yourself in to the police? You could surrender to the authorities?" Dean asked.

"That'll just get me killed faster," Zach said. "If I get locked up in a jail cell, I'll end up dead within a day. The Cause is everywhere, and I can't get safe."

"Zachary," Ashley said, her voice smooth and calm. "I can assure your safety. I have resources that will protect you from The Cause after you turn yourself in."

Zach wrenched her arm again and Dean took a step towards the two of them before a hiss of warning from Zach stopped him.

"Look, Zach," Dean pleaded. "Don't hurt her. She's done nothing to you."

"She can't be killed, Dean," Zach laughed. "I could shove this knife into the base of her brain and it would just send her away. I did some research into the Eldara trash living among us. All I can do is send her away for a hundred years or so. This body will die, but she'll come back again." He laughed wryly. "All I can do is hurt you for taking the wrong side in this fight. If I kill her now and send her away, you'll lose your ally and her help. That's what I'm here to do. I know I'm a dead man walking. I just want you to know some pain before The Cause catches up with me."

Dean's heart froze. He couldn't risk losing Ashley, even if she didn't really die, he couldn't lose her from his life. He had just found her.

"Zach please don't," Dean pleaded. "I'll help you. I can go to the Chief and get him to make sure the police keep you safe if you turn yourself in."

"I can't let you remove me from this location and time, Zach," Ashley said. "You will let me go.

"You can't tell me what to do, Bitch! I'm going to send you back to the hell you came from and there's nothing you can do about it," Zach hissed. His arm tensed and Dean watched helplessly as he knew that Zach was about to plunge the knife blade into Ashley's exposed neck. Then something happened.

Time seemed to slow, and light spread from around Ashley's outline. There was no other way to describe it. If was like all the light in the room intensified and concentrated around her. There was a flash, and a cry of pain, and Dean had to shield his eyes. When his vision started to return to normal a few moments later, he saw Zach was groaning on the floor behind Ashley, and she was standing over him shaking her head.

"Zach," Ashley said, standing over him. "The Eldara are not all beings of peace, though I am for the most part. But even the most peaceful of us are not without our defenses. I was never in any danger. You, however, are in a very dangerous place. It is clear you do not want our help, and I am not inclined to offer it to you anymore."

Zach whimpered on the floor, still somewhat dazed by whatever Ashley did to him. He looked up at her, fear in his eyes. "Are you going to kill me now?"

"I don't kill, Zach. I'm not like some of my more vengeful sisters," Ashley said. "I'm a healer. I also know that you are already near the end of your time here in this existence. You have chosen your path, and that last decision you made to try and kill me was the one that sealed your fate. I can do nothing for you at this point. I don't know how or where, but you will not live out the week."

Dean walked over to stand next to Ashley. She was speaking with an authority he had never heard from her before. It was as if she were receiving words from somewhere else as she spoke them. Her certainty in the pronouncement of Zach's fate was eerie.

Zach scooted backward on his butt, then climbed to his feet, swaying as he did so. He was not steady on his feet, and he stumbled some as he took another step back. He looked at Dean standing there next to Ashley, glanced at the knife on the floor in front of them. Dean took the hint and stooped down to pick up the blade from the floor.

"I don't believe in your words, your pronouncements," Zach said. His voice quavered. He didn't sound as if he believed what he was saying. "I'll come back and next time, you won't know what hit you." The former paramedic edged around the side of the room and then ran for the open door. Dean ran after him, but Zach was faster and he ran down the stairs and disappeared around the corner of the garage.

Dean stood in the doorway at the top of the stairs and looked out into the darkness for a while to make sure he was gone. Then he turned and went back inside, closing and locking the door behind him.

"We should call the police," Dean said walking over to the counter where his cell phone sat next to his wallet and keys. "They are looking for him and should know that he was here."

"It won't matter," Ashley said. "They will not find him. Anyway, he will not live for long."

"How can you say that?" Dean asked. "Did you do something to him?"

"No," Ashley said. She took his hand in hers. "When he touched me, I was able to detect some of his life force. I could also sense his connection to fate and this earthly timeline. His time here on earth is almost done. I don't know how it will happen, but he will be dead soon. I felt it as soon as he turned down our offer to help. Up until that moment, he had a chance to survive. That chance disappeared when he made his decision."

Dean picked up the phone. "I think we need to alert them that he was here. Even another hour still gives him time to hurt us or someone else." He dialed 911 and waited until the dispatcher's voice sounded. He gave his name and official designation to the dispatcher. She recognized his voice and asked what the problem was. He gave his report of the attack by Zach and requested police. He told them that no one was injured and that no ambulance was necessary. The dispatcher advised him to call back if Zach returned, to lock the door, and that an officer was dispatched to take a report in person.

Dean hung up the phone and looked at Ashley. A thin trickle of dried blood traced a line down the side of her throat where Zach had pricked her skin with the knife when he grabbed her. The bleeding had stopped, but the sight of it gave Dean a shiver.

Ashley saw his reaction, her hand rising to her throat. "I'm fine, Dean. I was in no real danger. When I sensed his final intent to take action, I reacted to defend myself."

"But he could have taken you away from me," Dean said. "That is something that I was worried about. He was right in that respect. I would have been devastated if something had happened to you."

"I'm alright, Dean," Ashley said. "Look, if it makes you feel better, I'll move into James' apartment building with you. I'm in no danger, but you are far too exposed and at risk here in this place."

Dean reached out and squeezed her hand. He had wanted her to say yes to his request to move, but he had not wanted the events of the evening to be the impetus for that move. He supposed he should be thankful that something had changed her mind, but the stress of seeing her in danger was almost too much to bear.

The two of them returned to the couch as they planned how they would move their things to the offered lodgings while they waited for the police officer to arrive. In the back of his mind, he wondered how Zach was going to meet his end. It was a strange thing to consider as they talked through their plans.

## Chapter 24

After the police took their report on Zach's attack of Ashley and left, Dean texted Brynne letting her know that they were going to take James up on the offer to move into his building downtown. She responded back quickly and said that James would have his assistant Celeste contact them to arrange the details. It was already late in the evening, and Dean and Ashley were both exhausted. The events of the last few days, from their trip to the lake to the long work day, and the meeting and attack by Zach, had all taken their toll.

Dean checked the lock on the door again for the third time after the officer had departed. He told them they would leave a marked police unit parked out front for the night in case Zach returned, but Dean was still scared of what could have happened, and what could still happen. Ashley sat on the sofa and watched him as he paced the apartment's perimeter. Dean checked all the windows each time he passed one to make sure they were locked and looked through the blinds into the darkness outside, but didn't see anything. Finally after a half hour of this he gave up and turned to look at Ashley.

"I don't know what to do," Dean said. "I feel helpless. I should have done something to stop him from hurting you." Ashley had gone to the bathroom and cleaned the dried trickle of blood from her neck. The small cut had stopped bleeding, but Dean could still see the mark on her neck and it seemed to taunt him that he was powerless to help his girlfriend when she had needed him the most.

"You need to calm down and sit still, Dean," Ashley said. "I'm fine, and I told you that I was never in any danger. I can protect myself. I have been in worse situations than this one and walked away without a scratch."

"Well, this time you did get a scratch," Dean said, pointing to her neck. He walked over and sat down next to her on the couch. "What if he had decided to push that knife home? Could you have stopped him before he did that?"

"I did stop him," she replied. "He was disarmed and left without anyone getting hurt. Zach was given a choice to determine his fate. He chose not to listen to my warnings. My conscience is clear, he was given a choice."

"But I let him in," Dean said. "I should be the one protecting you and not the other way around."

"You have watched over me," Ashley said. She laid a hand on his forearm as he sat next to her. "After I healed Zora, you took care of me while I regathered my strength. That was you taking care of me. This time was my turn. We are a team in this endeavor, Dean. We have to work together, but, more importantly, we need to trust each other to do what each of us can do."

"But I don't even know all that you can do," Dean replied. "I didn't know that you could zap him, or whatever it was that you did."

"I exposed my true form for a moment," Ashley said. "I am Eldara. In the old tongue, it means 'light ones' or 'made of light.' We assume corporeal form when here on earth and most of us choose never to reveal our true nature or form. However, were you to see me in my true form, it would overwhelm your senses. I simply used some of that power to overwhelm Zach's senses before he could take further action. If you look at the references to the Eldara over the millennia, you will see us defined as creatures of brightness, white light. It is why we are so often depicted with halos. That is the best way for those who have seen us or witnessed our true power and selves, to depict us."

Dean smiled. He liked finally learning something about Ashley's past and her identity as an Eldara. He knew she referred to stories in places like the Bible. Based on what he knew, it was likely an Eldara who stood in the empty tomb of Christ and told the women who came to prepare his body for proper burial that he had risen. It caused him to wonder if Ashley had ever appeared in historical scenes that he would recognize.

"So Ashley," he asked. "When are you going to tell me some of your past exploits in history? You must have some good stories to tell. I'm too wired to go to sleep just now."

"Unlike my sister and some of the other Eldara, I prefer to work behind the scenes," she responded. "I'm a healer, and that is the best way to enact healing. I helped others throughout history learn and become better healers. I try to avoid the spotlight. Some of my Eldara colleagues are not so humble. They like the spotlight, or rather to create a spotlight in which to shine. Gabriel is the worst of them, but he's a warrior at heart, so he's all about standing out in a crowd. It kills him that he can't appear in gleaming armor anymore. He hates that every army and soldier wears earth tones and camouflage now." She laughed quietly to herself. Her laughter calmed him.

"Come on, we need to go to bed and get some sleep. I know I am exhausted and you're tired, too. Everything will be better in the morning and we can work on getting ready to move into James' apartments tomorrow after work."

▭

DEAN AWOKE A FEW HOURS LATER, near dawn, to a chime on his phone. It was a message from a number he didn't recognize. He rolled over and looked at the screen and swiped to open the messaging app. It was from someone named Celeste who said she was James' assistant and that she had all the details arranged for him and Ashley to move in after their work shifts that day. He read the message several times as he cleared his head and then texted a reply that he had received it.

He rolled over to see Ashley lying next to him. She was still asleep. She slept so soundly most of the time that he was not sure how she heard her alarm to get up for work in the mornings. He looked at his watch and decided it was close enough to when he needed to get up anyway. He rolled out of bed and went out to the large living area off of the bedroom. He looked out the front window and saw the police cruiser still parked on the street outside his second-floor garage apartment. He shook his head and went to make coffee and some breakfast for him and Ashley. He also needed to pack up some clothes to take to the new apartment. The message from Celeste said that it was fully furnished and that James had the kitchens stocked with some basics so they'd have food.

He heard a small sound behind him and turned at the kitchen counter to see Ashley come out of the bedroom. She was wearing a pair of his boxer shorts and a gray tank top t-shirt. He marveled at her beauty, even first thing in the morning. Who woke up looking that good? His girlfriend, that's who.

"Stop ogling me and make me some coffee," she said as she approached. "I have to wake up and get ready for work."

Dean turned and started the single cup brewer to make her a cup of coffee. He felt her step up behind him and slip her arms around him and hug him from the back. He felt the soft firmness of her breasts press into his back as she squeezed him gently while he worked.

"Do you want me to make some eggs or do you just want cereal?" Dean asked as he turned in her embrace to face her.

"Cereal is fine," she said. "I just need that coffee to get started. Luckily I brought a spare set of scrubs to change into, so I don't have to stop by my apartment on the way to the hospital."

"I got a text from Celeste," he said. "She is James' assistant. She said that all was ready to go downtown. She said the apartments are fully furnished, and she will make sure there are some basics in the kitchen for us after work. I'll forward the address to you. She said to park beneath the building in the underground garage. The attendant already has our names, car descriptions and license plate numbers."

"Good," Ashley said. "The sooner we get you squared away there, the sooner we can both get back to focusing on what we need to do to solve this mystery."

Dean got out the box of cereal and filled two bowls while Ashley got her coffee squared away the way she liked it. She poured some milk from the carton into her coffee and then some more on the cereal in the bowls. She put the milk away in the fridge and then took her coffee and cereal over to the small round table nearby. She looked out the window.

"I see our police escort is still there," Ashley said.

"Yeah, I saw that, too," Dean said as he joined her at the table. "I will be glad when all this excitement is over with, and I can live my life without police calls and attackers in the night. Life was so much easier when I was just a simple paramedic with regular patients, even if those patients were far from normal."

Ashley chuckled. "Remember the ancient curse: 'May you live in interesting times.' That holds true now more than ever. And yet, if you hadn't had that excitement, we never would have met. I'm thankful for that, at least."

"Me too," Dean said. He thought about that as the two of them finished their breakfast in silence. He cleaned up the dishes when they were finished, while Ashley went back to the bedroom to get changed. She was slipping on her scrubs when he came in and started to change into his uniform shirt and navy cargo pants. He grabbed some clothes and additional uniforms and threw them in a large gym bag he had, and carried it over by the door. He glanced at his watch. The last twenty-four hours had been hectic, and the next twenty-four held even more change as he moved to a new home, even if it was a temporary arrangement.

Ashley came over to join him at the door. She had her bag and purse over one shoulder, and her car keys in her other hand. "Shall we?" she asked.

Dean opened the door and held it open for her while she proceeded him out and down the stairs to start the rest of their day.

He locked up and followed her. He kissed her goodbye briefly at her car and then he went to his pickup and threw his bag into the front passenger seat before climbing in himself. He waived at the police officer who returned the gesture as he drove by. It was off to another day at Station U, then on to the new apartment and the next step in their work to stop The Cause.

## Chapter 25

After a day of routine calls at the station, Dean got the directions to James' downtown building from Brynne and texted them to Ashley. He had thought he would be able to follow Brynne over to the apartment building after work since she lived with the vampire in his penthouse apartment in that same building, but she had some other errands to run and said she would catch up with him later, after he had settled in.

Ashley sent him a message that she was being held late in the ER due to an overflow of patients, so he was going to have to move in on his own. He said goodbye to Brook and Tammy, his relief crew at the Station, and headed out to his pickup. He dialed the directions into his phone's GPS, started the directions and headed downtown to his new place. He hoped it was only a short term move, but he also knew that he had no control over that.

As he arrived in the downtown area of Elk City about ten minutes later, he saw the building he was looking for ahead and on the right. It was a rather nondescript concrete building of modern design with lots of windows. It appeared to be about 15 stories tall and dominated the block on which it was situated. Because of one-way streets, he had to circle the block until he came in from the correct direction to access the underground garage. There was an enclosed attendant station with a uniformed security guard on the ramp leading down into the garage. As Dean pulled up to the gate, the guard stepped out of the enclosure with a clipboard in hand.

"Can I help you, sir?" the guard asked. He seemed bored and given the small workstation he came from, Dean couldn't blame him.

"I'm Dean Flynn," the paramedic said. "I'm supposed to move into an apartment today?"

The guard looked at his clipboard, using his finger to trace down the list he had there. "Here it is, Mr. Flynn," the guard said. "You will be parking in marked parking space number twenty-three. You'll get a card from Ms. Teal you can swipe after hours to get in and out of the garage. Welcome to the Nightwing Building, Mr. Flynn." The guard stepped back to his enclosure and pressed a button there. Dean waited for the gate arm to raise completely and then went on down to the parking area. There were two levels, but he saw the clearly marked numbers on the floor and his slot was on the first level, about one hundred fifty feet from the elevator. Dean pulled into slot twenty-three and slid the gear shift into park. He didn't want to live here this close to James and Brynne. It only reminded him of what was going on there in that relationship. He had told Brynne that he was okay with James occasionally feeding on her, but that wasn't true. It still bothered him. It bothered him a lot.

He got out of his pickup truck and grabbed the gym bag from the front passenger seat. He walked over to the elevator and once inside, Dean saw that he had been right. There were fifteen floors in the building. The elevator buttons read from P1 and P2 then one through fourteen with a level PH above that. Unless James had parking on the roof, that final PH stood for the penthouse. He punched the first-floor button marked L for lobby as Brynne had instructed, and the elevator door slid shut.

Once on the first floor, Dean walked to a security desk situated facing the street level front doors. The guard looked up and smiled as he approached.

"You must be Mr. Flynn," the guard said as Dean walked up to the counter. There was a bank of video surveillance monitors behind the large counter and desk, as well as a computer screen. "Let me call up to Ms. Teal and let her know you have arrived." The guard picked up the phone handset, dialed a number and murmured a few words Dean couldn't make out before hanging up. "Ms. Teal, Mr. Lee's assistant, will be right down. If you'd like to sit down and wait, she should be here shortly." The guard gestured to a seating area nearby in the lobby with leather and chrome chairs, and a couch, all situated around a glass coffee table.

"That's alright," Dean said. "I'll stand." He walked around the small lobby watching the darkening street outside as the sun set on Elk City. He was still looking at the traffic and pedestrians passing by outside when he heard a voice call behind him.

"You must be Dean," a friendly woman's voice with a deep southern drawl sounded from the direction of the elevators. Dean turned to see an attractive, pale woman with red hair in her late twenties, and dressed in a conservative pants suit with a blazer. She extended her hand as she approached.

"Yes," Dean said as he shook the woman's hand. It was cool to the touch and confirmed Dean's suspicions that she was a vampire like her boss. "You are Celeste?"

"I am," she said. "I'm so glad you took James up on the offer to stay here for a while, at least until the current troubles blow over. It's much safer for you that way." She looked around. "Is Ashley with you?"

"Uh, no," Dean explained. "She had to work late at the hospital. She'll be over in a few hours. Will that be a problem?"

"Absolutely not," Celeste said, smiling as she continued. "I'm sure you have already guessed, I am up all night anyway. We are on a nocturnal schedule here for the most part at Nightwing Industries. We tell our local suppliers and clients that it is due to our overseas investments and affiliates. I'll make sure the guards keep an eye out for her, and I'll have them call you, as well as myself, when she arrives. If you're comfortable doing so, you can come down and bring her up after I get you situated. I'm quite excited, actually. I've never met an Eldara before."

Celeste gestured to the hallway to the elevators. "Shall we go up and get you settled? I picked out two adjacent apartments for the two of you. You're on the fourteenth floor, just below the Penthouse where James and Brynne reside. I have a place on the same level. The view is quite lovely." She pushed the up button, and the doors slid open immediately. Once they were inside, she pressed the fourteen button, which flashed on and off. Celeste took a small keycard from her hand and waved it over the button, and the light turned solid and the elevator started upwards. She handed him two of the key cards in her hand.

"These are the keys to your room," she said. "As you can see, they also operate the elevators to the private floors, as well as access to the garage for entry and egress. I had two made in case you wished to share one with Ashley."

"Thank you," Dean said as he took the proffered cards. He didn't see a magnetic stripe so they must have chips embedded in them.

The doors slid open on a small vestibule with a table that had a colorful flower arrangement centered on it. He stepped out of the elevator and followed Celeste down the hallway to a door numbered fourteen-twenty-three. She waited while he waved one of the cards over the door plate and the small LED light on the door handle turned green. He turned the handle and stepped inside as he opened the door. It led to a furnished suite of rooms. To the right was a small kitchen area with a tall table and two padded barstools set next to it. There was a living area next to that, with a sofa and two matching chairs around a wooden coffee table. Across from the couch was a credenza with a large flatscreen TV on top. Next to the large, curtained window was a desk, a swivel desk chair, and on the desk, a computer monitor. He saw the computer tower situated to the right of the desk on the floor, partially hidden by the long window drapes. He turned to the right again and saw a doorway that led to a bedroom with a king-sized bed, dresser, two end tables, and two lamps. Another door off of the bedroom led to a master bath and large walk-in shower area. There was also a large walk-in closet against one wall.

"I hope this is to your liking," Celeste said. "James said to set you and Ashley up with the best we had to offer."

"It will be fine," Dean understated.

"The computer is hooked up to the internet if you need it, and I'll email you the wi-fi password for your phone or your own laptop as well," Celeste offered. "I took the liberty of having your kitchen stocked with a few things to get you started. Just the basics. If you need anything else, there is a small corner grocery two blocks away. The guard downstairs can give you directions if you need them."

"This is good," Dean said. "Thank you, Celeste. Please thank James for his generosity."

"I will be sure to do so," she responded. "He asked you and Ashley to come up later after you get settled. Your key card is set to access most of the building including the penthouse level. There is also a small fitness center on the second floor if you'd like to use it."

"I will talk with Ashley when she arrives, but I'm sure that we will be able to come up later," Dean said.

"Well, then," Celeste said, clapping her hands together and giving a nod. "If you are all set, I'll leave you to get settled. Here is my card. Call me if you need anything." She handed him a business card, then turned and left the apartment, pulling the door shut behind her with a click.

Dean looked around and then took his bag into the bedroom. He lifted it up on the king-sized bed and opened it, unpacking the contents into the dresser. He hung up his uniform shirts and noticed an iron and ironing board in the closet, as well as a small upright vacuum cleaner. He put the empty gym bag in the closet on the floor next to the vacuum. He turned and pulled his phone out of his pocket, snapping a quick pick of the bed and sent it to Ashley with a winking emoji.

She texted back that she would be leaving soon. Things had calmed down at the hospital. Dean sent a message describing the garage entrance and telling her that he'd come down to bring her upstairs once she arrived. She said she'd let him know when she was on the way. He put his phone down on the dresser along with his wallet and keys, and then changed out of his uniform into jeans and a T-shirt. He grabbed his phone, then went to check the kitchen. You never knew what you might get if someone else did the shopping for you, but Brynne must have briefed them. The pantry shelves had the cereal and toaster pastries he liked, and the refrigerator had his and Ashley's soda, beer and wine favorites. There were also the staples like milk, cheese, and butter. There was a loaf of bread on the counter and coffee pods next to the one-cup coffee maker.

He made himself a peanut butter sandwich, grabbed a soda and sat down to watch the TV, selecting the local news station. He wondered what the local and national news would do if they learned about the Unusuals living among the humans. Perhaps they did know and were part of the conspiracy to cover it up. He watched the sports, and then a syndicated sitcom came on that had him chuckling to himself when his phone buzzed in his pocket. He checked the screen and saw that Ashley was in the garage. He told her to come up to the lobby level and he'd meet her there. He slid on his sneakers and headed downstairs.

He showed up in the lobby and saw Ashley standing next to two large suitcases, talking with the guard. Clearly he had under-packed, he thought. Ashley turned and looked over at him as he approached. She said goodbye to the guard and pulled her suitcases over to him. She leaned in and gave him a kiss as he approached.

"Hi, Sweetie," she cooed. "This is exciting. Kind of like a holiday away."

"If you say so," Dean said. "I am just glad for the increased level of security here."

The elevator opened behind him and he turned his head to see Celeste emerge. She quickly crossed over to them and gave Ashley a slight bow.

"Eldara, I'm glad to have you staying under our roof," Celeste said in a formal tone. "I'm Celeste Teal and anything you need that is in my power to provide, I'll bring you."

Dean saw again that there was a hierarchy within the Unusual community. Ashley, and the Eldara in general, figured pretty high in that pecking order, based on the deference that Celeste showed her. The assistant held out two key cards to Ashley.

"Celeste, it is a pleasure to meet you. Please call me Ashley," she said. "Some of my brethren like all the pomp and circumstance, but I'm of a simpler mindset."

"I'm sure that Dean will want to show you around, Eldara, uh-Ashley. You're in unit twenty-four on the fourteenth floor, right next to his place," Celeste said. "James and Brynne hoped the two of you would come up later after you are situated. They'll contact you with the details when you're ready. I have to attend to another matter, but here is my card. Don't hesitate to call or text me if you need anything."

The vampire assistant nodded another small bow, then turned and headed over to the guard station while Dean took the two suitcases from Ashley and towed them back to the elevators. They were soon upstairs, and he was pulling the heavy bags into the apartment next to his, number twenty-four.

"What did you pack in here?" he asked. "We aren't going to be here that long."

"Oh, just a little bit of this and that," Ashley replied. "We might be here longer than you think, and I didn't want to have to go back to the other place every other day just to pick up some clothes and other things I needed." She walked around the apartment. "Ooo, this is nice. I could get used to living in a place like this for a while." Dean watched as she checked the fridge and saw yogurt and fruit inside, as well as the milk, butter, and cheese he found in his earlier. Clearly, Celeste knew something of what Ashley liked as well.

He went back into the bedroom and hoisted the two suitcases up on the bed so she could unpack them. He turned to see her stripping out of her scrubs down to her bra and panties in the doorway.

"Sorry, Sweetie," she said as she passed him. "I have to get a shower after the day at work I had today. Let me get cleaned up and then we can check and see if Brynne and James are ready for us to come upstairs."

"Can I watch?" he asked following her. "The shower door is made of glass."

"Watch is all," she said with a laugh. "I feel positively grimy. If you're nice, I'll let you scrub my back for me." He gave a growl he hoped sounded seductive, and she giggled and rolled her eyes. "Men!"

## Chapter 26

About an hour later, Brynne sent Dean a message to see if he and Ashley wanted to come up to the penthouse and meet with her and James. He returned a text saying yes, and he and Ashley headed up via the elevators. Using their key cards, the elevator took them up one floor to the penthouse level, and they exited to a hallway that led to a set of double doors with a doorbell button to the left.

Ashley reached out to push the doorbell button, but stopped as the doors opened, and Brynne smiled at them from the other side. This was the first time Dean had seen her out of her uniform work clothes and characteristic turtleneck. She was wearing a vintage black Led Zeppelin T-shirt and blue jeans. He noticed the two pinprick bite marks on her neck right away, but averted his eyes immediately. He wasn't really surprised by this, and drawing attention would only make things more tense and awkward.

"Come on in guys," Brynne said. "I'm happy you took us up on the offer to move in here for the time being."

Dean let Ashley enter first, then followed her. The penthouse apartment was impressive. The entry way led into a large open room with windows all around. He saw a kitchen off to the left as he walked in, and another hallway to the right that led off to the rest of the apartment, but the bulk of the space was one large room. James was seated in a large entertainment area with an enormous flat screen television mounted on the wall. He rose as they walked in.

"Ashley, Dean, I'm so glad you both are here," James said as he came forward. He shook Dean's hand in a firm grip, and then Dean flushed a bit as the vampire raised Ashley's hand to his lips to kiss as he bowed to her. He stood upright and gestured around. "Welcome to our humble abode."

"I have to say, James, I'm surprised by all the windows," Dean said. "It's beautiful to see at night like this, but I would expect it to be somewhat painful for you during the daylight hours."

"I have a special UV coating on the window glass. On particularly bright days, there are blackout shutters that I can close electronically," James explained. "I'm glad to have them though, and Brynne enjoys the sunlight. How can I keep her from it?"

"Thank you again for the offer of the apartments downstairs," Ashley said. "They are very well furnished, and I appreciated the efforts to stock the pantry for us."

"Celeste is most thorough, isn't she," James said. "She's been my assistant for more years than I can count. We often have visiting business acquaintances and Unusual VIPs in town who have need of a residence while they are here. It's part of what is expected of me as the head of our community in Elk City."

"Almost like the lord of the manor," Dean said. Brynne shot him a stern glance, but James chuckled.

"You are correct, Dean," the ancient vampire said. "It's exactly like the lord of the manor. Our traditions are very old, dating back to a time of feudal lords and fiefdoms. It is expected of me to provide some accommodations and a certain level of hospitality as the leader here. There are many things we hold over from the old times. We even have wars of succession in some areas still, although that hasn't happened here in the States for over a hundred years. Not since the war between the north and south."

"Are you still reminiscing about the good old days?" Celeste asked as she entered from the side hallway. "I thought I was the best thing to come out of the Civil War." She fanned herself with a hand, then laughed out loud and came into the room with a stack of papers and folders.

"You are, my dear, you are," James said. He took the papers she handed him, looked through them, then handed them back. "These will do fine, Celeste. Go ahead with the deal."

Celeste took them and nodded at the two newcomers. "I trust the apartments meet with your approval?"

"Yes, Celeste," Ashley said. "They are more than accommodating. They are already feeling like a bit of home. Thank you."

"Excellent," Celeste said with a smile. "I'm so glad you approve. Please let me know if you need anything. You have my card." She took the papers James handed her and headed back to the hallway into the back of the apartment.

Dean watched her leave, realizing that things like conversations with vampires reminiscing about the good old days over one hundred fifty years before had become commonplace in his life. When had that happened? He also realized that he didn't mind it. It was fun and exciting to learn more about the world. Imagine the things a history professor could learn from an ancient immortal being like Ashley or James.

"Dean," Brynne said, breaking the silence following Celeste's exit. "James is hoping that by having you here in the building, in close proximity to him, the two of you will be able to discover how you both figure into the current crisis. Perhaps it will give Ashley a hint on how to prepare for what is to come."

"I suppose that would be helpful," Dean said. "Did you tell James about Zach's visit to my apartment and his attack on Ashley last night?"

James looked alarmed, and Brynne shook her head. "I hadn't had the chance yet."

"I hope you were not harmed, Eldara?" James asked. "I would not have one of you injured while under my protection."

"I am not without my own protections, James," Ashley said. "It is not so easy to harm me, unless I wish to be. Regardless, I am well following the events of last night."

"I'm fine, too. Just in case you were wondering," Dean said.

"I'm sorry that my concern for the Eldara Sister does not match my concern for you, Dean," James chided. "She is a far more scarce resource in the world than a human paramedic. There are only so many Eldara in the world. To lose one, even for a short time, would be unfortunate in the extreme."

"I would not discount the importance of Dean's place in the world so lightly, James," Ashley said. "There is something central to this crisis that revolves around him, as well as you. There is a decision or action he will make. I'm not sure why it is him, but you are familiar with the way the humans and their free will are used as tools for the Gods' whims in their otherworldly struggles. Somehow this figures into their plans and Dean is central to that."

Brynne added her thoughts to the discussion as she relayed to James the details of the attack on Ashley and Dean in his home the previous night. "Zach was never the brightest guy. When I was working with him, I often wondered why he was assigned to me and Station U. It was never a good fit. It was one of the reasons I wasn't looking forward to training you, Dean. That opinion has changed, I'm pleased to say. Still, Zach's assignment to Station U makes more sense when you consider that Mike had something to do with his recommendation for the job."

"But Mike recommended me to the post as well, and that didn't work out for him either," Dean pointed out.

"I think that when the dim-witted Zach didn't pan out, Mike decided to try using a smarter student in the posting, hoping he could still guide you to see things his way after your first few weeks on the job," Brynne said. "I don't think he counted on how quickly you became acclimated to the clientele we serve. You have shaped up into an excellent paramedic and I think your probationary status will soon be released."

"Mike has never liked serving our community," James said. "His distaste for the Unusuals around him, though, dates back to when Brynne and I first met. Up until that point, he was simply doing his job, and he provided good care to our Unusual community. I don't think he allowed his distaste for the work to show until he realized that Brynne and I started dating. Then it became personal. He has carried this grudge for many years, but it is only lately that he has been emboldened enough to act upon it apparently."

"It has to have something to do with his meeting with this stranger that he alluded to," Dean said. "That seems to be what spurred the formation of The Cause and the initiation of the attacks on the Unusuals in Elk City." He looked at James. "Are there reports of other, similar attacks in other cities?"

"No, nothing like this is happening anywhere else. I checked for that right away," James said. "None of my counterparts elsewhere have had anything like this happen in their communities. They are most concerned about how we are handling things here, and there is a lot of scrutiny of what I am doing to protect my domain."

"What would happen if they don't like what you're doing?" Dean asked.

Brynne spoke up. "He holds his post under the authority of another who oversees the whole North American continent. If it is perceived that he can no longer fulfill his duties here, he would be replaced."

"So you all don't have elections like the rest of us?" Dean asked.

"No, I can be removed by my overlord if they think I'm not doing my job well enough," James said. "There are other ways to remove me from my position, including the challenge of ritual combat by one of my peers if they want my job, but that has not been done in a very long time."

"I'm wondering if your holding of the power here in Elk City is part of what is causing this to happen," Ashley interjected. "We know that Mike holds you responsible for what happens to Brynne. Perhaps his partner in this also holds some animosity toward you."

"But what does that have to do with Dean?" Brynne asked. "He's new to the city and new to the service of the Unusual community. It's almost like he's a wild card."

"An astute observation. That is why he is so important, Brynne," Ashley said. "Dean is the human part of the equation. His unpredictability and free will has been the center of this whole situation. He has been part of the attacks in some way each time. That makes him the crux, the pivot point for things. His decisions will impact all of this, somehow."

Dean considered that thought and didn't like what it said. If he had a decision to make, he wanted to know what he was supposed to do. A wrong choice could have a major impact on the whole situation, just like a bad diagnosis or treatment choice could impact a patient's life. Somehow, the correlation did not make him feel better.

"Let's ponder these things on another occasion," James said. "I would like to invite the two of you to remain for a late dinner with Brynne and me. We can talk about other things for the rest of the evening. We are glad to know that you are safe here with us for now. I am letting Kristof from Sabatani's operate a catering business out of my corporate kitchens downstairs while he rebuilds the restaurant. He offered to send up a dinner selection when he heard you two were going to be here to stay for a while. The food should be here soon. Until then, won't you sit down and join us for some lighter conversation."

James led the four of them into the main seating area where Dean and Ashley opted to sit together on a white leather love seat while James and Brynne took the matching couch. Dean never understood the penchant for white furniture. He thought it would be way too hard to keep clean. He thought about this as the conversation turned to more pleasant topics with Ashley and James comparing historical references and trying to see if they had known the same historical figures over the years. What a strange situation in which to find himself, discussing the relative sanity of Napoleon Bonaparte while they waited for dinner to arrive.

The important thing, as far as he was concerned, was that Ashley was here and safe from any attacks against him. The rest of this he was sure he could handle on his own when it came, as long as she was protected. He relaxed and settled back against the sofa, placing his arm around Ashley as he did. She looked up at him and smiled. It was all perfect. Nothing could go wrong as long as she was here with him.

# Epilogue

Mike Farver swirled the bourbon in his cup as he stared into the smoky depths. He looked up from his booth at the back of the bar in downtown Elk City. He glanced around to check if anyone was watching as a man dressed in a long, dark coat approached him. Mike took a sip of the bourbon, feeling the familiar warmth as he swallowed. He gestured to the seat across from him as the dark figure sat down.

"Michael, my man, you seem upset," the man said as he took his seat.

"You don't have to kill him," Mike whispered as he leaned across the table. "Zach is clumsy and foolish, but that is no reason to kill him."

"He has become a liability. That happened when he allowed himself to be identified in the video surveillance after the fire," the man said with a deep baritone rumble and just a hint of an accent. It might be Eastern European, Mike thought.

"Artur, we could just get him to leave town. That would get him out of the way just as easily," Mike said.

"He will be caught eventually, Michael," Artur said. "I promise,

I'll make it quick. He'll feel almost nothing. If he is caught by the authorities and talks, he will expose you. I cannot have that."

"So what do we do now?" Michael asked. "Zach was our contact with all the goons he had assembled."

"You will need to get their names from Zach. You have one day. Then we will take care of the Zach problem and lay a little trap for the paramedic, Dean Flynn. Zach will be the perfect bait," Artur said. "You get the contact information for the others so you can take over their operations. There is much we have to do while our meddling paramedic is out of the way."

"He won't stay that way long," Mike said. "I'm sure that bastard James will work to help get him out of trouble if we are successful. No matter how guilty he looks, he won't stay that way, not with James' resources to back him."

"That may be, but my plans will make sure he is no longer riding the ambulance at Station U." Artur paused as a waiter passed close enough to overhear them and then continued after the man had passed by. "You are sure he will be suspended if implicated in a crime, pending the outcome of the case?"

Mike nodded. "It is department policy in cases where a responder is charged with a felony."

"Good, then this plan will get him out of the way. As long as he is not responding to incidents and treating patients, my sources say he will not figure into our plans. Even the Eldara bitch can't help that." The bitterness showed in Artur's tone when he mentioned the angel.

"Then we proceed with our plans?" Michael said. "I thought that with the loss of Zach, we'd back off for a time and let things cool down."

"Oh, not at all, Michael," Artur said. "No, we will strike while the iron is still hot, and get the most from the upheaval this will cause to our opponents. James will never expect what we have coming next, and with his focus on helping Dean, he will be unprepared for our little coup."

Mike looked up and shuddered as he saw the look on Artur's face. He wondered again how he had gotten mixed up in this. It was

Brynne's fault. She had brought all of this on herself, when she chose that monster over him. And now she had dragged him into this unlikely partnership. Mike had to keep focusing on that betrayal. He must stay the course. He would do anything to bring James down. The old paramedic looked up at Artur and nodded, his lips pressed into a firm line on his face. The other man grinned. He saw that Mike had resigned himself to carrying their plans forward. Mike shivered a little as Artur let his fangs show in an evil smile.

Read on for a preview of Book 3 - *The Paramedic's Choice*

# JAMIE DAVIS

# THE PARAMEDIC'S CHOICE

*Extreme Medical Services Book 3*

Dean's eyes focused on the end of the gun barrel. He froze. He saw the finger tighten on the trigger, starting the squeeze that would fire a bullet from the chamber. That bullet would kill him. A loud bang and a flash announced the coming of the slug, but instead of the pain of the bullet striking his chest, he felt a jolt from his right, knocking him to the ground on the night club's lighted dance floor.

He sat upright in bed, jolted awake by the impact with the floor in the dream. It had been a dream, right? He looked around his room in the darkness. He was disoriented until he realized he was in the new apartment. A movement next to him caused him to look down and see Ashley lying in bed next to him. The dream receded into faint memory as he looked at his girlfriend. She was an angel — literally. She was a member of the Eldara race that served as the messengers and representatives of God among humans. She pulled the blankets up to her chin as she rolled over.

Dean climbed out of bed, still feeling the adrenaline coursing through his body from the nightmare. It had seemed very real, more real than most of his dreams, at least those he remembered. Dean tried to remember the details of the dream. It could be important. He hoped it wasn't prophetic. He didn't recognize the location but it was some type of nightclub. When he tried to concentrate on the face in the shadows behind the muzzle of the gun, the memory swam out of focus. Whoever it was, he knew they were determined to kill him and had almost succeeded. Then, just in time, someone or something had pushed him to the ground.

Walking to the kitchen, he poured himself a glass of juice from the refrigerator. He knew where he was now. He was in an apartment in the Nightwing building downtown, a guest of the Vampire Lord of Elk City. James Lee and his human girlfriend, Dean's supervising paramedic Brynne Garvey, had convinced Dean to move in here. That had come after a series of attacks on the Unusual patients he served with the other paramedics at Station U. Their patients were the hidden creatures of myth and legend that lived among their human neighbors, unknown except for a small group of humans who knew of their existence. Some of the more bigoted humans had formed a group of homegrown terrorists that decided to drive the creatures of nightmares from the community, striking with hate crime attacks against those served by the Station U paramedics. There was fear that Dean and the other paramedics were at risk.

He walked back through the dark apartment, sipping his juice. He peered through the bedroom doorway at Ashley sleeping there. He was so lucky that she had come into his life and provided him a level of stability he sorely needed during this stressful time. As well, there was the love, an intimacy they shared, that had filled a hole in his life. This Eldara Sister, one of a collection of mythical healers, was currently a nurse in the Emergency Room at the Elk City Medical Center. She had told Dean that he was integral to unraveling the mystery of the attacks happening in the city, and to ending them. He was supposed to do something, eventually. The problem was that no one seemed to know what that action would be. The attacks intensified, driving him and Ashley to move into two apartments here in James' secure building. Dean felt the pressure to end this drama but didn't know how.

He looked at his watch and snorted. He might as well stay up; he had to leave for work in about an hour and a half. Returning the empty juice glass to the sink, Dean gathered his uniform for the coming day and went in to take a shower.

As he left the station the night before, Brynne announced to him that he had reached the end of his probationary period as a new paramedic at Station U. That meant there was to be a brief ceremony at the beginning of his shift, including the presentation of his paramedic badge, replacing the probationary badge he had been wearing for the last weeks of training. He was proud of having that distinction. It meant that he was equal to Brynne and the others, and up to the task of taking care of their challenging patients - whether it be a fairy, a vampire, a werewolf, or a genie half-stuck in a bottle.

Turning on the shower and testing the water temperature, Dean knew he should be proud of this milestone in his career. That pleasure was tempered, however, by the fact he couldn't shake off the feeling of dread from that dream. He decided to let the warm water of the shower try to wash that feeling away. He stripped down and climbed in.

___

ASHLEY WAS JUST GETTING up when he grabbed his keys to head out to work. He wanted to leave early and stop by his old apartment to pick up some things he had left behind. There were some items that he might need if he stayed at the Nightwing apartment for any length of time. He really should have packed better the previous evening, but he had just grabbed a few changes of clothes and a uniform for the next day. He didn't think it would hurt to go back to his apartment and pick up things as he needed them.

He went over and gave Ashley a kiss good morning as she rose from the bed. She didn't have to be at work until seven AM, while his twelve-hour paramedic shifts started at six. She mumbled something about needing coffee and hoped he'd have a good day, then headed for the bathroom. He watched her go and closed the door, still amazed at his luck connecting with such an amazing woman.

He took off for his pickup truck, parked in the secure underground garage below the building.

Twenty minutes later, in his old apartment, he grabbed a small suitcase and started throwing clothing and some personal items in it. It didn't take him long, and he looked around at the spacious apartment he rented, situated over the garage owned by an elderly couple on the outskirts of town. The residential neighborhood was quiet, and his landlords were kind. He had to remember that he still needed to check in from time to time and help out with their yard chores. It was part of his lease agreement with them, but also something he enjoyed doing. Mr. and Mrs. Baxter had adopted him as if he were their own son and had in some ways taken the place of the parents he didn't have in his life anymore. Dean had been on his own for a long time and had thought he didn't need that kind of relationship in his life. The Baxters had proven him wrong.

Zipping up the full suitcase, he went out onto the small porch at the top of the stairs and pulled the door shut behind him, locking it and checking to make sure it was latched. It had just been a few nights before when the former paramedic Zach had attacked both him and Ashley in that apartment. It had been an act of desperation, after his actions as a member of the hate group, The Cause, had exposed him to authorities. The Cause was determined to expose the monsters living among the humans, and drive the Unusuals from their community. Zach was now being hunted by the police, following his exposure on surveillance video firebombing a local restaurant owned by a member of the Unusual community in Elk City. Based on his statements to Dean and Ashley during his attack on them, The Cause was displeased with him getting caught on camera.

Ashley had disarmed Zach, even while he held a knife to her throat, by using her innate Eldara powers to overwhelm him. The former paramedic had fled the apartment in fear. That attack had finally persuaded Ashley that she and Dean needed to take James and Brynne up on the offer of a safe place to stay downtown. Dean wondered where Zach was now. Ashley had announced to Zach during the attack, with startling finality, that his time on the earth was short, stating that The Cause member would not live out the week. She had told Dean that she sensed his lifeline shorten as soon as he made the final decision to refuse their offer to surrender and accept their help. Instead, he tried to kill Ashley. Wherever he was, Dean hoped he didn't do anything else dangerous or stupid in his desperation to change his fate. Grabbing the suitcase by the handle, Dean headed down the outside stairs and tossed it in the passenger seat of his white pickup truck. He glanced at his watch. It was time to head into work.

## Chapter 2

Dean pulled into the station parking lot about fifteen minutes early, then went inside to see the two nightshift paramedics, Brook and Tammy, seated in recliners, watching some syndicated, reality court TV show. He laughed because he knew they were hooked on the show, and they talked about it all the time.

"What's Judge Jane up to now?" Dean asked as he walked by. "Is she slapping down some idiot who thinks he doesn't have to pay his ex-wife's car payment or something?"

"You have no appreciation of what good entertainment is all about," Tammy quipped. "Judge Jane tells it like it is and she doesn't take any sass from anybody."

"Did you really just say 'she doesn't take any sass'?" Dean asked, laughing aloud.

"That's what Judge Jane calls it, and I don't know a better word to use than what she uses," Brook, the younger of the two, defended her partner then changed the subject. "Hey, how's the new digs downtown? Is the apartment classy?"

"It's nice, but it's not the same as being home in my own place," Dean said. "It's kind of like a high-end hotel suite, as in a fun place to stay, but I wouldn't want to live there."

"Wouldn't want to live where?" Brynne, Dean's partner and supervisor, entered the squad room, catching the end of the conversation.

"We were just asking Dean for details on his new place downtown," Tammy explained. "We wanted details on how the other half lives. You know, Brynne, like when you have a sugar daddy." Dean knew that Tammy referred to Brynne's boyfriend, James Lee. He was more than just wealthy. He was also the vampire overlord of all the Unusuals in the Elk City region.

"Oh, ha ha," Brynne said. "James is not a sugar daddy by any stretch of the imagination."

"He just pays the bills and gives you a free place to stay," Brook chimed in. "I don't know. If it walks like a duck and quacks like a duck … you know."

Dean jumped in. "You should see the penthouse apartment on the top floor, ladies, all full of artwork and fancy furniture, personally selected by an interior designer. I thought I'd stepped into a museum. Plus he's got a big screen TV that is as big as that entire wall," he said gesturing at the wall with the bookshelf and the station's small flatscreen television.

"Okay," Brynne said. "That's enough of that, Dean. Anyway, since your probationary period is over, we need to be ready for when the Chief arrives to present you with your new badge. He approved it effective today, and he will be here any minute to give it to you personally."

"Hey, congrats Dean," Tammy said. "I had forgotten that was going to happen this morning. It is well deserved, and about time."

"Yeah," Brook added. "Kudos. You've definitely got the right touch for this kind of work."

"Yes," a raspy voice said from across the room. "Congratulations, Dean. I should whip up something special for the occasion."

The voice came from a shambling, gray figure in the kitchenette area of the squad room. It was Freddy, a zombie and one of the undead Unusuals cared for by the Station U paramedics. He was also one of the best chefs in the country, or at least he had been. Unfortunately, Freddy had cheated on his voodoo priestess girlfriend and paid the price when she laid this curse on him. A few weeks earlier, when his trailer was burned down by The Cause, everyone had thought he perished in the fire. After it had been discovered by the paramedics at Station U that he had survived, they had decided to put him up in their station. Since then he had become the de facto housekeeper and cook for the paramedics there. It was a good arrangement for everyone, as long as he kept track of his digits and other body parts while he was cooking.

Dean murmured thanks to the congratulations from his friends. He felt the blush spread across his face at the praise, but he didn't care. This was something he had been waiting for, and it had finally happened. No longer on probation, he was now a full-fledged paramedic and member of the team at Station U.

Ari, the Chief of EMS for the Elk City Fire Department arrived a few minutes later, and in a very brief presentation, without much ceremony at all, handed Dean his new badge that read "Paramedic," without the probationary qualifier of his former shield. Everyone shook his hand and congratulated him again. The Chief left, waving off an offer to stay for breakfast saying he had an early meeting. He did tell Freddy that he'd take a rain check, stating that his favorite breakfast was Eggs Benedict.

Brook and Tammy came over and shook Dean's hand one more time. Then the two ladies grabbed their gear, including a takeout container of fresh breakfast from Freddy for each of them, and headed out the station door to go home.

Dean watched them leave, still basking in the glow of the promotion. Brynne broke his reverie. "Don't you have some bags to check at the beginning of the shift? Get them checked out and then I'll let you drive to the first call."

"Yes, Mistress Brynne," Dean said with a flourish and bow. "I'll get right on that." He headed out to the ambulance bay to get started on the shift work. He was going to get the chance now to trade off on most calls with Brynne. He would drive some and act as primary patient care paramedic on others. He climbed into the back of the ambulance and began to go through the bags to make sure that everything they'd need for the shift was available and in the right place. It did not take him long. Brook and Tammy had done their end of shift checks within the last hour, and everything was fully stocked and in its expected place. He was just finishing up when the alert tones sounded on the overhead speakers.

"Medical Box 423, injured subject from an assault. 1258 Sparks Road, Elk City," said the dispatcher over the radio.

Dean's head jerked up when he heard the address. That was his former street address. He hoped the Baxters were alright. Brynne popped her head around the open door at the back of the ambulance.

"Hey, Dean, isn't that your …"

"Yep, it's my address, or my landlord's," Dean responded. He finished zipping up the bags, storing them in their compartments. He then walked around to the driver's seat as Brynne climbed into the passenger side. She got on the radio and reported them responding, then switched to the med channel for additional information. The dispatcher came on and relayed that no additional was available, only that an injured subject was found in the garage, and that police were on the scene.

"I wonder why they called us?" Dean wondered aloud. "There are no Unusuals in the neighborhood that I know of and what are the police doing there? My apartment is in the detached garage. Could some former patient have sought me out?" Brynne leaned forward and keyed the siren on the ambulance dashboard to help move some of the early morning rush hour traffic out of their way as they sped down the road towards his residential neighborhood.

They saw the police lights first as they approached the scene. There were three police cruisers pulled up in front of the house and garage on the usually quiet residential street. Neighbors were standing on their porches and on the sidewalks nearby, watching as the police stood in the driveway. Dean pulled the ambulance out front between two police cars, positioned so they could easily pull out of their parking slot once they were ready to leave with the patient. It was important not to park in a way to get blocked in by other responding units. Dean climbed out, feeling a bit apprehensive as he saw one officer come down the stairs from his apartment above the garage. Brynne grabbed the bags and oxygen container from the side compartment while he grabbed the heart monitor and drug bag from inside the ambulance before joining her on the sidewalk.

The police officer who had just descended the stairs shook his head as he approached them. "I don't think you'll need that stuff. We just need you to go up and pronounce the guy dead so we can let the crime scene guys go in and do their work when they get here."

"There's a dead guy up there?" Dean blurted out. He rushed across the driveway and up the stairs with Brynne close on his heels. He did not hear her calling after him in alarm. Running up the stairs, Dean pushed open the door to the apartment he had left less than an hour before and saw that the place had been ransacked. It looked like there had been a fight. His kitchen chairs were pushed aside or overturned, and the sofa was shoved back from its usual position. A police officer was standing next to the sofa, and when Dean rounded the edge of it, he saw the body - Zach's body. There was the handle of a large kitchen knife protruding from his chest, and Dean could see several other stab wounds in the body from where he stood rooted to the spot. Brynne gasped from behind him.

The police officer turned and looked at them with a quizzical expression. "You guys act like you've never seen a dead guy before." He moved across the room to the doorway. "I have to get the digital camera out of the car. Make sure you don't move anything you don't have to. This is a crime scene, remember."

Brynne took a deep breath. "Dean …" She moved in front of him, into his field of vision, making him meet her eyes. "You need to go back to the ambulance. Go right now."

"But …" Dean started towards the body on the floor by the sofa, his sofa.

"No buts," Brynne said, firmly planting her hand in the center of his chest, stopping him from moving. "You go down and wait for me at the ambulance. I'll take care of things up here and be down in a moment." She finished in a whisper. "Don't say anything to anyone until I get there." She poked him in the chest to get his attention. He glanced back at Zach's body then looked down at his partner standing in front of him.

"Did you hear me?" Brynne whispered, poking him again to punctuate her question. "Go downstairs to the ambulance, and don't talk to anyone until I get back down there. Do you understand?"

Dean nodded, then turned and went back out onto the small landing at the top of the stairs. He took a deep breath then descended back down to the driveway to the ambulance. The police officer was returning with his camera and nodded at Dean as he passed. Dean hardly noticed. His mind was racing. How had Zach gotten back into his apartment, and who had attacked him? He had just left there a little more than an hour before. Everything had been normal. He had made sure the door was locked, and everything was secure. There were so many questions swirling in his head. He continued walking to the ambulance, his legs feeling stiff and wooden. When he got back to the emergency vehicle, he climbed in the back and replaced the heart monitor in its rack and put the other bags back in their compartments. Then he exited the back of the ambulance and sat down on the back bumper. He was sitting there with his mind racing in multiple directions when Brynne returned from the apartment. She walked over to Dean, took him by the arm and led him to the passenger side door of the cab.

"Get in," she said.

"But, I'm driving," he responded.

"No words, just get in. I'll drive back," she ordered. "We are going back to the station. Don't say anything, just get in your seat and buckle up."

He didn't understand, but followed her instructions and climbed into the passenger seat. He watched her walk over to one of the offi-cers on the scene. She exchanged a few words before coming back to the ambulance and climbing into the driver's seat.

"Put us back in service with a priority four patient," Brynne said as she put the ambulance in gear, slowly pulled out from between the police cars, and started down the street.

Dean picked up the mic and alerted headquarters that they were back in service following pronouncing their prospective patient dead - a priority four. A priority one patient was a critical patient, and then the numbers went down to four based on the differing needs each type of patient had for emergency care. A priority four patient was one who needed no care at all - usually, but not always because they were dead.

He placed the mic back on its cradle on the dash and looked at his partner. "Brynne, what's going on? Why was Zach killed back there, in my apartment? I was just there before I came to work."

"I know, Dean," she said as she drove, not taking her eyes off the road. "The police didn't know whose apartment that is. I asked. That gives us some time to come up with a plan. We need to get you back to the station, and we need to get you some legal representation before the police detectives put two and two together and come looking for you. You're being set up, Dean. Someone obviously wants to frame you for Zach's murder."

"But why?" Dean asked.

"It's a perfect plan, actually," Brynne said. "You get saddled with the murder of Zach and end up disgraced, or even in jail. If you are in jail or no longer working as a paramedic, maybe that means you can't do what it is you're supposed to do to stop the current attacks on our patients. Then you can't stop The Cause. They obviously have their own resources who have told them you are central to the situation here in Elk City. Someone decided to try and remove you from the picture."

"But I didn't do it," Dean argued.

"I know that Dean," Brynne replied. She looked his way with concern on her face. "I know that. You know that. We all know that, but to the police… Well, at the very least, this is going to look suspicious. They are going to tag you as a material witness or person of interest. At worst you're going to get charged with doing the deed. Maybe it can be passed off as self-defense, but that will take a trial to determine. In the meantime, you may be sidelined by the investigation, and maybe suspended or fired from the department."

They drove in silence for a while. Suspended? Fired? But he had just gotten promoted. He was wrapped up in these sad thoughts when Brynne spoke up again. "When we get back, you call Ashley and tell her what happened. If you don't get her, don't leave a voicemail. Just hang up. We don't need you recording your random thoughts about this anywhere the police can find it. I'll contact James. He'll know what to do, and should be able to get you a lawyer in the meantime." Dean had no words.

"We'll get through this, Dean," Brynne said as she drove. "We just need to keep our heads on our shoulders, think it all through, and plan carefully."

Dean just nodded. He was still in shock. He could still see Zach's lifeless eyes staring up at the ceiling as he lay on the floor next to the sofa with that knife sticking out of his chest. It was one of his kitchen knives. He recognized the handle where it jutted from his paramedic predecessor's chest. This was all spinning out of control, and he didn't know what to do. He hoped Brynne did because he was lost at that moment. He was lost and afraid that his whole life was slipping away. This shift had started with his promotion. Now, it may be taken away from him. He stared out the windshield trying to make some sense of it.

---

## Chapter 3

---

Dean left the ambulance after Brynne backed it into the ambulance bay, and started pacing back and forth in the garage behind the emergency vehicle. What was he supposed to say when he called Ashley? How had this happened? Who killed Zach in his apartment? There were too many questions swirling around in his head for him to figure out what was going on. He turned and went into the squad room to find Brynne finishing up a conversation on her cell phone.

"I will keep him here, James," she said. "You get him a lawyer, a good one. This is going to be tough to beat. The set up looked pretty solid. If I didn't know any better, I would think he did it." She looked up and saw Dean standing there. "Uh, look, I gotta go. Call me back when you have a lawyer for him and a plan."

"Did you mean what you said?" Dean asked. "That you could believe that I did this?"

"That's not what I said, Dean," Brynne replied. "I stated that if I didn't know otherwise, I would think you were a suspect. Believe me, if I thought you had done this, I would have reported you to the police right there on the scene." She glanced down at the phone in his hand and asked, "Did you call Ashley?"

"No, not yet," Dean admitted. "I don't know what I'm supposed to tell her."

"Tell her you're likely to be framed for Zach's murder and that you expect the police to come looking for you any moment," his partner said. "But, remember, don't leave a voice message if she doesn't pick up. Just hang up the phone."

Dean pulled up Ashley on his phone and pressed the send button to call her. He waited to hear her voice. She would know how to calm him and ease his anxiety. She always did. He waited and waited, and then it went to voicemail. He did as Brynne said and hung up rather than leave a message. Her smartphone would show he had called, so that was enough. She would call him back.

"Not picking up?" Brynne asked. "Okay, I'll text her and tell her to call me right away."

There was a knock at the station door, and Dean flinched. Brynne went over and looked out the window into the parking lot. Dean waited for her to tell him who it was. She turned and looked a little pale.

"It's the police, Dean," she said. "I'm going to let them in. Don't say anything, just request an attorney and then shut up."

"But why don't I just tell them I didn't do it?" Dean asked. "We work with these guys all the time at accidents and other emergency scenes. They know us." The police outside knocked on the door again.

Brynne headed to the door. "You don't say anything. They could twist anything you say to mean something different. Just stay quiet. Request an attorney. That's it." His partner held his gaze for a moment to let what she said to sink in, then turned to walk across the squad room to the parking lot door.

Brynne opened the door and stepped back as two uniformed police officers, and a plain-clothes detective with his badge on a lanyard around his neck entered the room. Dean recognized the two uniformed officers from the scene, and he knew them as the police officers from the law enforcement version of Station U.

The detective spoke up as he came in. "Dean Flynn? I don't think we've met before. I'm Detective Ricketts. I'd like to ask you a few questions. We are all a little curious as to why you didn't identify yourself as the resident of that apartment to the officers on the scene when you responded back there?"

Dean started to answer the question, to defend himself, but caught Brynne's quick shake of her head out of the corner of his eye and stopped himself. "Uh, I'd like to have a lawyer present before I answer any questions," Dean said quickly. Brynne nodded and gave a little smile of encouragement.

The detective seemed to notice the byplay. "If that's the way you want to do this. You know that asking for a lawyer only serves to make you look guilty in our eyes. It will go better if you just tell us what happened back there at your apartment."

Dean couldn't resist. "How would I know? I didn't even stay there last night."

"Well that might be true, but your landlord," the detective paused and pulled out a notepad and glanced at it. "A Mrs. Baxter, says that you were there just a few hours ago. She saw you go upstairs this morning around five thirty AM. Would you care to explain that? I could understand if you surprised a burglar. It could all just be self-defense."

"Dean, don't say another word," Brynne cautioned. "Wait for your lawyer like I said."

"Ma'am, I'll ask you to stay out of this," the detective inter-jected. "I have questions for you, too. I wondered why you didn't remain on the scene longer? I was surprised when you weren't still there when I arrived. It seems that you may have a part in this, too, since you tried to hide evidence."

"What evidence?" she shot back. "I only pronounced the victim dead. That was why we were called to the scene. Once that is done, we're obligated to put our unit back in service. We usually hang out on the location for a while when we have nothing better to do, but nothing says we have to."

"Did you recognize the victim?" the detective asked her. "O'Malley here says he does. Isn't the deceased your former partner at this ambulance station?"

"He is. But you didn't ask for his identity," Brynne replied. "I was just doing my job pronouncing death. I will let you all do the police work."

The detective sighed and motioned to the two officers. "Okay, if that's the way you two want to handle things. Dean Flynn, you are being taken into custody for questioning in the death of Zachary Castle. You have the right to remain silent. Anything you say can, and will be used against you in a court of law. You have the right to an attorney. If you cannot afford an attorney, one will be provided for you by the court. Do you understand these rights as I have recited them to you?"

Dean nodded as O'Malley and his partner came over and put a pair of handcuffs on him, pulling his hands behind his back. "Dean," O'Malley said. "This is protocol, that is all. Just come along quietly, okay?"

Dean nodded in response, feeling the cold weight of the steel cuffs settle on his wrists.

"I need you to say you understand out loud," the detective said.

"I - I understand," Dean whispered. He felt suddenly overwhelmed by the events and wanted to say something, anything to stop this from happening.

"Dean, don't say anything," Brynne reminded him. "I'll have James get the attorney to meet you downtown at the police station."

Dean just nodded. He didn't talk, he didn't say anything. This was all just too much to handle and process. He knew he didn't kill anyone, but he also knew how it must have looked to a police officer examining the scene. It looked like there had been a fight, and they knew that Dean had a connection to Zach. They also knew that he had been at the apartment earlier that morning. He didn't know how he was going to get out of this.

Officer O'Malley and his partner led Dean outside into the bright morning sunshine. Dean blinked and wished he had his sunglasses. Of course, how would he put them on? He was in handcuffs, after all. The two officers escorted him to the marked police car, opened the rear door, and settled him into the back seat. O'Malley leaned in and snapped the seat belt across him. They shut the door, and Dean was alone in the back of the police vehicle. It was a first for him, and he looked around. There was a metal grate that separated the back and front seats and the interior of the police car smelled of disinfectant, bad aftershave and old french fries.

Dean looked out the window and saw Brynne standing in the parking lot outside the station, talking on her cell phone. The two officers climbed into the front seats and started to drive him away to the police station. He watched Brynne talking on the phone, her eyes following the car as he left in the custody of the police, watching as he was taken off to jail.

Chapter 4

The process of being fingerprinted and photographed at the police station was humiliating. He wanted to shout out that he was innocent, but he knew Brynne's advice was correct. He refused to answer any questions and had waited for his attorney to show up to represent him. It didn't stop Detective Ricketts and the other police officers from talking around him about how it was always a good idea to cooperate with police and tell your story. He knew they were just trying to get to him. He gritted his teeth, kept his mouth shut and waited. It took several hours, but he was eventually taken from his cell to where a well-dressed man in a three-piece suit waited in an interview room. There was a mirror on one wall that he assumed was one-way glass.

"Sit down, Dean. Let's talk about your situation," the man said as he sat in the chair on the opposite side of the table. "My name is Mansel Hood. I'm Mr. Lee's personal attorney, and I'm here to be yours as well." He opened a manila folder on the table between them and looked over some papers before continuing. Dean looked around the room's sterile gray walls while he waited.

"Our focus right now is to get you out on bail while we figure out how to proceed," the attorney continued. "Mr. Lee told me to assume you are innocent of the crime in your apartment. I, frankly, don't care. The only thing I care about is that you don't lie to me. Understood?"

"So you think I'm guilty?" Dean asked, shocked. He buried his head in his hands. This was getting even worse. If his own lawyer thought he was guilty, then he was done for.

"No," Mansel said in a calm voice. "I said 'I don't care.' There's a difference. My job is to get you cleared of this crime. As long as you tell me everything you know, and answer every question truthfully, I have a good chance of doing that. If you choose to tell me whether you committed this crime or not, I only ask that you tell me the truth. Otherwise, we'll work on the assumption that you're innocent."

"Okay," Dean started. He tried to calm down, taking a deep breath before continuing. He cleared his throat began to speak, then stopped and stared at his hands for a moment. He looked up and met his lawyer's eyes. He noticed the irises were an odd shade of amber. This man was an Unusual of some sort, which made sense, given who he represented. "Mr. Hood, I will tell you now, and forever more, that I am innocent of this crime. I didn't kill Zach, leave him in my apartment, go to work and then come back to my apartment to pronounce him dead. It makes no sense. I'm being framed for this crime."

"I agree," Mansel said. He jotted a note on the yellow legal pad before him then continued. "That will be part of our defense, along with our expert testimony which will refute the medical examiner's estimate that the time of death corresponds to your time in the apartment before work. But let's not get ahead of ourselves. For now, we are focused on getting you released on bond, which Mr. Lee will guarantee. In a little while, we are going to go to court and face a judge. I'll talk with him and the district attorney some, and then you will say only what I tell you to say and nothing more. It's all just a formality at this point. You'll get your chance to defend yourself later on. For now, just follow my lead."

Dean nodded as he clenched his hands into fists. This was getting worse and worse. James was paying the lawyer, and he hated being in debt to anyone, let alone James Lee. Now he was going to owe James even more for bailing him out, on top of the attorney's fees. He listened to the words coming from his attorney, but they didn't register in his mind as his thoughts raced over the events earlier in the day. Mansel gathered up his legal pad and files and packed them back in his briefcase. He walked over and knocked on the door. A guard came in after a few moments and opened it. The guard came over and helped Dean stand up, leading him back down the hallway to the cells. The last words from the attorney stayed with him.

"Keep your mouth shut and wait for the arraignment hearing in a few hours," Mansel had said. "I'll see you there, and we'll get you bailed out of jail and back home." He made it all seem so matter-of-fact and straightforward. Dean hoped it was that easy.

THE JUDGE RAPPED his gavel and Dean sighed. One million dollars bail or one hundred thousand dollars bond for his release. That was what the judge had decided. That was what he was worth. Not that it mattered much. He didn't have the lesser amount, let alone the full million. He had resigned himself to going back to the city jail, when the attorney, Mr. Hood, announced that he would make the payment arrangements within the hour. He made it sound like he was paying the electric bill, and not a particularly expensive one.

Dean was led back to a holding area in one of the lower floors of the courthouse after the hearing. Dean didn't have to wait long. True to his word, Mansel showed up less than an hour later to pick Dean up as he was released from police custody. There was some paperwork to fill out to sign for his belongings, confiscated upon his arrest and intake into the system by the police earlier. By the time he walked out of the courthouse with Mansel, it was late, nearly eight in the evening. There was a black town car waiting at the curb outside the side entrance to the county courthouse. Mansel gestured to the car, and a gentleman in a dark suit jumped out and opened the door for Dean and his attorney. The driver then jumped in the driver's seat and started off. Within a few minutes, they arrived at the Nightwing Building downtown, just a few blocks away. The car pulled into the underground garage after the driver slid a keycard in the slot next to the gate. They stopped one ramp down, in front of the elevator doors.

"Dean," Mansel said as Dean climbed out and stood outside the back door to the town car. "I will be in touch regarding the next steps for the case. In the meantime, don't talk to anyone but me, Mr. Lee, Ms. Garvey or the Eldara about the events of this morning. Anyone else could be in league with our opponents. Understood?" Dean nodded, although he was still in a bit of shock from the day. Mansel said something to the driver and the car pulled away, leaving Dean standing there.

He was heading over to the elevators, planning to go upstairs to his temporary apartment, when his phone buzzed in his pocket. He pulled it out and glanced at the screen. James had texted him and asked him to come up to the penthouse level. He pushed the up button outside the elevator doors, scanned his keycard to gain access upstairs, and rode up to the vampire's apartment. Dean's shoulders sagged with weariness as he approached the double doors on the penthouse level and reached to ring the doorbell.

The doors swung open, and he looked up as Ashley rushed to him, the tall brunette nurse still dressed in her pastel blue scrubs from the ER. She pulled him close and hugged him tightly without saying a word. He looked past her shoulder and saw the grim faces of Brynne and James staring back at him. He squeezed his arms a little to return Ashley's hug and then released her.

"Dean," James said, gesturing inside. "Please come in. I know you have had a long day, but there is a lot we need to discuss. We will work to get to the bottom of this situation; I promise you. I have everyone working on it. Apparently, we underestimated our opponents, their will, and their intentions."

Dean followed James and Brynne inside the spacious penthouse apartment sitting atop the Nightwing building while Ashley trailed at his side, holding his hand in hers. The group went into the living room area and sat down. Dean and Ashley took the love seat while James and Brynne sat together on the matching white leather sofa.

"Well, I guess I can use my mug shot in my Christmas cards this year," Dean said, using humor to blow off steam. It was good to be out of the jail cell, but it was like his mind was still there. He felt locked in by the situation and didn't see a clear way out. The lawyer, Mansel Hood, had not given any indication of his thoughts, just telling Dean to go in and get some rest.

"Have you thought what you are going to do next, Dean?" Brynne asked.

"I don't know. I guess, since I'm out of jail now, I'll just go back to work while I wait for the trial," Dean said. He couldn't think of anything else to do but return to his routine. He noticed that his three companions were silent and glanced back and forth as if deciding who should speak up. Was he missing something?

"What is it?" he asked. "What aren't you telling me?"

Brynne started to say something and then stopped herself, looking from Ashley to James.

"Now you're all are freaking me out, and I didn't think I could be freaked out any more than I already have today," Dean said.

Brynne broke the momentary silence that followed his statement. "Dean," she began. "You are under arrest for a felony, a violent crime. The chief had to suspend you - with pay, but suspend you nonetheless, pending the result of the inquiry. You can't come back to work."

Dean felt his shoulders sag as if he couldn't be any more depressed by the day's events. Being a paramedic was all he had ever wanted since he had watched an ambulance crew save his girl-friend's life, after the car accident they were in had nearly killed her. Now, his career was being taken away from him, too. He found he suddenly was having trouble breathing, and his vision clouded with tears. He wiped them away, not wanting to show weakness here, especially in front of Ashley. She squeezed the hand she was holding in silent support.

"There's a bigger problem at hand here," Ashley said. "Since Dean's arrest, I have felt a shift in the balance of power in this struggle. When I said that Dean and James would figure strongly in resolving the situation here in Elk City, that has now changed. It's still a possibility, but the previous course of action has faded. It's much more tenuous in nature now. That concerns me because I still believe that it is the solution to these attacks and the push against the Unusual population here."

As an Eldara and messenger of the Gods, Ashley could sense the correct or best path for the good of a situation. She had earlier predicted that Dean and James were linked to some future event; some event that would bring the current attacks to a resolution, restoring what Ashley had called a balance to the region. That was why she had come here and attached herself to Dean in the first place.

"So, Eldara," James asked. "What do we do to change back to the future envisioned before?"

"I don't know, not yet," Ashley replied. "I can't understand what is different. We got Dean out of jail, and he is free for the foreseeable future. Maybe it has to do with him being discredited as a paramedic. People won't trust him now, because of what they think he did, perhaps?"

"That is not the case among my people," James said. "If anything, thinking Dean killed one of the attackers who had been preying on them would raise the opinion of him in their eyes."

"That's true, I guess. But what else could it be?" Ashley asked. She waved her hand in front of her eyes. "I can't see through this fog shrouding my other sight from another course of action."

"I think you are all missing the obvious reason for the change in the potential future," Brynne said, breaking into the conversation between the two Unusuals. "It's a simple change of a variable in the equation. Dean is suspended, probably for weeks. What if he had to be a working paramedic to take the action he was supposed to take, in order to resolve this conflict? What if, now that he is off the streets and not riding the Station U ambulance anymore, he will no longer be in a position to do or say what he was supposed to?"

Dean watched as they all looked back and forth and then at him. This was all a moot point from his standpoint. He wasn't a paramedic anymore. He couldn't ride in the ambulance and help out his Unusual patients. Right now, he didn't have any particular purpose in the world. He had nothing to offer to anyone, at least, not until this situation was resolved. He stood up, letting go of Ashley's hand.

"I'm grateful for all of your support, especially from you, James," Dean said. "I know that without Mansel Hood and your bail money, I'd still be in jail right now. It has been a long day, and I think I need to get some sleep. If I can do that, maybe I can try and get some perspective on this. I'm not giving up. I'm not quitting the fight, but honestly, I'm not up to figuring all of this out right now."

He started walking towards the doors back to the elevators. Ashley got up and followed him, with James and Brynne trailing behind. He pushed the down button and waited while his friends stood around him. Brynne broke the silence.

"Good idea. Get some sleep, Dean," she said. "James and I will keep working on this. We'll keep you and Ashley in the loop as we work through some possible solutions." She placed a hand on his shoulder.

Dean nodded, turned and entered the elevator as the doors opened. Ashley joined him, taking his hand in hers again. He looked at James and Brynne standing there watching him with the worry obvious in their eyes, even in James'. Strange, how his opinion of his partner's vampire boyfriend had changed over the last twenty-four hours. He did consider James a friend now, which was not something he could have said before the recent turn of events. He knew he would trade that friendship back in a minute if it meant he could get his paramedic status back and get back on the ambulance. The doors closed, and he was left with his Ashley, his Eldara angel. She gave his hand a little squeeze as if she knew he was thinking of her. At least she was still standing by his side through this crisis. He just hoped that would be enough to get him through it.

<hr>

## Chapter 5

<hr>

Dean woke the next morning to see that Ashley had already left for her shift at the ER. He had not slept well, but despite that, he didn't remember her getting up. He glanced at the clock and saw that it was already past nine in the morning. It didn't matter what time it was. It wasn't as if there was anyplace he had to be that morning. He lay there in bed for a while, staring at the ceiling, lost in his thoughts of the previous day. Why couldn't this all have been a vivid nightmare like the one he'd had the night before?

After about a half hour of ruminating about the predicament he was in, Dean grunted, rolled over, and got out of bed. He couldn't do anything to fix what was going on, and the people who were helping him were all doing what they could, so he just had to wait. But, it wasn't in his nature to just lie about all day. He got some breakfast, then changed into a pair of shorts and a t-shirt and put on his sneakers. James had an excellent gym on the second floor of the building. Maybe a workout would help Dean clear his head and order his thoughts. He grabbed his smartphone, earbuds and the key-card to the apartment, and stepped out into the hallway, nearly colliding with another individual in a dark suit.

"Oh, excuse me," Dean muttered. He was surprised because he

didn't know anyone else was staying on the private residence floor other than he and Ashley. James had said he kept the furnished apartments for visiting VIP dignitaries from the Unusual community.

"You should be more careful," the man said in a thickly accented voice.

Dean couldn't place the language of origin, but it sounded sort of Eastern European or Russian. The man was dressed from head to toe in a black suit. He wore a black shirt and tie as well. His skin was pale, and the paramedic immediately suspected he was a vampire. One way to be sure. He extended his hand.

"I'm Dean," he said, smiling. "Dean Flynn."

The other man extended his hand, and Dean grasped the cold hand in a firm handshake. He knew he was correct based on the lack of body temperature coupled with the pale skin. He was getting better at identifying Unusuals when he encountered them.

"Artur Torrence," the vampire replied, smiling as well. "You must be the young human paramedic about whom I've heard so much. I was passing through your city on the way elsewhere to conduct some business and decided to stop in and see what James had going on here in Elk City."

"I hope you've heard the good things," Dean said. "You don't want to believe everything you hear."

"I have only heard good things about you," Artur replied. "Though James was just mentioning something about a bit of trouble you were having. He also said that you were innocent of the charges leveled against you. I'm sure everything will resolve for you soon enough, one way or another."

Did Dean see the man's lips twitch in a smile there at the last part? He decided it was his imagination and responded politely. "From your lips to God's ears, Artur," Dean said. "I'd like this to resolve quickly, that is sure."

Artur snorted. "I'm not sure God's listening to anything from me, at least not for a very long time." He glanced at his watch and back at Dean. "I'm afraid I must be going. The hour is late for me, and I have dinner waiting for me in my rooms. I had her selected especially for my stay here. Perhaps we shall see each other again, eh?"

"Absolutely," Dean said. "I was heading down to the gym anyway. Enjoy your, uh, meal." Dean winced inwardly at the awkwardness of the way he said it. He was sure that the meal in question walked and talked just like him. There was a consensual arrangement with some human donors who would let vampires and other Unusual blood drinkers consume directly from them for a healthy fee. Dean smiled at the other man, forcing himself not to think about it. Artur nodded and turned, continuing down the hall-way, turning the corner and disappearing from sight. Dean watched him for a moment, then he shrugged and headed to the elevators to get his workout in and sort out his thoughts. He wondered if James had any other Unusual guests staying on the floor that he didn't know about. The elevator arrived, and Dean stepped inside, still wondering about the possibility of neighbors he wasn't aware of, and whether they too, knew about him.

▭

DEAN RETURNED from his workout an hour later. The exercise on the circuit training equipment of the building's gym had helped lighten his mood. Now he just needed a shower and to get cleaned up. He had to do some shopping. His old apartment was a crime scene now, and the police had confiscated his suitcase from his truck for evidence. He was going to need some more clothes before too long. He stepped off the elevator and started down the hallway to his apartment. Looking up, he was startled when he saw a young blonde woman staggering down the hallway towards him. She swayed and started to fall forward as he neared her. Dean reached out and caught her just in time as she fainted in his arms.

He lowered her gently to the ground, and as he did, he saw the bite marks on her neck and shoulder. They were fresh, red and ragged looking. Not the simple double pinprick marks he had seen with other vampire bites. These bites were more vicious, more like an attack than a willing feeding. The woman's eye's fluttered open as she lay there and she started to rise. Dean placed a hand gently on her shoulder and pressed her back down.

"Easy going there," he said. "You need to rest for a little bit. You've lost a lot of blood. Who did this to you?" Dean thought he knew, but he asked anyway.

"I just need to get back to my room downstairs. I'll be okay," the woman replied. "I don't want to be any trouble. I need this job."

"You need an ambulance," Dean said, pulling out his phone. "Let me call one for you and we can get you tended to. I'm Dean; I'm a paramedic, and you should get looked at in the hospital. What's your name?"

"Codi, Codi Beck," the woman said. "And you can't call an ambulance. Ms. Teal wouldn't like it. I'll be alright. I just need to get some rest."

"Celeste knows about this?" Dean knew Celeste was the vampire assistant to James. The redheaded southerner was charming and seemed kind enough. He found it hard to believe she would condone this behavior. He turned his attention back to his patient. "Do you always get drained like this when they feed off of you?"

"No, uh, this was different," Codi admitted. She struggled again to sit up and failed. "Lord Torrence is an honored and influential guest of Mr. Lee. I don't want to cause any trouble." Her voice trailed off as her eyes rolled back and then closed as she slipped into unconsciousness.

Dean knew he should call 911, but decided to call someone else instead. He looked down at his phone, opened the contacts app, and flipped through them, selecting a name. He tapped it with his thumb to dial the number. The phone on the other end picked up on the second ring.

"Yes, Dean," the smooth southern drawl on the other end said. "What can I do for you?"

"Celeste, you should probably come down to my floor," Dean said. "There's been an incident with one of your other guests and their dinner. I wanted to call an ambulance, but she insisted I don't. Maybe you can help."

"I'll be right there," Celeste replied. "Can you get her up and into your apartment? I can see you on the security monitor. You are close to your door."

Dean looked up and noticed the small black domes in the ceiling of the hallway. He hadn't paid attention to them before. "Uh, yeah. I think I can move her in there. Are you coming down?"

"I'm on my way now."

Dean put his phone back in his pocket. Then he reached down and picked up Codi and carried her over to his door. She groaned a little when he lifted her up but then fell silent again. Her skin felt cool to the touch. She was going into shock. He needed to get her warmed up. Struggling a little to get his key card out, he waved it over the door's panel and then opened it and went inside. He laid her down on the sofa and went into his bedroom and grabbed the blanket off the bed. She needed to be kept warm to reduce the effects of shock on her body. There was a tap at the door; then it opened, and he heard Celeste's voice as she leaned over him to check on Codi.

"How is she?"

"She needs a hospital and at least two units of blood," Dean replied. "She shouldn't be here in my apartment."

"This isn't the first time something like this has happened," Celeste said coming over to his side. "We are prepared for these things." She set a large medical bag down next to him on the floor, not unlike the ones he used on the ambulance. She was also holding a small, ultra-compact heart monitor, which she placed on the coffee table next to the sofa.

Dean opened up the heart monitor and attached the leads to the sticky pads and attached them to his patient. He applied the blood pressure cuff and slid the pulse oximeter sensor over one finger. He cycled the machine to start taking vital signs and then unzipped the bag. Inside were IV supplies and tubing, fluid bags, and some bandages and dressings. He began prepping her arm to get an IV line in place to get her some fluids.

There was a tap at the door as he was finishing up. Celeste went over to answer, and he heard a murmured conversation. The door closed, and the vampire assistant returned holding something out to him.

"Here, Dean," she said, holding out a bag of blood. "It's O-negative, the universal donor type. It's been screened and is safe to give her."

"I'm just a paramedic," Dean said. "I'm not licensed to give blood products."

"You're not a paramedic right now, Dean. You are suspended. You can do what you want," Celeste said. She said it as a matter of fact, not to be mean. Celeste continued. "This is what she needs. You know it."

Dean hesitated for a moment then took the bag from her. It was warmed already which should help, too. He read the label carefully, verifying that it was indeed O negative blood type. Then he took some more IV tubing out of the bag and spiked the bag before attaching the other end to replace the IV fluid tubing he had already flowing. The blood was better than straight fluids. He knew he needed to watch her carefully for adverse reactions from the blood. There should be none if the blood had indeed been screened for her but sometimes things were mislabeled. Celeste brought over one of the barstool chairs from the kitchen area and took the bag from him to hang from the back of the chair to keep gravity flowing the blood from the bag into the patient. Dean cycled the monitor again to collect another set of vital signs and then looked up at Celeste.

"Your guest was a little rough on her," he said. "Someone should have a conversation with him about how to treat people who volunteer to provide him with a meal."

"This is a delicate situation, Dean," Celeste said. "Artur Torrence is an old rival of James. Their relationship goes back centuries. To top it off, Artur is older than James, and there is a hierarchy that must be observed. Technically, James can't tell him what to do, even in his own domain like Elk City."

"And James let this guy visit as an honored guest?" Dean asked. "That's ridiculous! He nearly killed this woman."

"I'm sure James will have a word with him about it," Celeste said. "But there's not much he can do. He's not even sure what Artur is doing here. He is not the type to just drop in. Artur is up to something, but James is not sure what. He is afraid it has to do with the unrest in Elk City. It could be a sign from James' superiors that they are not confident in his ability to rule here."

"So Artur is here to take over?" Dean looked down at his patient, still unconscious on the couch. "I'm not sure I want this guy running things around here. I don't think it would be safe for people based on the way he treated Codi."

"That is an understatement, Dean." He waited for her to say more but she didn't.

The two of them fell silent for a while. Dean kept monitoring Codi's vital signs every five minutes or so and checking that blood was flowing smoothly. The bag was almost empty. Her color was getting better, and her blood pressure was coming up. When the blood bag fluid ran out, he detached it and reattached the plain saline solution and continued slowly giving her fluids. He was pretty sure she would survive this attack, and that was good. He didn't have any garlic extract to counteract the effects of the vampire potentially turning her if she had died. That couldn't happen unless she drank from him as well, but you never knew what went on in these types of situations. The paramedic turned his attention to dressing and bandaging the bites to her neck and shoulder while she slept.

Celeste watched him work. "You're good at what you do, Dean. I've never seen you at your job, but you seem to know what you're doing, and you do it well."

"It's all I've wanted to do for a long time, Celeste," Dean replied. "Of course, I'm not going to be doing it much while I'm suspended. Who knows, Codi might be the last patient I ever care for."

"I'm sure that is not the case. James has investigators of his own working on the case. Plus, your lawyer, Mansel Hood, is one of the best in the state. We'll make sure you get through this and back on the ambulance. You just have to be patient."

"I don't think I have that kind of patience," Dean snapped back.

"I've got nothing to do while I'm waiting for the disposition of my case. I've been suspended, with pay at least, but suspended indefinitely nonetheless."

"Well, maybe we can find something for you to do in the meantime?" Celeste proposed. "Let me talk to James. There are sometimes incidents like this one here in the Nightwing building. We always have different clients in town from James' various businesses and partnerships. You could be our on-call medical assistance in the time frame it takes to get this all straightened out and we get you reinstated."

Dean thought about it and knew that she was creating something here just for him. It was likely she did not really need it. It was a position offered just to keep him busy, but it would be something to do and keep his mind off his troubles. Plus he'd get a chance to keep his skills up and take care of people. "I guess I could do that. What would it entail?"

"I don't know. Let me talk to James about it. I think we could set up an office for you downstairs on the second floor. Once down there, you could help check on people like Codi here to make sure they don't go back to work until they meet the required rejuvenation of their blood levels. It would be only part-time, but it would be something to do."

"I think I would like that," Dean said. "Thank you."

"No problem, Dean," she replied. Celeste looked at Codi, resting peacefully on the sofa. "I assume you have her squared away?"

"Yes, I've got this. She just needs to rest," Dean said. "I'll sit with her until she wakes up and I will make sure she gets back to her room downstairs in one piece."

"Excellent, then I'll go and see what we need to do to get you set up in your new job."

___________________

## Chapter 6

___________________

Ashley called to check in with him at lunchtime. Dean was glad to hear from her. He told her about the patient on his couch and the conversation with Celeste. Ashley seemed alarmed when he told her about his encounter with the visiting vampire lord.

"Artur Torrence is in town?" she asked. "That's not good news. He thrives on chaos and death. I've encountered him before in my travels over the years. He must be sensing some weakness in support for James at higher levels. I've seen him come in like this in the past and try to take over things during a political disruption in the community."

"He's not a very nice guy either," Dean responded.

"You need to stay clear of him, Dean," Ashley cautioned him. "He is very old-school and wouldn't bat an eye at removing you from this earth if you get in his way. Because you and I are connected, there is some protection I can offer you, but it is not a certainty if he wants to do you harm."

"I can tell what he thinks of humans, Ashley. I've seen the way he treats his meals. Don't worry, I'm not going to cross him anytime soon. I just need to take care of the patients he leaves in his wake while he's here."

"Well that is good news at least," the ER nurse said. "I was wondering what we could find for you to do while you had this forced time off. I didn't want you lying around all day eating Cheetos while you waited for me to come home."

"I don't know; I think Cheeto dust is a good color on me."

"That is something no woman wants to hear from her man, Dean."

"I'm kidding!" he said, laughing. "I am glad I have something to do with my time, too. I'm not sure if it is legal since I'm suspended, but I don't think my patients will be complaining to the medical board about it."

"Have you had the news on at all this morning?" Ashley asked him.

"No, why?" He picked up the remote and put the local news station on the TV.

"There have been two more attacks since last night," Ashley replied. "Both were related to recent ambulance calls from Unusuals in the community. One was an assault on the person who called 911. A black SUV pulled up on the street, and a group of men jumped out and beat and kicked the caller until they were unconscious. They are in the ICU now. The second attack was another firebombing of a residence where the ambulance had just been. No one was home since everyone inside rode to the hospital in the ambulance with the patient, so there were no injuries, thank goodness."

"None of the Station U paramedics were hurt, were they?" Dean asked.

"No, but everyone is a little jumpy this morning," Ashley replied. "There were also more threats turned in to the local police and online announcements with links to web pages attempting to expose Unusuals in the community. Some people are starting to pay attention and ask uncomfortable questions."

Dean grabbed the remote and switched on the TV. A woman on the noon news was talking to another reporter on location somewhere within the city. They were covering the firebombing, as well as the assault in the daily report. This wasn't the type of attention the Unusual community wanted. Dean knew it was going to have repercussions. Since the attacks seemed to be linked to the station U paramedics, it was likely their unique patients were going to stop calling them for help. They would go back to what they used to do in the past, and try to take care of their medical problems on their own. It was not good for anyone concerned.

A groan from across the room distracted him from both the phone and the TV. Codi was waking up. He told Ashley he'd see her later and then crossed over to check on his patient. As he got there, she woke with a start, looking around in a panic.

"Easy, Codi. Easy," he said. He pushed the button on the heart monitor to cycle the vital signs again. "You're safe. Celeste and I brought you here to my place since it was close and I was able to get you some fluids and blood to replace what you lost. How do you feel?"

"I feel a little dizzy, woozy, like I'm not really awake," Codi replied. "I guess I owe you a thank you?"

"We can worry about that later," Dean said. "Let me take your blood pressure and other vitals again and then maybe we can see about getting you back down to your room, Okay?"

She nodded and Dean went about assessing her again. Her vitals were much better than when she had arrived. Once he had reviewed the readings, he unhooked her from the heart monitor and removed the blood pressure cuff and sensors. He took the IV out of her arm, applying a small adhesive bandage in its place, then checked the bandages he had put on her neck and shoulder. When he was done, he looked her over one more time.

"Let's sit you up slowly, and see how you feel. Then you can stand up and see how that feels. If you feel alright after that, I'll walk with you back downstairs to your apartment."

Codi sat up and looked around the room. "This apartment is much nicer than mine downstairs. Maybe I could stay here a while longer?" She placed a hand on his knee and looked him in the eye.

"I don't think my girlfriend would like that too much, Codi. Let's just get you settled back in your apartment. Maybe I can check in on you later to make sure you're alright."

She sighed and nodded. He helped her stand up and then walked next to her, ready to support her if she started to fall. She was a little unsteady but able to walk on her own. Dean led the way to the door and took her to the elevator where she pushed the button for the third floor. When they got to her apartment, just the size of a small, poorly furnished hotel or single-person dorm room, he walked her inside and helped her sit on the bed.

"I will be back close to dinner time and make sure you are still doing alright. My girlfriend is a nurse so she will probably want to check on you, too. In the meantime, you rest." Dean waited until he was sure she understood, then he left and returned to his place upstairs.

———

HE STEPPED out of the elevator on his floor and saw Artur standing outside his door. The vampire lord had assumed a relaxed pose, leaning against the wall opposite Dean's apartment door. He looked up as Dean approached.

"I wanted to thank you for cleaning up my mess, Dean," Artur crooned. "I thought she could make it on her own back down to her little dwelling below." His grin grew broader. "Perhaps I was hungrier than I expected."

"Perhaps you should learn some self-control," Dean quipped. He wasn't in the mood to play games with this bloodthirsty monster. Dean had learned a lot about Unusuals, and he knew that, for the most part, they were just people, folks who wanted to live their lives like everyone in the human population. He also knew that every group had their bad apples. Artur was one of those bad apples from the Unusual barrel in Dean's book.

"Perhaps you should learn to respect your betters, young man. I think you should reconsider how you speak to me. I am not one to have as an enemy." The grin was gone now. It had been replaced with a sneer.

Dean glared at the vampire, meeting his eyes for a moment, then the paramedic turned away to open his door. Artur reached out and grabbed his arm, only to hiss in pain and draw away. Dean was surprised, but not as surprised as Artur was. The vampire stared at his hand for a moment, flexing his fingers as if testing them after getting a jolt from an ungrounded electrical appliance. He looked at Dean and then closed his eyes and inhaled deeply through his nose. Dean stood and watched, not sure what was going on. After thirty uncomfortable seconds, Artur opened his eyes, took a step back, and gave a brief nod to Dean. It was the kind of nod one fencer gave to another after a touch.

"I had forgotten the Eldara and her involvement in this," Artur said in an offhand manner. "Miss Moore and I have encountered each other before. I knew there was an Eldara Sister in the vicinity. I had not realized it was she who was your protector. This information changes the direction of things. I will have to come at this problem from a different direction." The last part was not to Dean, but rather as if he were making mental notes aloud.

"You know Ashley?" Dean asked, not sure what was happening. Was this vampire threatening Ashley in some way? "You stay away from her, Artur."

"She has nothing to fear from me, young man," Artur laughed. "I have no desire to cross swords with her again, or her sister. Her insane sister is not in town, too, is she?" The vampire almost sounded concerned. When Dean returned a curious stare, Artur continued. "No, of course not. We'd all know if she were here. She is much more…direct, shall we say. Please pass my regards to Miss Moore. Perhaps we can arrange a meeting to discuss her purpose in being here. Let her know I will await her response."

Artur turned and hurried away around the corner to his rooms, leaving Dean standing in the hallway wondering what just happened. He looked at his arm where he still felt the steel grip of the vampire's momentary grasp. Even though Artur had let go instantly, it had been intended as an attack based on the force applied by the vampire's grip. What had Ashley done to him that had the power to hurt the vampire lord? Dean turned and unlocked his door, going inside while still pondering what had happened. It had been a curious day all the way around.

He was picking up the first aid supplies he had used to take care of Codi when his phone buzzed in his pocket. He pulled it out and glanced at the screen. It was Ashley. He answered with a swipe.

"Dean, is everything alright?"

"Yes, why?"

"I sensed a — well, some sort of attack on you," Ashley said. "Did something just happen?"

Dean told her about his encounter with Artur and the vampire's response when he grabbed Dean's arm. He relayed the message from the vampire lord for a meeting and the strange comment about Ashley's sister. That brought a surprised laugh from the other end of the phone.

"I don't think this is funny, Ash," Dean said. "I get the idea that you and he have some animosity towards each other. He stopped short of threatening you, but I got the sense that he doesn't like you very much."

"It's not funny, Dean," she replied. "At least not all of it. He's right, though. If my sister were here, things would be a bit more interesting. Direct is a good way to describe the way she works. In any case, I'm in no danger. I've told you before; I can take care of myself. But Artur's being here during this crisis cannot be a coincidence. I'm sure of it now, after this incident. He is mixed up with all of this in some way. I know it."

"What did you do to me that caused him to let go when he grabbed me? It was like he got a jolt of electricity or something."

"It is hard to describe. Because of our close physical relationship, my aura, for lack of a better explanation, extends partly to you," Ashley explained. "There are some negative plane Unusuals who can have their energy drawn away when they come into contact with my aura if I choose it. Some of that power extends to you. If one of them touched you with the intent to cause you harm, they would encounter a jolt of pain. Understand, they can still continue to attack you if they choose to ignore the pain. It would not drain them the way my direct aura would. They can also use a surrogate to attack you, so don't think this makes you invincible."

"I don't think I'll feel that way. My arm's going to have a bruise where he grabbed me."

"Exactly, so you should be careful around Artur. Knowing you, you made a rude comment to him, and being who he is, he didn't take kindly to it. Still, now that he knows I'm here, I don't think he'll take direct action like that again. But that is no reason to take any chances."

"Are you coming home soon?" Dean asked. He glanced at his watch. Her shift was over soon.

"I am getting ready to leave. I just need to do my shift report and hand over my patients to the next nurse on duty. Why don't you contact Brynne and see if she and James are available to catch up tonight? I think this situation with Artur requires us to look at this in a different way."

"Okay, I'll shoot her a text," Dean said. "See you when you get back."

He disconnected the call and went back to cleaning up the medical supplies and repacking the trauma bag Celeste had brought down. When he was finished, he texted his former paramedic partner about meeting upstairs in James' penthouse later that evening. It was strange how his life had changed over the last two days. He'd been charged with a crime, suspended from his job, pissed off a visiting vampire lord, and discovered that his girlfriend, and apparently her sister, were badass enough to scare off said vampire lord. Just when he thought his life couldn't get any more mixed up, it got even crazier.

# Chapter 7

Brynne responded to his text message almost immediately. She urged him to come up as soon as Ashley got back from the hospital and had a chance to change. James would order up some dinner for the four of them, and they could sit and eat while they discussed the day's events. Brynne had been out all day in the ambulance responding to the attacks on the Unusual community while Dean was here, in what was supposed to be a haven, responding to attacks of a different sort.

Ashley returned from the hospital and texted him from her apartment next door that she'd be ready in a half hour after she got a shower. He watched some of the evening local news and saw more reports of the attacks from earlier that day. The news anchorwoman even made a joke about the internet stories on monsters living among the people of Elk City. Dean shut it off. That was a sure sign that the attacks by The Cause were starting to have their desired effect. If the human population started wondering about what was going on with their weird neighbors, the Unusuals in the community might start getting exposed for real. Nobody in the Unusual community wanted that. They depended on their anonymity.

He got up at a tap on his door and opened it to see Ashley

standing there looking as beautiful as ever. She had changed from her ER scrubs into jeans and a loose-fitting blouse with a low-scooped neckline. His eyes lingered over the hint of cleavage there.

"Hello to you, too, Dean," Ashley said.

"Sorry, Ash. I'm just amazed that a gorgeous woman like you picked a guy like me to hang out with."

"Yeah, yeah. Flattery will get you nowhere, at least not right now," she replied with a wink. "We are expected upstairs, yes?"

"Yes, but I will take a rain check on that 'not right now,' okay?" Dean proposed.

"Perhaps, but let's focus on the things at hand, shall we?" She held out a hand, and they walked together to the elevators and headed upstairs to the Penthouse level.

Brynne had already opened the double doors to the Penthouse apartment when Dean and Ashley arrived off the elevator to the entry hall. She was wearing a pair of blue jeans as well, and had on a duty t-shirt with the Elk City EMS logo printed on the pocket. The t-shirt exposed her neckline, and Dean immediately noticed the double red pinprick dots there that showed where James had been feeding on her. It made him think back to the much more severe wounds on Codi he had cared for earlier. Was there a difference? Dean thought he had resolved his feelings about Brynne's and James' private arrangement, but the events from earlier in the day had brought them back to the surface.

"Won't you come in?" Brynne said. "How are you guys? Dean, I heard you had a productive day."

"Yeah, you could say that," Dean said as he and Ashley walked into the spacious apartment that looked out over the city around them. "I heard that there were more attacks associated with the Station U ambulance calls?"

"Yes," Brynne replied. "It's getting more and more dangerous. I am surprised by the speed with which things have ramped up, especially since they found Zach's body. I would have thought The Cause would have slowed down with the loss of one of their own."

James came over to greet them and said, "That might be true if they thought we were responsible for his death. Since we know that is not the case, I have to assume they have made this all part of their plan, including his murder. In that case, it would not slow them down at all." The vampire lord of Elk City led them to the dining area where the table was set and ready for dinner. They sat down, and as they removed the warming covers from the platters of food, Dean realized how hungry he was. He hadn't eaten since breakfast. The incident with Codi and the run-in with Artur had distracted him from needed sustenance.

They started filling their plates. Well, everyone except James, who sat back at the head of the table and drank from a white ceramic mug, setting it down on an electric warming plate between sips. Dean knew what was in the cup that needed to be kept warm. He preferred not to think about it. He returned his attention to his food and dug in. As the rest of them started eating, James broke the silence.

"Dean, I wanted to thank you for caring for Codi today. I do not like it when my employees are harmed in the course of their work for me. I'm glad you were available to take care of her."

"It was your guest who caused the injury," Dean said, finishing a bite of food. "I assume you had a discussion with Artur about this so that it won't happen again?"

James glanced at Brynne and Ashley, then looked his way and answered him. "It's not quite that simple. I cannot issue orders to Artur. He is my guest, not my vassal. Usually, a guest is more respectful of the hospitality of their host in our society. Artur, however, is more resistant to change than some others. He considers himself better than most of those he encounters."

"So there's nothing you can do to keep it from happening again?" Dean asked in disbelief.

"I have talked to him about it. He merely offered to compensate me for my trouble," James said. "Honestly, I didn't expect much more. Artur is much older than I, and I have no way to compel him to act differently."

"Maybe Ashley can do something," Dean said. "She's had dealings with him before."

James raised an eyebrow at this revelation. He looked at Ashley, and she waved a hand in front of her mouth while she finished a bite of food.

"It has had more to do with my sister than it has with me," she said. "We first ran into Artur during the Crimean War in the early 1850's. I was assisting Florence Nightingale with her work in the British military hospitals. My sister happened to be there, too, where she always likes to be, near a battlefield."

"Wait, I thought all the Eldara Sisters were healers," Dean asked. "Why wasn't she helping you in the hospital?"

Ashley smiled. "It's a common mistake when I talk about my sister. The Eldara Sisters are the healers of the Eldara. It's like a person having different types of jobs. The Eldara Sisters are our healers. It just so happens that I also have a twin sister. She's about as far from a healer as you can get. She is what you might call a Battle Maiden."

Dean and James both laughed when Brynne nearly did a spit take while she was drinking her water. After she had finished coughing, she gasped, "Your sister is a Valkyrie?"

Dean stopped laughing at Brynne and looked from Brynne to Ashley. "Seriously? A Valkyrie? The winged women of Norse legends who carry those who die heroically in battle on to Valhalla?"

"Yes," Ashley sighed. "You have to understand, my sister and I are very different. We are two sides of the same coin. She attends the fallen heroes on battlefields, personally ushering the most deserving of the fallen souls onward in their spirit journey while I heal the surviving injured and wounded. In the Crimea, there was a sudden surge in vampire attacks in the areas around the battlefields. Some of the wounded soldiers in the hospital died and were turned as well, so I went east to the battlefields to investigate. There I found Ingrid. She was looking into a sudden decrease in the available souls after the battles and took issue with Artur coming out at night and finishing off the wounded and dying on the field of battle, turning them into his vassal vampires. He, too, sought out the strongest and best among the warriors."

"Artur always fashioned himself as something of an armchair

general," James said. "It doesn't surprise me that he would want to associate with former warriors. So your sister took offense?"

"She took it personally and spent the better part of two months trying to hunt Artur down," Ashley said. "Eventually, Ingrid and I were able to track his vampires back to his lair. There was a confrontation in that country inn involving too many vampires to handle on our own, and we had to fight together to kill most of them. In the end, Ingrid confronted Artur, but he ended up getting away before she could reach him. She could have stopped him permanently had she caught up with him. In the end, he escaped and left the battlefield wounded to me, and those who were dying to her. She swore she'd never forget what happened. There have been a few other run-ins over the years where Artur had other close calls. He always managed to escape in the end."

"Your sister sounds like a bit of a badass," Brynne said with a chuckle. "Would she have staked him if she had caught up with him?"

"Oh, most definitely," Ashley said. "She is a powerful and capable woman. She wouldn't have used a stake, though. The Eldara can manifest heavenly blades of pure silver, wrought in the forges of the upper planes. With that in her hands, she would have been more than a match for even an elder vampire lord like Artur, had she been able to bring him to a fight."

James chuckled, "Artur has always been such a pompous ass. I would love to see him turn tail and run, and settle this thing once and for all."

Ashley looked around at the three others at the table. "Which brings us back to the matter at hand. Why has Artur shown up here, at this particular time? He is always working some angle. It has to be connected."

"James, you've known Artur longer than any of us," Dean asked. "He's your friend. What could he be up to?"

James held up a hand in response. "He's not a friend, Dean. I'm extending him hospitality according to tradition; that is all. He and I have never been what anyone would call friends. I thought it curious that he came here. We have never gotten along. I assumed he was just passing through on business and needed somewhere to stay while he accomplished his work. I thought he stopped here just to annoy me with his little slights like the attack on Codi. Now, I'm not sure." James pulled out his phone and tapped a message on it while the others watched. "I'll have Celeste look into what Artur has been up to while he's been here."

"I'm almost certain he is connected to what is happening here in Elk City," Ashley said. "It all makes sense now and perhaps is why I was chosen for this assignment, in this time and place, given my prior encounters with him."

"It gets tiring that your bosses can't seem to send you a direct message explaining everything to you up front. It would make things so much easier," Dean said.

"I told you, I'm a change agent. I influence things based on my instincts and impressions of the people I'm working with. If the gods interfered directly, there'd be no such thing as free will, ever. The most they can do is work through agents like the Eldara to help people realize their choices. In the end, though, it's up to them to make the decisions."

Brynne interrupted them, "But Artur has only been here for a week. How could he be involved? The attacks have been going on for several months."

The assembled friends at the table fell silent while they pondered that point.

James broke the silence. "Celeste will find out," he said. "She has excellent resources and contacts throughout the extended Unusual community. If Artur is up to something more than his usual unsavory business, she'll find out. In the meantime, Dean, she informed me that you might accept a position here to help with the health of our employees in the building. Have you made up your mind?"

"I think I would like that very much," Dean said. "I want to keep helping people somehow, and being suspended with nothing to do all day doesn't appeal to me. I'd rather keep busy while everyone out there decides my fate for me."

"Excellent," James said. "We'll set you up with a full suite of assessment tools, and I have a portable blood lab downstairs that we'll get set up for you."

"I don't know how to run something like that. I can use a hand-held blood analyzer like the iStat, but I'm not a lab tech," Dean said.

"Don't worry, we'll take care of all the training you need," James countered. "Maybe we'll get you so used to working here you won't want to go back to working for the city. I know I can pay you better."

"Anyone can pay us better," Brynne quipped. "I keep telling you that we don't do it for the pay, it's something we would almost do for free. In fact, in many rural areas, there are volunteer EMTs and paramedics who provide all the care on ambulances."

Dean listened as the conversation turned to healthcare reform and how people paid for that care. He thought about the possibility of staying here and working for James. He decided that, while it might make a nice distraction for him right now, it wasn't something he wanted to do long term. He belonged on the streets, caring for those who couldn't care for themselves.

## Chapter 8

The next two weeks went by for Dean in a blur. He got set up in an office on the second floor and familiarized himself with the equipment James purchased for him to use, or in some cases already had, for onsite medical care. He found out that at any given time, there were upwards of sixty feeder humans staying in rooms like Codi's in the Nightwing building. They were all there voluntarily and were compensated quite handsomely. There were males and females, and all were there to supplement the bagged blood supplies purchased to feed the vampires in James' coven as well as any visiting vampire dignitaries like Artur. The large number was important to maintain and monitor since it took time for the human body to replenish lost blood supply. While the fluid itself was replaced rather quickly just by drinking water and other liquids in the course of a few days, it took upwards of forty-five days to replace the life-giving cells in the blood that were depleted after a feeding.

Since the incident between Codi and Artur, Dean paid particular attention to any of his charges who exhibited any signs of additional injury or assault. They all came in once a week to get their blood tested, and he checked them over for signs of infection or illness. If he saw a fever, slow healing wounds or other symptoms of disease, he referred them to a nurse practitioner on James' payroll in a nearby medical office building. All of the feeders, as they called themselves, were pretty matter-of-fact about what they did. They were thankful that the testing could be done on-site by Dean. Previously, they had to go to a regular lab, and the technicians asked awkward questions about why they had to get tested so frequently. Some of the lab techs thought they were involved with the porn industry because of the frequent blood tests.

It didn't take long for Dean to learn that each of the resident vampires had their favorites, and a few of them called down frequently to see when their feeder of choice would be back on the menu. Dean would check the records and let them know when he thought they'd have replenished their blood based on what the hemoglobin and hematocrit numbers were. He was struck by how normal the whole situation seemed to him after just a few days. Once he was sure that no one was being coerced into being there, and that they were being paid very well for the services they rendered with their bodies every month and a half or so, he settled into the routine of testing and keeping records.

Artur seemed to have settled down too, at least no one else who reported to him had an injury indicating anything more than a vigorous bite. The worst of the wounds he saw were able to be closed with a butterfly bandage or even a mere band-aid. Still Dean knew Artur was up there. He was aware that Artur was plotting something sinister to undermine both James and the Station U program. He spent his downtime texting Ashley and Brynne, or surfing the web to find out what was happening with the latest attacks by The Cause on Unusuals. The attacks always seemed to coincide with a Station U ambulance call. Their Unusual patients were starting to realize that fact. The number of calls the unit received daily had dropped off quite a bit. They were all rightly afraid of being the unwitting victims of attack, and while they didn't necessarily blame the paramedics themselves, the Unusuals knew that it was often the ambulance that heralded the next assault.

Ashley was also worried about it and had taken to going out at night herself, somewhere, to try and track down the source of the attacks or attackers. Dean always asked to go with her but she refused, saying that she was traveling in a manner he couldn't, and he would not be able to keep up with her. The combination of her shifts at the ER and the late night forays into Elk City were starting to take their toll on her. She insisted that she didn't need any sleep in the human sense, but Dean also knew that when she spent her divine energy, she became fatigued. He had seen it firsthand for himself once when she had healed a wounded dryad with a septic infection on a weekend trip to the mountains. Her powers might be formidable enough to cause a vampire lord to be afraid to cross her directly, but they were finite and needed to be recharged from time to time.

The worst part was that he was unable to do anything about it. Ashley was worried, too. She had said before that he had a role to play in stopping the attacks and resetting the balance in Elk City. But, since he was put on suspension following the murder in his apartment, that link between him and the potential solution had faded somewhat. At least, that was the way Ashley had put it. He was still linked somehow, but it was now more tenuous and signaled to her that his chances of influencing things were diminished. Dean mentioned that change one evening when he convinced Ashley to stay in and not go out prowling Elk City for clues, or whatever it was she was looking for.

"What if getting me off the street, away from providing patient care for the Unusuals has been what changed my involvement in this whole situation?" he asked Ashley as they cuddled in the dark of his bedroom late one night.

"What do you mean?"

Dean continued the thought. "I mean, what if getting me off the Station U ambulance was the whole reason for setting me up for Zach's murder? You said that the link to my involvement changed in your eyes as soon as that happened. So what if it was all about taking me out of the equation on the streets? That would make it so I couldn't act directly to save my patients in a given situation, whatever that is."

"That makes sense," Ashley said. "But it could take months for the legal case to resolve and for you to get your job back. The way things are going right now, there aren't going to be any Station U patients left to call you, or at least not any that are willing to take the risk to make that call. The terror campaign and attacks against them are working. Brynne and the rest of the paramedics there are only taking about one call a day. Eventually, the city is going to see the drop-off and start asking you all to take regular EMS calls for humans. Once they start cycling you all back into the regular rotation, Station U as we know it will cease to exist."

"Okay, so we have that much figured out, but what can we do to change it?" Dean asked. "I can't get back in the ambulance unless we can somehow prove my innocence."

"It's one of the things I'm working on, Dean," Ashley said. "I've been trying to get a sense of where the connection between you and Zach is. Whenever I try to focus in on it, I'm just drawn to the center of the city and then the sensation dissipates. I know you're frustrated about this. I'm frustrated, too. It's almost as if someone is cloaking their involvement magically."

"Is there some way we can overcome that with a magic of our own or pierce the veil?" Dean asked. "If magic or some magical ability is being used, there must be a way to counter it, right?"

"It is not always that simple, Dean," Ashley replied. "There are hierarchies of magic out there. You need to know the kind of magic being used to identify the way to counter it. I'm not even sure if it's magic at all, just a suspicion."

"Is there a way we can find out?" Dean asked.

"Maybe," Ashley said. "It's not without its risks, though. Because it centers around you and your involvement in this, you would be the one to pay the price."

"That sounds ominous."

"Magic and magical powers all have a price, Dean," Ashley explained. "It's basic physics. Matter and energy cannot be created or destroyed, merely transformed in some way to another type of matter or energy. That transformation and the control of it comes at a cost. Just like my fatigue when using my powers to heal, those who deal with such magic and the use of their skills must pay a price to balance the energy equation. You will be asked to compensate them for that price they must pay."

"What kind of compensation?" Dean asked.

"I do not know," Ashley replied. "It varies and depends on many things including the way the individual caster feels towards you personally. If they don't like you, you pay more. If they like you, you pay less. If they like you a lot, maybe you pay nothing."

"So how do we go about doing this?" Dean asked. "I'll pay the price. I can't just sit here and watch while the whole Station U program gets scrapped, just because I did nothing to stop it."

"Be careful what you say, Dean," Ashley cautioned. "You do not yet know the price that will be asked. If the caster doesn't like you or doesn't care, your willingness to pay more will cause them to raise the cost. As to how we go about this process, I need to talk to James and do a little investigating on my own. If we are going to do this, I want to stack the odds of success in our favor for a change."

"So what do we do in the meantime?" Dean asked. "I'm going stir crazy stuck here in this building. At least take me out with you on your next nighttime excursion. Maybe having me with you will change the balance somehow. It's got to be worth a try." Dean leaned forward from where he was lying next to her and kissed her lightly on her shoulder. He had missed her on those many nights when she left to go out and search for answers. It had been over a week since they had spent any meaningful time together. "Come on. You know I can be very persuasive if I want to be."

Ashley laughed and turned towards him in bed. "I'll think about it. In the meantime, you can try very hard to persuade me. I give you my permission."

▭

BY THE NEXT MORNING, Dean was sure he had convinced Ashley to take him along on her excursion around the city that night. He asked her directly as she got up to get ready for her shift in the ER, and she looked at him for a minute then nodded in assent. He saw her smile when he jumped up and gave her a hug and kiss. This was the best news he had heard in a while. He was finally going to get out of this building and do something to take care of the city he had come to love and support for a change. He had gone for short walks during his days, in between his duties for James. However, he had never really had a purpose or destination for where he was going. Dean had quickly returned to the building to spend time in his room watching the news of the attacks, or surfing the web for the increasing reports of strange creatures living in the city. That was all he could do until now to try and get a handle on the events beyond his control.

Ashley showered and got ready for work while he made them some breakfast. She opted for just half a bagel with some cream cheese, yogurt, and some coffee. As soon as she was finished eating, she gave him a kiss and left, leaving him alone again. At least, this time, he had something more to look forward to. He decided to do some research on the origins of magic and how some Unusuals might harness it to help or harm him in his quest for answers. While he didn't have the extensive library of myths and legend they had at Station U, he did have the Internet, and he knew how to search for those same books online in website or eBook form. He found much of what he was looking for in the public domain section of the Google Books Library Project. The original Grimm's fairy tales were a good starting point, but he also looked for magic use in several Eastern, Asian, and African cultural myths, too.

A lot of what he read supported what Ashley had told him the night before about the price that must be paid for the use of magic. Some of the stories were more than a bit gruesome and disturbing in the prices demanded in pay for a magical intervention. He thought he would just meet a local witch, or priestess, or something, and they would conjure up an answer for him. Dean snorted at the thought. He should have known better, though. He had seen enough about what went on in the Unusual community over the last several months riding with Brynne at Station U to know that nothing would be that easy. He would have to be very careful about how he responded to whomever Ashley found for them to consult. One wrong word could commit him to a bargain he would not be able to back out of.

Dean wrapped up his research when he saw on his watch that it was time to head to the medical office downstairs to start his work screening and assessing the feeders again. He decided to ponder the potential price that would be asked of him while he went about his work for the rest of the day. How far would he go to resolve things here in Elk City? He would need to have a firm understanding of that for himself before Ashley returned later and they began their quest to find an answer to the magical block protecting their adversary.

Chapter 9

Dean was waiting in his apartment when Ashley returned from work. She texted him that she would be over after she showered. He was dressed and ready to go. He had been ready for more than an hour. He wanted to get moving to work around the magical block that was helping The Cause create havoc for his patients. Dean waited, pacing the floor and glancing at his watch until there was a tap at his door. He opened it and saw Ashley standing there in black jeans, a black t-shirt, and black leather jacket. Her hair was pulled back in a ponytail, and she had a grave look on her face.

"Are you ready for this?" she asked, as he stepped into the hallway to join her.

"I've been waiting for this all day. I'm ready," he replied. "Where are we going?"

"I reached out and called in some favors. It helped that you have built a reputation in the community for being a healer and caregiver to the Unusual population," Ashley said. "In the end, it was the Witch coven of one of your former patients that offered to cast the spell we need. It is not without risks and their leader, Asha, was clear to me that there was a real danger of a backlash against the coven - and us, with the casting."

"What sort of backlash?" Dean asked.

"Asha wasn't clear on that. My experience is that they will have to break some kind of barrier or shield, and the release of energy will rebound back on them. That is why they will ask a price."

"What price?"

"She didn't say," Ashley admitted. "I tried to nail her down and negotiate it with her, but she avoided my requests. She said the price would be determined when you arrived. Are you sure you want to go through with this? I cannot protect you from this. If you agree to the price, you will have to pay it. I can't interfere."

"I don't want you to interfere, Ashley," Dean said. "Don't you see? We have to stay the course. If we don't get to the bottom of these attacks, everything I've tried to become, all that the other paramedics at Station U have worked hard to accomplish, will be for nothing."

He matched Ashley's determined stare for a moment, then she nodded and turned to head down the hall to the elevators. He walked with her, side by side as they went to meet with the coven. They took Ashley's red MG sports car rather than his beat-up pickup truck. As she drove up the ramp from the underground garage and into the night, the evening air swept around them with the car's top down. The air felt good; cold and bracing as he stared straight ahead while she drove the convertible to their meeting.

After driving through the downtown streets and turning off towards a residential area of Elk City, Ashley arrived at a part of town Dean had not been in before. It was an older part of town with big, Victorian style homes on generous lots. The lights were on in the large home, and there were many other cars parked in the wide driveway in front of the detached four-car garage. Ashley parked on the street, and the two of them walked up onto the front porch, reaching the oversized, ornate, hand-carved wooden front door. The Angel reached up and rapped the cast iron knocker in the shape of a dragon's head. After a few moments, the door opened, and a woman, who appeared to be in her sixties with long white hair and a white dress, answered the door.

"Eldara, the sisters of the moon welcome you into our home," the woman said with a bow. She turned to Dean. "Paramedic Dean Flynn, you are known to us. You also, are welcome in our home. Please enter." The woman gestured gracefully, and Dean followed Ashley into the sizable foyer. He looked around and saw a sweeping central staircase that led upward. There were several sets of double doors off the entry hall, and they followed the woman to the right-hand doorway and into a large room with a wooden floor that had a large circular mosaic pattern in the center. There were chairs arranged in a circle around the ornate inlay. He had pondered for a moment before he realized it represented the night sky with a full moon. There was an open space in the circle of chairs and the woman led Ashley and Dean to that spot, then went to sit in the largest chair, directly across from where they stood. The other seats were already occupied by women who ranged in age from early twenties up to middle age. He was struck as well by the diversity of the women. There were two black women, an Asian woman, and several Hispanics in the group as well. There was even one woman who he couldn't identify because she wore a veil. She was notable as well because she was seated in a wheelchair.

"Eldara and Paramedic Dean Flynn, I am Asha Beales, the leader of this coven," the woman began after she sat down. She gestured to the group of women seated on either side of her around the circle. "We, the sisters of the moon, have considered your request for a divining spell to pierce a magical veil that conceals your opponents from you. It is not a request to be considered lightly. Once begun, the spell must be completed, and there is no way to determine if the power behind the veil you wish to pierce is beyond our strength until we begin the casting. Even if it is too strong for us to pierce, life force will be drained from each of us in payment for the attempt." She paused to let that statement sink in. Dean looked around at the women in the circle. All of their eyes were on him. He felt uneasy at the center of their attention.

"With that fact stated, the coven has agreed to consider your request and grant it, provided you are deemed worthy of the magical price to be paid." Asha gestured to Dean. "Paramedic Dean Flynn, step forward to the center of the circle and be judged."

Dean glanced at Ashley, and she nodded, her lips pressed together in a firm line, her green eyes turned somehow darker and more serious in her stare. She had warned him, and he had said he was willing to pay the price. Now was the time to step up and stick to his guns. He stepped forward into the center of the circle of Witches and faced Asha and the other sisters of the moon. Let them judge him. He was ready.

When Dean assumed his stance at the center of the circle, Asha spoke in a formal tone. "Let the judgment begin." Dean tensed and waited but for a full minute, nothing happened. Then a woman to his left spoke.

"Why should we risk our life force for this man? We are dedicated to the balance of power. Neither for good or evil, we represent nature and it's constancy of change, seeking to be like the waters of the rain which find their own level wherever they fall."

Another woman in the circle spoke up from his right in reply. "We have all felt the balance shift, though, sisters. There is no balance currently in Elk City. Our group has felt the effects of this directly, as you all well know. Are we not bound by that to take action?"

Dean didn't understand the discussion, but he knew from his reading and research that the Witches had a dedication to the balance of nature. They and the Druids were known for their belief that both good and evil had a place in the world, that they were both two sides of the same coin. It was similar to the belief that for life to exist and have meaning, there had to be death. Balance and all it stood for was necessary for existence in their view. He turned to his rear, as a woman behind him spoke up.

"Will one of our number vouch for this man so that we may know his character?"

He looked around as the women all stared at him. He met their eyes in turn as he looked around. An electronic beep caused him to turn and look at the veiled woman in the wheelchair. She had activated the motor and used a joystick mounted on one armrest to move the chair a few feet towards Dean. She tilted her head, and Dean could feel her looking up at him from her chair for a moment before she turned and looked around the circle.

"I will speak on behalf of this man," she said in a raspy voice. "I have seen his dedication and character displayed in his work as a healer."

Who was this woman? He looked at her hand and saw burn scars there where her skin showed beyond her long black lace sleeve. He realized then, in a flash of memory, who this woman must be. She was the Witch woman burned in an attack by The Cause in his first weeks on the job. It was where he had first seen and recognized Zach in the crowd, watching while he struggled to save her life with Brynne. What was her name?

"Vanessa," he said tentatively. "Is that you?"

"Yes, it is I, Paramedic Dean," she said. "I'm glad you remembered my name. I had not yet thanked you for saving my life." She looked around at the circle of women. "I say that we owe consideration of this man because of his actions on my behalf, a member of this coven. He has demonstrated his worthiness." She shifted the joystick and backed up to return to her place in the circle.

Silence settled in the room again. Dean waited. He wanted to speak up and help to convince them, but he sensed that it was not his place. This was a decision that they had to arrive at from within their group. He had already spoken by his prior actions, treating Vanessa for her burns months before.

Asha spoke from her position at the top of the circle. "We determine that he is worthy of consideration." Dean started to sigh in relief, thinking that was all, but then she continued. "There is still the consideration of price for our casting. Life force must be paid for with life force in kind." She stopped speaking and looked at the group, awaiting the response. Dean turned and looked around, trying to gauge the thoughts there. He didn't like the idea of giving up some of his life force for this, but he had decided he'd pay the price to stop the attacks, whatever it was.

He was surprised when Ashley broke the silence. She had stayed out of this, knowing it hinged on him and his responses.

"May I speak?" she asked, and all heads turned to her.

"You may speak Eldara," Asha said. "You do understand that you may not pay this price for him."

"I understand, but I have information that may impact your decision on the assessment of price," Ashley said. "Paramedic Dean Flynn has been determined to be a pivot point for the current conflict in Elk City. It is why I have chosen him as my companion. He must be left with the strength to act as he must if he is to return balance to the city. I have seen that without his intervention, the power in this town will shift in a way that darkness will rule here for some time to come."

"Thank you, Eldara," Asha replied. "We will consider this in our deliberations, but a price must be paid nonetheless. It is the way of such things. There must always be a balance, even in negotiations."

"I have a thought." Dean turned to see a middle-aged black woman with a colorful African headdress, stand and take a step in his direction. She paused after the first step. "May I approach and lay hands on you, Paramedic Dean Flynn?"

He nodded in assent and stood still as she came up to him and put a hand on his forehead and another over his heart. He could hear her murmur under her breath, but could not make out the words she uttered. It was as if the words dissipated as soon as they passed her lips. After a while, she removed her hands and stepped back, turning to face Asha.

"His eldest child will be a daughter," she spoke with the finality of pronouncement. "I propose we levy the price of life force for life force. He gives us life force for the future growth of our coven, to be weighed against the life force to be spent this evening." There were nods and murmurs of assent from around the circle. Dean wondered what the pronouncement meant and how that had anything to do with what was going on here and now. He was pretty sure he and Ashley couldn't produce a child based on things she had told him in the past. She wasn't human. If there was another woman out there for him beyond Ashley, he couldn't see it in the near future, let alone considering having children. This made no sense. He spun to look at Asha, and she spoke as if in response to his questions.

"Paramedic Dean Flynn," the Witch leader said. "We have agreed upon a proposed price for our casting this evening. Our sister, Udele, has determined that your firstborn will be a girl child. In exchange for our casting of divination tonight, you will pledge that child to this coven."

"You want my yet to be born baby for some sort of human sacrifice?" Dean blurted out in horror. "That's barbaric!" He had pondered many prices in his research, but this had never occurred to him. It was ridiculous.

Asha laughed aloud, as did many of the sisters surrounding him. "Dean," Asha said, her voice softening. "We are not monsters. You have such an open mind, but your human prejudices leap out from inside you despite your education. We ask simply that your child one day be educated here with us when she is old enough to begin school. She will live here and become one of us, thus replenishing the life force of the coven."

"How would I convince my future wife of such a thing? I don't even know who that person would be, let alone if they would agree to it," Dean said.

"That is your cost," Asha said. "The price we propose is like a precious diamond. It is hard, valuable, and multifaceted. It is not just your child that is the price, but also the effect on the relationships with your future wife and others." She held his gaze for a moment. "Will you pay the price?"

Thoughts flew through Dean's mind. Part of him wanted just to say yes. He couldn't wrap his brain around the concept of being a father, so it didn't seem real. But he had also seen many things in his short career with Station U to know that what Udele had seen in his future was going to happen. He would have a daughter someday. If he agreed to this, he would be bound to the coven to turn her over to them regardless of what his future wife, or girlfriend, or whoever would have to say about it. But if he didn't agree, they would be back to the beginning without any access to what was going on with The Cause in Elk City. Dean looked back at Ashley, then around at the circle of women, finally letting his gaze rest on Asha at the top of the circle.

"Yes," he said in a whisper. "I'll pay the price."

———————————————

# Chapter 10

———————————————

As soon as Dean agreed to the price, Asha asked him and Ashley to leave the room where the circle gathered. A young dark-haired girl of about thirteen years of age led them from the circle room back to the entry hall. She pulled the double pocket doors closed behind her and then led them through another doorway to a sitting room across the entryway. Once there she offered them refreshment, but neither Dean nor Ashley was in the mood for anything to eat or drink. She nodded and left them alone in the sitting room, where the two of them each sat in one of the chairs arranged around a central coffee table. There was nothing to do but wait for the response to what the coven found in their casting.

The two of them sat in silence for a time. They could hear a murmur of chanting coming from across the hall but nothing concrete. Dean looked up at Ashley and saw her watching him. She had a curious expression on her face.

"What?" he asked. "Do you think I should have said no, or negotiated a different price?"

"The decision was yours to make, Dean," Ashley responded. "I could not influence it one way or another, and I doubt you could have negotiated anything different. They rightly perceive that you have some innate power inside you. It makes sense. After all, fate has chosen you to have an important part in what is happening here in Elk City. In their eyes, that means your offspring will have power, too."

"But what was I thinking? I don't even know how I'm going to approach this when the time comes," Dean said, shaking his head. "What woman will give up her child to a coven of witches to raise as their own?"

"That will be something you will have to consider when you reach a point in life where you are ready to have children," Ashley said. "They will not take the child until she is of school age, and I suspect that you will be able to visit and watch over the child while she learns the ways of the coven and the Witches' life. The thing I am most interested in is the shift I felt when you agreed to their terms. Something major happened when you made that decision, Dean. We may not know what that change in the future is, but something is now different because of your promise to the coven tonight."

"Fantastic," Dean said throwing his hands in the air and leaning back in the chair. "I give up. Now I'm instrumental in some other otherworldly plan. Am I stuck in the middle of these things for the rest of my life?"

"That is up to you, Dean," Ashley answered him. "It has always been your choice. You can walk away and let events happen however they work out on their own without your intervention. You can do that anytime you want."

"You know I can't do that," Dean said in reply. "People are being hurt and maybe dying because of what is happening here. If I can do something to stop that, I have to do it."

"I know," Ashley said. She leaned forward in her chair and laid a hand atop his where it rested on the arm of his chair. "It is why I was chosen to be here to help guide you, and it is why I am attracted to you."

The chanting in the other room across the hall rose in volume and intensity. It made the hairs on his neck stand up on end as if the level of static electricity in the room went up exponentially. Who knows, Dean thought to himself. Maybe it did. He looked over at Ashley.

"What do you think they'll discover in there?" Dean asked. He was afraid that the answer to the question would not be worth the price paid to get it.

"We'll know when they have finished the casting and not before," Ashley said. "That is the way of such things. We must wait." She looked at him with a reassuring smile and a squeeze of his hand.

Dean got up and paced around the room, looking at the odd knick-knacks on the shelves and tables around him. There were crystals of various sizes and colors, a few tribal carvings of what appeared to be women, though some had animal heads on naked human female bodies. There were other items hanging on the walls, including some tribal masks from different cultures he couldn't name. He moved to the large built-in bookshelf on one wall and started looking over the selection of books. There were classic novels and stories, as well as old texts on biology and anatomy. It was strange, but there was nothing there on Witch culture, spells or anything like that. He did see a few familiar tomes on mythology and fairy tales that were similar to the ones kept at Station U for the paramedics to read and review about their patients. He took one of these down and sat back down in the chair across from Ashley.

"I guess I'll get some more reading done since I haven't been able to do any since I got suspended," Dean said. "Gotta keep my knowledge base up." He attempted a confident smile but wasn't sure he was successful. Ashley returned the smile and pulled out her phone to scroll through the apps there. All they could do was wait.

THE EXPLOSION WAS the first sign that something was wrong. The double doors across the hallway that led to the circle blew outward in splinters. Dean and Ashley both dove from their seats and took cover. There was no fire, just the force of an ice-cold wind that washed over them. Once it had passed, Dean was on his feet in an instant. He ran forward to the demolished doorway, followed by Ashley. He peeked around the corner into the room carefully, mindful of scene safety, as he'd been taught. The room was a scene of devastation. The blast seemed to have originated in the center of the circle, judging from the way the chairs, and their former occupants, lay spread out around the perimeter of the room. He heard groans from inside and that shook him out of his shock at the destruction he witnessed. He rushed inside, followed by Ashley.

Starting at the closest woman to them, he began working his way around the room, using a rapid assessment technique used for situations where you had a large number of patients to assess quickly. It allowed him to move swiftly and identify life-threatening injuries as soon as possible. He started moving left, and he saw Ashley head to the right, as they each started around the perimeter of the room. Dean soon reached the far end of the room and picked up the large, high-backed chair that had held Asha. She lay underneath it and started to rise when he lifted it from her.

"Stay still Asha," Dean cautioned. "Let me look you over. Then I need to call for help. We need several ambulances here for you and your coven."

"No," she said forcefully. "No ambulances! We will not draw a further attack on us here in our home. We have found the source of your enemy, Dean, and I will not subject this coven to further danger by drawing attention to us with a visit from your Unusual Paramedics. There are others who can help. I will call them."

Dean stepped back as she sat up and took a phone from her robes and dialed a number. He heard her relay her address and then she hung up. She looked around the room, a pained look on her face.

"Look I don't know who you called, but you need to get some medical attention," Dean cautioned. "Luckily everyone is alive, but there are several head injuries and broken bones to deal with."

Ashley arrived at his side from her assessment around the other side of the room. "Dean is right, Asha. I have done what little I could do. No one has died, but there are injuries that need tending."

"The witches have long been healers for our communities. We

have our own resources, as you know Eldara. While modern medical attention might help in some ways, in the current situation it would draw unnecessary attention to us if we were to call the Station U paramedics and 911. I have called others to come and tend to us. They will be here soon."

Dean didn't know what she was talking about regarding other responders. He had no idea who that could be, but this was what James and Brynne had feared would happen. The Unusual community was avoiding calling for paramedics when they needed help specifically to keep from drawing the attention of The Cause and another attack. He looked at Ashley and shrugged. She returned his gaze with a worried look on her face. He began back-tracking around the room, trying to make the women he had just assessed more comfortable, and started tending to the injuries as best he could based on his limited resources. A few minutes later, he was using a broken chair leg and strips of ripped tablecloth to splint a broken arm when a familiar voice sounded from the entryway.

"Oh, my God! What happened here?" said Gibbie in a high-pitched voice. Gibson Proctor was a middle-aged vampire turned community first responder after Dean and Brynne had trained him and a few others weeks before. He had apparently taken his community first aid training seriously and decided to help those in his neighborhood more directly.

Dean took in the frumpy vampire, dressed in his brand-new store-bought uniform pants and shirt. He carried what looked like a trauma bag and an oxygen tank bag as he stood in the doorway.

"Gibbie, what are you doing here?" Dean asked.

"Asha called me," Gibbie replied. "She said she needed help and to come fast. I picked up Kristof on the way here because it sounded like I'd need some help. He's bringing more bags in from my van. What are you doing here, Dean? I thought you were suspended?"

"I am," Dean said. "I was here seeking some help from the coven. Now they need our help. Let me see your bag and see what supplies you have." Gibbie handed Dean his trauma bag and set down the oxygen bottle on the floor. He looked around and then back at Dean.

"Dean, what do you want me to do?"

Dean handed the vampire responder a couple of packs of gauze and some rolled bandages from the bag. "Start over there and attend to any bleeding you see. Stop the bleeding like I taught you and then bandage the injuries. Ashley and I need to attend to the more seriously injured."

Just then, Kristof Algar, the owner of Sabatani's restaurant, and another of Dean's Unusual Community Emergency Response Training students came in the front door with additional first aid supplies in his arms. He looked around in surprise.

"Kristof," Dean said as he saw the gray-haired Djinn, or Genie, enter. "You help Gibbie with the bandaging." The man nodded and moved to help his companion. Dean wondered how Asha had known to contact them but decided that was a question for later. For now, he, Ashley, and the two volunteer first responders had their hands full with the patients at hand.

It took twenty minutes to treat what injuries they could between the supplies at hand and what Gibbie and Kristof had brought in with them. Dean stood in the center and discussed the situation with Ashley. The thirteen women who had been injured in the blast were all going to live. Ashley admitted to him that a few could use a CT scan to rule out brain bleeds from traumatic brain injury, and most had signs of at least a mild concussion. The blast had been significant enough also to cause a few broken bones and numerous bruises and contusions. All of the women refused to go to the hospital though, so that option was out for the time being. They needed to be reassessed throughout the night to make sure nothing developed, and he and Ashley decided to stay there at the home. They were still talking over the disposition of their patients when Gibbie approached holding his cell phone.

"Dean, I've got another call for assistance. I'm going to go, okay?"

"What do you mean you've got another call for assistance?"

Dean asked. "You mean other folks are calling you instead of calling 911?"

Gibbie shuffled his feet a little and stared at the floor in embarrassment. "Uh, well, yeah." He looked up at Dean. "People are afraid to call 911 anymore because of the attacks on the others. I decided to let it be known that I was available at night and that Kristof and the others from our CERT class, they take shifts during the day. If someone needs to call us, we will show up and try to offer what help we can." Gibbie dug in a pocket and then held out a business card to Dean.

Dean took the card and read it aloud so Ashley could hear. "Gibson B. Proctor, CERT, Volunteer Medical Responder." It had a cell phone number that Dean recognized as Gibbie's, and a stylized EMS star of life emblem.

"I got the cards made up online," Gibbie said. "I know this isn't what you told us to do when you and Brynne trained us, but this is different. Everything is changed now since you got suspended. Our people are in need of assistance, and they are too afraid to call the Station U paramedics anymore. Someone has to help them."

Dean didn't know what to say. He had trained Gibbie and the others to keep the vampire from freelancing just like this after he decided he wanted to do what Dean and Brynne did as paramedics. The Federal CERT training program seemed the perfect fit to make Gibbie feel like he was contributing and to build community resilience for situations of disaster and extreme need. This situation with The Cause was desperate, that was true, and there was a definite need. He looked at the vampire, in his brand new EMS uniform, and shook his head in resignation. He handed Gibbie back the card.

"Go, do what you can," Dean said. "Hopefully, you can do some good since I cannot. Call me, though. I want to have a talk with you about this. Maybe we can arrange for Brynne, or maybe James, to get you some better supplies and gear."

Gibbie grinned and nodded with enthusiasm while he picked up his bags. He called to Kristof, who waved to Dean, and the two Unusual responders left to tend to their next patients. Dean watched him go and wondered if things would ever return to normal here in Elk City. Asha's voice broke through his contemplation.

"Dean," the Witch leader called to him from across the room where she sat in her uprighted chair. "Come here. We were able to find out some things before the protection spell rebounded to strike back at us. The price was higher than we expected, but the bargain was struck, and we will hold to our end of it."

Dean and Ashley crossed over to the elderly woman where she sat amidst the devastation of the coven's casting chamber. She watched them approach and waited until they both stood in front of her before she continued.

"The conflict centers both at the fire department headquarters and somewhere downtown," Asha began. "We were able to penetrate the Fire Headquarters quite quickly. There were no substantial protections there. There are two individuals who oppose you there. One is known to you already, and there is a personal connection there. The other is still hidden. It is someone whom you have not met before and is also unknown to us. You will have to figure that person out on your own. We were also drawn to the building of James Lee. It was there we had to penetrate not only the defenses of a supernatural target but the defenses of the vampire lord of Elk City. We did not definitively identify the source of the troubles there, but it is one who is ancient, powerful, and evil. Also, the focal point of this ancient evil power is not on you, but on James Lee."

Dean started to speak and ask a question, but she forestalled him with a raised hand. "We can tell you no more. Our intrusion was detected, and the backlash of that attack followed us back here before we could discover more. You will have to make do with that limited knowledge." Asha paused and considered him for a moment before continuing. "Do not return to us for further assistance until you have paid the debt you owe us. We will await the time when that payment is received. In the meantime, we must see to ourselves. It will take us a long time to recover from this casting, and we must heal."

The paramedic watched as she stood and turned to check on her sisters, leaving him standing there with Ashley wondering what to do next. That there were two individuals at headquarters concerned him. He knew of Brynne's mentor and his academy instructor Mike Farver. He had some personal reason to be involved in this mess. The other had to be someone pretty high up in the department leadership. They were funneling private information to The Cause directly from dispatch. As far as the focal point at the Nightwing building downtown, he suspected that he knew the source of this ancient evil aimed at James. They had already voiced their suspicions to each other about Artur. The question was what they could do about it? The whole situation was so convoluted; it gave him a headache. Dean needed to talk this out with Ashley, Brynne, and especially James. Now that they had confirmed he was the ultimate target, they needed to figure out why Dean was so important to the situation with James. That didn't make sense at all. Dean had nothing to do with James aside from his working with Brynne. Looking to Ashley, he reached out and took the angel's hand and gave it a squeeze. They had come here looking for information and answers. They would leave without many answers at all, and a lot more questions.

# Chapter 11

After seeing to their patients at the Witch house one final time, Ashley drove them back downtown. Dean shot a text to Celeste Teal to see if James was available. James' assistant responded almost immediately. She said he would be in an hour or so and asked if everything was alright. Dean replied that he'd explain when they arrived back at the Nightwing building. He was glad it would take James an hour to free up his schedule. Dean wanted to clean up a bit and gather his thoughts.

Ashley drove in silence, leaving him to his deliberations. She hadn't said much back at the Witch house. She had told him that he had to make all the decisions there on his own, but he wanted to hear what she thought. He valued her opinion of him and his choices. As she pulled into the underground garage in James' building and parked, Dean turned and looked at her.

"What?" she asked. Ashley smiled and reached over to lay her hand on his. "You have something on your mind. What is it?"

"I want to know what you think of my decision back there. Do you think I did the right thing?"

"I don't second guess you, Dean," the Eldara replied. "You had the decision to make. Only you could make it, and if I had influenced you in any way then it would not have been just yours, it would have been mine too. I think you are more concerned about what I think about you, than the decision itself. All I can say to you is this - I have seen good things come about from both good and bad decisions. Over the years, I have seen people struggle to do the right thing for the wrong reasons and make choices that spelled certain disaster, only to have them work out in the end. You made a difficult decision, and the fact that it is so hard for you to reconcile that decision about your future, and your child, only shows me that you are a good person at heart. That pain and reconsideration of your choice doesn't make it a wrong decision, just a hard one."

"It wasn't easy, but I was thinking about the here and now, not the future," Dean said. "I wanted to fix the problem we have at the expense of a person's future life. On top of that, it's my own future daughter's life I used to pay that price. Doesn't that make me a monster?"

Ashley laughed, and Dean flinched back as if she were laughing at him. She pulled him closer and answered him. "No, I don't think you are a monster. You're just human. You made a decision that your daughter will be raised as a Witch. Some people decide their kids will be football players, or lawyers, or doctors. Those children grow within the boundaries set for them and are still successful. She will be what she will be. That will be between her and the Coven."

"I hadn't thought about it that way," Dean mused. He was quiet for a moment, mulling it all over in light of what Ashley had said. He smiled after a bit and said, "It doesn't make me feel completely better, but I guess I'm not as worried as I was." His phone chirped, and he glanced down at it. "Celeste says that James and Brynne are upstairs waiting. I texted that we needed to meet up about the recent discoveries."

"Well, then. Let's go upstairs," Ashley said, grabbing her car keys and climbing out of her classic sports car. Dean followed her to the elevator and headed up to the Penthouse suite. This was important. He'd clean up later.

▭

BRYNNE MET them at the door to the apartment on the upper floor of the Nightwing building. After greetings all the way around, they sat down and Dean explained the earlier events at the Coven's house. He omitted the part about his payment, but left everything else in, including the arrival of Gibbie and Kristof after the explosion. The part about the self-appointed volunteer responders brought a surprised chuckle from Brynne. Dean continued describing the events with the Witches and got to the part with the discoveries from the divining spell. He told them about the locus of the problem being in this building as well as at Fire Headquarters. Dean paused and looked at James and Brynne.

The two sitting opposite Dean and Ashley glanced at each other, and James sighed. He got up and walked to the large wall of windows looking out over the city skyline at night. The other three waited for him to respond. Brynne looked concerned.

"I've been looking into why Artur is here," James said. "I asked a few friends I have at the Minotaur's court in Washington, DC, to see if they had heard anything about what he was up to. The answers I got were vague and dodgy as if they didn't want to respond." The Minotaur and his court currently ruled over all of the Unusual fiefdoms in North America. James, the vampire lord of Elk City, turned around and looked at the three of them. "I'm afraid that we have stumbled into a coup for my position here as the leader of the Unusuals in the region."

"Then why in the world are you still letting him stay here?" Dean blurted out. "I'd have kicked him out as soon as I found out what he was doing."

Brynne spoke up. "It is not that simple, Dean. There are protocols, and not just for how high-level Unusuals expect to be treated when visiting another of their station. There are also considerations between vampires who are of a different rank."

"But you're the lord of the city; surely you outrank him," Dean said.

"Actually, I don't. He's older than me by at least a thousand years, maybe more, and he has held larger fiefdoms than I in the past," James said. "He could almost, but not quite, just come in and ask me to step down. As it is, he is working to discredit me with both my people and my superiors, while positioning himself to be the one chosen to replace me."

"And believe us when we say that you don't want someone like Artur running things for the Unusuals here in Elk City," Brynne said. "Artur is very old school. He still very much sees himself as an apex predator, and humans as his prey."

"Wait a minute," Dean stopped her. "I thought that sort of thing was pretty much finished. I thought we were all about trying to make sure that the two populations could live peacefully together without problems anymore."

James crossed the room and sat on the arm of the sofa next to where Brynne was standing. "Artur has been trying to garner a place in the new world for about one hundred fifty years. All of the progressives in the Unusual European community came to the Americas with the first group of European settlers and set ourselves up here very early. We saw an opportunity for something better than our adversarial lives of the past. Over the years, we made peace with the human governments, and helped create this enlightened, new world."

"Then the leaders from the old world in Europe saw what we were doing and tried to muscle their way in and take over control from those of us who had worked so hard to create this new society. We successfully pushed them off. It was in the 1820s, and that conflict was part of what influenced the Monroe Doctrine. The Americas would rule themselves, including the Unusuals who were here, and further European colonization and control would be discouraged."

"Wait, the Monroe Doctrine I learned about in grade school history was started by you and your Unusual cronies?" Dean asked.

Ashley laughed. "It's not that hard to believe, Dean. The human and Unusual communities have been living side by side for millennia. Sometimes peacefully, other times, not so peacefully. But they have always been parallel to each other in many ways. That is why so much depends on how both sides work together, even in the shadows. It is why I think you and James still figure to be the pair who influence the outcome of this problem in Elk City. I still see that connection. It is more tenuous since your arrest, but it is still there."

"So you see the conundrum, Dean," James said. "I cannot openly oppose Artur, any more than he can publicly come against me. But, he can work behind the scenes to discredit me. He is using the Station U program, which has some detractors among a few of the leadership, to undermine the perception of my control over this region. Unless we bring The Cause out into the open and stop them from continuing their attacks, Artur will continue to work his machinations to bring me down. There is nothing I can do to stop him directly. My hands are tied."

"Well if we can't fight Artur directly, and definitely not here in this building, then we have to reach out and fight back against him out there," Dean said, pointing to the nighttime skyline of the city around them. "If I still figure in this equation somehow, I can't do anything about it sitting here. I've got to get back out on the streets. It is where I belong, and it is where I can do the best I can do."

Brynne shrugged. "Chief Ari and I are trying to work something out, but your suspension is written in stone. You've been implicated in a felony, and until you are cleared, you're off the streets. Plus, it's clear from the Witches' divination that there is a force operating against you at headquarters, too."

"That has to be Mike Farver, doesn't it?" Dean asked.

"He doesn't have the pull to leak patient information about specific ambulance calls in the system," Brynne said shaking her head. "Someone else higher up is at work here. Maybe one of the other deputy chiefs or the Fire Chief himself? I'm not sure. We will have to tread carefully. I know it's not EMS Chief Ari, but he might have some ideas about who it is. Until that all gets exposed, you're still off the street, Dean."

Dean walked across the room to look out at the streets below. "I'm off the streets, yes, but officially only," Dean said. He had an idea, and he turned to face them so everyone could see his smile.

"What did you have in mind, Dean? That smile means you've got something up your sleeve," Ashley said.

"What did you and I do tonight at the Coven?" Dean countered.

"We were out, on the street, providing care. Okay, we were in a house, I know, but bear with me here. Yes, I am suspended from working in any official capacity, but nobody said I couldn't volunteer my time. I could be a Good Samaritan. Headquarters couldn't stop me from doing that, and I could do a lot of good. I even have a way to get the job done."

He looked around the room. There were puzzled looks staring back at him. Ashley suddenly started smiling. She seemed to have gotten the gist of what he was saying. He could see it in her eyes.

"Brynne, could you work through back channels and get me an old, spare heart monitor, and maybe put together a drug bag for me?" She started to speak, but he held up a hand. "I know that using meds and my paramedic-level skills puts me above the level of just a bystander."

"You could lose your license if you're caught," Brynne cautioned.

Ashley interrupted the two paramedics. "You wouldn't lose your state license if you still had a medical director overseeing your patient care."

Dean looked at Brynne and then back to Ashley. He wasn't sure where she was going with this.

"I'll talk with Doc Spirelli at the ER," Ashley said. "He has been following your case and knows you're innocent. I'm sure he'll write you a letter of oversight to cover your back, at least until you are off suspension."

"So," James said. "You can get back on the street. You can even act as a paramedic. How are you going to get dispatched when there are emergencies? You can't be on the radio with all the other paramedics. You are still suspended."

"Ha ha, James," Dean said. "You don't know what I know. I will have a secret ally." Dean pulled out his phone and dialed a number. He waited while the other three watched him and the phone rang. He put it on speaker as the phone on the other end picked up.

"Hello?" said the voice on the other end. "Dean, is that you?"

"Gibbie, my man," Dean said, grinning ear to ear. "I have a proposition for you."

# Chapter 12

It took two long days to pull everything together that Dean wanted in place for his plan. Brynne got an old, retired heart monitor/defibrillator from a storage closet at Station U, as well as a few old, beat up medication and trauma bags. Ashley got Doc Spirelli at the ER to order the meds from the hospital pharmacy for a "clinic" and she got trauma bandages and supplies from the ER storage that was used to resupply the ambulances. James wanted to get into the act and buy a new vehicle for the plan, but Gibbie put his foot down. He wouldn't take anything from James, refusing to be beholden to his vampire overlord for anything. It seemed odd to turn down the gift, but Dean chalked it up to some sort of vampire pecking order thing. He did talk Gibbie into letting James put new tires on Gibbie's white creeper van. At least they wouldn't suffer a blown tire while responding, and Dean insisted after he saw the condition of the bald tires on the first meeting he held to get organized.

Dean spent those two very busy days working part-time in the Nightwing clinic set up by James for the feeder employees, and the rest organizing his gear for the street. He also took a big step forward, banking on his success in beating his legal troubles and getting back on track in his career as a Station U paramedic. On her day off, Ashley took him downtown to a shop called Tattoo Icons. It was where all the paramedics at the station had gotten their permanent ultraviolet ink tattoos of the Station U star of life emblem. The tattoo was not visible to humans, but it could be seen by Unusual patients, and it would identify him as a paramedic specifically for them. Displaying it would let patients know that they could relax their guard and get medical attention from him when they needed it.

The owner of the shop, named Gareth, appeared Native American but was, in fact, a chupacabra - a shapeshifter variety from the southwestern United States and northern Mexico. He had long black hair pulled back in a braid and a big toothy grin that greeted everyone who entered his tattoo parlor. Dean learned that Gareth had moved to the east coast to be with his human wife when she got moved for her job. He set up shop here in Elk City more than twenty years ago, and had a broad clientele in the community, both human and Unusual.

This was Dean's first tattoo, and he was a little nervous, especially since he couldn't see what Gareth was doing with the invisible inks. He assured Dean that it looked great when he was finished, and Ashley agreed, nodding enthusiastically. He needed to keep the area clean for the next few days while the area on the back of his hand healed. He was given some lotion to use on it, too.

So, it was with a new and still healing tattoo that he couldn't see, some borrowed medication and gear bags, and an old refurbished heart monitor, that Dean got started on his counter-career as a volunteer responder. He stood with all the gear on the concrete around him, in the parking garage below the Nightwing building. He checked his watch for the fifth time, waiting for Gibbie to arrive. Ashley was there, as were James and Brynne. This plan had a lot riding on it, in more ways than one. The people served by the Station U paramedics still needed care even though they had become too scared to call 911 anymore, and Dean felt the need to get back out on the street. Plus, this seemed the best way to circumvent his suspension.

Dean heard a car horn that sounded like a European siren and

Gibbie's beat up white van pulled around the corner in the underground garage. The middle-aged vampire hopped out and approached the group with a huge grin on his face. He shook hands vigorously with Dean, hugged Ashley and Brynne, and bowed to James.

"Are we ready to get this show on the road?" Gibbie asked. He was bouncing on the balls of his feet, his naturally flamboyant nature taking control.

"Easy does it, Gibbie," Dean said. "You really need to tone this down about ten notches."

"I can't do that, Dean. When I get excited about something, the dial goes to eleven!" Gibbie said with a laugh. "I've got things set up with some of the CERT team you and Brynne trained. Some of them are going to work to take calls and act as dispatchers for us. Wim and Dora, the twin dryads from the class, are going to use a room and phone lines provided by Kristof at the newly remodeled Sabatani's restaurant to take calls from our patients."

The side door of the van slid open, and a girl's voice came from inside. "Hey, you guys gonna get us out on the road? I'm itching to get started. This is going to be awesome."

The owner of the voice leaned out and Dean could see Marian Gregory, a teenaged werewolf who was another of their CERT students. Her bright pink spiked hair stood out as much as her eyebrow and nose piercings. Dean lifted one eyebrow in question, looking at Gibbie.

"Oh, yeah, Marian is going to join us on the weekends and when she doesn't have homework during the weeknights," Gibbie explained. "That's okay, isn't it? You trained us to do this, so I thought it was alright to include everyone."

Dean looked at Brynne, and she shrugged. Clearly it was alright with her. They were all flying by the seat of their pants on this venture. He knew what she was thinking, though. They were already breaking so many rules, what did a few more matter? Dean knew he was working without a parachute here. He wasn't covered under any kind of liability policy, and if headquarters were forced to take official notice of his activities, that would be it. He'd lose his license as a paramedic forever, whether he had a piece of paper from Doc Spirelli or not, even if he was found innocent of the charges against him.

"Yeah, Gibbie," Dean said with a nod to Marian. "It's fine, but she has to keep her grades up. That's on you to check in with her parents and make sure."

"Oh, absolutely, Dean. I already told her that. Her mom and dad are happy to have her doing something constructive." Gibbie leaned in and whispered, "I think she has a boyfriend they don't like too much, and they want something else to distract her." The paunchy vampire turned and waved at Marian, who was still leaning out the side of the van. She rolled her eyes at them and ducked back inside.

"Well, it's time to go then," Dean said. "Let's load up." He handed the monitor and gear bags to Gibbie, who took them and walked back to the van to stow them. Dean looked at Ashley, leaned in and gave her a kiss.

"I'll see you later this evening or tomorrow morning, I guess," he said. He turned to James and shook his hand.

"At least I got you new tires so you won't go careening off some back road with a blowout," James chuckled, looking at the van. "As to the rest of that heap of metal, well, good luck to you."

Dean laughed and started over to the idling van. Brynne walked with him as he headed to the passenger side. Gibbie had already climbed back in the driver's seat, and Marian slid the side door shut.

"Remember, Dean, you call for help from the Station U medics if you get in over your head," Brynne cautioned. "Even with the danger from The Cause, patient care has to come first. They are all aware of what is going on and will do their best to cover for you if you have to call them."

"I'll remember, but we have to protect our patients, too." Dean opened the front passenger door of the van, and Gibbie reached over and slid some trash off the seat to make room. Dean shook his head. He was going to have to whip this bunch of misfit responders into shape if this plan of his was going to work. The first thing was to keep their response vehicle in order and without trash strewn everywhere. He would set Gibbie and Marian to that task when they stopped for gas this evening. Dean sat down and closed the door, waved again to the others assembled to see him off, and hastily buckled his seatbelt as Gibbie peeled out and drove the van out of the garage and into the nighttime streets of Elk City.

▭

THEY RODE in silence downtown for a few minutes, and Dean took some time to look around the inside of the old van. It looked like Gibbie lived in here, even though he knew the vampire had a basement apartment on the edge of town. There were balled up used blood containers littering the floor and crumpled Starbuck's cups, too. A glance over his shoulder showed Marian sitting on the edge of her seat, the eagerness palpable as she leaned forward to look out the windshield.

"Shouldn't you buckle up, too, Marian?" Dean asked. "There is a seatbelt law in Maryland, you know." He glanced at the driver. "You, too, Gibbie."

"Nah," the teenager said. "I regenerate, so I don't have to worry about it like you humans do."

"That's only if you survive the initial impact," Dean said. "You'll only regenerate if you're still alive. Besides, I don't want to be killed when your regenerative body gets thrown into mine during the collision. Same for you, Gibbie. Seatbelts are there to keep you in the driver's seat and in control of the vehicle, too. So buckle up, both of you, or I'll have you take me back to the garage."

Marian rolled her eyes and then slid back into the seat, buckling a lap belt across her hips. Gibbie pulled the shoulder strap around and across him and buckled up his belt, too. Dean nodded his approval and looked forward again. He had thought he had a handle on all the things he was going to need to do in this new venture, but he had missed some operational details. Gibbie had tried to fill them in, like getting the Dryad twins to dispatch calls for them, but there were still things they didn't know because there wasn't an institutional culture of conduct under which to run, the way there was in a fire department. He was going to have to build that from the ground up if he was going to be successful in what he intended to do.

The plan was for Dean and Gibbie to start providing some basic emergency medical care again for the Unusuals in and around Elk City. Because this would be seen as part of James' oversight for the region, there should be a significant surge of goodwill. Hopefully, that would offset some of the bad will associated with his inability to stop The Cause in their attacks. The hope was that by having Dean back on the street, he would be able to do whatever Ashley had foreseen for him and James in her visions. She said it was still unclear what that action was, but it was less likely to happen as long as he was cooped up in the Nightwing building. The other good thing about responding to Unusual calls for assistance through the CERT team's efforts was that it circumvented the regular 911 dispatchers and the fire department. Someone there was feeding info to The Cause. Because the members of the CERT team were such a small group, they could keep things closed down somewhat and respond to calls for help without anyone else finding out. At least, that was the plan.

A cell phone rang, and Dean looked on the dash where Gibbie had mounted a burner phone with Velcro strips. It lit up with a number Dean didn't know, but Gibbie obviously did. The vampire smiled at him and reached over to tap the respond button. It went to speaker mode and Dean heard a female voice he assumed was either Wim or Dora.

"Hello Gibbie-mobile," the voice said cheerfully. "How do you read?"

"We read you loud and clear, Wim, honey. What's the dealio? Do we have a customer?" Gibbie replied.

"You do indeed. This is so cool. I feel like a real dispatcher," Wim said over the phone. "Dora and I got headsets to plug into the phones. We have one to take calls and one to call you guys. And we have our laptop set up so we can follow you on the map, and give you directions if you need it. It's awesome.

"That's so cool," Gibbie said. "What app are you using to track us?"

"Uh, guys," Dean interrupted. "Stay focused on the job at hand. We have a patient to take care of …"

"Oh, yeah," Wim said. "Dora's on the phone with a guy who says his friend is overdosed. They're in a building down by the harbor downtown. He is being quite cagey with my sister on the phone, so she doesn't have a lot of info to pass on. Just that it's a guy, and it's one patient. Sorry."

"That's alright, honey," Gibbie soothed. "You gals are doing the best you can."

"Yeah, Gibbie's right," Dean added. "Just try and keep them on the line while we head that way. What's the address?"

Dean listened as she passed along the street address while Gibbie turned and headed to the harbor district. He entered the address into his phone's navigation app and started giving Gibbie directions based on the instructions he was getting but Gibbie just waved his hand in the air.

"I know the place, Dean. It's a skeevy vamp hangout for some of the most undesirable members of our community. Stay close to me when we get there, just in case." The vampire driver looked up in the mirror at their third partner. "You, too, Marian. These guys don't like lycans and other shifters much."

Dean felt the van lurch a little when Gibbie accelerated as they got on the cross-town freeway and headed off toward their first call as responders in the night.

# Chapter 13

The white van slid slowly down the street. Dean looked out the passenger window at the abandoned industrial buildings on his side of the road. They were mirrored by similar buildings on the other side. The multi-story brick structures were looming on either side of them in the darkness. The van slowed to a stop, and Gibbie slid the gear lever into park.

"That's the building right there," Gibbie said, pointing to the left.

Dean looked at the building on the corner. The flickering streetlight showed the painted bricks spelling out "Sherwood Distillery" on the side of the building's second floor. There was a giant smokestack standing to the rear of the lot, disappearing into the cloudy night sky's darkness.

"Okay, we need to be careful," Dean said. "Just like I taught you guys in our class. Scene safety comes first. Pay attention to where we are and your surroundings. If you see something, say something. We're each other's eyes and ears on the street." He unbuckled his seat belt and climbed out. Marian slid open the door on the side.

"Hand me the med bag. You carry the trauma bag and give Gibbie the heart monitor," Dean said. He took the bag she gave him and then led the three of them across the street and up the broad steps to the main doors. He reached out and tried them. They were unlocked. He heard Gibbie talking with Wim over the phone behind him asking for directions to the patient.

"Wim says they are on the third floor, towards the back," Gibbie relayed. "She says to watch out because the floor is falling through in the middle of the room. Stay along the walls."

"Great, no power, so no elevator and no lights, and we take the stairs," Dean said. "Okay, Marian, there are two Mag Light flashlights in the side pocket of that bag you're carrying. Hand me one and you shine the other one. I know you two can see in this darkness, but I am going to be nearly blind up there. Remember that."

The werewolf girl handed him a long-handled, black metal flashlight. He turned it on and started inside. There was a long hallway ahead of him with trash strewn across the floor. He looked to his left and saw an open stairwell door. He beckoned to the others and started upstairs, watching his footing carefully as the wooden stairs creaked under his weight with each step.

He heard Gibbie stumble behind him and the vampire whimpered a little bit. "Take your time, guys. Watch your footing."

"I just hate places like this. They give me the heebie-jeebies," Gibbie said.

Marian snorted, "What do you have to be afraid of? You're already dead. This place is awesome. You could have the most awesome rave here."

"I've always been afraid of the dark, okay.

Dean stopped and turned around, playing the light on Gibbie. "You're a vampire. Can't you see in the dark?"

"It's just shadowy, creepy places. I know I can see in the dark, but I know the darkness is still there."

Dean saw that Gibbie was terrified. He glanced at Marian and back to Gibbie.

"Let Gibbie hold the other flashlight, Marian. I need you up here with me so you can use your superior sense of smell to help us find our patient." He waited while she handed off the flashlight and came forward to join him. "Just make sure we aren't surprised by anything while we are here. You are going to be our situational awareness. Got it?"

"Got it, boss," Marian said. She had a big grin on her face as she moved to the front of the group. She started scanning the darkness ahead and behind them like a trained bodyguard.

The three responders continued up the stairs, taking their time and making sure of each step. It took precious minutes, but they finally reached the third-floor landing. The doorway to their right opened onto a spacious and open warehouse floor with columns spaced across it supporting the ceiling. The floor was littered with crates and broken furniture. Dean shined his flashlight around the room, but the light failed to illuminate the furthest corners of the huge room. He turned and looked at Marian.

"See or sense anything, Marian?"

The pink-haired teen drew in a deep breath through her nose and closed her eyes for a moment as if considering the scents she was taking in. Her eyes opened, and she pointed to the right, across the room. "There," she said, the excitement coloring her voice. "I smell vampire and human over there."

Dean entered the room and shined his light in the direction indicated by his teen colleague. He could almost see the far wall. There was an extensive bank of windows there. Then a bit of movement at the edge of the light caught his eye.

"Hello, I'm a paramedic. Did you call us? We are here to help," Dean calls into the darkness.

At first, there was silence; then a voice called from the shadows. "Over here, they are over here. Please help."

It was a woman's voice, and Dean motioned to the others to follow him as he moved in the direction of the voice. Soon his flashlight beam fell on a trio of figures. Two were lying on a mattress, and one was standing next to it. It was a woman, scrubbing her hands together in frustration.

"Please help us," she called as the paramedic and his team approached. "I think they overdosed."

Dean continued closer and started assessing the scene in front of him. There is an old, tattered mattress on the floor with a man and woman lying on it. They both looked homeless, their clothes a mismatch of items and layers. They both looked pale and apparently unconscious.

"I'm a paramedic," Dean said again as he approached. He held up his hand showing the new tattoo. The woman glanced at his hand and then looked back at him. She gave him a relieved smile, and he caught a hint of her elongated, sharp canines.

"I told him not to drink so long, but he didn't listen, now he's taken too much and won't answer me. She has just stopped breathing, too."

"What did they take?" Dean asked. He knelt down next to the pair on the mattress. He motioned to Gibbie and the vampire responder started unpacking the wires of the heart monitor and getting out the blood pressure cuff.

"She likes heroin, so Bryce got her a hit in exchange for letting him feed on her while she was shooting up. It's been fine every other time. This time, though, we got the stuff from a new supplier. It must have been too strong because they both went out almost immediately. It scared me, so I called a friend, and they called you guys."

Dean looked at her. "What's your name?"

"Mya."

"Okay, Mya," Dean said, using a calm and soothing voice. "We are going to do the best we can to help Bryce and your other friend. Do you know her name?"

"We just call her Red," Mya said. "I don't know her real name."

Dean looked back to his patients. He knew what to do for opiate overdoses, but was unsure how to assess the effects in a vampire who didn't breathe at all, unless it was to talk. The opiates suppressed the respiratory system and depressed the central nervous system. They also caused pinpoint pupils of the eyes.

The girl was breathing way too slowly; he could see that. Her ragged, snoring breaths were not regular. He leaned forward and shined his light in her eyes and then in Bryce's. The pupils didn't change. They remained tiny points of black in the irises. Dean decided to treat her first, then the vampire.

"Marian," Dean said. "Get out the naloxone, two syringes, two needles, and two nasal atomizers from the med bag." The naloxone was the drug that would counteract, temporarily, the effects of the heroin. Marian started digging in the medication bag and handing the requested items to Dean.

Dean drew up a dose of the drug in each syringe and then attached the small silicone rubber cone-shaped atomizers to them in place of the needles. Leaning over his patients, starting with Red, he used a syringe on each and sprayed the atomized drug with half a dose in each nostril. The medication would be absorbed in the nasal mucosa and into the bloodstream. He waited for the drug to take effect. It would have been a faster effect with an IV injection, but that would have taken too much time to get started. She was an IV drug user so her veins would be crappy and hard to access. Vampires had little, if any blood flow, so they were hard to get an IV line in as well.

Bryce started to come around first. His hand moved to brush against his face, then he sat up suddenly, leaned over and vomited blood onto the floor next to him. Dean knew that was the effect of the sudden withdrawal from the heroin. The naloxone worked by suddenly blocking the drug's access to the body's opiate receptors. Bryce also started shaking with tremors, but he was wide awake as he looked around the darkened room at the figures hovering over him. Dean showed his tattoo to the newly recovered patient and the recovering vampire saw and nodded. Mya rushed to his side and hugged him.

Red was slower to recover, but her breathing soon became easier, more even and deeper. Her eyes fluttered open a minute or so later. Dean had Gibbie get a set of vital signs on her while the paramedic went and attached the heart monitor leads to check her heart. She looked up at him as he did it.

"Red," Dean said. "I'm Dean. I'm a paramedic, and I'm here to help you. Do you remember what happened?"

"I think so," she said looking around. "Did I pass out?"

"Yes. I think the heroin you were using was stronger than you expected or you overestimated the dose," Dean explained. "I've given you a drug to counteract it, but it's only temporary. You will need more medical attention."

"I don't want to go to the hospital," Red said, a frantic tone coloring her voice. "Can't you stay with me here and watch me?"

Ordinarily, Dean would have said no. When he was working on the Station U ambulance, the protocol was to transport and put the unit back in service to take care of the next person. What was the protocol here? He guessed he'd have to make it up as he went along. He had plenty of the drug to give until the heroin wore off for both of them. He and Gibbie and Marian were safe right now, so that was not an issue. Dean looked around at his team and then back at his patients. He'd never get them to go to the hospital, and he didn't have an ambulance to take them in any way. He would have to stay and continue to monitor them, giving additional doses of naloxone as needed.

"Okay, Red," Dean said. "I'll stay for a little while with you and Bryce until you are clear of danger. Maybe we can talk about you and what drew you to start using heroin in the first place. I want to give you some IV fluids, too. You've lost some blood during this situation." Dean looked at Bryce, who gave a grim, tight-lipped smile. He looked back at the human girl, and she nodded.

"You aren't going to call the police, right?" she asked.

"No, that's not my job unless you do something to hurt me or my companions. As long as we are safe, we will stay, and there will be no police," Dean soothed his patient's concerns. "Now let me get that IV started. You'll feel better with some fluids."

Red nodded and lay back on the mattress while Dean got started with the IV preparations. Her veins were going to be crappy, but he'd find something. Gibbie started assembling the IV fluid bag and tubing, handing the flashlight to Marian. Dean's time training some extra skills in his CERT class was paying off. His team knew how to assist him, and it smoothed the process of care. He was able to get fluids started for his human patient. Then he turned back to Bryce.

"How do you feel?" Dean asked.

"Better now," Bryce replied. He looked at the vomited blood on the floor next to him. "I guess I got that out of my system."

"At least for now," Mya snorted. "When are you going to stop using, Bryce. Feeding on junkies just to get high? It's disgusting, and it almost killed you."

Dean stayed silent. He wasn't an addiction counselor, and he had never considered something like this before with an Unusual patient. Addiction was a huge problem for all communities, though there was little he could do to control it other than just respond and treat the addicts. Sometimes a paramedic could encourage someone to seek some professional help, but that was all. Dean turned his attention back to what he could control since he couldn't stop the addiction itself. He and his CERT team started taking vital signs and monitoring both patients, wary of the need for the eventual follow-up dose of the drug that could save their lives.

## Chapter 14

It was nearly dawn when Gibbie drove him back into the garage at the Nightwing building. They had dropped Marian off at her home hours before, at around midnight. She had school the next day, and they wanted to make sure she paid attention to her grades, as well as her desire to be a paramedic someday. Dean did leave her with some praise for her work that night, along with a warning to keep her grades up if she wanted to keep coming on the emergency response calls with them.

Gibbie pulled his white van to a halt near the elevators and slid the gear lever into park. He looked at Dean with an exhausted glance. Dean knew he looked tired, too.

"Good night, boss," Gibbie said as he smiled at Dean. "It was a good night, wasn't it?"

"I think we were successful," Dean said. "We saved a few lives, and we were able to let people know that we were out there to help them. I still wish they would call the real 911, but for now, this will have to do." He climbed out of the beat up van and then opened the back to grab the med bag. "I'll get Ashley to grab us replacements for what we used tonight, Gibbie. Will you please make sure to plug in the heart monitor batteries, so they are recharged for this evening?"

"Got it, charge the batteries," Gibbie said with a thumbs-up. "You get some sleep. I'll see you after dark tonight."

Dean shut the door, stepped back and waved once as Gibbie pulled away and out of the garage. He was exhausted. The first call had been stressful enough, going into that abandoned building. The other three calls they ran over the course of the night had been more routine for EMS calls. An elderly weretiger woman had an asthma attack and had run out of her medications. Dean had administered a breathing treatment for her and then called in to Ashley to see if social services could arrange to have her meds delivered the next day. Then there was an injury sustained by a new vampire who thought he could just jump from a roof and fly away in bat form. Luckily he had fallen into some bushes below that helped break his fall. There was a broken leg that Gibbie helped him set and splint. That would be healed by morning, but it had needed to be attended to before it would heal properly. Gibbie explained to the newbie that his powers would take a few years to develop fully and to take it easy.

The final call of the evening was a young fairy family in the Barrens mobile home park with a baby who had had a febrile seizure. This was a type of seizure brought on by a sudden fever. It was rarely life threatening to the child, but Dean knew it was scary as hell for the parents who witnessed it. Dean stayed on scene for a while, counseling the parents after giving the baby a dose of liquid acetaminophen. He advised them to get some acetaminophen to help keep the fever down until she was better. He also urged them to see about getting a pediatrician. He would get Ashley to refer one who was Unusual friendly. The seizure was unlikely to happen again, but if it did, he recommended they drive over to the ER and get the baby checked out. The mother hugged him as they packed up to go, thanking him for being available to help them. He knew she meant that he was able to help without bringing the risk of additional human attacks. He told her to let her friends and neighbors know he and the CERT team were available for a while, and that they were working on fixing the whole system to get them safe 911 services again. Thinking back about the night, Dean thought that overall it had been an exciting first evening with the new team. Plus it just felt good to be out on the street helping people again.

Dean pushed the button for the elevator and was waiting for it to arrive when a black sedan with tinted windows pulled into the garage and parked in one of the VIP slots nearby. Dean watched it stop and then Artur climbed from the driver's seat. He gave Dean a half grin and helped two young ladies from the back seat and walked over to the elevator. Dean wondered if he should warn them what they were in for, but decided to keep his mouth shut. Now was not the time to challenge the ancient vampire. The elevator doors opened, and Dean stepped inside and held the doors for the other three. He pushed the button for their common floor and waited quietly as the doors closed.

"What's that you're holding, Dean," Artur asked. "Missing your time on the streets and carrying an ambulance bag around with you?" The sneering sarcasm in his tone infuriated the paramedic.

"If you must know, I was out all night providing patient care on my own so that people can still get the help they need." Dean shut his mouth as soon as he said it, but it was too late to take back what he had said. He saw the vampire's dark eyes narrow as he looked down at the battered and used medical bag.

"Well, well, well," Artur said. "I suppose people couldn't have expected to keep you on the sidelines for long, provided that was what they were trying to do. You should be careful, Dean. I'm sure your opponents have nothing personal against you, but if you insist on pushing forward with rash and irresponsible actions, things could get … uncomfortable."

"I'm a paramedic," Dean said. "Uncomfortable is what we train for." The elevator doors opened, and he gestured for the trio to step off first. Artur nodded and led the girls from the elevator.

"Don't say no one warned you, young man," Artur sneered. "I'd stay and deal with your rashness myself, right now. But, as you can see, I'm famished and must get to my dinner before bed. Don't worry, though. I know how to clean up my own messes now. Ta ta."

Dean stared at them in anger and almost missed his chance to get off the elevator behind them as the doors started to close on him. He interrupted the sensor with a wave of his hand and reopened the doors, stepping out into the hallway. The trio had already turned the corner at the end of the corridor and were out of sight. Dean walked down to his apartment and decided to place a call to James' assistant Celeste to warn her about the two girls with Artur. He was pretty sure the vampire would abide by at least some of the rules of hospitality. He would probably not do anything overt to expose James, like leaving two dead bodies to be found near the building. Probably. Still, it was a good idea to warn her just in case. He shut his apartment door as he placed the call upstairs before going to bed to get some sleep.

▭

HE WOKE as Ashley placed a kiss on his cheek. He rolled over in bed and looked at the clock on the nightstand while hooking an arm around his girlfriend to pull her close. It was five o'clock in the evening already, and she was in her scrubs to go back to work in the ER for another night shift. He looked up at her, the green-eyed beauty staring back at him. She leaned back in for another kiss.

"I thought I'd stop over and wake you up, sleepyhead," Ashley said between kisses.

"Why don't you stay a bit and help me fully wake up?" Dean proposed.

Ashley laughed and pushed him away, rolling out of bed. "None of that," she said wagging a finger at him. "I have to get to work. I just wanted to get you up for the night's activities. I got your text about the medication replacements. I'll get the script for them, and you can swing by the ER later. I'll meet you in the parking lot with them since you can't come in. How'd it go last night anyway?"

Dean sat up and pulled on a t-shirt and shorts. "I think this will work out pretty well, Ash. Gibbie is pretty good as an assistant, once you get past his more unusual quirks and flamboyant reactions to everything. Marian has the makings of a pretty good EMS provider, too, if she decides to stick with it after high school."

"That's good," She said. She kept talking as she went into the living room. "I've wasn't sure after you went out last night. I expected an immediate shift in my premonitions that would indicate we were on the right track. It didn't happen until this morning just after dawn. I was at work, and suddenly I sensed a change in the possibilities of the future. It all seems to have realigned. Did you do something this morning at the end of the shift with Gibbie?"

Dean shook his head. "We had our last call at about four AM. We just drove around for the rest of the night and Gibbie dropped me off. I got back here around dawn." Then Dean thought for a moment. "Unless ..."

"Unless what?"

"Unless it had something to do with my running into Artur this morning on my way up in the elevator. I thought I had screwed something up, and let the cat out of the bag when I lost my temper with him." Dean explained about the interchange between him and Artur in the elevator and beyond.

"You shouldn't have tried to push his buttons, Dean," Ashley said. "He is dangerous, old school and vindictive. If James or I aren't with you, he could just end you without so much as a shrug, even with my residual protections in place." Her concern showed in her facial expression, worry lines crinkling her forehead.

"I guess I figured that the rules of hospitality applied here in James' building," Dean said. "I thought maybe he couldn't hurt me while I was here. I was just so pissed off that he was flaunting the two girls at me when I knew what he had done before."

"Well, whatever you did and why you did it is beside the point now," she said. "That encounter with Artur changed something in the chain of events here. It has reset the course for us, at least partly, in our favor. You just need to be extra careful out on the street at night. Now that he knows about what you are doing, there are going to be situations that might not be what they seem on the surface. There will be opportunities to get at you. I'll do what I can to protect you from afar, but you need to pay attention to what you're doing and what's going on around you. Okay?"

"Okay," Dean said. "I'll be careful out there. I'm not going to stop, though. It felt good to be out helping people again, and the patients are glad they have someone to call for help. We've got to keep pushing forward."

"We will, but it will be for nothing if anything happens to you, so be careful."

"I will, I promise," Dean said.

Ashley came over and gave him another kiss before heading for the door. "I'll see you later when you stop by for the meds."

Dean watched her leave, then turned back to get ready for the night with Gibbie and Marian. He was excited by the news from Ashley, that what they were doing had shifted her premonitions back on track. It meant that this was the right thing to do to fight The Cause. It helped that it felt like the right thing to do anyway, just helping people. He headed to the shower and thought about what else he could do to get under Artur's skin while he was out serving the community tonight.

## Chapter 15

That night Dean and the crew went out and rode around for several hours without any calls for help. It gave them all a chance to get to know each other better and for Dean to work through some procedural things for them to keep track of that would have normally been taught in the academy. They worked out that Dean would always grab the med bag while Gibbie got the monitor and their teenaged helper, when she was able to come out with them, grabbed the trauma bag with the bandages and dressings.

He was reviewing the extra gear in the trauma bag when the first call came in. Dean glanced at his watch. It was near midnight. Dora had taken the dispatch phone this evening while her sister answered calls from their emergency callers. Dora told them they were getting called for a traumatic amputation at the city park on Broadway. The Broadway Park was about thirty acres of open parkland that included baseball and soccer fields, as well as playgrounds and a community pond. When they pulled into the parking lot, a figure shielded its eyes from their headlights while waving to them. Dean got out and approached the figure, realizing he knew who the person was when he got there.

"Freddy?" Dean asked. "What the heck are you doing here this evening? Is everything alright?" Freddy, the Zombie chef for Station U's paramedics, stood there, shielding his eyes from the van's headlights.

"Hi, Dean. I am fine. I'm here for my weekly meet up with the other zombies of Elk City. It's our full contact Ultimate Frisbee night."

Dean knew he must have looked ridiculous when he did the double take and just stared at Freddy. There was a zombie Ultimate Frisbee league, and this was the first he heard about it? He was still looking at Freddy when something flew in and thumped him the chest. Dean bent down and picked up a Frisbee, then dropped it like it was a hot rock when he realized it was smeared with blood. He hastily reached into his pockets and fished out a pair of exam gloves, pulling them on. Gibbie and Marian were walking up to join him in front of the parked van.

"Glove up, guys. This one is going to get a little messy," Dean cautioned.

Freddy bent down to pick up the Frisbee and carried it with them as he led the trio of responders out onto a dark field. Dean and Gibbie turned on their flashlights and trained them on the path in front of them. It wasn't hard to keep up. Freddy didn't move very fast. Dean picked up a step and caught up with their leader.

"What happened? Why are we here?" Dean asked. "Dora said something on the phone about a traumatic amputation."

"We play here once a month or so, at night so people can't see who we are. To anybody walking by on the path, we are just guys playing Frisbee in the dark. Sometimes it gets a little rough. A few of the guys are pretty competitive by nature. Anyway, tonight, when two of the guys were reaching for the same Frisbee, they grabbed, held on, and then pushed off of each other with the other arm. One came away with both the Frisbee and the other guy's arm. It's happened before, so nobody was too concerned, but Dirk is all about keeping his parts together. He just wouldn't wait for the end of the night to get his arm reattached."

"Seriously," Dean said, chuckling a little. "Good thing you guys can't feel it when stuff falls off. That would nearly kill anyone else, Unusual or human. So, where's the patient?"

"Just over here. By that tree up ahead."

At this point, as his eyes adjusted to the darkness, Dean could see people stumbling around in the field nearby. Clearly the game went on despite the injury. He looked ahead and could now make out two figures, sitting by the tree Freddy pointed out. He played the flashlight on them as he approached. Both of them had the mottled skin and dry, musty smell that indicated zombie. One was cursing a blue streak while the other patted him on the shoulder with one hand. He was holding a detached arm in the other. They both looked into the light, squinting. Dean came up and handed his light to Freddy.

"I'm Dean Flynn. I'm a paramedic. I think one of you is in need of some help?"

"Well I'm glad someone is here to help," said the figure missing an arm. "All Ricky here can do is apologize and whine about how sorry he is."

"Well, I'm here now, so let us see what we can do," Dean said. "What's your name?"

"I'm Dirk, and I used to be the best player here. Now I'll be forever known as the armless wonder."

"Look," said Ricky, "I said I was sorry. You could have let go of the Frisbee. I got there first. But you decided to fight me for it and hold on until your arm came off."

It looked like the two of them were ramping up to another argument. Dean held up a hand to calm the two of them down. "Okay, okay guys. That's enough. Dirk, let me take a look at that shoulder and arm. Sometimes, with zombies, we can reattach things that fall off."

"I certainly hope so," Dirk said. "I've got to have a chance to show Ricky up before the night is over.

Dean moved around them and crouched down next to Dirk to look at the stump of his arm where it came off at the shoulder. He could see that it was cleanly off at the joint. That should help. If it hadn't been too long, in theory, he could reattach the arm, and the zombie tissue would reconnect over time, making it usable again. The outer wound around the skin would not heal, though. That meant it would always be prone to dropping off unless he could come up with some way to hold it there. Tucking his flashlight under one arm, he turned to Ricky and held out his hands for the detached limb. When Ricky handed it to him, he was surprised by how heavy it was. He turned it and looked at it, trying to realign it in his mind. Dean tried to think of a way to hold the heavy limb in place. Medical adhesive tape would not be strong enough to hold it for long, especially when Dirk started moving it as the tissues reconnected.

"What are you thinking, Dean?" Gibbie asked. "Can we help?"

"I need to come up with some way to reattach this arm sort of permanently or it will detach itself randomly and not stay in place. If we don't figure it out, we'll just end up having to keep coming back here once a month and putting it back on."

"Wait here," Gibbie said. "I think I have something that will work." The frumpy, middle-aged vampire turned and headed back to the parking lot while Dean and Marian waited with their patient. Dean looked back to the parking lot where the van was parked under a street light and watched as Gibbie retrieved something out of the back of the van and came jogging back over to them. Dean handed his flashlight to Marian and took the small, plastic tackle box Gibbie handed to him.

"What is it?" Dean asked, flipping open the latches.

"It's my sewing kit," Gibbie said.

Dean stopped and stared at his friend, then flipped open the lid and looked inside. He wasn't much with a needle and thread, and this definitely was outside his scope of practice as a paramedic. Still, it sort of made sense.

Gibbie leaned over, shining his flashlight into the box. "I thought we could use a curved upholstery needle and some upholstery thread. That's pretty tough stuff." He reached past Dean and selected a large spool of thread. It did seem more substantial than the other thread selections. Dean took the spool and unwound about a foot of the thread and tried to break it by pulling with both hands. He could not pull the upholstery thread apart. In fact, it cut into his fingers and hurt him without even stretching. This might work out after all.

"Find that curved needle, Gibbie and thread this on it," Dean said handing him back the spool of tough nylon thread. He turned back to his patient. This was going to be tricky. He had never sutured a patient before and especially not all the way around an entire arm. It was going to be all about getting the positioning right before he started.

"Marian, come over to this side and hold the flashlight so I can see the wound in Dirk's shoulder," Dean instructed his teenaged aide. "Keep the light aimed so there aren't any shadows while I'm working."

"Got it, boss. This is awesome. Wait until I tell my friends at school about this," she said, bouncing on the balls of her feet with excitement.

"No, Marian. You are not going to tell anyone. You will not talk about this with anyone but me and Gibbie," Dean said, stopping his consideration of the patient to look up at her from where he crouched. "That's one of our first rules, right? Keep the patient's private stuff, private."

She nodded and seemed to deflate a little bit. Dean noticed and added with a smile, "It is pretty awesomely cool, though. I agree." He turned back to his patient. "Dirk, I will need you to sit very still. I don't think this will hurt very much, but it might get uncomfortable sitting still while I finish up."

"I'm not doing anything else," Dirk replied. "Do your worst. And by that I mean do your very best, please."

"This is new to me but I plan on putting my best effort forward," Dean said. "Okay, let's get started." He held out a gloved hand, and Gibbie handed him the curved needle with the upholstery thread ready to go. "Gibbie and Ricky, hold the arm out straight from the shoulder so I can work all the way around it. Try to move it as little as possible." He leaned forward and decided to work on the underside first to practice his stitches where no one would see it. Hopefully, they would get better as he worked around to the top. He reached over and started inserting the needle through the skin on the underside of the arm and then hooked the needle around through the skin of Dirk's armpit, pulling the thread through. Gibbie had tied a knot at the end of the thread, and it pulled to a stop at the skin of the arm. One stitch was done, and about a hundred more to go. This was going to take a while.

Dean took his time, and it did, indeed, take about a half hour to work his way carefully around the whole arm. When he was finished, he took the flashlight from Marian and leaned in to inspect his work. It didn't look half bad, considering his lack of experience. He handed the light back and looked up at the aide.

"Marian, get a triangular bandage out of the trauma bag. We need to fashion a sling for Dirk. It will support the arm, and hopefully, things will start reconnecting inside." He was not an expert on the animated dead, but it was supposed to work that way once things were reattached. He waited while she dug in the bag and then came up with a plastic-wrapped cloth triangular bandage. He took it out of the packaging and folded it, tying a loose knot with the two long ends. He had Gibbie bend the arm at the elbow and slowly bring it down to Dirk's side, watching the stitching on the top of the arm as the skin stretched and pulled when he manipulated the arm. It looked like everything was holding together. He slid the forearm through the sling and then had Dirk duck his head as he passed the knotted loop over his head. Dean leaned back and checked his work.

"Dirk, try and wiggle your fingers," Dean said.

They all looked at the hand at the end of the previously detached arm. Slowly, the fingers started moving. Dirk tapped each of his fingers against his thumb, one at a time. He looked up at Dean with a big toothy grin.

"You did it," Dirk exclaimed.

"I'm glad it worked as planned," Dean admitted. "You will need to take it easy until the connection is stronger. All that is holding that arm on right now is the stitching, so be careful with it going forward. I would not try to play any contact sports with it until a few days have passed. Based on you moving your fingers, though, I think that you are on the mend."

Dean stood up and looked around in the darkness. He could hear the game still going on out there, though he couldn't see a thing. Dean was pleased with himself and the CERT team. He had pulled this one off, all on his own, without Brynne looking over his shoulder, giving him her advice on what to do based on her experience with Unusuals. It felt good to be able to come up with unconventional solutions on his own in these types of strange situations. He looked around at Marian and Gibbie as they cleaned up their mess and packed up their bags.

"Gibbie," Dean said. "Excellent job. Thinking of using that upholstery thread and the needle was ingenious. You, too, Marian. You held that light steady the whole time. I couldn't have done this without you, either." He saw them both grin ear to ear in appreciation of his praise. He knew it was important to share the credit with his team at times like this. It helped build their bond and improved everyone's ability to improvise and think on their feet when they knew their hard work was appreciated.

They carried the gear back to Gibbie's van, and they were all feeling great. Gibbie climbed into the driver's seat with Dean on the passenger side next to him. Marian assumed her usual position dead center of the seat behind them. They drove off into the night to seek out their next patient in need.

---

# Chapter 16

---

The rest of the week went quickly for Dean and the rest of the CERT team response crew. The word was getting out to their prospective patients that there was another resource to call for emergency medical assistance in the Unusual community. Dean could sense the relief among his patients and their families when he talked with them about their problems. He did what he could to help each of them, but was frustrated because most did not want to go to the hospital for fear it would draw The Cause's attention to them or their families. He would need to come up with another solution that could bring more definitive care to them in their homes. He was only a single paramedic, and could only do so much for these people with his limited resources.

He was not able to even do lab tests like he had done before on the Station U ambulance. They had not been able to get him an iStat portable hand analyzer. There were no extra ones lying around. They were a new tool and were pretty expensive. He mentioned it, though, to Celeste on one of the meetings with her that week. The vampire assistant pulled out a tablet computer and looked something up, telling him she would see what she could do.

Ashley was trying to put together a group of nurses who were aware of the Unusual community and were willing to do some volunteer work on the side. She hoped they might go out and do home visits on the numerous chronically ill patients to try and take care of problems before they became emergencies. It was hard because of the volunteer nature of the work, and the fact that almost all of them were pulling extra shifts in the ER due to a shortage of qualified nursing staff. She promised him she would put something together, though it might take some time to get organized.

In the meantime, Dean and Gibbie and Marian were getting a real sense of teamwork going. He learned what he could rely on each of them to do on arrival at the scene, and they both asked good questions after each call to try to improve their efforts. He couldn't ask for a better sense of professionalism from any paid EMS provider, and these were volunteers. Each response improved on their teamwork and patient care and Dean was pleased with the progress his team was making.

It was all going so well that Dean and the others started worrying about what The Cause was going to do in response. They had to know what the CERT team members were doing, even if they didn't know everyone involved. In fact, Dean himself was the only one that Artur and the rest of The Cause knew about. That wouldn't last, of course. The lack of a response from their opponents put Dean on edge. He and Ashley, along with James and Brynne sat down over dinner to discuss it and the possibilities for protecting the team when a problem did arise. Dean didn't want anyone getting injured or attacked because of his rebelliousness; especially a teenage girl.

"I get the sense that Artur is getting more and more frustrated as time goes on," James said, sipping from his usual mug of warmed blood. "He is supposed to be here on a business trip to expand some new business plans in the Elk City area. That means he is forced to meet with me to go over the supposed business ventures he is proposing. I must say that it is kind of fun to watch him fume as I expound on the way you have circumvented the attacks on our population."

"Do you think that is wise?" Ashley asked. "I mean, we know it is him at the heart of all of this now. He too, must know that we are aware of his involvement. Is it prudent to push him to further action?"

"Ashley, you know the political machinations of our people as well as I do," James replied. "He would never tip his hand openly to me, even though he knows I know that it's him behind all of this. We each must let it play out to the end. Artur sees himself and me as the chess masters, moving our pawns and other pieces around the board. It wouldn't be proper to take direct action."

"Oh, great," Dean said between mouthfuls of dinner. "I'm now a pawn to be moved about in this deadly game you and Artur are playing. Jeez, James, I'm feeling kind of used here."

"There is a difference, Dean," James said. "That is how he sees you. I see you as a valuable colleague and teammate. Artur has no such loyalty to his supporters and followers. If this fails to work out for him as planned, he will just leave. He has no connection that we can tie to this so he will walk away and let his peons take the fall for his ambition."

"That is what he has done in the past," Ashley said. "Every time his previous plans have started to crumble, he cuts out and leaves his followers to take the brunt of the response to his machinations. At least, that has been my experience."

"What about you, Ashley?" Brynne asked. "Can you sense anything new, now that Dean is back on the street?"

"All I can say, based on what I can feel, is that you are all on the right track here," the Eldara Sister said. "It also feels closer, somehow. The turning point or event or whatever is on its way. Maybe not tomorrow, or even next week, but soon."

"Well, I guess that's good to know," Brynne said. She didn't seem too convinced of what she was saying.

"It is," Ashley confirmed. "If you look at these as a timeline and progression of events, we have pushed the events forward in a way that seems to be in our favor. I think that if we continue on this path, we'll come up with a further solution and draw this situation to a close."

"I don't think Artur is the type to give up on this without a fight," James said. "He will have something else in his plans, I'm sure. He is not stupid, or without significant resources."

Dean considered that and wondered what else The Cause had planned now that they had stopped the Unusuals from calling 911 for help. He and his undercover medical team could fill some of that gap, but there were people out there in trouble, and they were doing without help out of fear, and that was not right. It all had to stop. They had to finish this and draw Artur out somehow, to make him show his hand so they could expose both him and his helpers in the Fire Department headquarters. He looked at his watch. It was just after eight in the evening. He had told Gibbie to pick him up at nine o'clock tonight to allow time for this dinner meeting.

Just then his phone buzzed in his pocket. In fact, everyone's phone went off within seconds of each other. He looked down and saw it was Gibbie calling. He picked up and heard Gibbie's frantic voice on the other end.

"Fire, Dean. There's a fire. A really big fire."

"Hold on Gibbie. Slow down. Where is there a fire?" Dean asked.

"The Barrens, Dean. The Barrens is on fire," Gibbie said.

Dean heard the others talking earnestly, each into their own phones. He took the phone away from his ear to listen to what the others were saying.

"… I'll be right in, see if the chief can free up a second ambulance for us to staff," Brynne said.

"… I can be at the ER in about twenty minutes," Ashley said.

"… Tell August I'm on my way," James said. He must be talking to the leader of the Barrens, Dean thought.

They were all getting calls about the same thing. A massive blaze at the trailer park would have multiple injuries and need a ton of resources to treat those injured, both on the scene and at the hospital. This was serious and had many implications. Many of those who inhabited the Barrens were fairy folk. It would be hard to hide their true nature from the uninformed among the EMS, fire and hospital staff if there were a lot of injured. A distant shout coming from his own phone brought him back to the conversation with Gibbie.

"I'll meet you down in the garage as soon as you get here. Do you have Marian with you?" Dean asked.

"I have Marian, and I'm picking up Wim, Dora, and Kristof on the way to you. I figured we needed all hands on deck for this one," Gibbie replied.

"Good idea, Gibbie," Dean said, commending the vampire's forethought. "Okay, I'm getting finished now, so head to the garage at the Nightwing building and I'll meet you there." Dean hung up the connection as the others were doing the same.

James looked around at all of them. "I assume that all of you were alerted about the fire at the Barrens?" He waited for the nods he anticipated before continuing. "That was August, the fairy leader of the Barrens. Three SUVs pulled up about a half hour ago, and about ten humans jumped out with Molotov cocktails. They used them to ignite every trailer they could reach quickly and then took off again. The trailers are packed so close together that they are all starting to burn. There are a lot of injuries."

Ashley nodded. "I heard from the hospital. They are calling in all the staff they can and holding others past their shift in anticipation of the injured arriving there. If the injured arrive in large enough numbers, there's going to be no way to hide their nature from the nurses and doctors who are not aware of Unusuals living here."

"Chief Ari is sending regular ambulances in addition to the Station U crew," Brynne said. "He wants the off-duty Station U paramedics to come in and help run interference and talk the other paramedics through what they see with the injured so that everyone gets the care they need."

"Gibbie has gathered the entire CERT team and is on the way to pick me up," Dean added. "We will be able to help, too. We can't worry about hiding things. We need to focus on patient care and getting the worst injuries to the hospital quickly."

"Agreed," James said. "We have to assume that there could be more incidents tonight. I'll get Rudy to alert the pack in case there are other attacks. We can't let this happen again if we can help it. I'll meet you all over there as soon as he and I hook up." Rudy was James' second in command and the werewolf leader for the Elk City pack. "I'll have Celeste remain here and coordinate. If any of you need more resources, call her, and she'll know where to reach me."

They all stood as a group. Dean and Ashley headed to the elevators and downstairs to their apartments to change. He gave her a quick kiss at the door of her place. She hugged him briefly and urged him to be careful, then went in to change into her scrubs. Dean quickly changed into his EMS gear, the navy pants with pockets to hold his assorted small tools like his trauma scissors and penlight. He grabbed his stethoscope from the counter, went back into the hallway, and headed down to the elevators.

Once he got to the garage, he didn't have to wait long before Gibbie arrived. The beat up white van pulled to a screeching halt in front of him, and he climbed inside, barely closing the door before the vampire pulled away, peeling out of the garage in a screech of tires. They were still too far away. This was always the worst part of responding to a known serious injury. You could only drive so fast, especially in a civilian vehicle like this one. The problem was, the patients often couldn't wait.

Dean turned in his seat to see the rest of the team seated behind him, all grim-faced, though Marian bounced a little in her seat in anticipation of the excitement to come. She gave him a little smile when she noticed him watching her. He returned the grin, trying to reassure her before he returned his attention to the road in front of them as Gibbie drove into the night to the outskirts of town. The Barrens housed the poorest and most vulnerable of the Unusual community. They couldn't defend themselves and offered no threat to anyone. He hoped they weren't too late.

Chapter 17

As they got closer, Dean could see the glow of the fire over the trees, and they all started to smell the smoke from the burning house trailers. Gibbie pulled into the gravel parking lot and dodged the van around the fire engines there to park on the far side of the lot. Dean took in the scene. There were trailers on fire as far as he could see. Figures darted in the shadows, outlined in the night against the flames. The firefighters were hard pressed to address even the closest of the mobile homes' flames. There was no way to get all the way into the woods and deal with the blazing homes towards the back of the trailer park.

Dean saw the Station U ambulance parked near the chief's vehicle. The doors were open, but the crew was nowhere in sight. As he watched, another two ambulances arrived. They would be regular crews and unprepared for patients with wings, fangs or any other type of Unusual signs. He turned to his team seated behind him. Their eyes were wide as they took in the scene through the windshield.

"Okay," Dean said, calming his voice to help calm them. "This is bad, but it is not hopeless. Our job is to bring some sort of order to the chaos. The first thing we need to do is separate the injured into groups like we taught you in class. Work in teams of two. Send those who can walk out to the parking lot. Have them gather here near Gibbie's van. Gibbie, you will stay here and check people in as they arrive. That will keep them out of the normal responders' way. If you find someone who is too injured to move on their own, have one of the uninjured stay with them and then seek out one of the paramedics or firefighters. I'll be roaming and checking on you after I check in with the chief on the scene. Got it?"

The team nodded back to him. They got out. Wim and Dora heading off with their responder bags in one direction, while Marian and Kristof headed in the other, circling the outskirts of the fire ground. Dean looked at Gibbie. The vampire nodded. Dean turned and headed over to the command vehicle to check in and tell the on-scene chief that his team was there and what they were doing.

Dean waited while Chief Compton, the deputy fire chief for the whole department, gave a few orders over the radio. He cleared his throat behind the chief to announce his arrival. The deputy fire chief looked over at Dean, surprise showing in his eyes and he spat on the ground.

"What are you doing here, Flynn," Chief Compton growled. "Haven't you caused enough trouble with the department? You're supposed to be suspended."

"I brought the CERT responders that Brynne and I trained. They know the community and might be able to help out with getting them to seek help and medical attention," Dean replied.

"I don't care what these freaks decide to do. I'm just here to put this fire out before it sets the whole forest ablaze," the Chief snapped back. "I don't want to risk good firefighter's lives here."

Dean was taken aback by the vitriol in the Chief's response. He was saying that property was more important than the lives at risk here. The incident commander turned his attention back to the radio and barked another command while Dean considered what was happening.

"Don't worry about response teams, Operations," the Chief said. "I have it on good authority that most of these trailers are abandoned. Just surround and drown the flames, so they don't spread to the woods. Also, return the other ambulances, we won't need them here. One ambulance from Station U is enough."

Dean was shocked. If the Chief wasn't trying to save lives with his crews and telling his firefighters not to search for survivors, the number of injured and dead residents would soar. He looked at the Chief, the incredulous look on his face evident because the other man just leered in response and turned back to the command table deployed from the back of his SUV. Dean was pretty sure he had just found the leak in the fire department that was helping The Cause. The deputy fire chief was perfectly placed to listen in to every 911 call and radio dispatch. It would be easy for him to send The Cause to the scene to intimidate the Unusuals who called for help.

He backed away, then turned and walked back to Gibbie's van. He grabbed the trauma bag and started back towards the blazing trailer park. Gibbie began to ask him what was going on, but his stark stare stopped the vampire's words with a look. If the Chief wasn't trying to save lives, he would have to tell the other paramedics from Station U what was going on and try and come up with a plan with them. As he got closer to the flames, he found the Station U crew from the ambulance. Brook and Tammy were soot-stained and haggard already from caring for their patients. They had spread out a large tarp on the ground and had their patients spread across it.

Tammy looked up and surprise registered on her face in the darkness as he walked up to her. He set his bag down. She was trying to comfort a crying fairy girl of around twelve. Her wings were badly burned, the fragile insect-like membranes charred and melted from the heat she had encountered escaping from her home. She sobbed in pain as Tammy used some sterile water to try and douse the ragged edges that were still smoldering.

"What can I do?" Dean asked. "I just talked to the Chief, but I don't think you're going to get much help from him. He's written off the whole scene as a loss, the residents included."

Shock and anger showed on her face as she realized what he

was saying. "I'm just trying to deal with the ones we have here. These are the ones who can walk themselves out. I haven't even tried to go into the scene and try and treat anyone else," Tammy said.

"I have my CERT trained team here. They are circulating around the edges and sending the walking wounded out to Gibbie's van over there," Dean said. "The Chief returned the other ambulances, you know."

Brook came over to get more supplies from their bags. "We heard over the radio. We're on our own, I guess." Dean could hear the bitterness in her voice. "We need to get some of these to the burn unit, but I don't want to leave the others here."

"Brynne is supposed to bring another ambulance. Chief Ari was going to let her sign one out from the motor pool. I can't believe she'll just turn around, no matter what the radio response says. I'll call her and tell her to proceed in," Dean said. "We can also load some others into Gibbie's van. He can carry six or seven." He took out his phone and dialed Brynne's cell phone. She didn't pick up, so he left a message with the details of what he knew and told her to proceed to the scene.

He watched as Brook and Tammy moved from patient to patient there on the tarp. Then he looked into the nearby fire scene. He knew where he was needed.

"I'm going to head in closer and see if I can round up any others who can get out to you. There might be others who need care but can't move, too," he said. "Gibbie has more supplies if you need them, over in the back of the van. We loaded up from the stash at the Nightwing building."

Dean turned and started walking carefully towards the burning buildings. The heat coming off of them was intense. He didn't have any kind of protective gear so he couldn't enter any of the smoldering ruins, but he could look for survivors who might have made it out. As he was walking through the edge of the scene, he encountered August Beche and his wife, Helena. They were standing there, looking at the fire with tears in their eyes. He laid a hand on August's shoulder as he passed. Their eyes met, but Dean had no words to counter the sorrow and fury he saw there. He gave a grim smile and continued his search.

He was picking his way past one smoldering building when a groan to his left drew his attention. He trained his flashlight on the area and saw a blackened hand reach out from what he thought was a pile of rubbish. Dean rushed over, picking his way around the smoldering patches of grass. He carefully pulled a blackened blanket from the lump on the ground and saw a figure curled in a fetal position. It was a fairy woman; he could tell because of the wings that were wrapped around her. The male fairies didn't have wings. There were bad burns all over, and the wings were blackened and charred even through the blanket. She must have used it to shield herself from the flames while escaping the home.

"My name is Dean," he said, kneeling next to the woman on the ground. "I'm a paramedic, and I'm going to try and help you." He wasn't sure there was much he could do. The burns were extensive, and he was surprised she was alive at all.

"Paramedic Dean Flynn," the gravelly voice rasped. "It fits that it is you who found us. Little Flynn will be glad that you are here to save her since I will not be able to be with her much longer."

"Nura?" Dean asked. He knew this woman. It was the fairy woman whose child he had helped deliver. It was the first baby he had delivered, and it had been a fairy girl. It was one of the proudest moments so far in his short paramedic career. The family had named her Flynn after him and declared that she would grow up to be a paramedic like him. He looked around. Where was the baby? She would be about three months old by now, not old enough to crawl away yet. He gently reached out and rolled the charred figure onto her back. The wings crumbled away where they were wrapped around her abdomen, exposing the baby she held there. The child wasn't moving.

Dean reached out and checked the infant's pulse along the upper arm. There was a pulse, but it was too slow, and the baby didn't appear to be breathing. He carefully picked the fairy infant up, wary of the wings on her back and leaned forward. He tilted the head back slightly to open the airway and covered her mouth and nose with his mouth, blowing life-giving air into the infant's lungs, one puff at a time. He continued for a few minutes and felt the infant stir in his grasp. He checked the pulse, and it was stronger and faster now. His intervention had done the trick.

"I brought her back, Nura," Dean said. There was no answer, and he looked over at the mother lying on the ground next to him. She was staring vacantly at the dark, cloudy sky overhead. She didn't blink. Shifting the baby in his grasp, he reached over and checked the mother for a carotid pulse on her neck. He detected nothing. Sighing, he gently slid the eyelids closed and stood with the baby. Flynn started to cry a little. Dean's experience with babies was limited, but he knew he needed to get her somewhere warm and dry.

He started back out of the charred trailer park towards the staging area in the parking lot. The movement seemed to help soothe the baby. He checked her over while he picked his way around the charred obstacles in his way. She might have some minor, first-degree burns, but her mother had done a good job of protecting her from the heat. Aside from some smoke inhalation injury that would be expected in a fire, she appeared to be fine. Holding her close, he reached the parking lot and the area where Tammy and Brook were tending to the injured.

Brynne had shown up and brought two other Station U paramedics, Bill and Lynne with her. Chief Ari, the director of EMS for the fire department was there as well. He was arguing with the deputy fire chief, probably about the decision to turn around the responding ambulances earlier. Their shouts were audible to anyone within fifty feet of them. It didn't seem as if the EMS chief was getting anywhere with his points. As Dean walked up to the others, he saw Chief Ari storm off, back to his SUV.

Dean looked around, trying to see where he could put the infant, or with whom. Bill noticed his arrival first, the grizzled old paramedic chuckled and gestured in his direction with a bloody gloved hand.

"Look what the cat dragged in," Bill said. "I knew you wouldn't be able to stay away from the action for long, bud. Where'd you get the baby? Is she okay?"

Brynne looked over and noticed him. She came over after finishing taping off the end of a bandage wrapped to a woman's arm. She held out her hands to Dean, and he handed her the baby.

"It's baby Flynn, Brynne," Dean said. "Her mom didn't make it, but she was able to get the baby out alive. I had to ventilate her a little bit, but otherwise, she seems alright despite the fire and smoke inhalation."

"Let's check her oxygen levels and get her some supplemental oxygen anyway," Brynne said. "She probably inhaled a lot of carbon monoxide and other chemicals in the blaze. Better to be safe and err on the side of caution until we can get her to the hospital for some lab work. You did good, Dean."

It felt good to be working alongside all of his Station U colleagues again. This was where he belonged. All he had to do was beat the murder charge, and he could return to his job taking care of his special patients.

"Anything else on what happened?" Dean asked.

Tammy looked up from where she was taking a set of vital signs. "It seems several SUVs pulled up, and men dressed in black exited the vehicles. They were carrying bottles and started running down between the trailers, lighting the cloth wicks in the Molotov cocktails and tossing them into windows and doors before racing back to their vehicles and leaving. Most people were caught unawares, and you know how these trailers are. There's often only one main doorway out. I'm sure a lot of residents were trapped inside unless they could climb out a window. Who knows how many are dead here in the remains of the trailers."

"I heard Chief Ari yelling. Are we getting any more ambulances to transport the injured to the hospital?" Dean asked.

"I don't know," Brynne said. "Deputy Chief Compton refused to call the Red Cross either. They would be useful to help get shelter for the displaced survivors here. He claimed it was to protect their secret, but I don't think that's it."

"I don't think so either, based on my earlier run in with him,"

Dean agreed. "Brynne, he might be the leak at headquarters. I think he's the one slipping The Cause their information on our emergency calls from 911 dispatch."

"That would make sense," Brynne said. "He has all the access he'd need to get that job done and shut us down with the attacks." She started back towards the other patients with the baby. "Come on. Let's get these folks sorted out. We need to decide who has to go to the hospital and who can be treated here."

Dean followed her into the group of injured fairy folk. He stopped at the first one he came to and started his follow-up assessment, glancing at the triage tag Brook or Tammy put on him earlier. Triage tags had different colored stripes on them to allow follow-up responders to identify the level of injury quickly for the patients. It gave him the information he needed with its color-coded stripe and the boxes checked off. Dean settled into the familiar patterns of assessment and documentation as he moved from patient to patient. Even with six Station U paramedics on the scene, this was going to take a while.

# Chapter 18

The six paramedics, working together, were able to get through the sorting of the remaining patients in about ten minutes. So far, they had ten that needed to go to the hospital in the first load, most of them for severe burns. The challenge was they only had two ambulances and the hospital was 20 minutes away. It would take them hours to ferry all of them there taking them two at a time. Brynne made an executive decision. She said that since this was a major mass casualty incident, normal transport rules didn't really apply. They could take multiple patients per ambulance and perhaps do it all in two trips. Since he was still suspended, Dean was not eligible to ride the ambulance to the hospital so Tammy and Brook would take one, with Brynne and Bill taking the other. Dean and Lynne would stay behind and tend to the patients remaining at the scene until more help could be rounded up for them.

Right before they loaded up the first round of patients, Dean's phone chirped in his pocket, and he checked the screen. It was Ashley. He swiped to answer and heard her voice on the other end.

"Dean, what's going on?" she asked. "We have extra staff here expecting a ton of patients, but no one has arrived yet. Are there no survivors?"

"There are survivors, Ash," Dean said. "The first round of patients are inbound now. You should be getting a call on the med radio soon with a heads-up on what is coming. We had a run in with a chief officer who didn't want to waste ambulances on the freaks living here." He heard her gasp of shock over the phone line. Dean filled her in on his suspicions about Deputy Chief Compton.

"Are you safe?" Ashley asked after hearing his report.

"I am," Dean reassured her. "It has been touch and go, and we have several severely burned patients here. We figured out how to get the ten most seriously injured and some of the walking wounded loaded up and get them there in two round trips with the ambulances we have."

"Alright, I'll tell the team assembled here," Ashley said. "Be careful. This could be the beginning of a whole shift in what The Cause is doing. This was a pretty large-scale attack and is very different from what they've done in the past with just one-on-one attacks for the most part. It could mean they are ready to act against you and the other paramedics directly."

"I will be careful and keep my eyes open. I've got to get back to work. I'll see you later." Dean ended the call and looked around as the two ambulances pulled away. They were able to get three injured patients on each ambulance with one paramedic in the back and also putting one of the less severely injured patients in the front passenger seat with the driver. They should be able to get the moderately and severely injured patients into the hospital in two trips as planned. The remaining patients were bumps, bruises, and minor burns. He figured he and Lynne could help them. His CERT team members were there as well, and they were bringing in residents who had fled to the woods surrounding the trailer park during the attack. There were a few minor injuries there too, but the CERT trained folks were tending to their wounds pretty well.

He looked over at the command vehicle with its back lift gate up. The Chief was standing there overseeing the mopping up operations for the firefighters. The fires had died down as they consumed the fuel that made up the wooden trailers. There were some minor patches of flames here and there, but the firefighters in a brush truck could be seen working their way around the perimeter of the trailer park, dowsing areas of flames in the grass and brush as they found them. Some of the responding fire companies were already packing up their hoses and cleaning their gear in preparation to head back to their stations. It wouldn't be long now until they were left alone with this group of displaced patients and residents - people without homes and nowhere else to go.

Dean was starting to bend his mind around ways to get the remaining people here some shelter arrangements when two dark SUVs pulled into the lot. It was still dark out, and the windows were heavily tinted so Dean couldn't immediately see who was in the cars in the blinding headlights. He saw backlit figures exit the two vehicles and come towards him and the rest of the team. It wouldn't be The Cause returning, would it? He was about to assume a defensive stance when he realized it was James and others from his organization in the city. Celeste was there, as was Rudy. The four other large individuals who exited from the second vehicle were probably pack members there to act as security for their leaders. That group spread out and stood guard. Dean sighed in relief.

He walked over and shook James' hand as the vampire leader approached. James was looking around in the darkness, taking in the smoldering ruins beyond where Dean stood. Dean had to remember that it was as bright as daylight for James' enhanced vision, and he could see things the paramedic could not. James stood there and took it all in for a moment then looked at Dean.

"Is it as bad as it looks?" James asked.

Dean nodded. He took a moment and filled him in on their transportation plans for the patients, as well as his concerns for the remaining residents and survivors. James listened and nodded as Dean went down the list of needs. He gestured to Celeste, who was standing nearby, tapping notes into her tablet computer.

"Did you get all of that, Celeste?" James asked. She nodded and the vampire lord of Elk City turned back to Dean. "You all did a good job here, Dean. I think Celeste and I can find places to relocate the survivors in the short term until they can rebuild. Do we know how many perished in the fires?"

Dean shook his head. He looked back at the former trailer park and thought of Nura. How many others like her were lying around and in the remains of the mobile homes? He wasn't sure they'd ever recover all the bodies or identify them all.

"All we know, James, is that we've swept the area several times at this point for survivors, or for those who just ran away from the flames," Dean said. "There might be a few more we haven't found, but we can't be sure. My CERT team can all see pretty well in the dark, and they said they can't find anyone else. There are about five more severely injured and another four or five who need treatment. They'll be taken to the hospital when the ambulances return from their initial runs. In the meantime, the rest will all need a place to stay for the rest of tonight and beyond. I estimate that it's about sixty or seventy people. Where will you put them?"

"There are some motels on the edge of town owned by Unusuals," James said. "I've already been in contact with them, and they have plenty of room open to take the residents in. It will be a little tight for everyone concerned, but it will have to do until they get their homes built again."

"Who will pay for that?" Dean asked. "These people had little or nothing to begin with."

"I will," James said. "I own the land on which the mobile homes rested. It will fall to me to do something with this space now that the existing Barrens is no more. Perhaps I'll build some affordable housing apartments here to replace the way they lived before. They don't need trailers and caravans anymore. It is about time they shifted from their ties to the nomadic past. None of them have moved their trailers in years. It's time they recognize that they've put down roots here in this community."

James looked around at the expectant faces of the displaced residents around him and back to Dean. "Is August Beche or his wife here?"

Dean looked around, too, then shook his head. "I ran into them earlier. They were in shock from the events of the night. They didn't come out when I told them to leave. I don't know where they are now."

A woman lying on the ground nearby spoke up. "August and Helena ran back in many times to help others escape the fire. They pulled me out of the back window of my home and carried me here. I have not seen them in some time."

"Thank you, madame," James said. "We will look for them and lend them aid if it is possible."

Dean leaned in a little closer and lowered his voice. "If that is what they were doing, it may be likely that they were overcome by the smoke or heat and did not survive."

"I know, Dean," James said. "But we will look for them or their bodies anyway. It is the least I can do since I could not prevent this tragedy from happening to them."

Dean went back to tending to the gathered patients and survivors. While he was working, Gibbie and the rest of the CERT team came over together. They had been working hard, and it showed in the smudges of ash and soot on their faces and clothes. Gibbie seemed alright, but Wim, Dora, Kristof, and especially Marian all looked wide-eyed and a bit traumatized. It was likely that all four of them had seen their first dead bodies this night. Dean finished what he was doing and walked over to where the small group of civilian responders stood, a little apart from the assembled patients.

"How are you all?" Dean asked. The exhaustion showed even more, close up.

"We've scoured the woods all the way around the perimeter three times," Gibbie said. "We found people the first two times, but there was no one left to rescue by the time we made the third circuit."

"At least no one left alive," Marian muttered half under her breath. Dean heard her comment and knew that his guess about what they may have seen was correct. They needed to talk this out and get their feelings to the surface.

"Look," Dean said, his voice lowered to a near whisper so only the CERT team could hear him. "I know that this was a tough one for you guys. We are almost done here, and we'll be getting wrapped up to leave soon. Head over to the van and gather our gear, then take a break. There's some water bottles in the back of the van. Drink something and take a load off. I'll be over as soon as the ambulances return from their run to the hospital and load up the next group for transport. Okay?"

He met each of their eyes and registered their nods of agreement before he let them go. This was his team, and it was his job to help them through these difficult responses and traumatic experiences. He and Brynne had taught them back in their CERT training that sometimes patients died no matter what you did. But that was a dry lecture on managing stress and difficult situations taught in a classroom setting. This was something else. It was real, and he knew the smells, sights, and sounds of the things they encountered this evening would stick with them all. The smells especially were even more pervasive than the visual images burned into their memories. At least, that was the way it was for him in situations like this. He'd have to spend some downtime tonight de-stressing them. It was important to encourage them to talk about what they experienced this evening. He hoped he could draw them out and get them to talk about it. For now, all he could do was wait until it was time to pack up and leave.

## Chapter 19

The van ride back to the city was quiet after they left the scene of the fire. The CERT team members were subdued by what they had witnessed that evening. Dean knew they needed him to do something about it. He wondered aloud if there was a place they could go and get a bite to eat, sit down and talk. It was nearly three in the morning, and all the restaurants were long closed. He didn't want to go to some diner and talk. Dean felt like it needed to be something special.

"There's always The Irish Shop downtown," Gibbie offered.

Dean knew the place. It was an Irish gift shop in the main street shopping district. He'd never been inside, but he was pretty sure it didn't have a restaurant, at least not one that was open this late. He told Gibbie as much.

"No, we just use the portal there and visit the pub on the other side. They should be up and serving a nice Irish breakfast by now," Gibbie said, checking his watch. "They are five hours ahead of us, so it's like eight o'clock over there."

"Wait," Dean interrupted. "There's a shop downtown with a magical portal leading to Ireland? Don't you need a passport or something?"

"Not if you don't leave the pub," Gibbie said matter-of-factly. "It's just there as a convenience to the owner. He's a leprechaun who set up shop over here. He needed a connection to the homeland to keep his magic juiced up."

"Well, if that's the case, that would be perfect," Dean said. "To The Irish Shop, driver."

Dean sensed the mood lighten as the rest of the group anticipated this side trip for breakfast. It would be perfect for their after-action debriefing. He looked back at the group seated in the seats behind him. Marian had resumed her normal position on the edge of the seat, leaning forward in the pose he expected from her. When they left the Barrens, she had been slouched back in the seat just staring at something on her phone screen. The dryad twins, Wim and Dora, started chattering about what they would get for breakfast. Kristof smiled back at him, and even Gibbie was showing signs of good cheer, humming quietly as he drove back to the city. Dean decided it was a good sign of life with the whole team that they were excited to do something new together after the events earlier in the evening.

Gibbie drove them downtown to the shopping district. The Irish Shop was located next to the old Elk City Pharmacy and Lunch Counter storefront downtown. Gibbie pulled up on the curbside parking out in front of the specialty gift shop. At this hour, street parking was not a problem. The vampire pulled out his cell phone and selected a number from his contacts. He waited for someone to pick up on the other end.

"Dougie?" Gibbie asked. "It's Gibson Proctor. I wanted to take a few friends through the portal for a pleasant, peaceful Irish breakfast."

A pause and Gibbie took the phone away from his ear and rolled his eyes. Dean could hear the voice chattering on the other side. When it stopped, Gibbie started talking again.

"Dougie, I really need this favor. We just got done helping out with the Barrens fire and could use a break. I've got one of the Station U paramedics with me." He paused again, then continued after a glance around at the whole group. "There's six of us total.

We're parked right out front." Gibbie tapped to break the connection and replaced the phone in his pocket. He looked at the rest of them. "We're all set; he'll be right out to let us in."

Dean and the rest of the CERT team climbed out of the van and walked around to stand and look into The Irish Shop's plate glass window while they waited for the owner to come down and open up. Dean could see a sea of green items with shamrocks on them. There were also some attractive Irish lace and linen items draped on a table there. He saw some Irish jewelry, too. Perhaps he'd come back during regular hours and pick up something there for Ashley. It would be nice to get her something out of the ordinary. This place fit the bill. He was still window-shopping when the lights came on, and a figure moved through the showroom to the front door. He was easily six feet or more tall, with a shaved head and a surly look on his face.

The team moved over to the door as the man unlocked it and then stood back as Gibbie pulled it open and held it for them to enter. The ladies nodded to the man in greeting as they passed him and stood inside the entrance. Once Kristof, Gibbie, and Dean entered, Gibbie introduced them all.

"Dean, this is Dougie, proprietor of The Irish Shop."

Dean stuck out his hand, and the shop-owner shook it. "I'm surprised," Dean said. "I expected, uh…"

"Someone shorter, perhaps?" responded the man, his thick Irish brogue evident right away. "I know, I'm not what you'd expect from a leprechaun. I'm half human, and that is the half that decided to show up in my size. Believe me, I hear it all the time from my full-blooded brothers and sisters."

"I didn't mean anything by it," Dean said. "Seriously, no offense." He held his hands up in surrender.

"Don't you be worrying about it," Dougie said. "It's not like it's something I haven't heard before." He turned to look at Gibbie. "What happened at the Barrens? I saw a brief something on the news last night, but the coverage wasn't much. I figured it was being covered up to keep away from human eyes."

"It's bad, Dougie, bad, bad, bad," Gibbie said, shaking this head. "The whole neighborhood is a total loss, and there are a lot of bad injuries. Plus, we haven't accounted for everyone yet either. No one is sure how many dead there are."

"That's not good," Dougie said. "I heard through the grapevine that it was another attack by those human thugs." He looked briefly at Dean. "No offense intended."

"None taken," Dean replied.

Gibbie continued. "We saw a lot of things tonight, bad things. Dean here thought it might be a good idea for us to sit and talk about it a little bit before we all went home for the night. I thought sitting in an Irish pub like Mulligan's over breakfast might be a good change of pace."

"I suppose it might be at that," Dougie said, smiling. "A bit of the Irish morning sunshine can brighten any soul. Alright, follow me."

The large half-leprechaun led the group back to the rear of the shop. They went behind the sales counter to the back of the store and into the storage area for the store out front. There were shelves lining the walls with all sorts of knickknacks, and boxes stacked everywhere. The most notable thing in the room was the large, bright green door set in one wall. It was the sort of green that was the color of new grass shoots coming up in the spring. It was also hard to stare at for any length of time. Dean found he couldn't look right at the door for long without seeing it sort of waver or move, with a haze coming over it like you saw on a distant highway when it was baked with sunlight on a hot day. Dougie took a large iron key from his pocket and inserted it into the keyhole below the door's antique white porcelain knob. Turning the lock, he removed the key and handed it to Gibbie.

"When you come back, Gibson, leave the key on the counter by the cash register and make sure the door latches out front when you leave," Dougie said. "I'm going back to bed. I'm not a creature of the night as you are."

The team members all murmured their thanks as the shop's proprietor left them standing there. Then they all stood back as Gibbie pulled the door open. On the other side was a small room with a worn hardwood floor. On the other side of the small wooden room, there was a plain, six-panel wood door set in the far wall. Gibbie gestured for them to enter and he came in behind them, closing the green door. He then worked his way through the group to the front as they all waited for what was next. Gibbie grabbed the handle of the other door, smiled at them all and opened it.

Dean's eye's widened in surprise. He wasn't sure what he expected to see, but it wasn't a bustling pub common room with sunlight streaming in the windows at the far side of the room. As they went through the door and closed it behind them, a woman with an apron tied around her waist walked by with a tray of food. It smelled delicious. She looked at them in passing and gave a smile.

"Just take a seat anywhere, folks," she said. "We don't stand on formality here at Mulligan's." Obviously, she was used to people coming in through that entrance. Gibbie led them to a table away from the windows and the bright sunlight shining through them. That direct sunshine would be painful, if not fatal to the frumpy vampire. Gibbie took a seat at the back of the table, settling into the shadows against the wall. The other five sat down around the rest of the seats at the round table with him.

"This is nice," Marian said. "I didn't know this was here."

"It's not technically 'here' in Elk City," Gibbie explained. "We're in Dublin."

Dean looked around and soaked up the old-world aura all around him. This was what he would think of, if he were to picture an Irish pub or restaurant. The name of John Mulligan was painted on one wall near the ceiling next to the bar. The place was full of people, and he could hear the Irish brogue in the English spoken all around him. There were people seated at the bar eating, as well as at the tables along the wall where they sat. He was still looking around when the cheerful waitress came back; this time empty handed. She looked at the group of them.

"Americans?" she asked. They nodded. "I'm Wendi. We are always happy when Dougie sends his friends over to visit us. When you go back though, make sure you tell him not to be such a stranger." She winked at them. "Now what can I get for you?"

Gibbie spoke up before the others could answer. "Wendi dear, my friends will all have the full Irish breakfast. I'll have a nice cup of hot tea."

Wendi looked him over and leaned forward so as not to be overheard. "We have several blood types on the menu if you'd like, sir. Unless I miss my guess, that might be more to your tastes."

"That's alright, I'm not that hungry," Gibbie said. "Just the tea is fine."

"Suit yourself," she said. "I just don't like sending anyone away from here hungry, that's all. I'll be right back with your breakfasts. Tea all around for the rest of you, too, or would you prefer coffee? Our barista is quite accomplished. Better than that overpriced Starbucks stuff."

"I think coffee would be nice," Dean said. Wendi nodded and went back to the kitchen to get their orders started. He would have to remember this place. Maybe he could bring Ashley here sometime when things calmed down. He looked around at the CERT team. He was happy to see they seemed much more relaxed. This change of pace had been a perfect choice. Gibbie had been right, and Dean would have to remember to tell him that later. He let the small talk continue, listening as the twins shared their thoughts on the best local Elk City night spots for young adults while Marian listened, perched on the edge of her seat, as usual. He caught Gibbie's eye at one point and nodded his approval. The vampire returned his grin.

It didn't take too long for Wendi to return with their breakfasts. Each of them got a plate full of food including two fried eggs, pork sausages, fried potato hash, and toast. When the plate was set in front of him, Dean's stomach growled loud enough for the others to hear.

"Someone's hungry," Wendi said with a laugh. "There's more where that came from, so eat up. We don't like to send anyone away without a full belly." She set the steaming coffee cups in front of each of them and left a small bowl full of sugar and sweetener packets, along with a small white pitcher of fresh cream.

They all dug into their plates as soon as the waitress left. Gibbie sipped his tea and watched as the others devoured the food in front of them. Dean knew that nothing made him hungrier than a long stressful shift of high-energy calls. They all had burned through their reserves that night, and the food was recharging them while he watched. He let them settle into some normal conversations as they ate. They chatted about life in general until their plates were empty. Dean decided it was time to debrief them and talk about the events of the fire.

"I'm glad you're feeling a little better," Dean said. "The addition of some calories back to your systems, as well as some fluids, is healing. That's normal. It's also normal to have some residual bad feelings, or sad thoughts about what you all saw tonight at the Barrens. Gibbie is a bit older than the rest of us, and he has seen the most so I'll ask him to go first and share his thoughts and feelings. You don't all have to take a turn - but it helps, I assure you." Dean looked to Gibbie and the vampire nodded.

"I am not new to death and dying," Gibbie began. "I am a vampire and, on top of that, I'm more than four hundred-years-old. I've seen people die in a variety of ways, from illness and disease, as well as from injury. Saying that, though, I have to say that tonight is one of the more horrific things I've ever seen. Maybe it's because fire is one of the few things a vampire has to be afraid of, or maybe it's because the smell of burned flesh seems to stick with you for a long time. All I know is, what I've seen tonight will stay with me for a while."

"Thanks, Gibbie," Dean said. He looked at the others. "I'll go next while you all decide if you want to take a turn." He then proceeded to tell them about Nura and how he found baby Flynn. He had tears in his eyes by the time he was finished, and the others were struggling with tears of their own. "Would anyone else like to go next?"

Marian spoke up before either of the twins could answer. "I'm just mad. I mean I'm really pissed off." She leaned forward and continued with a harsh whisper. "I want to find the people who did this, shift to wolf form, and tear them to bits. I don't think that they understand what could happen to them when they came after one of the pack. Those fairy-folk aren't technically part of the pack, but they might as well be. If they came after us directly, it would be a lot different than attacking a community of fairies. That is what I have to say." Her eyes had taken on a feral gleam while she was talking, and he thought he saw her canines elongate, and her fingernails start to lengthen to claws. Dean needed to calm her down, or there was going to be an incident with a teenaged American Werewolf in Dublin.

"What you are feeling, Marian, is completely normal," Dean said, trying to soothe with his voice. He hoped it was working. "I'm angry, too. I want to change what happened. I want Nura to live to see her baby grow up, maybe to be a paramedic like me. Anger is part of what you should be feeling right now. I'm glad you shared with us." He finished with a friendly grin at her.

She nodded and returned his grin with one of her own. She seemed to calm down a bit, but he would have to watch her closely to make sure she didn't carry this inside for too long. He knew adolescent lycans were pretty volatile. Brynne had taught him that they were difficult to control and often lacked the self-restraint to keep from shifting in stressful situations. He had not considered that when taking her out on patrols in the evenings. The stress from this night's incidents could add to that volatility. He would have to say something to her parents when he and Gibbie dropped her off. Wim cleared her throat, and Dean looked at her with a smile.

"I think that I was most upset because I could see it happening to me," the dryad said. "The trees all around the Barrens, and in among the trailers were crying out in pain from the fire. Many were injured like the people."

"Yes, I was most upset by the trees," Dora said. "I mean, the dead bodies were awful, but all I could hear was the trees crying out in agony. Is that wrong?"

"There isn't any right or wrong in this, Dora," Dean said. "We all respond differently to this type of thing. Some of us feel anger, some fear, and some, sorrow. You are more connected to the trees and feel their pain in this event. There is no right or wrong answer, and your feelings may evolve or change over time as you talk with others about this, and you should try to talk about it. I'm not asking you to violate patient privacy. But you can describe your feelings, and how what you saw makes you feel while your brain tries to process it all. That's what I want you to take away from this breakfast and debriefing. Plus, remember that my door is always open for you if you decide you need to talk one on one some more with someone who was there with you."

They all looked at him and nodded in understanding. At least, that is what he thought they were showing. They could all still be in shock. He wasn't a trained counselor and was nearly as new to all of this as they were. He would keep an eye on them moving forward and check with James to see if other, professional resources could be made available. Wendi came around then and took their empty plates, asking if they wanted anything else. He suggested that they would just like the check. It was time for them to all return to Elk City and the problems that they had left behind there. At least they had gotten away temporarily. It was a start.

# Chapter 20

Their return through the magical portal to The Irish Shop in Elk City was uneventful. They had spent an hour and a half in the Irish pub on the other side, and it had created the desired effect as far as Dean was concerned. The team was laughing and joking with each other again, and the haunted looks they had before breakfast were gone for the most part. He wasn't so naive as to believe that the trauma was completely healed. They were going to need more time to process what they had seen at the Barrens fire, but this was a start for them to realize that their lives would go on, that they could go on.

Gibbie turned the large iron key in the big green door to lock it behind them and placed it on the counter next to the cash register as Dougie had requested. The vampire said he was going out to warm up the van and asked Dean to make sure the shop door was latched behind them when everyone else left. The three women were chatting about their trip to Ireland and what they were going to tell family and friends as they walked out the shop's entrance to the street outside. Kristof followed them out. Dean double-checked that they had left nothing behind and then pulled the shop's door closed behind him, tugging the solid door until he felt the latch click. He checked to make sure it was locked and was turning to walk across the sidewalk to the van when chaos erupted on the street around the team.

Two black SUVs raced up and screeched to a stop next to the van, and six men dressed in black pants, and black hooded sweatshirts jumped out. They tossed a loop of shiny, silvery cable around Gibbie's neck. The tubby vampire shrieked in agony as his hands went to his neck to try and pull the loop free. Dean saw smoke coming off the cable where it contacted his skin. Four of the men pulled at Gibbie and shoved him into the open back lift gate of one SUV while two others were wrestling with Marian. The teenager screamed at first, and Wim and Dora's screams of fear joined hers as the two dryads shrank away from the violence.

Marian's scream turned into a long, ripping snarl as she started to shift in front of Dean's eyes. He had never seen a lycan shift so quickly. To his knowledge, it took a full minute or more most of the time. This transformation only took a few seconds as her hands sprouted talons, her face elongated, and her mouth sprouted large canines. The transformed teen werewolf turned and bit down hard on one of the men's forearms. It was his turn to scream in fear as he let go, clutching his arm and staring at the bite in horror. The other man let go of his grip and backed away, but not fast enough. Marian's clawed hands swiped across his face and chest, leaving bloody slash marks through the sweatshirt and across his face.

The two wounded men backed away and then stumbled over to their SUV. They struggled to climb over each other to get back inside, away from the angry werewolf racing up behind them. The other black-clad men had finished loading Gibbie into the back of their vehicle. When they saw that the fight had shifted, instead of coming to help Marian's would-be abductors, they opted to load up into their own vehicle. As soon as the last of them had climbed in, before the last door was closed, both black SUVs peeled out with screeching tires, driving away into the night. Marian chased after them for half a block, howling at the escaping attackers. It had all happened so quickly; Dean had barely taken two steps from where he had stood at the door to The Irish Shop. The dryad twins were huddled together in fear next to Gibbie's van, Kristof had moved over to comfort them, and Marian was stalking back towards them, half in wolf form and half in human form, snarling and growling the whole way. Dean moved out into the street to intercept her.

"Marian," Dean said, trying to adopt a soothing tone, despite his racing heart. "The danger is past. You can return to human form. Can you hear me? Listen to my voice."

He kept talking as she walked up to him, her wolfish face tilted to one side as if questioning his words. He kept up the running dialog, trying to talk her back down. She stopped a few feet from him and stared at him for a moment, then, with a whimper, shifted back to human form. She collapsed to the street, sobbing, tears flowing down the restored teen girl's face. When Wim and Dora saw she had shifted back, they ran over and crouched to comfort her.

Dean stood in the street in front of Gibbie's van and looked around in the darkness. There were no other cars in sight. No other signs of danger to his team. Not that there needed to be. The Cause had come prepared to kidnap a vampire. That metal cable must have contained a silver alloy of some sort. It was toxic to vampires and leeched away their strength as long as it was in contact with their skin. As prepared as they were for Gibbie, they obviously weren't as prepared for a shape-shifting teenager, and judging from the looks on the one man's face, weren't properly inoculated against Lycanthropism, the disease that caused shape-shifting. Marian's bite had almost assuredly infected him. Dean wondered what The Cause did with members who became Unusuals. Whatever it was, it probably wasn't a good thing.

Dean took out his phone and dialed 911, telling the dispatcher that he had to report a kidnapping. He stayed on the line, giving the details of what he had seen while he waited for the arrival of the police units that were on the way. Wim and Dora helped Marian stand and took her over to the van. Dean saw Gibbie's keys lying on the street next to the driver's door. While he talked to the dispatcher, continuing to answer the questions she had on the other end of the phone line, he walked over and picked up the keys. He could hear sirens in the distance, coming closer. Soon, a police cruiser with lights flashing and siren blaring, turned the corner, drove up and pulled to a stop in front of the van. Dean notified the dispatcher on the phone that the police had arrived and was advised to hang up the phone and talk directly with them.

Dean recognized the officers as part of the Unusual police unit. He waved to them as they approached. They looked around, then the driver, Officer Jimmy Shorter spoke.

"I thought you were suspended? What are you doing out and geared up tonight?" he asked.

"Hi, Jimmy," Dean said. "I was out advising a CERT response team at the Barrens fire earlier tonight. We came back here and parked to regroup following that incident before dropping folks off at their homes. Most of my team was pretty shook up by the traumatic event. We were ready to pack up and head home for the evening when two black SUVs pulled up and a group of men kidnapped one of my team members, almost getting a second one before she fended them off."

He pointed down the street from which the police had arrived. "They drove off down that way when they left. The whole thing happened pretty fast. It couldn't have taken more than a minute from start to finish."

Another police car pulled up followed by an unmarked sedan with a flashing blue light on the dash. Dean surmised the second vehicle would be a supervisor or detective. The two officers left his side to walk over and talk to the ladies. Dean watched the unmarked police vehicle for a moment and then felt his shoulders sag when he recognized the detective who climbed from the driver's side. It was the same detective who had come for him following the finding of Zach dead in his apartment.

"Mr. Flynn," Detective Ricketts said as he approached. "I would have thought you'd want to stay out of any sort of police trouble considering the actual charges on the table against you."

"I am innocent of those accusations, Detective Ricketts, and this attack was unprovoked and a complete surprise to us," Dean said. He supposed that distrust and suspicion was a job requirement for people in Detective Ricketts' line of work, but that didn't keep Dean from adding a tinge of anger to his response. He recounted the kidnapping again for the detective, stressing that he was afraid for Gibbie's well-being. If The Cause had him, then Gibbie was in severe jeopardy. The detective wrote some notes on his spiral notepad, told Dean to stay put for the moment, and then went over to interview the women. Dean pulled out his phone while that was going on and called Celeste. She would know the best way to get ahold of James if he wasn't home. Dean was sure he was still out managing the efforts to get the Barrens refugees some place to stay.

"Hi, Dean, what can I do for you," the redheaded vampire said in her characteristic Southern drawl. "Is everything okay?"

Dean gave her the rundown on the rest of their evening since leaving the Barrens fire. He told her about the kidnapping of Gibbie, and the attempted abduction of Marian. She listened until he finished giving his report.

"Okay, I'll pass that along to James, as well as Rudy. As pack leader, he'll want to know that one of his pack was attacked directly and bit someone. It's not something they take lightly."

"It wasn't her fault," Dean interjected. "She was being attacked, and they were trying to kidnap her, too."

"I'm sure they'll take her age and inexperience into account," Celeste said. "It's just the lycans, like the vampires, take turning a human into one of them very seriously. It is drummed into them from a young age that if you bring someone into the fold, you are responsible for them. This was an extreme case and situation, but that is likely one of the reasons she is so upset."

"Well, that's good to know," Dean said. "I still don't think she had a choice. I'll tell Rudy as much myself when I see him."

"I'm sure he'll want to talk to you and Marian, when you get back," Celeste surmised. "When will you be able to return the team to the Nightwing building? Based on this attack, I think James would like to see all of you. He wanted to thank the team for their work at the fire. Now I think he'll want to find out what he can do to get Gibbie back."

"We should be finished here shortly. There's really nothing else for the police to do," Dean said. "There isn't any evidence or stuff like that to collect. I think once they get finished talking with Marian, Wim, and Dora, the detective will let us leave."

"Okay, text me when you're on your way," Celeste said and then she disconnected.

Dean pocketed his phone and walked over where Ricketts was wrapping up his interview with the dryad twins. He gave each of them his card and urged them to contact him if they remembered anything they didn't tell him already. Ricketts turned to Dean and walked with him a short distance away.

"Do you have any idea how they found you here?" Ricketts asked.

"What do you mean?" Dean replied.

"Well, it looks like they targeted you specifically if this was The Cause," the detective explained. "Did you see anyone following you after you left the Barrens?

"No, it was pretty deserted. It was like three AM when we finally left. There weren't that many cars on the road."

"So, they either found you by chance. You know, recognized the van, and waited for you all to leave the shop where you stopped. The alternative is that they tracked you here somehow. Any thoughts?"

Dean pondered the detective's line of reasoning. How could they have tracked him and the CERT team when they didn't know who they were or even what they were doing? He and Gibbie had gone to great lengths to keep the group separate from the Fire Department in every way. They had set up their own dispatch system and locations. The only recognizable thing was Gibbie's van. Perhaps someone saw the van at the scene earlier with the Barrens fire and put two and two together? He knew that Artur was aware they were operating a response system on their own. He could have put The Cause on the lookout for them. If someone recognized him at the Barrens and saw Gibbie's van, they would have targeted them. He told Detective Ricketts of his suspicions.

"We will look into that," Ricketts said. "It's an interesting theory. Do you know how we can get in touch with this Artur character? Maybe we can rattle his cage and get him to give up some information."

Dean snorted a laugh, "I don't think that Artur is easily 'rattled,' and he is not going to have anything to say to you. He is way too old and sharp to be tripped up in an interrogation. You're welcome to try, though. I guess it can't hurt. Maybe the increased scrutiny will pressure him to leave Elk City. You can get his contact information from James Lee or his assistant Celeste."

"I have to talk to him, at least," the detective said. "We have to give it a try, and we will also look into his background. Maybe some of his business dealings will lead to a connection to The Cause. Look, I don't think you did anything wrong here. As for your other legal problems with Zach's death, the evidence points to you, but it's too easy. You have a reasonable alibi that almost clears you, and we know that something bigger is going on here in the city. We just want it all to stop. Things used to run smoothly here, and everyone lived together and got along. Now we've got attacks on the streets, arsonists fire-bombing homes, and bigots trying to run people out of town. It's not right. I just wanted to tell you what I thought."

"Thanks, Ricketts, I appreciate that," Dean said. "I just want to get back out and start doing my job again. There are a lot of people, Unusual and otherwise, who are not getting the medical attention they need. We could be serving them. Instead, we are running around and dealing with the attacks and the fear. Hopefully, you can uncover something and get things ironed out."

"We're trying," Ricketts replied. "I have everything I need. You all can head home if you want. We will try and review the traffic cameras, as well as any security cameras in the area. We will see if we can figure out who took your friend and where they took him."

"Thanks," Dean said. He took Gibbie's recovered van keys out of his pocket and climbed into the driver's seat, starting the vehicle. He waited while the ladies and Kristof climbed inside and buckled up. The whole situation made him angry. He had brought them here to help defuse the tension and stress. They had taken on a lot of that when they responded to the Barrens fire. Now this attack had destroyed any headway he had made with the team on dealing with their stress. They were back where they started before the trip to Ireland, and he didn't have any more tricks up his sleeve to talk them back down. He did the best he could engaging them in conversation while he headed back to the Nightwing building. Marian's parents met them in the underground garage. Her dad came around to the driver's side of the van to talk with Dean as soon as he got out.

"I'm upset, Mr. Flynn. Upset that my daughter got caught up in this," Marian's father said. "We had hoped that her interest in this would keep her out of trouble, not get her in more trouble and attacked by those human monsters."

"I don't blame you for being angry, Mr. Gregory," Dean said. "I'm upset about this as well. I'm glad she is safe, but I'm very upset that she was forced to defend herself in such a direct way. I assure you that she bears no responsibility for this. In my opinion, she did what she had to do to avoid getting kidnapped like our friend."

"That may be true, but I hope you understand that she will not be coming out with you for a while," Mr. Gregory said. "I will be keeping her home and close until this whole mess with this Cause blows over."

Dean nodded. He understood completely. He was glad she could afford to sit on the sidelines. No teenager should be mixed up in a mess like this. "I understand. Hopefully, we can get her back engaged with this work after we solve this current situation. I'll make sure that we let you know what is going on."

The two men shook hands, and Dean walked with the others over to where James and Rudy waited to talk to them. He stood behind the group while the leader of Elk City's Unusual population praised them for their work and told them that he was working with authorities to get Gibbie back. He then offered all of the CERT team a ride home with his personal security team to ensure their safety. Dean just wanted to go to bed and get some rest, like the rest of the team. On his way to the elevator, Celeste said she'd make sure to call him later in the afternoon in time to come up to the penthouse for a planning dinner that evening. He said he'd be there and pushed the button to take him up to his floor. It was time to put this night to bed.

## Chapter 21

The dinner meeting that night was sedate, to say the least. Dean, Ashley, Brynne, and James all sat around the table in the penthouse apartment of the Nightwing building in silence, the only sound being the occasional scrape of a fork or knife on a plate. The aftermath of the Barrens fire and the later attack on Dean's CERT team were on all of their minds. Twenty-eight bodies had been found in the search after the fire was contained. Of the injured, four or five more might still succumb to the burn injuries they sustained getting out of the burning trailers. It was a devastating loss for the Unusual community, and it took the attacks by The Cause to a whole new level.

Domestic terrorism was a real problem, Dean knew, but for some reason, the situation in Elk City had avoided Federal attention. Perhaps because it was directed at the Unusual community and not the human community. Still, Dean found it hard to believe that the national leaders could so easily afford to turn away from the attacks of the previous evening. They couldn't just let local authorities handle it, could they? Dean believed that they had made a grave error. It was the underserved and voiceless who needed the extra protection, and any Federal involvement now might be too little, too late anyway.

Dean listened when they gathered for dinner as James told them that the FBI was sending a small task force including Alcohol Tobacco and Firearms (ATF) investigators to look at the fire. He was afraid the incident would cause the Unusual community to dive deeper underground and avoid further contact with human government services, but he, as the leader of the Unusuals in Elk City, was obliged to welcome the Feds in and make sure he and his underlings cooperated with them. The Federal team would be made up of agents who were aware of the Unusuals and their presence in the U.S. population, that was certain, but what was their mandate? James wondered if they were just sent to make sure the incidents didn't spill over into the human community. Dean knew one thing for sure: in light of the fire and the number of dead and injured there, they didn't care about the abduction of one vampire responder. That was a local problem.

It infuriated Dean that no one seemed to be looking for Gibbie. Anything could be happening to him right now. They could be torturing him, or maybe even already have staked him, ending his undead life. Dean clenched his fist and thumped it against his thigh in frustration. Ashley laid a hand on his fist, her fingers coaxing his hand to unclench and relax until her fingers interlaced with his. A gentle squeeze caused him to look at her where she sat next to him at the table. She gave him a tight-lipped, grim smile. He looked around at the others at the table. James was staring into the contents of his plain white mug, cupping the container of warm blood in two hands. Brynne was chewing a bite of food while she looked off into space somewhere out the windows at the nighttime skyline of the city. Everyone was stuck in their own, although similar, thoughts.

"I think we should initiate our own search for Gibbie," Dean said. He decided to break the silence and say what he hoped they all were thinking. "We can't just sit here and do nothing."

"I'm not sure there is anything we can do," Brynne said. She set her fork down and looked around at the others. "No one knows where they are staging their attacks from to begin with. All we know about them is they drive dark SUVs, but heck, there are hundreds of those driving around the city."

"I can't believe there is nothing we can do, though," Dean continued. "Isn't there some sort of magical search we can do, some way to divine their presence?"

"We used that route once, Dean," Ashley said. "It pointed us to Fire Headquarters and confirmed Artur's involvement. It did not uncover their hideout, though. The coven is still recovering from the blast, and even were they receptive to trying again, they will be unable for some time to make the attempt to pierce whatever concealment charms Artur has put in place."

"I still refuse to believe that there is nothing we can do to help," Dean said. The police were no help. If there were a magical concealment spell on the hideout, humans would not be able to locate it. The police would literally drive right by it and see nothing. Dean knew that, but it didn't resolve his feelings of helplessness.

"We have to be patient, Dean," Ashley said, giving his hand a reassuring squeeze under the table. "I sense no change in the future possibilities; there is still a major event to come that will require both you and James to act. That has not changed."

"Still no clue as to what that event might be Ashley?" James asked.

"No, it is still hidden, but that is not unusual to me. I'll not know it is directly imminent until almost the moment the event happens," Ashley replied. "I can steer you and advise you on what I think you should do, but I'm not sure what effect any action you take will have until after it is done."

Brynne snorted a sarcastic laugh. "So we can have help, but not help that really gives us any real assistance. Typical."

"Brynne," Ashley said. "I'm not here to tell you what to do. I'm a support network, to make sure you can make the choices required of you all when the time comes. But it still comes down to free will. You must arrive at your decisions on your own, without interference."

The female paramedic held up her hands, exasperated. "Ashley,

I'm sorry. I'm not attacking you, I'm just frustrated like Dean and James are."

"No offense taken," Ashley said with a smile.

"So," Dean interjected. "We are back to square one. We have no inkling what is happening and who we need to be dealing with next. Gibbie is still taken and needs our help. We have to do something more than sit here and bemoan our lack of solid plans."

"We may have a lead to follow-up on," said a male voice from across the room. The group looked over towards the entrance to the penthouse apartment. Dean experienced a glimmer of hope as he recognized Rudy, the werewolf pack leader, and James' second. Rudy was leading the Unusual side of the investigation, informally at least.

"What do you have, Rudy?" James asked. "Do we know where they are staging their attacks from?"

"Close, boss," the werewolf said with a feral grin. "I've been following up on the attack last night and the abduction of our friend. I decided to go and talk with each of the CERT team members who witnessed the attack. I started with the twins, and they didn't remember anything different from what they had told the police. But, when I went to chat with Marian, I could tell that she was holding something back from me. I wasn't sure what it was, but I could tell that there was something. I eventually had to go all alpha wolf on her to compel her to tell me what she was hiding. She told me about this." He held up a smartphone, triumph showing in his face.

"Whose phone is that? Is it hers?" James asked.

"No it's mine," Rudy answered. "But it is not the phone itself that is the clue. It is what is on the phone. Our little counter-culture wolf-child hacked Gibbie's phone when he wasn't looking. She wanted to follow the CERT team calls at night, even when her parents wouldn't let her out. She installed a spyware app on Gibbie's phone so it would send its location to her phone. Not only that, but she also can remotely access the phone's camera and microphone."

"But that means that we can tell where Gibbie is, right?" Dean said, holding back his rising excitement.

"Maybe, Dean, maybe," Rudy answered. "We have to take this slow. I've installed the spyware client on this phone, and I've got a team working to follow-up on the information I have so far. It can give a general GPS location and then we need to see if the phone can send video and audio of his surroundings, provided the phone is still on his person."

"If you have an approximate location, we should still go there and see what we can find," Dean said.

"I already have a few of my more discreet pack members following up on it. Let me find out more about what we are facing. Then we can know who and what we are going after. There's no upside to just rushing in. That is how people get hurt, Dean."

"How long will it take to get your people in place?" Brynne asked.

"They are on their way there now, but they have to take their time. It's in the warehouse district, and there is not a lot of traffic down there this time of night. A car driving by at night would be noticed, so they need to be very careful how they approach the area." Rudy looked at James. "I just wanted to give you a heads up, James. If we find Gibson, what do you want us to do? I heard they had silver chains on him. That will affect us, too. I don't want to lose anyone else trying a rescue."

"Why can't we just call the police?" Dean asked. "They aren't allergic to silver."

"Think about that for a moment, Dean," Rudy said. He paused before going on, letting that sink in. "If we involve the local police, we involve all the local authorities. That includes the leak we suspect is going on inside the dispatch and response system of the city. I think we are going to have to extricate the hostage ourselves without local help. Calling the police will only serve to alert them we are coming and give them the opportunity to foil our attempt – or worse."

Dean sat back in his chair. He hadn't thought about that. He knew there was a leak inside headquarters somewhere. Since the events on the fire ground the previous evening, he now suspected it was deputy fire chief Compton. The bad news was that the chief could monitor police frequencies as well. If he was the leak and he overheard a police operation heading to the site of The Cause's safe house, he could warn them to bug out, or prepare to repel the assault on their hideout.

"Dean, at least we know more now than we did a few minutes ago," Ashley said. "We were just saying we had nothing to act on. Now we have a possible location of The Cause, and that means for Gibbie, too. Be patient, it will work out."

"What did you tell Marian when you figured out what she had done?" Dean asked Rudy. "Does she know that what she did could help us?"

"I told her that it was very fortunate, even though it was a violation of personal privacy," Rudy said. "We lycans are an honorable people, Dean. I'll not have sneaks and thieves in my pack. I impressed that on her. She was appropriately chastised over it."

"You should reward her, not punish her," Dean exclaimed. "Sure, she overstepped her bounds and invaded Gibbie's privacy, but when you look at what it enabled us to do, it turned out alright. We should teach her the right things to do, but encourage her to expand her skills in this area. It's a useful skill, especially in today's security conscious world."

"The ends don't justify the means," Rudy said. "At least not to me." He shot a glance at James and Dean got the sense that he and his leader had had this discussion before.

"I agree with Rudy that she took the wrong actions, and they worked out for us this time, mostly due to luck," Brynne said. "I do think that we should talk with her and encourage her to develop these skills further. The world is changing and having an Unusual with this type of security and computer expertise could be a good thing. James, you have scholarships you give out to members of your community. You should think about sending her to a top-notch computer programming school. She could become a huge asset to you and the rest of the Unusual community."

"You may be right," James said. "We will look into that when this all blows over. It could be a moot point if we don't make it through this intact. I may not be in a position to award anyone a scholarship unless we catch a break. Let's hope the information she enabled us to find works in our favor." He looked up at his second. "Keep us in the loop, Rudy. We'll be here if you find out anything."

"Will do, boss," the werewolf replied. "I'll get you hourly updates by text message and call you directly if we find anything solid on Gibson's whereabouts." He nodded to the rest of the group, turned, and left them sitting over their dinner while he headed back down the hallway towards the elevators.

Dean and the others looked around meeting each other's eyes. The mood had changed. They had a solid lead, and things were not quite as hopeless as they were a few minutes before. There was a chance they'd get their abducted friend back. Dean started to eat with renewed vigor. He was hungry now, and he might need the extra energy if they ended up going on a rescue mission to retrieve Gibbie. He thought about what he might do if he encountered the attackers in person again. He wasn't a violent person, but these guys needed to be stopped, and a little vigorous persuasion might go a long way to stopping the attacks and finding out who was controlling them from the top.

They knew it was Artur on an unofficial level, but it would be much better if they were able to turn up proof of his involvement. That would force him to drop his plans, lest they be exposed to the higher Unusual leadership. Dean got the sense that, while they did turn a blind eye to some of what had been going on, if James came forward with direct evidence against Artur, he would be forced to back down and would be discredited. That was Dean's goal. It wasn't just to stop the attacks. It wasn't just to discredit and expose Mike Farver and Chief Compton at Headquarters; he wanted to make sure that the one who was ultimately responsible was punished. If they proved Artur was at the heart of it, he wanted to hurt him as much as possible.

# Chapter 22

Dean and Ashley left dinner feeling much better than when they had when they arrived an hour and a half earlier. As they stepped off on their floor, they laughed at a shared joke Dean brought up on the elevator. Their laughter stopped when they turned the corner of the hallway and saw Artur coming the other way.

The vampire looked at them with a puzzled expression, then assumed a sly smile and said, "I am surprised to see you two in such good spirits. Surely there are things to be concerned about this evening that don't merit such elated behavior."

Dean knew the vampire lord was fishing for information. He wanted to know what they were up to in their efforts to counter him. Dean should have just passed the creature by without responding, but he could not resist taking a dig at the old vampire.

"Artur, we're on to you, you know. We will stop your efforts to destroy what we've started here." Ashley laid a cautioning hand on his arm to stop him, but Dean kept going. "And when we get finished foiling your little plot here in Elk City, I am going to enjoy hunting you down and helping some friends of mine drive a stake through your heart."

The vampire's eyes narrowed to slits, but the grin never left his face. He and Dean stood nose to nose in the hallway outside Dean's apartment. Artur looked first at Dean and then turned his attention to Ashley. "Perhaps you should teach your trained puppy some manners towards his betters, Eldara. He needs a leash to keep him in line."

Dean lurched towards the vampire at the insult, but Ashley barred his way with her arm, demonstrating surprising strength as she stopped his advance without much effort at all. Dean stopped and looked at her. It was like he had run into a chest-high iron bar.

She shot him a glance and said, "If you lay hands on him, Dean, my protection is negated. As long as you do not initiate violence against him, my aura extends over you. Remember that you are a healer, not a warrior."

Artur smirked at the exchange. Dean could see he thought he had won the encounter, and struck at the pair with more of his smug words. "It's too bad your girlfriend's protections can't watch over everyone you care about, Mr. Flynn. If you are not careful, you might lose your entire little response team." He finished with a wide grin, exposing his sharp, elongated canines. The grin abruptly disappeared with Ashley's next words.

"My sister sends her regards, vampire. I would think that you would steer well clear of any Eldara and her friends, considering how anxious she is to have words with you again."

All semblance of calm humor was wiped away from Artur's face. Dean now saw something else in his eyes. Was it fear? He couldn't be sure, but their adversary took a step backward before he stopped at the wall. His eyes darted up and down the hallway as if looking for something, or someone.

"No," Ashley said. "She's not here. At least, not yet. She has another task to complete, but she wanted me to tell you that she hasn't forgotten the Crimea, or Antietam, or Saigon for that matter. If I were you, I'd conclude my business here quickly. I don't know how soon she will be finished with what she is doing, but I'm assured she will be coming here next."

Artur looked thoughtful for a moment. "You are telling the truth. I know you cannot lie, but why tell me this? Is it perhaps because you want me to hurry my plans for Elk City?" He paused and matched Ashley's determined stare for a time before continuing with a dismissive wave of his hand. "I care not. My plans are all in place and will proceed with or without me at this point. I will be leaving town soon anyway. Nice try, Eldara." He waggled his finger in the air at her, then moved past them in the hallway gliding towards the elevators.

Dean watched him go and when the vampire turned the corner, started to say something, but Ashley laid a finger on her lips and shook her head. She took him by the hand and led him the rest of the way down the hallway to their adjacent apartments. Dean took out his keycard and unlocked his door. She pushed past him inside and pulled him in after her. Once the door was shut, she waived a hand in the air over it and then turned to him.

"We can talk now, no one can hear us," she announced. She looked squarely at Dean. There was anger in her eyes. "What were you thinking out there? You can't take him in a straight up fight. Artur would tear you apart before I could do anything to stop him. My protection is very specific and peaceful in nature. Were he to attack you first, my lingering aura would cause him great injury. Even then he would destroy you with little thought if he wanted to. He knows he would heal eventually."

"I couldn't let him just walk by without knowing what I want to do to him," Dean argued. "He needs to know that I'm on to him, and I will hunt him down. That was not an idle threat."

"Men!" Ashley said, throwing her hands in the air and walking across the living room to the large window. She turned and glared at him. "I just told you that you aren't powerful enough to stop him on your own. He is a very ancient vampire. James and Rudy together would be hard-pressed to best him, and the two of them are extremely powerful."

"But you could take him, right?" Dean asked.

"I've told you, Dean. I'm a healer," Ashley explained. "My

powers give life; they don't take it. I can defend myself, and to a limited extent, defend you from his attacks, but that is all."

"But he seemed very afraid of what your sister could do, would do to him."

"That is different," Ashley said. "Ingrid is a warrior angel, a Valkyrie. Her powers are all about fighting and strength and war. She would defeat him handily, and make it look easy. That is why I invoked her here. I wanted him to think she was aware of where he was based on her previous encounter with him. It was enough to get him to back down."

"So, she's not coming?" Dean asked.

"Oh, she is coming now," Ashley said with a laugh. "I told you. I invoked her. When I told him my sister sends her regards, it connected her to the conversation. I could feel her amusement as she sort of jumped in to overhear the conversation. Based on the response I could sense from her, she is definitely on her way. She has a very old score to settle with Artur."

"Well good, then she'll take care of Artur for us," Dean said.

"No, Dean, we don't want that. Ingrid brings a certain, uh, level of turmoil, shall we say. When she visits somewhere, it is usually because of a war and the chaos that war brings with it. She can be much more direct than I have to be under normal circumstances. No one notices when strange things happen in a war zone. When she gets here, it is going to take all my energy to keep her from razing the center of town trying to get to Artur."

"Oh," Dean said. "I didn't realize she had that kind of power. When will she get here?"

"She's somewhere in the Middle East right now," Ashley said. "People have been fighting each other there for millennia, so she likes to hang out there. I did sense she is annoyed, so that means she has to finish some task there before she can leave to come here to renew her feud with Artur. My guess is it will be somewhere between a few days to a few weeks until she arrives. That means that we have that long to finish what needs to happen here before she gets here and really messes things up. Like I said, she is anything but subtle."

"And this is my fault?" Dean asked. "What did I do?"

"You provoked Artur. That made me take steps to get him to back down," the Eldara explained. "Now events are in motion that I have no control over and the future, which was cloudy already, is now so dark as to be invisible. You and James are going to be forced to make your decision early, maybe in the next two or three days. Beyond that, I can see nothing anymore."

Dean considered what she said. He was startled by her worry about the coming of her sister. It took a lot to get her to worry; in fact, through all of this going on since he had known her, he couldn't remember her being truly worried about anything. Even so, he wasn't sorry he provoked Artur to take direct action. If it got the vampire to step up his timetable by bringing Ashley's sister into it, so be it. He wanted all of this to end in Elk City. He wanted things to go back to normal where he could just be a paramedic again. People he cared about were getting hurt. It had to stop.

Dean met her stunning green eyes. "All I know, Ash, is that the sooner we get rid of Artur and The Cause, the sooner we can get people back to getting the help they need from the paramedics at Station U. Is that wrong?"

"No, sweetie, it is never wrong to wish for things to be better than they are," Ashley replied, her eyes softening with her smile. "I often forget that being human brings a sense of urgency of purpose that those of us with a longer life-view don't have. It is one of the things I cherish about you all. You want to cram so much into your brief lifespan, to try and accomplish every potential task set in front of you. It is an admirable quality to have. Look, let's get to bed and get some rest. That way we'll be ready to see what we can do once Rudy and his security team have some information we can act on," Ashley started to head into Dean's bedroom.

"I'm not that tired, Ash," Dean said. "I slept all morning after last night's course of events."

"Well, then," she said, looking back over her shoulder with a smoldering glance. "I'll just have to figure out a way to wear you out so you can sleep better."

DEAN WOKE up to the sound of his phone buzzing on the nightstand. He was curled around Ashley in bed. He rolled over, careful not to jostle his sleeping partner. Picking up the phone he saw it was Celeste. He swiped the phone screen to answer.

"Go for Dean," he said, his voice cracking from lack of use.

"Hi Dean, it's Celeste," the voice on the other end said in her characteristic southern drawl. "Rudy's team thinks they've found Gibbie. He wanted me to let you know, in case you wanted to be in on the rescue."

"You bet I do," Dean said, jumping out of bed and to his feet. "Where should I meet him?"

"Rudy is waiting downstairs in the garage," Celeste said. "He wants to leave quickly, can you get downstairs in ten minutes?"

"Easily. In fact, tell him I'll be there in five," Dean said. He hung up and started to get dressed, pulling on pants and looking around for a shirt.

Ashley stirred and rolled over, propping up on one elbow, watching him. "What is it?"

"They think they found Gibbie," Dean said. "Rudy is waiting downstairs for me. He asked me to go along on the rescue attempt."

"That sounds risky; please be careful," Ashley said. "I can't come along; I have to get ready for work. Text me as soon as you know anything. In fact, text me every hour or so, so that I know you're alright."

"Got it," Dean said. He leaned over to grab a quick kiss from Ashley. She latched on to him and planted a sensuous kiss on him that left him breathless.

"That is to make sure you know how much you have to live for," Ashley said shaking a finger at him. "Don't go doing anything stupid. Let Rudy's goons take the chances. They regenerate."

"I'm perfectly happy to let them take the lead, Ash," Dean said after catching his breath. "I'm going to consider myself tactical medical support. I fully plan on being back in this bed with you later tonight. Deal?"

"Deal," Ashley replied. "Alright, go and bring Gibbie back safely. I'll be watching for your updates."

Dean left the room, grabbing his trauma and med bags, along with the heart monitor. He didn't want to keep Rudy waiting. Gibbie was depending on them.

Rudy was in the underground garage of the Nightwing building, sitting in a black Ford Expedition. The engine was idling, and the werewolf leader was on his phone as Dean approached. He loaded the medical bags in the back seat and climbed into the passenger side, buckling the seat belt as he settled in. He looked to Rudy, who held up a finger while he continued talking on the phone.

"Okay, don't do anything until I get there unless there is a change in the situation, and the hostage is in imminent danger," Rudy said. He glanced at his watch. "I'm ten minutes out." Cutting the phone's connection, he looked to Dean as he slid the SUV into gear and started up and out of the garage. "We've been checking the warehouse district once we were able to track Gibbie's phone. We were able to narrow it down to one particular building, and my team has been casing the place carefully while monitoring Gibbie's situation. They're saying they have plans to move him to the roof at dawn and have a vampire barbecue."

"We can't let that happen," Dean said. He was alarmed at the werewolf's matter-of-fact manner.

"We think it's an idle threat," Rudy replied. "They could have killed him by staking him at any time. I think they want something from him. Information or something else. I'm not sure, but we're not taking any chances. We plan to go in just before dawn, or sooner if it looks like they are moving Gibbie to the roof."

"How many people are there?" Dean asked. "Do they have weapons?"

"Guns don't concern me so much as the presence of silver, Dean," Rudy said. "We know they used a silver chain or cable to subdue Gibbie in front of The Irish Shop when they abducted him. If they have other silver items, such as silver-infused bullets or arrows, we could be in trouble."

"I brought my med bags and gear," Dean said. "I'll be there to help if you need it."

"That's good, but let's hope we do this without any trouble or at least a minimal amount of it," Rudy said. "I would like to catch these guys and turn them over to the police with some information on their leadership. That way we can try and put an end to The Cause once and for all. I've tried to impress that on my guys and gals. They are all out for blood. They all have heard about what happened at the Barrens. It's going to be hard to keep them from ripping these terrorists apart, limb from limb."

Dean shuddered at the thought of a pack of angry werewolves loose in a warehouse full of humans they were mad at. He looked at Rudy as he drove. "Can you keep them under control?"

"I hope so," Rudy answered. "My pack leader bond is strong, and I can compel a lot from a pack member, but once the action starts, instincts take over. If they lose control, if we start taking losses in the assault on the building, I'm afraid that all bets are off."

"Let's both hope it doesn't go that route," Dean said. "It will only prove to their enemies that Unusuals are the monsters they believe they are."

"I know the risks, Dean," Rudy said. "I want this to end as much as you, and to get Gibbie back. I want to take out the opposition and move forward peacefully. I have a family and children. I want them to grow up and realize their full potential without worrying about what some human might think about their shapeshifter side."

Dean thought about that as they continued to the location in silence. He had only met Rudy a few times. He forgot that he was a person who had a family like everyone else. He had hopes and dreams and wanted the best for his kids just like every other person did. They were different, sure, but they were also very much the same. It was important to keep that in the front of his mind even though he already knew it deep inside. He continued to think about it as they drove through the deserted early morning streets.

***

DEAN CROUCHED by the corner of a building staring across the dimly lit street at a large, two-story warehouse where they thought Gibbie was being held. He checked his trauma gear over one more time and looked behind him to make sure that his assistant was where she was supposed to be. Marian nodded and showed she was holding the heart monitor and his med bag in both hands. He had been surprised to see Marian on the scene with her father when he arrived a half hour earlier. Apparently, they had needed her hacking expertise to open the connection on Gibbie's phone, and she refused to show any of the adults how it was done. Dean was glad to see her. He knew he might need an extra pair of hands. This was a tactical assault, and he would need her if he ended up with a bunch of trauma patients later on.

Her father was glad to have something else for her to do and someone to keep an eye on her. He clearly wanted to participate in the assault on the building but didn't want to leave her unattended. Dean's proposal that she join his team for medical support was a perfect solution for everyone concerned.

"Marian, they should be about ready to go in, can you see anything?" Dean asked. "My human eyes are only picking up shadows and darkness."

She moved up to crouch next to him and looked around the corner. "I got your back, bossman," the teen werewolf said. She peered up at the roofline across the street. Dean followed her gaze, and for a moment thought he caught a flicker of movement. Then he wasn't sure he saw anything as the shadows swirled around whatever he saw, or thought he saw.

"What do you see?" he asked.

"They found a window on the second floor that was unlocked or that they were able to break open quietly," she replied. "I saw four of our team go in that way. I think the others are trying around the other side. I don't see anyone else. Wait, something is happening."

Dean turned his gaze down to the street level. He heard the distinctive pops of gunfire. Muzzle flashes from the shots lit up the first-floor windows. He tensed and waited. There had been a flurry of shots and then silence. Then he heard another two, no three, pops that sounded farther away, deeper inside the building.

Marian was leaning forward as if straining against an invisible rope. Her head turned this way and that as if trying to look everywhere at once. Dean laid a hand on her arm to attempt to calm her down. She jumped and turned to look at him with a feral snarl, her eyes glowing red in the darkness.

"Easy, kid," Dean soothed. "You need to take a breath. One thing we can't do is go rushing in there and not pay attention to our situation. Remember scene safety. I know that with guns involved it's less safe than we'd like, but that is all the more reason to keep ourselves calm and grounded. When they call us in, we are going to walk, not run over there and start doing our jobs. The fastest way to screw up is to start rushing. We bring order to chaotic situations; we don't add to it, okay?"

"I'm sorry, Dean," she said. "You're right. I'll keep myself in check. Thanks for the reminder." She jerked her head around and looked back at the building. "I just heard someone inside say the word 'medic.' I think they are going to bring us in soon."

As if on cue, the door in the side of the building across the street opened, and they saw Marian's father stand in the opening and wave to them, gesturing for the two of them to come over. Dean shouldered the strap for the trauma bag, then he and Marian dashed across the street and followed Mr. Gregory inside. Dean looked around, scanning his surroundings as he entered. The large warehouse room on the other side contained scattered crates and pallets stacked to the ceiling. There were large concrete columns that supported the roof around the room. He didn't see anyone.

"How many injured?" Dean asked Marian's father as they picked their way around the obstacles on the floor.

"One of the pack took a bullet wound," the werewolf replied. "Based on the pain and the bleeding we think it was silver coated or a silver alloy. Three of the six humans are down. We caught two others more or less intact. The last one is holed up in the office upstairs using the vampire as a shield. Rudy is talking with him now, trying to get him to surrender."

"Let's look at the gunshot wound first, then I want to look at the 'more or less intact' humans, too," Dean said. The werewolf nodded and turned towards a set of stairs. As they got closer, Dean heard a male voice.

"I can't stop the bleeding, it's soaking through everything I have put on the wound." Dean could finally make out figures in the darkness ahead clustered around a shape on the floor. He approached with Marian and her father, then handed the father the large flashlight he had stowed in the trauma bag. Mr. Gregory switched it on and played the light over the scene where the figures stood.

Dean saw a man on the floor writhing in pain. He was extremely pale. Another figure was pressing a blood-soaked cloth against his arm above the elbow. Dean set the trauma bag down, took in the amount of blood pooling on the floor and dripping from the makeshift dressing and made a decision to go right to the use of a tourniquet. He had a combat application tourniquet in the oversized cargo pocket of his duty pants. Pulling it out and ripping open the Velcro strap, Dean wrapped it around the injured man's upper arm, lacing the end through the buckle and pulling it tight.

"Ouch," the man said, looking sharply up at Dean.

"I know that hurts, but it needs to start out tight, or it won't clamp down tight enough to stop the bleeding," Dean said. "I'm Dean, the paramedic, what's your name?" He tried to make conversation while he worked to distract the patient from what he was doing.

"I'm Morgan, Morgan Gregory," the patient said through gritted teeth.

"He's my uncle," Marian said chiming in from beside Dean. "What can I do?"

"Take over on the arm here and try and control the bleeding. Apply another layer of gauze over what is there and press down hard just like I taught you," Dean said to his helper. He turned his attention back to his patient. "Okay, Morgan. I've got the tourniquet in place here. Now comes the hard part. This is going to hurt while I tighten this down but it has to be done to stop the arterial bleeding in your arm. Alright?"

"Do what you need to do, I'll deal with it," Morgan said.

Dean nodded. He started to twist the windlass stick built into the tourniquet. As the twisting pulled on the fabric of the strap, it tightened the strap. Morgan groaned in pain. Dean watched the blood dripping from the soaked dressing slow and then stop. He latched the windlass in place with a smaller built-in Velcro strap to keep it from unwinding and then looked at Marian.

"Keep the pressure on the wound for another few minutes. Then you can wrap it in place with a pressure dressing," Dean said. "I'm going to start an IV and get some fluids started in case we need them to keep his blood pressure up."

He dug around in the trauma bag and compiled IV supplies, to start the IV on the other arm. By the time he was finished, Marian was finished with bandaging the dressings in place on the injured arm. He double checked the wound and saw the bleeding had indeed stopped. One patient down and tended to, now to check on the others.

"Where is Gibbie being held and where are the humans you said might be injured?" Dean asked Marian's father.

"They're upstairs," he replied. "Two have some scratches and bruises, and maybe a concussion. We are waiting for an opening to remove them from up there to down here. The third one got bitten pretty badly on the shoulder. He got away from us and is holed up with the vampire. He is threatening to kill him if we don't leave. Rudy is trying to talk him into surrendering."

"Damn," Dean said. "Do we know if he's armed?"

"There's plenty of loose and broken pallet wood around in here. I don't think it would be hard to come up with a makeshift stake," one of the assembled pack members said. Then he suggested, "Maybe we could just wait until he passes out from lack of blood."

"Except with that bite, time is ticking down," Dean said. "I need to give him a Wolfsbane injection soon, or he's going to end up a pack member. I don't think Rudy will want that." The surrounding growls from the pack members told him they agreed with him.

"Take me upstairs to Rudy," Dean said. "I might have an idea."

Chapter 24

Dean was escorted upstairs, while Marian remained on the lower level, monitoring her uncle's condition. Two of the other pack members carried Dean's bags and monitor for him. He entered the second floor that looked much like the first floor, except the there was a row of doors that led to windowed offices along one wall. He guessed they were there so managers could see onto the warehouse floor and monitor what was going on. He heard Rudy talking to someone in a loud, clear voice, his strong baritone carrying throughout the large, open space of the warehouse's second floor.

"Look, you've got nowhere to go," Rudy said. "Come out now and we can help you, we promise we won't harm you further."

"No, I have no reason to trust monsters like you," a muffled voice said. "One of your rabid buddies bit me. He bit me! I know what's going to happen now. I have nothing to live for. I don't want to become one of you."

Dean moved towards the voices and saw Rudy standing by a stack of wooden crates, his eyes focused on one of the enclosed offices. He could see a pair of shadowy figures inside the darkened office through the large plate-glass window set in the wall next to the door. Dean moved up next to Rudy and looked at the office. It was unlikely that any of the pack members could get inside in time to stop the man from killing Gibbie if he was determined to do the job, even if they shifted and moved at top speed.

"Can I talk to him?" Dean asked. "I might have something that can talk him down. Make him have something to live for and give up."

"Take it away," Rudy said with a wave of his hand. "I'm no hostage negotiator. I would much rather take a direct approach and charge in there. But I also know what that would mean to our friend in there."

Dean nodded and moved around in front of Rudy.

"Hello inside the office," Dean called out. "My name is Dean. I'm a human paramedic. Can you tell me your name?"

There was no answer.

"Look, I understand you are injured, that you were bitten," Dean called out again. "I want you to know that no matter what you think, there is a way to keep anything from happening to you as a result of that."

"You're lying," the shaky voice came from inside the room. "I know that it's just a matter of time until I turn into a freak like those other monsters out there. I'd rather die." There was a shriek from inside the room and then Dean heard Gibbie's frantic voice.

"Dean, he's got a stick, and he is sharpening it with a pocket knife. Get me outta here."

"Everybody needs to calm down," Dean said trying to project his voice without sounding like he was shouting. "Tell me your name. I told you mine." There was silence for a bit then the voice answered.

"I'm Eric." The voice sounded exhausted. Maybe he was losing blood, Dean thought.

"Okay, Eric, I'm not lying about helping you," Dean replied. "I have a drug that can reverse the shape-shifting effects of the bite, but I need to administer it quickly after the bite for it to work."

"How do I know you're telling me the truth?" Eric asked.

"I'm a paramedic, a healer, a medical professional and a human," Dean replied. "I don't lie to my patients. You are my patient. I came here to treat anyone wounded during this rescue. That includes you, too."

"You're him," Eric said.

"What?" Dean asked.

"You're the one that we helped the Chief frame for Zach's murder," Eric explained. "Why would you want to help me?"

Dean paused. As much as he felt vindicated by hearing Eric's admission, he was angry, hurt and emotionally engaged. That made it tough to be a professional in this situation. If he were an armed tactical medic and he had been in the lead elements of the assault on this building, he might have even been called upon to injure or kill this person. Now he was in the difficult role of trying to help him. Why was he interested in helping this guy? Letting Eric become a werewolf, turning into a creature the man had dedicated his life fighting against, would be a fitting punishment. But that wouldn't be the right thing to do. Dean was a healer. Being a paramedic and helping people was all he had wanted to be, if he stopped doing that, even for a moment, just because he was angry — well, that made him no better than them.

"Eric, all I can tell you is that I'm here to help you. I also want to rescue my friend. We can accomplish both things here. You sound tired. Is your wound still bleeding?"

"Yes, I can't do much with one hand to stop it," Eric said.

"I think you need to let me come in there and stop that bleeding. Once I do that, I can give you the medicine that will stop you from getting the disease that causes shapeshifting. That's what it is, you know. It's just a disease. They aren't monsters. They are just people who got a type of virus, and have adjusted to living with a long-term illness."

"We don't really see it that way, Dean," Rudy whispered behind him.

"Shhh," Dean said lowering his voice. "I'm trying to talk him out of there. We can talk about your lycan culture and history later."

Eric was quiet for a few moments, then he responded. "I don't want to become like them. I don't know. You could come in here and do anything to me. How do I know you are telling me the truth?"

"Eric, at the end of it all, I can't give you any guarantee beyond my word, my promise that I want to help keep you from dying, or developing the shapeshifting illness," Dean said. "Think of what you've heard about me. Have you heard anything about me that denies that I work hard to take care of my patients, whoever they are?"

Another pause in the conversation, then Eric replied. "Okay, but if anyone comes in, it is just you alone. If I see anyone else, the vampire dies."

A hand clamped on Dean's shoulder. "No, Dean, it's too risky," Rudy whispered in his ear. "We have no way to protect you."

"Ashley told me that I had to make a choice," Dean said to the pack leader. "That I would have a decision to make that would solve the problems here in Elk City. I think maybe this is it. I am a healer first and foremost. I need to go in there and tend to the wounds of a man who is my enemy, no matter how I feel about him personally. I have to do this."

"If anything happens to you, James and Ashley will have my head on a stick," Rudy said. "If you're wrong, and this goes south, you are dead, and another decision you were supposed to make never gets made, then we are all screwed; you know that, right?"

"I'm not wrong in making this decision," Dean said. "This may not be the choice Ashley is talking about, but I have to try and save that man - enemy or not. Plus, you heard what Eric said. He has the information I need to clear my name in Zach's murder. He knows about the plan to frame me. This has got to be the solution Ashley foresaw."

"It's your head, so it is your decision," Rudy said. "We will be just outside. We are still listening in over Gibbie's hacked phone. If you need us to rush in, just say the word 'banana' in a sentence. We will try to do our best and rescue you."

"Banana, really?"

"Sorry. I'm hungry; food is on my mind," Rudy said with a shrug.

Dean almost laughed, then stifled it and turned back to the office. Raising his voice again, he said, "Eric, I'm coming in alone. I'll come up and open the door slowly. I'll have my trauma and medication bags, and a heart monitor, okay?"

"Okay," Eric called back. "Just move really slow when you get to the door."

Dean shouldered his bags and picked up the heart monitor. He stepped out from behind the stack of crates. He half expected to hear a gunshot and feel the punch of a bullet. But that didn't happen. He took a deep breath to steady his nerves and walked over to the door to the office holding Eric and his hostage. Dean slowly turned the knob and opened the door. He looked inside.

In the back corner, away from the windows, stood a man not much older than himself. He had blonde hair, and if Dean had met him under other circumstances, might have been the kind of guy Dean would have thought nothing about on the street. The man's shoulder was oozing blood, and the bite had shredded his shirt so that Dean could see tendon and bone exposed there. This was Eric, and he must be in a lot of pain, not to mention going into shock from blood loss. Dean knew he had to work fast.

Eric held a sharpened wooden stake over Gibbie's chest, but his hands were shaking. Gibbie was seated in a chair wearing nothing but a pair of boxer shorts. There was a silver cable around his neck that wrapped around his chest and down to his feet. Dean could see red welts in the vampire's skin where the metal cable contacted it. That had to be painful for Gibbie, but he was silent. His eyes were wide, though, and seemed to plead with Dean to get him out of this predicament. Dean shot him a grim smile.

"Eric, I'm Dean," he said from the doorway. "May I come in?"

"Yes," Eric replied. "But close the door behind you."

Dean followed the instructions, taking a few steps forward and pulling the door closed behind him. Dean moved a little closer, taking his time until he was about five feet away from the pair in the room's corner. He set the bags and heart monitor down on either side of him. He pointed to Eric's shoulder. "That looks painful, and it's still bleeding like you said. Let me tend to it and give you the medicine I talked about."

"What is it?" Eric asked.

"It's a wolfsbane extract," Dean said. "It will act as a counter-agent against the virus you probably contracted when you were bitten. I don't know the full numbers, but nearly everyone bitten by a shapeshifter contracts the disease unless the extract is administered within an hour or so. When we get you to the hospital, we can get you the follow-up doses you need."

"I don't want to become one of them," Eric said, his voice falling to a whisper.

"They don't want you in their pack either, not this way," Dean said. He smiled. "The shapeshifters are a proud group, and they wear their disease as sort of a badge of honor. They don't let others in unless they feel they've earned it in some way. This happened as a result of a fight, and they would like very much for me to heal you, so you don't turn." Dean knelt down and slowly unzipped his medication bag. He had prepped a few syringes for this likely occurrence, and he held one of them up for Eric to see.

"May I?" Dean asked. "I'll give you this shot and then I can do something to stop that bleeding."

Eric looked at Dean, then at Gibbie. He lowered the stake he was holding on his hostage and sank into a chair just behind him. He nodded to Dean. "Go ahead. I guess I have nothing to lose."

Dean walked over and pulled the other guy's t-shirt sleeve up, exposing the deltoid muscle of Eric's uninjured arm, giving him the injection after quickly swabbing the skin with an alcohol prep. He stepped back to his bag and looked at his patient. "I'd like to dress that wound and stop the bleeding next, but it's going to hurt. May I give you some morphine to help with the pain first? It might make you sleepy. It is your choice."

Eric just nodded. He seemed resigned to the situation now. Dean drew up some morphine and gave him another injection in the same shoulder. He rubbed the injection site with his gloved fingers to hasten absorption of both of the drugs.

"I'm going to give that morphine a minute or so to start working, Eric. Okay?" Dean asked. Eric just nodded. Dean hoped that the drug would help to sedate him. The opiate painkiller had some euphoric effects as well as helping to manage pain. After a few minutes of silence, Dean gathered a trauma pad and some four-by-four gauze pads from his trauma bag and started to tend to the wound, packing the gauze in tightly to stop the bleeding, and topping it all with the trauma pad which he held in place with direct pressure from his hand.

Erik winced a little but otherwise watched the paramedic work in silence. He looked up and met Dean's gaze. "I didn't think you'd do it. I thought you'd try some sort of trick. Why?"

"I told you. I'm a paramedic," Dean said. "It's my job, or at least it was until I got suspended for a crime I didn't commit. You sounded like you know something about that? You said the chief killed him, and you helped him frame me for the murder?"

"It was awful," Eric said. His eyes welled up, and he looked like he was about to cry. "Zach had been caught on the security camera setting the Sabatani's fire. The chief told Zach that he had to leave, that he couldn't stay in Elk City. But after Zach left the room, the chief told us he could serve another purpose. When Zach came back after packing up his stuff so he could take off, we held him as ordered and called the chief, waiting for him to arrive. He showed up and then — then he just walked up to Zach, pulled out this big knife, and he just stabbed him while we held on to him. I didn't expect that. None of us did, but what was I supposed to do? Then the chief had us wrap up the body and sneak him up to your apartment. It was easy enough to stick him inside and put your kitchen knife in his chest."

"But he was your friend, part of your group," Dean stated. He stepped back and looked at the other man. "How could you do that to him?"

"I don't know. I guess I was just in too deep at that point," Eric replied. "I didn't know how to get away. We had done so many bad things at that point. I knew that what happened to Zach, well, it could happen to me, too."

"You keep mentioning the chief," Dean prompted. "Who do you mean? Do you know his name?"

"I heard Zach call him Chief Compton once," Eric said. "I think that was his name. We just called him the chief because he and the other fireman, Mike Farver, would show up sometimes in their fire department uniforms. It was like they wanted us to know they were connected to the top, you know?"

Dean listened as Eric started to talk about everything. He talked about the attack on the witch, the assault on other patients, the setting of the Barrens fire. He tied himself, and this group in the warehouse to everything that had happened. Dean hoped that Gibbie's phone caught it all and that Rudy had the recording still going. This was everything they needed to stop The Cause. When Eric was done talking, he sighed.

"What's going to happen to me?" he asked.

"We are going to turn you over to the police, and you can tell them what you told me. Maybe they'll offer you some sort of deal." Dean secretly hoped the police did not do that, but he didn't know much about how such things were done. "In the meantime, can I get those silver cables off my friend? He looks like he's in a lot of pain."

Eric nodded, and Dean started to work Gibbie free of the silver cable. He soon had them worked loose enough for the vampire to slip out from under them and extricate himself. Gibbie stood up and turned to look at his captor.

"Won't he attack me?" Eric whined looking at the vampire standing over him. "He's going to kill me."

"Oh, honey," Gibbie said, rubbing at his sore wrists. "You are not my type, believe me."

# Chapter 25

Dean walked outside to the street and took a long breath of fresh air. He needed to settle his nerves after what had happened in the warehouse. The police were on their way. Rudy had called them. He wanted them to handle the situation once Dean had settled Eric down and released Gibbie. Dean heard the sirens in the distance coming closer. He hoped this would finally rid them of the problem with this hate group in the city. He wanted things to return to normal again.

Eric had known nothing of Artur. In fact, he had refused to believe Dean when he brought the vampire lord up. He told Dean there was no way any of them would take orders from any of those creatures. Dean knew it was too much to hope for to be able to tie him directly to all of this. Ashley and the others had told him that Artur was a careful planner with lots of experience at intrigue and insulating himself from direct involvement. He should be happy enough with what they recorded about Zach's murder. There was now plenty of evidence about what the chief did to Zach, and how they framed Dean. Marian checked the phone's connection and confirmed that the recording was complete. She even made sure it was saved to the cloud with a back-up just in case. Once the police heard the recorded conversation and talked with Eric directly, it should clear his name completely regarding the murder charges against him.

He pulled out his phone and called Ashley. He wanted to hear her voice. It always calmed him to talk to her. He also wanted to see if she thought he had completed his quest - that the decision to treat Eric and save him instead of attack him had to be what he was supposed to do. It must be the choice she had talked about. Dean wanted to see this finished and know that everything was done. He got her voicemail and left a message that he was okay, then disconnected the call. He would have to get an answer to his questions later. Most of all he wondered if Ashley would leave Elk City now that the reason for her presence was resolved.

The first police cars arrived, and he was hustled off to one side as their response teams entered the building. He also saw two ambulances arrive. He recognized U-191 as it pulled to a stop nearby. Dean saw his friends, Bill and Lynne, climb out of the Station U ambulance. They saw him, and each nodded to the other as they set up to take care of the patients he had started care on.

"Flynn," He heard a voice behind him. He turned to see Detective Ricketts. "I don't suppose I should be surprised to find you here. You seem to be mixed up in this up to your eyeballs."

"Detective, I'm here as a contractor with a private security team sent to investigate a corporate kidnapping," Dean said, using the cover story Rudy had worked out for him at the beginning of this operation. It covered him from getting in trouble for operating as a paramedic while suspended by the fire department.

"Private contractor, huh?" Ricketts snorted. "I'm sure you have the paperwork to back that up so I won't even ask."

"The most important paperwork should be the paperwork to drop the charges against me. I believe you will find that everything I have said about my innocence is true. We have recorded evidence and an eyewitness to clear me," Dean said. "The security team has all of it inside the warehouse, as well as whatever other evidence you discover inside. We recovered Gibbie, too."

"I'm glad your friend is alive and well. We shall see about the rest of it. Let me do my job and process the evidence," the detective said. "You should stick around, though, in case we need to ask you any questions about this highly unusual, private security operation inside city limits."

"I'm not going anywhere," Dean said. "I'll be right here if you need me."

The detective nodded, left a patrol officer with Dean, then went inside the warehouse. Dean was not sure what it was about him that the detective did not like. He had thought Dean was guilty in the murder of Zach and didn't seem inclined to change his opinion about him, despite Dean's protestations of innocence. He guessed that was related to the detective's experience in his job as a police investigator.

Dean waited and watched as a lot of police and assorted evidence-gathering crime scene techs entered and left the building. Eventually, he saw Bill and Lynne bring Marian's Uncle Morgan out on a stretcher. Marian walked beside him to the ambulance, then climbed into the front seat. She looked around and gave him a little wave before she closed the door. Dean was sure she was excited to ride in a real ambulance. It looked like Bill was driving. Knowing him, he would probably let her run the siren on the way to the hospital. Dean laughed at the thought and hoped the people on their route had ear protection handy.

A pair of paramedics from Station twelve came out. Dean knew them only by sight, not by name. They had Eric strapped on a stretcher. His hands were handcuffed to the side rails, and a pair of police officers walked next to him. The paramedics loaded him up in the back of their unit, then one officer and one paramedic climbed in the back while the other moved to the driver's seat. Soon that ambulance pulled out and drove away, too. Dean took out his phone and texted Bill. He needed to tell the docs about the werewolf bite on the second patient. They would need to run a secondary infusion of wolfsbane once Eric arrived to make sure that Dean's initial loading dose worked. He was finishing up the text message when his phone started ringing. It was Ashley.

"Dean," she began as soon as he connected the call. "Are you alright?"

"Yeah, I'm fine," Dean replied. "We got Gibbie back safe and sound, and only one of the team from the pack was injured taking the building. It looks like he'll be okay. Bill and Lynne just left with him to take him to the hospital. Also, there's a second patient inbound with a werewolf bite. I started an initial dose of wolfsbane, but he'll need the subsequent infusion. He's one of the members of The Cause."

"I'll make sure the Unusual medical team is involved with both inbound patients then," Ashley said.

"Does anything feel any different?"

"What do you mean?" she asked.

"I thought maybe you'd feel something change," Dean explained. "I had to treat The Cause member, a guy named Eric. He ended up confessing to everything, including how they killed Zach and used his body to frame me. He also named Deputy Chief Compton as the one who did it. I thought maybe this was the choice I needed to make - that it solved the issues here in Elk City."

"Maaaaybe," she said elongating the word as if thinking while she said it. "The future seems, uh, I don't know. Brighter somehow? Does that make sense? This might have been the thing you had to do. Or it might just have set other events in motion that have solidified the future so that your choice is more certain. I feel like you are still tied to James in some way. I think your real choice still lies before you."

"Well that's disconcerting," Dean said. "I was hoping this whole mess was over. I guess not."

"Don't lose heart, sweetie. This has got to be a step in the right direction," Ashley reassured him.

"I hope so," Dean replied. "I just want this to be over." Dean saw Detective Ricketts exiting the building and come his way. "Hey, I've got to go. I'll call you later." He disconnected the phone call and waited for the police detective to come over to him.

"Well, Mr. Flynn, I reviewed the recordings your people inside made," the investigator began. "I still have to interview the suspect who was taken to the hospital, but it appears that you may be innocent after all. I'll notify the district attorney of my findings once I complete my investigation. There are no promises, and I will be thorough following up all the leads, but I thought you should know it looks good for you getting off the hook for this homicide."

"Thank you, detective," Dean said. "I appreciate it." The two men shook hands and the detective turned and went to confer with a group of police officers standing nearby. Dean looked around, then walked back over to Rudy's SUV. It was his ride back home, and he didn't want to miss it. He was exhausted and just wanted to get some sleep. The sun was just starting to come up. He leaned against the vehicle and watched the police activity around him, wondering if everything would ever be normal again. He decided, after thinking on it a bit, that normal was not something real. It assumed that things never changed, when in reality, they changed all the time. Dean realized that it was probably a better idea to wish for change that moved more slowly. It was better than the alternative.

Rudy came out of the warehouse with a few members of his team behind him. He stopped to talk to a group of police officers, then headed over to where Dean was standing.

"We are finished here, Dean," the pack leader said. "What do you say we head off and get a bite to eat? My treat."

"That sounds like a good idea," Dean said. He wanted to get home, but the mention of food caused his stomach to rumble, and he realized he was hungry after all the action of the evening. "You pick."

"Hanks Diner is not too far away," Rudy proposed. "You like that place, right?"

"Hanks is a great idea," Dean said. He was already thinking of a big breakfast he could order there. It wasn't Dublin, but it would do. Dean climbed into the SUV as Rudy got in and fired up the engine. A nice meal was going to hit the spot. Rudy drove out and headed off into the early morning traffic.

DEAN LEANED back in the booth and let out a satisfied sigh. His plate was wiped clean as he mopped up the rest of the chipped beef gravy with a final piece of toasted wheat bread. He popped the last piece of toast into his mouth and closed his eyes as he chewed, enjoying the flavors. He opened his eyes as he swallowed, when his breakfast companion grunted in pleasure. Dean watched as Rudy dug into his second steak and eggs breakfast plate. The pack leader had put away more food than Dean had thought possible. He ate like a, well, wolf. He knew it was because the lycans burned a lot of energy, especially when they shifted and maintained their wolf forms. Their metabolisms were amped up well beyond the normal human range.

Rudy took a bite and looked up at Dean. "I had a long talk with that detective back there. Did he come out and talk to you?"

Dean nodded. "Yeah, he told me he was probably going to recommend dropping the charges against me. He sounded disappointed though, which bothered me."

"Don't get upset," Rudy said, taking another bite. "It's a side effect of the job, I think. Most cops get invested in finding a suspect for a crime, and when they find one they think is their man they have trouble letting go of their resolve that that person is the guilty one. Once he has a chance to pick up another suspect, he'll let it go."

"Any word on what they plan on doing with Chief Compton?" Dean asked.

"From what I heard, they already had a judge working on a warrant for his arrest, and to search his office and home," Rudy said. "They may have already picked him up. They are also going after Mike Farver. The police collected all of the phones belonging to The Cause members in the warehouse. One of the idiots didn't even have it locked with a passcode and it looks like there are pictures from the Barrens fire taken while they tossed the Molotov cocktails into the homes there. There are pictures of Mike on the scene with them. I'd say that these guys have a lot of explaining to do. They aren't going to see the light of day for a long time."

"What did the police officers say about the ones you had to kill on the way in?" Dean asked.

Rudy looked up and seemed shocked. "We didn't kill any of them, Dean. What makes you think that?"

"Well, Mr. Gregory said that you had three of the humans 'down' and I assumed that meant they were dead," Dean explained.

"No, Dean, we didn't kill anyone. I made sure everyone knew that we had to be careful of that," Rudy said. "They were all rendered unconscious with a knock to the head, or a quickly applied sleeper hold. They will need some medical attention, but will all survive. I suspect they will all start talking and will turn on each other once they are under police interrogation."

"Well, that's good news," Dean said. "I wish we could listen in on their police interrogations. I'd like to hear what they have to say."

"James and I have been promised a full report at the end of the day," Rudy said. "It's a perk of his position in the Unusual community, along with the nature of this particular investigation. We should know most of what the police know by later on tonight."

Dean looked down and saw that Rudy had finished off his steak and eggs. "Ordering more?" he asked.

"No, that's enough for now," Rudy laughed. "Man, I was hungry. It's good to get some food on board after a night like that. If you want to head out to the truck, I'll get the check."

Dean nodded and stood to leave, smiling as Daisy, the waitress, came by with their bill. The last twenty-four hours had been hectic. It was going to be good to get home and get some sleep, especially sleep that didn't have him thinking about what a life in prison would be like. He left the diner to stand in the parking lot on a bright sunny day - a day that looked better than any day had for the last several weeks. Dean was looking forward to the change of pace.

## Chapter 26

It took two days for all of the details to shake out following the pack's raid on The Cause's hideout and Gibbie's rescue. On the second day, Dean and his lawyer, Mansel Hood, appeared in court before the judge where the district attorney officially asked that charges against the paramedic be dropped. Dean shook his lawyer's hand and walked out of the courthouse a free man for the first time in over a month. He looked at Ashley waiting at the curb to pick him up in her little red sports car. Dean walked down the marble steps of the city courthouse and climbed into the MG next to his girlfriend. The two of them headed off to a congratulatory dinner that James and Brynne had arranged.

They arrived at the newly renovated and restored Sabatani's restaurant a half hour later to actual applause. Dean blushed at the attention from everyone there. James had invited the whole CERT team, the Station U paramedics, including their spouses or significant others, and others Dean had become close to over the last few months. A cold glass of beer was placed in his hand, and then Brynne hushed the crowd and offered a toast.

"To Dean Flynn, station U paramedic, healer, and hero, it's not so bad a world as some would like to make it. But whether good or whether bad, it depends on how you take it. Dean, you've taken the world, good and bad, taken what it has given you and left it a better place. May you continue to do so for many years to come. Cheers!" She raised her glass to Dean, and the others echoed with cheers and kudos.

Dean nodded in reply and mouthed a 'thank you' to his partner. He looked forward to working by her side again. She had been a good mentor and had stood by him through all of the accusations, attacks, and their aftermath. He respected her not just as a good paramedic, but as a good friend. He noticed James at her side. He realized that he didn't harbor the feelings of unease about their relationship that he held for so long. They seemed right together. The two of them fit as well as any couple he had ever known. Dean didn't realize when that shift in his viewpoint had happened, but he could see now that he had been wrong to distrust the vampire and his intentions with his partner. He would need to let them both know how he felt. He had not always been positive about how he felt about their relationship.

James had rented the back room at the restaurant, and the food was laid out buffet-style on tables all around the room. People gathered in small groups, standing and seated at tables and Dean was able to roam from group to group with Ashley on his arm. Friends and colleagues all greeted him, each offering their praise, and in some cases, their thanks for his actions. The whole evening was a blur of conversations that left Dean a bit overwhelmed. Eventually, the dinner wound down, and as the servers started to clean up the dishes and silverware, Dean found himself seated at a table with Ashley, Brynne and James looking at a room now empty of guests.

"James, I want to thank you for this," Dean said. "It has been an amazing night. I never realized so many people were involved in this whole chain of events."

"It's the least I could do, Dean," James said. He raised his characteristic white mug of blood. "You earned it."

Brynne took a sip of her wine and said, "So, does this mean this is all over?"

"There have been more arrests, and Chief Compton made a full confession after he saw the evidence presented against him," James said. "They found the knife he used to kill Zach hidden in his home. It still has blood residue on it. They are still waiting for the DNA testing to come back, but I suspect it will tie the chief to Zach's death. It looks like The Cause's whole operation has been rolled up. Artur left town without a word last night. I'm sure we'll need to keep an eye out for him going forward, but for now, he's gone."

"I only wish they had caught Mike Farver before he disappeared," Brynne said. Police had gone to arrest the fire academy instructor but had been unable to locate him. Dean heard that it looked as if he had left in a hurry, and all attempts to track him down had been unsuccessful so far.

"It might take time," James said. "But they'll catch up with him eventually. Compton exposed Mike as their leader, the man with all the plans, so he must be the one who ties everything to Artur."

"Maybe Artur has something to do with his disappearance?" Dean surmised. "Maybe his body will turn up. Artur has to see him as a major loose end."

"That's a definite possibility," James said. "Still, he's gone and is the police's problem now. For us, it is all in the past." He looked around at the others. "I feel like celebrating some more, shall we wrap up the evening with some drinks and dancing?"

"That sounds like a great idea," Ashley said. "Are you thinking of Sensations and the Loft?" She was referring to the popular and secret Unusual-only club that existed upstairs from the main human nightclub below.

James nodded and Dean was excited all over again. He had heard of the Loft at Sensations from his companions, but he had never been there. Only Unusuals and their escorted guests were allowed upstairs. It was supposed to be pretty spectacular. The four of them got up and left the restaurant together, turning right and walking down the night streets of Elk City for the few blocks it took to get to the nightclub. They joked and laughed. It all was very normal, and Dean was glad to experience it. The two couples had become close over the events of the past weeks.

When they arrived at Sensations, the bouncer nodded to James and unhooked the rope blocking the entrance to let them right in, jumping the line of partiers waiting outside to enter. James led them through the room to the back corner of the club. There was a nondescript door there guarded by another large muscular man. He nodded to the vampire lord and opened the door for the group. Beyond the door was a hallway leading to a broad staircase that Dean assumed led up to the Loft. At the top of the stairs, they were greeted by cheers again as the Unusual revelers above responded to their arrival. Dean saw many former patients in the crowd, and he nodded to them as he passed by. A waitress led them to a table in the center of the room, roped off with velvet ropes and brass poles. The group slid into the circular booth and ordered drinks.

Dean looked around in wonder. The Loft at Sensations was one of the few places where the Unusual community could be themselves, letting their true natures show through without fear of discovery by the humans who surrounded them most of the time. There were spiral staircases in each corner of the room leading up to a balcony that surrounded the room. A woman on the balcony leaned over the edge, and he thought she was going to fall to the floor. Just as she tipped over the edge, gossamer fairy wings spread out behind her, and she glided effortlessly to the other side. She climbed gracefully over the wrought iron railing to the balcony on the other side of the room.

Brynne laughed at his reaction. "I was the same way my first time here, Dean. It's pretty amazing isn't it?"

"Amazing doesn't cover it," Dean replied. "This is awesome." He sat back and continued to look around the room, taking it all in. He tried to avoid staring, but he saw so much that caught him by surprise. He saw a vampire couple in a nearby booth, each feeding on a human of the opposite sex. He was concerned, but then they stopped drinking and the two humans, dressed in shorts and gray tank tops, just got up and walked back to a door set in one wall. He knew that they were paid very well for their donation of blood, and would be checked out medically before being sent on their way for forty-five days until they could donate again if they chose to do so.

He was still scanning the room when there was a commotion by the door. Then multiple pops went off, barely heard over the thumping dance music. Curious, he looked in that direction. His gut tightened. Lately he had heard plenty of gunfire and recognized it. His suspicions were confirmed when screams erupted, and more shots sounded. Dean saw bodies lying on the nightclub floor. People started running away, and the crowd between them opened up to reveal a figure walking towards the center of the room, holding a semi-automatic handgun stretched out in front of him. It was Mike Farver.

Dean started to stand up, but James was faster, his vampire reflexes and strength propelling him at the attacker. He'd almost reached Mike, and Dean was sure he would take the man down when Mike's other hand raised and displayed a large silver cross in James' direction. It was as if the vampire had slammed into an invisible wall. He bounced backward and slammed to the floor hard and stayed there. Dean stood up and moved out of the booth to stand in front of the two women.

"Mike, what are you doing?" Dean said. "Are you crazy?"

"No, I'm not crazy, Dean," Mike said still walking towards them. "I'm disappointed in you, though. You betrayed your race, and your training to heal people. I mean real people, not these monsters. And now all the hard work I put in is done. Everything I did to keep us humans safe from these parasites is for nothing."

Dean saw James starting to rise from the floor, but Mike did, too. He thrust the cross in his direction and it knocked the vampire back to the floor. Brynne started to move to her boyfriend's defense, but Mike pointed the gun in her direction, and she stopped.

"I'm most disappointed in you, Brynne," Mike said. "This all could have been avoided if you had just listened to me in the beginning. I tried to warn you what getting attached to this creature would do to you, but you ignored me. Not only that, but you got me fired from the job I loved, and they shuffled me off to the Academy. I was a laughing stock to everyone. Everyone knew you chose that monster over me."

"Mike, there was never any you and me," Brynne said. "We

were partners. You were my trainer, my mentor, but never were we going to be anything more. You had to know that."

"I soon realized that you were being brainwashed to turn your back on your humanity. There was no other explanation," Mike countered. "I knew there was only one way to make it right. I had to get rid of James in a way that would make him leave - leave here and also leave you. The Cause was well on its way to achieving that goal. Then Dean here screwed it all up." He swiveled the gun to point back at Dean.

Dean put his hands in front of him. He didn't know why. It wasn't like they'd be able to stop the bullets. Maybe Ashley could do something. He half turned to her behind him. Mike laughed at his reaction.

Mike sneered. "Do you think your little angel-girl can do something to save you from what is to come? She knows what I'm prepared to do. If she moves a muscle, I cut you all down."

Ashley's voice sounded from behind Dean. "I may not act in this case, Michael. This is a situation where human action and free will must carry out to their own ends. Know this, though. Your fate is not yet sealed. There is still time to change your path."

Great, now Ashley decides to step back and let the humans play without interference, Dean thought to himself. He knew she operated under her own set of rules, and this situation was apparently one of those times she was unable to act or interfere. It was one thing to know the intellectual reasons for things to happen, but was something else to live in that situation and feel helpless to change the events happening to you.

Mike laughed after Ashley finished her announcement. "I don't need your warnings, Eldara. I know my fate, and it is already sealed. My goal here is to finish something I could not accomplish when I started all of this in motion years ago. Brynne, I couldn't save you from yourself no matter how many ways I tried. Now I only have one option left, and that is to save your soul." Mike turned the gun back on Brynne and fired two shots, striking her in the chest with enough force to knock her all the way back into the cushioned booth behind her.

## Chapter 27

It all happened so quickly. Dean never had a chance to stop it or do something heroic like jump in front of the bullets. He just stood there and watched it happen. He wasn't alone though. As Mike took his attention off the cross in his other hand, James leapt from where he had been lying on the floor. He struck Mike's back, knocking the man to the ground. With two hands, he snapped Mike's neck with a twist of his head.

The struggling body stopped moving instantly, and Dean knew that Mike was dead. The danger from Mike was gone, but that wasn't Dean's primary concern. He immediately turned his attention to Brynne. There was dark blood staining the front of her green cocktail dress where the bullets had entered her chest. She was struggling to get up as she coughed up a mouthful of blood. Dean ran over and clamped two hands over the wounds in her chest, applying pressure. There wasn't anything else he could do. He didn't have any of his gear with him, and with chest wounds, there wasn't much he could have done even if he had her in the back of his ambulance.

"Someone call 911," he shouted. "Get help here now."

James was kneeling at his side, holding Brynne's hand. "Dean, do something. What do you need? Anything, I'll get it."

"There's nothing I can do, James," Dean said choking away tears. He turned his attention back to his partner, now his patient. "Brynne, you need to stay awake and hold on. Help is coming."

"God this hurts," she whispered, then she coughed again, and more blood came out of her mouth. "It's alright, Dean. I know what this means and what you're trying to do. It's not your fault." She blinked once and then closed her eyes and didn't open them again. Her breathing became more ragged.

"Wake up, Brynne," Dean said, shaking her a little. She didn't move. She was breathing shallowly, and that was the only sign of life. Dean turned and looked at Ashley. She just shook her head.

"Dean, I can do nothing in this place and time," Ashley said. "I'm so sorry. The time of your choice is upon you, and I may not interfere in any way. This is it. The choice is yours." Tears fell down her cheeks as she held his gaze for a moment, a grim smile on her face.

Dean looked back to Brynne. What choice? He had no choice. There was nothing he could do to save her. The ambulance was not going to get here in time. She needed an operating room in a trauma hospital, and even then they would be hard-pressed to save her life given the location of the wounds. The bullets had almost certainly pierced her heart and lungs, and likely one of the great blood vessels leaving the heart. That would account for the amount of blood she had coughed up.

Ashley had said the choice was up to him, but what choice was there? He was dumbfounded. Ashley had told him that he would have to make a choice to resolve the situation here in Elk City - a choice that he and James would somehow have to work together to make. He and James. Dean looked at the vampire sitting to his left. He was holding Brynne's hand and stroking it almost lovingly. No, not almost. James loved her. Dean did not doubt that at all. He wasn't some sort of monster; he was a man. He had his differences, but at the center was a man who loved a woman - a woman who was dying.

Then it hit him. There was a decision that needed to be made and it had to be made now. Dean looked back up at Ashley, a question on his face. She knew it now too. She smiled at him and nodded. That was the confirmation he needed. Dean looked at James and gripped the vampire's shoulder. James turned his own red-rimmed eyes towards Dean, questioning the interruption of his grief.

"James, you need to turn her."

The vampire just looked at the paramedic in front of him and seemed to not understand the words. Dean nodded toward Brynne, dying on the floor next to him. Her breathing was almost gone. There was no more time. "James, listen to me, you have to turn her. There's no other option. If we want to save Brynne, you have to turn her into a vampire."

James looked from Dean to Brynne and then back again. "Are you sure?" James asked. "I promised her I would never turn someone against their will. I've always held the belief that becoming one of us should be a choice, and not something randomly thrust upon someone like it was with me."

"I'm sure," Dean said with finality. "You two love each other. There is no other way to make this all work out. That is my choice, for Brynne, my friend and colleague. You must change her; I know she would want it. James, you have to do it right now, before it's too late. She's almost dead, and then it will be too late."

James looked at Brynne one more time and then nodded. He held his wrist up to his own mouth and bit down hard to open his vein. Once his vampire blood started to flow, he held up Brynne's head and placed the wounded wrist over her mouth. He leaned down and said, "Drink, my love. Drink so that you may live again."

Dean looked at Brynne and couldn't tell if she consumed any of the vampire's blood or not. There was no change at all. She was already pale from blood loss. James held his wrist in place whispering to her for the last few minutes of her life and beyond. Her breathing had stopped, and Dean slumped back on his heels from where he knelt next to his former partner. James howled in pain, stood, and stumbled away from where Brynne's body lay on the floor.

Ashley came forward and placed a hand on Dean's shoulder then crouched down and placed her arms around him. She whispered in his ear. "It was your choice to make for her, and you made it. Do not be sad for Brynne. It would have been what she wanted."

Dean couldn't fathom her words. He hugged her close while he looked at the body of his partner, his mentor, and his friend. It was his choice to make, but he must have taken too long. The choice hadn't become clear until it was too late to save her. She was laying there, no signs of life at all, just a finger twitching here or there. He was overcome with grief.

Wait. Dean broke the hug with Ashley.

He looked intently at his partner's body. Did he see her fingers twitch or had that been his imagination? He watched her hand again and this time saw a definite movement, of her whole hand this time.

"James," Dean called. "Get over here. I think it worked."

The vampire rushed back to Brynne's side, and there was renewed chatter among the onlookers from the nightclub crowd. James picked up one hand and gripped it. Dean watched in wonder as the grip was returned. Then he saw Brynne's eyes flutter open. She looked around at everyone watching her and then at James. She sat up and her free hand flew to her chest, probing around before she pulled away the top of her dress to peer down inside. A look of surprise showed on her face, and she looked up at James where their eyes met. James nodded.

"It was Dean's decision. His choice," James said. "He made the choice for you. I hope you are not angry."

Her voice was hoarse as she responded. Dean saw her look over and meet his eyes. "No, I'm not angry." She hugged James close for a moment and then leaned back, smacking her lips. Dean saw the newly elongated canines in evidence in her mouth. "I am thirsty, though." She looked at Dean, and he leaned in to give her a hug, too. James' arm barred his advance.

"She is too new," James warned. "She would not be able to

control herself." He snapped his fingers. "A cup of O negative, quickly please."

Dean looked at Brynne and shivered as she gave him a feral grin in return. He shrank back from her hungry gaze. He looked at Ashley, horrified. What had he done to her? Ashley shook her head.

"Do not blame yourself, Dean," the Eldara said. "She is different, but she is still the Brynne you knew. Give her some time to acclimate to her new condition and you will see that she is the same as she always was."

James nodded in agreement. "It will take a few weeks to understand what she has become and what she must do to make sure she does not harm others. I will be by her side and make sure the changes are managed, I promise."

A server appeared at the edge of Dean's field of vision. She handed James a white mug that he held to Brynne's lips. She sipped slowly at first, unsure of what she was drinking, then gripped the mug with both hands and drank quickly, tipping the cup upward to drain it to the last drop.

"That was delicious," she said when she was done, handing the cup back to James. "But it did taste sort of, I don't know, off somehow?"

"That is because it was not taken directly from the source," James explained. "It will take some time before you will be able to do that on your own without risking the life of the person who is donating. You will have to trust me until then."

"If you say so," Brynne said. "It did make me feel better and I'm not so hungry." She held a hand out to Dean, and he looked to James for advice.

"She has fed, so it is safe," the elder vampire said. "Just maintain some distance for her comfort."

Dean reached out and took the offered hand. Brynne gripped it, and he winced at the force of her squeeze. She let up when she realized what she was doing.

"Sorry, I guess I don't know my own strength," she said. "Thank you, Dean, for making the choice for me. It was the right thing to do. I mean, I feel awesome. I can hear, no, I can feel every heartbeat in this room, imagine the paramedic I'll be."

James sighed, and Dean and Brynne both looked at him. "Brynne, you cannot go back to that life. At least, not for quite a while. Being a newly turned vampire will make it so that you cannot be around sick, injured or helpless humans or others. With the blood and their helplessness, you would find it difficult to resist feeding upon them. I'm sorry. It will be a few years before I would trust you to go back to that work."

Dean looked back and forth between James and Brynne, realizing what the older vampire was saying. Brynne could no longer be his partner at Station U. Her transformation would prevent it for a long time, perhaps forever.

"It's okay, Brynne," Dean said. "I'll still come up and visit from time to time. I promise." He knew that it was a small consolation. Brynne loved being a paramedic. He had not thought about that when he had made the decision to change her. Of course, the alternative was death. Ashley had once said that everything magical in life came with a price. This was part of the price that must be paid for saving Brynne. He would lose her as his partner, and she would cease to be a paramedic.

Voices at the doorway interrupted them as the Station U paramedics and police arrived at the club. There would be a lot of explanations and statements to be made. Dean hoped that when all of that was done, they would finally be able to lay this whole episode to rest. The trauma of the evening washed over him, and he started shaking as the adrenaline drained from his system. He wanted to go back to making normal life-and-death choices, the kind a paramedic made every day. It certainly didn't involve watching friends die then turn into vampires. Paramedicine was what he had trained for, and that was what he longed to be again. He stood up to tell Bill and Lynne what was happening as they rushed across the floor to where Mike lay. There was a lot he needed to tell them about the new normal, because this was as normal as it was going to be ever again.

---

'Normal' is a lie. It is a word that Dean decided was used way too much. He had been hoping for the past weeks and months for everything to get back to normal, even a new normal. He thought that if he solved the problems facing him and his patients in the Unusual community, everything would go back to being the way they were. Nothing, however, was the same. Nor would it ever be. He pondered this as he drove to work through Elk City in the early morning hours of what should have been a 'normal' Monday.

It had been four weeks since the incident with Mike in the night-club. That night would be forever burned into his memory. Dean knew he would always wonder if there was something he could have done differently to save Brynne. He had visited her several times, always chaperoned by James or Celeste for his own safety. Brynne said she was doing well, acclimating to her new reality. She told Dean that she was glad he had made the choice on her behalf, the choice that she be transformed into a member of the undead. He knew her too well though, and saw that the change brought with it regrets and things she missed as a human. James told him that it was a common reaction to the change in lifestyle required for new vampires. She was just adjusting to her new normal.

Dean snorted under his breath as he drove. There was that word 'normal' again. He thought about it more as he pulled into the parking lot at Station U. There was no normal. It was fiction devised by people living in the past and not looking towards the future. Dean had learned the hard way that change was constant, and that you could accept the changes thrust upon you, or work to enact changes of your own that were more agreeable. He had been a literal agent of change and was determined to be more proactive in shaping the changes around him in the future.

The past few weeks had brought more change for him than he could ever have expected. Chief Ari had praised him for his perseverance to serve his patients and recommended him to take the two-week paramedic preceptor course. It was unusual for someone as new as he was to take that class, but the Chief had said it was well-deserved. Then, while he was out of town attending the preceptor course, he had received a cryptic text message from Ashley. She said she had something urgent to attend to, and had to leave town. He had not even had a chance to say goodbye or learn when she would return. Her phone was turned off and untraceable. Now he was driving to the station to start his first shift as a preceptor, and was getting a probie of his own to break in. Another new guy to show the ropes in the world of the Unusual community and extreme medical services. It was not a return to normal at all.

Dean strode into the station break room to a flurry of greetings from paramedics staffing the previous shift, Brook and Tammy. The two women were packing up their things after their twelve-hour shift and he knew they looked forward to getting home. Tammy had her kids and husband to see off to school and work respectively, and Brook probably looked forward to having the bed to herself after her husband left for work. There was something to be said for the value of a good day's sleep after working all night. He returned their greetings and thought of his own empty bed. He missed Ashley and wondered when she would return.

"Hey, Dean, you ready for the new probie inbound this morning?" Brook asked. "At least you'll be able to sympathize with them since you can easily remember what it was like to be one yourself."

"Yeah, Brook," Dean replied with a chuckle. "I have that going for me. I think my best bet is to work under the mantra 'what would Brynne do?'"

"How is Brynne anyway?" Tammy asked. "We were going to call and schedule a time to stop downtown and visit her since she's can't go out in public yet."

"She's well. I saw her yesterday," Dean replied. "I think she would like seeing you guys. She misses her old friends and colleagues. It has been a difficult transition for her, though James said that it is all going the way it is supposed to go."

"Well, he's the expert," Brook said. "We've got to follow his lead, Dean. I'll call on my way home and set it up for us to drop by this afternoon before we come back to work. Does that work for you, Tammy?"

Tammy nodded and picked up her purse. "We'll cheer her up. I want to hear what the sex is like now that she and James don't have to hold back with each other."

Dean and Brook both laughed. Tammy always fantasized about what it would be like to date an Unusual, even though she and her perfectly human husband were infatuated with each other. She loved to hear tales of her colleagues' escapades.

A tap at the parking lot door interrupted them, and Brook opened the door and then stood back to let the new arrival in. It was Dean's new probationary paramedic, Barry. He had a few years' experience under his belt in a nearby system as a regular paramedic for humans. He had applied to Elk City's community paramedic program and had impressed the leadership with his drive and ingenuity. That was what they had told Dean when they described him. He was about the same age as Dean, stood about five foot, ten inches tall and had blonde hair. He smiled as he entered and walked over to Dean extending his hand.

"Hi, you must be Dean," the new guy said. "I'm Barry, and I'm excited to be invited to join you guys in this community paramedicine program. I didn't know there was another program aside from the standard community program. No one seemed to have heard of Station U, no matter who I asked."

Dean saw Brook and Tammy share a look, and then they both burst out laughing, waving their goodbyes and leaving him alone with the new guy. Barry watched them leave and turned back to Dean.

"What was that all about?" he asked.

"They're women, so who knows," Dean said. He knew the new guy would figure it out soon enough. Best to get him acclimated to the station and go over the ambulance in case they got a call. There would be one on the radio system sooner or later, so it was best to be prepared. Since the roundup and arrest of all of the members of The Cause, Station U's ambulance calls had returned to normal.

"So, Barry, what's your favorite fantasy novel?" Dean began as he led the new guy out to the ambulance bay to get oriented on the ambulance. Barry had so much to learn.

DEAN SAT in the office workstation getting some much-needed paperwork done and reviewing email updates from headquarters. Barry was out washing the ambulance, a daily chore that was especially needed in these spring months, as every bug in the world came out from its winter hiding place to splatter on their windshield. The new guy's first day was a slow one, and there had been no calls on which to get him squared away with the type of patients they served. Dean was pondering a way to break the ice with him about their patient population's unique natures if they didn't get a call soon.

Barry came into the squad room and looked at Dean. "Hey, you should come check this out. A totally hot brunette in a vintage red sports car just pulled into the parking lot. I don't know why she is way back here in the industrial park. She must be lost and looking for directions or something.

Dean jumped up and ran to the parking lot window. His heart leaped in his chest as he saw Ashley's MG convertible parked outside next to his white Ford pickup truck. She was getting out of the car. He raced out the door and ran up to her, spinning her around and planting a kiss on her. He felt her pause for a moment then pull him closer, her mouth opening and the kiss deepening. This was hot, though Ashley wasn't usually this into public displays of affection. And when did she get that tongue-stud? He thought they were hot and all, but it was not something that he expected Ashley to do.

Dean's eyes sprang open in surprise when he felt her hands groping for his belt. What the …? He forced himself to push back from the kiss and stare at his girlfriend in consternation. He got a further surprise as he took in her new look. Ashley was clad from head to toe in black leather, from the high-heeled boots to the tight-fitting jacket zipped up just far enough to expose her ample cleavage. She had new silver earrings piercing her left ear all the way from the lower lobe to the top of the cartilage. There was a nose piercing, too, with a small ruby stud showing on the right side. She was wearing a lot more makeup than she usually did, too. Then it hit him.

This wasn't Ashley. Ha!

"Hello, lover," said the voice with a definite British accent. "You have to be Dean. My sister has always preferred a certain type when it comes to men."

"Ingrid?" Dean asked, using Ashley's twin sister's name for the first time. "What are you doing driving Ashley's car.

"Surprised?" she said with a laugh. "Not as surprised as I was. I was in the middle of something important, but family is family. Am I right?"

Dean just stood there and looked at her. What was she doing here? Where was Ashley?

"Look, Dean, much as I would love to take you inside and finish what we started out here in the parking lot, we've got a lot of talking to do. Ashley's in trouble, and it's going to take both of us to get her out of it." She hooked a finger for him to follow her as she strutted past him, across the parking lot, and right by the dumbfounded Barry holding the door open for her as she entered the station.

Dean stood there, watching her go inside, wondering again what happened to his normal life.

---

Ready to keep reading? **Get Extreme Medical Services Vol 4-6 in one box set!**
or
Read on for a preview of Book 4 - *The Paramedic's Hunter*

# The Paramedic's Hunter
## Preview - Chapter 1

The wounds were severe, at least that was the information coming in from the dispatchers over the ambulance's radio. Dean drove quickly through the nighttime streets of Elk City. He made good time but drove with due regard to safety and all traffic laws. It didn't do the patient any good if the ambulance wrecked on the way to the scene.

The call was for an animal bite. The dispatcher said that the caller was having difficulty stopping the bleeding. There were numerous bites to the patient. Dean worked hard to stay focused. He was distracted lately, ever since he found out his girlfriend, Ashley - an actual angel or, as she preferred, Eldara, had been abducted and was still missing. It was important for him to find her. It was also important for him to make sure he cared for his patients. He redoubled his focus on the on the dark nighttime residential streets in front of him.

Dean glanced over at his new partner. Barry Winston had been an experienced paramedic before he applied for the special Station U community paramedic program in Elk City. He had been unaware, just as Dean had been in the beginning, that their patients were not normal people. In fact, their patients were not human at all. The Station U paramedics responded to calls for emergency medical aid from what other people would call the creatures of myths and legends. Some might even say they were the monsters of nightmares.

Dean had come to know different. They were just people who were trying to live their lives alongside their human neighbors, without anyone knowing how different they were. Barry had been shocked at first, but was coming around. He was adjusting better than Dean had in the beginning. Barry was already a pretty good paramedic and that, plus a predisposition for reading fantasy and science-fiction books, had helped him overcome his cultural biases.

Barry operated the siren while Dean drove, changing the tone of it when they entered an intersection. Once they were through it and speeding down the road on the other side, he looked over at Dean. "What do you think caused the bite? It sounds serious. Could it be a shapeshifter like a werewolf or werebear?"

"Not sure, yet, Barry," Dean replied as he drove. "Whatever it is, it does not sound like a casual bite. Also, most shapeshifters are very careful about who they bite and infect with Lycanthropy. The disease is a blood borne illness and they take it seriously when someone is brought into their pack. It doesn't sound like that kind of bite. Whatever it is, we will see soon enough."

Dean turned the ambulance onto another residential street and started looking at the house numbers as the headlights illuminated the mailboxes lining the street. He was looking for number eleven-ninety-four. He knew he was getting close, and started looking on the right for the even-numbered houses. Most of the houses were modest ranch style single-family homes with large front yards. The street was lined with trees and didn't have any streetlights. Both of these things contributed to deep shadows and only a little moonlight filtering down to the ground.

He saw a flicker of movement ahead and turned the ambulance toward the shoulder of the road to shine the headlights onto one of the lawns in front of them. He saw a person crouched over a figure sprawled on the ground. The crouching individual, a middle-aged man, shielded his eyes from the glare of the headlights and then gave them a frantic wave. This had to be their patient, and the nine-one-one caller. Barry put them on location over the radio and was acknowledged by the dispatcher's voice in return.

"Careful on this one, Barry," Dean cautioned. "Whoever or whatever bit this person might still be in the neighborhood."

"Got it, Dean," his partner responded as he climbed down from the passenger side of the ambulance.

Dean grabbed the large flashlights from the compartment behind the driver's door on the ambulance, then he went around to the rear, climbed inside and got the heart monitor and oxygen bags out of the back. Walking around to the passenger side, he handed one of the lights to Barry. His partner had grabbed the trauma and medication bags from the compartment on his side of the ambulance. They hung off his shoulders by their straps. Switching on their lights, together the two paramedics walked across the lawn to the patient and caller. Dean shined his light around the yard to check for the creature that caused the bite. He had an itch between his shoulder blades and wished he could see better in the dark.

When they got to the side of the patient, the two paramedics saw she was an Asian woman in her fifties. Her entire shoulder on her left side was laid open so that Dean could see bone and tendon underneath. There were also deep slashing wounds to her abdomen. No wonder the caller couldn't stop the bleeding. It was a wonder she had lived long enough for the ambulance to arrive.

Because he was still on probationary status, Barry took the lead, with Dean observing and in support. The newer Station U paramedic held out the back of his right hand so the male caller could see it, and shined his light on it. That would reveal the hidden, ultra-violet ink stamp placed there. It showed the Station U paramedic emblem. It was invisible to humans, but it could be seen by their patients and other Unusual community members. The man nodded as he saw the fresh ink stamped there and he visibly relaxed. Dean showed his right hand as well. His mark was a more permanent UV tattoo of the Star of Life emblem. If Barry worked out in the long term, he would probably get one, too. All the Station U paramedics did eventually.

"Thank the Gods you are here," the man said. "My wife, she was attacked by some sort of demon-made-flesh."

"I'm Barry, and this is my partner Dean," Barry said as he set to work. "We are going to help your wife the best we can, okay?"

"Thank you," the slight Asian man said. "I'm called Yamo, and my wife is Akiko. Please help her. I did what I could but I'm not as powerful as she is."

Barry nodded as he started controlling the bleeding, slapping large, absorbent trauma pads over the wounds. Dean started collecting and assembling the IV supplies so they could get her some fluids. She had to have lost a great deal of blood.

"What sort of Unusual are you?" Dean asked. He had been unable to figure it out just from looking at them, or from anything that was said so far. That was normal. Sometimes you just had to ask.

"We are Hakutaku," the Asian man said. The woman groaned as Barry continued to work on her, packing her significant wounds with gauze and trauma pads. The groan distracted the man from Dean's inquiry. He knew a little of the Japanese and other Asian myths. The Hakutaku were healing spirits, and generally considered helpful and non-threatening. They were rumored to be related to the Chinese Bai-Ze spirits. It was times like this that his study of the extensive library of myths and legends back at Station U came in handy. It also explained why she was still alive. Her husband must have used some healing magic to sustain her.

Dean shined the light around in the darkness to check the area around them again. "Sir, did the attacker run off, or is it still out there nearby? Do you know what it was? Tell me what happened."

"I don't know," the man said. "We go for a walk every night. We love this neighborhood and enjoy the quiet after dark. It is a good time for contemplation and rejuvenation. Tonight, though, the natural world around us, was upset for some reason. We sought to understand why as we walked, but could come to no conclusion. We strive to bring healing and balance to both individuals and the world around us. This time we couldn't figure what was wrong. That was when the demon jumped out and slashed at Akiko. I was able to conjure a burst of light energy that drove it back. It screamed and ran off into the darkness. I turned my attention to my wife. I haven't seen it or heard it since. That was about fifteen minutes ago."

"You keep saying 'demon,'" Dean said. "What kind of Unusual being was it? A lycan? Another variety of animal shapeshifter?"

"No, no. You do not understand," Yamo said. "I think it was an Oni, a type of Japanese demon. I am sure of that much. I don't know how it got past the wards and entered this world. It must have sensed our true nature and set upon my wife right away. She's the stronger of the two of us."

The hairs on Dean's neck stood up. He had never encountered a demon before. He knew they were the evil opposites of the heavenly Unusuals like the Eldara. Those angels fulfilled the roles of messengers and agents of the gods of good and nature. The demons served another group, who sought to tear the world asunder, or so legend said. They were confined to the netherworld and kept there by a series of wards set in place millennia ago. An Oni was an Asian form of demon, though there were many varieties. Some were intelligent, but others were much more dangerous because of their unpredictable animal natures.

Shining the light around the yard, the paramedic saw nothing but the house and the trees and grass. He turned his attention back to the patient and her husband. If there was an Oni on the loose and attacking people, it would need to be dealt with, but that was a matter for someone else. He and Barry were here to care for this patient. They had to get her to the Elk City Medical Center trauma team.

⊏⊐

THE ONI DEMON, called Tegu by its lord and master, watched from the roof of the house nearby. It had been easy to climb up there and watch for the arrival of its true target. Tegu had been told that it would know the one it was to kill by his aura, and the stink of an Eldara on him. The Eldara, the messengers of the gods, were the most hated of the adversaries faced by demon-kind. The master was right. As soon as the strange, loud vehicle arrived and the occupants climbed out, the Oni noticed saw the white glow surrounding the driver. He was one of those touched by one of the hated Eldara. That was the demon's target. The man would not be without some sort of magical protections, so the demon watched and waited for the right opportunity to strike. He must kill this man. The master had ordered it.

DEAN FETCHED the stretcher from the ambulance and took it over to where Barry was finishing up his treatments to Akiko. She was semiconscious, only occasionally groaning in pain when Barry was forced to move her while binding her wounds. He had stretched out the clear plastic from a roll of plastic food wrap and had wrapped her chest to seal the wounds and help prevent what was commonly called a sucking chest wound. The lungs required a closed system to work effectively. When air was able to rush into the chest cavity without having to go through the mouth and nose, the lungs could not inflate properly. This was one of the causes of a collapsed lung. By wrapping her wounds in airtight plastic, Barry helped seal the wounds and prevent air from entering the chest cavity by another route.

Once the stretcher was rolled up next to her, the two paramedics carefully lifted her up onto it and then began loading their other gear up and around her so they could roll the whole package of patient and gear back to the ambulance in one run. Dean pointed to the ambulance and told Yamo to go get in the passenger seat of the ambulance's cab while they loaded his wife into the back. The two paramedics then rolled her over to the back of the vehicle. They took care on the uneven ground to avoid tipping the top-heavy load.

When they arrived at the back of the ambulance, Barry lifted the head end of the stretcher up and Dean helped him retract the wheels and roll it into the back of the ambulance. Considering his route to the hospital, he closed the doors and started to walk around to the driver's side of the ambulance.

TEGU SAW its opportunity as the two paramedics separated. Its target was alone at the rear and turning to walk to the front of the vehicle. The demon leapt down from its perch on the roof of the Hakutakus' home. This would be the chance to finish off the target for its master. It would be satisfying to kill one of the agents of good. Even if this human was just another minion, it would be satisfying to serve its master this way. As Tegu scrambled from the roof to the ground, the demon failed to notice another dark form detach from the other shadows at the corner of the house, following after it. The hunter was also the hunted.

Ready to keep reading? Save 40% - **get Extreme Medical Services Vol 4-6 in one box set!**

## Also by Jamie Davis

**Get a free book and updates for new books.**
**visit JamieDavisBooks.com/send-free-book/**

—

### Eldara Sister Series

*The Nightingale's Angel*

*Blue and Gray Angel*

—

### The Huntress Clan Saga

(A 6-book Urban Fantasy series starting with)

*Huntress Initiate*

—

### The Broken Throne Series

(A 5-Book Dystopian Urban Fantasy

starting with)

*The Charm Runner*

—

### The Accidental Traveler LitRPG Series

(with C.J. Davis)

(A 6-book Epic Fantasy Series starting with)

*The Accidental Thief*

—

### Lone Wolf Squadron Scifi Series

(A multi-book space opera series starting with)

*Marshal the Stars*

—

Follow on Facebook for updates, news, and upcoming book excerpts

Jamie's Fun Fantasy Readers Facebook Group

# Help the Author

**I Need Your Help ...**

Without reviews indie books like this one are almost impossible to market.

Leaving a review will only take a minute — it doesn't have to be long or involved, just a sentence or two that tells people what you liked about the book, to help other readers know why they might like it, too. It also helps me write more of what you love.

**The truth is, VERY few readers leave reviews. Please help me out by being the exception.**

Thank you in advance!

Jamie Davis